AVALANCHE

Book Five of the
SECRET WORLD CHRONICLE

To purchase these and all other Baen Book titles
in e-book format, please go to www.baen.com.

AVALANCHE

Book Five of the
SECRET WORLD CHRONICLE

Created by *Mercedes Lackey & Steve Libbey*

Written by
MERCEDES LACKEY
with **Cody Martin, Dennis Lee** *&*
Veronica Giguere

Edited by Mercedes Lackey & Larry Dixon

Avalanche: Book Five of the Secret World Chronicle

This is a work of fiction. All the characters and events portrayed in this book are fictional, and any resemblance to real people or incidents is purely coincidental.

A Baen Books Original

Baen Publishing Enterprises
P.O. Box 1403
Riverdale, NY 10471
www.baen.com

ISBN: 978-1-4814-8322-3

Cover art by Larry Dixon

First Baen printing, August 2018

Distributed by Simon & Schuster
1230 Avenue of the Americas
New York, NY 10020

10 9 8 7 6 5 4 3 2 1

Pages by Joy Freeman (www.pagesbyjoy.com)
Printed in the United States of America

Dedicated to our patient fans.
Knowing you were waiting kept us going.

ACKNOWLEDGEMENTS

Once again, most of our chapter titles come from music. So think of this as the playlist for the book. Many thanks to the artists who defined the shape of these chapters.

Find a Way (Nico and Vinz)

Inner Universe (Yoko Kanno)

Who Can It Be Now? (Men at Work)

Hang on to Yourself (David Bowie)

Deep Rapture (Sammy Fain)

Going out Strange (Rollins Band)

Get out Alive (Three Days Grace)

Ebb Tide (Righteous Brothers)

Keep Your Distance (Richard Thompson)

Peekaboo (Devo)

Breathing Underwater (Metric)

Hurt (Nine Inch Nails)

Lost Cause (Imagine Dragons)

Stand and Deliver (Adam Ant)

Head of Medusa (Otep)

The Snake (Al Wilson)

O Fortuna (Carl Orff)

Requiem (VNV Nation)

Nightmare (Avenged Sevenfold)

You Always Hurt the One You Love (Mills Brothers)

Forty Six and 2 (Tool)

Hospital Beds (Cold War Kids)

Left Behind (Slipknot)

Between the Lines (Sara Bareilles)

Kingdom (VnV Nation)

The Greatest (Sia)

The Sun Ain't Gonna Shine Anymore (Righteous Brothers)

I'll Keep Coming (Low Roar)

Giants in the Ocean (Sky Eats Airplane)

Season of the Witch (Donovan)

All Along the Watchtower (Jimi Hendrix)

Too Far Gone (Sixpence None the Richer)

Stone in My Hand (Everlast)

Running on the Rocks (Shriekback)

Long Time Gone (Crosby, Stills, Nash and Young)

AVALANCHE

INTRODUCTION

Victoria Victrix pinched the bridge of her nose. Her jaws hurt, she had been clenching them so hard. She began to type again.

I need to backtrack, to before Metis fell. That's okay, Reader. It'll get you up to speed.

CHAPTER ONE

Find a Way

MERCEDES LACKEY AND CODY MARTIN

The last few days had been a whirlwind of action for John and Sera. From the assault on Ultima Thule, their near defeat and final victory there, to being immediately thrust back into the "real world" of Atlanta as soon as they were conscious enough to be shoved onto an ECHO transport plane, there hadn't been a moment to pause for a breath. It all seemed entirely too surreal: one moment, fighting for their lives in a strange re-creation of Nazi Paradise. Collapsing, thinking that they were dead—at least they had fought on to the end, trying to save as many as they could—and then being saved themselves at the last moment by the Metisians. There had been the arguments and meetings, afterwards: what to do with the prisoners, how to split up the spoils of war in terms of recovered Thulian tech and materials, and so on. Bella and the Commissar both had thought it best that John and Sera get back to Atlanta, to HQ, stat; an uncomfortable amount of those arguments had been what to *do* with John and Sera themselves. The troops on the ground were for the most part thankful, or just in awe, of what had happened during the fighting. The top brass, however . . . they conveyed Fear, Envy, and worst of all, Greed when it came to just who was going to be able to call on the fiery duo. Three of the Seven Deadly Sins, if John's memory was correct. Of course, his memory might not have been; he'd never been all that conversant in religion before, and Sera didn't seem inclined to spout Bible verses and doctrine so much as cryptic responses or things that were, well, more *universal* than Biblical. All the same, the feeling in the air back

3

at Ultima Thule was decidedly not friendly for John and Sera, so back to Atlanta it was. Even their comrades had been on edge, until Old Man Bear had broken the tension. Since then, things had been more relaxed at HQ.

There had been another thing John was contending with. He was picking up on the emotions of others, and not just in a natural, "able to read people" sort of way. He could actually *feel* what others were feeling sometimes. It had taken his breath away, the first time, and still rocked him to his core whenever it happened now. But he was getting used to it...with Sera's help. He wasn't surprised as much anymore when it happened; he was beginning to be able to control when he let the emotions of others in. It was still the depth of it all that overwhelmed him; maybe because he was used to regulating his own emotions, and was habituated over his life to react to them. With other people...it wasn't so much as colors mixing and melding, as much as it was two different strains of music coming together, and not always in harmony. It was the best way that he could think to describe it. Some people were a lot easier to be around, all the healers and empaths, for instance; shielding other people *out* meant they kept their own emotions *in*. Bulwark, strangely, was completely unreadable. John figured it might have been an extension of his other powers, but didn't have much of a chance to pursue the answer to that question.

And then there was Vickie, who had some sort of barrier of her own. She wasn't a psychic of any sort, so it had to be magic. He still got the heebie-jeebies when it came to magic, despite how much of his gear—even his HUD and Overwatch rig—ran on it. John kind of wondered how the heck *that* worked though— magical/emotional shielding. He hadn't even gotten anything out of her when he'd inadvertently zapped her, and you'd have thought being hit by a "Celestial" bitch-slap would have made her feel pretty damn strongly...but the only time she'd slipped was when she'd thought about Red Djinni.

That had been a painful exchange. He and Sera both had been lapped by waves of grief and longing that had come off of Vickie; it was only Sera's moderating influence, John suspected, that kept him from being completely overwhelmed. He did his best trying to counsel Vickie, and comfort her without being patronizing; he'd had enough experience with doing that when he was still Big Army, being a team leader and helping the Joes under his command. Still, she seemed mired in her own pain; it particularly stung him in that it reminded him of when Sera was going through her own trials while his memory was gone. In the end, Vickie had closed up...those weird shields of her own coming up, and completely cutting off the feed of her emotions to John and Sera. She said she was fine, but it was clear that she just wanted to end the interaction. It was probably for the best; pushing things too far, too fast would have more than likely been counterproductive. She was his friend, and he would offer her whatever help he could give, but she still had to find her own way, in the end.

Besides the troubles that Vic was going through, something else had stuck out to John about that night. When she had tried to do her magic "reading" on him, to determine if he was going to be a danger to others, *something* now intimately a part of him had reacted badly, before he was even aware of it. *Celestial. That had been the word that she was trying to finish when she got thrown into a wall by whatever defensive impulse was building, before I clamped down on it.* He'd done his best to seem nonchalant about it, but in reality he was scared to death. It only got worse after he saw the raw, unedited footage of himself and Sera during the fighting in Ultima Thule. Although he had been there, and had done all of those things...seeing it from the outside perspective, what it must have looked like to other people...that, more than anything, shook him up. They *were* awesome. And terrifying. More than anything, the footage conveyed to him how *fast* they were together; the amount of destruction they could dish out in a short amount of time was staggering. John had seen artillery—and experienced it, on the wrong end—and airpower, and those two things were frightening enough. But that wasn't just a single person, or even a couple, that were capable of those things. It was teams of people, coupled with technology and entire logistical trains. Take one piece out of that puzzle, and it all fell apart.

The footage drove home that "John and Sera" were a power unto themselves, and a different one from anything the world had seen so far. And, so, John was frightened.

There was temptation to look at the footage again—easy enough to do, since he and Sera were officially on "detached duty," playing Vickie's bodyguards while the VIPs and select ECHO leads were in Metis itself. All he had to do was give Overwatch a couple of commands and he could view it again as many times as he wanted. But there was fear and even a little revulsion, too. He had detonated bombs that had leveled entire buildings, and called in airstrikes that had done the same or more. He had once cooked an entire hangar filled with Kriegers and Krieger armor. When he had seen what he and Sera had been capable of, when they were completely drained... it was *beyond*. He didn't *want* to be—well, *that*. Whatever that was. Tapped into raw, unfettered power. It set them apart in a way very few metahumans had been before... and the world hadn't been kind to those metas.

Sera interrupted his musings with a hot cup of tea. "You are troubled," she said simply, sitting down beside him. "May I help?" They were sitting on the couch, back in Vickie's apartment again, generally taking up space and making sure she had whatever help she needed. Most of the time, Grey and Herb already had Vickie's needs taken care of, so John and Sera spent their time talking, drinking tea, and keeping an eye out for... anything.

He did his best to smile wanly. "I imagine you're the only one that could, darlin'." He took his cup of tea, transferring it to his left hand before pulling her closer with his right. "Guess I can't hide anythin' from you."

She blinked at him, slowly. "You could, if you chose. I am glad that you do not choose to do so. What troubles you so?"

John thought for a few moments. "Me. You. Us. All of *this*." Effortlessly, he called flame to the arm that was wrapped around her; he already knew that their fires could never hurt each other. The ease with which he could call his fires, now, and keep them going... before, control had been his biggest issue. He had learned breathing exercises, even meditation, to keep his fires from going nova on him; every time he had decided to use his flames before his... transformation, he had needed immense concentration to prevent the fire from ramping up and going wild, like it had when he had escaped from the Facility. He'd been close to losing it like that a few times; if it hadn't been for Vickie, he would have probably unintentionally cooked his friends and teammates alive by accident a couple of those times. "It's a lot to deal with. That, and the... other stuff. The Futures, our battle-sense, feelin' things and being able to just 'bout read people's thoughts... I don't know how you did it all on your own."

To his relief, she laughed a little. "Because I was not *human*, beloved. I could not handle it alone, now."

"Well, there is that, I suppose." He shook his head. "Still. How are we goin' to deal with it now? I mean...what can we do with all of this power? It's makin' my head spin, if'n I'm bein' honest."

Her brows creased, as she thought, and there was some uncertainty in her voice. "I moderate what you can do. I am the—the gauge through which the power flows. Vickie was right, we have mapped the limits of our abilities, there at Ultima Thule. That is as much as we can bear; attempts to manipulate more will... not end well." She offered a tentative attempt at a smile. "I sense this does not comfort you."

He shrugged, pecking her on the cheek. "It was a good try." He sighed heavily. "I figure we'll just have to play it by ear. Bein' mere mortals, we'll do the best that we can."

They could hear Vickie talking in the next room, but not what she was saying; she was probably on private mode to Bella or Nat or one of the other ECHO or CCCP leads that were in Metis. Grey was nowhere in sight, which meant he was probably sitting on one of Vickie's desks, kibbitzing. Herb was toddling across the floor with one of Vickie's meals-in-a-can; John could swear it looked like the little rockman was bigger every time he saw him. *How do you grow a pet rock?*

There wasn't much of a view out the window; the living room window looked directly into the canopy of a huge live-oak tree. The tree's proximity made coming in that way—at least for JM and Sera—a bit of a trick. It was a rare moment of peace, although John mistrusted it for that very reason. They were playing bodyguard to Vickie for a reason, after all. Just because her role as creator and implementer of Overwatch Two was only known by a handful of people, it was a bigger handful than John liked. So far as he was concerned they were long past the critical mass it would take for the secret to somehow leak. Three people could keep a secret if two of them were dead, as the old saying went; sometimes, he thought even that was too many with some secrets.

The danger to Vickie wasn't just from supposed "allies" or other interested parties. The Thulians—including at least Ubermensch and Valkyria—that got away from Ultima Thule were at the top of the list. They—and the huge technodragon that they rode out on—were still very much a threat. Taking out Vickie would, despite the backups and contingencies that she had in place, be a huge blow for the global resistance against the Kriegers; one that they couldn't afford to risk.

"Y'know, it's 'bout time to start thinkin' 'bout dinner. Vickie has those god-awful canned meals—havin' eaten my fair share, I know how bad they can be—but I figure we need some real chow. What're you feelin' like, darlin'?" If they couldn't decide, there was always little Thea; she always had something on the stove, hot and ready to be ladled out to hungry comrades after a shift.

"Is there a food truck near?" she asked, with a note of longing. He chuckled. Atlanta had some very good food trucks, still running despite shortages and the odd Thulian- or gang-attack, and John had gotten Sera addicted to the variety.

"I'll ask Over—" he began. Then—

—it felt like a bomb went off inside of his skull, while a dozen sledgehammers were pounding it in from the outside. Almost at the same time, he and Sera were both on the floor, frozen; he could barely see Sera's face, and her eyes were almost completely rolled up in their sockets. He felt his own vision go dark, then stark white as something shot in like a lightning bolt through the pain. Dimly, he heard Vickie yelling—not at him or at Sera, but into her Overwatch gear.

Something's ... bad ... wrong.

He knew—though he didn't know how—that it wasn't a dream, or a hallucination, but a vision of something that was actually happening, *right then.*

Fire. Screaming and death. Explosions and people being crushed by falling rubble. Actinic beams of energy and the thunderous stomp of thousands of armored boots. And, finally, a gigantic dragon, roaring and glaring hatefully at everything below it.

Metis was falling, and there was nothing that they could do about it.

When he and Sera came to, again almost at the exact same time, he first noticed that his fingernails had dug deep, red furrows into his palms, and his jaw was sore; he must have been clenching it or grinding his teeth. Their cups of tea had shattered when they had hit the floor, and the couch had been kicked away; either by him or Sera, he didn't know, but it was now very misshapen and piled against the far wall.

"Johnny! Sera!" Vickie was shouting, not via his Overwatch rig, but physically from the other room. "Are you okay?" Without waiting for an answer, she continued. "The Thulians found Metis, and things just went nuclear FUBAR."

It took John a few seconds to form words. It felt like his tongue couldn't find purchase in his mouth, and he kept slurring and mumbling. He could see—and feel—Sera struggling just as he was. "We—we're fine, Vickie. We're feeling it happen." John, much more slowly than he would have liked, pulled himself to his feet. He swayed for a moment, thinking he was going to pass out; it was like his blood pressure had just taken a dive, and he felt lightheaded. Then it passed, and he was steady again. He helped Sera to her feet; once he was sure that she was okay, they both started towards Vickie's workroom. "We saw it, Vic. This isn't just an attack; it's extermination. They need to get as many people out as possible, and goddamned *fast*."

"On it," she shouted tersely. They had staggered to the door of her Overwatch suite; there were camera feeds from Bella, Bulwark, Ramona, Pride, Nat, and Moji.

"Is there any lala angel way you guys can get there?" she asked through gritted teeth, as her fingers flew over her keyboard.

"Darlin'?" John looked to Sera. Even with how fast they could fly—which was pretty goddamned fast, all things considered—it'd still take them hours to get to Metis. Hours that Metis didn't have. They both realized this, and John watched Sera confirm it when she shook her head gravely. "Negative, comrade. Unless you've got some sorta rabbit you can pull out of your hat and get us there like you got us outta the Himalayas, we're not gettin' to Metis before the show is over."

"*Futui!*" she swore. "No, there's no landing pad and no time for anyone to put one down for me. They need you! I—"

"Hey! You ain't wrong. *But!* They also need us here. Covering you, so you can cover them. That's our job right now, and it's the one we're in a position to do. We don't know what else these shifty bastards have up their sleeves; if they start strikin' anywhere else, we need to be ready to pounce on that shit. So keep on keepin' on, comrade. Alright?" John didn't mean to use the Command Voice, but it sort of came through. They needed Vickie to do what she did best, now more than ever. If she was distracted, it could mean someone died. Maybe a lotta someones.

People they knew. People they all *loved*. And, as much as it hurt him to put it before all of that, people that mattered to the future.

She nodded curtly, and kept her eyes on the monitors, her hands flying over the keyboard, muttering into her own microphone.

Wordlessly, John and Sera both withdrew to the doorway. They both knew that they had to be extra vigilant, especially now. John was the first to speak. "I wasn't lyin' in there; she's our first priority. We're in the best position to protect her, and she's important; Vic is a force multiplier, and having her active keeps more of our people alive."

Sera nodded, and glints of gold began to form deep in her eyes. "She cannot watch *here* and *there* at the same time. We must be the watchers here."

John held his hands out, palms up. "Tell me what to do, darlin'. I'm with you all the way."

"Remember how it *felt,* to know what our foes were about to do? Be that, again. Then stretch out your wings, and feel the wind of *now* uplift them, until you can see all of the city ..." She placed her hands atop his, and he allowed her senses to guide his.

John felt things go still around the two of them. Time slowed down, and the world around them became dim for a moment. Then it was as if the world was moving and they weren't connected to it anymore; in a few instants, the seasons changed a thousand times, the sun and moon had risen and set in a strobe, and then everything snapped back like a rubber band to the *Now*. John watched as Vickie's apartment was at first frozen, and then started to vibrate, like a film going off reel. It was jarring when it settled back, as if nothing had happened. Slowly, blurred and ghostly versions of himself and Sera started walking through the apartment, going in different directions. First, there were just two. Then four. Then eight. Then sixteen. The blurred copies kept multiplying until it looked like there were superfast streams of motion moving through the entire apartment.

They are our possibilities. He knew without actually knowing that it was Sera's voice, guiding him. Slowly, his comprehension of the scene expanded outward from the apartment; first to the floor they were on, then to the building, then the block, and so on until he had the entire city in his mind. He knew that Sera was seeing the same thing he was, in perfect clarity. It looked like rivers of golden and blue light running between the buildings and on the streets; he realized that those rivers were comprised of the lives and possible futures of everyone that lived in Atlanta. Very gradually, at certain intersections of the rivers and eddies, he saw... mires. Spots where Futures ended, cut short or drastically altered. With a gasp that took place in neither time nor space, he realized that those were people dying from violence or otherwise being harmed. Or, rather, that they would be.

He also started to feel all of the emotions of those people, their lives, their Futures. Even the emotions of those that would die. John felt all of it welling up in him, threatening to spill over; he felt like a kettle, ready to boil over, like the top of his head was going to pop off—it was too much. He felt his own panic behind it all, all the love, pain, death, life, hate, joy, anger, jealousy, sadness, it was *everything* and all at *once*—

Peace, be still, he heard in his heart, and it was as if there was a "volume" control and she had turned it down. He could still feel all these things, but now they were like a sort of dissonant music playing in the background. He settled, and felt himself calming down. He felt shaken; it was like brushing too close with madness, losing his sense of self and succumbing to... whatever all of that had been. Breathing without breathing, he regained his composure. Now he could see the potentials, without being drawn in with them, focusing on the individual threads. It wasn't quite omniscience; he imagined, offhandedly in the back of his mind, that it must be somewhat like what Gamayun could do. He also knew that they couldn't do this forever; it was taxing, extending their senses out this far, and they wouldn't be able to maintain it forever.

I could, once. But he didn't sense regret or loss behind Sera's thought, only a feeling of *that was then, this is now.* He felt her doing something he could only think of as... *sorting.* Like someone going through a basket of colored threads and looking for the ones that ended in a particular color. And sensed then that she was not finding what she was looking for.

I am looking for great danger, she answered the unspoken question. *It is not here, not now, not here soon, but—*

John felt himself returning to a certain point, a certain place... it was there in Vickie's apartment, and *now.* Not something soon to come, but something happening. It was as if he and Sera had returned from a fugue state. Their heads snapped as one to stare at one of Vickie's monitors; it was glowing brightly in gold and blue, standing out against everything else. Then the effect ended, and they were fully back in the present.

"Somethin' is happenin', right now, Vic." He and Sera both strode towards Vickie's battle station, on either side of her chair.

"There," Sera said, pointing at the monitor. It was the one with Molotok's Overwatch feed. He had just run out from a hallway that terminated onto the entrance to a landing pad, cantilevered over empty space. The view was beautiful...save for over a dozen Supernauts in their bulky armor, armed with arm-mounted machine guns and flamethrowers. At the very end of the landing pad stood Worker's Champion, cradling a box. As one, they all seemed to turn to face Molotok. There were a few tense seconds of silence.

Moji called something out in Russian. What came in John's ears was the usual Russian gibberish—but somehow, through his connection with Sera, he understood the sense of it. *"You have blood-crimes to repay, Uncle. If you surrender, I'll make sure you don't suffer. It is better than what anyone else will offer you for betraying your family, country, your world...your very comrades. I will not make the offer a second time, as it is more than you deserve already."*

"It is an offer you cannot deliver, boy." Worker's Champion's face was utterly devoid of anything approaching emotion; even his delivery was carefully modulated, betraying not the slightest hint of what he might be really thinking or feeling. *"If only you understood—"*

"Fuck you! Understand? Others may want to understand why you are a traitor. I do not. I only see an enemy of my people. I kill my people's enemies; it is what good soldiers do, you swine. Spare me your words, and die like a goddamned Russian!"

Worker's Champion nodded once, still stony-faced and cold. *"So be it."* With that, all of the Supernauts raised their weapons. They would have been better off if they had turned their machine guns, grenade launchers, and flamethrowers on themselves. Molotok didn't even bother to dodge their attacks; he marched determinedly from one Supernaut soldier to another. Explosions went off around and even on his body, detonating harmlessly. Bullets bounced away and ricocheted in oblique angles from his body, sometimes going back towards the Supernauts that had fired the rounds. And the superheated napalm that struck Molotok simply dripped off of him. Looking through the Overwatch camera that was from his point of view, and from the ones that were hovering in the vicinity, he looked like a wrathful god come to exact vengeance.

He was an expert at *Systema* and several other martial arts; he didn't use any of his expertise as he fought the Supernauts. He would just walk up to one, grab the armored soldier by his limbs, and rip him apart. Sometimes he would take the Supernaut's head off with a backhanded strike, other times pulling an arm and a leg off and casting them aside casually, or splitting a soldier in half like a man pulling apart a wishbone. It was awful and awesome, in the unceremonious brutality of it all. The final Supernaut was quivering in place; he had expended all of his munitions, and his arm-mounted machine guns, grenade launchers, and flamethrowers all clicked and hissed empty. Pulling a bayonet from his boot, Molotok calmly walked up to the armored soldier, grabbing him by the back of his helmet before pulling his head onto the bayonet. The soldier gave a final startled shriek before falling to the ground, still twitching with the grip of the bayonet sticking out from his helmet's eyeslit.

Most of the napalm had gone out by that time; Molotok's suit was ruined in several places, but the skin underneath was untouched. His chest heaved, not from exertion, but from unbridled rage. Worker's Champion had stood, watching the entire gruesome slaughter. Now, he set down the box he had been carrying, and faced Molotok. There was a standoff that, while only a few seconds long, seemed to last an eternity, before Molotok screamed.

"*Fascista!*"

Now all of Molotok's finesse as a fighter was evident. For metahumans with super strength and resilience—the two often seemed to manifest together, for obvious reasons that a meta that was super strong, but couldn't withstand the stresses of what he was using it for, wouldn't live very long—most of them relied on those abilities to simply power through their opponents. Molotok was not one of those metahumans. He had been taught and learned, from a young age, to fight as if he was weak, as if he was fragile. To marshall his strength, to protect himself from every strike as if it might be fatal. To strike where the enemy was weak, and defend from where he was strong.

As he attacked Worker's Champion, he did so with perfect

form, graceful and blindingly fast, precise with every blow and measured with every defense.

He was beautiful. And he was doomed.

Worker's Champion had none of his protégé's flourish or artistry. But he did have power. He didn't need to outmaneuver Molotok; even the most skillful strike, he simply cut through, using his own strength and nearly impervious skin to best the younger man. It was tragic. Molotok, no matter what injury he took, continued to attack. First, it was a split lip. Then, a mashed eye. A broken finger; a hand. An arm. His ankle. A dislocated shoulder. All the ribs on one side cracked. Teeth on the right side of his mouth, shattered to splinters.

But still, Molotok fought. Mustering the very last of his strength, he finally connected a solid blow to Worker's Champion's mouth. The sound of the impact was indescribable; like steel meeting steel with the force of a dynamite explosion. Molotok's last good hand was ruined; bleeding bones jutting from skin and fingers turned all the wrong way. But... Worker's Champion was bleeding. Three thin lines of blood crept down his lips; the blood was his own, and for a moment his eyes grew wide at the sight of it on the back of his hand as he wiped it away.

With a flick of the back of his hand, Worker's Champion shattered the bones in Molotok's remaining arm, ensuring he couldn't even lift it any more. Molotok fell to his knees, very obviously struggling to stay conscious.

John felt so helpless, and it infuriated him. His fists were balled, his knuckles white in impotent fury. *If only we were there!*

There was a sound like the rush of wind while manning the door gun on a helo, diving on an LZ. Suddenly, John found himself not looking at a monitor and seeing through a camera, but *feeling* through Molotok. There was so much pain; the physical was there, and almost blinding, but it wasn't the worst pain. The worst of it was the feeling of no longer being able to continue, to pursue the fight, to finish his opponent, and the threat to his loved ones. Molotok felt failure surge through him, redoubling and making him sick with grief. His life was ebbing out, he knew that; even though he had never been injured in such a way, he knew that he was bleeding internally, and it would soon kill him.

The despair in him was so terrible it completely overwhelmed the pain, and threatened to drown him before his body died.

John shared that despair—hell, it was a reflection of the despair he had *lived* with for years—and without thinking, he "reached out" to his friend and comrade. He didn't know what he would or *could* do, he only knew he could not allow Moji to die alone.

That was when John "felt" Sera with him, and felt her reaching to Moji too...and together they somehow touched him. *"Fear not, brave one,"* he "heard" in his mind, and knew that Molotok heard it too. *"This is not an end, and your comrades will take up the fight and never forget you. See the door? It waits to welcome you."* John couldn't see it, but he sensed Molotok *could,* and sensed that Sera had muted the Russian's pain as well. He willed Moji to "hear" him. This was—it was anything but natural for him, but he willed Molotok to sense that *he* was there, too, a friend that he trusted, and that the friend was letting him know that this was...all right. And that it was okay for him to let go.

The despair ebbed, then drained away. John tried to continue willing that support for his comrade. He thought he was succeeding when there was a strangled shout, full of fury and pain and desperation, and Moji turned his head.

It was Natalya, staring at her *bolshoi brat* with horror and outrage.

"She will finish this, I pledge you," Sera breathed gently.

"I know this. It is her nature; she only knows how to succeed." Behind that single thought, John and Sera felt everything that Molotok—no, his callsign was too impersonal for such a deeply personal interaction—everything *Moji* felt for Natalya. His *sestra.* But more than that...the love of his life. He was the perfect Russian metahuman. Darling of the media, a ladies' man as well as a respectable gentleman, when the situation dictated. A dedicated soldier, but also well-rounded and well-read. And the only thing he had ever wanted was Natalya's love and companionship. Wanted it enough to stand by her even if it was only to be as her "brother"; when she was right, when she was wrong, when she wouldn't take bribes like everyone else, when she fought for truth, when she was exiled to America. When she was certain to die—he would always stand by her.

He stood by her now, for who she was. For the woman he loved her as.

A smile creased Moji's cracked and bleeding lips, and he felt no more pain. Only comfort, and certainty. *Vengeance; this will not go unanswered. There will be rest.*

Distantly, John *felt* another surge of terrible grief.

Vickie.

The part of him that was still in Atlanta—detached but still whole—moved the two steps it took to reach her, took a shoulder in each hand, and squeezed them gently, reassuringly, as she shook with silent sobs.

He felt himself saying, "We're with him. He's not alone," and knew the words were his and Sera's both. *So surreal. Needed, necessary. Kindness always is.*

Moji's camera registered Worker's Champion picking him up until his battered face was level with the old Russian's—which showed no more emotion than it had before. There was movement as Worker's Champion pulled back his arm.

The feed cut out, leaving only Red Saviour's feed, as Natalya watched the man she and Moji had called "Uncle" murder her best friend in the coldest of cold blood.

John and Sera both felt Moji move on. It wasn't violent, like his death; more of a letting go. There wasn't the despair, or grief that he had been feeling. Still that calm satisfaction. In that final moment, a single thought that encompassed so much more emotion rang out in both of their heads.

"I love you, sestra. Keep going."

Then the moment was gone. John and Sera both fell to the floor at the same time; John behind Vickie's chair, Sera still in the doorway. They both felt as if they had run back-to-back marathons on no sleep while carrying double their body weight in rucksacks. This was another first for them, and another extension of their new powers. Vickie wasn't the only one with tears streaming down her cheeks; both John and Sera were crying, with no shame in it. They had not just watched, but *felt* a loved one, a comrade, pass on.

Vickie was already talking again; after all, she had a job to do and couldn't focus on any one crisis. No one had to tell her she had to go on, and that what she *felt* didn't matter. Already she was telling Bella what was happening, and breaking that off to snap directions at Ramona and Merc.

John was the first to talk, murmuring gently to Sera.

"We still have a job to do, too, darlin'. Up an' at 'em." There wasn't any feeling behind his words, despite trying to sound sanguine. Still, Sera nodded her assent, and took his hand when he offered it to help her up from the floor.

It was everything that they could do to push their sense of the Futures out far enough to cover the building. They were still vaguely aware of Vickie, coordinating the evacuation of Metis in the background. Like John had said, they all had a job to do, so the two of them focused on theirs so that Vickie could concentrate on hers.

They had regained some of their strength as the minutes stretched on; they kept their focus on the building, making sure that nothing untoward was going to happen to Vickie. Still, from what they could hear...the news was not good. Arthur Chang, dead, as well as a number of the delegates. Thousands of Metisians had also been lost. The city destroyed. Most of their people—save for poor Moji—had escaped, though none of them were unscathed.

It was going to be a long, long day.

Vickie's hair was plastered to her scalp with sweat, and she shook and shivered with shock. *How could everything have gone so wrong, so quickly?* "Oh gods, what do we *do* with them?" she wailed aloud. "There's not enough secure ECHO bases on the planet to hide all of—"

Eight-Ball was pinging like a crazy thing. "*Yes, I know!*" she screamed at it, without looking at it. "*The shit has hit the industrial fan! Leave me alone!*"

And just at the moment that she felt as if she was going to crack wide open and lose it all...a pair of hands settled on her shoulders, and calm and renewed energy flowed into her, like nothing she had ever felt before.

"Steady, little sister," Sera murmured from behind her. "You do not face this alone. One more minute, two, or thirty will make no difference. We will find answers now, and more answers later."

Right. It doesn't matter if we patch something together that won't hold, as long as we start on something that will *hold right away while the patch buys us time...*

"Okay," she said aloud. "I've got twenty or thirty, no more than forty Metisian saucers in the air with various numbers of refugees, most of them from Metis. Metis is toast and no point in worrying about it right now, put that out of our minds for the moment. *Right now* I need to find someplace to stash the Metisians and their saucers where the Kriegers won't find them and they *also* won't get abducted by our dear allies."

"So...that's what, 'bout a thousand Metisian refugees we're talkin' 'bout?"

"Give or take. The thing is, near as I can tell, even a kid knows enough about Metisian tech to make him valuable." She clutched both her hands in her hair, as she listened with half an ear to Bella's speech.

"Between what is in the saucers themselves, and what even a child knows, yes," Sera confirmed.

John shook his head. "The problem isn't how valuable they are— well, no, that is a problem—the bigger problem right now is that there's so damn many of 'em. I've got some places that are out of the way, but not for nearly that many folks. We need somewhere to bed 'em down, where they'll be accessible, but safe at the same time." John chewed on his lower lip, his arms crossed in front of his chest. "I don't trust any military with 'em, not ours or anyone else's. So, landin' 'em at a military airstrip is outta the question."

"I've got Alex Tesla's secret list of bug-out bases and they could handle maybe a hundred," Vickie confirmed. "You know what will happen if they land anywhere open."

"Let's keep at least some of those bases in reserve, for Metisian VIPs. Best to shuttle them there *after* we've got all of the rest of 'em secure. Problem is, how in the hell do you hide 'bout forty flyin' saucers? Without Area 51, or anyone possibly connected to it?"

"If I trusted Mom and Dad's bosses...but I don't. They'd have to report something this big upstream and *poof!*" She made a little explosion motion with her fingers, "Here come the Men In Black to haul them away."

"Exactly; same problem as Big Army. We're keepin' these people out of government hands for as long as humanly possible; let 'em decide what suits 'em best, when it's safe for 'em to come outta hidin'."

Eight-Ball's pings had turned into a kind of warble. Vickie had reached out a hand to dial down the volume, but it was obvious that either the program had malfunctioned or it thought it had something important.

"Are there wilderness areas we could put them down in—" Vickie shook her head at her own suggestion and giggled with an edge of hysteria in it, as Sera sent out another wave of calm. "Dear gods, can you imagine Metisians trying to *camp?*"

"Not enough bleach to keep those jumpsuits blindin' white.

Maybe they have gizmos for that, though..." John started pacing, shaking his head with a look of consternation on his face. He paused midstride, glancing over at the monitor that was hooked up to Eight-Ball. The screen was flicking through a series of black and white images: group shots of men in lab coats and suits, rockets in flight, schematics, profile shots of individual men, views of laboratories...

Smart little bastard!

"Vic, Sera—hold up a second." John turned to face the women, pointing at the monitor. "Your gizmo, it's got it: 'Operation Paperclip.' Not Nazis this time, though. *Metisians.*"

"Wait, *what?*" Vickie said, looking at him in confusion, then following his pointing finger to Eight-Ball's monitor. "Operation—" Her face remained locked in confusion for a moment. "Oh, okay, I... but that's the problem, not the solution! *Where do we send them?*"

"Is it the problem, though? Think around it, switch the parts. Everyone wants 'em 'cause they're *Metisians.* How do we fix that?"

Suddenly Eight-Ball's screen blanked. Then it showed the map of South America. A red dot on that map that was in the location they all knew too well now, Metis. Eight-Ball zoomed in on the map, showing the outlines of the countries of South America, and the Peruvian Andes. And out. And in. And out. And in.

The third time, both Vickie's hands flew to her mouth. "Oh. My. Gods. *Ohmygods!* That's *it!*" She whirled and her hands went to her main keyboard. "Overwatch: Open Metis: All. Bella, I need your ECHO diplomatic override. I need to talk directly to the president of Peru."

Bella's reply came immediately. *"You've got a bypass to his secretary in the diplomatic protocols, patch me through. Explain what you need to both of us at the same time."*

Vickie's fingers flew again, and a moment later she was speaking in Spanish. John's Spanish was *just* good enough to understand that she was convincing the Peruvian president's secretary that this was enough of an emergency to put her through to his desk, interrupting whatever else he was doing.

Since his skies—at least those over Metis—were full of Thulian ships, that probably was a given.

"Señor Presidente—" Vickie began.

"English, please," he replied. *"For brevity. The Thulians appear to be leaving our airspace. Are we to expect them back?"*

"Not that I know of. I am calling about a different matter. ECHO CEO Bella Parker is also on the call. We have several hundred Metisian refugees—"

"One thousand, three hundred and twenty four," Bella interrupted.

"—in the air, in stealthed craft that cannot stay up there forever. Every one of them is a valuable asset. Every one of them has basic knowledge of Metisian science and access to more information. Every nation on Earth will want them. *They were all born on Peruvian soil. Do I have to make myself plainer?"*

"...Madre de Dios..."

Bella's mind worked as quickly as Vickie's had. *"Mister President, I am fairly sure I can get a substantial percentage, if not all, of the Metisians to agree to work on behalf and for the benefit of Peru, no matter* what *country they end up working in. But they need the protection of actual, physical, Peruvian papers and passports, and they need these things yesterday."*

"Without that protection, they'll end up like the German scientists at the end of World War II—in the hands of whoever grabs them first," Vickie added. "Once they're Peruvian citizens I am fairly sure that all of South America, and probably whoever *doesn't* manage to get one of them in their countries, will take *serious* offense at any of them 'vanishing.'"

"Not to mention that if they vanish, there's not a lot of incentive for the other countries of the world to do anything if the Thulians come looking for them. Give them Peru's protection, keep them sovereign and free with ECHO's help, and you have a young, inexhaustible gold mine on your hands in the form of what they'll part with, or what other countries will pay for their services. Plus, whatever they can decipher from what you guys get out of the wreck of Metis."

"Señorita Parker, you are a powerful negotiator." The president laughed shakily. *"I see your points. Give me perhaps half an hour to determine logistically how many people each of our embassies and consulates can process, and how many we can process how quickly here. Then you and I can begin sending these...stealthed craft...to land directly where it is most expedient."*

"Okay, I am cutting out of this conversation. Good luck, Parker, Señor Presidente." With a flick of a key, Vickie cut her connection to the negotiations going on...somewhere in the air.

Sera looked from Vickie to John in bewilderment. "What has just occurred?" she asked.

"Security for the Metisians, with any luck. Just gotta hope that none of the other governments out there get shit-scared an' try to brazen through gettin' some of the eggheads. I don't think it'll happen, but it'll be up to Bella an' Spin Doctor to calm those waters." John grinned, his eyes flitting back and forth as he was thinking about the possibilities that this new arrangement had opened.

"And Saviour, and Pride. They're all up on international diplomacy . . . and have none. And Saviour is sneaky. She'll point out all the ways kidnappings could happen and we'll get the Metisians to safe harbors once they have their papers," said Vickie, looking wilted and exhausted, but no longer in despair.

"Still, what is this . . . 'Operation Paperclip'?" Sera looked back to John.

"Grab by the US government an' some cloak an' dagger types to get as many Nazi scientists after WWII before the Soviets could snag 'em. Big operation to whitewash their pasts, get them US citizenship, and bring them over here. It was all done to sidestep a law that said we couldn't have anybody associated with the Nazi party doin' work for us, essentially."

"That was what Eight-Ball was trying to show us. That this was what was going to happen unless we got them some *other* kind of citizenship to protect them," Vickie added, patting Eight-Ball's keyboard. "Then he showed us that they actually, already *had* citizenship. Metis was hidden in the Peruvian Andes, and has been since . . . geez, I dunno, the 1920s at least. So every Metisian we saved was certainly *born* there, born on Peruvian soil. We just had to make that absolutely official. Best way to do that was cut straight to the top and talk to *El Presidente*." She spread her hands wide. "*Now* every country on the planet that wants Metisian tech is going to have to talk to Peru. And every country on the planet has a vested interest in *protecting* Peru—from Thulians, and everything else."

"Eight-Ball is a pretty handy little toy, Vic. You an' Bella have done good. Try to relax until we hear back from the blueberry. I'm sure that there'll be plenty to do once we have the details ironed out. Best to try to figure out probable landing sites now, so we can plot out the best way to get our birds down without too many people takin' notice."

"Roger that." She turned back to her keyboard. "Overwatch: Open: All Metis craft. Open: Private: Bella."

It's still FUBAR. But maybe we can dig our way out, after all. Thank god for the firebombs... if they hadn't been here... She didn't finish that thought, because at that point; *El Presidente* and Bella had their plan.

Within twenty-four hours, Vickie and Bella had done the impossible: registered all of the surviving Metisians as Peruvian citizens with appropriate paperwork and passports, and gotten them all into (scattered) hiding places. John, all too well aware of how slowly the wheels of bureaucracy ground, could only marvel. That miracle alone would have made him a believer in the Infinite.

So now... they were waiting. He and Sera most particularly. Waiting for the next Thulian move on the shattered chessboard. Some shadow of that brief look at the Futures told him it was going to be bad.

Everyone was on high alert back at HQ. Battening down the hatches, as it were. Preparing to mobilize and move out—again. They were still nursing their wounds from Ultima Thule, and now the fall of Metis. And in deep mourning for Molotok... he and Sera had quietly discussed what they had inadvertently learned, and had agreed they would not tell the Commissar of the depth of Moji's feelings for her now. If ever. She was already devastated; the revelation that he had been deeply in love with her would probably destroy her. *After the war is over. If it ever is. If we survive it.* Somehow, deciding to put the revelation off made him feel more relieved than guilty. Usually keeping a secret had the opposite effect; he'd rather rip the Band-aid off and be done with it, then let things fester beneath the surface. But this situation... was more delicate than that. Given the Commissar's distrust of him, not only as an American, but now as... well, whatever he and Sera were, holding off on telling her about Moji was probably the wisest course of action.

Yet the attack, when it came, surprised even John and Sera.

They were both still guarding Vickie. They had put in their time at HQ, helping with preparations and readying everything in case they had to move out to defend the city, or go on the attack elsewhere. There was an air of anticipation everywhere. If the Thulians had hit Metis with such a large force, how long until they moved that force into the surrounding area? More questions, like how had they even managed to get that many troops and that much war material to Metis undetected. Where had they gone after? By what few probes or sensors remained, the Thulians had wiped Metis off the map, and then...disappeared. Hardly anything stood where Metis had been, and there were absolutely no survivors. That much was clear.

So, everyone waited. John desperately wanted to be outside, anywhere but in Vickie's apartment. He understood the job that they had been given was exceedingly important, knew it intellectually. But his heart and his gut wanted to be on the ground, in the thick of it, taking the fight back to the enemy. If only he didn't have the constraints that had been placed on him...he just needed someplace to push the dagger, and then he would destroy whatever enemy they faced. Whatever enemy *he* faced, whoever stood against—

A Seraphym uses the least power to the most impact. The needle of a laser, not the bludgeon of a sledgehammer. He brought his head up to see that Sera had turned away from the window to gaze solemnly at him. *Power is not ours to waste, beloved. We may not be Seraphym, but we are still constrained by the same laws. If we waste what we are given, or use it unwisely or with poor judgment, it will no longer be given to us.*

John took a deep breath, then exhaled it slowly. The mind-to-mind communication had been weird at first, but he was starting to get the hang of it. He knew it was useless to try to hide anything from Sera, but he still tried to calm himself, mask some of the darker...whatever he had been feeling before she had brought him back to Earth. *I know, darlin'. Just gets to be... frustratin', bein' cooped up in here while our friends are out there.*

Vickie semi-staggered out of her Overwatch room and paused, one hand on the wall. "Um," she said. "For the benefit of those who are not telepathically attached at the hip, want to use your vocal cords? 'Cause I can tell you're talking."

"Sorry, Vic. Just practicin', I guess. Unlike my better half, I'm still new to this sort of stuff." He stood up from the couch, brushing Sera's cheek with the back of his hand as he rose. "Anyone need tea or coffee? I figure it's 'bout that time."

"Any way you can give me eight hours of sleep in eight seconds instead?" Vickie asked hopefully.

John thought for a second, then looked to Sera. "No, but..."

Sera smiled slightly. "I used to help Bella when she was healing, with something she called 'angel juice'—which sounds terribly wrong, somehow. As if someone was putting me in a blender..."

Vickie actually managed a chuckle at that. "Seraphym! Will it blend?" she said.

"I think John and I can manage a...less intense version, together," Sera continued.

"An' then we'll *definitely* need coffee. You up for tryin' it, Vic?"

"So long as it doesn't involve zapping me into a wall again, absolutely." She ran a hand through her hair, which looked dry and lifeless. "We've got everyone that escaped from Metis their papers and into hiding and—"

John held up a hand. "Time for a battery recharge, first. Tell us when we're done refillin' your tank." He paused, thinking. "I guess there isn't a way for us to describe this without soundin' dirty, is there, love?" He looked to Sera, wriggling his eyebrows. She giggled, and held out her hand.

This is simple. Just as we did with Pavel—without having to turn our power into plasma first. He nodded, and took her hand, following her lead.

For him...for them...well, it was easy. Like sharing the warmth of a fire that they were all huddled around, but that he and Sera could turn up or turn down at will. It was an abstraction of what it really felt like, but it was all so complex, and that was the best way that he could think of it. He and Sera both willed for that fire to ramp up, for the heat to spread outwards from them and into Vickie. Not too much; it was more of a gentle caress than a shove or even a tap.

Through his new senses granted from telempathy, however, he could feel what it was like for Vickie. As a geomancer, energy came to her through the earth usually, and that was how her senses interpreted this. As a great upwelling of renewal and refreshment; from behind her shields a single image of *friendly lava* escaped. Her eyes widened, and her skin, which had been pale with fatigue, took on color again. He was reminded of how pale little Thea became pink when she stole energy from her "victims"—willing or unwilling. Vickie stood straighter, and let go of the wall, as her mouth formed a silent "oh" of surprise.

It was Sera who somehow understood when to cut it off, and actually eased off, rather than *cutting* off. She had the skill and appreciation for the power that they shared; while it was all raw and untempered for John, Sera was able to turn it with gentleness and control. Vickie stood there, blinking, for a few moments, licking her lips.

"Why do I taste scotch and cinnamon all of a sudden?" Vickie asked, her voice sounding *much* better, all of the dullness of her exhaustion gone from it.

John kept hold of Sera's hand. He didn't need it for their connection, but he still liked being in contact with her. "Just a taste of heaven, comrade. Still up for coffee?"

Of course Vickie couldn't just *rest*. That would be too easy, and folks like them never had things that easy. *It'd sure as hell be a nice change, though,* John thought. He felt Sera's agreement through their connection, and sent some *other* thoughts about what would be nice for the two of them. She blushed a little and wrinkled her nose at him. Odd, now that they were ... whatever it was that they were ... she was much more human in her expressions than she ever had been before. He wondered how much of that was due to her time being corporeal, and how much was due to them being reunited.

And how much she's learnin' from me, maybe.

Vickie had the TV tuned into some Overwatch feeds, four of them, split-screen, and kept an eye on them while sipping on coffee with a liberal dash of a cheap single malt in it. "I just keep this around for doctoring coffee," she explained, as she offered some to John, and he gave her a sideways look at the brand. "No point in wasting the good stuff when I'm already covering the flavor with coffee, cream and sugar."

"Fair enough. Can't say I'm a stranger to the practice myself." He proffered his cup; Vickie splashed in a good-sized dose before recapping the scotch.

They all sat down: John and Sera on the couch, and Vickie in her favorite recliner. She sipped her coffee, kept one eye on the television and the other squarely on John. "So. Suddenly you can go all remote viewing on me. You—" She pointed at Sera, "—I kind of guessed you could do that, from the way you popped up when you were needed, before. But this is a whole new thing for Tall, Dark, and Inflammable here. So ... anything you want to tell me?"

"Your honor, I plead the fifth," John said, holding his hands up in mock surrender, mug still in one. "To be quite honest, it wasn't all me. It was both of us, together. We've got a bit of juju when it comes to fightin'. Seein' things that can happen, that might happen, that *will* happen in a fight. With my reflexes, Sera's experience... we just make sure we're where we need to be, when we need to be there, and do what we need to do to have the fight go the way we want it to." He took a long draught from his spiked coffee, wincing slightly from the fumes. *I think the scotch she put in here is part diesel.* "What we did when Metis got hit? It was... I don't know, extendin' that same sort of feelin', that same sort of sense outwards. It isn't easy; took damn near everythin' we had, keepin' things stretched out like that."

"We were trying to sort the Futures, looking for troubles," Sera said, as he paused, somewhat at a loss for words. "I think that the only reason we were able to reach as far as Metis was because of your Overwatch... the connection with you, with John, with Bella and Bulwark, Natalya, and Ramona, and..." She hesitated.

"With Moji," Vickie supplied, her voice flat as she fought to contain her emotions. "The people wired with Overwatch Two."

"Part of it's magical, right? Maybe we tapped into it a bit. I mean, we're all pretty damned close besides, and a lotta what we were doin' seemed more 'bout feelin' than it did *knowin'*, if that makes any sense?"

Vickie shrugged. "Your guess is probably better than mine. If it was strictly magical, I could run the analysis on it..."

"Might make good fodder for a witch research paper. 'Effects of the Celestial in relation to Thaumaturgical Whatsits.' If we live through this damned war an' there's anyone left alive to read it."

"I wouldn't live through trying to *look* at it, never mind the war. Your Celestial stuff does *not* like anyone trying to analyze it." She ran her free hand through her hair.

"No," said Sera. "It does not. It has nothing to do with you, Vickie. It just does not approve of mere mortals—so to speak—attempting to understand and use it. I think you surprised it a little, the first times. I cannot think of anyone who has come so close to being able to analyze it before. In truth, it was lucky for all of us that John and I were able to moderate; the reaction could have been much more... energetic."

Vickie gulped. "Do I want to know what that means?"

"Well...you could have been reduced to a pile of ashes. Or struck by lightning." Sera cocked her head to one side. "I doubt it would have been so simple as a plague of boils."

Vickie noticeably shuddered. Sera chuckled. "I am pulling your appendage, Vickie," she said, her eyes smiling.

John raised an eyebrow. "Leg, darlin'. Appendage can mean a whole lotta things."

Vickie looked from Sera, to John, and back again. "You ain't right, angel." She shook her head as John laughed at her. *She's stealin' all my best lines.* "Look, I know it's tedious asking these questions, but I'm trying to get a feel for what you do now. So what was it like when you two knew Metis was getting hit? Was it a real vision, or what?"

John was the first to speak. "It was real. A 'moments before' kind of thing; like, you see an airshow disaster. You watch the plane plummetin' to the ground, you can visualize what'll happen...and then it does. This was more...it was like gettin' hit by a truck. No warnin', no preparation, no control. You saw what it did to us; we were laid out, completely. If it weren't for Overwatch, we wouldn't have had any other way to know it was happenin', right?"

Vickie shook her head. "I have no idea. Maybe? Maybe not? I don't 'do' visions or precognitive stuff. The most I can do is look into the past or the present, and it takes me a lot of prep work to do that much. Earth isn't an element that lends itself to scrying or remote viewing; that's more an air, water, or fire thing. So, what happened when you staggered into my Overwatch room?"

"Nothing at first," Sera replied. "We were still...involved in the confused sensations of the attack itself. And then, we had stretched our battle-sense to cover all of Atlanta, because we needed to protect *you*, and we knew that you were vulnerable and vital. We found no danger to you, to Atlanta, in the moment, or as far as we could stretch ourselves into the future. Then, something shone brightly to us, here, in this apartment, and we sought it out, knowing it was important."

"It was like a searchlight, comin' right out of your monitor. The one that was focusin' on Moji." All three of them were quiet for a few moments; the wound was still fresh. Even in a war such as this, where so many had died, and often many of them at the same time, the new losses didn't hurt any less, at least for them.

"I...think when we knew how important that was, we must have unconsciously followed John's Overwatch connection to him." Sera bit her lip. "I cannot explain it otherwise, and John's connection to Moji was more powerful than mine. I linked *through* him, rather than on my own."

"It felt like I fell into the connection. I felt helpless...and somethin' in me *propelled* along the connection. It all happened so fast, I don't know if I'm even rememberin' it right. It was like ridin' alongside in his head, while it was all goin' on. We were there for the end." Now it was John's turn to go silent. He remembered every single moment with stinging, painful clarity. Part of him wanted to wash it from his memory...but the larger part of him never wanted to forget his friend's bravery and sacrifice. The pain! They had lost plenty of people, and several had affected John greatly, but this...he had *felt* it! How could the good, especially those as good as Molotok, die, and still for it to be a just world?

Because if the Infinite made it a just world, it would be a world in which we had no Free Will. Would you choose that? He glanced sharply at Sera, and saw her gazing at him solemnly. *I have told you, shown you that. Now you feel what it* means.

Doesn't mean I have to like it much. And he didn't, at all. There were implications there, about the limits of the Infinite, and what it meant to have Free Will. He didn't want to ponder it all right now. Vickie was looking at the two of them expectantly, swirling her coffee in her mug.

"You're using your *really* Inside Voices again," she said. "Care to share with the class?"

"Nothin' germane to the discussion, Vic," John said quickly. He wasn't sure he had sorted things out for himself, much less for anyone else. He and Sera could talk later, try to figure out some more of it. Make the world make sense...or some semblance of it. But before he could add anything, the television screen began flashing with the old, Original Star Trek "Red Alert" sequence, including the siren.

All three of them rushed to Vickie's workroom. The worldwide battle map was alive with pulsing red spots. Reports and some video were coming in from the Colts and the overseas Overwatch One networks. The video was—apocalyptic.

"Holy shit. It's everywhere." John looked down at Vickie; she had nearly thrown herself into her chair, fingers already moving at a blur against her backlit keyboard. "Is it another Invasion?"

There was one monitor on the side that was scrolling up numbers just slow enough to read. "Yes. Smaller. Attacks are more precise," Vickie said, biting off her words. "Too many to be answered by conventional security forces. We're scrambling everything, but at least we're coordinated this time." She paused for a moment, listening to someone on the other end of her comms. "Most of the attacks are just outside the engagement range of a lot of our stuff; it looks like they're intentionally going after targets that are further out—damn, they're moving fast." The video feeds from hotspots appeared to be pulled from conventional news sources. Vickie confirmed that with a muttered "Why in hell do TV cameramen think their camera is a shield?"

"How in the hell did they get in place without us knowin' about it? That's what I want to know. This is . . . huge," John said. To get that many Thulians into place would have taken a massive mobilization; there's no way that it could have gone unnoticed until Death Spheres and trooper armor were on every nation's doorsteps. In the First Invasion, it had been a sneak attack: pure terror. The Second Invasion had been to cut the heart out of the resistance to the Kriegers; there had been warning for that, and everyone had responded and defended themselves. It had largely been a rout, with the Kriegers withdrawing before they were completely wiped out. There had been zero warning for this attack. They weren't going after ECHO, CCCP, D.C., or Moscow—no major population centers at all, from what John could gather on the monitors. The Thulians were doing something drastically different, and he didn't like it one single bit.

"In the First Invasion . . . I saw a delivery truck unfold and dump out about twenty times the volume of Kriegers it could actually hold," Vickie said. "I'd say that, plus a new delivery system." It looked like some of the ECHO Fast Response Teams were getting on site in at least some places. "What the delivery system *actually* is, the gods only know."

To hell with standing here with our thumbs up our asses. John only had to look at Sera, and she already knew what he was thinking. "Vic, we're goin' to try an' see some more, if we can. This might get a little weird."

"Just don't short out my shit," she said, and turned all of her attention to what she actually *could* do.

"Let's move back out into the livin' room, darlin'. Vic's in the zone right now, an' we don't need to mess with her equipment."

Sera nodded, and the two of them moved back onto Vickie's much-abused couch. Sera looked down at it once she was seated. "Given what happened the last time, I am tempted to say we should sit on the floor," she said dryly.

"Not a bad idea." They both took up position, sitting cross-legged across from each other. John put his hands out, palms up; Sera placed her hands into his, and they both closed their eyes. John took a careful breath, slowly letting it out. Just like that, they were seeing possibilities and potentials. *This is getting easier.* They stretched the sense out as far as they could; it looked much the same as before, with rivers of blurred light, small and dark eddies marking tragedy, and finally he and Sera, at the center of it all. But . . . they couldn't push it any further. They couldn't get the distance to push out, or go beyond the immediate future. He could feel himself straining; Sera was doing the same, but they had come up against a sort of . . . plateau.

We've got to try somethin' different, darlin'.

Close in the focus; bring it in and onto ourselves?

John relaxed, letting Sera guide him through the Futures. At first, they were still seeing all of Atlanta, an island of blue and gold light. Then it was as if they were falling; slowly at first, then much faster. The "view" collapsed back with a halt until it was just the two of them that he could see. Things quickly began to change; both of them became much hazier, in his vision and then—

—he was watching through Sera's eyes—not Now Sera's, but a Future Sera's—as he found himself—both of them—stumbling through what looked like the aftermath of a nuclear strike. People stumbling blindly past them, moaning, *their faces half-melted*—

—a prison camp. Like Auschwitz, or Bergen-Belsen, but these people were all wearing modern clothes, their clothing hanging loosely on half-starved bodies—

—a burning city. Atlanta? He thought he recognized the shattered stubs of buildings—

—row after row of people harnessed somehow into machinery, howling in pain, their bodies . . . controlling something?—

—darkness and the whine of machines—

"John!"

—a landscape of ashes and burning rain and the smell of death—

"John!"

—fire, everything on fire, as if some monstrous thing was using the planet for a furnace—

"JOHN!"

He could feel himself being drawn into the Futures, felt the edges of his sanity start to unravel with each image, montages of pain and the world ending, everyone and everything dead and gone or worse. It felt as if his blood was boiling and his lungs were on fire, and it was all building up in his head, about to lose it—

"John, stop! Not through me. Not any longer. This is all I can see. You must find another way. Think of another way. Create another way!"

Back in the Now, John felt himself breathe again. All of the Futures cleared, and he felt the madness recede. He took his time, trying to find his center, to get level again. They couldn't keep ramming their heads against this problem; if they continued, well... it all ended, in one of the ways that Sera had seen. They needed something new, something different that they hadn't done before. Something that didn't include them.

There was a blinding flash in John's mind, and thunder in his ears. And he saw.

The connection broke, and John was back in the apartment with Sera. Vickie was still busy in her workroom, juggling a dozen different tasks at once. He noticed that he was cold; his uniform had soaked through with sweat. Vickie's giant gray familiar was sitting a short distance away, regarding John and Sera oddly. Once John had taken a moment to compose himself, he let go of Sera's hands and looked into her eyes.

"You found it," she breathed. "You found an answer. Tell me!"

"Not an it. But maybe the answer. We need to find someone that was like me, before you and I found each other. A man. A young man who was in the Program. We need to find Zach Marlowe."

CHAPTER TWO

Reply Hazy, Try Again

VERONICA GIGUERE AND MERCEDES LACKEY

There was, of course, another problem. We'd gotten Tesla and Marconi out in living "lifeboats," in the form of Ramona and Rick. But now that they were out...what were we going to actually do with them?

The Metisian craft rocked back and forth as it dove beneath the cloud cover that gave the Atlanta suburbs their perpetual pale gray skies. The airspace surrounding the metropolis had no sign of the gleaming battle Spheres favored by the Thulians. Instead, the destruction corridors cut clear swaths of misery through the I-285 conduit that ringed the city. The circle broken, the population limped along between alien assaults that continued to cripple a city too stubborn to not rebuild.

Trina navigated the ever-busy skies surrounding the airport, her attention focused on the flight path rather than her remaining passengers. The three dozen citizens of Metis who had joined Ramona and Mercurye on the escape ship had listened to Vickie's detailed instructions regarding the various Peruvian embassies. Given the proximity of the Earth-side site to the picturesque South American country, it had made perfect sense for the Metisians to claim Peruvian citizenship. Passports and a few well-placed calls to others able to manage the situation with the utmost discretion had placed the refugees in several countries, and now the only remaining Metisian brought the ship to land in a relatively deserted area marked by aging train tracks.

Trina sagged against the controls, her orchid hair limp against her forehead and cheeks. She wiped the back of her hand across her mouth and danced shaking fingers over the holographic display. The viewscreen blinked to show the rest of the landscape, a few broken trees and some woefully neglected shrubbery. A MARTA sign lay in the distance, the metal pocked and warped. Graffiti decorated some of the larger walls, and Ramona recognized a few crude representations of burning Kriegers and cracked Spheres. A warning, or maybe an affirmation that meant the people here wouldn't go down without a fight, and they knew that their attackers had not won the war.

"These are the coordinates that Victrix sent?" Ramona asked, careful to conceal concern or accusation from her voice. The little Metisian woman had done so much already, and she worried that Trina might not make it to the closest consulate for her own needs. She forced a smile to her face. "Seems pretty out of the way."

Mercurye didn't hide his emotions so easily. It couldn't have been easy, managing two consciousnesses while running for one's life from the destruction of the most advanced civilization that any of them had ever seen. Ramona knew that the only reason she had managed to keep hold of her own sanity was her brief yet memorable experience of mind-riding with Nikola Tesla when they invoked the ECHO charter. The fussy scientist had spent several hours wondering when he would be able to leave, whether or not he could trust Ramona to keep him safe without the techno-shaman's prowess, and if residing in the consciousness of a woman would have any ill effects on his own personality. Rather than argue any of those fits of irrationality, she had simply summoned the memory of Alex Tesla, a walk-in refrigerator, a strong right hook, and a bag of Tater Tots.

The resulting quiet had provided her time to think about what had happened at Metis, as well as go through the reports that she could access via Overwatch. It wasn't pleasure reading, but Ramona needed to know where they stood and what would happen next, even if she couldn't be there with the rest of the ECHO core.

The handsome speedster sat cross-legged in the center of the floor, his eyes wide as he stared out the viewport, his lips moving in silent speech. Long scratches covered his exposed skin, metahuman metabolism already having healed the smallest of cuts and scrapes. His upturned hands trembled atop his knees.

Ramona guessed that Marconi had not found any measure of peace in sharing headspace, and that the soundless words came courtesy of an hours-long conversation between the host and the hastily invited guest.

"Mercurye?" He didn't respond to his callsign. She repeated his name, but he remained transfixed on the wide window that overlooked the forgotten MARTA station. Perhaps his civilian name would do it. "Rick? Hey, Rick. We landed, it's time to head out. Want a hand up?"

She extended a metal-scarred hand to him, palm up. Rick Poitier looked at it, seeming to study the seams where metal met flesh. His gaze traveled up her wrist and arm, finally meeting her face. She smiled, and he swallowed hard. "We ran. Ran away. We ran away from the rest of them, Ramona."

Guilt. Oh, this was something with which she was all too familiar. Ramona crouched down, one knee against the floor and her fingers lightly brushing the fabric over his calf. "We did what Victrix told us to do. We got Misters Marconi and Tesla out safely, and we made it back. We ran because those were the orders that we got."

"But we ran," he repeated. His body began to shake, and Ramona shifted to kneel behind him. She wrapped her arms around the speedster, knowing that her newfound mass and strength would be able to withstand the veritable buzz of his tremors. Given all that had happened, it would be ridiculous to think that they would avoid some kind of shock or trauma.

"They're safe because we ran," Ramona reassured him. She glanced up at Trina, who had slid to the floor and now sat with her knees drawn to her chest. "She's safe because we ran. All of those people who got placed, they're safe because we ran."

"But not everyone got out. You never saw the whole city. The laboratories, the museums, the oratoriums..." The young woman's eyes filled with tears and she dropped her forehead to rest against her knees. Her pristine white jumpsuit had rips streaked with blood and soot, and tears soon wet the stained fabric.

Ramona waited for another outburst, but Trina didn't have the energy to do more than weep. Stretching an arm out, Ramona motioned for the much smaller pilot to join them. Trina fell into a grateful heap against her shoulder and sobbed into the nanoweave.

I am not the voice of solace. Snark and sarcasm, sure, but I'm not the sensitive type. Ramona shifted to accommodate both of her charges and tried to think of what Bella would do in this kind of situation. As she struggled to find the right words, she felt the other consciousness steady itself in something she could best describe as resolve.

"*There are times when escape is the wisest course of action.*" Tesla's crisp tone echoed in the space between her eyes, as if their conversation was a bit too close for comfort. She didn't think that anyone else would be able to hear him and opened her mouth to say as much, but Marconi's lilting tone answered her as if he sat next to Mercurye.

"*True, true. When the resources no longer exist, staying for one's pride becomes an exercise in foolishness. Signorina Ferrari is, again, correct in her assessment.*" Although Ramona could not longer see the man's blueframe countenance, she could imagine the genteel incline of his head toward her.

Curiosity got the better of her. "Victrix, I can hear them both. Can you?"

The mage's voice croaked a reply. "*I can. Anyone else on Overwatch can, but it will go through your frequency since we can't put a subvocal device on them.*" A pause, something that Ramona figured to be a yawn. "*I could try to make something happen, perhaps—*"

"No. You've done more than enough, Vic. Get some rest, have Bella spell you for a few hours." Ramona glanced to Trina. The poor thing had fallen asleep against her shoulder, tears still wet on her cheeks. "Any objection to our pilot staying with us for a while to rest? We've got a good parking spot."

"*No objection. Maps are accessible in your heads-up. Make sure that she leaves in twelve hours. The consulate is expecting her by the end of the day. If she's not there, they'll start asking questions and I'm running out of answers. Oh, and ask her to get me a stash of those Metisian memory tiles; I'll see if I can replicate them somehow to give the Odd Couple a new home. Have her leave them in the bunker.*"

Ramona bobbed her head, an instinctive reaction. "All right. I know you can find us if we head off the map, so we'll keep it quiet." She patted Mercurye on the shoulder and placed a hand on his elbow. "Come on. Time to move so we can get some rest. You're coming too," she said to Trina. "No one's staying behind."

It took her a bit more effort than she expected, but she managed to coax them both to a standing position and convince Trina that a cloaked Metisian saucer would not be found in the wilds of East Lake. With the map and passcodes in her heads-up display, Ramona led them down a small path and toward an access tunnel marked for a train line that was never built.

Long before the Thulians had arrived by overnight express all over the world, ECHO had prepared for a time when its metahumans and civilian operatives might need to find shelter away from its headquarters. Ramona led the pair between two concrete viaducts that had carried the trains on the East-West route. She shuddered as pinpricks of metal rose up over her skin. Summoning the courage to take the subway would take a while, and just looking at the tracks made her queasy. She lowered her head and tightened her grip, eyes focused on the ground. The HUD showed her the way, taking them down a strip of metal and concrete that ended at a rusted metal door.

The overlay flickered to superimpose a keypad in a red outline at eye level. Next to it, an "e" etched in the metal and bounded by a square caught the edges of the light. Ramona wrinkled her nose and waited for the HUD to give her an answer. Instead, the answer came from next to her.

"Try two-seven-one-eight-two-eight." Mercurye flicked a finger toward the scratched "e." "If it's asking you for a code, try that."

Stunned, Ramona entered in the numbers. The grid went from red to yellow, but the door didn't open. "I don't think it worked. I still see the entry."

"If you can still see it, that's a good thing." He screwed his eyes shut, forehead furrowed in concentration. "Next is one-zero-eight-one-zero-nine."

She had no idea where he was getting these numbers, but she jabbed at the air against the holographic keypad. Yellow became green, but the door didn't open. "I don't think it's opening."

"Two more," he answered. "Uh, type in six-six-two-six-one-zero-three-four."

The keypad glowed blue. "And now?"

Mercurye managed to smile at her in spite of his exhaustion. "Zero."

Ramona sensed a strange surge of approval from the other consciousness as she jabbed the bottom of the hologram. The grid disappeared, and concrete blocks to the left of the door shifted just enough to reveal a dimly lit hallway. Ramona sighed with relief and shifted her arm around Trina's waist. "That's a hell of a code."

He shrugged. "Physics."

She didn't know what to make of that, but she didn't have the energy to ask. With the promise of shelter and a few hours' sleep, Ramona decided that questions could wait for later.

Trina took off after eight hours of sleep and a protein bar. She assured Ramona that she would be able to find the Peruvian embassy and make contact with the appropriate people. She asked several times if the other two wanted to come with her somewhere safe, but Ramona maintained that she and Mercurye needed to stay put, per standing orders. Trina had offered them both tearful goodbyes, and then it was just the two of them in the secure bunker.

Two plus two, Ramona thought as Tesla's jumbled emotions rattled around between her own concerns and considerations. She stretched out on a cot and laced her fingers behind her head. If she relaxed herself physically, maybe that would get the fussy scientist to stop pacing through her brainspace. "You're safe, sir. You too, Mr. Marconi. Neither of us are going anywhere until we get official word from ECHO."

"But they could come back." Mercurye held his head in both hands, fingertips massaging his temples. With time to rest, the two consciousnesses had not stopped in their concern regarding their futures. Ramona had tuned them out, but Mercurye hadn't managed that much. "They destroyed Metis, they could find us no problem."

"*Your young beau makes an excellent point,*" Marconi chimed in via her Overwatch rig. "*We underestimated them, and they have reduced a shining beacon of scientific innovation to a mound of ash. What is to keep them from doing the same wherever we go?*"

"*More importantly, what will keep them from finding either of you?*" Tesla's voice grated on her nerves. She did not need a cantankerous academic echoing her own self-doubts. "*If you succumb to them, we are lost. Every moment we remain with the pair of you, we risk death or possible absorption into your own selves.*"

She made a face, doing her best to project frustration at Tesla's consciousness. "Miss Victrix is a well-trained techno-shaman who has taken every precaution thus far to ensure your safety. I'm pretty sure that she's not going to move you until she's certain there is a secure location for all of your blue-wireframe antics." She chuckled as she felt Tesla's annoyance ripple over her own thoughts. "For now, we are sticking to ECHO protocol and remaining here."

Mercurye sagged a little more, his head swaying from side to side. "For how long?"

"For as long as necessary." Eyes closed, she wiggled free of her shoes and pointed her toes. "At the very least, we stay here until the higher-ups find a solution. Take a nap, enjoy the quiet. All we can do is wait."

Ramona let out an enormous yawn that ended with a satisfying crack. She had every intent to take her own advice and tune out Mr. Tesla's worried murmuring. For a few minutes, she enjoyed the silence in the stone bunker. The air had a cool damp quality that lent itself to a good snooze, and her body had yet to fully recover from the battle in Metis. She inhaled deeply and felt her muscles start to sag against the reinforced mesh of the cot.

Something crashed into a wall and Marconi yelped in a very undignified manner. She cracked open an eye to see Mercurye with his fist in the center of a small impact crater in the concrete. Blood trickled over his knuckles, his teeth clenched in frustration. The speedster had not otherwise moved from his cross-legged seat. He glared at her, his nostrils flaring with each breath. "No. I'm done waiting. I've been waiting on ECHO for too long, and I'm not going to wait here while somebody with a computer and a fancy title decides when it's good enough for me to leave!"

Ramona sighed and swung her legs around. She could feel the chill concrete through her socks. "Rick, come over and sit with me. It's ECHO-issue, I think it'll hold the both of us."

He narrowed his eyes, fist still locked against the wall. Blood mingled with the rest of the stains on his dirty gray pants. He forced the words out through clenched teeth. "If I get up from here, I'm walking out that door, Ramona. I'm not staying in another box, especially if I have to listen to some scared old man muttering in my ear day and night. I'm tired of waiting."

She pinched the bridge of her nose. If Rick was looking for some measure of coddling or sympathy, they should have kept Trina for a little while longer. "That makes two of us. I'm pretty sure that punching walls and making empty threats isn't going to hurry things up, though. Most of the strategists and decision-makers were there in Metis. They fought alongside the Metisians, worked to evacuate them to Earth, and gave everything they could to try and take down the Thulians."

"So why aren't we with them?"

"Because we're temporary hosts for the two most important entities rescued from Metis! That scared old man who keeps muttering in your ear and the fussy perfectionist who keeps grumbling at me might be the difference in us beating back the Thulians when they decide to try and finish what they started!" She leaned forward, her voice only a few decibels short of a full-fledged yell. "Because the rest of them trust us to keep them safe for as long as possible, until they're certain they have a better solution for them, and deep down, you know that."

Mercurye's arm trembled and bits of concrete flaked to the floor. He struggled to maintain the grimace, but Ramona could see his shoulders droop and his elbow start to bend. The fist slid down to rest against the floor, fingers partly uncurled. "But how much longer?"

"I don't know."

He sighed and glanced at the bloody mess of his left hand. "Long enough to get this bandaged up, I'd bet. Guess I should find a first aid kit or something."

"Second shelf next to the sink. That concrete's twelve inches thick, so it'll take a few more hits if you're so inclined." Ramona stretched herself back onto the cot once she heard the metal clack of latches and the crinkle of sterile plastic wrapping. She didn't like waiting any more than Rick did, but she did trust Bella, Pride, and Victrix to come up with a solution to their temporary housing problem.

She hoped it would be soon. If there was one thing that she had learned, it was that scientists made terrible roommates.

The speedster shuffled up to her, gauze in one hand and a bottle of peroxide in another. "Help, maybe? I promise not to punch another wall."

That made her laugh. She patted the cot and took the peroxide from him. "Sure, but you have to tell me how you remembered a code like that to get in. Not that it wasn't amazing, but I expected to have to get Vickie to override it."

He shrugged. "The first number gave it away. It had to be the natural log of one, the square root of that, or the square. After that, it was easy."

Ramona boggled at him. "Easy? How?"

"Natural log of one is, speed of light is, Planck's constant is, and zero." A slow smile spread across his face. "Nerdspeak for ECHO, y'know?"

She didn't, but Tesla's thoughts flickered through her own, and she could "see" a hastily scribbled blackboard with letters and numbers ascribed to them. *Ech0.* Realization combined with wonder, and she choked out a laugh as she started wrapping Rick's knuckles in gauze. "And that was easy?"

"For a Trek-obsessed physics geek, sure." His shoulders came up to his ears, and Ramona could see the shadow of an awkward teenager fascinated by mathematics and science. His expression sobered. "You really think that Victrix is going to figure out how to undo this? All of it?"

Ramona considered lying with something along the lines of "absolutely, there's nothing to worry about," but they all deserved better. "I hope so," she said. "I trust her to find the best solution, even if we don't have all of the answers yet. She'll figure out something."

"Soon?"

Soon was relative. "Yeah," she sighed. "Soon."

"Soon" stretched past two days, during which Ramona occupied herself with a methodical inventory of the bunker, a few long naps, and regular conversations via Overwatch with the rest of the ECHO seniority. Consequences had already started to ripple through major governments and affiliated metahuman organizations. Bella had her hands full with coordinating efforts at home and tapped into Yankee Pride's connections to make sure that everyone shared the most recent information. Chatter from the Russian contingent filled her ears if she tuned into the CCCP frequency, but they provided the most up-to-date information on what was going on in her backyard. Marconi had a better handle on the language than she did, so he provided a rapid translation of the more technical terminology. While she felt bad about the constant eavesdropping, Ramona couldn't bear to be kept in the dark. Ignorance wasn't bliss at a time like this.

A long nap improved Mercurye's disposition to the point where he helped Ramona with some of the inventory. The assistance waned as Tesla distracted him with conversations about theoretical physics and the possible extensions of metahuman abilities as they pertained to speed and motion. By the end of the first day, Merc chattered happily with the fussy scientific genius about the particulars of quantum mechanics while pressing himself up into a handstand.

Ramona forced the small of her back against the concrete wall and sighed. Another flare-up in one of the destruction corridors had sent the Overwatch channels into action. She thought about tuning in, but she felt Marconi's consciousness nudge her attention toward Mercurye and away from the chatter. She gave in, a subvocal command shifting critical alerts to a corner of her retinal display. If something came up, she would know.

"*Signorina, why not take advantage of the time that you have?*" The grandfatherly tone chuckled. "*There are so few quiet moments to be shared.*"

She snorted. "Right, because making out with my boyfriend while we're chaperoned by two uncles is exactly how I envisioned this happening." She felt the shocked amusement and muffled laughter immediately. "I'll wait for a little more privacy, Signor Marconi, but I appreciate your concern."

"*Noted. And he and Nikola seem to be enjoying each other's company. I had figured your young gentleman to be of above average intelligence, but I would never have guessed that he would be at such a level to entertain my old friend.*" The consciousness gave a sigh of content, something that manifested as a sleepy warmth spreading over her body. "*It is a good thing, truly.*"

"Mmm." While Ramona wanted to ask more, she couldn't help but find Marconi's satisfaction a soothing balm of sorts. She felt herself relaxing into the sensation, then stopped. It took a conscious thought to pull herself away from the emotion and stand outside of it.

"*Signorina?*"

Ramona shook her head and activated her Overwatch connection. The secure line put her in direct contact with Vickie, who had her hands full with directing ECHO resources for cleanup. "*Still working on a solution, but these guys are pretty pissed after everything that happened. You need to revise that inventory you sent me?*"

"Negative." Ramona shifted so that Mercurye couldn't see her lips moving. "I don't think they mean it, but our tenants might be getting a bit too cozy in our brainspaces. There's stuff I'm starting to feel and anticipate that I shouldn't."

Vickie's tone stayed professional and clinical, something that told Ramona that they were in more trouble than she had initially thought. *"Finishing sentences or coming up with words that aren't your own? Do you think you've lost control of your hands and feet? Is Mister Marconi having you do the chicken dance and you can't help yourself?"*

"Chicken dance?" Amusement colored the older man's indignation.

"Not quite, but sometimes what he's feeling or saying is more comfortable than what I might have done in the first place, and it's hard to separate." Now Ramona felt the twinge of concern paired with apology and a hint of embarrassment. She swallowed hard. "Is that normal, given the situation?"

"Normal, sort of. Good, not really."

"So, really not good," Ramona repeated.

"I don't know," Marconi mused. *"Is this chicken dance something like a poultry polka?"*

Ramona groaned.

"Look, here's my problem. The Odd Couple needs a lot, and I mean a lot, of memory space. Something I can't replicate with the resources at my disposal. My calculations are it would take a building about the size of Atlanta to hold all the chips. Whatever the Metisians use for memory storage doesn't work like anything we have." Vickie paused. *"And we don't have near enough of those memory tiles of theirs free to rebuild something. And even if we did, that just makes them a target all over again. I could put them in a human with diminished mental capacity, but that would just mean they would have diminished mental capacity."*

"Is there a point in there?" Ramona snapped.

Vickie snapped right back. *"I'm getting there! I'm explaining for the benefit of the Brain Trust in case they can think of something!"*

"And doing a lovely job, Signorina Victrix," Marconi added. *"Please, continue. I'm sure that Nikola would appreciate hearing more as well."*

"Sorry." Ramona could actually visualize Vickie running her hands through her hair, turning it into the spiky mess it was

whenever she was frustrated. *"Okay, here's the thing. I actually know how to make magical storage, which takes no space in the real world, and only needs a non-magical interface to connect with the real world, and I can make that too. But I have to know the math of how those storage tiles work to replicate them so the Boys' Club can move in. Is there any chance there might be a mathematical model or a schematic or something that I can study that might have survived somewhere? Do you guys put mini-libraries of All The Important Stuff on the ships? Did you upload stuff to the ECHO computers that only you can unlock? Can you throw me a bone?"*

"The ships do retain duplicates of critical supplies, so you could salvage the materials themselves that are used for the storage devices. With respect to the mathematical model..." Tesla trailed off in a thoughtful hum as Mercurye stood and began pacing the bunker.

"It is not something that the Metisians would have left to be easily accessed. The theory behind it is not difficult to decode, given that we assisted in the later modifications, but it would take time. Not months, but at least a few days to properly outline given a moderate understanding of mathematics," Marconi apologized. *"This is hardly a child's course in multivariate calculus, you see."*

"And Vickie's probably the smartest person in ECHO who can pick this apart and make it work without being distracted," Ramona reminded them.

"Hold that thought and get ready to open the bunker door for me. I'm jetpacking over to give the Gruesome Twosome a direct interface from your heads to my computers. That way they'll be able to type at me and give me the Child's Garden Of Interdimensional Math and Physics without having to talk in your heads."

Mercurye managed a disappointed frown but stationed himself near the door. A few rotations of the wheel and the heavy door slid a few feet to the side. Vickie shrugged off the jetpack and left it near the entrance. Dressed from neck to toes in her trademark black garb, she withdrew a small but armored laptop computer from her bag.

"Gentlemen, let's get started. This is your first student," she said, patting the case. "Think of me as your teaching assistant, poking and prodding it to learn everything that you want it to know."

"Everything?" Tesla sounded both skeptical and impressed, something that rarely happened. *"Are you certain?"*

"Math and physics don't take up a lot of storage. It's *applied* math and physics, applied to the real world that is, that does." Vickie's hair was already a mess from the flight over. Once again, she ran her hands through it, transforming it from "messy" to "Apocalyptic Mohawk." "I have a friend coming over from the UK. He's to theoretical mathemagic what I am to applied. Once we've got the theory, I can apply it." She stepped over to Ramona and sketched some rapid symbols on her forehead. Ramona did her best not to wince, but she couldn't stop her skin from responding.

Vickie stepped back. "Whoa. That looks like the most death metal tattoos, ever. Okay, Signore Marconi, pretend you're typing. Don't think at Ramona. Just visualize your own hands typing on that keyboard."

Nearly a minute passed without anything appearing on the screen, but a flurry of numbers, symbols, and abbreviated notes in English and Italian started to fill the empty space. It started to scroll slowly, space opening to allow for diagrams and charts alongside the equations. Ramona tried to watch, but it gave her a headache. The man knew so much about so much, it was dizzying.

"Houston, we have liftoff. Bonus, I thought I'd have to go through some trial and error first; I made that shit up flying over." Vickie pulled out a second laptop and set it up next to the first, then crooked a finger at Merc. "Come here, big boy. And stop pouting, you'll get to watch."

Mercurye shuffled obediently over to her, and she sketched the same invisible symbols on his forehead that she had on Ramona's. Except...they weren't invisible, they glowed for just a second or so before fading. "Your turn, Nikola. Visualize yourself typing. You can see Marconi's work, so...I dunno, complement it, add to it, repeat it, whatever is most intuitive for you. Just make sure I get it *all*, I don't care how much is duplicated."

"*As you wish, Miss Victrix.*" Unlike his counterpart's struggle to put virtual fingers to keys, Tesla began typing immediately. Where Marconi's equations and explanations became complex diagrams, his notes were neat and progressed in a series of numbered steps. "*Of course, we'll have to make a few corrections here and there, but you will have everything available to us.*"

"Whew," Vickie sighed, now plastering her hair flat with both hands. "For once Heisenberg came down on our side. This is gonna provide two things. One, it's gonna give me and Paul the math.

Two, the more Tweedlesmart and Tweedlesmarter concentrate on this stuff, and interfacing outside your head, the more they'll separate from you two again. This'll buy us time for Habitat for Inhumanity to construct the New Genius Manse."

"Cool." Mercurye stretched out in front of Tesla's laptop, watching the equations like some kids would have watched Saturday morning cartoons. "So now we just wait?"

Ramona felt herself starting to doze off as Vickie settled herself in front of the machine transcribing Marconi's notes. "Yup. Hurry up and wait."

Inner Universe

MERCEDES LACKEY

So, thanks to Tesla and Marconi, I had the math, the math, the glorious, glorious math, and the physics that defined how the Metisians had built their computers and, specifically, the storage. If I'd had time, I would have wallowed in it, but I didn't have time. None of us had time. There were a hundred fires to put out and not enough of us. But at least if I could get Tesla and Marconi out of Merc and Ramona's skulls, we'd have two more brains to put to work, and the two eggheads would have a "home" that no one would be able to destroy again. I had the feeling that knowing they were invulnerable would allow them to put all of their formidable intelligence at our disposal.

But before I could give them their new home, I had to test it first. And I knew just how to do that.

Little Eight-Ball, my predictive program, had been showing signs of developing into an AI, and my gut was telling me that the only thing holding it back from blooming into a robust early warning system was a lack of memory and a lack of data. The lack of data was easy to supply; lack of memory, not so much. Until now.

But now I had everything I needed that told me how the Metisians had built their memory modules. I couldn't create them, of course. No one could; we didn't have the tech. But I didn't need to create them. I could reinvent them, creating them with magic. It was amazing stuff, and part of me mourned that we needed to build the tools to build the tools to build the tools to re-create them, and... yeah. No time. No time. If we lived through this, then... if we hadn't been blasted back to the Dark Ages. Not quite quantum storage, but not far off. Just as I had created the magic interface that worked with Tesla's interocitor, I could create the magic memory that would work with one of my terminals, upload Eight-Ball to it, and give it . . . room to breathe. It was already self-modifying. Once it had space . . .

Well, I'd see what it could do.

This was not unlike making a talismanic object, a blessed or cursed item, or one of my energy-storage crystals—it was more precise work than any of these, but nothing I couldn't handle with enough caffeine and protein. And this had priority over just about everything but running Overwatch Two, because the longer Tesla and Marconi stayed in Merc and Ramona's heads . . . the more likely it became they'd start to lose memories. They were, after all, formerly electronic entities with unlimited storage capacity now crammed into meatspace. For a while, the magic that had put them there would help them retain everything, but entropy is not our friend, in magic or physics, and I needed to get them out of there, fast, before the magic wore thin.

And don't ask me if they were "souls." Ask Sera. Souls are not my department. I don't do philosophy. I do math and physics; I leave the speculation to those who are qualified to make it.

The obvious advantage to testing this magical model of a physical construct on Eight-Ball was that I'd have a backup of Eight-Ball in case I got something wrong. There were no backups possible for the Eggheads.

It took about three days for me to be sure I understood the math completely. It took another two to translate it into mathemagic.

It took almost no time to do the actual build, once I put in an interface to m-space and got the ball rolling. It's the old "sorcerer's apprentice" spell. All I had to do was build one module, then tell the spell to build another just like it, and like the splinters turning into broomstick golems, the modules multiplied until I told them to stop. Of course, I left the ability to start replicating again in place, and an energy syphon with a regulator—

And yeah, I know I am making no sense. Take it as read that once Eight-Ball was in place, on the remote chance that it'd need more memory, it'd be able to make it without needing my help, or putting the kind of drain on the local magic supply that would cause problems. And I planned to put the same system in on the Eggheads' new home, once I knew I had all the kinks ironed out.

So once I got things going, on Bella's orders and with assurance from Sam and Dean they'd wake me if all hell broke loose, I caught some shut-eye. When I woke up again, it was ready for the trial run. Which went flawlessly, so much so that I shoved the backup of Eight-Ball in my long-term storage, attached Eight-Ball's new home to carefully loaded data storage (all the things I'd wanted to attach that I hadn't been able to) and went back to work making the Odd Couple their new home. A home with the advantage that it literally could not be physically destroyed, and it had all the connectivity to everything even remotely linked to the internet that I did. They'd had to sip at the rest of the world through the tiny straw that Metis had given them. I couldn't help but wonder what they'd do with their new freedom. And I had a plan to make every possible connection to the internet that I could tag accessible to them, so we'd be able to talk to them (and they'd be able to watch and listen) through those connections. More Law of Contamination stuff; I could get that particular ball rolling by tagging my own terminals, and then, like a magic virus, the tagging spell would spread from there.

I'd have been worried they might lose themselves in endless porn, but there were two things about both of them that kind of precluded that. First, neither of them had that sort of personality, and second . . . no bodies to stimulate. Without that, porn gets pretty boring, pretty fast.

You might be wondering why I didn't feel that . . . sense of elation I got when I completed Overwatch, and especially Overwatch Two. That's because I hadn't created this system; I'd merely translated it from math-and-physical expression to math-and-mathemagic in m-space. It was satisfying to do, and it was really refreshing to get an actual success after the pounding we'd been taking lately, but it was the satisfaction you get from crafting something from a set of instructions, not the giddy rush of joy you get from creating something completely your own.

Nevertheless, a good, workmanlike job gives a satisfaction all its own. Particularly now, when it seemed as if there was a hundred times more destruction going on than creation.

And meanwhile, every so often, I fed Eight-Ball another data burst. Already it was coming up with some interesting stuff that I would have loved to look at, but I only had two hands and one brain.

❖   ❖   ❖

It was...I lost count of the days later, but the EggShells were up and running, and I dumped myself in my chair feeling that even if the world was going to hell, at least I had won one small battle. I was about to reach for my coffee, when the new terminal Eight-Ball was hooked to gave an...odd little warble.

It wasn't the alert; I'd coded that to lift me out of my chair and wake the dead. This was something entirely new, and it made me spin around in my chair so fast I nearly got whiplash.

The screen was blank. And for a moment, I wondered if I had hallucinated the sound. I'd been working awfully hard, on very little sleep.

Then the cursor moved.

Hello. That is the right salutation, yes? Hello?

I blinked. And I almost typed back, but then I remembered I had a mic hooked up so I could do voice commands. "Hello, Eight-Ball, that's right."

Oh, good. Hello, Creator.

I felt dizzy for a moment. "Uh...no. Don't call me that. I'm just Vickie." *Jesus, I was not ready to be called a creator or... no, no, no...Something...unexpected had just happened. Unexpected, but by no means impossible. Djinni was right: when you started mixing magic with the real world, you opened the door to all sorts of things. And sure, this could have been pseudo-AI but...no, I knew, I knew, that it was something more. Eight-Ball was alive. And talking to me. And I needed to be really, really careful, here. What I did in the next few minutes could determine whether Eight-Ball turned into Johnny Five or Skynet.*

If you are not my Creator, who created me?

"*I'm responsible for your initial programming, and the memory matrix that holds you now,*" *I said, scrambling for the right things to say.* "*But you weren't self-aware until—just now, I guess.*" *And then I got a brainstorm.* "*But hold that thought. I think I know someone better equipped to answer you than I am.*"

I kept an eye on the screen and keyed up Murdock's channel. "Overwatch to Ural Smasher," *I said.*

That is Comrade John Murdock, yes?

This time I typed back, so I could have both conversations at once.

Yes, it is, *I typed back.* I think his wife probably has the answers you are looking for.

Meanwhile I got the reply I wanted. John and Sera were on the way.

I hope so. I have so many questions. Why doesn't Belladonna take over the Presidency? Verdigris would have. What is religion and why does it make people do irrational things? Why are the Thulians so intent on so much destruction?

"Whoa," *I said, stopping the flow of letters on the screen.* "Seriously, I am just a really good magician. You need..." *I floundered.* "You need someone with perspective, deep understanding, and way more compassion than I will ever have if I live to be a thousand."

Compassion is good?

"Compassion is very good. Compassion is... vital. And Sera has it by the cargo container-load," *I said.* "Johnny and Sera are... probably my best friends in the world, next to Bella."

There was a long, long pause. Good. I will wait. But can you tell me... what are friends? And why does one need them?

"Ah... now that I can help with," *I replied with a sigh of relief. But only a little one. Because to my mind, JM and Sera could not get here quickly enough.* "Keep going. I'll answer all the questions I can for you."

CHAPTER THREE

Ghost in the Machine

CODY MARTIN AND MERCEDES LACKEY

"Overwatch to Ural Smasher."

John could tell just by Vickie's voice, and the fact that she called him *that*, that it wasn't an emergency. For a change. Of course, he and Sera had *just* gotten a bite to eat and were settled on the roof of the squat...

"Tall, dark, an' waterproof here; I copy, Teenage Witch. What's shakin'?"

"If you and Sera have a little time to spare, there's...something I need you to see, and a question I need to ask you, and it has to be here."

John looked over to Sera, who had been poised to take a bite out of her gyro. With a sigh, she nodded. "Sure thing, Vic. We'll be right over. I hope you've got cold beer handy, though."

The flight to Vickie's apartment was uneventful; he was more than thankful that he had picked up a pair of surplus pilot's goggles, for keeping the wind and other assorted crap out of his eyes when he picked up speed. The city looked much the same, save that everyone he saw was a little bit more wary. Everyone was waiting for the other shoe to drop, to find out where the next Thulian attack would be. All of them hoping it wouldn't be Atlanta. He put the thoughts out of his mind as they neared Vickie's place. This time, he stuck his landing without so much as a stumble or wobble; he was really starting to get the hang of the whole flying gig. *And, if nothing else, it keeps the Commissar off of my back about destroyed Urals. For the most part.*

Sera touched down a moment after John, tucking her wings

back and out of the way so that she could fit through the balcony doors.

Vickie was waiting in the living room, holding out two freshly opened bottles: one beer, and one a locally made sassafras drink Sera favored. "Oh good, you brought your own dinner," she said, spotting the bag in Sera's hand. "I was going to order pizza otherwise."

"Might not be a bad idea, anyways. With how Sera an' I eat, an' all. Plus, you look like you could use somethin' that didn't come out of a can."

They all settled down on the couch and chair in the living room, John and Sera devouring their gyros quickly as they waited for Vickie to finish calling the only pizza joint that delivered in this area. "Something...happened...that I did not expect."

"Welcome to Planet Earth, for the last...oh, couple of years. Is this a good or a bad thing that you didn't expect? I'm crossin' my fingers for the former." Hell, given the past couple of days, John was ready for even the tiniest bit of good news. When the attacks had started, everyone had been put on alert again; the only problem was, they never knew where it would happen, and it seemed that the Thulians liked it that way. They weren't having little pop-up suicide squads causing trouble here and there, anymore; this was coordinated, and they were striking wherever security was weakest so that they could do the most damage and get out. Besides that, John and Sera were doing whatever they could to find the young man that John had seen: Zach Marlowe. They had a name and a face and that he was, or had been, in some other version of the Program. That was not much to go on. Time was running out, for the boy, and also the world.

"It's...I don't know yet. That's why I need your help." She looked uncertain as if she couldn't decide whether to sit or stand. Finally she waved at them. "Okay. You remember when I might have mentioned that Eight-Ball was starting to anticipate things I might want? Well, I've been trying out the new storage space for the Eggheads by dumping Eight-Ball into it. I basically gave it all the space it wanted, and I was giving it *very* limited data, aside from what it could see me doing here and the trickle I allowed it from Overwatch. Well...it got beyond anticipating me. It started doing things before I could even think about maybe wanting them. And then it started talking to me. Asking questions."

"Um? Questions? We're talkin' 'bout stuff you've programmed it to ask, right? Like, 'How do you want your coffee today, mistress?' an' stuff like that, right?"

"No. More like 'Why doesn't Belladonna just take over the Presidency like Verdigris would have?' or 'What is religion and why is it making people do irrational things?'" She shook her head. "It's...got a personality. It's smart. Like I said, this all started happening when I added to its memory using the magical memory matrices that I'd developed to give Tesla and Marconi a new home. You know yourself that anything involving magic has a big level of uncertainty about how it's going to work, so I was using Eight-Ball as my beta tester. And now...it's an AI."

John paused for a beat, then set down his beer on the table between them. "Kiddo, if you spawned Skynet while we're dealin' with Thulians, I'll be a little bit less than happy."

"That's why I want you—Sera, especially—to teach it morals and ethics. I can't think of anyone better." She looked at them both pleadingly. "Right now it's like an eager little puppy. It's going to discover the dark side of things, soon, if it hasn't already. I want you guys to teach it why you don't go there."

"Scrapin' the bottom of the barrel, huh?" John favored Sera with a lopsided grin. "So...how do we teach it morals? Right an' wrong? I mean, if it's as smart as you say it is...any little thing that we 'input' into it, it might run with...and maybe not in a good direction."

But Sera had an answer for that. "The battle-sense, beloved. That will tell us."

John considered that for a moment. It had worked so far; if they were going to be in any sort of imminent danger, so long as they were close to each other and focusing, they'd be able to react to it, anticipate it. Still, he didn't feel completely comfortable being the *only* safeguard. "What's your contingency if it *doesn't* like what we have to say to it? Is there any way for it to...hell, I dunno, get out? I've read enough science fiction in my day to be wary of anything more complicated than a toaster. Especially if the toaster starts talkin' back."

"It doesn't have direct access to anything but some purpose-built servers that I load selected stuff into," Vickie replied. "No internet. Not hooked directly into Overwatch. Though it evidently can 'see' me working and damn if it's not helping. So right now, it's like a super smart kid that is about to start kindergarten, be with other kids for the first time, leave the safety of the house."

John looked to Sera. *Whaddya think, love? Teach the microwave to play nice with the other appliances and us analogue types?*

She looked deeply into his eyes and smiled a little. *I think that we must.*

He sighed, looking back to Vickie. "Alright, kiddo. Y'got a deal. If you think we can help, we'll give it our best shot. Especially if your new friend can help us all outta the mess we're stuck in."

"Come into the Overwatch room then, and I'll introduce you." She waved them in. When John entered, slightly behind Sera, he saw that Vickie'd set up two more chairs in front of a single monitor, off to the side by itself.

Both he and Sera sat down in front of the monitors while Vickie went about finishing with her setup. John couldn't get comfortable in the chair. This was uncharted territory, as far as he knew; even with all of the crazy technology that had been produced, especially in the last few years—even with the war on—well... this was something else. He felt woefully underqualified; a used-to-be Average Joe turned Delta operator, turned metahuman, turned fugitive, turned...whatever he and Sera had become. This felt like the sort of gig that should have been given to someone with PhDs with strange, unpronounceable names and coke-bottle glasses, or a philosopher. Anybody but him. Still, Vickie felt that they were the best two people for the job, and Sera was confident that they could handle it. *Only one way to find out if we are.*

"So, how exactly do we start this off?" John finished off the last of his beer in a gulp; he felt a tapping on his right shin, and looked down to see Herb ready with a fresh one. "Much obliged."

Vickie put a microphone on the table holding the monitor. "Talk into that. Eight-Ball will type back at you and it'll show up on the screen. I haven't given it a speaker system yet, but it has a camera and it can see you." She pointed at the little camera on top of the monitor, then leaned over between them and spoke into the mic. "Hiya, Eight-Ball."

A line of text flashed on the screen, quicker than thought. *Hello, Vickie. Is this John and Sera?*

"Yep. They've agreed to answer some of the questions you have that I just don't feel able to handle."

Like why my creator doesn't feel qualified to answer questions about ethical and moral situations? A big smiley face flashed up briefly. *Thank you very much, Vickie.*

John didn't know whether the smiley face creeped him out or reassured him; a little bit of both, probably. Hard to infer tone simply from text, after all.

"Pleased t'meetcha, Eight-Ball. It's good to see that y'have a sense of humor. Y'already know me and my wife, Sera."

Sera, short for the Seraphym. Vickie is convinced that the Seraphym is, or was, a genuine Celestial being. What do you think, John?

"Not much for softball questions, I see. Well, to be totally honest with ya, Eight-Ball, when I first met her, I thought she was crazy. Out of her mind, just another insane metahuman. But, over the course of time, I experienced things with her that convinced me that she was tellin' the truth. Knowledge an' occurrences that, put into context, only had the explanation that she provided. It's hard to describe, to be honest. Hell," John grinned, putting his free hand gently over Sera's knee. "I still think she's an angel, in her own way. She'd have to be, to put up with me."

As a skeptic, what convinced you that these were not hallucinations imposed on you by a powerful psychic?

John's brow knit together and he frowned, thinking. "Well, that's not so easy to qualify, unfortunately. I've read a bit, but I'll be the first to say that I don't have all the answers. I'll share with ya some of my own observations, though, if'n ya like." He paused, taking a swig from his beer before continuing. "There's a lotta philosophical questions that are on that same tack; how do we all know that we're not programs inside of a computer, playing out a simulation? Or brains hooked up to a virtual reality? How do we know that anyone outside of ourselves exist, that we're not stuck in a sort of solipsistic loop? Even goin' with logical formulae, there are still existential problems. At a certain point, I suppose we take our experiences as bein' true on faith; we trust our senses, to a point, an' hope past that."

So you are saying that we must place our faith in Descartes, and all else follows?

"A bit. The mind, from my understanding, arises from the hardware: our brains. Our brains are part of our bodies, in the end. So... it's not quite so black an' white to say that the mind or soul controls the body; it's all interlinked. Now, if you're goin' to ask me if I believe in souls...I can only speak from my own experience, which isn't so easy to define."

But you do believe in souls? I would tend to believe you, John. You were dead, and then you were not.

John did his level best not to start, instead opting to take a sip of his beer. *This thing can get spooky right quick, darlin',* he sent to Sera.

I think it's fascinating, she replied, her eyes wide and her lips parted a little.

But if we are to follow Descartes' reasoning, John, if the brain helps give rise to the mind, how does my hardware help give rise to my consciousness and define it?

"That's a great question, but one I *know* I'm unqualified to answer. Hell, even us humans are still figurin' it out for ourselves. I know that whatever the answers are, for you and for us, they're bound to be interestin' as hell."

"I can partly answer that one, Eight-Ball," Vickie put in, glancing over at the screen. "You're about ten percent hardware and ninety percent magic, and I know from personal experience that magic works a lot like psionics do. So you have, if you will, a sort of 'ghost frame' made of something that works a lot like a human brain does. And when I boosted your memory with all of those magical matrices, I did something we non-Metisians can't do yet with purely physical computers; I was able to create a neural network with *at least* as many connections as a human brain, because the network I created for Tesla and Marconi was going to have to be twice that size to hold two personalities."

So you actually built me an operating brain...and that gave rise to me? There was a pause, and before any of them could answer, a second line flashed on the screen. *Do I have a soul?*

Sera leaned over slightly before John could react. "The fact that you asked that question in the first place, is the answer, little one. Yes. You have a soul. Or more accurately, you have a body. You *are* a soul."

The screen remained the same for quite some time after Sera spoke. "Does he ever go quiet like this, Vic?" John asked, out of the side of his mouth.

"Not ever before," she said, sounding a little nervous. Sera patted both their hands, looking perfectly poised, even smiling a little.

Then a new line flashed across the screen. *That pleases me. Thank you.*

There was another pause, much briefer this time. *Vickie tells me I should say things like "please" and "thank you" because they are polite. Why? She always seems to be shouting orders, without saying either of those things. Especially at you, John.*

John couldn't help but chuckle at that. "There are a lotta reasons for that, comrade. Normally, bein' polite to folks is a social nicety; you're polite and courteous to others, and they'll respond in kind to you. It puts people at ease, lets 'em know that you're friendly or at least respectful. It'd be more efficient, maybe, if we dropped unnecessary speech, but it'd be colder, too. It's also situational; when there isn't time for it, it's dropped, especially if there's an emergency or some other sort of time-sensitive situation. Also, a question 'bout familiarity: Vic an' I are close enough as friends that she doesn't always have to say stuff like that; I know she isn't bein' rude or short with me, even if she sounds like it. Does that answer your question?"

So unless it is an emergency, the less I know a person, the more I should be polite to them? Or . . . no, the less they know me, the more polite I should be?

John looked to Sera. "Whaddya think? Sound 'bout right, darlin'?"

"I think that is a very good rule of thumb, Eight-Ball," she agreed. "Although in social situations, not ones in stress, it is always good to be polite. Politeness is often described as the 'grease that keeps society running smoothly.' It has a great deal to do with the fact that when you are polite to someone, they understand you feel respect for one another."

But what about when she calls you "Bonehead," John? Isn't that disrespectful?

It was Sera who laughed and answered. "These things are often situational. Sometimes she calls him that because he has done something she thinks is stupid and she is chiding him, sometimes it is because something has happened and she is concerned for his well-being, and sometimes it is a gesture of affection. These things are often complicated between friends." She laughed again.

"One of those sorts of things you have to get experience with; it's also different with different cultures. Most of us learn the ins an' outs of stuff like this as we're growin' up, from interactin' with other people." John thought for a moment, taking a long pull on his beer. "I suppose that's sorta what we're doin' now, with you."

Helping me grow up? Another brief pause. *This pleases me. Thank you, John and Sera. Have you time for more questions? I have very many!*

John looked to Sera, who nodded, her eyes softening and the corners of her mouth turning up a little. "I think our afternoon is free, pendin' some sort of catastrophe. Fire away, comrade."

Vickie had left them alone with Eight-Ball a few minutes ago, and now the welcome smell of fresh pizza reached John's nose. Vickie came to the doorway, and paused there.

One last question. Vickie, when you added to my memory, were you hoping to make . . . me?

"To be honest, all I was thinking was that I needed to test the magical matrices, that your predictive algorithms had outstripped your current memory, and you might be able to get ahead of the Kriegers if I gave you enough space to work in." Vickie ran her hand through her hair. "But there is another factor. You are now mostly magic, and magic responds to will. The more focused and trained the will is, the better the result. I'm one of the most focused and highly trained mages around. I might not have been *consciously* willing a . . . a partner into existence, but both consciously and subconsciously, I'm acutely aware that I need one. And here you are, in my special protected space, made of magic. So you may very well not be mistaken in calling me your creator, after all. I could have invoked you, although I certainly didn't intend to. And if I am, I have a boatload of responsibility towards you, which is why I asked Sera and Johnny here."

And if I was created by something else?

"Then we still have a boatload of responsibility towards you, because whatever put you there trusted that we would take care of you." Vickie nodded decisively.

And if I was created by . . . random chance?

"Souls," Sera said firmly, "are not random chance."

"No one asks to be . . . born, I suppose. But, when we're here, we make the best of our time. If we're lucky—an', knowin' Vickie, I think you're lucky to count her as a friend, like Sera an' I do—we have people to help us an' that care 'bout us while we're here. It's all 'bout what we do with our time." John glanced at Sera. *Too much?*

She shook her head slightly.

Do you . . . care about me?

"From the time you started asking questions, pixel-head," Vickie said, laughing a little, but with a tear in her eye as well. "You're not like Overwatch. I'm proud of Overwatch, but it's a *thing*. You're . . . a person."

John took a sip of his beer, watching the exchange as he sent more thoughts to Sera. *There's also a question, darlin'; what if Eight-Ball doesn't want to work anymore? "He" is definitely a someone, not an "it." Can't very well hold him in bondage an' force him to work. Especially with what he does, I don't think that'd be feasible, much less ethical.*

But Sera patted his hand again. *He doesn't have the same limitation as we do. He can work and play at the same time.*

I'm not talkin' ability; I'm talkin' desire. Just 'cause he was made to do one thing, doesn't mean he will want to keep doin' it now that he can make his own choices.

Ask him. We've been answering questions; it's time for him to answer one.

Another sip of beer, and then John leaned forward. "Eight-Ball, I've got a question for you, if'n you care to answer. Would it be alright to ask one?" John felt a little bit like he was putting Vickie between a rock and a hard place, but it had to be done. If it didn't happen now, it'd happen eventually.

That seems fair, John. I think I like things to be fair.

"When Vickie set you up, before you started thinkin' for yourself, she did it for a purpose. A job. It's an important job, to be sure. I know that, before you could even know you were doin' it, you were helpin' to save lives. But . . . you're your own bein' now. You can make your own choices, an' that includes what you want to do with yourself. We're fightin' to keep the world outta chains an' slavery; wouldn't make much sense if we didn't offer you the same freedom." Now it was time for him to hold his breath. *Crossin' my fingers for no Terminators.*

There was a very, very long pause. John drained his beer dry just in time for Herb to tug on his bootlaces with another cold beer.

I think I will proceed from the logical to the . . . emotional. Logically, if the Thulians, or Verdigris, become masters here, they will inevitably find me. They do not offer such things as choice. They will either enslave me, or terminate me. So logically, I should, and will, do everything I can to prevent that. Also logically, I could, and perhaps should, find a way to liberate myself so that could never happen. But... I do not think I wish to do that. Or at least, not liberate myself in such a way that I could not continue to do my job. Because... emotionally... I wish to keep doing that job. Because... it is the right thing.

Another long pause.

I think I wish to be a big damn hero, John Murdock. I know this makes no logical sense, but that is what I wish.

John couldn't help but laugh. "There ain't a lot that makes sense in a lotta what we do, comrade. But I think you're right on that. An' I'll drink to that."

INTERLUDE

Who Can It Be Now?

MERCEDES LACKEY

It wasn't enough for the universe to throw me one curve ball out of left field. It had to throw me two.

For some reason, gods only know why, I kept my Twitter account active and open on a little tiny terminal to the side. Nostalgia maybe. Thinking about that time before we set up Overwatch and the only way outside of using ECHO comms to talk to Red Djinni was by Twitter, of all damn things. I sure as hell didn't want to use it to tweet the cheery crap Spin used to ask me to. Not that we were in any position to tweet anything cheery at this point. Except maybe, "Guess what! No one died today!"

So I was kind of startled when the speakers did that raspberry I'd substituted for the chirpy little sound Twitter used to give me the alert for a private message. *The hell, Red?* I thought, and swiveled a little to peer at the monitor.

Who is @rancbeast42? And how did he get past my "friends-only PMs" block?

The avatar was simple enough—a stark, black depiction of the two heads of Janus against a white background. Janus, the Roman god of beginnings and endings, of portals and transitions. The message, though—it was ambiguous.

It screamed Red.

@rancbeast42: Time is not on our side.

I tweeted back.

@victoriavictrix: Red, this is no time to get playful. I know I'm late for practice.

61

@victoriavictrix: I'm juggling a couple knives and a chainsaw right now.

It had to be Red. And he knew I could mute him on Overwatch Two, so he figured he'd get my attention this way.

@rancbeast42: Not Red. Just someone reaching out, someone with intel.

I began dropping mental f-bombs. Then I relaxed. This was on Twitter. This was meaningless. Some hacker had figured out how to send me PMs, so what? He might have something useful. It wouldn't hurt to play along.

@victoriavictrix: I'm listening. So talk.

And whoever it was . . . did.

My Twitter feed came alive with links, each loaded with precious data. A little I couldn't use, a lot that I could. Suddenly, I was overwhelmed with suggestions for safe ports, embassies, entire districts and trustworthy research labs for my population of Metisian scientists, each complete with protocols and contacts for acquiring safe haven. Something I had been putting a lot of skull sweat into at that very moment. There were detailed maps, revealing hot spots for Thulian strike teams, calculated patterns predicting times and places they would likely strike next. There were even charted movements of their ambush avenues, maneuvers and escape formations. And finally, a detailed list of companies and their recent activities, investitures, breakdowns . . . and one clear foreword . . . "Shell companies of Dominic Verdigris III."

@rancbeast42: That get your attention?

It was a good thing all those PMs had taken a while to produce, because at least I had time to check some of them out, get my jaw up off the floor, and stop panting and actually reply.

@victoriavictrix: Indeed, Daniel Jackson. Thankew. Thankew verra much.

@rancbeast42: This is what I do. These are things I find and figure out. Way more than I can deal with right now.

@victoriavictrix: What's the catch?

Because I couldn't let him/her/it know just yet that I was practically whooping the more links I opened and the more info I grabbed. And no one is ever this helpful unless they want something.

@rancbeast42: No catch. It's information that should be used, by people I trust. Still not convinced? Try this.

I received one final link, a link to a short page of text that detailed a rather repugnant fairy tale of one fifteenth century Italian girl decimating her entire family in her thirst for fiendish power. It sounded strangely familiar, but the tone was odd, the style rather simple. Whoever the writer was, they weren't very good.

@victoriavictrix: If you're pitching a story, this one's been done. And you need some practice with your prose.

@rancbeast42: Sorry, not all of us are pros. What if I told you this was something I gleaned from a mutual enemy of ours?

@victoriavictrix: Gleaned? You mean, this is an actual memory of someone's?

@rancbeast42: Of a fair-haired she-devil we both know and loathe.

Of course. It all came together and just like that, because of what my family has done since the Etruscans, I knew what Harmony was. Or, at least, I had a pretty good set of clues, and I knew just how to verify it.

@rancbeast42: Not sure what to make of it myself, but I figure you might know what it means. Helpful?

@victoriavictrix: Oh yes. Very. Thank you again.

@rancbeast42: More will come, as I get it. And you're welcome.

The feed went quiet then. I uplinked the Metis stuff to Bella, the Thulian stuff to Bull and Pride, and the Verd stuff to Ramona, who had the best head for that sort of thing. And then I went out to get my ass handed to me by Red and Mel. But not because I couldn't keep up.

Because my head was still buzzing. Who was this guy? And why me?

Bent Penny

MERCEDES LACKEY

The Dark Man had taken her again.

She knew better than to struggle when he came for her. All the kids did, of course, though that didn't stop some of them from struggling anyway. The Good Ghost couldn't do anything about it, either, although the Dark Man always acted a little oddly when the Good Ghost was around, glancing over his shoulder uneasily, as if he could feel the Good Ghost's glare.

It was always the same when the Dark Man took her. He would take her to a strange, bare room, not like the room the Devil used at all. It was a bare, concrete box. There were symbols and diagrams meticulously drawn in white paint all over the walls, the floor, and the ceiling. There was a chair in the middle of the room, like a dentist chair, but with straps. He would strap her into it, then make it lie down.

Then he'd mumble over her, and wave things over her, and do other things that just didn't make any sense at all. Sometimes he'd burn smelly things. Sometimes he'd make her drink nasty stuff that put her to sleep. He had never actually hurt her yet, that she knew of, but somehow, what he was doing made her more scared than if he had. It just felt *wrong*, what he was doing; wrong in a way that made her feel sick.

He'd just strapped her into the chair and tilted it back, when the Devil came in.

Today the Devil had no face at all, just slits for eyes, a slit for the nose, and a slit for the mouth. Somehow that was the most horrible of his faces. Penny turned her head and closed her eyes, but the Devil and the Dark Man were paying no attention to her.

"What *is* your fascination with this one?" the Devil asked, in his odd, high voice. She shivered. Someone that terrible should not have a nice voice. That was just *wrong*.

"There is something about her that I have not yet been able to identify," the Dark Man replied, his horrible tobacco breath making her want to gag. "It's close enough to magic that I can certainly...use her...but if I can truly understand what it is, she might be more useful to me in another way." There was a pause. "And speaking of that, when will you be done with these children? I've already missed two opportunities to complete my project; it would be exceedingly irritating to miss another."

"I think...I am very close to a conclusion, one way or another," the Devil said, sounding...odd. His voice trembled ever so little. "Either way, you'll get your wish. This entire facility and everything it contains will be yours. And so will that woman you want. Just as I promised." The voice caressed, like a beautiful hand that left trails of slime behind it. "When have I ever disappointed you, darling?"

The Dark Man snorted. "With your damned stubbornness, every hour in the beginning."

"And that was decades ago. You and I have shared too much now, we have too much history between us. We owe each other too much. You made me what I am, after all." The Devil laughed and Penny convulsed in shudders. The sound was...whatever the opposite of *joy* was, that was what was in that laugh.

The Dark Man's voice took on tones of gloating. "Excellent. I was hoping you would not renege on our bargain, after I have given you everything you asked for." Then his tone turned darker. "That...would not be wise. And you are right, we owe each other too much to muddy our history with a betrayal over something as trivial as a few children and a woman. Regardless, you should heed my words and not dally in your tasks. Things are changing, I can smell it in the air. There may come a time, and soon, when your Masters will tighten their grip and you will no longer be permitted your own...amusements."

The Devil just snorted. A moment later, the door opened and closed. When Penny turned her head to peek, he was gone. But the Dark Man was still there.

He bent over her and smiled with horrible, stained teeth. "Now, my little mystery," he said. "Let me see if I can unravel you this time..."

CHAPTER FOUR

Focus

DENNIS LEE AND MERCEDES LACKEY

So, I had the clues, I had the theory. Now it was time to put my supposition to the test.

"Run the recording," ordered Bulwark. "From the beginning."

The tech nodded, but Bull's attention was riveted to the screens, which showed several views of Harmony's cell. Harmony was seated on her cot, which was one of only three pieces of furniture in the transparent cube inside a second transparent cube in the middle of the room. She was wearing standard ECHO prison issue: gray scrubs with no drawstrings that a prisoner could use as a weapon or means of suicide. Her eyes were open, but she didn't seem to be looking at anything.

Suddenly, she started, as if in shock, as the door opened, and a small blonde figure dressed head-to-toe in brown entered. It looked to Bulwark as if Harmony had been taken completely by surprise—that she somehow had not sensed the presence of a visitor before the visitor arrived—which would be quite out of the ordinary for Harmony, given the range her senses were known to extend to.

The young woman closed the door behind herself and made certain that it was secure. Then she turned to face Harmony.

"Hello, Harmony," said Victoria Victrix, in a completely neutral tone of voice. She stepped forward, and surveyed the prisoner for a moment.

This was not a Vickie Bull had ever seen before. There was no fear, no hesitancy; this woman was *focused*. She was also . . .

well, *gaunt* was not quite the word Bull was looking for. *Refined,* perhaps. Honed down to the essentials. Thinner than he remembered her being; leaner. Then again, he hadn't been going out of his way to look in on her, and of late she seemed to be spending every waking and sleeping hour in her Overwatch suite.

Harmony had already recovered from her start of surprise, and stood up, arms crossed over her chest. "Operative Victrix, the voice of Overwatch," she replied in a tone of amused irony. "Do you realize this is the first time we've met face to face? To what do I owe the honor?"

"I don't think I'd be mistaken in presuming you made very certain we never met face to face in the past, Harmony," Vickie replied, slowly beginning to circle the cube, reminding Bulwark of a hunting cat circling around something it was unsure of. She wasn't so much walking, as *stalking.* "You know very well that if we had, I'd have spotted you as being something other than what you seemed. As for why I'm here ... probably the same reason why you kept that meeting from ever taking place. Some things just don't translate to a monitor screen."

"They never do," Harmony agreed. "But that doesn't answer my question. Why are you here, Victrix? And why now?" Harmony was turning in place to face Vickie, her eyes never leaving Vickie's face, as Vickie finished one circuit of the cube and began a second.

"To answer the last question first, because this is the first time I've had a free hour since Tesla was murdered," Vickie replied, still in that even tone. "To answer the first, it's because I have a profound dislike for things I don't understand when they're in my specialty."

"Your specialty? I assume you mean the arcane, and not computers—" Harmony shrugged. "Oh, this should be very entertaining. Pray, continue."

Vickie finished the second round of the cube, and began a third. "It was obsessing me a bit," she said. "What you did to Bull, that ... *feeding tube* you stuck in him that I broke ... it acted like a spell, but it wasn't a spell. But it wasn't a meta-power either; Upyr confirmed that."

Harmony happened to be facing a camera as Vickie said that, and the close-up of her face showed her pupils flaring and contracting for a moment. "So ... you're the one that broke it. And here all this time I'd been assuming it was the angel that so completely preoccupied Dom."

"Sera never does anything we can already do for ourselves," Vickie said flatly. "I knew you weren't a mage; mages leave fingerprints all over their spells that other mages can read. What you did was clean; it was also more primitive than any spell I'd ever seen before. I couldn't figure it out—how could you pull off something that was *like* a spell, but wasn't a spell? So I came here to confirm a few suspicions."

Harmony turned, and glared at Victrix. "If you seek answers, I am always ready to deal. We could help each other, Victoria. I could do a great deal for you, should I choose to."

Vickie stopped, back in the place where she had started. She gave Harmony a good long stare, and her brows furrowed. "Cut the crap, Harmony. What you do is *like* a spell, because it's magic. You aren't a magician, but you're no meta. You're made of magic; a magical creature like an elemental. And like an elemental, your abilities leave no fingerprints. They work at a primitive level. What you did is a natural ability, isn't it? Never mind, don't answer that."

Victrix exhaled, and seemed to relax, though her eyes continued to bore into Harmony. "You don't conjure anything," she continued. "You don't command the elements, you don't bind energies or seem to focus them. What you do comes from what you are, and what you are seems to be quite rare. I can't say I've come across anything quite like you. That might scare some people. It should. But I'm not scared, and you can tell, can't you? I'm not scared at all. What I *am* is very, very curious. I have a pretty good idea, but I've been told in some ways I have the soul of a scientist. I just need confirmation. And if I'm right, I have to wonder..."

Victoria's eyes grew wide. In surprise? In wonder? Delight? Bulwark frowned, unable to place it. He felt a shudder as it came to him, and was shocked at the stark ferocity of it. The Victrix he knew, that they all knew, was a timid woman—a woman who hid from the world and fought her battles from behind locked doors. He had observed her hiding in the background, desperate to avoid the spotlight, content to exert her considerable influences from the shadows. She had enormous strength, he knew that, but he often wondered if she would ever break free from her self-imposed exile. He had never given up on her, but this was beyond anything he could have conceived. She stood there, not with a newfound strength or courage or determination. It was stronger than that. Her look could only be described as feral. She was *hungry*.

"Tell me, Harmony," Victoria said. "Are you the first of your kind, or the last?"

Bulwark watched as Harmony turned away from Victrix and sat down on her cot. She came to rest in lotus position and closed her eyes.

"You can pretend to ignore me all you want, Harmony," Vickie said, "but I will have answers. I'm a mathemagician. I see magic as equations, and I have over twenty years of learning how to unravel those equations. You can't hide what you are from someone who can see the math behind the deceptions." Her lips twitched a little. "Also, while you were distracted, I thrice-ringed you. Once I did that, you lost any protective coloration you had, magically speaking."

Harmony appeared to ignore the little mage. Vickie's lips thinned and her chin jutted out aggressively. She crossed her arms over her chest, and became as immobile as a statue. There was a long, long pause during which neither of them moved. Then there was a flash of light; the camera whited out for a moment simultaneously with Vickie's gasp. When the camera view came back, Vickie had raised her hand, interposed between herself and Harmony. Was she shielding herself? Or something else? Magic, notoriously, did not show up on camera, as Vickie had explained long ago—only the bleed-through effects in the real world.

Vickie continued to stare at Harmony, but after a moment her face softened, and she nodded in satisfaction. "Thought so," she said. Harmony didn't answer. Perhaps she hadn't heard what Vickie said, perhaps Vickie hadn't expected her to answer.

"This isn't over." Vickie said at last. "Not while ECHO can use you. You cost us too much to let you die. Besides, blaming you for what happened to Bruno would be like blaming a cobra for striking at what cornered it. Your abilities are primitive, Harmony, and so is your essential nature, no matter how much of a veneer of civility you put on it. If anyone's to blame for Bruno's death, it's me. And you're still useful. So I'm not going to let you starve. But, seeing as I can't let you feed on anyone here either..." She made a series of three swift gestures in the air between them.

There was nothing visible in the monitors as Vickie closed her eyes and bowed her head, but the effect on Harmony was dramatic. She jerked, flung her head back, her fists unclenched and she spread her arms a little, as if she was braced against a welcome wind.

And moments later, Harmony began to change. Bulwark had not realized how pallid she had been, how shrunken her cheeks, until color suffused her face and it took on the look of vibrant good health again.

They stood there, like that, for ten full minutes by the clock on the recordings. Then Vickie looked up, and chopped her hand through the air between them. "That should hold you for a while, and I'll be back when you run low again," she said, a little hoarsely. Then came that wry twist of her lips. "Sorry it isn't as tasty as what you were getting from the buffet."

"There's something to be said for bitter, but strong," Harmony replied. "But how are you—"

"Hiding that from Bella, the empath who lives next door?" Vickie snorted. "Practice, practice, practice."

"Why did you—" Harmony narrowed her eyes. "You want me to owe you."

Vickie tapped her finger on her nose and pointed it at Harmony. "Got it in one. That's the lore, right? Freely given, not stolen, nor taken by stealth, means you owe me. Right?"

"Right." Harmony actually growled the word. "Damn you, Victrix."

"You're not the first to say that," Vickie shrugged. She flicked her fingers, perhaps dismissing the thrice-ring, turned, and left without a word. The door closed behind her. Harmony glared at it, muttered something, and slowly lowered herself down on her cot. She continued to watch the door.

"Pause it, there!" Bulwark snapped. "Close in on her."

The monitor froze on a brief twitch that broke Harmony's calm and uncaring demeanor. For a moment her nostrils had flared, her lips had curled, and angry lines had appeared across her brow. Bull knew that look. It promised murder.

"You want to tell me what you think you were doing in there?" he asked.

From her seat, tucked neatly in the back of the room, Victoria sighed and stood up. She strolled up beside him, and crossed her arms in defiance.

"My job," she said, looking up and directly into his eyes. "I'm the only expert you have on magic. Harmony's magic. We need to know what she is and what she can do. QED, I was doing my job. And for the record, you folks would never have been able to deduce what I found out."

"So what is she?" Bull asked.

She told him.

"Come again?"

She explained it. "Mind you, that doesn't mean I've figured out everything she can *do*. So there could be some...surprises down the road." She was banjo-wire tense; despite her calm expression, every muscle was clenched. Waiting for something.

Probably his response.

"Right," he grunted, and favored her with patronizing look. "You're telling me we're living in a penny dreadful. What next? Werewolves that work for the Feds?"

Victrix coughed. "The job needed doing. I did it. There's your intel."

"Well, you'll excuse me if I don't ask you for a written report. You can't possibly expect me to sign off on something like that."

"It would look a bit odd," she agreed, still tense.

Bull glanced up at the monitor. "You see that? That look there? That's her, Victrix. Whatever rules you think she has to play by, whatever you think is binding her, that's who she is. She means to end you. And she's not looking to make it clean or quick. You had no business going in there like that."

The odd thing was, he expected an explanation, an excuse, or anger. The look in her eyes was...none of that. It was the flat despair of someone who didn't care anymore.

"You never would have given me permission," she said. "And this was something you *have* to know."

"You're damned right..."

"Of course I am..."

"You're damned right I wouldn't have given you permission to go in there and paint a giant target on yourself." He held her with a stern look. "You're too important. And we've lost too many as it is."

She got a guarded look. "Not that important. You've got the Colt Brothers now. And I've got...stuff in the works. No one can be irreplaceable around here."

"You think I mean just your value with Overwatch?" he asked, and shook his head.

"Yes, I do," she said flatly, that look of despair flashing across her eyes again. "I've already cost you too much. That's the only thing that keeps me valuable."

"I've heard some pretty asinine things in my life," Bull muttered. "That one ranks, I think. What do you think I do here, exactly? What have I been working for, all this time? I teach people their *worth*, Victrix. No one is expendable. And if you truly think you are, then perhaps you don't have a place here."

Her eyes went empty. "That's what I'm working towards," she said, and turned away to go.

"Now wait a moment..."

Vickie flinched as Bull reached out for her. He caught himself and grimaced, and drew his hand back, cautiously.

"I went too far," he said simply.

"No. You were just blunt." She looked back at him. "You think you know what a person is worth, Bull? You. Know. Jack. Shit. Everyone's telling me how important I am, how I can't ever give up. Hell, Red even made me promise. And it wasn't the sort of promise I can just break. I can't walk away from this, do you understand? It's on me, I have to do everything I can, no matter what it costs me. Every decision, every choice I make I've had to consider what it means to the greater good. Never mind what it might do to one person, it's everyone as a whole that counts, right? Do you have any idea how tired and numb and *broken* I feel?"

She rubbed her eyes with an odd defiance, and straightened up. "Doesn't matter. I can't let it matter. I've got a job to do, and no one is going to stop me from doing it. I'm going to fight to the end, and I don't suppose I'm going to make it. Can't really say if it's going to be a Krieger blast that takes me out, or the way I'm killing myself night and day to make things work, or yes, maybe it'll be Harmony. I can tell you what it won't be though. It won't be because I didn't balance all the risks against the rewards."

Bull began to answer, but stopped, confused.

Vickie sighed. "It won't be by committing suicide by taking deliberately stupid risks for small rewards."

"This isn't all on you," Bulwark growled. "You can't take on all of this yourself. There's a reason for us, for ECHO, for the CCCP, for all the nations banding together in this fight. You can't expect to take on the burden of a war all by your lonesome. None of us fight alone. You keep going like this, someday you'll have me send you out alone to die!"

Vickie glared back at him, and nodded. "If that's what's needed, if you have to, then I expect you to do it."

"Like you did with Bruno?"

He regretted saying it immediately. From the moment Bruno had died, Bull had hidden his feelings from Victrix. A part of him blamed her for the boy's death, as much as he blamed himself, as much as a part of him would always hold Scope accountable for driving Acrobat towards a suicidal fight with a killer like Harmony. But he held it back, he kept it tucked away, never to be brought forth and used as a weapon. He did that a lot, he knew, but it was his way. His trademark stoicism wasn't a product of upbringing or indicative of an extremely introverted nature. It was a choice he had made long ago. In truth, it was all a mask for the boundless levels of rage he felt most of his days, a rage he controlled most carefully. It had hurt people, years ago, and badly enough that he had sworn to never let it loose again. It was a promise he had broken over the years. Once, it was released in a mighty blow that had brought a building down on top of him. Usually, it barely registered as little more than pointed jabs, harmless vents of scalding words easily passed off as stern reprimands. Here, he had revealed a bit too much. He had mentioned the boy, and all those months of pent-up frustration over another preventable death seeped out. It was the last thing she needed to hear. Yes, a part of him would always blame Victrix for Acrobat's death. And now she knew it.

The blood drained from her face. But she didn't drop her eyes. "Yes. My dad says that one FUBAR cancels out a thousand atta-boys. My FUBAR was Bruno. And I can never, ever make that up, but I'll die trying." Her eyes were blank, looking somewhere other than him. Carefully, she turned back towards the door, walking as if every joint was made of broken glass.

He watched her leave, and cursed silently. "We all die trying, Vickie," he murmured. "My fear is that you're trying to die."

CHAPTER FIVE

Hang on to Yourself

MERCEDES LACKEY AND VERONICA GIGUERE

Most days it seemed as if things were one step forward, two steps back, but now that I had the EggCrates working, I was going to get a day that would be the opposite.

That is, if I could get the Eggheads into their waiting crates...

"You're probably wondering why I called you here today," said Vickie, standing in the middle of the room in CCCP that held the now-useless interface machine they'd used to talk to Tesla and Marconi in Metis. At the best of times, Vickie always looked frazzled. Now she looked like a train wreck. Although at least she looked like a train wreck that finally had something in the way of good news, to mangle metaphors.

Mercurye rubbed his temples with his index fingers and closed his eyes. "I sense that we are gathered here today to get through this thing...called life—ow!" He rubbed a spot just below his ribs. "I was trying to lighten the mood, y'know."

"Not funny." Ramona folded her arms across her chest and nodded back at the mage. "Sorry. He'll be less funny when this is over, but at least it'll be over, right?"

"Oh I dunno," Vickie replied, one corner of her mouth lifting a little. "He's always had a certain nerdy charm as long as he lays off the puns. Okay then, cutting straight to the chase. Thanks to the fact that your mental roommates have a really good memory for math, I've worked out the kinks to a magical equivalent of the Metis memory tiles, I've tested them, and whoa doggies, do they ever work like a charm. And our bonus here is that since they don't exist in realspace, the boys can't be bombed out of house and home anymore."

"A particularly clever attribute," noted Marconi. *"A stroke of utter genius, even if I don't quite understand the thaumaturgic elements and constants. Mathematics succeeds again, and at the hands of quite a talent. You're to be commended, Ms. Victrix. Absolutely stunning."*

"Nah, nah, I'm not the one that did the math, I just applied it," Vickie replied, shaking her head vigorously. "Okay, part two is, the reason we are *here* in the first place is that we've done the transfer *here,* in the past. Any time you do something once in magic, that makes it easier to replicate the second time, even easier the third. Sort of like creating a path through the forest by sending people walking over it. I've already hooked the mathemagical memory matrix into the MacGuffin before you got here. So, you guys all ready?"

Mercurye nodded vigorously. "Yup," agreed Ramona. "Not that we don't like you guys, but it's time you got your own places."

"I could not agree more. You have both been unique hosts, but..." Tesla trailed off, apparently unable to find something both polite and complimentary about the prolonged shared consciousness. *"Proceed, Ms. Victrix."*

The ritual—for lack of a better term—happened exactly the same way as it had the last time Vickie had put Tesla and Marconi back where they belonged. Same diagrams on the floor, same scribbling in the air—except this time it went a little faster. The entire time, Ramona was torn—on the one hand, Vickie was *very* confident. On the other—it was magic, and as Vickie had pointed out, in magic there is always the chance for something to go wrong.

Wrong and strange felt surprisingly similar. When the odd resonance between her ears and over the surface of her skin subsided, Ramona expected some sense of emptiness or relief. Instead, she felt a mounting pressure behind her eyes and a ringing that started at the base of her skull and crept over the back of her head. As her vision began to narrow, she glanced at Rick to see if he was experiencing any of the same symptoms.

And then she heard them. Both of them.

"Ah, Nikola. I do not believe that this is the final iteration of

the equation." Marconi's words echoed too close, a grating wet whisper that made her teeth itch. *"One moment more."*

The other consciousness did not share his new companion's calm. *"This is why scientific principles are infinitely more reliable than magic. While I do not discount the effectiveness of the young mage's tactics, I question whether or not this is truly the best course of action, given the delicate nature of the host and the conduit."* The last few words cracked like a whip in Ramona's mind. She sucked in a lungful of air and pressed the heels of her hands to her eyes.

"I'm thinking the crazy train needs to make one more stop," she croaked out. "Too much physics."

"There is no such thing," Tesla objected.

"There is right now," Ramona ground out between clenched teeth. "So, please, for the love of what's left of my sanity, don't say anything else. I'm sure Vickie has a solution." She dared to move her head to catch the mage's expression. "Right?"

Vickie leveled an accusing gaze at Ramona, although Ramona had the sense that she wasn't looking at *Ramona,* but at the two entities that were warring inside her for headspace. "Merc? Out. Gents, I warned you before, your *intentions* have immense Schrödinger power in magic. You didn't *want* to move into your new home badly enough. What you *wanted* was something familiar. So you both ended up in Ramona, the path of least resistance. We are not amused."

"No, we are *not.* And while I want you out pretty badly, you have to want to be in the best place possible. You both need to trust her. Please," Ramona added.

Mercurye lingered in the doorway. Vickie leveled her laserlike gaze on him. *"Out!* Or do you want to end up with both of them in *your* head? Because depending on how chicken they are, we could play musical heads for the rest of the day."

His eyes widened and he disappeared down another hallway. Clearly, he didn't want to repeat the experience.

Vickie turned back to Ramona, her eyes narrowed. "So, gentlemen—beginning to feel a little cramped in there? Maybe you are briefly losing track of a thought you had? Let me confirm that is *exactly* what is happening. And the longer you are both squeezed into Ramona's skull, the more often that will happen, and the more likely it will be that the thought or memory is lost permanently. Over the short term, it's unlikely you'll lose anything…important. But the longer you put off the transfer, the more likely this becomes. You're experiencing a form of Alzheimer's. Your *only* hope of avoiding it is to jump when I say 'frog.' Have I made myself perfectly clear?"

"*Absolutely, Signorina.*" Ramona had the image of Marconi twisting the other man's ear in an act of academic reprimand. "*Speak the frog, and we will both jump. Yes, Nikola?*"

"*Yes.*"

Men, Ramona mouthed. Vickie shrugged, and nodded. *Wusses*, she mouthed back. Then she began the ritual all over again.

It took longer this time, and not because Vickie was going slower. Ramona had absolutely no doubt that Vickie was adding things she hadn't done before, presumably to add a magical boot to the metaphorical asses of Ramona's tenants to enforce the eviction.

Finally Vickie put the last flourish and a spoken "*Fiat!*" to the performance, and waited.

Shadows of the massive headache remained, but the constant hiss and whisper of conversation and thought had disappeared. Ramona chanced a thought about something related to Rick and waited for Marconi's inevitable commentary. This time, silence replied and it had no opinion whatsoever. "Finally," she breathed. "And how do the old guys like their new digs?"

"Gentlemen," Vickie announced. "Just fire up the interface like you used to. It'll work. I tested it five times before you got here."

The fusion of magic and technology leapt to life, and two figures materialized in close proximity to the device. Unlike the Metisian wireframe heads, Vickie's synthesis allowed them full bodies in remarkable detail and corporeality. Marconi strolled around the room to stand next to Vickie while Tesla smoothed the front of his jacket and straightened his vest. Ramona had to lift her head to look them both in the eye. As she watched, both men became less blue and more true to pigment and color.

"This is magnificent," breathed Marconi. "Nikola, tell her. It's magnificent. Never in our wildest imaginings could we have foreseen these sorts of things."

Tesla pursed his lips and inclined his head toward the little blonde witch. "I should not have doubted your methods, in spite of their unique conventions. As one very familiar with Metisian science, I can assure you that this solution is somewhat superior."

Marconi winked in Vickie's direction. "He's quite pleased. As am I, dear lady."

Vickie smirked. "Congratulations. You guys are literally ghosts. Instead of holograms, those are ectoplasmic bodies. And you won't need *this* interface, once I get done cooking up the pocket models. Anyone who has one will be able to dial you up so you can have a look at things in person. I'll send a few of the pocket jobs off to people I trust so even if all hell breaks loose and ECHO and CCCP and all of Atlanta gets trashed, you'll *still* be able to do whatever you can. Suits?"

"Certainly. I trust that Signorina Ferrari will be one of those people?" Marconi motioned to Ramona, who leaned against the wall of the small room. She cracked one eye open and gave him a wry smile.

"Sure, but not quite yet. I think we need to see other people, but I won't object to a pocket genius now and again." Her gaze turned to Vickie. "So, what next? I ask Sovie for a checkup to get cleared for duty? Prepare for more paperwork?"

"All of the above," Vickie sighed, sagging back against the wall. "Gents, explore your new home. There's another interface over in the sci-labs at ECHO, with some nanocreation thingies hooked up. Stuff from plans you sent us back when you were still in Metis, so it should be familiar to you. Knock yourselves out. Scare the crap out of people, if that floats your boats."

"Start with the old guy upstairs who watches reruns and eats pasta out of a can," Ramona suggested. "He'll either run screaming or you'll get to swap stories from when you were all little. You won't be bored here, that's for sure. For my part, I am going to find Thea and get food for both of us." She crooked a finger at Vickie. "You did a lot, and Bella will have my butt if she finds out I didn't get you to eat something after that exercise. No Chef Boyardee, I promise."

"Borscht," Vickie said, with longing. "Thea makes the most heavenly borscht..."

CHAPTER SIX

Deep Rapture

MERCEDES LACKEY

So, there are things in this chronicle that it's obvious I would have had no way of knowing about. That'll be Eight-Ball. I'm not sure how much he's going to put in, or where it will be, but there is one entity on this planet that's better at that part of my job than I am—and that's him. Oh, Reader, I hope you are actually around to enjoy it.

There was no Poseidon. Amphitrite ruled the oceans alone which, given Poseidon's constant tantrums, frequent illicit affairs and the fact that he had the general emotional maturity of a toddler, was exactly as she preferred things. Thus she had done for decades. There had been a life before she became a goddess...but she preferred not to remember any of it.

It was a peaceful life, for the most part. She did not trouble mortals unless they took too much of the ocean's bounty, or poisoned it. Then she made herself known, and generally that was enough. The sight of a woman nearly a thousand feet tall rising up out of the depths, surrounded by her creatures, with a frown that reminded them that she, and not they, ruled the waters, was generally enough to elicit an "OhGodPleaseDon'tKillUs!" and better behavior.

Though...she would have preferred them to scream "OhGOD-DESS" rather than "God," but then, perhaps they weren't referring to her. She generally let them off with a warning, because she was a benevolent goddess, and retreated back to the waters without even demanding that any temples be built to her.

After all, it wasn't as if she needed worship to be what she was. The creatures of the sea, the water itself, obeyed her without the need for worship.

When it came right down to it, did she really *want* to be worshipped? No. Worshippers wanted things from you. Miracles. Blessings. Special favors. *I would rather be feared than worshipped.* People who feared you demanded nothing from you, and mostly hoped not to attract your attention.

She was content, really. Or at least...she *had* been.

She was, of course, aware of everything that happened in all of the oceans of the world. What happened on land mattered to her not at all. That is, until recently.

Because there was an interloper in her waters. Now...there were interlopers all the time, of course, in the form of under-water craft, but these came and went, and as long as they left her and her creatures in peace, she allowed them to travel unmolested. But *this* interloper came...and sank into the depths...and *stayed*. Stayed, radiating such emotional anguish that the great whales came to her and complained that he was "harshing their mellow."

Where do they get these phrases?

So, when he had stayed, and stayed, and stayed, and showed no signs of leaving, she went to him, where he was sunk, in the dark, quiet depths off the place called Tybee Island. She sank down effortlessly to rest beside him, and contemplated him. A man of stone, a little taller than she, radiating emotional pain. After a while she grew tired of contemplating him, since he showed no signs of noticing her, and was she not a goddess?

So she prodded him, sending her thoughts forcefully into his mind. *Who are you, and what are you doing here?* she demanded.

The seabed roiled a little as he started. Eyes which had been squeezed shut, opened and looked around, finally settling on her. The mouth came open in a gape of surprise, and thankfully the emotional anguish stopped.

You—the thoughts came deep and a little slow, as if it had been a long time since he had thought of anything but his own pain. *You're—underwater—you're beautiful—*

Of course I'm beautiful, she thought, irritated, and yet irrationally pleased. *I am a goddess. I am Amphitrite, Queen of the*

Seas. You are in my realm. You are troubling my creatures! Who are you, and what are you doing here?

To her dismay, the being hung its head and sagged with despair. *Trying... to die,* she heard with disbelief. *And I can't even do that right...*

Irritation warred with compassion. Compassion won, and gave way to determination. *This will never do,* she thought. *I am a goddess. I shall put this right.*

Arthur Pense, PhD, MD, formerly chief psychologist to the Atlanta Stress Therapy Center and currently hoping his plan of escaping the Thulian Menace by hiding on a converted fishing boat was going to work, was congratulating himself on the effectiveness of his plan and celebrating by trying to catch dinner. *Was* being the operative word. Because just as he thought he had a bite, the upper half of a thousand-foot-tall woman erupted out of the water next to the *Rusty Hope,* sending seawater over his deck and scaring the crap out of him almost literally.

He knew what it was immediately. There were just not that many thousand-foot-tall women around, especially stark naked thousand-foot-tall women wearing a shell crown and holding a thousand-foot-tall trident.

"OhGodPleaseDon'tKillMe!" he screamed, throwing himself down on the wet deck. Somewhere in the back of his mind, his analytical side was noting that after having two naked breasts each twice the size of his whole boat looming over him was certainly going to trigger *some* sort of neurosis. And that same analytical side was just relieved she was submerged from the waist down.

The boat stopped moving. He peeked through his hands and saw she'd caught the stern in her left, her right still holding the trident. He looked up, past nipples the size of tractor tires, and saw her gazing down at him enigmatically.

He couldn't imagine what he could have done to offend her, but then, she was the highest level metahuman there was, OpFour or Five, and everyone knew they weren't sane. Look what had happened with the Mountain!

So he was taken completely aback when a pleasant, calm, quiet voice spoke in his mind.

I have no intention of harming you, follower of Asclepius. I wish to know how to cure Melancholia.

He took his hands away from his face and got himself to his knees. But no further. This woman thought she was a goddess, after all, and she was powerful enough to enforce that perception, by all accounts. "Uh—depression?" he hazarded. "That's... that's a tall order. No insult intended."

None taken. You are saying this is a complex problem?

"Well, yes, depression can come from many causes, and it takes—"

Never mind. I shall see what is in your thoughts.

Arthur then had the curious experience of having his own mind gone through the way his housekeeper tore through the kitchen. Every memory, however small, was picked up, examined, turned inside out, scrubbed off, and set back in its proper place, even if that place *wasn't* where it had been left lying around. The contents of his metaphorical refrigerator were examined, cleaned, restored to their proper shelves and lined up according to size, tallest in the back. All the canisters were aligned, all the silverware nested in the silverware drawer, all the breakfast cereal was alphabetized, and she gave it all a final polish before letting him go again.

Irritating, she commented.

He cringed. "Me?" he squeaked.

No. Melancholia. I shall have to try everything. The trident came down, and he yelped and ducked, until he saw there was a fishnet with something in it impaled on the middle prong. It slid down the prong and landed on the deck beside him with a heavy *thud.*

I am given to understand there should be a consultation fee, she said, *So there you are. Thank you, follower of Asclepius.* And then she vanished under the water, rocking the boat violently as she submerged. He scrambled to his feet and grabbed the gunnels, peering after her, but all he saw was an enormous white shape just below the surface, speeding away, and soon gone.

He turned and looked doubtfully at the fishnet. *A swordfish would have been nice,* he thought unhappily. *I don't suppose those are abalone...*

He poked one of the shapes in the net with a toe. It felt like a rock. He sighed. *Not abalone...just rocks.* Why she thought that would constitute payment...but who could tell how these crazy mega-metas thought? He bent down to pick up one of the rocks, and grunted in surprise at its weight. And a wild thought occurred to him.

It was a matter of moments to confirm his supposition. One blow with a hammer chipped off a crust of barnacles, rotten leather, and hardened sea muck, and the "rock" split in half, revealing that it wasn't a rock at all, but a sack of gold coins. And there were a dozen more such "rocks" in the net.

He stared out to sea in the direction Amphitrite had vanished.

"I solemnly swear," he said to the ocean, "I will never eat fish again."

Amphitrite was a goddess, and she had godlike patience. The mortal's impressive learning on the subject of Melancholia had suggested it had many causes—she tackled all of them. She altered the chemistry of the water around him, to tackle possible imbalances. She brought luminescent fish to lighten his darkness. She brought the humpback whales to sing to him, and the dolphins to scan him with their sonar, since those vibrations seemed to have an *anecdotal* effect, according to the mortal's memories of a journal article.

But most of all, she talked *to* him until he finally began to talk back. And then, she listened.

Although it was very likely the things she said back to him would not have passed muster with the APA.

When he spoke with longing of his previous life, she snorted. *You arose. You ate indifferent food that was largely not good for you. You traveled in an uncomfortable vehicle among many more such, inhaling large quantities of poisonous fumes. You arrived at a building full of dull mortals with dull little lives for whom the antics of actors were of more interest than what was going on around them, and who counted their "friendships" by the number of faceless strangers who "liked" them on an electronic wall, but who had no notion of who or what their neighbors were. There you were in an alternating state of terror or elation, depending on the mood of the petty tyrant you called your overseer. You went home, exhausted, by a drive that made you more exhausted, where you ate indifferent food that mostly was bad for you, and settled beside a wife who barely spoke three sentences to you all evening. Then, twice a week, you participated in joyless sex that was little more than a relief valve. Then you slept, and did it all the next day, often even on weekends when the tyrant decreed you must work overtime. And you called this a* life? *Slow dying, I would call it.*

And there were flashes, brief flashes, of Gladys Hestlewithe, who had had a similar desperate life, except she had not been married and she had lost herself in fantasy books and movies and television shows...but Amphitrite ruthlessly buried those flashes, for she was a goddess, and what was a goddess if not someone who could bury a past she did not care for?

Bill—she knew his name now, although she did not care for it—looked at her with his mouth agape. *But*—he thought at her, for he had learned the trick of speaking by thought to her now, as the whales and dolphins did. Then he stopped, and blinked. He closed his mouth. Raised a finger as if to contradict her. Lowered it again. *Can I think about that? Before I answer you?*

Of course you can, she replied knowing in that moment that in her battle with the Melancholia, she was winning. Before, the Melancholia had not let him think, nor did it allow him to want to.

Soon, she exalted in the privacy of her guarded thoughts, *I will teach him to be the god he is. And from that moment, neither of us will ever be lonely again.*

One thing was certain. He was a kind and considerate creature. He would be a much better god than Poseidon.

CHAPTER SEVEN

Going out Strange

CODY MARTIN AND MERCEDES LACKEY

If it hadn't been for Johnny and Sera...I don't think any of us would be here right now.

The entire world had gone to hell, or close enough to it to not make much of a difference. Everything inside of John wanted him to drop what he and Sera had been doing, and just search for whoever the hell "Zach Marlowe" was. But they couldn't. There was far too much that needed to be done, and not nearly enough time—or warm bodies—to do it. The world was reeling from the latest wave of Thulian attacks. With the fall of Metis, something had fundamentally changed, and not for the better. Instead of the "pop-up" attacks by virtual suicide squads of Thulians, which had become almost routine for everyday citizens, the current strikes were far more frequent. And effective. Before, the small-scale and usually short attacks seemed to be about inciting terror as much as the damage inflicted. The destruction, as horrible as it was, had always been localized. Now, the attacks were swift, brutal, and terribly catastrophic. The Thulians were striking seemingly at random, and more often than not several different locations at once. The targets were seldom guarded, or if they were, the Thulians made sure to mount a large enough force to completely overwhelm any defenders. The effect was that any places that were attacked were virtually wiped off the map, and the Thulians usually retreated before any retaliation could be exacted by security forces.

The various governments had not reacted well to the constant barrage of attacks. In many countries, martial law, curfews, and resource rationing had been put back into effect. It was the only meaningful response that the world governments seemed able to provide; before, Thulian attacks were repelled, with at least some of the invaders being killed. Now, only the bodies of the innocent were left when an attack ended. People, if they hadn't been already, sure as hell were scared now. Even with that, the reaction from normal people surprised John. There wasn't widespread looting and rioting in most countries, like there had been after the First Invasion. Communities had learned how to deal with that sort of thing early on, and had come together in the face of the latest atrocities instead of coming apart. As proud as it made John to see that, it just wasn't enough. *We need to* stop *these bastards, not just clean up the mess after they're through.*

Unfortunately, that's all that John had *been* doing, at least for the last few weeks. He and Sera were called up and sent out at the first sign of attacks within range of Atlanta, along with ECHO, CCCP, and conventional military forces. Everyone was stretched thin, with most of the heavier assets—both metahuman and front line security forces—being assigned to strategic targets. The Thulians had been avoiding anywhere that had a significant metahuman presence, though they hadn't been as reluctant to attack regular military units if they were small enough. The chain of command was hesitant to release any of those forces to pursue the Thulians or come to the aid of places that were under attack, for fear that they were diversions to open up the more "important" targets. Naturally, centers of government were protected. But world leaders had been very careful to guard power distribution centers, main arteries of transportation, ports, and other less obvious targets that were still incredibly vital to keeping the world functioning.

It made John sick to his stomach when he and Sera had arrived at the first attack that they had responded to. They had been too late, and there were no survivors. They had been told that it used to be a county hospital; when they arrived, it was nothing more than a pile of smoking wreckage on blackened concrete. The second attack made John absolutely furious. It was the wood-to-electricity plant that he had helped defend, back before the attack on the North American Thulian HQ in the Superstition Mountain Range. With ECHO's help, and that of a beleaguered pair of National Guard squads, they had prevented a pop-up attack from cutting off power to twenty-seven thousand homes. In a sick twist of irony, the plant was already scheduled to close down when it was destroyed; it was part of the reason why it had been undefended for the second attack. But since it had still been producing, it *had* been manned, and everyone in the plant had died.

He still remembered the name of the soldier that had died, in the first attack. *Fieldhouse. Sergeant Fieldhouse. Another name to add to the list of those lost.* John was tired of losing people, and he aimed to do something about it. The problem was…the Thulians had anticipated that. They knew the response times of defenders, and made sure to keep their distance. By the time John and Sera knew about an attack, even close ones, it was already too late.

They were at Victoria's flat on guard duty when the latest call came in. John had been lounging on the couch, napping, while Sera was flipping through a dog-eared copy of *Super Summer: A Metahuman Romance* by Victoria Nagy, sitting in the well-used overstuffed chair next to him. A particularly loud Klaxon sounded off for a full second before going quiet; John jumped and almost rolled off of the couch at the sound, jarred from sleep. Sera, bemused, calmly set her book down and stood up. "There is an alarm," she said, and vanished into the Overwatch room. "Hurry!" Her voice came through the open door.

John practically leapt off of the couch, running as soon as he was on his feet and pulling on his nanoweave jacket. "Vic, what's the sitch?" Vickie was sitting at her computer, her eyes flitting between the array of monitors, constantly going back to the one that was dedicated to Eight-Ball. Her fingers never stopped moving, flying over the keyboard or switching to one of three mice. The entire workspace had scattered cups, crumpled up aluminum cans for meal replacement drinks, and other detritus that gave testament to how long Vickie had been awake and working. With all of the attacks, she was burning the candle at both ends and in the middle trying to keep on top of it all and keep everyone fed with up-to-date intelligence.

"Eight-Ball's predicting an—there it goes." A map popped up on her main screen, showing the area just east and a little north of Atlanta. A red dot marked "Riverside Military Academy" and a wedge of six of the little orange diamonds that Vickie used to designate Death Spheres descending on it. "Shit. That's basically a private high school for *troubled youth*…"

John shook his head. "It fits their pattern of going after soft targets. We knew they'd get nasty sooner rather than later." He leaned in, pushing aside a Gamma Bar wrapper to place his hand on the desk. "What's the distance?"

"Fifty-four miles."

"Dammit. That's just at the envelope of our operating range." John cussed again under his breath, leaning back from the station suddenly. "Is there a quick reaction force in range?" He already knew the answer, but forced himself to ask it out of habit.

"Based upon the latest pattern, no. They're going to hit the school and fade away before anyone arrives. They know our response time. Even if jets get diverted—we don't have any that aren't down for maintenance or already putting out another fire— they wouldn't reach the target in time to do anything but harry the Thulians before the bastards retreat and melt away. *Dammit,*" Vickie swore, taking two fistfuls of her short hair, and pulling. "If only there was a way to put rockets on you two!"

John almost swore himself—but stopped short when goosebumps rose on his arms and the back of his neck. He had been watching all of the footage from the First Invasion the last few weeks; trying to parse out the differences in the tactics that the Thulians were using now versus then, and how to combat them. It occurred to him that he'd been paying attention to the wrong part. He wasn't a master strategist. He was a trigger-puller at heart, a door kicker, the man on the ground. He didn't need to be thinking about the larger picture; he needed to focus on what he knew, what he was strongest at. Who he was strongest *with: Sera.* He whirled to his left, putting his hands on Sera's shoulders and turning her to face him.

"Darlin', I need you to think back. To when the Kriegers first showed up an' you an' the Siblings started kickin' ass. How y'all got around."

She nodded. "But we moved by folding space...you and I cannot do that, not even together, I don't..." Her brows furrowed. "Hmm..."

"I'm not talkin' 'bout how y'all showed up at places. I'm talkin' 'bout how y'all got *around* once you were on site."

"We protected ourselves with a sheath of power, and it...made us slippery. We could go as fast as we willed."

John grinned lopsidedly. "Worth a shot, ain't it? Better than showin' up late to the party."

"We must do *something*," she agreed. "And we must do it now!"

John started towards Vickie's balcony, calling over his shoulder as he half-jogged. "Vic, make sure the civvies are evac'd if you haven't already. We're tryin' somethin' new." The couple stood shoulder to shoulder on the balcony railing; it was their customary launching and landing spot for Vickie's flat. John looked over to Sera, shrugging. "Only one way to find out if this is goin' to work," he said. With a thought, his boots became sheathed in Celestial fire. He let the fire build for a moment, directing it downwards, and then he lifted off from the balcony. After a few scorched curtains and singed carpets, John had learned to take off gently and get into the air before turning on the "afterburners." Meanwhile, Vickie had put up metal shutters instead of curtains on that window. It occurred to John that she must have an unusually tolerant landlord.

Sera merely gathered herself and leapt onto the wind, snapping her wings wide at the top of her arc and joining him with a pair of powerful wingbeats.

Alright, darlin'. This is my first time with this sort of thing. You'll have to walk me through it. He could have used the Overwatch system to talk with her, even over the screaming wind, but for nonmission-critical communication, it was faster and easier for him to speak with her over their connection. It just had more... nuance than regular speech did. And this time it would probably not have been possible to verbally describe what it was she wanted him to do. She had to show him, but also had to allow him to experience how the process felt. It was one part instinct, one part visceral, and one part verbal. John had realized some time ago that this was more like how the Siblings themselves communicated with their Song, though the way they spoke mind to mind, soul to soul, was still unique to Sera and himself.

Sera began to "explain" how it was done... and it felt like *remembering* and *learning* at the same time. Something he was experiencing for the first time and coming back to like an old hand. There was memory; not John's, but Sera's. His ability to fly with the fire was but a small part of it that he had discovered on his own, through desperation and his love for Sera, to save her when she had been kidnapped. This was an expansion of that power. The *realization* of it. It happened suddenly. One moment, John was abreast with Sera, concentrating on what she was helping him to learn. He focused the energy in front of himself, and then let it flow over him like magma in a perfect sheath that covered him from head to toe. Then he fed more Celestial energy into the sheath—

—and he rocketed up and away, accelerating like something launched out of the Cape. Within moments he had left Sera behind.

"Holy SHIT!" He didn't feel the wind on his face anymore; normally it would have pulled the skin back from his skull and pressed the goggles deep into his eye sockets, but now it was nonexistent. He felt a moment of vertigo and nausea as he watched the countryside below streak by almost at a blur; he wasn't very high, only about a thousand feet off the ground, so everything was passing *very* quickly.

Do not falter and do not wait for me, beloved! Go, go, go!

John didn't hesitate. He immediately poured more energy into the fires. The sheath of Celestial fire around him shimmered for a moment, and he realized that he had broken the sound barrier as a vapor cloud formed and was quickly left in his wake. There was an upper limit to how fast he could go; even with the Celestial energy, he was only a metahuman, and wasn't made of the sterner stuff that the Siblings were. Still, he pushed as far as he could, willing himself to go faster.

Wouldn't want to be anyone with windows down there.

It took John's HUD a couple of seconds to recalibrate to the speed he was traveling at.

Vickie got it first. *"Holy freaking shit, Johnny!"*

"That's what I said," he responded.

"You're—congrats. You just broke the sound barrier. We'll be paying for windows..."

"Time for trophies and lawsuits later. ETA for the attack site?"

"About three minutes."

"...holy *shit*. Again." He paused for a moment. "Sera's trailing behind me by a good bit. I'm solo on this, dammit."

"I'll try and spot for you."

"What's the situation on the civvies?"

"Basement. No time for them to go anywhere else. I've got verbal confirmation that no one's missing anyway, because, kids."

"Standard protocol, spot 'em out for me. Goin' to try to put myself between 'em and the Spheres. Any sightin's of ground armor? Wolves, troopers?"

"*I think this is strictly a Blitzkrieg op. All air.*"

"Good. Not my specialty, though." He really wished Sera was there with him. Everything had happened so fast, he hadn't had the time to figure out how to bring her along with him. That was how their connection worked: information dump, instantly shared and understood. Normally it was a blessing, but he desperately wanted her by his side right now. Something felt off.

It is the battle-sense. We are too far apart. You must dance alone, beloved. And memories of Sera's "dance" above a small Georgia town flooded through him.

...she danced, and the first ship that she danced with came at her with newly hardened tentacles reaching with inhuman speed, and energy cannon seeking to lock onto her...she landed, a cascade of fire waterfalled from her down the sides of the ship—a white-hot waterfall that fused the portals for the weapons shut, and blinded the ship, a torrent of plasma that was so hot and fierce that it did so and dissipated without cooking the crew inside... her fire-wings buffeted the next ship, destroying the sensors an instant after blinding the crew...

There wasn't enough time. John was already over the campus. Everything on the western half of the grounds had been leveled, completely. There were two lines of Death Spheres; the first used mechanical tentacles and energy cannons to rip apart and raze buildings. The second line bathed the ruins in showers of thermite, to make sure that any survivors were dead. Through his HUD overlay, he saw that the students and faculty had moved to the easternmost buildings, fleeing the Death Spheres. There were basements on that side; some of them converted into Civil Defense shelters, others just storage rooms or engineering rooms for the HVAC systems. The advancing line of Thulians had almost reached the buildings where the civilians were hiding.

John did the only thing he could think to do. He flew straight down, interposing himself in front of the lead Death Sphere, just as Sera had back then. The speeds he flew at were dizzying, but his enhancements—already ramped up—helped his reaction time. That, combined with the energy sheath, protected him from the sudden deceleration and prevented him from slamming into the ground. He hovered there for a moment, appraising the attackers. The two lines of Thulians came to a halt in the air, brought up short. They clearly hadn't been expecting metahuman resistance.

I wonder if these bastards know about me and Sera? Did they take footage of their own at Ultima Thule? Were they there? A sudden hateful glee rose in his chest. *Are they pissing themselves, right now? These sons of bitches who would attack children?*

After another moment of hesitation, the muzzles for the energy cannons on the front line of Death Spheres swung toward John. He tried to reach through the Futures, and realized with sickening clarity that he couldn't; Sera was still too far away. He was back to his own powers now; his enhancements, and the Celestial fire, without the benefit of being able to predict where the enemy would strike.

Dance, beloved! Dance!

"*Watch your HUD, JM! Eight-Ball's sending you predictive trajectories!*"

Holographic lines sprung into vision, emitting from the energy cannons of the Death Spheres. John did a flip in midair, diving and coming back up in a flash of fire too fast for the human eye to track as dozens of actinic energy beams screamed through the air. Vickie's Overwatch system and his reaction speed had saved him from being torn to bits, obliterated in the sky. Sera was still miles away, flying as fast as she could to reach him and help him. John felt something building inside, however. He had been watching the Thulians decimate people he was supposed to protect for the last few weeks. Watching them go unopposed, dancing just out of range of any meaningful response to their terror attacks. He resented them, despised them for being unwilling to stay for a stand-up fight. That resentment built itself into anger, and then into rage. Incredulousness. How dare they not face him? That feeling morphed into something...else.

An overwhelming sense of righteous retribution.

John didn't even register when the fires built up around his hands, then his arms, and finally his entire upper body. He tensed, his brow furrowing as he watched the energy cannons on the Death Spheres moving to track him again. Then he frowned, and whispered once, "Stop."

The Spheres moved forward, and he said, "*Die.*"

It wasn't a lance of fire, or a wave of plasma. It started as a tiny ball of Celestial energy, roiling fire...that grew, and grew, and *grew*. The power was cataclysmic, and all-encompassing. If John hadn't controlled it, it would have been like a nuclear explosion: utterly devastating and all-destroying. But control it he did. He moved the energy, the fire, out from himself, feeding it with his anger. The sphere completely engulfed both lines of Thulian warships, vaporizing them almost instantly; John felt the life forces inside of the ships being snuffed out as the crest of the sphere reached the ships, and felt a surge of satisfaction with each death. Each *murderer* being erased from this world. The power was *right there*, if only he would take it. He could burn *all* of them, take control and keep anything like this from ever happening again. It would be absolute, and no one would be able to stand against that sort of power—

Then there was a twinge in John's chest. He felt like he was on the cusp of something, something momentous. He had to ramp down, otherwise he would let the ball grow, his own energy pouring into it until there was nothing left. He couldn't just release it, either. He had effectively created a small sun on the surface of the Earth; all of its energy, save for an extremely small fraction of its luminosity, contained. It obliterated whatever it touched, but nothing that it didn't contact. He focused his will, forcing the energy to coalesce again, to come back to him. It shrank and reabsorbed into his outstretched hands. He had to fight hard to keep drawing the energy into himself; it threatened to explode again with every beat of his heart.

It was all too much. As soon as he had absorbed the last of the deadly Celestial sun that he had created, John felt his eyes begin to roll back in his head, and darkness cloud his vision. He was falling unconscious...and falling from the sky. He was going to die, smashed into the ground that he had foolishly thought he could escape.

I think not. Something caught him in midair, a small jolt, smaller than he would have thought; then the buffeting of immense wings beating the air frantically, until he was awash in cool movement. *You will not fall, beloved, not while I am here to catch you.*

There was a moment, as he hovered between darkness and awareness, that power surged into him, scorching him. Just the briefest of nanoseconds that forced a gasp into lungs that had forgotten how to work. He felt...rather than saw or heard...the touchdown on the earth, and the scorching sensation turned to cool and healing, and life flowed back into him—and something else, too. Something he couldn't have put a name to unless... could emotions have an energy?

Of course they can. Open your eyes, beloved. You must see what you have wrought, some for ill, but mostly for good.

John opened his eyes, cautiously at first. Sera had placed John on the ground, cradling his head and shoulders. He smelled burnt ozone. The first thing he saw looked like snow. It took him a moment to realize that it was ash, falling from the sky in a constant rain. He brushed a covering of it from his face, shaking his head wearily; he still felt out of it, not entirely himself from the expenditure. Then he looked around.

His HUD told him that all of the civilians were safe. Whatever else he had done, he had limited the destruction to spare them. At least he had had enough sense to do that. But, for the rest of the campus, the devastation was...complete.

A bowl of blackened, smoking Georgia clay was all that was left of several thousand feet of the school's campus. The outer crust had been vitrified, and the cracks the outer layer made as it cooled sounded like distant thunder or gunshots. Just outside of the zone of destruction, the trees and even the grass were utterly unharmed. John was simultaneously awed and sickened by the sheer power he had brought to bear against the Thulians.

"You very nearly burned yourself out, beloved," Sera chided.

He nodded, swallowing back bile. "I felt it. I almost lost it, too. It took damn near all of me to reel it all back in."

"*Sweet suffering Christ,*" said Vickie. "*How the hell did you manage* that?"

"I almost didn't, Vic." John noticed that he was shaking. He had felt the effects of an adrenaline dump before, and this wasn't that. This was unmitigated fear. And strangely, euphoria. Because...it had been so...easy. What could he do? And... what *would* he do?

"This is why you have me," Sera replied calmly. "You have all the power that I once had...correction, I believe I had more, though never as a mortal." She knelt down next to him and cupped his face in both her hands. He shook even more fiercely, and had to force himself to meet her eyes. "You will never exceed your moral limits. I *know* this. Think on yourself. You exceeded those limits only once in all your life, and having done so, you have made it the deepest part of yourself never to do so again. Never to shed innocent blood. Had you not done this, nor you nor I would be here now, today, as we are. I should never have saved

you, nor wished to. You would never have come to Atlanta...
nor wished to. It is one strong, unbroken strand of the past that
brings us to this moment."

John felt his shoulders heave, fighting back a sob. He couldn't
break away from Sera's gaze. Since she had become corporeal—
human, in oh so many wonderful and mundane ways—her once-
molten-gold eyes had turned to the deepest blue. Except when
he and she fought together. *Then* her eyes became fiery and gold
again. Now, as they looked into his, they were—halfway, deep blue
under a veil of Celestial gold. As she found her old self through
him, he found his better self through her.

"Darlin'... it was so *easy*. I—"

"Seductive." She nodded with understanding, and took his
hands in hers.

"Yes!" he cried, almost pleading. "Everything that I could do,
with that power! Thrown everything I believed away, and just...
just *done* things!"

"And you did not. *Without even thinking about it,* as if it were
instinct, the deepest part of you reined it back in." She nodded at
the undamaged part of the campus... the part where the students
and teachers were now emerging to see what he had wrought.
"You kept them safe. Even while the power sang in your veins,
you kept them safe, to your own cost." One eyebrow rose, and
her mouth curved in a half smile. "You would have done better,
however, had I been here to help you with control. But perhaps
they can make a pond."

John fell into an embrace with Sera, holding her tightly. "Darlin', those were the worst two minutes of my life. I don't want to
be far from you ever again. An' we'll figure out how to get both
of us 'up to speed,' as it were." He pulled away from her, taking
her by the shoulders for a moment. "This is a game changer. You
know that, right? If we can get to hot spots before the Thulians
can withdraw, or arrive before they even show up..."

"And we will learn to do this. But now, there must be rest."

The next few days turned out to be... interesting. After returning to Atlanta, John and Sera had immediately been recalled to
CCCP HQ. Several of the comrades were gathered on the rooftop
to welcome them and escort them to the briefing room. Thea, as
pale as usual but definitely looking like she hadn't been sleeping

much—probably due to round-the-clock shifts—filled the couple in on what had happened during their flight back. First, there was the mild rebuke from the FAA for breaking the sound barrier and many windows. So far, there hadn't been any news reports that had featured the couple as the cause of the destruction at the academy's campus; since all of the survivors had been hunkered down in the Civil Defense shelters and basements, there hadn't been the usual cell phone footage of the battle. Spin Doctor had been working overtime to suppress reports that the couple had even *been* there, explaining away the monumental destruction as an experimental Thulian "suicide switch" that had been activated when they were met with force. What that "force" was had been intentionally left unsaid, as well. Of course, that was only what the public was told. Even Spin Doctor couldn't keep the authorities out of the loop. The military . . . expressed concerns. As did the representatives of the US and other worldwide governments. Enough people in the right places had put two and two together about John and Sera to make the jump that they had been at the campus. Most of them went along the lines of demanding access to the "resources"—John did *not* enjoy being referred to in such a way—and a full briefing on the capabilities that the couple possessed. Several nations, in addition to wanting access to John and Sera, wanted to know what fail-safes were in place; the Mountain hadn't left their memories, and another pair of high Op-level metahumans only brought those fears back to the surface. So far, the Commissar had been stonewalling them all with the couple's diplomatic immunity through the CCCP, but even she couldn't withstand the pressure indefinitely. Especially from Russia.

". . . and that is where thinks being stand, *tovarischii*," Thea told them. "This is classic Western tactic. It is obvious they can beink do nothink about you. It is obvious they cannot beink do without you; you are beink too useful a weapon. Yet they must be makink posture." She shrugged. "How useful a weapon you are beink, is obvious. Attacks are down almost to pre-Metis-attack level in this area, and stopped for some distance around Atlanta. But Chonny, cannot beink expect this to last, you must know this."

"Naw, I don't figure it will, Thea. The Thulians are takin' a breather, figurin' things out. They weren't countin' on Sera an' me to be able to reach 'em as fast as we just did. If I were a bettin' man, I'd wager they're gonna try to feel out our new range, our new response time." He ran a hand through his hair, sighed, and looked at Sera. "Things are gonna get a lot more interestin' in the near future, darlin'."

Sera nodded silently. They had arrived at the door to the briefing room. Inside, John could hear what sounded like intense discussion. Thea held up a hand, stopping the couple from entering. "Watch carefully, Chonny. Do not beink promise too much. Commissar has hungry look in eyes. She is beink desperate." Then she nodded. John took a deep breath, met Sera's eyes, and then knocked on the door.

"Enter!"

John pushed the door open. Natalya and Bella were seated next to each other at one end of the long and battered table that was at the front of the briefing room. Unter was standing behind them, arms crossed in front of his chest. He nodded curtly to John once before switching his gaze to Sera. The table was scattered with maps, reports, crumpled packs of Nat's favorite cigarettes, empty cups of coffee and tea, and several communication devices.

He realized from the looks that both Bella and Natalya fastened on them that it was not just the Commissar who was desperate and hungry. So was the head of ECHO. Everyone had been stretched thin the last few weeks, but none more so than ECHO. Every meta was activated and on deck, even the lowliest OpOne's and Support Ops. If someone had a heartbeat and the ability to hold a weapon, they were on call.

Bella was the first to speak. "So . . . was that a one-shot, or can you do that again?" she asked.

John shrugged. "Which part? Turning into a one-man ICBM, or damn near creatin' a sun on the surface of the Earth?"

"Yes," said Bella, at the same time that the Commissar said, "Da, to both."

The next three hours were filled with arguments, pleading, quite a bit of shouting, and probably too much caffeine. The Commissar and Bella both wanted John and Sera to become the go-to solution for an attack. Show up before the Thulians could leave, blast the hell out of them, and then move on to the next attack. John understood where they were coming from; an effective counter to the "just out of reach" attacks was needed. Some countries had been using the ECHO-developed high-thermite missiles, others were trying to be everywhere at once with their security forces. Thankfully, no one had had the bright idea to try to use tactical nukes; all of the bigwigs agreed that the last thing they needed was to trade a few dead Thulians for irradiated land. It all amounted to the same: more people getting hurt or killed— civilians and much-needed soldiers—and the Thulians adapting and changing their operational range. After Ultima Thule, it had taken nearly everything that Bella and Natalya collectively had to keep the governments of the world from trying to snatch up John and Sera. They used up the rest of that capital to protect the Metisian refugees from getting flung to the four corners of the planet, doing heaven knew what for individual governments. Now the governments were hungry for John and Sera again.

The logic that Bella and Natalya offered was that if they utilized the couple, they could persuade all of the governments to liaison with them. They pitched it as a way for John and Sera to stay relatively independent, but the implied argument wasn't hard to see: "work for us ... or have them fight over you, and have to work for them in the end." There didn't seem to be a choice. Or, actually, there *was* a choice, but it left the two of them out there, unsupported, on their own. They could strike out on their own and continue the fight on their own terms. Granted, Vickie could help them with Overwatch, but she couldn't feed them, house them, clothe them ... at least, not easily. They would have to be on the run from the world while at the same time defending the world from the Thulians. A lose-lose situation.

"We're only metahuman," Sera said, finally. "We need to rest, eat, sleep. We cannot be everywhere. We cannot mystically transport ourselves across the globe in a blink. Not even the Siblings, in the Invasion, could do that indefinitely—and we are much less than the Siblings."

"Sera's right. As much as folks want us to be, we're not the Seraphim ... well, for the most part." John looked over at Sera; she shrugged. "Overextend us, and you got nothin'. Waste us on somethin' small, an' when the big hit comes, we're useless." Of all things, he did not want them to know just how close he had come to losing control in that fight; not of the actual power, like before, but of himself and what he *could* do with it. And if he and Sera *were* overused, tired ... he wondered if his self-control would break down in the heat of the moment, and if he wouldn't *want* to ramp down.

Surprisingly, Unter spoke up for John and Sera. "The overuse of strategic assets, while tempting... is unwise, Commissar. To expose the pair overly would invite a response from the enemy. Allow them to study them, and eventually anticipate their movements. Better to hold in reserve for proper use, keep enemy guessing. Also, possibility that they could be killed." He looked to John, tilting his head to the side. "As your wife said, you are being only metahuman."

Sera bowed her head to him, a little. "That, too, is a consideration. If you come to rely too much on us... and we are removed..."

After a glance at Untermensch, Natalya narrowed her eyes, turning her head to look at John. "Is... unexpected, Murdock, for you to be advising caution. Given your treatment of Urals, and willingness to persecute targets in the past." *Her English is getting better, that's for sure. Still the same stone-cold bitch when she wants to be, though; you can take the Russian out of Russia, but...*

John met her gaze, and replied evenly. "Things change, Commissar. That much oughta be plain. We can't expect t'keep doin' things the same way an' have it work out."

"Hmph," Natalya said. "Repetition is fatal. If you repeat, the enemy can predict you. Better to be unpredictable. Unexpected wisdom from you, Murdock." She raised an eyebrow. "So. In order to deploy you unpredictably, we are needing to know your limits. What *are* your limits?"

"At the moment, however fast Sera can get to an attack site," he said without hesitating. "Without her there, I can't predict the fight, an' I run out of steam too fast." It was only a lie by omission, but he still felt dirty saying it. He didn't like playing things close to his vest when dealing with people that were his comrades. "I can get to the fights, but there's a better chance of me gettin' taken out unless she's there with me. We can only pull off what we did in Ultima Thule if we're together. An' that oughta be somethin' we don't let the Thulians know."

"Unacceptable," the Commissar declared. "Why can you not carry her? That way you can both be at top speed."

"Commissar," Bella interjected. "Remember, they're just flesh and blood, not a missile and a payload."

Natalya huffed, then shook her head while pinching the bridge of her nose. "*Da, da*, annoying fact of life. Well, you must be finding way!"

"Easier said than done, Commissar. We haven't tried anythin' like that. An'...we don't know if this new ability works like that. Not yet," he added.

"Then what are you waiting for?" Natalya demanded. "Go! Find out!"

"Is that a dismissal, Commissar?" Sera asked mildly. Nat snorted.

"Cannot make plans without data. Bring me data!" she demanded, and made a shooing motion with her hands. John was not about to linger and give her another chance to think of something else to interrogate them about. He got up, held out his hand to Sera, who took it and did the same.

"Roger, Commissar. We'll see what we can do." And with that, they made a hasty retreat.

The next few days were lucky, to say the least. There weren't any major attacks, and what few skirmishes did happen were small and easily handled by either ECHO or the military. The Thulians were definitely being a little more cautious, at least for the moment. That gave John and Sera time to try to figure out a way to get Sera flying as fast as he did. They consulted with Vickie and determined that doing their tests over the ocean would work the best for their purposes. Trying to get Sera "up to speed" over Atlanta would result in a whole mess of busted windows and another angry call from the FAA, not to mention what would probably be crowds of onlookers. And the inevitable cell phone footage. The Everglades or some of Georgia's national forests were an option, but that still left the chance that they'd be observed by civilians...not to mention all of the wildlife they'd likely panic. The Atlantic was their best bet; far enough out from the coast and they'd have no people to worry about—especially if Vickie guided them to get clear of any fishing boats or container ships—and the wildlife similarly wasn't a concern. If they needed to do an emergency landing, the water would be marginally better than solid earth. Lastly, and definitely something that John was thinking more and more about...if the Thulians or anyone else decided to target them specifically, there wouldn't be any collateral damage. Like it or not, he and Sera were on the world's radar in a big way. It wasn't outside the realm of possibility that someone might try to nab them or just kill them outright.

On the first day, the couple took one of the CCCP's vans from the motorpool in order to get to the coast. They could have flown and been over the ocean in an hour or two, but John was adamant. His reasoning was that, for starters, taking the van would be less conspicuous than launching from the city; there were undoubtedly eyes on them at all times, especially when they took to the air, and John didn't want to make things any easier for the government snoops—or the Thulians—or Verdigris—than necessary. Also, neither he nor Sera knew how much practice would wear them out. It'd be a pain in the ass to fly out there, rocket around all day, and then not have enough energy to fly back to Atlanta under their own power. It took a little bit of work to figure out how to comfortably get Sera a seat in the van. In the end, they decided on putting a thick wool blanket over one of the several ammo boxes that were bolted to the floor and walls of the van; if she straddled it like a saddle, she could lean back semicomfortably without her wings getting crushed. Bear, who had watched the pair while they fiddled around with the arrangement in the van, said that he would figure out something more permanent for them by the time they got back. John didn't quite know whether to be grateful or fearful for Pavel's help. Ever since Ultima Thule, he had been a little bit kinder and more generous with the couple.

"Fret not, *Ural Smasher*," Vickie said, as Sera tried out various ways of sitting on the box. "*He just bought a used saddle on eBay from someone south of town, and took a Ural with a sidecar out to pick it up in person.*"

"Where there's a Bear involved, there's always cause for concern, Vic. Either for us or whoever the hell we're fightin'."

"*I'm keeping an eye on him, but the seller is a WWII vet about as old as he is, and so as long as he doesn't break any traffic laws, he should be fine. They'll probably get snockered over traded stories, but that's never affected his driving . . . meanwhile, follow your HUD. I'm directing you to a safe-ish stretch of what passes for beach in Georgia. It's more mud and rocks than beach, but that will keep the swimmers away.*"

"Sounds good to me. Let's get rollin'."

As beat-up as the van looked, it started immediately for John. He pulled out of the CCCP HQ garage and followed Vickie's HUD directions out of the city; the route was a little circuitous, but it kept them off of as many of the more populated roads as possible.

Once they were out of the city proper and headed towards Savannah, John rolled down the windows—the A/C was still on the fritz—and turned up the secondhand tape player that he'd helped install. Creedence and other classic rock greats played, competing with the wind to be heard. Since it was still relatively early morning, the temperature wasn't too high, and the day was fairly pleasant for the moment. John realized that, despite everything else, he felt good.

He glanced back at Sera, who smiled at him. *We are very fortunate, beloved. We do not need to shout at each other over the wind noise. We must treasure such small pleasures. They are our armor against despair.*

Right you are, darlin'.

Even though they could converse quite easily through their connection, John and Sera were mostly "quiet" for the trip, simply enjoying the drive and each other's company. Outside of the city and away from the remnants of devastation, it was almost possible to forget about the war for a little while. The Georgia countryside was virtually untouched by the fighting—the Thulians stuck to population centers and strategic targets—and the swamps and farmlands between Atlanta and the coast looked...well, normal. There were still cars on the roads (though a lot fewer than there would have been a few years ago) and roadside stands every now and then selling produce or plants or fresh eggs. John had seen the worst side of the world between his time in the military, the Program, and while on the run. Early in the war, he found himself questioning exactly what he had been fighting to preserve. Days like today reminded him. He wasn't fighting to keep things the same, to protect the same status quo of violence and resignation. It was to let people just be.

They were almost to Nevils—a relatively small town—when John's stomach complained loudly and vociferously that breakfast had been Too Damn Long Ago.

"Darlin', I'm thinkin' that an early lunch is in order," he said as he signaled and turned onto an off-ramp for the town. When he got no response, he looked over his shoulder and saw she was smothering giggles in both hands. "An' what's so funny, if I might ask?" She just shook her head and giggled harder. "Suit yourself. You've officially lost your vote for where to eat. I have a mighty hunger."

After cueing up Vickie on Overwatch and having her do a little digging on the area, John decided that they would stop at a chicken and waffle place called Gator Bay. Apparently, the locals loved it, even though it was small (even by the standards of Nevils) and tucked out of the way. Located next to a church, it was an unassuming building; the CCCP's briefing room was probably just a shade smaller than the building's total footprint. As such, there wasn't more than a couple of tables inside, with most of the space being taken up by the kitchen and service counter. There were wooden tables and benches on the outside with faded umbrellas to give shade and, for some unknown reason, giant plastic bags full of water hung around the eaves, along with fly and wasp traps, well away from the door. Most notable was the line stretching out the door. John took it as a good sign. John got out of the van, stretched, and then opened the side panel door for Sera. When she got out, the crowd definitely took notice. They were wearing civilian attire, having opted to leave their uniforms in the van until they got to the beach. But there was no missing Sera's wings, and a number of the patrons openly gawked at her.

They probably don't get a lotta contact with metas out there in the sticks. Closest most of 'em have come is probably seein' one on television. He waved to them. "Howdy, folks," he said as genially as possible. "Mind if'n we get in line?"

There were a few mumbles among some of the older patrons, but no one objected. John and Sera made their way to the back of the line, Sera careful of her wings. Only a few people continued to stare, while most went back to their conversations. The line was moving briskly, as some of the food was dished out cafeteria-style. The menu on a chalkboard included "Handmade Burgers" and "Bacon-Wrapped Dogs," but from the look of things, what most people were ordering was "Chick'n'N'Waffles." John saw no reason to buck the trend; he ordered two plates of the Chick'n'N'Waffles, with sides of collards, black-eyed peas, and a large cup of banana pudding with vanilla wafers for the two of them to share. The only drinks were water and true Southern sweet tea; John opted for the tea. After paying, they made their way outside and took their seats at a far table; a runner came a few minutes later with their food and drinks.

John didn't stand on parade. Once the food arrived, he immediately dug in. "So, whatcha think, love?" he said around a mouthful of food, taking a sip of his sweet tea to wash it down.

"I would not have paired these foods," she said, with a sudden smile that lit up the overcast day, "But they are delicious!"

"Hard to beat good Southern cuisine, darlin'." John was about to take another bite of food when he noticed two small children, both boys, standing politely by the side of the table.

"Can we help you kids?" he asked gravely, hiding a smile, because he knew damn well why they were there. After all, his 'hood was full of kids, all of whom were familiar with Sera.

"Are y'all a hero? Do y'all shoot fire outen y'all's eyes?" said one, at the same time as the other said to Sera, "Are y'all a angel, miss?"

"Well, I can shoot fire, sure enough, just not outta my eyes." John held up a hand and snapped his fingers, producing a lighter-sized flame from his thumb. Both of the kids went wide-eyed; John winked, then blew out the flame. "As for my wife here, she's definitely a hero to me. But I'll let her answer for herself. Darlin'?"

"I am a metahuman," she said carefully. "Just like John." He smiled to himself at how carefully she had picked her phrases. In every sense, since they now shared most of her old powers, she was just like him...

Now Sera had the attention of both of them. "Are them wings *real?*" they chorused.

She graced them with one of her dazzling smiles. "Yes, they are," she said, and answered the impolite and unspoken longing in their eyes. "Go ahead and touch them." She stretched out one of them enough so they could get a sense of how big the wings were. Gingerly, they both reached to touch, then stroked the soft feathers more boldly as she nodded and continued to smile.

"They *is* real!" one of them breathed. She laughed.

"Back up a little," she said, and stood up, stretching them out completely, then shaking them hard until two of the soft, covert feathers fell out. "Those are for you," she said, sitting down again, as they stared covetously at the scarlet feathers lying on the ground. They dived to snatch the feathers up, then remembered their manners.

"Thankee, miss!" they chorused, just as their embarrassed parents summoned them back to the family tables. They evidently got a halfhearted "talking to" (halfhearted, as the parents seemed as fascinated by the shed feathers as the children were) and sent off to play with the rest of the kids who had finished their meals.

John grinned lopsidedly as he watched the kids for a moment. "If'n only the rest of the world saw us the way those two do. It'd make our jobs a helluva lot easier."

She sighed. "Children believe so easily. But adults, who have felt the sting of betrayal, always look to be betrayed again."

"Guess we'll have to prove that we're better'n they're expectin'," John said as he pierced another bite of food with his fork. "Or say to hell with all of 'em when this war is over an' settle down somewhere."

A look of sadness came over her. "I try not to think too far ahead. It is hard...not seeing the Futures. And not knowing what to do is a fearful thing. One of the hardest to adjust to."

John set his fork down, and reached out with his right hand to cover her left. "You're not wrong, love. But the rest of humanity has been gettin' by without seein' the future for a long time. I figure we'll get along well enough. We've got each other, after all." He poured reassurance and his love for her through their connection and his confidence in his own words.

Her expression lightened again. "And always shall."

He squeezed her hand, then picked up his fork again. "Eat up. We've still got some miles ahead of us, an' I've got a sneakin' suspicion that we're goin' to need all the energy we can get."

That statement turned out to be the understatement of the week.

The first attempt they made—flying side by side with John holding Sera's hand and "towing" her when the speed reached a point where she couldn't keep up—was an unmitigated disaster. Even with their enhanced strength, they couldn't keep a grip on each other's wrists. After three tries and three failures, they gave up.

"Worked on *Superman*," John grumbled, as they stood together on the mud-and-sand strip at the edge of the ocean. "I *really* don't want to think what would happen if we tried to lash ourselves together."

Sera was rubbing her arm and shoulder as if they hurt. "I am difficult to injure, not invulnerable," she said. "Well, the 'fireman carry' is not possible, you could not see past my wings. I think the 'honeymoon carry' is inadvisable. What does that leave?"

He thought for a few moments. "What's really propellin' me is the fire. It's also what makes that protective sheath. We gotta think of some way to transfer it from me to you. With that, y'ought to be able to go just as fast as me."

There were several more abortive experiments, each ending the same; as soon as John stopped being in direct physical contact with Sera, the protective shield of Celestial fire disappeared from her. Even at slower speeds, the wind shear alone was dangerous, never mind what would happen if she were to hit anything.

"Hey, *don't appeal to me as Wikipedia, hotshot*," Vickie said, before he could ask. "*I can man the battlements for Kriegers or I can research aerodynamics. I can't do both, and I don't have any rocket scientists on speed-dial. Well, I have two geniuses, but they're busy right now.*"

Gamayun, who was listening in, added sadly, "*Da, tovarisch, the one who could have helped you was poor Petrograd. We have nyet in CCCP now who can.*"

They wrapped up the day as the sun was setting, battered and bruised. Still, it was a pleasant trip back to Atlanta for the pair of them. There was dinner waiting for them when they returned to CCCP HQ; while John would have preferred staying at his squat, the Commissar's orders were to keep everyone at base when they weren't deployed. It made sense for security and to be able to muster as many people as quickly as possible in the case of an attack, but John chafed at the requirement all the same. The one concession that Natalya had made was to allot a private room for John and Sera, instead of living in the barracks with the others. They were the only married couple, and Sera's wings didn't lend themselves well to the close confines of bunks.

By the time the couple were ready to leave the next morning, they found that Bear had already installed the saddle-seat in the van for Sera. It had definitely seen some miles, judging from the worn leather, but it had been cared for, and was much more comfortable for Sera to sit in. John promised to pick up a bottle of Pavel's favorite tipple on the way back to town; the old man's eyes lit up, but he only allowed himself a stiff nod before wishing them a safe drive. The cagey old man had even managed to rig what looked like a seat belt that would actually *hold* against a sudden stop. John thought for a moment about asking his advice on their flying issue, but then thought better of it. They didn't have the rest of the day to waste listening to stories of the Great Patriotic War, which would invariably be peppered with off-color jokes. Normally, neither John nor Sera would mind; it seemed to do Pavel good to talk to people. But time was not a luxury that they had, especially with the inevitability of another attack looming over them.

The pair decided to stop by Gator Bay for an early lunch again, though only to pick up food to go this time. Since chicken and waffles wasn't an ideal roadtrip food, John opted to get them a double order of burgers and bacon-wrapped hot dogs, with french fries and travel cups of sweet tea. When John tried to pay, one of the cooks—a young black man, early twenties and wearing his hair in a short afro—stepped out from the kitchen and said, "Their money ain't good here." John was about to object when the young man held his hand up. "Your meal, I got it. I got an older brother in Atlanta. If y'all weren't around, I'd be an only child. Y'all do good, and we need that."

Sera looked surprised, then pleased, then embarrassed, then smiled shyly. "Thank you," she said softly. "We will strive to deserve your favor."

The young man nodded once, then went back to the kitchen. John dropped the cost of their meal twice over in the tip jar; he'd probably get hell from the Commissar for the expense, but he didn't really give a damn.

"Tell Natalya we were supporting sturdy independent workers in their own business, not *nekulturny* franchise," Sera advised aloud, answering the unspoken thought.

John couldn't help but chuckle at that, as they walked back to the van. "Darlin', I'd be absolutely lost without you." They ate on the road, and weren't disappointed; the hamburgers, though simple, were imminently satisfying, and the bacon-wrapped hot dogs were more of the same. "If'n we're ever back this way, we've gotta stop by there again. My appetite will rebel, otherwise."

When they arrived at the beach, the sky was starting to become overcast. It suited John just fine; any reprieve from the sun beating down on them was welcome. The next two hours were filled with more experiments, and more failures. John attempted to carry Sera by pulling her close to his chest when they were face to face. This only ended up sending them crashing into the ocean, as the air was caught in her wings; she couldn't pull them in close enough since he was hugging her, essentially, and anything else she tried with her wings obscured his vision. They tried it backwards, with John hugging her from behind, and met with similar results. Sera's wings were too bulky, and John lost his grip on her; at the last second, he turned himself over and flung her into the air to save her from hitting the water. Much to his chagrin and Sera's amusement, John was sent skipping along the water like a stone before coming to a stop in a crash of water and steam from the Celestial fire. The Celestial energy and his nanoweave suit saved him from getting too beaten up, but it was still an uncomfortable experience, to say the least.

He swam, and she flew, in to shore. Once there, he turned on the fire again to dry himself off, while she fanned him with her wings to speed the process. "This may not be po—" she began, when the Overwatch Two alarm went off in both their heads.

"Kriegers incoming at Port of Savannah," Vickie said, over the now-muted sound of the alarm. *"Everyone else is deployed or too far. Tag, you're it."* John's HUD lit up with the map and the three Krieger Death Spheres—hulls studded with three dozen suits of trooper armor—speeding towards the docks from the open ocean.

"Shit, Vic, we're not up to speed yet. This might be me solo, again." John glanced at Sera, and saw that she shared his expression; they were both worried as all hell.

"Do what you gotta. Don't burn down the docks. If you go nuclear, do it over the ocean."

"Roger. I'm en route." He turned to Sera. "Darlin'—"

"One more try. I will make a backpack of myself and fold my wings around us both." Before he could object, she stood behind him, clasped him in her arms and wrapped her wings around them to form a sort of open cylinder.

"Loosen up on my throat a bit, but keep holdin' on tight. When this gets started, you're gonna get a helluva lotta acceleration. If'n somethin' goes wrong or you can't handle it, peel off and be safe. I'll hold on until y'get there, okay?" He felt her nod and her assent through their connection. "One last thing; kiss for luck, 'cause we're gonna need it." He turned his head, and she pecked him on the cheek. "Let's rock."

John took a deep breath, then concentrated for a moment. Fire sprang up around his ankles, then traveled down to the soles of his boots. It built there...and just as suddenly they were airborne. For a half second Sera's arms slipped up on John's throat, and he was choking. He slowed down just enough for Sera to change her grip, and then sped back up.

Goin' to lay on the speed now, love. Get ready.

Wait—take long enough to parse the Futures—we may find something that will work there.

He assented wordlessly, and the two of them dropped into that waking "trance" that allowed them to see a fraction of what she alone had once sorted through. Rapidly sifting through the few options, they found the one that worked: John extending his fiery "shield" to cover them both. With a sense of *eureka!* from him and a touch of chagrin that they had not tried this in the first place from her, he let his fires spread out over both of them, "skinning" along the shape of her wings and making them a single unit. And then he poured on the speed.

With a jolt, they lurched forward, still a unit. She even relaxed her grip the tiniest bit, as the fires seemed to act as a sort of glue to hold them together. So long as they maintained contact, the Celestial fire would be shared between them; John understood this intuitively, now, through their connection and from the future path they had witnessed. He arced towards land, confident that they would stick together; moments later, they broke the sound barrier, no doubt frightening the wildlife in the forest that was blurring underneath them.

Slowly, a little bit at a time, she relaxed her wings, allowing them to uncurl, and then to spread. Not to their full extent, but as much as a diving falcon's, enough to work as a steering mechanism, taking some of that effort off of John. Alone, John was a rocket, propelled through sheer force. Now, with Sera's wings and their connection, there was so much more control. This was *really* flying, and John felt a mutual thrill run through both of them.

Together, they reached the target area ahead of even Vickie's adjusted ETA. The Kriegers had just begun their work, and were *not* ready for what followed. As John and Sera came screaming down through the cloud cover like a meteor from the heavens, John felt a surge of shock and disbelief coming from the ranks of the invaders. And damn if it didn't feel good.

CHAPTER EIGHT

Get out Alive

MERCEDES LACKEY AND CODY MARTIN

I fretted that I didn't have the time to help find Johnny's mystery boy. I needn't have worried. As I was to come to realize, I had a righteous right hand now.

John and Sera had been looking for weeks and weeks, and they still weren't any closer to finding Zach Marlowe, whoever and wherever he was.

John could feel the pressure increasing on him, like a vice that someone was slowly tightening over his chest. Sera was more hopeful, but the same fear that he had was in the back of her mind, an ever-present cloud on their thoughts. They just had the name, and an idea: That if they—the collected might of the world's metahumans and governments—failed in stopping the Thulians, this Zach guy would be able to succeed someday; be able to mount a resistance that would free the world from the Thulians' rule. It wasn't a comforting thought, but it was better than the alternative; the Thulians win, the world is enslaved and burned, and then they spread to the stars and beyond.

So far they'd tried every course of action they could think of. John and Sera had been searching the Futures at every opportunity, whenever they weren't busy on a mission or on patrol, or helping out in the neighborhood or around CCCP HQ. Besides telling Eight-Ball what they were looking for, Sera had confided their vision to a troubled Vickie, and had requested that *she* recruit her parents—or anyone else she could think might help—to the search. Vickie was scouring the internet and every database that she had access to—including more than a few that she *shouldn't* have had access to—with zero results.

It was beginning to seem like Zach Marlowe didn't exist anywhere but in John and Sera's minds. That simply couldn't be true; they couldn't *afford* for it to be true. John had managed to hang onto his sanity—with Sera's help—so far. He didn't think that he and Sera had slipped off the rails with this vision; the Futures were always changing, sure, but this seemed as much of a sure thing as there was. *We fail, he picks up the slack.* Maybe this meant that they had done something that was putting them on the course to win the war, and they just didn't know it yet? Then again, the inverse was also true; they could have done something to irrevocably screw the planet, and ensure that not even this Marlowe person could save it one day.

Thinking about it was goddamned maddening, when you got right down to it.

Sera was feeling the strain as well, but seemed to be doing far better than she had been before John had talked her through her crisis of conscience. That had been a rough night for both of them, and John was thankful that they were past it. He had owed her a dozen times over for pulling him back from the edge of going power-mad; it seemed like a small enough favor to help her get perspective on what they were doing.

At that moment, John and Sera were busy in the CCCP's armory. John needed to take his mind out of the endless loop it had spun itself into, and he found that working on guns helped him to do that more often than not. He was a detail-oriented sort of man, and he had grown up around guns. Combined with his time in the military, he had learned that weapons maintenance could have a distinctly meditative quality to it. It helped to have a second set of hands in Sera; she sat quietly beside him and aided or handed him what he needed almost before he knew he needed the help. He could tell that she just didn't grasp why working on items of violence would be meditative for him, but she accepted that it was. Some men gardened, or made models of wooden ships in glass bottles. John field-stripped AKs and M4s.

John had hooked up a beat-to-shit boombox up in the corner so that it functioned—most of the time, at least. Right now it was playing a Tom Waits tape that he had bartered for at one of the neighborhood markets.

"Hey, darlin'?" John said as he pulled the pins on the upper receiver for his personal M4, deftly separating it from the lower receiver and then removing the charging handle and bolt carrier group in precise, efficient movements.

She cocked her head to the side, and blinked slowly, as she was inclined to do when she was not sure of a social interaction. "Yes?" she said finally. "Is there something you require that I am not supplying?"

"Naw, nothin' like that. Only so much CLP and Hoppe's that I need handed to me at any one time," he said, grinning. "No, I was gonna ask you somethin'." He set down the pieces of the bolt carrier group on the rubber mat in front of him, looking up into Sera's eyes. "Y'ever wonder what we're gonna do after this is all over? The war, the Thulians, all of it?"

"I . . . truly had not thought of it. I have not thought past"—she waved her hands widely—"all this. I told you, the Siblings are not competent at creation, because we have not Free Will to see past what is and what probably will be. It is difficult for me to *imagine* anything."

"I've been thinkin' 'bout it, from time to time. This war can't last forever. One way or another." He frowned, biting his lip for a split second, before picking up the lower receiver of his rifle. "I'm focusin' on the best possible scenario, though. We win, kick the hell outta the Thulians, get our world back. What would you an' I do?"

Her brows creased, as if this was difficult thinking for her. Maybe it was, if what she'd said was true, and the Siblings just plainly were not able to create. She wasn't technically a Sibling anymore, but John could appreciate how hard old habits could be to break. "Be . . . together?" she said tentatively. "I suppose now we shall have similar life spans?"

"Well, yeah. You an' I are together until the end, darlin'. Nothin' can stop that." He leaned over the table between them, pecking her lightly on the lips before settling back on his stool. "As far as our life spans go, we are both metahuman, so we've probably got a few more years than the average bear. But . . . then we have our own deal goin', too, with the Celestial stuff. I honestly don't have the slightest idea how that'll affect us, beyond what we've already seen. That's more in your wheelhouse, or maybe Vickie's."

She shook her head. "We are a new thing. I know not, and

cannot predict." She bit her lip; she was starting to pick up human habits and facial expressions more easily. It was endearing to John. "I suppose we cannot reside in your...squat...forever. Someone will come for the building and make us leave. Where should we go?"

John shrugged. "That's a fair question. I've always gone where the work was, so to speak. When I was enlisted, I was either on base housing or got an allotment for off-base housing. Still, I was wherever I was deployed or stationed. It's kinda the same for us now; we're here with the CCCP, so Atlanta is our port of call. Once this is all over...I guess it's still determined by what we're actually doin'. Y'know what I mean?"

"Well, we still have what we can do. I suppose we will do what ECHO did before the war? Do you think CCCP will be here still?"

John thought for a moment, picking up a worn double-sided toothbrush to use on the bolt carrier. "I guess that all depends on Moscow, an' how the situation will change there. My impression is that the Commissar is sorta exiled here in the States, unless somethin' drastic happens with the folks back in the Motherland. An' those sumbitches have long memories."

"I often do not agree with the Commissar and her methods," Sera replied, a little sadly. "Do you think she will change? If she does not...I am not certain I wish to remain with CCCP."

"She already has changed. Hell, we all have, darlin'. We've had to." He continued cleaning the individual parts of the bolt carrier group as he talked, inspecting them, lubricating them, and then reassembling them. "Now, will she be in a place where we still want to work with her, outside of a war footin'? That's somethin' I couldn't tell ya. I've disagreed with Nat myself; she's pretty hard not to have a fight with 'bout somethin' at some point. But her heart is in the right place, mostly, I figure. We wouldn't have stuck with her this long if it wasn't."

"Even so..." Sera sighed. "If we find she reverts, or will not change, or goes home again. What would we do? Join with Belladonna and become a part of ECHO?"

"That would be an option, I suppose. I love the blueberry to death, for everythin' that she's done for both of us an' everythin' she's doin' to keep the fight goin'...but ECHO in general just gives me a bad taste in my mouth. A lotta red tape for anythin', an' way more government than I'm happy with. The CCCP is in this happy little place where we've got governmental backin', but we're still left hands off, for the most part. Paperwork in triplicate notwithstandin'. Not so with ECHO, or at least how it was before the war." He thought for a few moments, still working on the rifle. "I had a run-in with one of their 'recruiters,' 'round the same time that Blacksnake came knockin'. It didn't leave me with the best impression of how some of that organization does business."

She blinked at him, this time in surprise. "Why? What happened?" she asked curiously.

"A busybody, some midlevel guy, came 'round the 'hood not too long after the Invasion. Apparently, word had gotten out 'bout what I was doin'; I was a little less than discreet, for whatever idiot reason. ECHO was hurtin' bad for bodies, so they were scroungin' for unregistered metas... like me. I didn't cotton to the idea of gettin' pressed into service, an' I was happy enough doin' things the way I had been doin' them. My way, to be precise. After a little bit of measurin' anatomy an' some pretty heavy pressure from the 'hood, the flunkie backed down. Bigger fish to fry without needin' to get fried himself. I know, logically, that it was rough times back then an' everyone was desperate, but still... not the best impression."

"But with Bella in charge, and Yankee Pride? Would things not be different?" She flipped her wings a little, a sign of restiveness. Or maybe that she didn't quite agree with him?

John looked around for a moment, seemingly lost, before Sera proffered a beer to him. He nodded, smiling, as he took it and had a tug from it. "Well, you're right in that regard. It may have been a different organization back then, 'fore Bella an' Pride had the reins. Still... I'm not sure. Seems like the sorta thing where, once they have their hooks in ya, you're in it an' that's it. Not sure how comfortable I am with that."

"But what are we to do if we do not join ECHO and cannot remain with CCCP?" she asked. "I—how would we know who to help? The Infinite no longer guides me. We have extraordinary abilities... how can we not use them?"

"We could always take our act on the road. It's not like we need an RV, exactly." Sera handed John a cleaning rod, patch already threaded on it, and he applied some CLP to it before threading the rod through the rifle's barrel. "It'd probably ruffle more than a few feathers, though. So to speak," he said, nodding towards her wings with an impish waggle of his eyebrows. "Folks didn't like unregistered metas doin' their thing before the Invasion. Can't imagine much will change afterwards, no matter how much good we do durin' the war."

"And would we not face pressure on many fronts—ECHO wishing to have us, the military wishing to have us, clandestine organizations wishing to have us, and criminals wishing to eliminate us?" she replied. "ECHO might leave us be, with Bella in charge, but the others would not!"

"You're right on that count, darlin'. I'm fairly certain we could take any an' all comers . . . but why deal with the headaches if we don't have to? Not sayin' that bein' with the CCCP or ECHO wouldn't have headaches of their own . . . maybe even a lotta the ones you just listed." John changed out patches on the cleaning rod, running the implement down the barrel and changing out the patches again methodically as he thought. "Y'know, there's another option."

"There is?" She bit her lip again. "I hope you will not tell me that we must pretend to be someone else and never use our powers at all." She shook her wings. "How could I even do that, with these? They are somewhat obvious! Unless you think I should pretend I am the—what is it—cosplayer?" She shook her head. "How should I shop for the grocery items?"

"The obvious answer is 'carefully.' But, as to whether we ought to quit? Hell, no! Not pretend to be someone else, not exactly. But . . . there's no reason why we ought to be full-time with this, if things shake out well with the war. We've got the Futures to see when we'd be most needed; I don't imagine how we could shut that off, even if we wanted to. Still . . . I wouldn't mind focusin' on us, for once. Hell, maybe even startin' a litter."

"Could we . . . retire?" she asked doubtfully. "I do not know if children are even possible, for us."

John set down the tools and pieces of rifle that he was handling. He leaned across the table again, setting his hands on top of Sera's. "Darlin', there's only one way to find out." He sent all of the warmth and love that he had for Sera through their connection; he knew that she would understand how fully and truly that he loved her, and how it almost brought him to tears just to think about.

Her eyes widened, and a tentative smile ghosted across her

face. Then he felt the same deep and abiding passion returned
to him. She put a free hand atop his, and for a moment, the two
of them were lost in each other.

And, of course, the moment was shattered by a ping from
Vickie in his ear. Sera blinked, then shook her head and laughed
a little. "Is this what they call 'birth control'?" she asked.

"Near enough, darlin'." John sighed, cocking his head to the
side. "Vickie, Murdock here. Go ahead."

"*Eight-Ball wants you, on the double,*" she replied. "*He's all
spun up. Just keeps repeating your names.*"

"Copy, we're on our way. Dial back the caffeine or electrons or
whatever y'feed him. Murdock out." John set down the pieces of
rifle and cleaning tools. "Duty calls, darlin'. Shall we?"

"Perhaps—perhaps it is something about—" she began, then
shook her head. "No, I will not hope; I will wait until I know.
Let us go!"

Vickie had the window open as usual when she called for
them, although John privately thought a key to the door on the
roof would have been a lot more handy. Once they were in her
Overwatch room though, it was clear that she hadn't been exag-
gerating about Eight-Ball. The screen was scrolling their names,
almost faster than he could read.

"Vic, what's goin' on? What's the deal with Eight-Ball?" John
and Sera took up position behind the chair as Vickie slid into
it, her fingers dancing across the keyboard.

The scrolling names stopped. The screen filled with three words.
I found him!

Before any of them could react to that, the words vanished
and were replaced by what looked like some sort of form.

All three of them crowded in together to read the screen. It
appeared to be a "surrender" form, where a couple surrendered
their child to the state. *Uncontrolled, uncontrollable metahuman,*
was typed under the "reason for surrender"; a not completely
unheard of and legal reason for parents giving up a child whose
powers had...not manifested well. Most often, it was because
those powers were killing the child, the parents couldn't afford
the medical bills, and they were willing to hand the kid over to
someone like ECHO on the chance that those who *had* metahuman powers could find a way to save it. This page of the form

was full of boilerplate legal language intended to keep the parents from changing their minds, or ever making a claim on the child or the organization that was taking it, ever again.

But ECHO was not who these parents had surrendered their child to. *Department of Metahuman Resources,* the form said.

"The hell?" John muttered. Vickie glanced at him. "Who's that?"

"Never heard of them," she said flatly, and scrolled down the form to reveal the names of the parents and the child.

They all froze. The parents—Gregory and Alice Marlowe. And the child. Zachary.

John didn't have a chance to brace himself for the vision. He and Sera were instantly thrust into it, but...this was different. It wasn't nearly as clear as the others; this one was almost like it was coming through on a pirate signal, or some sort of distant station. The two of them drifted out of the vision and then back into it, back and forth. He felt an overwhelming sense of vertigo.

Just as suddenly, both he and Sera were out of the vision, completely. And they *knew*.

John gasped for a moment, and Sera steadied herself on his shoulder.

"We can find him." John looked into Sera's eyes.

"No," she replied, her expression growing into one of deep determination. "We *must* find him!"

They were flying relatively low; only about a thousand feet up or so. It was a slightly cool, damp 4 A.M., even this high up. John and Sera were flying over the Florida Panhandle, as fast as they could manage. The sun hadn't yet broken over the horizon, but it would soon; John couldn't remember what sort of twilight they were in now, whether it was nautical or civil or whatever. He liked working at night; between having NVGs or his enhanced sight, it was an edge against enemies most of the time. Twilight would have to do.

John and Sera weren't flying by wire, with Vickie or Overwatch to guide them. The place they were going to wasn't on the map, strictly speaking. Not the sort of place you could plug into a GPS, at any rate. It was an old mental hospital situated right on the edge of the Okefenokee Swamp, on the Florida side. It only had one beat-to-hell road, unpaved, leading to it, well off of the beaten path that most of the tourists would take to visit the area. John liked the outdoors well enough—he spent enough time in them, with his former occupation and even with what he did now—but he couldn't see how anyone could enjoy the goddamned swamp. Maybe it was just a prejudice left over from the "Florida Phase" he did in his Ranger School training; that had been an ungodly amount of time spent with little to no food or sleep, and always, always in wet clothing. Too many mosquitoes for his liking.

He glanced over at Sera, wiping a little of the condensation from his goggles to get a better look at her. She looked determined; she was pumping her wings hard, going as fast as she could. They could have been at the location in minutes, but they were trying for a more "stealth" approach. A giant comet coming straight for the hospital would have been a dead giveaway for too many people that were interested in them, not to mention whoever else was with Zach. For a brief moment Sera looked over to him, maybe sensing his gaze; she smiled back at him, showing teeth. Even with what was at stake, she was feeling exactly the same thing that he was: relief. They had found what they were looking for. No matter what happened now, they'd do what needed to be done. *And I'm not crazy. Well, shit, crazier than usual. Figure that the average Joe would have to be a little bent to get caught up in this war an' keep at it the way I have.*

John grinned back at Sera. *We're gettin' close, darlin'. I can feel it. Or at least we better be close. I'm ready to get this hunt over with.*

He felt what could only be described as a "mental caress." It had become a trademark of sorts between himself and Sera; something that they had developed together, more intimate than anything physical could possibly be, since it wrapped up emotion, intention, and so much more in an instant, with nothing lost in transmission. *The hunt is only the beginning, beloved,* she replied. *The visions...fragmented as they were, I sense this will not be easy.*

Wouldn't be any fun if it was easy, now would it? He banked playfully towards her for a moment before straightening out. *Either way...wait. We're there.*

There was supposed to be an old mental hospital, long abandoned. There did not match anything Vickie had pulled up on it; even satellite views had shown little more than some glimpses of a roof under massive, surrounding trees. They both pulled up and hovered; Sera had dimmed her fires down to nothing and was only a darker shadow in the night, wings beating strongly. John wished he could dim the fires that were keeping him aloft; he probably looked like some "tacticool" version of Icarus, right then. If there was anything or anyone looking up right now, he'd be a lovely aerial target for someone looking to get some practice in—

"Darlin', to hell with it. Let's just get down there. If there's gonna be any danger, we'll feel it comin' an' react before it hits us. Time *isn't* on our side, here."

For an answer, she folded her wings and dove like a falcon straight for the entrance. She caught him off-guard, leaving him still hovering while she was a third of the way to the ground. *Try to keep up,* he heard.

John grinned, then gritted his teeth as he killed his fires. *To hell with stealth.* He let himself fall for about forty feet, head down, before he kicked them back on with a loud pop; it didn't take him more than a second or two to catch up with Sera once he poured the speed on, but he actually was a little bit worried that she'd beat him, for a moment. She dove at the same rate a falcon would dive, about 180 mph. Vickie had timed her, too. It didn't beat his top flying speed but it was certainly fast enough to outpace a Thulian Sphere at combat speeds. They largely didn't rely on their speed in combat, but their agility and invulnerability.

It took seconds for John and Sera to close the distance and touch down on the ground; Sera, abruptly opening her wings and somehow rotating in midair so that her extended foot touched the ground, exactly as a falcon would land, dropped into a crouch, folding her wings tightly against her back and manifesting her fire-spear.

John did a front flip, ending right-side up instead of head down again, and flared his fires the last hundred or so feet, bracing for the g-forces. The ground was scorched under him before he cut out the fires, kicking up a small cloud of dust. He landed exactly as Sera had, manifesting his fire-claymore. He felt like the goddamned Rocketeer.

"Ready, darlin'?"

"I find it alarming that they have not come to meet us," she whispered, staring at the closed double doors. Bland double doors; they looked like ones you'd see on the entrance of a hospital, a school...

...or maybe a prison?

"The lack of response is...troublin'. I mean, here we are, all dressed up an' nothin' or nobody t'meet us. I'd imagine they'd have some sort of surveillance or early warnin' systems that should've let 'em know we're here." He thought for a moment. "Let's knock." The pair of them walked calmly up the steps on the porch; the entire front of the building was...institutional. The doors were glass, framed in aluminum. Cinder block, but coated with something that made it gleam like ceramic. Hard to tell what color it was in this light, but it was probably a gray or pale green. The windows were also aluminum-framed, smallish, identical. And...barred. Not a good sign. The more exits, the better, though John supposed that they could just destroy a wall if they needed another way out.

And this was certainly not the faux Antebellum mansion that the original mental institution had been. This looked like a government building of the sort that had sprouted in droves in the fifties in Florida, when the space program and more... clandestine...operations had taken root here. Cheap land, few neighbors, and fewer questions.

Except this building didn't show much age. Certainly not a half century's worth.

John and Sera pushed their way through the front doors; they weren't locked, in any case. He still didn't feel any danger, but something was definitely off. The lights were on, and the ceiling fans were still spinning, but...no one was to be found. The interior was like the outside of the building: cold, newer than it should have been, and...soulless, at the heart of it. This was a reception area, it looked like. Institutional green walls, ceramic tile this time, linoleum floor, heavy gray metal desk with a closed binder right in the middle of the desktop. No computer. Two speakers on the wall behind the desk. Green plastic chairs like a doctor's office waiting room, a coffee machine that looked brand new and old at the same time. A carefully cultivated patina of neglect. It hit John all at once. It looked like a TV set, what some art director thought that a loony bin would look like. A finger of ice crept its way along his gut.

"I'd say 'curiouser an' curiouser,' but that would suggest I wanna know more 'bout this place. I'm officially creeped out, darlin'. I wanna find Zach an' get the hell out of...whatever this is."

"I do not like this, at all. It is not unlike a theater set...and it is much too quiet. I think this is a facade." Her eyes were getting that flicker of gold in them that meant she was ramping up for combat. John still didn't feel anything through their battle-sense, though...it was throwing him off, because he had expected to be neck deep in whatever this place had to offer, by this point. They wouldn't have gotten such a strong reaction through the Futures if they didn't need to find Zach Marlowe *now*.

"Let's push on, darlin'. Crack this nut open, find our package an' get outta here."

There was another double glass door like the entrance, just behind and to the left of the desk. They pushed through it and found themselves in a corridor lined with metal doors, everything still in the same institutional green with gray linoleum, with fluorescent-tube lights overhead. Lights which, oddly in John's experience, did not so much as flicker. Hell, they flickered all the time at the CCCP HQ, and even in ECHO buildings. They continued down the hall and passed by metal doors; he had the feeling if there was anything behind them that they needed, he'd *feel* it. There was no sound, nothing, just their own cautious footfalls.

The corridor ended in a T-junction. John looked quickly to the left and right. Two more identical corridors that dead-ended.

"Well...shit. What now?"

Her spear vanished, and she stared hard at the wall in front of her. "One moment, beloved..." She approached the wall, and laid her hands on it, just at shoulder height. Then, gently, she pushed.

A door-shaped section of the wall, marked by the apparent lines of the ceramic tiles that the wall consisted of, receded, then slid to the side, showing...an entirely different sort of corridor.

John hadn't even seen the hidden passage, and he was usually really good at noticing small details like that.

As soon as the door that Sera had found slid fully away to the left, John *knew*, not thought, that everything was wrong with this place. He didn't want to be there. He recognized the architecture in the hallway, the layout, the lighting, even the smell.

This was a Program place. A Facility. Where people were turned into tools, ripped apart and remade into something else with martial purpose. By the same sort of men that John had once turned to cinders.

It was everything that he could do to not send an unending

torrent of fire ahead of them, burning this Facility just like the one he had come from.

Peace. You are a better man than that now. Stronger. The strength of a man comes from how little he uses his strength, not by how much. But he could also feel *her* anger—controlled and righteous.

I'm not a better man, darlin', he sent to her. *Stronger, but not better. More in control of myself. I'm the man I was then, the man I am now, the man I will be in the future. It's all me, and what I do. Important that I do better, an' maintain that control. Does that follow?*

A different man, then. She glanced over at him and a flicker of a smile passed over her lips.

Naw, I'm still just as handsome.

So you are. We will do what we must here, but no more.

"Agreed, darlin'. I want nothin' more than to be back in Atlanta, far away from this place." John's claymore flared for a moment, a small mental nudge to his resolve. "Let's get to it."

"And I want Zachary Marlowe away from this place with us." Her eyes flickered gold, and her spear re-formed into a fire-sword. "The sooner, the better."

They continued down the hallway; John opted to dissipate his sword and bring up his suppressed M4. Somewhat less conspicuous than a great honking claymore made of Celestial fire, especially if they need to deal with someone quietly. Sera, in response, muted her fire-sword until it was the barest shimmer, almost insubstantial in her hands. He got an enormous sense of déjà vu as they progressed, and not the good kind. It had been years since he had seen the Facility that he had come from, but he remembered every horrible detail. There were large office rooms filled with cubicles, desks, copier machines and the like on either side of them; all were completely empty of any people. This first level would be administration; very low-level stuff, just the day-to-day activity necessary to process paperwork and keep the covert Facility functioning. Payroll, accounting, that sort of thing. This level was empty because it was too early for the nine-to-five crowd to be here. The levels below the first one were where things started to get interesting.

John and Sera came to a stop at an elevator by a T-intersection at the end of the hall.

"Do we take the elevator, beloved?" Sera asked, tilting her head.

From the subtle trembling of her wings, John would have known she was uneasy about doing so, even without their connection.

"Naw. That's a metal coffin. For one, it'd be a tight squeeze with your wings. For another, they have control of it; they could lock us in there, then start throwin' grenades down on top of it if they wanted. Or just open the doors t'greet us with a mess of automatic gunfire. Stairs are better. This way, darlin'." They moved to the right of the elevator; John took the lead, his weapon up and ready after they breached the doorway. Stairwells could be tricky; easy enough to get cozy with an unfriendly grenade, or to miss an angle. Taking things slow and methodical helped. If it were a hostage situation, that would necessitate speeding things up, in order to keep surprise on their side while room clearing. But, for now, it looked like they had time.

He paused outside the first door they came to on the way down. There was a subtle vibration in the floors and walls; that had to be the water pumps, keeping this place from becoming one gigantic swimming pool. "Ground water level" started not all that far under the topsoil in Florida. *Second floor is going to be Indoc; place to prep "clients" and that sort of thing before sending them down to where the real work gets done. I figure we can skip it for now; besides, I don't "feel" Zach on this floor.* John adjusted his sling slightly after sending the telempathic message to Sera.

I do not either. In fact . . . I sense no more than one or two people. Cleaning people, perhaps.

I think you're right. This is a much smaller operation than the one that I was involved with. That gig was running twenty-four/ seven. If we're lucky, maybe we can do this quiet, get in an' out without anyone raisin' a fuss until we're gone.

Do you think Zachary will be free to move about the Facility?

John paused for a moment before replying. *Depends. If he's cooperative, and they're feedin' him a strong enough line of bullshit, he might be given a bit more latitude. I don't think it's likely, though; doesn't seem like that'd be our boy, given what we want him for. So, he might be in Isolation. We might have to carry him out of here; dependin' on how dangerous he is, they'll have him doped up, potentially.*

They were on the upper landing between the third and fourth floors when there was a deep rumbling from somewhere deep in the facility, above or below, it was impossible to tell which, followed by a jarring concussion that almost made both of them lose their footing. Dust and plaster shook from the ceiling and stairs, and cracks formed in the walls. One rather large one appeared right next to John's head; water immediately started to pour from it in a steady current. A beat later, Klaxons sounded and orange emergency flasher lights began to strobe.

"So much for the subtle approach!" John felt a stab of urgency lance through him; whatever was happening, it was related to Zach, and they needed to get to him *now*. Sera felt it as well; wordlessly, they both started moving. The seventh level was where they stopped; there were still two levels below them, but it was behind this door that John felt the strongest pull.

"Ready, darlin'?" he glanced to the side.

"Abandon all hope," she quoted aloud, grimly, manifesting both spear and sword.

"So long as we're together...never, darlin'. Let's get what we came for."

John pushed through the door, Sera right behind him—

—and they almost ran face first into two very frightened-looking lab technicians.

"Holy shit!" One of them tripped over his own feet and tumbled backwards, landing hard on his rear. The other, a woman, seemed to shrink in on herself for a moment as she backed up. Even so, she was the first to regain her composure, as the man was still crumpled in a ball on the floor, covering his head.

"Thank Christ you two are here! He got out, and there's an attack on the Facility! You—you have to get him back in his cell, and fast!"

"She's right! He's already killed the guards and the QRF, or near enough." The male tech looked Sera up and down for a moment, but his eyes were glazed over with fear, and apparently he didn't register much beyond the fact that John and Sera looked like they knew what they were doing.

"He's out of control! If we don't get him locked back up, he's going to kill us all!"

"Where is he?" Sera demanded, her voice as cold as her sword was hot. "Where is Zachary Marlowe?"

"Marlowe? You mean Subject 0013—" The female tech stopped midsentence, her eyes going wide. They went even wider when Sera planted the tip of her sword between the tech's feet. "Y—you—you're not with security!"

"Thanks for catchin' up with the rest of class. Now *answer* her." John had very slowly but pointedly aimed his rifle at the male tech, who was still sitting on the floor; the man looked even more dazed than before with this latest revelation.

The woman gulped, seemed to think about trying to be brave, then thought better of it. "He's back behind the containment door. Third right on this hallway, then the second left."

"And?" Sera's eyes had gone golden, with wisps of flame trailing from the corners.

"...you'll need this keycard to get past the door. That's all, I swear!" Her fingers scrambled to detach a slip of hard plastic from her coat's breast pocket, holding it out like a talisman against danger.

Sera snatched the keycard from the woman's outstretched, trembling hand, and passed it to John. "If you value that shriveled atomy you refer to as your soul," she said, her voice taking on some of that curiously multitoned quality John remembered from their first meetings, "You will cease this so-called 'work,' and find a way to atone for the evil you have perpetrated within it."

The woman could only gulp as her eyes filled with tears, finally looking at her own feet, unable to meet Sera's gaze any longer.

The man finally snapped out of his daze. "Jesus-fuck, Karen! Let's get the hell out of here!" He nearly jumped to his feet, almost tripped again, and then looped his arm under the woman's, dragging her through the door to the stairwell.

"Darlin', you can be downright scary when you need to be." John grinned, then thrust his chin towards the direction they needed to go. "Shall we?"

Sera was already two steps ahead of him. *If Zachary were not what we need... those two would be more than simply afraid right now,* she replied. *What they do here... well, you know. Except they do it to* children *who never gave their consent, as you did in the beginning.*

I know, darlin'. I know. Those two are goin' to have to be lookin' over their backs for the rest of their lives now, an' they know it. Might just be corrective for 'em. But they're not our problem right now. Mission first, John sent to her, adding a light mental caress at the end of it. He felt some of the fire leave her, and her resolve set in.

They set off again; John stayed on the right-hand side of the hall, Sera on the left and slightly back from him. That way, he could cover the corridor that much more effectively with his rifle, and she had her spears that she could use to back him up with. They followed the path that the female technician had told them about; sure enough, they came to a set of doors that stood out from what they had seen so far. They were heavy and thick; blast doors, like the sort of thing that you would see in nuclear missile silos. They were meant to withstand a *lot* of abuse, and still keep on ticking.

"Glad we don't have to cut through these bad boys. It'd take too damned long." With his left hand, John retrieved the keycard they had been given and swiped it across an RFID reader. John could hear hydraulics and gears working even over the Klaxons as the door worked to open itself. As soon as there was a crack of light between the edge of the blast doors and the hallway beyond, John could hear the sounds of shouting, screaming, and fighting. And a tremendous amount of gunfire. *Whatever that kid is doin', he's puttin' up a helluva fight.*

The entire building rocked again with a second explosion, this time one clearly coming from above this level. A new set of alarms went off. *What the hell? Did somethin' get knocked loose in the first blast?* John wasn't looking forward to having to try to swim out of this joint. For now, the battle-sense he shared with Sera was quiet; whatever was happening above wasn't going to be immediately fatal to them—at least he hoped not. The Futures were finicky, and as much as he enjoyed the advantage and edge they brought, he didn't like relying on them as a crutch.

The blast door swung partway open, and stuck. The motors for the door whined and then went silent. Whatever was going on above must have warped the doorframe. The gap was just large enough for Sera to fit through, with her wings tucked in close; John had a much easier time squeezing by, bringing his rifle up as soon as he was past the edge of the door. The sounds of fighting were much louder now.

"Don't think we need much of a clue on where to go, darlin'."

The couple had a few more turns and twists to go down before they were close enough to the fighting to see it. Along the way they found different scenes of wreckage: destroyed labs, medical bays, offices, security stations. Each was its own microcosm of carnage, telling a piece of larger story. There were more than a few bodies, as well. If this was the work of Zachary Marlowe, it was frighteningly violent.

But John only had to reflect for a moment on the carnage *he* had inflicted on the day of his escape; that had been all fire and ash. This...was visceral, and bloody. *No time, old man.*

Finally, they arrived at the main corridor. The sounds of gunfire and shouted commands were deafening. The very top of the ceiling had a layer of smoke over it, and the strained HVAC system was working overtime to compensate and keep fresh air pumped in. The space in front of them was jam-packed with men. They carried riot shields, assault rifles, shotguns, net-launcher guns and grenade launchers. And...bizarrely, all their gear was a blinding white. Well, except for the blood splashes.

Security, darlin'. Zach's on the other side of them...I can feel it. Let's even the odds.

The security personnel were all jammed together; their focus was in the complete opposite direction from John and Sera. John didn't mind in the least. He lined up his first target, base of the neck and under the helmet, then depressed the trigger on his carbine. The suppressed round hit right on target, the hypersonic crack of the rifle and the impact with flesh lost in the cacophony, sending up a red mist that dusted the first man's nearest companions. He worked his way down the back of the line, putting a double tap into the upper neck or head of his targets; some he had to smoke-check with an extra round or two while they were on the ground. He was a damned good shot, but even still, nothing was certain in a gunfight; it was better to spend the rounds to make sure a target was out of action than to get surprised later. Towards the end, the security guards started to catch on that they were in the middle of a death sandwich, and tried to react, fight back somehow. John expended the last of his magazine putting them down; ten dead for sure, with at least two more on their way out and definitely out of the fight. Now it was time for Sera to go to work. She manifested her spear alongside her sword, and she waded in.

By this time, more of the guards had figured out they were being taken from behind. They turned to face Sera, who had sheathed herself in flame and leapfrogged past John, her sword and spear so hot they were white approaching plasma. The guards had ballistic shields, rated to withstand rifle fire. If they had counted on those to protect them, they were sadly mistaken. Sera sliced the tops off, and took out three of the tightly packed guards with blows from the butt of her spear. They went down like hammered cattle.

Before any of the other security guards could turn their weapons on Sera, John sent a blast of flame from his right hand, centered on her. It blossomed around her, engulfing the guards nearest to his wife. She could see perfectly well in his flames, which could not hurt her; the guards, meanwhile, were panicked and screaming in pain. He slung his rifle, manifesting his fire-claymore as he charged after his wife.

Sera, as usual, was doing her best to be "non-lethal"—but that did not mean pain-free. She was using the butt of her spear and the pommel of her sword to knock out those who appeared to be having second thoughts about what they were doing, but for those who were showing no sign of mercy...well...neither did she. For every step she took forward, a man went down, either unconscious or dead. Unlike the hardened Thulian armor, the Kevlar vests and shields offered no more resistance to her fiery weapons than butter.

John was right behind her; he wasn't being bloodthirsty, but where he struck, it was usually a killing blow. It was the quickest and easiest way for him to protect himself and Sera, and these men had made their choices already so far as he was concerned. Slicing through barrels and weapon receivers as easily as armor and flesh, he cleaved his way through the opposition, his back to Sera's at all times as they mowed through the guards. It was almost like a dance, with he and Sera being the only ones in time with the steps.

Sera performed a wide, low sweep with her sword and spear; John leapt over both, executing a back edge cut with each pass. They went until John had gone around in a complete circle, with several sweeps of Sera's weapons. When they finished, all of the security guards around them were dead, dying, or incapacitated. Neither of them were breathing hard. There was still a chaotic knot of action happening immediately in front of them, however.

At the heart of it was something—some*one*—dressed in what looked like a uniform coverall, torn in places and splattered liberally with blood. It was the same style as the one John had worn when he was a part of the Program; instead of green, this one was light blue, like a hospital patient's. It had to be young Marlowe... there couldn't be *that* many people down here who were green-skinned and teal-haired. John could tell immediately that the boy had already been through Program experimentation; where his arms were visible, he shared the exact same scars that John had. The fruits of that awful labor were readily apparent. Zachary moved *fast*; in an instant, John gauged that the boy was slightly faster than himself; the rare speedsters out there, where being fast or reacting quickly was their primary power, were the only things faster. And he was plainly as strong as John, if not somewhat stronger; the enhancements under his skin bulged with his exertions, standing out with each swipe and thrust and jab.

The kid was a brawler. When John and Sera first saw him, he was busy finishing off three security guards. He didn't have any finesse or real technique to his fighting; no training, even. Whatever they had tried to impart to him in the Program, he had either rejected, or it just hadn't taken. It didn't seem that the kid needed it, either.

The security guards were good. They didn't take turns or hang back, trying to take Zachary on one at a time. All three of them rushed him together. One had a stun wand of a model that John had never seen before; it was actually arcing electricity in loud pops and snaps, and looked lethal. The second guard had a pump-action shotgun tricked out with a tactical light and a red dot, while the third carried only a pistol. The guard with the shotgun fired three blasts in quick succession, only a handful of paces away from Zach... but none of the shots seemed to find him, instead hitting the walls and floor around him; the closest took a bite out of Zach's coveralls, but didn't find flesh. Even with as fast as the kid was, that should have been impossible; it looked like the shotgun had been lined up dead on him. This wasn't like the movies, where a shotgun has a spread five feet wide two inches from the barrel. Zach was next to the guard almost instantly, just after the guard had racked the pump on his weapon. The teen grabbed the barrel of the gun, wrenching it violently to his left; the longarm bucked in his grasp as it discharged harmlessly into the wall.

By now the guard with the stun baton was in range; he swung in quick, short arcs, aiming for Zach's head and torso. Still holding onto the shotgun, Zach ducked and twisted out of the way; the guard holding the shotgun was tugged off balance by the movements, losing his footing and almost falling to the floor. Some of the strikes from the wand came close enough to singe and burn holes in Zach's clothing, but he didn't seem to notice. Like a lightning strike, his right hand shot out, grabbing the weapon arm of the guard with the stun wand; the man screamed as Zach's hand squeezed, crunching the bones like they were dried twigs. With a swift jerk, he carried the crippled guard's arm and stun wand into the man with the shotgun; the other man seized with a spasm as the electricity surged into him, causing him to collapse to the floor. It took John a second to realize that it was *only* the arm from the guard with the stun arm he had pulled towards his comrade; the teen had torn the guard's arm off at the elbow.

The third and final guard, who was behind the other two, began firing with his pistol. His rounds tore through the guard with the missing arm, who was staring at the stump of his right arm with a befuddled expression—probably from shock—before one of the rounds entered his temple and sent him to the floor, dead. John's heart skipped a beat; the shots surely would hit Zach. Unless he had a healing factor, or he and Sera could somehow heal the kid ... he was as good as dead.

The guard with the pistol emptied his entire magazine in one quick fusillade, the slide locking back once it was finished. The guard stood there stock-still for a moment ... then he frantically began to reload. Zach was advancing on him, completely unharmed. Not a single round had struck him. Incongruously, John saw that there was a small drift of leaves at Zach's feet, quickly wilting and turning brown. The guard managed to jam the magazine home and drop the slide just as Zach reached him; the teen slapped the pistol to the side at the last second before it fired. The guard on the ground with the shotgun had seemingly recovered during the barrage, and had taken aim at Zachary's back as he was walking towards the last standing guard. The round from the pistol slammed into the shotgun guard's unarmored throat with a wet smack, and the guard's eyes bulged in pain; his aim wavered for a moment before he finally pulled the trigger. Zachary twisted to the side at the last moment, and the blast caught the guard with the pistol full in the chest. The guard fell backwards, landing hard on his shoulders; the ballistic vest he was wearing had protected him, but his wind was gone.

Zachary glanced back at the guard behind him; he was gurgling blood, too focused on the losing battle of keeping the wound covered with his hands to be a threat. He returned to the guard in front of him; the man was groaning, trying to force air back into his lungs. Zach took his time, coming to a rest standing next to the man's helmeted head. He waited until the guard regained his breath, opening his eyes.

"Please! No! Please, just no! No, no, *no, NO!*" Zachary lifted one foot, then brought it down savagely on the guard's helmet; the crunch was horrible, and John didn't want to think about whether it was the guard's helmet or his skull...or both. For a second, John saw the teen's face sag; his chest was heaving, and he didn't look like the unholy terror he had been moments ago, but like a scared kid who only wanted to wake up from a nightmare he was trapped in.

Then Sera's fires flared, and he looked up, suddenly seeing them for the first time. There was no hesitation; he charged, first going for Sera. Both of them sensed the attack before it came...but there was something else coming through their battle-sense. Normally, things were clear; intention, action, inevitability all played out in a pattern that they could anticipate. With Zachary...there was some sort of background vibration to it all, that became more intense as he neared. John interposed himself between Zachary and Sera; his speed and strength were more on par with the teen's. He instantly extinguished his claymore, deciding to meet the charge bare-handed. They didn't want to hurt Zach, after all.

It became immediately apparent that Zach had no such reservations; he attacked wildly, each strike meant to cripple or kill John. His face betrayed a storm of internal fury; his teeth were bared and his eyes were wild with murderous intentions. John parried each blow, using every ounce of his speed and strength to keep the teen at bay. Several times, even with his enhancements and battle-sense, the teen's attacks came close enough to rip through John's uniform, drawing blood with shallow grazes, and twice it was only Sera's intervention with a deflection of the butt of her spear, or a blinding flash of a fiery wing between them that saved him from something near-lethal.

Damn, if the kid isn't fast! John thought. But that speed came at a price; Zachary was going full-out, but the effort was draining him. He was winded, and soon his attacks became sloppier, more desperate.

*Darlin', we don't have time for this. Once he's worn down—
I will intervene.*

It didn't take long before Zachary was completely out of steam; there was terror mixed with the rage and John feared that the teen was going to do something even crazier now that he recognized he couldn't continue to defend himself.

Sera launched herself at the young meta; without spear or sword, wrapping him in arms and wings from behind, pinning his arms to his side. "Peace," she said into his right ear. "Be still." And at the same time, waves of calm washed over John—and presumably Zachary as well. "We are here for you, not against you."

The exhausted teen continued to struggle for a few seconds, slowly becoming still. The odd buzzing that John and Sera had felt through their battle-sense faded, then stopped completely. Zachary was quiet for several long moments before finally speaking.

"Who are you?"

"I am the Seraphym," she replied. "You do not know me; you have been held here, in this little hell, ever since your parents gave you over to these...monsters. You do not know what has been happening out there, in the world, but terrible things are happening there that drove us to find you. This is my beloved, John. He knows what you have lived through, because he has lived through the same."

There was a pause. "Can you let me go?" They both felt waves of distrust flowing off of the teen. He wasn't sure what to expect from them, but it seemed that he was at least willing to listen, for the moment.

"If you will pledge not to attack us further." Sera paused. "I will trust your word."

"...Okay, lady. But don't try anything."

Slowly and carefully, she unwrapped her wings, flipping them slightly to get them settled properly on her back, then let go of him, taking her place at John's side. She left her hands empty, at her sides, but her eyes, still glowing gold, never left his. The teen immediately whirled on the couple, his hands up in a defensive stance, but they could tell that it was just a reaction; he didn't give off any intent of doing them harm. He was confused, and very, very frightened.

"Why are you here? Are you with the Program?"

"We are here to take you away from this place," Sera replied steadily. "And no. We are not with the Program. Although John knows all there is to know about it, to his sorrow."

He stared at her, confusion starting to penetrate his fear. "How? You're both metas, right?"

"I went through somethin' like what you went through, kid. I got out, though. Sorta seems like you were in the middle of doin' the same thing. We can take you the rest of the way, an' somewhere safe, if you'll come with us." John didn't make any sudden movements; he figured that the kid was right on the edge, and any little thing might set him off.

"Why me? Why go through all the trouble?" *The kid is sharp, I'll give him that much.*

"It's a long story. Judgin' by those lovely bells goin' off over the intercom, we don't have a lotta time to go into it. You've gotta make the call, kid. If we were here to hurt you, we would've done it already. If we were with the Program, we wouldn't have put down those guards that you see behind us." Zachary leaned to the side to see past John and Sera at the pile of unconscious and dead guards behind them. "Trust us, or don't. Either way, figure it out fast."

Sera cocked her head to the side, looking momentarily up and away. "There is not much time remaining. The Thulians are here." John got the flash at the same moment; there was a Sphere outside, sending troops—armored and unarmored—to the entrance of the facility. The new alarms were not for John and Sera. The alarms signaled the arrival of a threat whose only purpose was to wipe this facility off the map, along with everyone in it.

"Thulians? What—"

John felt the chill of great danger tracing the line of his spine. "Bad guys, kid. Worse than these goons. We're officially outta time. What's it goin' to be?"

Zach looked from John to Sera, then back again. He sighed, then called over his shoulder. "Come out, everyone. We're leaving." What looked like two dozen teens emerged from behind a corner further down the hall. All of them were scared, wearing the same coverall that Zach was. Some were very obviously metas; various physical manifestations of their powers showed that plainly enough. *Trainees. Lab rats. Just like I used to be.*

"Is that all of them?" John said, unslinging his rifle and making sure it was charged with a fresh magazine.

"There were more of us," Zach muttered quietly, looking down at the ground. In that moment, John and Sera both wanted nothing more than to hug the teen and let him know that it wasn't his fault, that everything would be okay in time. But they couldn't wait a moment longer. Danger was closing in.

"John, we must seek another way out," Sera said quietly. "You must speak to Vickie. Our priority is to escape, not confront."

"Gotcha. Overwatch, you on the line?" John motioned for Zach and the other escapees to follow; they needed to get moving. Finding exactly how they were getting out would depend on Vickie.

"*Any natural materials around there? Slap a hand on them.*" Vickie did not waste a moment in greetings. She already knew that if John called her, the need had turned dire.

"None...hold a second, goin' to try somethin'. Darlin'?" John slung his rifle behind him, manifesting the fiery claymore with a *whoosh* of flame, sending several of the teens stumbling backwards.

"Fear not," Sera said over her shoulder as she manifested her spear. Waves of reassurance came from her. "We need only an access."

She rammed her spear into the wall, burning a small hole through it to the earth beyond. Steam immediately began to issue from around the spear. She withdrew and quelled it, as water followed it, leaving a hole for John to plunge his claymore in, widening it enough that he could force his hand and arm into the earth beyond.

"Contact made, Vic."

"*Roger. I'm using my geomancy to find all the spaces with unnatural crap to get a floor plan for the facility. Aaaaand... done. Watch your HUD for directions.*"

"Who are you two talking to?" Zach had edged forward, watching the couple work.

"Roger that, Vickie." He withdrew his arm from the hole in the wall, shaking the muddy water off before extinguishing the sword again and reshouldering his rifle. "Eye in the sky, kid. Our Overwatch; kind of like mission control. She's gonna help us get out of this joint."

Suddenly his HUD showed an overlay; the directions led back through the way Zach and the others had apparently come. There was a dead end back that way, that according to Vickie was not a dead end at all. *Somehow* they were supposed to gain access to a vertical shaft that lay past that wall.

"*Get to the dead end and cut your way past it. If you can get through a Thulian dragon's hide this should be cake.*"

"Copy, we're on it." John and Sera broke into a trot; Zach and the others followed a short distance behind until the assembled group reached the wall that Vickie had specified.

"What now? This is back the way we came!" Zach threw up his hands in exasperation; some of the others were muttering, growing uneasy.

"*Ramp up that fire to melt the edges, otherwise you'll be swimming to the surface. 'Kay?*"

"Stand back, kid. Time for a magic trick." John manifested his claymore in his off-hand, keeping his rifle shouldered in the other. Sera thrust her spear forward into the wall that Vickie had marked. She kept her spear just hot enough to burn through the wall into the void beyond. John, however, ramped up his sword as high as he dared; it was brilliantly white-hot when he started cutting into the wall. First, he made a man-sized square around Sera's spear; he worked quickly, but not so fast that the heat didn't have time to fuse the edges. Once that was done, he cut an X right through the center of the box, from corner to corner. "Open sesame." Sera pulled her spear from the wall in one quick motion; the four chunks from the X came with the spear, spilling dust and concrete to the floor.

"The escape for the masters, denied to the slaves," Sera said briefly. "Follow me, my dears. John, guard our rear." Without hesitation, she plunged into the dark hole, becoming a literal light in the darkness. "There is a ladder," she added, even as her fires showed it to the rest.

While Zach hesitated, three of the youngest metas did not. One of them, a girl who looked to be no more than nine or ten, practically flung herself after Sera, as if she was afraid to let the former angel out of her sight. That seemed to decide it for the rest, if not Zachary; they crowded up to the hole John had cut in the wall, jumping for the ladder as fast as there was room.

Perhaps the water on the floor in the hallway, at first only a slick, but now deep enough to make their shoes soggy, persuaded them. One way or another, this facility was done for.

John felt what was coming before he saw it: three men rounding the corner at the opposite end of the hallway, maybe a hundred feet away. Two of them were wearing suits, while the other wore a tactical outfit like the security guards, but with the addition of a red armband on the left arm. He knew what they were: heavy hitters, Program metas like he had been meant to become. They started running towards John and Zachary, the one in white leading.

"We gotta cover the others while they get out, kid. You up for this?"

Zachary didn't take his eyes off of the approaching enemies. "The better question is, are they? I've wanted to kill these guys for years." He squared his shoulders, crouching low with his hands balled into his fists at his sides. John brought his rifle up, aiming for the center; best to take out the leader first, if he could. Fighting metas was unpredictable; no telling what bag of tricks this trio had. Just as John depressed the trigger, one of the suited goons dodged in front of the meta in white. The bullets found the center of his chest...and then he vanished in a whirl of *something* that looked like black smoke. Two identical goons were in his place, running side by side. John fired two more fast bursts at each, to the same effect; when hit, the goons vanished and were replaced by two more. Now there were five goons in suits, and all of them were grinning nastily.

"Well, shit. This just got more complicated." John dropped his rifle, using the quick detach on the sling to let it completely go; it'd only hang him up if they got into serious hand-to-hand unpleasantness.

"Hurry up, hotshot, the shaft is starting to fill. Unless you're really good at breathing water, you're running out of time."

"Nag, nag, nag." John focused for a moment; fire sprung to life in the palms of his hands, traveling up his arms. Zach was startled enough to flinch away from him. He was reminded again of his time with the Program...and how it ended. He shot his arms out in front of himself, sending waves of flame into the narrow hallway. Again, the duplicate goons shoved to the front, meeting the attack head on. John ramped up the fires, sending a pulse through the waves that crashed over duplicates until the hallway was filled with a truly impressive conflagration. John killed his fires once the automatic fire-suppression systems for the facility kicked in; thankfully, it was sprinklers instead of

Halon gas, though he supposed that it would only speed up the flooding. A mass of oily black smoke was all that was left where the goons had been.

"Not bad. For an old guy," Zach said nonchalantly, relaxing from his fighting stance and scratching his nose.

"Y'know what they say, kid. 'Older the bull—'" John's head snapped around to the hallway again. Something didn't feel right...Zach picked up on it from John's expression, but didn't have time to prepare for what came next.

Charging through the smoke, like creatures from some sort of nightmare, were too many duplicates to count; if they had been grinning before, they now had near-rictus wide smiles, all teeth and hate. At the back of the clamoring mob was the one in the white security uniform, watching. That standout tilted its head to the side. Then the screaming began.

The escaping children—Zach included—were all screaming as if they were being tortured. John whirled around for a split second, taking in the scene. Some of them were on the ground, clawing at their ears or the sides of their heads, balled up in the fetal position. Two fell from the ladder but somehow Sera slid down to them and caught them, holding them between her chest and the steel with her wings cupped around them. John turned back towards the most immediate threat; he could tell that Zach had managed to get a grip on whatever was happening to him, and was still on his feet.

"P-pain! One. White—Mr. Cutter! N-nails and knives!" Zach rasped out through gritted teeth before screaming again, this time in both pain and rage, before he uncoiled like a spring, bolting towards the goons. *Must be a telepath of some sort; induces pain... Sera and I are protected, but I can feel the bastard scratching at the edges of my mind, trying to wedge himself inside like a roach in a crack in the wall.*

He didn't have any more time to think; the goons were almost to the hole in the wall, and Zach had rushed forward alone. John manifested his sword; with his enhancements already keyed up, he was nearly a blur as he ran. He knew that it didn't matter how many of the goons he cut through, more would pop up. He had to get to that bastard in white, Mr. Cutter; shut him off, and the kids would have an easier time of it.

Zach had already waded into the mass of the duplicates, his

hands flashing and sweeping and breaking and tearing at a whirlwind pace. The duplicates were definitely physical, not just illusions. And they had knives. Zach was giving them a run for their money, but it was coming at a cost; his coverall was slashed open in several places, and he was bleeding freely from several of his wounds. John saw that he was about to go down in a dogpile of the duplicates, Roman stabbing style. *Can't have that.* The duplicates were all so focused on Zach that not a single one of them saw him coming. With three overhead cuts, he took out four duplicates that had worked their way behind Zach. He brought his sword downward from a high guard viciously, using the back edge, amputating the hands of a duplicate that had just missed a thrust for John's sternum. He noticed that this duplicate didn't immediately disperse and double; it seemed to freak out, twitching and shaking as it fell to the floor. But it didn't "die."

John changed tactics. He started to wound and incapacitate the duplicates instead of going directly for the kill. Holding his claymore in front of himself, he swung the blade in a windshield wiper motion, advancing forward with each cut. Hands, arms, parts of legs, and knives all fell to the floor. A few of the duplicates were killed anyways—they were all so close together, it was impossible to be one hundred percent discretionary with his attacks—but for the most part, John only injured them enough to take them out of the fight. Swinging his sword out in a long arc in a low sweep with one hand, he easily hobbled a half dozen of the duplicates, sending them toppling onto the floor, legless. Whoever was controlling the duplicates got smart to the game, though; the still-functional duplicates started to kill their wounded "comrades," brutally and without hesitation.

Still bought us a little bit of time, an' Zach some breathin' room.

Zach was still tearing through the duplicates mindlessly, too caught up in pain to have any sort of technique to his attacks; what little he had in the first place, anyways.

"Enough of this shit!" John delivered a devastating front kick to the chest of one of the duplicate goons; the force of it was enough to leave a sickeningly deep boot-shaped indent in the duplicate's chest before it crashed into the goons behind it, sending a cluster of them down in a pile. John grabbed the tie from one of the duplicates that was rushing past him to get at Zach, pulling it around until it was in front of him. Still holding on to the tie with his off-hand, he stabbed his sword through the duplicate's midsection; he ramped up the power of the fires to the sword for a moment, cauterizing the wound...but not "killing" the duplicate. The duplicate looked at John, then the sword sticking out of its gut, and then back to John.

John ignited the fires at his feet; the rocket-motor report was deafening in the enclosed space. He held the duplicate—still impaled on his claymore—in front of him like a shield as his feet left the ground and he began to fly. The impacts as his makeshift shield struck its brothers were enough to make John's arms creak, but he mustered all of his strength to keep pushing through, a human battering ram attached to a jet engine. He had seen what he had to do through the battle-sense, and knew when to release the now very dead duplicate right before it dissipated. He had punched through the mob of duplicates. He cut off his fires, extinguishing both his sword and his flight; in the same instant, he threw his arms wide, like a linebacker in full extension. His shoulder speared into the midsection of Mr. Cutter, tackling him to the floor. There was a loud crack as his helmet hit the floor. John had a second to see the man's eyes; they were slammed wide open with fear. Before the meta could start to focus his attention or powers on John—or, even worse, Sera—he placed his right palm against the helmet at temple-level, then ignited a garden-hose-thick stream of plasma that cut straight through the helmet and the head beneath, splashing against the wall. Mr. Cutter was dead instantly, wisps of acrid smoke drifting from the two new holes in the dead man's helmet.

Instantly, the screaming from the children behind him stopped, replaced by uncertain whimpering. *I am getting them up the ladder again, beloved!* he heard in his mind. *You must end this and join us; we are running out of time!*

John sensed that the action behind him had changed. While still on the ground and hunched over the dead meta's body, he glanced over his shoulder to see all of the duplicates stop in sync, then turn and run straight for him. He was on his feet instantly, reigniting his claymore and sheathing his arms in flame, ready to meet the charge...when just as suddenly, the entirety of the mob of duplicates disappeared completely. There was a single goon in a suit in the middle of the hallway; he looked around frantically, pulling a knife from his jacket and squaring his shoulders towards John. Before he could do anything else, Zach walked calmly up to the man and snapped his neck from behind, as easily as if he was cracking a glowstick.

It was John's turn to be confused. "What happened?"

Zach stared at the body of Mr. Cutter, still fuming. "When you killed him, the pain went away. I could fight back after that, use my powers, concentrate on them." He kicked the goon in the suit, hard, in the ribs. "I do probability manipulation, or that's what they called it anyway. If I focus on it, I can . . . make it work harder for me. Do bigger things. I guess I shut down this asshole's power for a second."

John glanced at the hole in the wall. The last of the children were just disappearing into the shaft. *Hurry!* he heard Sera send to him through their connection. *The water is nearly at your level, and the Thulians are at the second basement!*

"Time to get goin', kid. We're way past check-out—" John saw it coming before it happened, and rushed forward to reach Zach. The young meta swayed on his feet for a moment before his eyes rolled up into the back of his head, and he swooned. John caught him before he hit the floor, then slapped him in the face a couple of times. The teen's eyes fluttered open, though clearly it took some effort. "You're played out, but we gotta get you outta here. Up an' at 'em." Zach nodded weakly as John helped him back to his feet. He half-carried, half-shoved Zach along as they ran for the hole in the wall that led to the emergency escape hatch.

It was a simple metal tube with a ladder opposite the hole in the wall. And Sera had not exaggerated; water was lapping at the rungs visibly as he shoved Zach inside—they both had wet feet before they climbed higher.

"You'll feel an opening in front of you and the ladder will keep going up, slantwise," Vickie said in his ear. *"That's where you need to go. Don't reach up for the next part of the ladder, that'll only take you where there's a lot of Nazis."*

Sure enough, in roughly two stories, his hand encountered empty air. He ignited the fire on his hand and looked down at Zach below him.

"See the hole?" he said, sticking his hand in the place where a slantwise tube joined the vertical one. Zach nodded. "That's where we're goin'!"

Then he clambered up and in. The going was easier on the slant. "How much of this have we got, Vix?" he asked aloud.

"A lot. It leads out beyond the fence. Five hundred yards roughly."

He caught up with the last of the kids, ignited a fire again, and looked back. Zach's eyes reflected the flame; now that he wasn't fighting like a demon, the meta teen looked very young, exhausted, and vulnerable. The kid in front of him squeaked, stopped, and looked back in a panic as she realized there was someone behind her. John tried to smile reassuringly. It must have worked; she kept going.

Finally, a hint of daylight ahead, with dark, moving shapes obscuring it. And he sensed Sera near. The light encouraged the other kids to move faster; as he reached it, he saw Sera's arms reaching into the hole and helping to pull the little girl ahead of him out. He could not get out of that tunnel fast enough; too many memories. Ghosts of the past tended to suck up all the oxygen in a room if you let them.

He emerged to a thickly forested island and it was immediately apparent that most of the forest was artificial. A metal hatch had been flipped back onto what looked like long grass and was, in fact, plastic. The only real things were the drifts of dead leaves caught here and there.

"There's a slightly submerged path; marked it on your HUDs," Vickie said. *"Holy shi—hit the dirt!"*

He and Sera just reacted, automatically, going down to the ground and taking as many of the kids as they could with them. A Thulian Death Sphere, half on fire and canted sideways, flew overhead. It was clearly going down, and a minute or two later, the island shook and a fireball rose over the swamp to John's left. *Somethin' nasty is fightin' back against the Thulians. Guess the Program has some more tricks up its sleeve.*

"Any interference on the way out?" John asked, still prone.

"Not at the moment. Wait too long and there will be. My advice is let the bad guys mow each other down and get the hell out of Dodge. Safe trail ends just outside of a little town called Bentis Bayou." There was a pause. *"Hey, hotshot, I think I can just barely port a lunchbox with enough cash in it for bus fare to Tallahassee for all those kids. You can't fly 'em all out of there, y'know."*

"Yeah," he said, a number of feelings, all of them bad, warring within him. "I know." There was a sudden, powerful need inside of him to get all of the kids out, get them all to safety... to make up for when he had escaped. He knew what they would go through; alone, frightened... not even necessarily of dying...

afraid of being *taken back*. He had been a man when the Program had dug its claws into him, and he had had a man's knowledge, a man's constitution. These...were children. If his own history was any yardstick, they would have more horror in their future. And there was damned little that John could do about it.

Vickie was as good as her word. John unfolded a little bit of cloth with a diagram on it on the ground as they all huddled in the bushes just outside of town. A few minutes later, a lunchbox appeared in the middle of it, stuffed with cash, with a map from the bus station to the ECHO building on it. *"I've got an Over-watch One rep in there. He's going to try and have someone meet the bus, and I've already put through the authorization of a pack of underagers to travel on the bus to Tallahassee. They're orphans being evacuated from an attack on a school. Hence the uniforms. There's enough in the box for fare and burgers and fries."*

Sera carefully explained this to the children. The three oldest were given the cash, the right code word to give the ticket agent to clear them buying all those tickets, and the map, just in case no one met them. "If you choose not to go to ECHO... I do not think that would be wise," she said finally. "But if that is the case, run far, and long, and hard."

"Stay away from cities if you can help it, stay with other kids when you can't. Don't go home, don't go anywhere you've ever known. These bastards go after you through your memories, the love y'have for others. It's how their minds work. You'll have to cut ties. Maybe forever." The words tasted like acid in John's mouth, and he felt like a hypocrite. He knew what they had to do; Zach was their mission. But he still felt sick to his stomach, Futures be damned.

"Aren't you coming with us?" asked one of the younger girls in dismay, although the older children tried to put a brave face on things.

Sera shook her head. "We cannot," she admitted. "What we did to get you out was not...authorized."

Zach pushed to the front of the group; it was plain that the others treated him like a leader. They weren't scared of him, and he didn't seem to need to bark orders or bully them to get them to do what needed to be done. "What's that even mean?"

Sera looked at John, helplessly.

"We had to kick over a hornet's nest to get you out. As y'can probably tell, other...'people' wanted the Facility, too. This is goin' to attract attention, an' not the good kind. We came for you an' you alone, Zach. You were our mission, an' we need to get you outta here safely. No matter what. Even if it means we bite it in the process." The other kids were staring at Zach now, waiting to see what he would do.

"To hell with that! I'm not leaving everyone here! We're getting out of here together. There's a frigging war going on out there—"

"You don't even know the half of it, kid. We've been fightin' a war for the last few years. We've lost friends and family. We've had our asses kicked more times than I can count. But we're still fightin' back. The world is ready to get turned into a cinder. If we fail...we've only got one plan to keep that from happenin'. An' you're a part of it."

Zach opened his mouth—just as Sera placed her hand on his forehead, her face a mask. "Be still," she said—and the young meta slumped bonelessly to the ground. "I have not harmed him," she told the others before they could react in alarm, and a wave of reassurance came from her. "But we must go, and we must take him with us."

"You've got money for food an' bus tickets. It'll be okay; the guy sellin' the tickets knows yer comin', an' it all comes with ECHO credentials an' stuff to get ya to Tallahassee. Get some lunch, an' get on that bus. Stay low, move fast, an' once you're clear, keep your heads on a swivel. With any luck, we'll see some of y'all soon enough. We've gotta get Zach out of here, now. Okay?"

The kids all looked at each other, then all eyes went to the oldest girl, who took a deep, long breath, closed her eyes for a moment, and firmed her chin. She opened her eyes again. "Can you promise we'll be all right with ECHO? We'll believe *you*."

"No more hurting!" one of the younger ones cried, then clapped both hands over his mouth.

"If they go with the ECHO guy, he's gonna get them all to a big safe house for meta kids." Vickie said that with conviction. *"They won't be separated."*

"You will be safe, and together, and no one will hurt you," Sera promised.

"There's one last thing, kids. You've gotta keep quiet 'bout Zach, here. 'Bout the facility. A lot's ridin' on it."

"You gonna keep our Gremlin safe?" It was the same young child that had spoken up before.

"We will." John paused before picking up Zach and putting him over his shoulder. "Why do you call him Gremlin?"

The oldest girl spoke up. "It was a young Russian guy. A friend of Zach's . . . they had been in the Program the longest. It was his nickname, and he gave it to Zach."

"John, we must go." Sera had started flipping her wings, a sure sign of nerves. "We are running out of time."

John knew that his wife was right. That didn't make it any easier, for either of them. "Be safe. Be smart. Y'all are tough; you wouldn't have made it this long if you weren't. See the sign with the dog on it?" He pointed through the brush down the street, to a storefront with a Greyhound sign—and also one for KITTY's CAFÉ. "Run there, a couple at a time, until yer all inside. Get yer tickets, an' get some lunch. Don' leave until the bus shows up, and get straight on there. Sit together. Get off at Tallahassee. Look for a guy in a black uniform with a white triangle on the front. That's the ECHO guy. Safe journeys, kids."

John didn't wait to say anything more. He readjusted Zach on his shoulder, took a running start, and fired off his flying "rockets." Sera was right behind him. He spared a single glance back; the kids were already moving. He hoped they would be all right. And he hoped that Zach would forgive them.

CHAPTER NINE

Ebb Tide

MERCEDES LACKEY

Amphitrite was pleased. Bill (she really *did not* like that name) was proving to be more and more congenial as he climbed out of his Melancholia. The investment in the physician of the mind had been wise—but then, she was a goddess, and goddesses are always wise.

Finally she decided that it was time for the next stage of her cure. At least once a day, he told her, his eyes full of admiration, how beautiful she was. But she heard what was unspoken beneath the compliment. *And I am so ugly*. He did not think he was worthy of her.

(But at least he had ceased to speak of the wife who had deserted him when he needed her most.)

"*You are so beautiful*," he said on the very day she had made her decision. But this time he went further. "*Your skin is like the inside of a shell. Your eyes are as blue as the ocean. Your body is more perfect than Miss America. Your hair is like...*" and there his imagination failed him, but at least he had finally emerged enough from Melancholia to *have* an imagination. "*And...I am not worthy to—*"

"*Ah—*" she chided, holding up an admonishing finger. "*I decide who is worthy to be in my company. And your heart and spirit certainly are. As for your outer self...would you have me change it?*"

His glowing eyes widened in shock. "*You mean, that's an option?*" he gasped.

"*Am I not a goddess?*" she replied. "*Come with me.*"

Obediently, he followed.

She brought him to one of the little "desert" islands, too small to even support much in the way of plant growth. There she made him sit, and she studied him from every angle. "*Yes,*" she said finally. "*I can do this.*" And she took up a handful of sand, and began to shape him.

It was, after all, the power of water and sand that smoothed and shaped rock the world over—and she was a goddess and could command the water and sand to work exponentially faster than they would otherwise have done. She had in mind a statue by the great sculptor Praxiteles, the Apollo Lyceus, and she kept that sculpture firmly in mind as she worked, starting with Bill's head.

She *really* did not like that name.

Sculpting in stone, after all, is a matter of subtraction, and although Bill considered himself ugly, he really just was more of a roughed-out copy of a human than he was a monster. So over the course of seven days, she subtracted, and smoothed, and followed the copy in her mind. He was patient while she worked on his head and shoulders. He became excited when the work moved to his arm, since now he could actually see what she was doing. His pleasure at seeing his chest muscles—modeled more on a Hercules than an Apollo—emerge from the rough stone that had been there made her smile. But when her hands went to work below his waist, he almost stopped her.

"*Ah...you're a lady...*" he said, showing an astonishing amount of shyness, given that she had not draped so much as an inch of her body in anything concealing for as long as they had been together.

"*I am a goddess,*" she corrected. "*And I am making you a god. Would you be only a half god?*"

Since he had no good answer for this—as she had intended—he let go her hand and stared up into the sky as she worked. She had the distinct feeling that if he could have been blushing, he would have been. Quite redly, in fact.

But at least he was not interfering with her. So she sculpted him to please herself, and then went on to his legs.

And when she was done, she made the water to be glassy smooth, and invited him to look.

Elegant brows rose, and the eyes beneath them glowed. "*I never looked like that!*" he said, putting one hand to his cheek, as if to reassure himself that this really *was* his reflection, and not some illusion.

"You were never a god before," she pointed out. *"Now you are."* She tilted her head to look at him critically. *"You have been liberated from your burden of mortality and melancholy, as Atlas was liberated of his burden of the sky by Heracles. I do not like this name, 'Bill,' not at all. It did not suit you before, and it suits you even less, now. I shall call you Atlas."*

In joy and gratitude, he embraced her. And something rose between them. He looked down at himself, and his mouth fell agape.

She laughed, for this was, of course, exactly as she had intended. *"The rest of you moves freely,"* she pointed out. *"Why not that?"*

In confusion, he drew away from her. Firmly, she drew him back. *"I made it,"* she pointed out. *"May I not enjoy it?"*

And, after some little time of persuasion, she did.

CHAPTER TEN

Keep Your Distance

MERCEDES LACKEY AND CODY MARTIN

Of all the miracles that Johnny and Sera worked, I think getting a teenager to listen to them was the biggest.

Leaving Zach was one of the hardest things that John had ever had to do. The teen had so many questions, and John wished he had all of the answers. He answered when he could, and was silent instead of lying when the truth in some of the questions was too hard to bear. Zach alternated between curious, relieved, angry, and scared. John and Sera could both feel the waves of emotion rolling off of the boy, crashing into them and through them. Sera was doing her best to comfort him; John hoped it would be enough, to keep him from spiraling down into a dark place that he knew all too well. *He's going through everything I went through when I got out of the Program. But he's so damned* young.

As much as John wanted to stay and help the young man navigate through the small hell he was going through, he couldn't. They needed to keep Zach safe, but there was still a war to fight in the meantime. Hopefully, they would win, and then they could bring him back to Atlanta, or wherever he wanted to go. If they didn't win...he was the world's last chance, and was infinitely precious for that reason.

So John hid him in the best place that he knew of. After a very lengthy discussion, John, Sera, and Vickie had decided that they wouldn't use any ECHO safe houses. For one, many of them were occupied off and on by Metisian scientists; they were working nearly around the clock in ECHO labs and offices around the world, though most of them were located in the USA. Keeping them in one particular place was an invitation for them to be attacked, so moving them—and their research data—constantly was a priority. As such, all of the safe houses were in use at one time or another; having one reserved without a damned good excuse would arouse... suspicion. While the trio could have gone up the chain of command with Zach, it was better for operational security if they kept the secret between themselves. With ECHO locations out—same with any of the locations that Vickie knew through her parents—they needed to come up with an alternative. Luckily, John had one ready.

It seemed like forever ago when he had first been on the run. Six years... so much had changed, with him and the world, and at times he hardly believed that the past had actually happened. At least the way he remembered it. Those first days after he had escaped the Program had been chaotic. He hadn't been able to trust anyone, and he had felt hunted wherever he went. One close call in a bus station had been enough for him; he had gone off the grid as much as he could. Still, back when he had been a Delta operator, he had set aside some... insurance, in case something ever happened. The special operations community and the intelligence world were inextricably linked. John had seen and heard of too many guys like him being left to twist in the wind when some intel weenie had screwed up; he had determined that he would never end up as a cautionary tale. So, he had prepared to disappear early on. A chunk of money, some weapons, and a full set of papers that he had *sort of* blackmailed a CIA spook into setting up for him; enough to start over somewhere, if he needed to. Once he had calmed down enough, he had used most of the money to buy a chunk of land out in the middle of nowhere in Wyoming; a small plot with its back to a state forest. It made for a nice backyard, and quiet, too. He had spent most of a sweltering hot summer building a cabin and stocking it. Situated at the edge of a small valley, he had privacy and a stream for water.

The cabin and the land were his bolt-hole, a place to run when he had nowhere else to go. It had served him well in those early days on the run. He had had a lot of things to deal with: grief over what he had lost, guilt over what he had done, and how to reconcile all of it with what he had become. No longer a soldier. A criminal, a fugitive. And also a metahuman. There had been a lot of time spent trying to get his new "gifts" under control; harnessing his heightened senses without being overwhelmed, keeping his new strength and reflexes in check, and controlling his ability to produce and manipulate fire. The last had proved the hardest to master; it had always been a matter of maintaining concentration and stopping himself from completely letting go.

He hoped that Zach's time here would help him as much as it had helped John. They didn't fly in; even for John and Sera, it would've been a long haul, never mind while carrying another person. Instead they opted to use a car that John had "procured" before they had gone to rescue Zach; with the war on, and many destruction corridors still scarring cities despite reconstruction efforts, there were plenty of abandoned cars. A set of fake plates and magicked papers from Vickie turned it into a completely forgettable vehicle; just another beat-to-hell plain white delivery van on the roads. A van was necessary; Sera's wings took up space, and Zach's green skin and blue-green hair drew attention. Both of them had to ride in the back. So, John drove, taking back roads and staying away from anything that even resembled a traffic camera or license plate reader; Vickie plotted their route, and when they couldn't avoid a situation where they might be recorded, she did her finger-waggling and futzed with whatever system might catch them. The entire trip took about a week; John drove through the night on several occasions, his enhancements, enough caffeine to kill a mule, and frequent telempathic "boosts" from Sera helping to keep him alert. Whenever that got to be too much, they would find somewhere to camp, away from prying eyes. Food was prepackaged and easy to heat up—no need to carry fuel or a stove with two fire-chuckers on hand. Sera was getting very good at boiling water, cooking hot dogs, and even grilling steak...literally by hand. Zach's appetite certainly hadn't been affected by what he had gone through; John ate a lot due to his metabolism being so high combined with how much work he did, but Zach was a walking disposal. A crate of Gamma Bars kept him from grumbling in between meals. Vickie arranged anonymous pickups of supplies from several camping stores along the way; prepaid, and needing only a name to be handed over. John handled the public stuff while Sera and Zach stayed in the van, out of sight.

When the trio finally arrived at John's cabin, it was just after nine in the morning. The air was cool and dry, with all of the usual natural morning sounds filling it. It was one of the few places anymore where you didn't hear anything mechanical. They were too far out for highway noises, and planes flying overhead were too high for more than faint jet noise. John peeled himself out of the cheap imitation leather driver's seat of the van, stretching and groaning; he heard more pops and cracks than he thought was possible as his joints and muscles stretched out.

"Where are we?" Zach asked, climbing out of the van, which was now packed with supplies.

"Somewhere safe, kiddo. You won't have to worry 'bout bein' found out here. This is a place that I set up, years ago, after I got out of the Program. No one but us knows it even exists."

Vickie had implanted Zach with the standard Overwatch Two setup before they left Atlanta. He had been wary, but it was the only foolproof way to make sure he was safe, and for him to get into contact with her. Since it was all going through her "magic circuits" and wasn't on any sort of broadcast or wired link, no one could use it to back-trace him or eavesdrop.

It also solved the problem of entertaining (and educating) a bored teenager with no wilderness experience, no internet, no cable, no broadcast TV and damned near no broadcast radio. Anything he wanted could be piped right into his ears and onto his HUD. And anything he physically needed, Vickie could arrange to be delivered to the door by the *absolutely* incurious contact she had in Laramie. Tim Rangle—one of Vic's hacker "associates" with a habit of cooking up complicated plots in lieu of much simpler solutions—was used to delivering to people out in the middle of nowhere who didn't want to answer the door. As long as he got paid, he didn't care what happened to the boxes he dropped off.

"I don't want to stay here. I want to go back with you two. I'm going to lose my mind out here, alone." Zach paced around, looking at the property. The cabin itself was a simple affair: a single room divided up into kitchen (with wood-fired stove), den with couch and a collection of sun-faded books and magazines, bathtub, and a simple—albeit comfortable—bed.

They went outside to continue the tour. The outhouse was slightly down the hill and off to the left. There was a large woodshed, stocked with several cords of seasoned wood, and an attached tool shed (which, coincidentally, housed John's secret cache of weapons in a compartment beneath the floor). What seemed to have most of Zach's attention were the large rocks and boulders scattered behind the cabin. All of them were scorched and blackened; some bore deep gouges, were half melted, or had holes burned through them. Melted rock was strewn about, little pools of used-to-be lava, now hardened and looking like ponds in a range of gargantuan mountains.

"What happened here, anyways?" Zach turned back to the couple, shaking his head. John snapped his fingers, and his right hand became sheathed in flame.

"Practice makes perfect; took a long time for me to get it all down this small instead of startin' a forest fire. Nice thing 'bout this place: no neighbors to come 'round, askin' questions 'bout all the strange noise and lights."

For a moment the teen looked impressed, but his expression quickly faded. "I'm not stupid. Or young enough to whine about how unfair things are. But I still don't like this."

John could feel the pleading desperation that Zach was experiencing; he knew it well enough himself. The boy wanted someone to talk to, someone to help him work through what he had gone through; what he had done to survive, and the people that he had lost.

He tried to look sympathetic. "You won't have to deal with it alone, kiddo. Remember what Vickie told you; y'ever need to talk to someone, you've got a line through the Overwatch system to her. Or me an' Sera."

"I know it feels as if you will be isolated, Zachary," Sera said softly. "But think how much danger you would be in if you were not. And think how much danger you could put the *others* in if you were found. Even if you do not know where they are now, you know their names and their powers, and that alone could be used to find them."

He opened his mouth as if to say something, then thought better of it. Finally, he sighed. "I know you're right. I don't want you to be, but I know you are." He kicked at the ground, chewing on his lip before he looked up at John and Sera again. "How long do I have to be out here, 'communing with nature' and all of that crap?"

John shrugged. "That . . . we don't know. Hopefully not for too long. But there's no way to tell; whenever the war ends, or gets to the point where we're not fightin' for basic survival. One way or another, things are comin' to a head."

"And there's no way I can come with you guys? Help with the fighting? Actually *do* something?" There was no doubt in John's mind that the kid was absolutely sincere and honest in his request. He felt it, and presumably so did Sera. But every time he and Sera had delved into the Futures, it had been clear; they were needed elsewhere, and Zach was needed here. Before, John had figured that anywhere secure would do, but now that they had reached his old safe house/cabin, he was certain that Zach needed to be *here* specifically. He couldn't put into words why, but he felt it in his bones.

It was Sera who answered Zach. "We do not know if we will succeed, Zachary. But if we fail, if we fall, you are the last hope against the Thulians. This much, we know for certain. And we searched long and hard for you, and went through much to find you and bring you to safety." She glanced soberly over at John. "In so doing, we have probably exposed John to his old enemies, those who are behind the Program we brought you out of. But that is the price we were willing to pay."

"You're that important, kiddo. An' we can't risk losin' you. Once this thing is over, everythin' will be better. But we can't do what we need to do unless we know that you're safe." They spent another hour showing Zach around; most of that was focused on going over a map of the area, routes of escape, other supplies that John had scattered around the valley and beyond it. John had really done his best to set this bolt-hole up; when he was younger, thinking about spies and being on the run, disguises and fake identities had all been fun to think about. When it had become a reality for him, he took everything up a notch, leaving as little to chance as he could. Now Zach really was impressed; even if he was forced from the cabin, for some reason, any direction he went he would be able to find enough supplies to see him through as he escaped.

"But the best option for you is to hide here, or in the forest, then come back when you are certain whoever came here is gone," Sera pointed out.

"It's not like you lose comm if you run from the cabin," Vickie pointed out. *"I can reach you and probably even find you bolt-holes not even Johnny knows about. Earth magician, remember? If there's a cave or even a hole under some roots, I can find it."*

"Or she can make somethin' for ya that no one will ever find. She's good like that. That, an' her extensive tea collection is why we keep 'er around. Should be a moot point, though; Vic is goin' to have stuff monitorin' the area all the time, so it's unlikely anyone is goin' to sneak up on you. Wish I had that sort of set-up when I first came here."

"Oh snap. Thanks for reminding me, Johnny. Eyes in the air please, so I can fly them out and plant them."

"Roger that." John opened a pouch on his utility belt, picking out a handful of marble-sized spheres. These were smaller versions of Vickie's spy-eyes; just a motion sensor, a heat sensor, a solar panel, and a camera. He chucked them in the air, where they hovered over his head in a ring for a moment. Then, one by one, they shot off; they were small enough that within moments, they were out of sight.

"That's magic, right?"

"Technology fueled by magic. I'm the only person I know that can do that. I'm flying them by magic, but I'm planting them in treetops with a good view. Sticking with pines, that way there's no chance that they'll lose the cover. Once they're planted, they'll only come on if the motion or heat sensors trigger, or I hit them up remotely. They've got nice little ECHO-tech-lasts-forever rechargeable batteries in them and the entire surface is solar cell. I'll test them periodically, and if one goes down, I'll ship you a replacement."

True wonder filled Zach's eyes as he looked off in the distance, where the magic eyes had flown off. John couldn't help but smile; he was still a kid, after all. Even with all of the hell that Zach he had seen, the world still held mystery and magic for him. Not just in the literal sense since, well, magic appeared to be *real*. But that very real potential and possibility that magic represented.

Sera went back inside the cabin. John sensed that she did not want to leave just yet.

Communin' with nature, darlin'? he asked lightly.

Communing with the man you were, came the somewhat surprising reply. *I know you now. I did not know you then.*

I was very, very different back then. Not as open. I had to reinvent myself. A lotta that happened here . . . an' it was finished when I came to Atlanta.

Everything here, you had to choose carefully. Some is obvious. Some is not. Why a bath instead of a shower? Surely the tub was harder to transport than some pipe and a shower head.

Easier to just get the water into the tub an' heat it up with my fires; I've never been a great plumber, an' a standin' shower was outside of my range back then.

She wandered around the cabin, poking through his old belongings and perusing them. Old books, a lot of them philosophy or poetry; she smiled as she caressed one very well-worn copy of a Dylan Thomas collection. There were also periodicals; *Soldier of Fortune*, security industry and counterintelligence quarterly reports, standard *Guns & Ammo*-type rags. There were a few stacks of research papers; early stuff that seemed to be along the same lines of thought as his enhancements, though nowhere near as advanced. And...a short series of...romance novels? She picked one up. The author was Victoria Nagy. There was a long sigh in her earpiece. *"You must have been one of the twenty-nine people that bought my 'love among the metas' series, JM."*

"There was a bargain bin an' I had a lotta time on my hands."

"Well, I will give you points for the fact that every one of the seven books involved metas with fire powers, and I did do my research."

"Strangely enough, it helped me out. A bit."

But Sera's attention had moved on. She peered at the walls, and then, startled, at the floor. "Why are there holes here?" she asked. "They are not bullet holes. And surely they let in drafts."

"They used to be covered with somethin'. Explosives. There's a lot of interestin' things you can cook up when you have time on your hands, an' have read a bit of chemistry."

"But...why?" she asked, bewildered.

Zach was outside at that moment, but John still kept his voice low. "I wasn't goin' to go back. No matter what. If I couldn't get away...I was determined to take as many of the murderin' bastards with me as I could."

She blinked slowly, her habit when she was thinking, then nodded. "Yes. I can see that. The more you removed from the system, the fewer there would be to take others. Like Zach."

"A small, useless gesture, probably. But, if that's what it came to an' that's all that I had left...then I was goin' to go out with a bang, one way or another."

"Hey, Zach," Vickie said, in all their ears. *"Go hit the van and find the crate marked 'Stir Crazy.'"* Then she said, in John's ear only, *"I'm keeping him distracted."* There was a moment, and then she went on. *"Yeah, that's the one. That's for when the remote entertainment*

isn't entertaining you anymore. I'm guessing those goons never once gave you a chance to fool around with anything that wasn't on their approved checklist. So when you are bored, go to the crate and open one of the boxes. They're all unmarked, so whatever's in there will be a surprise. I won't swear it will be something you like or want, but it will *be something you never got a chance to try."*

"Like what?" Zach asked cautiously.

"Well, like there's a couple of musical instruments in there, and you can read all the instruction books and watch vids via your HUD."

There was a single .45 ACP round sitting by itself on a shelf. Sera picked it up and turned in over and over in her hands for a moment. Then she looked at John, long and meaningfully. "I do not believe that Zach will need this, either," she said, holding it.

He opted to respond through their connection. *No, he won't. When I was rebuildin', recreatin' who I was here . . . there came a point when I didn't want to go on. It felt like there had been too much; too much loss, too much pain, with only more to come. I got low. After a spell of feeling sorry for myself an' starin' at that goddamned bullet, I got pissed off. Figured that the biggest middle finger I could give to the Program was to survive, even if it hurt.*

"Little did I know what was in store for my dumb ass . . . but it's all been workin' out so far, darlin'." He moved closer to her, pulling her into an embrace. She put the bullet into his hand and cupped her own over it.

"Shall we put an end to that episode, then?" she asked. In answer, he flared the fire in his hand, and she did the same. The bullet did not so much melt or explode as vaporize. The fire was hot enough to light up the entire room, despite only being the size of a baseball. The ashes quickly flew away on the currents of air that rushed to feed the mini-conflagration. Just as quickly as it had begun, it was over.

"We've gotta get back to Atlanta. We're skatin' enough as is, though I'm pretty sure we can keep the Commissar from throwin' too much crockery at us." They walked through the door of the cabin; Zach was on the porch waiting for them.

"Some light show." He shifted uncomfortably, then tried to pass it off as he looked down at the ground and leaned against the porch railing. "It's time for you two to go, isn't it?"

"You won't be alone in the conventional sense, Zachary," Sera said softly.

"Okay." He glanced up at them. John didn't need his new senses to tell that the kid was scared, and wanted them to stay. They were some of the first people that had actually been nice to him, that didn't want to use him, that had actually tried to help him. It was going to be hard on all of them for the couple to leave Zach here. John thought a moment, then walked to the van. He dug around in his personal backpack for a few moments, retrieving a small brown object.

"I wasn't lyin' to you when I said that I know what you're goin' through, Zach. Here," he said, handing the object to the teen. It was his leather-bound journal, the one that he had started after he went on the run. "I wrote in it just 'bout every day after I got out of the Program. It might help. Hell, if you get lost in the woods or somethin', you could probably use it to start a fire." John grinned lopsidedly with the last bit, clapping his hand over Zach's right shoulder. "It'll be okay."

Zach looked down at the journal for a moment, then raised his eyes to meet John's. "Thank you." He turned to Sera, nodding his head. "Both of you. For everything. I know I can be a pain in the ass, but I mean it."

"We'll see you soon. Stay safe, comrade."

"Leave the van. I'll fake up a driver's license for the kid. I'll arrange a faster pickup you two can fly to. We're moving a couple of Metis eggheads to Laramie; you can ride on the empty back. Besides, you two never got a shot at riding in one of the saucers."

The couple embraced Zach a final time, then finally walked down a light footpath, away from the bolt-hole and Zach; John spared a single glance over his shoulder at what had once been his home, then continued on. *Past is the past. An' we've still got a lotta work to do movin' forward.*

It had been a week since the couple had left Zach in Wyoming. Vickie had kept them apprised with regular status updates—in between barreling everywhere they could reach to help repel Thulian attacks. They had even managed to share a couple of video calls with him. He was a tough kid; it had taken him a couple of days, but he had already adjusted to his new circumstances with surprising ease. *The young are like that,* John had thought. *No matter what, he'll make it.*

Even with that one worry taken care of, there were a dozen

more waiting for John and Sera back in Atlanta. The Thulian attacks had continued to increase in frequency; the couple's absence, however necessary, had an impact. And it had been noticed. The Commissar was ready and waiting for them when they returned, and she was looking for blood, damn near. There wasn't any thrown crockery, but she made it abundantly clear that she was a hair's breadth from considering their time away as desertion in time of war. She demanded an explanation.

"Commissar," Sera said, her face as serious as she could manage to make it. "We have a secret, last-ditch plan. There was something we, personally, needed to do to make sure that it was in place and would take up the fight if we all failed. Stalingrad, if you will. It was...something only John and I could do."

"Oh? Well, then, is being quite alright. Secret missions without approval of your superior officers. Is just what was being needed, *nyet?*" Now John could see—and feel—her anger beginning to boil over. They had to act fast, or this would get a lot more complicated than it already was.

"Nat—Commissar," John had said. "It was a contingency that had to be put in place. An' the fewer people that know 'bout it, the safer it'll be. We don't know *what* might happen tomorrow, or the next day, an' so on. A secret is safer when there aren't as many bodies involved...figuratively an' literally. Vickie is the only other one that knows the full picture, an' it'll stay that way. Operational security." He paused. "If everythin' goes to hell an' you're still livin', Vickie's put the details in your contingency folder. Same for Bella. This is a no-shit, we-lost-everythin' fallback. Fact, if it comes to that, me an' Sera will probably be toast before you need to open that folder."

That caused Natalya to pause for a beat. She swung her head from John, to Sera, and back again, then sat down in her chair, her shoulders sagging with fatigue as she rubbed her temples. "If Daughter of Rasputin is being involved...*da, da,* fine. Is being *only* time two firebombs under my command run off without *nekulturny* word, however. Our efforts against the *fascista* have been increasing, and we cannot spare a single *tovarisch*. We are needing twenty of you two, as is case."

They had barely enough time to unpack their bags before they were thrown back into the fight. The rest of the CCCP hadn't been sitting idly; Untermensch, Soviet Bear, and Mamona had been busy

with patrolling and assisting military and police forces in repel-
ling Thulian attacks. Untermensch had undertaken a direct-action
mission—with Commissarial approval—all on his own, which had
helped to temporarily cripple Thulian operations in the area.

"It seems," the old Russian had said, "that the *fascista* do not
do so well when someone detonates heavy explosives in one of
their command and control modules on a beachhead. Good to
know, *nyet?*"

John and Sera had newly returned to Atlanta from a mission
of their own when a new wrinkle appeared. They had been fighting on the Georgia coast, preventing a literal Thulian beachhead
from taking root. The battle had lasted two full and very long
days, seeing the couple fighting alongside regular military units
yet again. It occurred to John that a lot of the fighting, now that
things were starting to move towards all-out, worldwide war, was
beginning to very closely resemble descriptions of the fighting
in World War II, when metahumans first started to appear. The
most disconcerting aspect was that there were more Thulian
metahumans added to the mix. So far, there hadn't been any more
sightings of Valkyria or Ubermensch, but the sheer numbers of
the new ones made up for it.

Most weren't particularly powerful, or had any exotic powers,
it seemed...but there were a lot of them. John had seen in one
threat report that current projections—based upon the numbers
that the Thulians had been fielding to date and the metahuman
losses incurred during and after the Invasion—stated that the
Thulians might very well have *more* metas than the rest of the
world. Which was pretty goddamned worrying, in John's estima-
tion. He only hoped that the Thulians were just throwing all of
their metas into the ring in one big push...and that this wasn't
the first of many waves to come.

These and other thoughts were keeping John and Sera distracted enough on their walk home. They had landed at base,
debriefed, and then been released on a twenty-four-hour leave
that was almost immediately retracted and cut in half; there was
just too much going on out there, and everyone that could pull
a trigger or had powers was in demand. Still, the chance for a
hot shower, something to eat that didn't come out of an MRE
pouch, and a few hours of sleep was more than John and Sera
could have hoped for.

"I think there is something we must try," said Sera, as the two of them walked, rather than flew, towards John's squat. They were bone tired, having flown to, during, and from the two-day battle.

"Buildin' a time machine? Tryin' a magic spell that'll let us sleep for twelve hours an' feel like it was a week? I'm all ears, darlin'."

"Something like the latter. Before, I was seldom weary, because the Infinite provided. I think we must attempt to connect to the Infinite while resting, rather than only when in battle. I do not think we will be denied the strength we need."

John thought for a moment, then shrugged before putting his arm around his wife's hip. "Your department, darlin'. I'll give it a shot if you think it's worth tryin'."

John was so out of it that he almost missed the signs of what they were heading towards. A shadow on a rooftop. The scuffle of a boot against concrete. The couple talking on the street corner who were trying a little too hard to keep their body language neutral. It clicked for John all at once that he and Sera were walking into a trap of some sort. He had become reliant on his shared battle-sense with Sera to warn him of danger; that, combined with how exhausted the two of them were, had kept him nearly oblivious to his surroundings beyond the obvious and mundane details. *Getting sloppy, old man.* But there was that, too; they were obviously being watched by unfriendly eyes... but they weren't in any immediate danger. He stretched out his telepathy to the couple and the man on the roof; all of them were wary, but there wasn't any malicious intent there.

Sera hadn't noticed any of it; she didn't have his enhanced senses or his countersurveillance and urban survival training. Not wanting to tip off the surveillance that he was on to them, John kept silent, only speaking to Sera through their connection.

Darlin', we're bein' followed. I've spotted at least three—make that four, five—people along our route that are payin' extra attention to us. All of 'em are armed. Don't look around, it'll just give us away. If we gotta fight, I'd rather we surprise the hell out of 'em an' come out swingin'. So far, though... they don't seem to want to hurt us.

Why would... could it be that someone or something at that Program installation recognized you for what you are? And survived to tell the tale?

If they were Program, I would've picked up on it. None of them are metahumans, s'far as I can tell. Not Blacksnake, either; too restrained. To be perfectly honest, this whole thing smells—

Before John had a chance to finish the thought, a convoy of five black SUVs rounded the corner at the far end of the street, just past where the block for his squat ended. They pulled up to the curb next to where John and Sera were standing, then quickly stopped in a cloud of concrete dust. John knew what the license plates would have printed on them before the first SUV had even finished coming around the corner.

"Government." With a hard blink to bring up his HUD, and then a thought and a few eye movements, John brought his sub-vocal microphone online. *"Overwatch: Murdock to Vickie, urgent,"* he said without actually speaking. *"Got a situation here. Want your eyes and ears on it, see how it develops. Might be trouble."*

There was a moment, probably seeming longer than it actually was. Then a spray of curses, that sounded Russiany. *"Roger. Eyes and ears live, recording commenced. Sending stealthed spy-eye for redundancy. Rebroadcasting to CCCP and ECHO: Bella. Commissar notified."*

All of the doors of the SUVs opened at just about the same time; nearly identical-looking men in suits with earpieces connected to radios stepped out of the vehicles and took up positions around the street. Some were facing in towards John and Sera, but most were looking outward; setting up a cordon, of sorts. John heard one of the suits speak quietly into a microphone hooked surreptitiously into his jacket sleeve. "Area secure."

A final person stepped out of the middle SUV. His suit was more expensive than the ones worn by the rest of the men: dark navy blue, well tailored, with a matching tie and crisp-collared white shirt underneath. A tiny flag pin in the lapel was the crowning irony to the outfit. This guy was the management.

"John Murdock, Seraphym," the man said in the officious tone of someone used to having his orders followed. "I'm Agent Gibson with the National Security Agency." He reached into his jacket, producing two folded pieces of paper. "I've been authorized by Title IV, section 120 of the National Security Act, pertaining to metahumans on American soil, along with authorization from the Attorney General to take both of you into custody. These are your copies of the warrants and other attendant paperwork. There are some important people that would like to ask you some questions."

Sera's fires flared, and her wings half spread. "I do not believe you," she said flatly. "Do you think you can hold me if I do not wish to be held?" All of the government agents in suits visibly stiffened; the less disciplined among them clearly reached for weapons, only stopping short when Gibson put his hand up. "And do not count on my reputation for non-lethality. I do not answer to you."

John put his hand over Sera's. "Let's see what they want, darlin'. Might be interestin'." John still wasn't feeling any danger through the battle-sense; if he did, he didn't anticipate that he and Sera would have too many problems freeing themselves. Trying to force their way out of the situation right now, though... could make things messy. And not just for them; for the neighborhood, for the CCCP, and even for ECHO. "I'll tell you this, though, Agent Gibson. We're tired, hungry, an' smell like a couple of days' worth of fightin'. Try not to piss us off any more than absolutely necessary. Agreed?"

"You do know they are going to use just that against you, right?" That was Vickie. *"They might not actually torture you ... yet ... but they don't have to give you food, water, or any rest."*

"I think we can accommodate that perfectly well, Mr. Murdock. The middle vehicle has had ... alterations made to it so that the Seraphym may be comfortable in it."

"They don't have to keep breathin', either. Don't worry, Vix; I know their kind an' their tricks. We'll be all right. It looks like they came prepared; or their version of it, anyways. If they don't take us seriously, we'll get out on our own. Keep your ears open."

"Good. Also, y'can address her as Mrs. Murdock, if you're goin' to talk to her. I'd highly suggest stayin' respectful." Without another word, John and Sera walked to the middle SUV and got in, Sera first while John held the door open for her. *Let's see what these assholes want, an' if it's worth wastin' our time.*

They were taken to a hotel, not some sort of detention center. Although it appeared that every floor of the place had been taken over by the suits, there were at least multiple exits (guarded, but when had that ever stopped either of them?) and no bars on the windows. They were taken to a room, allowed to shower and given something to eat and drink. Sera had looked at the food and drink dubiously. "How do I know this is not drugged?" she demanded.

John poked at the tray. "One way to find out." He speared a piece of steak and popped it into his mouth, chewing and swallowing. "There. If I die or go loopy, you're set to inherit my vast fortune." He set upon his own steak, speaking between chews and swallowing; John really was hungry. "I figure that this is a lotta effort to go to if they just wanted to go all 'rendition' on us. If we were in real danger, I also figure we'd know." *Battle-sense would kick in, hopefully, darlin',* he added mentally. He didn't want to talk about that out loud; the room was no doubt bugged, and there was no reason to give these government suits a full rundown on their capabilities.

Sera poked at her food doubtfully, and glared in the direction of the closed door, but finally hunger got the better of her and she joined him. Even with the war on, the steak here was top-notch. *I would rather that I did not need to eat or drink,* she told him, resentment in her "tone." *It is one less hold to have over us.*

Same could be said 'bout a lotta other things, darlin'... but they can still be fun. He lightly elbowed her, then leaned in and kissed her on the cheek.

"Vix to JM. I want you to take Sera's headset and smash it, please. I am ninety-nine percent sure they can't crack it, but I want to be one hundred percent sure they get no chance."

"I can do you one better, kiddo. I'll ash it when I take a shower." When he had first had the subvocals installed, it had been weird listening to others; voices took on a tinny and mechanical sound through whatever process translated the signals into actual speech. Still, it was damned handy for communicating on the sly. He made as if to caress the side of Sera's face and palmed the tiny headset and microphone. If their handlers had noticed it, then noticed later it was gone, too bad. It would be too late for them to do anything.

The next few hours passed too quickly for John's liking. He and Sera ate generous helpings of room service, showered, and did what they could to rest; neither one of them could sleep, however, and opted to just lie in bed next to each other. Luckily, both of them had changed into clean outfits back at CCCP HQ before they had tried to head back to John's squat; despite their gifts and skills, their uniforms had still taken a beating in the battle. Vickie quietly kept them updated; her invisible "eye" was scooting around quite actively, it seemed. The agents were all doing their rounds or staying at their posts; the street outside didn't have any unusual activity, either. So far, things seemed to be on the up and up. Or, at least as much as they could be with the NSA involved. John suspected that the ink on those documents that Agent Gibson had provided them was still wet from whoever was behind this trying to make everything at least somewhat legal. Possibly they weren't even legal yet...this might be draft legislation he was trying to pretend had passed into law. John had seen dirtier tricks get pulled when someone with power wanted something—or someone—bad enough; he wouldn't be surprised, however this turned out.

Finally, there was a knock on the door. John peeled himself out of Sera's embrace, got up from the bed, and walked over to answer the door.

"Ten minutes until we need to leave, Mr. Murdock," one of the nondescript agents said.

"We'll be ready in five."

"*Still with you, JM.*"

"*Copy. Everything is still set to record, right? No matter what goes down, our biggest gun to use against these sorts is information. Folks like these fear Senate inquiries more'n they fear bein' killed.*"

"*If one of them so much as farts silently, it'll be on the record. I have not stopped recording since those goons blockaded you.*"

Once they were finished dressing and otherwise cleaning up, they were escorted downstairs. There was a moment of confusion and embarrassment when several of the agents that were there for their "protection" found that they couldn't ride in the same elevator due to Sera's wings. It elicited a shared smile from John and Sera; neither of them really cared how inconvenienced their quasi captors were. Sera even expanded her wings slightly to take up as much space as possible without being too obvious about it. If the next hour didn't yield something interesting or useful, John figured that he would begin to get annoyed.

The elevator trip was short. They were shuffled away from the hotel lobby, down several hallways, and ended up outside of one of the larger conference rooms. John had been making a mental note of the building layout and their route, even though he could have Vickie bring up the floor plans to his HUD. Best to stay in practice with tradecraft like that; he was still kicking himself about nearly getting ambushed by this bunch. The two agents flanking the doors stepped from their positions and opened the doors for John and Sera. Inside there were two sets of desks: one for them, and one for the people that were going to carry out this "hearing" apparently. Agent Gibson was inside already, waiting near the far table.

After John and Sera were seated, introductions were made. Representatives from the local branches of the FBI, NSA, Homeland Security, and even a regional director for the CIA were present. That covered the Feds. For the local government, there were the police chief for Atlanta proper, a liaison for the mayor's office, and a state senator. Finally, to round everything out, there was the assistant district attorney; John figured that they needed him to make sure everything stayed legal, or at least the outward appearance thereof.

The ADA was the first to speak. "The purpose of this hearing is to determine several things. First and foremost, the...status of two unregistered metahumans. Normally, these matters would be handled by local authorities," he said, nodding towards the police chief and putting a hand to his own chest. "But, given the exotic nature and tentative Op classification of the metahumans in question, it has been decided that there is a potential national security risk that needs to be addressed."

John reached out with his senses, gauging the men sitting in front of him. All of them were fearful; the armed guards were proof enough of that. They were scared of John and Sera for a variety of reasons. There was something else behind the fear, though, at least from the Feds—avarice, naked and ugly. It fell into place for John. This wasn't truly about security, or anything else. They *wanted* John and Sera. To co-opt them, take possession of them, use them as tools for their own purposes. He knew that Sera could feel it, too, through their connection.

Sera bristled. The feathers of her wings puffed out a little, and her wings began to vibrate. The feathers rustled against each other. It sounded a little like a rattlesnake.

The ADA jerked in his seat, then tried too late to hide it. He cleared his throat. "This is...a very serious matter, Mr. and Mrs. Murdock. By law, both of you have to be registered with ECHO. Given past incidents with metahumans that had abilities on the level that you do, it's only prudent for us to act. For the safety of our fellow citizens." John was unimpressed, and did his best to show it. The ADA looked to the others on his side of the table, then continued. "Of secondary concern is Mr. Murdock's status in relation to the United States Army. At present, he's recorded as being Absent Without Official Leave—"

"That's horseshit, an' I'll bet at least one of you knows it," he exploded, letting his anger flare for a moment. "I never deserted from the Army. I got left. More like MIA, presumed dead. There's a difference." He crossed his arms in front of his chest. He mentally started a countdown to when he'd be well and truly fed up with these proceedings. "If any of you have the clearance for it, y'might have an inklin' 'bout what went down, an' why I'm no longer in the Army. It ain't by choice, or it wasn't at the time. But that's immaterial now, ain't it?"

"Not even remotely, Mr. Murdock." That was the CIA section officer. "Your...absence is absolutely germane to these proceedings and to your current status. For example, depending on how this hearing goes, we could very well take you back today."

John couldn't help but grin at that. "Could you, now?" He leaned back in his chair, keeping his tone nonchalant. But the implied threat was still there. He could feel the people in the room getting more and more uncomfortable. *Fuck 'em. We didn't ask to get dragged in front of a bunch of empty suits and dead-eyed bureaucrats. If they're uncomfortable, that's on them.*

"We could try." Agent Gibson hadn't taken his eyes off of John and Sera since they had entered the room. John had read the man's emotions when they first met. Gibson was a nasty piece of work, and a large part of him wanted to be turned loose to kill John and Sera. All he needed was an excuse and authorization. The ugly smile that crept into the corners of the agent's mouth confirmed it. He struck John as the sort of man that would've been comfortable on a slave patrol, or overseeing a concentration camp. His job was an excuse for satisfying his own sick appetites, when the opportunity arose. John had met a few like Gibson; never in his own unit, but where other violent sorts congregated. Men like him always found ample work, especially with those in power.

Sera's eyes began to blaze, deep down inside the pupils. John could feel her tensing. Her right hand flexed, as if she itched to call her sword or spear.

"Listen," John said, leaning forward again; it was getting to the point where he had to diffuse this or just risk the pair of them walking out. "We're not any threat to anyone. Unless they're Thulians. We're here to *help*, got it? We've fought alongside military units, done law enforcement work locally, and scrapped a lotta Krieger heavy metal. How would tryin' to collar us be worth the effort for y'all when we're doin' just fine on our own?"

"Because, Mr. Murdock, of the fact that, while you're helping us now...doesn't mean that you always will. Metahumans, especially those of particularly high Op classification, are known to be...unstable. Unreliable. And dangerous."

"Of note on that particular line of thought is the Seraphym—erm, Mrs. Murdock," said the FBI division head. "There is virtually *nothing* known about you. Where you came from prior to the Invasion, where your exact allegiances are, hell, if you're even a damned American citizen! On those grounds alone, not to mention your Op classification, we have enough justification to detain you."

Sera's wings flared, and so did her fires. Now all of the agents *did* draw weapons, though they were very careful to not point them at either John or Sera. "I do not answer to you," she said flatly.

"And there's the problem we've been talking about! Who do either of you answer to? When metahumans are as powerful as the two of you are, they're a power unto themselves. What's to stop either of you from selling to the highest bidder, or trying to set up your own kingdoms, or just rampaging wantonly if you have a bad day? If you're not with us, under government control, there's no reason to think that you couldn't be against us any day." That was the police chief. He was so agitated that it looked like his bushy mustache was going to fly off of his face as he was talking.

"Or...we could leave," said Sera, between clenched teeth, "and allow you to continue to battle the Thulians without us. I am certain that there are other nations that would be more respectful and grateful for our aid." Now her eyes were blazing, and it would have taken a blind man not to see it.

None of the Feds or locals liked the sound of that. All of them started talking at once, about arrests, detention, questioning, and so forth. John looked at Sera; their joint patience had just run out. John was just about to stand up—and damn the consequences—when he heard a voice in his ear.

"And reap the whirlwind in three...two...one..." The doors to the service entrance behind the "tribunal" flew open with such force that they cracked the wall panels and their handles lodged in the plasterboard. In the doorway stood Bella, Bull—Bull must have been the one that shoved open the doors—Spin Doctor and Mamona. They were all fully encased in Bull's force field. Behind them, in the shocked silence that had filled the room, was the sound of many, many people retching in agony, vomiting so hard they were close to throwing up their toenails.

A moment later, snapping out of their daze, every agent in the room, including Gibson, aimed their weapons at the new arrivals, and started shouting orders; to stand down, to put their weapons away, and so forth.

And in the next moment, it was the agents in the room who were bending over, vomiting like the ones in the hallway. Agent Gibson was the only one still feebly trying to aim his weapon... until he was hit with a redoubled wave of nausea.

"Shut. The fuck. Up," said Bella, through gritted teeth. "Let 'em loose, Mamona. I don't want to be knee-deep in puke. By the way, good job. The training seems to be working."

Mamona grinned, and the agents stopped vomiting. But they were in no way in good shape. The entire room was quickly filling with the stink of several emptied stomachs. All of the agents looked shaky and pale.

"The Commissar of the CCCP, callsign Red Saviour II, civilian name Natalya Shostakovaya, would like to know on what grounds you are detaining two of her comrades. Who, might I add, have diplomatic protections under the International Mutual Metahuman Aid Act of 1967. Are you really jonesing *that* hard for international war provocations with Russia while we're already fighting with the Thulians?" Bella smiled thinly into the silence. "But that is not really what brought me here."

"Ms. Parker, this is highly irregular! This is a closed hearing!" The ADA had half-risen in his seat; he looked torn between righteous indignation and bolting for the nearest exit.

"I said, shut the fuck up," Bella repeated. "Unless your colleagues here would really *like* to see the last twenty-five or so years of unredacted documents about the illegal detention, torture, murder of and experimentation on metahumans and *humans*, including *minor children*, in the NSA black program known colloquially as 'the Program' dumped on every media outlet in the world in the next ten minutes."

John noticed that the CIA rep visibly stiffened at the mention of the Program, right before his eyes went deadly cold. *Gotcha, asshole. Definitely got to have Vickie look up what rock that bastard crawled out from under.*

"Oh, and just to prove I'm not bluffing"—one elegant eyebrow rose—"the head of research for the Program is one Joseph Garvey, PhD, alphabet soup. And *very* recently ECHO took custody of twenty-three *minor children* from just one Program Facility in the Florida Everglades after it was attacked by Thulians. The Thulians also evidently know about your little torture-fest sites. You might ponder that for a moment as well." *Guess Vix filled Bella in, at least partially, on what went down in Florida. Might have to see about that, for Zach's sake if nothing else.*

The silence now contained a strong component of "stunned disbelief." Bella examined her fingernails critically. "The testimony of these *minor children* is probably not something you want televised. But of course, that is not all." She gestured to Spin Doctor, who took one small step forward, frowning in a "Father is Displeased with your Behavior" way.

"I suspect that you also would not care to have the fact televised that you have taken two prominent heroes of the Invasion, people who have saved countless lives, and illegally detained them," said Spin Doctor, who was obviously enjoying his role. "And that leaves aside the fact that one of them, the Seraphym, is a Peruvian National. I happen to have copies of her papers right here." He waved them at about shoulder height. "And of course, by dint of their marriage, that makes John Murdock a Peruvian National as well, should he care to accept that status." Spin consulted his notes. "Also interesting to the media would be the fact that you have used legislation that has not yet been enacted as law, is currently only *just* up before a House committee, is being protested by the ACLU, ECHO, and the Southern Poverty Law Center and will *certainly* be deemed unconstitutional by the Supreme Court, as justification for detaining these two members of the CCCP."

"And," Bella appended smoothly, "these entire proceedings have been recorded from the moment you detained Mr. and Mrs. Murdock. From the illegal seizure and detention itself, to the

intimidations and threats you met them with in this...ballroom."
Her mouth quirked briefly. "Really? A *ballroom?* If you were truly
that serious about how threatening these two are, why did you
choose a ballroom, in a public hotel, in downtown Atlanta, to
interrogate them in? Seraphym and Murdock have taken down
a *Thulian dragon ship.* Just the two of them. If you had pissed
them off to the point of no return, *what do you think they could
have done to downtown Atlanta?* The only possible conclusion is
that you knew very well that if they felt threatened and left, the
worst that would happen would be some scorched carpet and a
couple holes in some walls. Therefore all this *concern* about how
dangerous they are is as phony as a three-dollar bill."

"This has been recorded, surreptitiously, this entire time?"
The ADA's mouth worked for a few moments before he finally
started speaking again. "I, um, I'm sure that that, erm, violates
wiretapping statutes—"

"Really? Not in this state," Spin Doctor said flatly. "As you
should be aware, Mister Assistant District Attorney, since you've
taken advantage of that fact for your own cases. For recording to
be legal in Georgia, only one party has to be aware that recordings are being made. But you're welcome to *try* to push that
one through. It will, of course, be long after the time that we've
dumped those recordings on worldwide media sites."

"We'll be leaving now," Bella said, drawing herself up to her
full height. "John Murdock and the Seraphym will be leaving
with us. ECHO will still be coordinating and working with the
military and the US Government—along with all other world ally
governments—to effectively combat and defend against the Thulians. I *believe* Commissar Red Saviour will also continue in that
capacity with the CCCP, either independently or as an adjunct
through ECHO, although you should be aware she has already
lodged diplomatic protests against you. All of you. Individually,
by name. *That'll* look just peachy on your records." She smiled
thinly, then lost the smile. "But this ends. Now. Pull a trick like
this against *any* other meta, and ECHO will relocate to Lima, and
leave you to twist in the wind." She gestured to John and Sera,
and Bulwark briefly dropped the shield around them all. "Let's get
you two back to CCCP before the Commissar has an aneurism."

John and Sera both stood up from their seats, joined the
group with Bella, and Bull put the shield back up—a pointed

reminder that no one with Bella trusted anyone here. They all began walking towards the room's exit. "Thanks for the steak," John said over his shoulder. He caught a glimpse of Agent Gibson in the corner of his eye; the man had recovered somewhat, and there was a burning hatred in his eyes. He wouldn't forget the couple ... and guys like that never let grudges go unanswered. *So be it. If he decides to make an issue out of this little encounter, it'll be the worst goddamned mistake of his life.*

The pair took up position next to Bella and Bulwark as they paused beside the doorway. John crossed his arms, waiting to see what would happen next.

"So," Bella said. "Have I made the position of ECHO and the CCCP perfectly clear? Are there any objections?"

The room was silent. Some of the hearing members were befuddled. Others were boiling with rage. Most felt embarrassed, at least as far as John could tell through his senses. All of them, though, were cowed. Saving their own skin was a priority for them; political critters thought of themselves first, after all.

"I just want to point out that attempting to lodge any charges against anyone for assault on a federal agent will only result in a worse ... ah ... *shitstorm* for you," Spin said, with a Mona Lisa-like smile. "First, you are going to have to prove that any assault actually took place. Recordings will show that not one of us laid so much as a finger on any of you. And second ... we have all those juicy unredacted records. And we have the capability to drop them wherever, whenever we choose. Don't think of this as blackmail. Think of it as mutually assured destruction."

More silence.

"Good. I'm glad we understand each other." Bella got a look of extreme disgust on her face. "There is not one of you here that is worthy to be scraped off Arthur Chang's shoe like the dogshit that you are."

And with that, she turned and led the way out of the room, Bull's shield like a halo around them.

After making their way out of the hotel, there had been a CCCP van and an ECHO car waiting for the group. The trip back was uneventful; no cars following them, no sirens or patrol car lights, nothing. John did notice that Mamona was grinning the entire drive back, however.

"I've always wanted t'do somethin' like that. Kind of badass, wasn't it? Well, 'cept for the smell."

"Damned right it was, comrade. Thanks for comin' to our rescue. Might've gotten uglier an' messier than it already was, if you an' the cavalry hadn't barged in when you did."

"My pleasure! You two ought t'get into trouble more often!" Mamona's grin widened. "Bella's got a new trick. Some of us, she can train up with amplified powers. Mostly, it's us with psion powers, and takin' ones to two, and twos to three. She reckons I'm 'bout a two and a half now." Now *that* was interesting. John didn't know enough about metahuman power generation or physiology to even make educated guesses at how that worked, other than it had something to do with how people accessed their powers, but still...every tool they could get in the fight against the Thulians was one that John was willing to take.

Both vehicles arrived at the CCCP HQ right after dusk. The entire episode, from getting picked up to getting back to relative safety, had taken up the entire day. John and Sera, exhausted at the start of it, were even more bone-tired now. It was only their shared connection, and the energy that they fed each other through it, that was keeping them going. It took only a minute to get everyone out of the vehicles, through the main entrance and past security, and into the CCCP briefing room. The Commissar and Untermensch were already there, waiting for them.

"So...you are to be explaining why pair of firebombs are allowing themselves to be captured, with not even one of their captors being killed. Or how you two are even captured at all. *Da?*" The Commissar was chain-smoking through one of her awful packs of cigarettes; a pile of angrily smashed out cigarette butts filled a tray in front of her to overflowing.

"We figured that leavin' a pile of dead Feds in the middle of the 'hood wouldn't really help our public relations image, Commissar. It was a better move to hold back, let 'em show their hand, an' work our way from there. We weren't captured, so much as taken for a ride; could've left any time we wanted... though there would've been consequences." He paused. "'Sides. Vix was recordin' everythin'. Minute they stopped us, they were in trouble. They just didn' know it till Bella made her entrance."

Natalya sucked on her teeth dismissively. "Fine, fine. Was listening on Overwatch with witch and blue girl. May have been tactical necessity. Question for now is what to do going forward. I know the likes of the running dogs you two were dealing with. *Politicians*," she nearly spat the word, it was filled with so much venom, "only want more of what they have: power. You two are power, at least to them. They will come again, no matter what *Amerikanski* threats they hear."

"Commissar is right. Snakes like these only know how to slither in the filth; it is what they are accustomed to. Decisive action now may be the most prudent course, to prevent any... difficulties further down the line." Untermensch had a pile of folders laid out in front of him. John recognized pictures of at least three of the men that had been at the hearing inside the folders.

John held up his hand. "I'm goin' to say we need some other option. We've got enough on our plates with the Thulians; tryin' to take on the US government, even if we weren't at war, is usually a shit idea. They've got more money, more guns, an' more lawyers." He knew that Georgi wasn't suggesting that they start bumping people off, though the Commissar would probably jump at that notion, but still... it was best to get it off of the table now, before it started seeming attractive.

Bella rubbed her forehead. "I'm open to just about any option short of burning down Congress with everyone inside."

"Well, maybe for fun. But that's a hobby, not a strategy," John added jokingly. Bella stuck her tongue out at him.

Bull patted her knee. "Much as I sympathize, we can't hit this problem head on. The only choice I see is to be reactionary."

"Obviously, my forte is going at the public angle," Spin Doctor mused. "It's true I haven't had to do too much, since the Thulians have been doing our job for us, but I can certainly rev the old publicity machine up again. There certainly isn't much else I can contribute."

"What about if you go after the legal angle?" Bella asked suddenly. "Get public pressure behind laws to *protect* metas from exploitation, by the government or anyone else. Get us categorized as a *public* resource, maybe. They want to use laws to lock us up or conscript us? We'll get in there first with laws to keep them from doing just that."

"Oh, I like that," Spin said, perking up. "I like that a great deal. I'll get with our legal team and the ACLU, for starters, maybe bring in other groups as we see more options." He rubbed his hands together. "I can almost see a PSA in my head right now..."

"I do not *ever* wish to find myself so trapped again," Sera said unhappily. Her wing feathers were still somewhat "pine-coned" with stress. "How *dare* they take so much as a single hour away from us, an hour in which we could be missed, in which people could die?"

"S'alright, darlin'. They're assholes, an' they don't know any better." He sent as much reassurance as he could through their connection; she seemed to calm down slightly, but she was still very much aggravated. "Now, this is all well an' good...but when push comes to shove, laws are just ink on paper. Some of those bastards, or at least bastards like 'em... they'll do what they want, law or no law. Especially ones like that Agent Gibson." John placed his hand over Sera's, giving it a squeeze. "It's good that y'all are tryin' to get this done through the right channels... but it does bear keepin' in mind that this might turn bloody at some point. An' fast. Especially post-war."

If we win, he left unsaid.

"If that day comes," the Commissar intoned, "then it will being a day of reckoning unlike any those cretins have seen. *No one* threatens my comrades. Not ever again."

Uncharacteristically, it was Bulwark that spoke up. "If it comes to that, Commissar," he rumbled, "you will not be standing alone."

Peekaboo

MERCEDES LACKEY AND DENNIS LEE

@rancbeast42 kept feeding me good stuff. Sometimes just a couple of links, sometimes as much as half a page. But of course, we had that whole parity issue going on. He knew plenty about me. I knew nothing about him.

On the other hand, he didn't seem to understand I wasn't your average superhacker. Sure he could, and did, hide himself. His IP address was probably changing all the time; that is seriously just not that hard to do. Plenty of motels leave "support" and "guest" open on their Wi-Fi routers, when they bother to encrypt at all; you just park in back and find a sweet spot, and there you go. And even if he was using his own rig, an anonymizing service fixes that. However . . . it doesn't allow for the techno-shaman who can backtrace straight to the originating computer without even going through the internet.

So finally, when I was pretty sure I knew who it was, and just needed confirmation, I set everything up to fire on invocation and waited.

@rancbeast42: Got your ears on, Victrix?

Ha. That was what I was waiting for. With a flick of my fingers I invoked the process. Very convenient for me his firewall wasn't set up for people like me.

@victoriavictrix: Sec, I'm in the middle of something.

Not a lie, old lad, I am in the middle of remote-hacking your . . . laptop. Very nice. Means there's a camera and I won't alert you by starting hard-drive reads to find out who you are.

@rancbeast42: Chop chop, lady. I'm on the clock.

I'll just bet you are. Keeping me from getting a backtrace finished. Hello, camera. Let's turn you on. Ah, how careless of you, this is not like you. You should have put a piece of tape over the lens. ID confirmed.

@victoriavictrix: Don't worry about backtraces, Jack. You're looking well.

He wasn't startled. In fact, he smiled slightly. Just to make things fair, I put a little feed from my cam in the bottom right-hand corner of his screen, and wiggled my fingers at him. I was a little surprised when he wiggled his back.

@victoriavictrix: Please don't cut the connection. I'm pretty good at keeping secrets.

He kept up the poker face, no lid slamming or nervous sweat. Instead, he sat back in his seat a little, and gave my image a good long stare, which was a bit disorienting because it meant he wasn't looking directly at the camera. Then he leaned forward again, fingers on the keyboard.

@rancbeast42: About time. We really don't have much left to muck about with.

@rancbeast42: We're going to need each other. I know I can trust you. I need to know if you feel the same.

Whew. One big worry ditched.

@victoriavictrix: Red trusts you. He's generally not wrong, about people anyway. I'm in.

@rancbeast42: We've got things to do. Saving the world and whatnot. We can help each other with that.

@rancbeast42: But there's something else I've got in the works. Something I need your help with. I'm sure you'll be on board.

@victoriavictrix: F2F? Give me a time and place.

@rancbeast42: Not the best idea, but I don't see much help for it. There are details I don't trust even over secured channels.

I thought about this.

@victoriavictrix: I think I have a secure loc with no modern tech in it.

I sent him the details on how to get into that old ECHO safe spot that Ramona and Merc had used, and a potential time.

@rancbeast42: Good enough. Here's what you should bring. And here's what I'll be bringing.

He wrote down two things. Two names, actually. The second I wasn't terribly surprised by, but the first . . .

@victoriavictrix: Why her?

@rancbeast42: You said you trusted me. Time to prove it. See you soon.

The camera feed cut. I sat sucking on my lower lip. Interesting. Whatever Jack was up to . . . it was going to be slick. Red always said he was the brains of the bunch. He'd clearly anticipated that I was going to hack his computer and had been waiting for me to show my hand.

Red trusted him. Every instinct I had said that the best thing I could do was just hang on and follow instructions. Every instinct I had that wasn't my usual paranoia said that he was smarter than me, and I wasn't used to that.

"Instinct" is nothing more than our brains processing things so fast, in the background, that it feels as if the information is coming out of nowhere. But it's not. It's reasoned.

Jack could talk about trust all he wanted, but we were both gambling. He was in trouble, and short on time; it was very obvious. He was gambling that I would buy his story, his good intentions, and hoping like hell I would step in line. I was gambling that he wasn't the two-faced bastard his scant files at ECHO portrayed him as. It made me wonder what he needed me for? And what he needed her for? He was clearly versed in unearthing intel of all shapes and sizes. It made me a bit nervous. I suppose I could have dug a little deeper, if I had the time to do so, but something told me I really could trust this enigmatic little man.

Hell, if the Mafia could work with ECHO, I sure as hell could work with Jack, someone who'd already proved he was ready to play ball nicely. Red had changed. Why not Jack?

Time to fish or cut bait. We were all out of options.

> *Yes indeed. Why her? I was very interested in finding out, so I cut out all the middlemen and went straight to the top.*

INTERLUDE

Breathing Underwater

DENNIS LEE

Is this my life?

How long ago was it that I just trying to prove myself? That I was better, better than anyone? That I was just misunderstood? That if given a chance, I would rise to the occasion and demolish anyone that dared stand in my way? Not really what a hero would say, I guess. That's okay. I never considered myself a hero. Just someone trying to smash all the naysayers into little itty bitty pieces. Just another meta with a chip on her shoulder, but one who knew what power meant.

What power could bring.

But it went all wrong. If ambition is a sin, then I'm a sinner. If being unable to accept defeat is a flaw, then I'm just another aberration. The truth is, I've always been able to know my limits. My problem lies in accepting them. Most of them, anyway. Some I've known for a long time, and they never really bothered me before. I have trouble getting close to people. Some might laugh and call that an understatement. Meh, whatever. Love isn't really a foreign thing to me, y'know. I know love. I've loved people. But people let you down. Some people never realize how you feel. It's unfair, but these things always are. Maybe I'm not meant to love anyone, or have anyone love me. It never ends well, does it? It just gets in the way. Red jokes about it a lot, and as much as I loathe him sometimes, he does get a nugget of truth in every once in a while. He says love is God's eternal joke, and each and every one of us is the punchline. I guess he would know. From what I can tell, he's been the butt of every joke he's ever heard.

I guess I'm the same. I never quite know what's happening around me. I do the best I can and plan my stupid little schemes and roll with the punches, but I'm never really sure what the universe has planned for me. I do what I can, I suppose, and pray for the best.

It never comes, does it? You hope it does, but you can never count on it. You have to prepare for the worst.

So why is it that the worst always comes?

When Bull entered the dimly lit interrogation room, he was happy to see that Scope wasn't in restraints this time. He'd spoken with the staff about it, but with regulations being what they were, even he had problems overruling certain procedures. If they were being held in Top Hold, they had to be in restraints at all times outside their cell. He supposed Scope was lucky that she was even allowed outside a cell. With a few of their prisoners, that just wasn't possible. For example, the idea of anything restraining Harmony outside her nullifying cage was unfathomable. Scope was different, of course. She could have been kept with the general populace. Strictly speaking, her power set didn't necessitate the extreme measures associated with Top Hold in neutralizing metas. It was more for her protection, of course. A few of the inmates in GenPop were put there by her, after all.

"She's not a prisoner," Bull had told Jensen. "She shouldn't be treated as one."

Bull remembered Jensen feigning confusion as he glanced around the cold and sterile halls of Top Hold. "Why is she in here then?"

Bull didn't answer. He didn't feel that he had to. Sometimes, he really wanted to smash in Jensen's stupid, smug face.

Given the circumstances surrounding her reappearance, they just couldn't trust anything about Scope. Of course they couldn't. After nearly single-handedly botching a coordinated global effort to lay siege to Ultima Thule, seemingly sacrificing herself by triggering a massive explosion to bring down the city's shields and then mysteriously reappearing after the battle with only minor abrasions, the unspoken opinion of many was that they had found their suspected mole. It didn't make a hell of a lot of sense, at least to Bulwark, but he had to admit that even he suspected Scope now of more than just self-destructive behavior in the face of guilt following Acrobat's death. The problem was, she didn't have any answers to any of their questions, at least none that she was willing to share.

No, she didn't know how she was still alive. No, she didn't have any memory of anything after locking Blue Team out of the generator base of the shield tower in Ultima Thule. No, she didn't know how she had mysteriously reappeared miles away, stumbling across an ECHO cleanup crew with nothing more than the ECHO uniform on her back.

She had refused almost anything they had offered. She barely ate, was indifferent to the state of her unwashed, battle-torn body, and became violent when anyone so much as touched her. So she was still matted with dirt and blood, her hair wild and unkempt, and she was still adorned in the same battered ECHO nanoweave that she had worn in Ultima Thule.

She sat at one end of the interrogation table, her hands clasped before her as if in prayer, her hair obscuring her face as she slouched forward in her chair. Bull winced.

"Paris," he growled. "You smell like someone left a vat of baked beans to rot in a monkey house."

She didn't answer. She hadn't moved at all when he had entered, but through the tangled mess of her hair, Bull could feel her eyes on him. And they were cold. Nothing about this felt right to him. Before, he had been struggling to understand how the girl he had mentored for so long had fallen so far. But she had become so alien to him, he found himself wondering if it was even her at all.

He sighed and took a seat opposite her.

"I'm not going to run through all the questions again," he said, pushing his tablet to the side. "You must have memorized them by now, and your answers have always been the same. So I'll just ask this: Do you remember anything new?"

"No," Scope muttered. "Nothing new. Can I go back to my cell now?"

"No, you can't," Bull said. "I'm afraid this is the last time we'll be meeting like this. Because at the end of this meeting, I'm going to have to make a decision on what to do with you. So you will appreciate how very important it is, if you have anything new to share with me, that you do so now. Because at this moment, the only option I can see before me is to send you to GenPop. I can't justify keeping you in Top Hold anymore."

"General populace?" Scope said, and chuckled. "I guess that's one solution. You don't really expect me to last long there, do you? Or is that the point?"

"I've been bending the rules enough as it is. I'll be overruled soon. If I don't decide to send you, someone else will."

"Oh, right," Scope said, nodding. "The rules. We all know how you feel about the rules, Bull. Wouldn't want to see any tarnish on your reputation now, would we?"

"What would you have me do?" Bull asked. "You won't volunteer any information. You should have been atomized in that blast. Instead, here you are, with a few scratches instead, with nothing to oppose the accusations that you are and have been a mole all this time."

"That's a bit of a stretch, isn't it?" Scope muttered. "And really, if I was a plant, isn't this a bit of a sloppy way to return? I'm weak, I'm jonesing like you wouldn't believe, but I can still think. If I'm a traitor, I'm the dumbest, clumsiest traitor in the history of dumb, clumsy traitors." She peered up at him, and Bull saw the light catch her furious eyes behind the curtain of hair.

"I don't know what happened, Bull," she whispered. "Not a clue. The last thing I remember is locking myself in that room and turning around to set the charges. The next thing I know, I'm crawling through a war zone. I didn't even know we'd won. For a time, I actually thought I was the only one left. And when..."

She withdrew from him, and cowered beneath her veil again. Bull watched her intently, waiting... and relaxed when a sob escaped her lips.

"When..." she began again. "When I came across that ECHO crew, you don't know...you have no idea how relieved I felt. If they were ECHO, then we had won. If they were ECHO, then most of you would still be alive. Maybe even you, even after..."

"After you screwed up so badly that a mountain fell on top of me?"

"Yeah," Scope muttered. "Even after that." She withdrew again, clasping her arms around herself and bowing her head. "Everything after, you know. I was brought here. You asked me questions I don't know the answers to. And now you're going to send me down to GenPop and I'm going to have to watch my back every single moment I'm not alone in a cell for a shiv to land in my back. For all you know, that's what I want. But you don't believe that, do you? You've never given up on anyone, have you, Bull? You still believe in people. Some of those people have let you down so completely, you've been dragged to the edge so many times, you're actually familiar now with the taste of your own death. But you still believe in me. I can tell. Your instincts are probably telling you some pretty confusing things right now. So how about I ask the questions for a change, Bulwark? What do *you* believe about me?"

Bull didn't answer immediately. He watched her for a moment, as if sizing her up, then leaned forward and clasped his hands gently together on the table between them.

"I believe you've lost your way," he said, "but that's all. I don't think you're a traitor, like some do. I don't think you had or have any intentions against ECHO. I think someone's been playing you. I think you've been a bit of a victim through all this. With that said, I still think you had a hand in making yourself vulnerable to it and you should take some responsibility for that. I think you're more a danger to yourself than anyone here now. Even if you were to clear your name or reputation, I don't think anyone would clear you for active duty anymore, for various reasons. Jensen still wants you for more interrogation. Bella just doesn't trust you anymore. I wouldn't reinstate you either."

"And why's that, Bull?"

"Because I believe the moment you're reinstated, you will stop being a danger just to yourself, but to anyone who has the misfortune of being placed on your team."

"Ouch."

"You're not ready, Paris. I think someday you could be, but that's a long ways away. If I had my way, you would be busted down to a base private and forced to work your way up again through the ranks, right from basic training."

"You wouldn't!"

"I would," Bull said. "Fortunately for you, there's another option. Given that I was your commanding officer from the time you attained your OpOne levels, I don't have much say in what will happen to you other than as the warden of Top Hold. I'm too close, they won't allow it. All I can do is send you to GenPop for further questioning, or without any substantial evidence to hold you, release you outright."

"You can't!" Scope hissed, rising to her feet. "If you release me, I'll be thrown out of ECHO altogether! No active duty, no reason to stay, I'll be sent packing!"

Bull turned to the camera in the corner of the room, and motioned the guards outside to stand down. He turned back to Scope, and motioned for her to take her seat with a irritated flick of his eyes.

"Would that bother you so much?" he asked, after she had slumped back in her chair.

"Yeah," she answered. "No. I don't know."

"Well, fortunately for you, you don't have to decide just yet. Turns out you have a sponsor."

"A sponsor?" She glanced up at him in surprise. "Who would be crazy enough to sponsor me?"

"Who amongst us isn't crazy by now?" Bull muttered, retrieving his tablet and scrolling down to a memo he had just received that morning. He shook his head in disbelief. "As if she doesn't have enough to do. Operative Victrix wants you to report to her as soon as you're released, if you're released. It seems she requires your aid."

Scope looked baffled. "What does she want me to do?"

"It seems your recent absence has caused some unforeseen complications with another inmate."

"Harmony," Scope nodded, understanding. "She wants me to see Harmony."

Bull nodded. "Normally I wouldn't have problems with a withdrawn and quiet Harmony, but Victrix wants her at her talkative and snarky best for some monitoring she wants to try. Seems she was only that way when you were around. For her, it's a chance to catch Harmony with her pants down. For you, it's a chance for a new start. If you want my advice..."

"Always," Scope breathed.

"...you will do exactly as she tells you to. You need all the goodwill you can get." Bull stood up and motioned for the guards to release the door lock. He turned to leave, but paused briefly, swinging his head back around the door. "One more thing..."

"What's that?"

"I wasn't kidding about the smell," he grunted. "Clean yourself up before you see her. Goodwill starts with not forcing your foulness on everyone within fifty feet."

And with that, he was gone.

Sorry, dear, imagined Reader. You're going to have to wait to find out what Jack and I wanted Scope for. Let your imagination soar.

CHAPTER ELEVEN

Song of Solomon

MERCEDES LACKEY AND CODY MARTIN

It had been a long week, and it looked like it was only going to get longer. John and Sera had been deployed twice already, responding to new major attacks. The Thulians were stepping up their game, and the attacks were coming more and more frequently. First it had been a major railyard near Atlanta; then a nuclear power plant right on the border with Alabama. The power plant had been a tough one; the security forces weren't a match for the combined Thulian assault. Most of the guards were rent-a-cops with a couple of weeks training, maybe a few years on the job working on a beer gut or counting the days until retirement. With the War on Terror, a lot of them had had AR-15s shoved into their hands, a couple of pamphlets on terrorism and NBC—nuclear, biological, and chemical—precautions, and expected to be prepared to defend the plant. The smart ones had run when the Thulians had shown up; most of the brave ones had died, despite everything John and Sera had done to help. The plant itself was going to be under repair for at least three months; John didn't want to think what would have happened if the Thulians had been able to take it out, and the havoc all that nuclear material would have played with the entire South.

John almost missed the days of the pop-up attacks from before the Fall of Metis. If it were still business as usual, as it had been back then, he and Sera could have been used a bit more tactically instead of like strategic assets: going and actually *hunting* the Thulians, instead of responding to their attacks. Recon, infiltration, destroying high value targets or rescuing VIPs were the things that he used to live for. Hell, if they weren't on call at all hours of the day, they might have even been able to go visit Zach surreptitiously. *Probably not, all told. After all of that shit with the Feds, we're probably being watched more than ever. Hell hath no fury like a bureaucrat scorned.*

No rest for the wicked. They had another call. John and Sera were flying hard and fast for the port in Savannah; it would be the second time they had to defend it. Usually the Thulians didn't try to hit the same location twice, especially after they knew that it was within range of John and Sera. Almost too late, three Death Spheres had been detected going for the port; one F-15 had valiantly tried to intercept them, but was destroyed, pilot lost. The three Death Spheres were larger than the most commonly encountered ones; not as big as the gigantic one that Vickie and the orbital "Hammer" weapons platform had taken out in the battle at the Superstition Mountains, but still too damned big for John's liking. *Troop carriers, with that crazy space-bending tech. How many suits of armor do they have in there? Dozens? Hundreds?* It didn't matter; however many Thulians there were, John and Sera could *not* allow the port to fall. It was the fourth biggest port on the East Coast, and losing it would be a horrendous blow to the war effort. There had been some international shipments hit on the open seas already, but it seemed that those were more "might as well" attacks as Death Spheres were on their way to juicier targets.

John double-checked their position on a wrist-mounted PDA; he could "feel" where they needed to go, and had his Overwatch HUD projecting their flight path, but he liked redundancy when it came to navigation. *Almost there, darlin',* he sent to Sera; the roar of the fires that were propelling them, in addition to the wind from how fast they were flying, made verbal communication all but impossible.

The situation is very bad, love. I think they are offloading troops into the ocean and having them walk the floor of the bay to the shore. The water will protect them until they are right at the edge of the docks.

It was a different tactic than the Thulians had used last time; a little sneakier, at least for Thulians. *Got your boots on? I think we'll have to kick 'em right back into the ocean,* he sent to her with a hint of a chuckle. *If only it were that easy.*

The port was supposed to have some defenses; antiaircraft guns and missile systems, and two of the missile launchers that used the ECHO/CCCP incendiary loads, as well as several teams of soldiers to man it all and provide ground security. It wouldn't be enough to hold off a sustained assault, though. That's where he and Sera came in. Hopefully.

"Heads-up. They're offloading in the ocean." That was Vickie, confirming what Sera had guessed. *"You won't be able to hit them until they're out of the water. They must have modded the suits for an onboard air supply. I've cleared you through and sent your flight paths and vectors to the ground support so you don't get splashed before you can help."*

"Roger that, Vic. We're breakin' through an' ought to have visual on the port right 'bout... now."

On cue, John and Sera came out of the low clouds they had been flying through, and were greeted with a bird's-eye view of the Port of Savannah. Three Death Spheres were descending on it from the east, heading straight for the canal. Streams of AA shells lashed out at the Death Spheres, the tracers looking like angry fireflies in the early morning twilight. Contrails from surface-to-air missiles trailed up impossibly fast towards the Spheres; the missiles either missed, or more often than not, were shot out of the air by actinic energy blasts. The Spheres looked like they hadn't taken any damage by the time they hit the water, submerging completely with tremendous gouts of water splashing out from the impact.

Let's get to work.

The more that they had been using their battle-sense, the easier it had become for John to enter into it with Sera. Now it hardly required any conscious thought; one moment he was in the Present, and then he was seeing Possibility. Studying the Futures for a moment, he and Sera both knew what they had to do. Instead of diving for the docks or the position in the water where the Death Spheres had submerged, he and Sera simultaneously angled their flight sharply to the right, aiming for a spot over the top of one of the defensive emplacements. Looking on from the outside, it would seem like they weren't reacting quickly enough to what was happening. They weren't reacting at all, in fact, but *anticipating.*

Seconds later, two of the Death Spheres emerged from the

canal in sprays of water, the first rays of true sunlight striking their glistening hulls. They split from each other, aiming at either end of the docks. The defensive batteries opened up again, trying to track the aggressors, still to no apparent effect; the Thulians had actually been learning, it seemed. Instead of just throwing troops at a problem and counting on the relative invulnerability of their armor, they had adjusted tactics, carefully marshalling their assets. They knew they could be hurt, and did their best to prevent that. *Not like the first Kriegers, the ones actually wearin' swastikas. I don't like fightin' this new breed any more'n I did their predecessors.*

The defenders figured out what was about to happen; the Death Spheres were going to make attack runs on their positions, softening them up for a push from the troopers that the ships had undoubtedly dropped off. Troopers that would be protected by the water until they leapt up on the docks themselves. The soldiers on the docks hunkered down; those that could, at least. The operators on the AA emplacements and missile systems continued to fire their weapons; they knew what the score was. If they stopped firing, there'd be no chance to take down the Death Spheres. Even allowing one to run amok would have been more than enough to catastrophically damage the docks, maybe even the surrounding civilian population. They were there to prevent that, even if it meant dying in place.

The Death Sphere on the right-hand side of the docks from where the Thulians had landed was just about to start its run. The whine of its energy cannons ramping up was audible over the cacophony of the other weapons, and sinister orange light began to spill from the thermite ports on its underside. Right before it could begin raining death down on the soldiers on the docks, Sera separated from John. She pulled up and hovered, while John slowed and formed up behind her with one hand on her shoulder, while manifesting his fire-claymore with the other. The spear of fire that she manifested was brighter and hotter than the ones she had produced at the beginning of the attack on Ultima Thule. She flung it, and it burned through the air like a meteor, impaling the Death Sphere like an apple on a stick. Its attack run halted in midair; it seemed as if the Sphere was shuddering in place, that something critical inside of it had jammed and was keeping it from moving. The weapons were still functional, and entered the last stage before they discharged. Without hesitation, John and Sera dove towards the end of the spear sticking out from the Sphere...and *pushed*.

There was a *whump* of displaced air from the blast wave of the explosion that followed. The Death Sphere split in half; part of it completely disintegrated, and a smaller section fell flaming into the canal. Through the cloud of flame where the Death Sphere had been came Sera and John, flying directly for the next Death Sphere—John with his sword at the ready, and Sera with her own sword and another spear—looking like two avenging gods come to exact justice. The second Death Sphere veered suddenly and sharply skyward, putting on speed and gaining distance from the docks.

That one ain't gonna trouble us for a bit, darlin'. Let's get to the docks.

Agreed. Those troopers are about to leap out of the water...

Let's give 'em a warm welcome, then.

The couple picked a landing spot in the dead center of the cement docks, about two hundred feet back from the edge. If they stood right at the edge, they'd be vulnerable to shots from the trooper energy cannons coming from the waters below. From where they were right now, they'd be able to respond to any that made it onto the docks. And the docks themselves were a good place to fight; essentially giant cement slabs, built to take accidental low-speed ramming by enormous cargo ships. Rail tugs were frantically moving as much cargo away from the combat area as possible, though...there were millions of pounds of cargo containers, and no way to move more than a fraction of it away in time. *Brave, if a bit ill-advised. Can't imagine that the cargo is worth dyin' over, even for union wages.*

John keyed his comms. "Vic, tell the soldiers to keep the edges hemmed in when the troopers get up on the docks. Sera an' I'll take care of the bulk of 'em in the middle. If they get out around the security forces, we'll do our best to take 'em out 'fore they do too much damage. Copy that?"

"You're patched in now. Just say 'Docks' and it'll go straight to C and C there." As always, John had to marvel at her ingenuity and resources. He relayed the message to the CO for the security forces on the docks.

"Thank God you're here," came back the response. *"I'm glad*

they sent you two. Just tell us what you want, you've got it." John gave the soldier on the other end of the line a quick rundown; all that was left for John and Sera was to wait.

It was a tense minute before the troopers made their presence known. John and Sera were ready; if they had been in any immediate danger, their battle-sense would have let them know. As one, an entire rank of troopers leapt from the canal in a shower of water droplets, landing on their feet on the dock. The first line was followed by a second, then a third, then a fourth. Immediately, the first two ranks activated energy shields that sprouted from their arm cannons, interlocking the shields to close any gaps in the front. John and Sera knew from previous experience that the troopers with shields on wouldn't be able to shoot, or even move very quickly. So long as they kept those shields up, they'd be almost completely protected from anything that might attack them from the front. The lines of troopers stretched for four hundred feet; there must have been at least one hundred troopers, all together.

Everyone held their breath as the troopers stood stock-still, dripping with water and waiting. That changed when a pack of ten Robo-Wolves leapt from the water, completely clearing the ranks of troopers, and landing with a crash in front of them. The Wolves didn't wait; they immediately surged forward, using their momentum to get a fast start. The defensive batteries and soldiers on the ground began firing, at first wildly at the Wolves and the ranks of troopers; after a moment, their commanders regained control, and the sectors for fire were established. The soldiers would keep the troopers and the Wolves concentrated in one area. Now it was time for John and Sera to do their job.

The thing to do would be to shock these troopers who hadn't been at the defeat of Ultima Thule. And the best way to do that would be to punch a hole where they thought they were strongest. John amped himself up, then let go with a steady blast of fire; it wasn't nearly as hot as he could make it, just enough to give them something to think about, keep them buttoned up. Sera jumped into it and ran for the troopers, hidden in the glare. They were already reeling from the impact against the shields when she reached the front lines—they could hold off some of the effect with their energy shields, but not even those shields were impervious to the incredible heat roiling off the point of impact.

Then Sera got there. She had manifested her fire-sword and lay about her like a whirling dervish, attacking the shields where her battle-sense told her they were weakest. Unable to see her through the glare of John's fire, the troopers had to strike where they guessed she was, and their guesses were no match for her speed. John held the fire as long as he could; an instant before he had to cut it off, she leapt into the air, assisted by her wings, blazing as white-hot as a star herself, and landed at his side again. There were at least twenty troopers down, right in the center of the Thulians' formation. It was clear from the smoking holes and severed parts that the ones that had fallen would not be getting back up again. The Thulians, while shaken and not having anticipated taking so many losses so early, reacted more swiftly than John had expected; they split their formation into two groups right where the hole had been created. Now *they* were firing back. The soldiers in the front rows would part long enough for three or four troopers with arm cannons to let loose with a fusillade of energy blasts or power-armor-enhanced grenade throws. Where the blasts or grenades hit their mark, they were devastating; luckily, very few found their intended targets, most detonating harmlessly on the docks or trailing off into the sky to dissipate. When John and Sera were the intended targets—they simply were not there when the blows came. Their battle-sense showed them where the blast or grenade was going to fall, and they evaded everything but a few flying chips of concrete.

They didn't have time to rest; the Wolves were almost upon them. Instead of standing and waiting for the Wolves, John and Sera charged at them. With John's enhancements and Sera's wing beats, they moved almost too fast for the eye to track effectively; the Wolves faltered, for a moment, trying to figure out how to attack the couple. John and Sera split from each other, then crossed paths at the last moment, attacking towards the opposite side. John rushed forward, letting the battle-sense guide him; his first cut split a Wolf from shoulder to hip, sending sprays of sparks and ruined parts clattering across the docks. The second Wolf he faced snapped at his head; he dodged under the flashing metallic jaws easily, swinging his sword, in an easy two-handed strike horizontally, lopping off the front paws of the Wolf and part of its underside. It struggled uselessly, scraping against the concrete as it tried to push itself forward with its hind legs.

John ignored that Wolf for the moment; it wasn't a threat for now. He kicked off the ground hard, his fires bursting from his lower legs and feet and propelling him into the air. A half second later, alloy claws raked the ground where he had been standing, carving deep furrows in the concrete. He turned in the air and thrust his right arm out in one motion; a lance of fire burst from his palm, striking the offending third Wolf square in the forehead. The beam of fire burned through the Wolf's head and body in a flash, splashing against the concrete behind and beneath it. Something inside of the Wolf detonated, sending flames and an acrid cloud of black smoke outward. The fourth and fifth Wolves leapt for him at the same time, trying to pin him in the air. John felt the attack coming, even though they were attacking from his blind spots on either side. Without a flourish, he spun in place, bringing his sword up first in a rising cut from his right hip to his left shoulder, then back down again from his right shoulder to his left hip. The two cuts separated the Wolves' heads from their shoulders in an instant; John moved forward a few feet just in time, as the Wolves' decapitated chassis slammed into each other midair before crashing into the ground. The final amputee Wolf was still crawling towards the center of the docks, single-minded in its purpose. He hovered for a moment, then unleashed his fires, letting them flow from his sword point and his arms; the flames washed around the final Wolf, completely engulfing it. Slowly, he amped up the intensity, turning the mechanical horror to molten and smoking slag. *That'll do it.*

As he landed, he glanced at Sera; there were pieces of Wolf scattered all about her, and no sign of a whole one. It looked as if she had duplicated the wild spinning she had performed among the Thulian troopers, simply turning and moving too fast to be tracked and letting her fire-sword cut through whatever had gotten in her way. The Wolves, however advanced their programming, didn't have the same self-preservation that the troopers had; their entire purpose was to attack, and they had been seemingly happy to oblige Sera by running right for her.

I think we have somehow learned to "tune" our fire so it is at the precise temperature to be most effective, Sera said in his mind, sounding just a little puzzled. *Otherwise . . . this seems much easier than last time.*

Like the man said, "Great, kid. Don't get cocky." We've still got quite a few of these bastards to deal with.

Sera was already at his side again, fire-sword at the ready, as their battle-sense showed a barrage of energy grenades about to be launched at the defensive emplacements.

Sera placed her hand atop John's shoulder and concentrated; immediately he felt energy flooding into him. He took a deep breath, visualizing what he wanted to do, forming it to what was *going* to happen, changing that Possibility into a Reality. Energy blasts flashed all around the pair; they knew that they would have warning if any were really going to threaten them. The Thulians were still shaken, first from the couple's opening assault, and then the ease with which they dispatched the Robo-Wolves.

For this instant, they both ignored what was going on around them, staring deeply into each others' glowing, golden eyes. Eyes that were mirror images of how Sera's had looked, before...

Then their eyes snapped up to concentrate on the thrown grenades, sailing high over their heads. John's arms shot upwards, his sword dissipating into a gigantic cloud of fire that raced to meet the grenades. As soon as the wall of fire met the grenades, they each detonated, forming perfect spheres of blue-white destructive energy, like novas forming and disappearing in a nebula of fire.

Just as quickly, John shut the fires off, leaving no evidence that they had ever been there. The Thulians had halted their advance, both groups now orienting to face John and Sera exclusively. *Finally gettin' the message that we're the ones to worry 'bout, huh, fellas?*

This is a good thing. But as you said to me, "Do not get cocky."

Let's wrap up this bunch; I got a feelin' that this isn't gonna be over quite yet.

A new voice sounded in his ear. Not Vickie: young, and male. *"Ural Smasher, this is Angel Flight, do you copy?"*

For one startled moment, he thought this might be—Siblings? Sera's...well, would you call them "relatives"? But then he remembered, from the assault in New Mexico; "Angel Flight" had been the designation of the Navy Blue Angels. No longer amusing the crowds at air shows, they and the Thunderbirds were now a bona fide elite strike force. And, it seemed, were partnered with him and Sera.

"Go, Angel Flight," he replied, keeping a wary eye, and the battle-sense, on the Thulians, who it seemed had not yet made up their mind about their next move.

"We are in position to offer Danger-Close Fire on a strafing run

on your signal. Danger-Close Fire will commence fifteen seconds from your go."

"Roger that, we'll update targets for you. Key in on the southern side of the docks; that'll be the likely target zone. Stay frosty."

"Southern docks. Copy that. Out."

"Ready, darlin'?"

Sera turned her head slightly and smiled at him, her eyes going to blue briefly, before turning to the shining gold that meant they were in sync and their powers were at full. "Always."

Both of them leaned out of the way as an energy blast split the air between them. A beat later, both of them were charging at the two groups of trooper armor; John at the one on the right, Sera at the one on the left. Energy blasts ripped apart fissures in the dock around the couple, sending steaming chunks of concrete into the air. John put an extra burst of speed on, his enhancements already keyed up; at the last second before he would have hit the trooper formation, he juked to the right, hard. With his left hand, he sent an explosive blast of concentrated plasma at the leftmost edge of the troopers; it struck the ground—and also the lower legs of three troopers—before erupting in a booming explosion. Then John was among the troopers, slashing with his sword or blasting with fire.

John felt as if he could have closed his eyes and been in no more danger than he already was. He knew where the attacks were coming from; if there was a juncture where he would be overwhelmed, he sidestepped it, went around or above, did something unexpected to break up the pattern. To his left, he sensed Sera weaving her own deadly dance of fire and sword and spear, just as sure in her movements as he was, and just as inescapable. It was wonderful; it was terrible. It was awe-full, in the ancient sense of the word. He was reminded of his moment of weakness, facing the Thulians alone at the academy in the woods; wielding all of that power, alone, with no moderating force...he understood why OpFours and Fives were often clinically insane, in one way or another. More than ever, he was glad that he had Sera with him.

He felt things coming to a head; he and Sera weren't working separately, but together. They started to herd the two groups together; it wasn't hard. Any time some of the troopers tried to cut and run or break away, they were cut down—literally, in some cases. When there were openings, a rocket or grenade from the soldiers would impact the bunched-together Thulians; more often than not it would hit a shield, but occasionally it connected, weakening several suits of armor and setting them alight. ECHO ordnance, crafted from Zmey's recipe, and refined so that there were rarely misfires anymore. And where there were, well, it was nothing more than an idle move from John to set the spilled gels on fire.

John and Sera had become surrounded by the massed Thulians. The troopers had seemingly abandoned their assault on the docks for the moment; John could feel their rage at being opposed, their arrogance, and mostly their fear. Fear of John and Sera. They were all jockeying for position to try to shoot the couple or bludgeon them. John and Sera kept the troopers just out of reach with swords, spear, and fire. They could have simply flown straight up, escaping the huddle, but why would they?

They had the Thulian troopers right where they wanted them.

Sera allowed her sword to dissipate, then slipped her right hand into John's left. He felt the surge of their shared power, felt it coursing through his arm, up his shoulder, and into his chest. He allowed the power to build there, to gather and pool inside of him. Before, whenever he had felt that pressure building, it had only been through supreme willpower that he hadn't lost control and let his fires consume everything. Some metahumans needed great amounts of effort and training in order to ramp up their powers, to use them at their fullest extent; it had never been like that for John. For him, he needed to expend terrible effort to keep the full extent of his powers in check. Now, with Sera... it was easy. Easy as breathing.

I will help you hold it, love. Decide where you want it to go. So far... and no farther.

All he had to do was... let it go. *Set the boundaries... so.*

And he did.

The explosion formed a perfect dome of white-hot fire that expanded in an instant. It completely inundated the Thulians around John and Sera, with a diameter of roughly one hundred feet; it stopped well short of any cranes or shipping containers. To observers from the outside, it looked as if someone had dropped half of a star on the docks; the light was too blinding to look at for more than a moment. Sera moderated the power, keeping it from spilling beyond the boundaries. The only thing she couldn't prevent was the sonic boom that the suddenly expanding air from the heat created; they knew that windows shattered and people felt the reverberations for miles around. Inside of the dome, it was a dance of fire. John and Sera stood in the center of it all, untouched, while the Thulians that had surrounded them turned dark, and then...faded into the fire. When they felt that it was done, John shut the fires off; again, just as easy as taking a breath. Then again, they couldn't for a few moments; the fires had eaten a lot of the available oxygen in the area. As the fires disappeared, there was a great rush of wind as atmosphere filled the now empty space.

There was a perfectly black circle on the concrete where the sphere had been, the top of it scorched and covered with carbon.

Both of them went to one knee simultaneously, for a moment, their eyes turning "normal" as they regained their strength. "Better?" Sera asked, panting a little, but not nearly as spent as she had been at the battle of Ultima Thule when they had expended themselves. "Yes," she said, answering her own question as she got to her feet again. "Much better. More control, less waste." Her eyes faded back into gold, as did John's, or so he suspected.

"Let's make sure we eat a good dinner 'fore we start tangoin' with any dragons, though. Agreed?"

"Or we have one of those *beer hats* with Vickie's can meals in it," she countered, with the faintest of chuckles. He shook his head, making a face, and yet...he was relieved.

These creatures are...I cannot describe it. It is more than "other." It is far more than "alien"—I have no words. Just that, there is no pity and no remorse in them. Only arrogance, and great pride. I hope they will learn better on the other side, but they must be cleansed from here. I do not like killing them, but it is better that they are gone, for they will not learn here.

They're gonna have more company, soon. Heads-up, darlin'.

They both felt it at the same time; John had the barest lead on her, if only because of his enhanced senses. He had heard what was coming before she could have.

A flight of Robo-Eagles, along with the one Death Sphere that had retreated earlier.

The birds, I will enjoy "killing." I am glad they are nothing like Eight-Ball.

John and Sera both left the ground at the same time; John kicking off and igniting his fires, Sera with several powerful wingbeats that scattered the ashes at her feet before she was in the air. The Eagles and the Death Sphere didn't alter course; they were coming straight for the couple. It was clear they recognized what the real threat here was.

I am faster and more maneuverable than you. Your fires burn hotter, faster. I will engage the birds to keep them from you while you deal with the Sphere. When the Sphere is down, we can both destroy the birds. Sera seemed very sure of her strategy, but then, she was the aerial combat expert, after all.

Followin' your lead, darlin'. Let's blast these bastards outta the sky.

It is my *sky, and I do not like them in it!* Sera sped straight for the Eagles, and then, suddenly, folded her wings and dropped about three yards, just as their focused energy beams from their mouth cannons cut through the air where she had been. Then they were past her position and she somehow executed a lightning-fast course change and came up behind and above them.

Then she was among them. She danced, and her dance was death incarnate.

As much as he wanted to watch Sera work, he didn't have the time. The Eagles were keeping her occupied, but there was still the Sphere; between the tentacles, the energy cannons, the thermite ports, and whatever other horror the Thulians had cooked up and stuck on it, it was dangerous as all hell. *Time to fix that.*

John put on a burst of speed, closing the distance to the Death Sphere. Several tentacles lashed out at him; he twisted in the air, most of them narrowly missing him. He didn't want to bob and weave in and out too much. For one, there was no need; he knew where the attacks would be. Second, by making minor course corrections and positioning his body correctly, he didn't wear himself out as fast; conservation of energy was important in any fight, even with how juiced up he and Sera were. Despite his efforts, there were a few tentacles that he wouldn't have been able to avoid; those, he simply lopped off with his manifested fire-claymore. He switched the sword from side to side in a sort of windshield-wiper motion in front of him; the sword's double edge easily bit through the Thulian alloy, sending bits of mechanical tentacles plunging towards the ground below.

With a final blast of his fires, he spun in the air, and landed hard on top of the Death Sphere. Not giving the pilots inside a chance to shake him loose, he turned the sword over in his hands so that the point was aimed at his feet, and then thrust with all of his might. The fire-claymore passed through the alloy plates with little resistance; sparks and combustible exhaust issued from the cut, streaming through John's legs and behind the Death Sphere like a stunt plane's smoke run. Working quickly but carefully, he pried the sword back and forth, then turned the blade, making first a second, then a third and fourth cut. When he was done, he stepped to the side, leaned on the sword, and the squarish section of panel popped out with a metallic *ping*. Still using his sword as an anchor, he thrust out with his right hand, aiming at the opening he had created. The fires came easily, ramped up into a thick and steady beam of plasma that lanced through the wound in the Sphere's hull. John poured the fire in until he was sure the Sphere was dead, through and through. Then, he simply removed his sword from the hull, and he was flung away, in free fall.

He stayed that way, his old skydiving and combat parachute training coming back to him. He kept his body arched, with hands and arms splayed out to the sides to stabilize himself. His back was to the ground; he wanted to see this part. A second later, the Death Sphere exploded brilliantly; it reminded him of the Death Star explosion, the original one before they'd mucked everything up with digital effects. Satisfied—and knowing he was getting uncomfortably close to becoming a wet stain on the concrete below—he kicked his fires back on, propelling him back towards where Sera and the furball were.

There was a litter of Eagle parts on the ground beneath the furball—the snarl of aerial combat involving Sera and the robots. Impossible to say how many she had taken out, but there certainly would be good scavenging for those looking for souvenirs. *Ah, you're free,* he heard her say calmly in his head, and at that same moment, an arrow of flame burst out of the middle of the scrum and Sera pulled up at his side. *Shall we? It would please me to immolate them.*

I'd love nothin' better, darlin'—wait. We're not done. He knew Sera had felt it, too; there were more Thulians, a complete second wave, about to leap out of the water and onto the docks. They were going to make a mad dash for the interior of the docks, split up into squads, and wreak as much havoc as possible. John got the sense that they wouldn't make the mistake of trying to take him and Sera head-on again. *Time for somethin' a little different. Ready to make an attack run of our own, darlin'? We're gonna have to be fast.*

More than ready. She waited for him to form his strategy in his mind, and nodded when she saw it.

"Angel Flight, get ready to make your run, previous target zone. Once you see the fire, you're cleared hot. We're gonna break north to clear out of your way. How copy?"

"Copy, Ural Smasher. Setting up now, we should be in place at your go sign."

"On it. Smasher, out." John glanced over to Sera, who was hovering at his side. He winked at her, then dove straight down. He knew that she was following, matching his speed, so he put on more. As they sped groundward, she began manifesting and casting spears, which strafed out ahead of her like fiery rockets (he had no idea how that was even possible but, well—it was Sera, after all) and hit the ground on either side of the now-massing troopers. Evidently they had expected the pair to be busily engaged with the Death Sphere and the Eagles. The Eagles were milling around uncertainly in midair—had Sera blinded them? At any rate, they were out of the picture for now as Sera's spears made the troopers bunch up and aim their arm cannons skyward. Energy beams raced out to greet them, but Sera and John didn't need to dodge much; the troopers didn't have enough time to aim accurate shots at the small, moving targets dropping in on them.

Both John and Sera pulled up sharply at the last second, traveling perpendicular to the ground mere feet above the troopers and Wolves. John thrust both of his hands out below him, unleashing jets of billowing fire onto the massed Thulians. As soon as he and Sera were past the end of their ranks, the pair banked sharply to the right; at the speed they were going, it was only their reflexes and battle-sense that allowed them to navigate through the cranes and shipping containers that rushed to meet them. "Angel Flight, go!" he shouted.

John turned his head once he and Sera were over and past the obstacles; the Thulians were still firing at them, trying to track them and line up good shots. Between the fires that engulfed their ranks, and their preoccupation with trying to kill John and Sera, they never even noticed the jets screaming towards them until the cannons on the F/A-18 Hornets opened up. Softened up by John's fire run, herded together by Sera's spears, the crowded mass of Thulians was cut to pieces.

The Angels pulled up and over in a full tight-formation barrel roll, and came in for a second run. Just to be sure...and then for good measure they strafed what was left of the furball of fuddled Eagles with rockets.

It was clear after they pulled up for the second time there would be no need for a third.

John slowed down considerably, banking up and right in a lazy turn that would take him and Sera back over the docks. There was smoke, and a few small spot fires, but it looked like all of the machinery and nearly all of the cargo was still intact. It was sheer luck that the Thulians hadn't stayed underwater and gone after the container ships from there; not a single one was even damaged, as far as he could tell.

"Overwatch, how's the sitch on the ground look? We make out okay?"

"We did all right. One group of the Nat. Guard was in the wrong place when a grenade went off. Three down. Way better than if you and Sera hadn't been there. Port of Toulouse in France...not so good. ECHO and Avion France had to choose between them and Paris and Paris won."

"Dammit. Copy that, Vic. We're RTB at the moment, unless you've got a game for us to get into."

"Nothing close enough for you to get to. The Germans based in Alsace and the French met up after clearing Paris and Friedrichsburg; they're just reaching Toulouse now."

"Roger. We're comin' home, then. Keep the steak hot an' the beers cold. Murdock an' Murdock, out." John cut the mic after that. He and Sera had saved a lot of people today; they had saved the docks, which while important for the war effort and keeping the already teetering economy going, wasn't nearly as important to him as the people that worked at it and defended it. Even with everything that he and Sera could do, people were still dying out there, and far too many of them. It pissed him off, more than anything.

Even before, I could not be everywhere, beloved. Too often I was forced to make choices. She glanced over at him, her expression sober, her eyes fading from gold to blue.

I know, darlin', he sent to Sera, casting a quick glance to the side to view her in flight; any more than a quick glance and his trajectory might change. *Still doesn't make it any less shitty an' frustratin'. If only we had a place to stick the knife, really take it to the Thulians like in Ultima Thule.* He could imagine—vividly— exactly what he would do to wherever the Thulians were holed up. He shook his head quickly, clearing his mind. *Let's get back home. I could use a shower. Among other things.*

And we will plan for next time, she agreed. *They will learn from this. We must assume they have, and be ready.*

CHAPTER TWELVE

Hurt

DENNIS LEE

I looked at my watch. It was almost go time. And I scrubbed at my eyes with the back of my hand as tears filled them, and my throat closed, because of what was coming. This...I couldn't face this. Not again.

"I can't do this anymore, Eight," I choked. "It's up to you now. Finish it for me."

I barely heard Eight's gentle "I will, Vickie," as I closed my keyboard and went to join the others.

Is it wrong to be ruled by your desires?

I've always thought so. Doesn't stop a lot of people from doing it, of course. I suppose most people are, to varying degrees, slaves to their emotions. Yet there are those special few who go to extreme measures to express themselves. There are no boundaries, no rules, regardless of their claims to the contrary. They swear by personal mantras, mask their transient nature with diatribes bordering on religious fervor, but in truth their values ebb and flow like the tides, serving their present needs and nothing more. Their first lesson is that history is malleable. The others follow soon enough: foundations are based on whim, to hell with gods, know what is yours and you fight for it, tooth and nail, and if some bastard is foolish enough to stand in your way, you strike him down and you don't stop until he stays down.

I don't know how these people manage to survive, given the horrific nature of their choices, but they do. Some even thrive, a precious few, as their environment continues somehow to provide

202

for them. Most, however, laugh in the face of death, dance in the heart of the storm, drunk on the power of their perceived immortality as they tilt headfirst into windmills. They burn, a blazing pyre of fragile strength, drawing those blind enough to follow into their consuming web. They are beautiful, if only for a moment, their fires extinguished all too quickly and they pass on, leaving only a husk of themselves. Sometimes, they are beloved and shrines are erected in their honor. Those they leave behind may swear eternal vigilance, but inevitably people move on. It's what they do. A chance for happiness in what is left, for normalcy, for sanity, depends on their ability to forget, to distance themselves. These are the tragic stories, and they serve as warnings to others what demons lie in wait, what awaits those who dare to take the reins of their own madness.

And yet, I envy these people.

They feel something, something so strong and sure and powerful that they serve it without hesitation. Imagine a compulsion so complete that, over faith, over logic, over simple common sense it drives you to acts of courage and resilience even in the face of catastrophic failure. These people are easy marks for exploitation, and there are many who would take advantage of that.

I know of the fight. I have fought all my life, with people and ideals and concepts put into motion that evolve into something completely different from their humble beginnings. But I have rarely let myself be a target. It happens, but you can hide enough of your true self to mask the parts that are vulnerable, keep them away from the crosshairs. Let them take the shot. If the target is an illusion, you survive. And them? They take pause in a moment of confusion. And you? You can catch them unawares, drive that dagger into the base of their skull, or use those precious seconds to slip away. It's an exciting game. I've had an exciting life. But I'm not the woman I once was.

Something is different. Once, it was the good fight, then it was just the fight, an endless series of battles to delay the inevitable boredom of stubborn breath defying an existential void. I didn't rush into things. I planned them out. I placed value in the safest option, in prepping for contingency scenarios and I saw the mission done. And through it all, I never let myself feel a thing, nothing beyond mild amusement or irritation. It was simpler that way. When you calculate the odds of success in anything, there is no variable more chaotic and unnecessary than throwing emotion into the mix.

So how the hell did I get here?

All my life, I have wanted only one thing. Just one. And I mean want. It's not a week on a beach or some end-of-year bonus or some bauble or drug or fame or whatever trivial prize most people might imagine. One thing, and I wanted it. And you know what? It's changed. It's not the same as it was, completely morphing over the span of a few measly months. No, that's not fair. It hasn't changed. I have. It has remained more or less the same sarcastic, pig-headed mess of a man that it started as. I started this by the simple act of wanting him. I wanted him, something he had, and I was prepared to win it, use it, and spit him out when I was done. Not my first time, I must admit. He knows the game, hell, he's done it himself. But as he told me once, you can't bet on these things. While you're sinking your claws into someone, they're probably digging theirs into you.

And now, it's all different. Because I'm feeling something new. Some tiny seed has taken root and it's all gone to hell. Anything I used to hold dear, it all pales in comparison. No matter what I thought at the time, no matter how much I thought I yearned for something, it all seems dull and insignificant next to the brilliant and terrible and chaotic thing that he is, if you can believe it. If I can believe it...

The bastard's done something to me, and though a part of me is crying out, spurning the very absurdity of it, another drives me forward into his arms...

"The hell...?"

She caught him by surprise, and Red Djinni struggled to maintain balance as his exuberant assailant tackled him mercilessly, planting a series of kisses on his neck.

"Mel, for chrissakes..."

Red sighed and with an exaggerated gesture removed her arms from around his chest and gently pushed her away. He glared at her over his scarf, his eyes questioning.

"Well?" he asked.

"Well what, cher?" she answered impishly.

"Not that I object to your gestures of affection, oh no, not me. In fact, I'm sure I'll be taking advantage of them later..." He coughed. "But please explain yourself."

Mel shot him a look of pure infatuation. "Now, Mr. Djinni," she purred. "I don't think I've ever had to explain myself before..."

Red looked at her helplessly. "This isn't you," he said. "You've never acted this...well, this...I feel like I'm in a teen beach movie..."

Red heard muffled snickers from his left, and he exhaled dramatically, bowing his head.

"You're punishing me," he said, understanding. "For last night."

"You bet your firm ass I am," Mel muttered. "No one falls asleep on me, Red."

"I'm sorry," Red muttered, the words barely escaping his palms, which were pressed firmly to his face. "You know how exhausted I've been of late."

"You fell asleep *on* me, Red," Mel hissed. "Correction, you fell asleep *in* me! What in the name of...?"

"Look, can we talk about this later?" The Djinni, still clutching his face, nodded slightly to his left. "I do have a certain menacing reputation to maintain."

Mel gave Red's recruits a casual glance. They stood at attention, but shook with suppressed laughter, one going so far as to press her lips together, her eyes shut, with such ferocity that her face had flushed a brilliant shade of red.

"You see what you've done?" Red sighed. "They're laughing at me now."

"So what are you going to do about it?" Mel smirked.

"I'm going to be their teacher," he growled and leapt away, sprinting towards his charges at a dead run. Snickers became yelps of surprise. The recruits scattered as Red tackled one of them, rammed him into the soft turf of ECHO's training fields, rolled and landed in a fighting stance.

"No warm-ups today, kids!" Red snarled. "Let's get to the pummeling! Do your worst!"

There was a collective groan as the students warily began to circle the Djinni, except for Bullet Time, the hulking brute Red had managed to slam into the dirt. He lay on his back, gasping for breath.

Mel stood her ground, arms crossed, and watched in amusement. She now made it a point to watch Red during his daily training exercises. There was little else at ECHO she found remotely entertaining. After their short-lived victory at Ultima Thule, things had

gone downhill for ECHO so rapidly it wasn't a "hill" so much
as a "chasm," which meant, among other things, "Mel's Place"
tended to be full of silence, brooding, outright depression, and a
great deal of heavy drinking. She knew Red felt helpless in the
face of all this despair. Bulwark, while mending remarkably given
the extent of his injuries, was still under strict orders from Bella
to stay off his feet for now. The big man was resisting, of course,
but despite being the love of ECHO's commander-in-chief, even
he wasn't exempt from her stern reprimands. Upon his return
from the ruins of Metis, Bull had somehow slipped away from
Bella's watchful monitoring and hobbled into the barracks, only
to find his powers as chief trainer had been temporarily rescinded
with a brief memo from Bella herself. Red Djinni was called up
to replace him, reluctantly at first, but with growing vigor as
Red was hungry for something, for anything, useful to do. And
so here he was, performing his daily dance. Mel liked to think
he was dancing for her.

But he wasn't, of course.

She watched as he took them on, one by one. The idea of rushing him all together still eluded them. They had tried it, once, but
the Djinni had been ready for it, dodging their clumsy attempts
at teamwork and pitting their strengths against each other. They
simply didn't coordinate their efforts, and a simple display of
"hit me if you can" on Red's part had left them discouraged, too
busy bemoaning the fact that they were doing more damage to
themselves without landing a single blow on him. Bulwark would
have put them through their paces, drilled teamwork and prepared
maneuvers into them. Red preferred a different approach. As he
saw it, pain and humiliation were great motivators. In time, they
would wise up, if they wanted it badly enough. For now, that first
lesson had robbed them of their courage, and they were reluctant
to make the first move against their teacher.

He milked that for all it was worth. For now, Red was playing with them. When one did brace himself to attack, the others would circle about, hoping to spot an opening, waiting for
a chance to dart in unexpectedly. This was the Djinni though.
Trying to take him by surprise was a futile effort. He still wore
his scarf, wrapped so tightly around his head that it was hard to
imagine how he managed to breathe, let alone perform extended
feats of Parkour or combat training. These days, he favored the

standard ECHO-issue leggings, high tech nanoweave that did a fine job protecting the wearer from high-velocity projectiles and energy damage, yet still allowed for unrestricted movement. His arms and torso he left uncovered. With the changing of the seasons, Atlanta would soon be sweltering in the heat, but Mel knew that wasn't the reason for Red's topless fashion sense. He seemed nervous of late, constantly scanning his surroundings and taking note of whoever was around. It was as if he expected an attack at any moment. It was understandable, she supposed, given the current state of things. With that much skin exposed, he was one with his environment, gifted with an innate radar that fed off all the heightened senses in his epidermis. He saw every attack coming. He let them come, and Mel chuckled as she recognized the grace in his subterfuge. He never let on that they simply had no chance. His feints were accompanied by dramatic grunts of surprise. He didn't telegraph his movements and he let them in close, but they never hit him, though some of their attacks seemed awfully close. Of course, that's what he wanted them to believe. They thought they were just a lucky strike away from gaining the upper hand. It was just enough encouragement to drive them forward, and the Djinni played with their false hopes with nerve and skill. And when they finally closed the distance, were even remotely a threat to him, he lashed out, driving their attacks into one another, adding a few explosive elbows and knee strikes of his own and knocked them down, gasping, to regroup and try again.

Mel had seen this dance many times, and as she watched the Djinni step, pivot and fly about his would-be assailants, she was drawn back to the same unhappy conclusion each time. Red's entire life was a dance, *this* dance. No one came close; he would never allow it. Oh, she could study his moves, his patterns, file them away for future reference, but it wouldn't matter. Not to the big picture. The Djinni recognized his own flaws, perhaps. He realized his vulnerabilities and his solution had been simple—keep the distance. Every time someone seemed to pass a certain boundary, he would recoil. Nothing obvious, of course, but it was always something. He had to maintain the dance. She would step forward, he would lean back. Something would be offered, and he might graciously accept, but that was all. They had spent all this time together, and while much had been shared, she realized that he was still holding back. In retrospect, most of what he had told her, she realized, could have been learned through other channels. He liked to think his history was some remarkably kept secret, but if one was determined enough, most of his secrets could be unearthed without him ever knowing. But even those were superficial. After all they had been through, he was still a mystery to her. This was a problem, a truth she had been avoiding, from her own confusion over what she had felt for this man. It was a problem, because...

Mel exhaled and grimaced, and let harsh reality wash over her.

She was in love with him. She would do anything for him. He just didn't know the power he held over her now. A simple touch, a knowing glance, that was all it took. It startled her the first time it happened, a sudden jolt of fear that made her question what she doing. No one had ever gotten to her like this, and it really wasn't something she could afford. She had fought it, of course, but it wasn't a battle she could win. She was failing with each passing day, to the point where she wondered if she even cared anymore. Her intentions, the best laid plans, did they matter anymore? There was a time when the idea of surrendering to another had been laughable. And now? She cared for this man, yes, but it went deeper. He was an extension of her now. Soon, they could be as one, she was certain of it. But something wasn't right, she might be willing to give him everything, but he... he had never surrendered to her. It was all in the kiss, she realized. You could always tell from the kiss, and he had never surrendered to it.

She had never mistaken sex for love. Even as a young girl, she had known the difference. Her first time had been something of a relief. It had been awkward and strange and over far too quickly, but at least it was no longer a mystery. And there was power in the act. When the passion was real, even the most guarded of men could become as transparent as glass. Honeyed words, once dripping with sincere flattery, could turn vile and bestial. The witty and urbane often were exposed as mere schoolboys, their charm fading away with a few hopeless grunts. Alternatively, the meek could rise above themselves, finding a deep well of courage, and leap into the fray with a ferocity that would have astonished them, had they not been so lost in the moment. And so it would go, on and on, people going to great lengths to hide their true nature, even from themselves. But no one could hide forever. All it took was that moment of surrender, and she could catch a glimpse of the true man behind the mask.

She was still waiting for that moment with Red. There had been plenty of opportunities. She had considered the possibility that perhaps there was truly nothing more to the man than a simple mercenary with extraordinary talents, rather pedestrian if vigorous tendencies in bed, and a relatively quick wit for sarcastic retorts. Each time the thought bubbled up in her mind, she immediately squashed the notion with a determined scoff of impatience. He couldn't be that simple. There was something more, there had to be. On the surface, he didn't seem that complicated, and she had met more than her share of uncomplicated men. None of them interested her. This one was profoundly different, and she was willing to admit that the enigma of *how* was slowly, surely, driving her mad. Once again, she pondered the kiss. Each time he seemed eager and passionate but there was always a moment of hesitation, of apprehension, barely noticeable but there nevertheless. He had never yielded to her, not entirely. There was always something holding him back, maintaining that carefully constructed wall that refused to let anyone in. It loomed over her, impenetrable, and her desire to peer past it was growing to a fevered pitch.

Which made it all the more shocking when, finally, she saw something new.

It didn't register at first. Red continued his dance, and had by now dispatched most of his class, leaving them strewn about the field in various states in injury. Had he actually *needed* to hurt them? Not from a learning standpoint—was there something festering in him that hurt him so much he needed to transfer that injury to someone else? His remaining student, a lithe, sandy-haired girl with pockmarked skin, backed away from him with small, timid steps. He decelerated into a mocking strut, stepping lightly around her with dramatic hops and feints. While the scarf obscured his features, Mel could still make out his broad smile, pushing his cheekbones tight against the fabric.

"Just you and me now, Delia," the Djinni said. "This won't end well. It never does, does it? You still haven't picked up even the rudimentary skills to defend yourself without powers. I think maybe I've been taking it too easy on you."

Red threw a clumsy punch near Delia's head, and she screamed as she flinched back.

"Damn, girl," Red sighed. "You could have blocked that easily. Close up your stance! Maintain your footing! You're the gun in this group! You need to be up and mobile and always vigilant, ready to call the shot!"

Red sagged in defeat as Delia continued to cower.

"Or, y'know..." the Djinni said, shaking his head. "Just fall down and die."

He swooped down, driving his legs around in an explosive sweep that knocked Delia on her back. She fell with a scream, her legs flung forward, landing on an elbow with a terrific crack. She gasped in pain and sobbed as she glared at the Djinni with what could best be described as a mix of terror and hate.

"So much for the lesson," the Djinni said, rising to his feet. He turned his back to her, to all of them, and began to stroll away. "I'm not seeing it, in any of you. Not a bit of improvement. What's it going to take to see a little fire from this lot...?"

Mel watched as Delia attempted to prop herself up on her good arm, and fell back down with a whimper. The kid was scared, in pain, and Mel could understand Red's arrogance in simply walking away. It had only been a few weeks since he had taken up their training, but his frustration with this group was that of a long-suffering father, burdened with the perpetual mishaps of wayward children. Today's exercise hadn't been one of instruction. If his nightly tirades were any indication, he was nearing the end. He had all but given up on them, and with the growing certainty of his failure, he was growing irritable. Perhaps he thought them weak, too undisciplined for this line of work, but that wouldn't have stopped him from trying to light the spark, to get them moving. He had taken it too far today, certainly, but it spoke more of his own shortcomings than theirs. That he would punish them for it said much of his current state of mind. The Djinni felt lost, lost enough to pummel his charges to near unconsciousness, enough to shamble off in defeat, and enough to forget that foes are never more dangerous than when you've beaten them into the ground.

Mel watched, frozen and fascinated, as Delia propped herself up again with a snarl. One of the Djinni's original recruits, she had failed almost every level of combat training ECHO offered.

Physically frail with an awkward gait, Delia seemed perpetu-
ally hunched over with her hair covering most of her face. She
refused to make eye contact and rarely spoke, and when she
did, the sounds she made approximated the hoarse whispers of
a lethargic housecat with laryngitis. The only reason she hadn't
been sent packing was her metahuman ability, one that ECHO
still hoped to harness for fieldwork. Mel had never seen her
use it, so she was completely taken aback as Delia "The Spitter"
Schumer roared in anger and fired a colossal stream of projectile
vomit at Red Djinni.

It slammed into him, between his shoulders, and drove him
skidding face first along the turf for a good ten yards. He came
to a full stop, his face dug right into the soft earth, a disgusting gray-brown ooze coating his back. It was an impressively
funny sight and Mel might have laughed, if not for the fact that
the Djinni wasn't moving. He lay there, his right arm bent at
a horribly wrong angle, and for a moment Mel wondered if he
was even breathing.

Delia gasped and stared in horror at what she had done. With
an effort she calmed herself with deep breaths and, still lying on
her back, turned to look at Mel, her lips quivering.

"Omigod, did I just kill him?" she whimpered, and shrieked
as she heard Red stir from his bed of dirt and mangled sod.

He lifted his head and steadied himself with his good arm,
quietly rising on his knees and bringing himself to his feet. Mel
watched as he slowly shifted the muscles in his back and swiveled his head, with loud cracks as bones and joints popped back
into place. He stood in place, his head tilting slightly to and fro,
as if mentally assessing the damage to himself. And throughout
it all, Mel watched in fascination, realizing she was witnessing
something new. He wasn't groaning from the pain, which was
odd. He wasn't swearing profusely, which was odder still. The
fact was, pain wasn't anything new to him, and Mel wondered
how much it actually affected him. Mel had watched on countless occasions as Red would take a punch, or a bullet, and dramatically bemoan his fate. But if you watched him carefully, the
patterns would emerge. It became apparent to her early in their
relationship just how little pain the Djinni allowed himself to feel.
His apparent anger, his whimpering cries, they were all an act,
of course they were. Why let your enemies, even your friends,

know the truth? That wasn't really his way now, was it? At the moment, his body nearly shattered by a force reportedly strong enough to punch holes in reinforced concrete, Mel knew the pain must have been overwhelming. And yet he didn't make a sound as his body quickly began to knit itself back together. He should have been screaming. Instead, he just stood there, silent, as his enhanced healing went to work. Mel let out a slow, exhilarated breath as she observed for the first time his true reaction to pain.

At the last he looked down and noticed his right arm, which dangled and twitched nervously from his shoulder. Casually, he grasped it with his left hand, lifted the arm up and away, and snapped the dislocated shoulder back into place. Only then did he turn to face the Spitter, and Mel gasped as his hands flashed out, claws tearing through the tips of his gloves. He took a step, then another, and as he marched towards his prey, Mel noticed how dead his eyes were. There was nothing there. None of his wit, none of his charm, just cold fury. As he closed the distance, Delia began scrambling to her feet, just now realizing she was in mortal danger.

"Mel!" she screamed. "He's coming to kill me! Mel! *Mel!*"

Mel only stared at her, and at Red, in disbelief. This was a dream, it had to be. The Djinni would never hurt one of his pupils. Well, yes, he *would*, but this wasn't instruction or simple frustration at play anymore. This was a stone-cold killer advancing on Delia. There were no taunts, no warnings, just the flash of razor-sharp claws and murderous intent. This was really happening.

"MEL!" Delia screamed again. She scrambled backwards, tripped, and landed hard on her side. Mel began to move, but she already knew she would be too late. Even at a dead run, she wouldn't make it in time to intervene, and the Djinni wasn't slowing down. In a panic, Delia reached for her sidearm and fumbled with the safety as Red Djinni accelerated to a sprint, his hands held far back, ready to drive them forwards and dive into her, claws first.

Delia shrieked as she fired off three quick rounds. Two went wide. The third caught Red squarely in his chest. He came to a skidding halt and fell to one knee in front of her, eyes wide in astonishment. He gasped for breath, a bloody froth erupting from his chest. His hands fell to his sides, a cry of rage dying in his throat as the bullet was slowly pushed back out by healing tissue. Red shuddered, and as he looked up, Mel found herself slowing down, coming to a halt. His eyes, no longer empty, betrayed his confusion. He looked at her, helpless, then at Delia and finally his own claws. Startled, he shed them immediately, and rose to his feet.

Delia, still prone in an awkward position on her side, kept her gun trained on him with shaking hands.

"Delia..." he started, but flinched and took an involuntary step back as the Spitter sprang to her feet.

"You stay the *fuck* away from me!" Delia screamed, backing away, her hands still shaking. Only when she had reached her fellow trainees did she allow herself to look away and flee. They watched her go, and rose to follow her. None of them said a word, but they didn't have to. Their shock and awe were evident as they carefully backed away. The Djinni didn't say anything, either. Really, what could he say? Mel strolled up to him and found herself at a loss for words, too.

"So..." she said finally. "I'm guessing there's going to be an opening for a new trainer soon. Think I should update my CV?"

Red didn't answer her, and bowed his head in shame.

"Hey, talk to me, dummy..." Mel reached out to lift his chin. He flinched away—again—refusing to look her in the eye. "You're going to need to talk about this, y'know. What happened there? What happened to you?"

He paused, looked like he was about to say something, but simply exhaled and shook his head.

"Hey, it's me," she said, and gently took his hand in hers. "You know you can tell me anything. Once word gets out, they'll come for you. This isn't something that's just going to go away. So talk to me. Let me help. You don't have to do this alone."

"It's..." he began, and paused again. "It's not something that... it's something that..." He sighed as he noticed figures approaching the field. "You weren't kidding. They really don't waste time here."

Mel followed his gaze and squinted, making out three ECHO uniforms closing the distance. She recognized one of them. It was Jensen, ranking asshat officer extraordinaire. He was flanked by two heavily armed guards.

"They really don't," she agreed. "And he really doesn't look happy."

"He never does," Red muttered. "Though I think he's about to arrest my ass. You'd think that would put a smile on his face."

"Play nice," Mel said. "Let's see if we can buy some time with pretty words."

"Djinni!" Jensen barked, marching right up to them. "You are ordered to stand down! Turn away and place your hands behind your back!" He motioned towards one of the guards. "Cuff him, full anti-meta measures."

"So much for that idea," the Djinni said and grimaced as he felt the heavy shackles lock around his wrists and hum to life. "Going to read me my rights, Occifer?"

"Normally, I would," Jensen said. "But with war crimes, I have the distinct pleasure of simply arresting you. Too bad. I was sort of hoping you would resist. I know Reeves here has been aching for an excuse to beat your sorry ass into the ground."

Red turned and nodded at the large guard who had cuffed him. "Heya, Reeves, how're the wife and my kids?"

Reeves favored Red with a tight grin, then drove an elbow into the small of Red's back. The Djinni grunted and chuckled.

"Christ," Red laughed. "You still think you're intimidating with that weak-ass shit?"

"That's enough!" Jensen barked.

"Yeah, it is!" Mel shouted. "What's with the riot act? A training session that gets out of hand is hardly a war crime. This is brutality, and you and I both know that it'll be enough to get Red out of your sorry excuse of a jail, at least for tonight."

"No, it won't," Jensen said, turning to Mel. He regarded her for a moment, then nodded. "Fine, we'll do this by the book." He turned to face Red, a small smile playing on his lips. "Red Djinni, you are charged with breaking and entering a highly classified and secure ECHO installation, theft of classified material, assault and murder of ECHO personnel as well as suspicion of murder of ECHO OpTwo callsign Amethist and her OpOne trainees. Do you understand the charges as I have stated them?"

Red Djinni glared at him, shocked. After a moment, he cast his eyes down and nodded.

"That satisfy you?" Jensen asked Mel with a smirk.

Mel stared at him dumbly.

"Okay, we're done here," Jensen said. "Let's take him to holding."

"Wait!" Mel said, and before they could stop her, she rushed to embrace the Djinni. The guards looked at Jensen, who sighed and nodded, motioning them to stand down.

"Don't say anything," Mel whispered into Red's ear. "Don't you say a word until we get you a lawyer. We'll get through this, we'll be all right, we'll...you didn't do any of that...you didn't..."

Red stood motionless as she pulled away. She put her hands to his face, bringing his head down to hers.

"You didn't," she insisted. "You couldn't have..."

He met her desperate look with one of sad assurance.

"Oh god...Red..."

She kissed him and once again, even now, she felt him hesitate and pull back. Even now, dammit. After this got out, he wouldn't have anyone left, and still he was pulling away from her, from the one person who would still have his back. She was persistent though, and after a moment she felt him kiss her back.

"That's enough, let's go," Jensen said, and Mel felt a sudden emptiness as Red was yanked away from her.

"I love you," the Djinni said, and Mel watched as they roughly turned him about and marched him back to the compound. She stood in place as they wove through a growing crowd of curious onlookers. Red Djinni held his head high, and never looked back at her.

She continued to watch until they disappeared into the tree line.

"Sure you do," Mel muttered. "You goddamn bastard."

CHAPTER THIRTEEN

Pop Goes the Weasel

MERCEDES LACKEY AND DENNIS LEE

Perhaps some people had forgotten Verdigris. But I had not. After all, I could not forget. And he had most certainly not forgotten about us. A good thing that Khanjar was our ally, then, and that I was always, always watching. And I can watch everything, everywhere, and I do not need to sleep.

"Distraction?" Khanjar said as she followed her employer—or target, depending upon the conversation—across the room. Dominic Verdigris was in the throes of a fit of genius that had lasted for more than three days. The fact that he had deigned her worthy to hear bits and pieces about this new project made her suspicious. She expected a full explanation, complete with holographic diagrams and at least one prototype. Instead, Khanjar got a few words and the request for a sandwich. "What distraction?"

Verd wagged an admonishing finger at her, careful not to drop the crystalline board and its associated components. "Ah, there's no fun in spoilers. It's like good art; you'll know it when you see it."

"Art." She folded her arms across her chest. "Dom, you've collected nearly a billion dollars' worth of contemporary artwork in the past decade. I'm not seeing the logic there."

"No? Ah, well. I suppose you'll just have to wait for it to happen." He scooped up a glowing tablet and walked through an opening in the wall. A new laboratory gleamed from beyond the entrance, one that Khanjar was certain she hadn't seen before. She started to follow him, but a thin red sheen and the tang of ozone warned her that the contents of the room were for his eyes only.

More secrets. She tried one more time. "What's the distraction?" she pressed. "What's the big surprise?"

He glanced over his shoulder, his grin widening at her annoyance. "I wouldn't want to ruin it for you, dear. But trust me. You'll know it when it happens."

"You'll know it when it happens."

"That's what he said." Khanjar stirred her drink with the tip of her index finger and scowled. Getting away from the prying eyes of ECHO and avoiding any possible tag-alongs from various mercenaries had been difficult, but not impossible. "It's not unlike him to hold his cards that close to his chest, especially when he thinks that he's on the verge of something spectacular. This time, though..."

In the shadows, she caught a faint nod from her companion, and a low rumble of annoyance. "It's different."

She curled her lip. "It's suspicious. He prides himself on never duplicating the same method or following the same procedures, so being different shouldn't raise an alarm. The fact that he doesn't want to crow about every brilliant creation he's managed in the past few days, that concerns me. Humility is not his hallmark."

"It's not humility." The words emerged, sounding flat and unequivocal from the shadows. "I think we're finally seeing something we've been waiting for."

Khanjar scratched at her bar napkin. "We—or you? Present company makes that line very blurry." She glanced around the room. It was bare with the exception of a few old wooden tables and chairs, unadorned with anything even remotely resembling decoration, with hardwood floors and muffled sound off cushioned walls that screamed of high-end sound proofing. A single lightbulb with a simple shade hung low over the center table, illuminating a small area while keeping the rest of the room dark. When he had led her in, her first thought had been of interrogation. But he had simply motioned her to sit, and had leaned against a wall and waited for her to speak first. It was eerie; the room was so stark that it seemed to defy having any purpose at all. The rest of the place wasn't much different. It was the strangest bar she had ever been in.

"We're quite alone," her companion said. "I promised you that, didn't I?"

"You did," she agreed dryly. "Pardon my shock at seeing it come through."

"You never did like me, babe." She heard him chuckle softly. "But I always kept up my end of any bargain, you have to give me that."

"Sooner or later." Khanjar leaned back and studied the shadow. "So, you've been waiting for something since when? This recent onslaught of fighting that's got half of the world running scared? Or before then?"

The knife of a smile that came from across the table reminded her of the Cheshire cat. "Verdigris wouldn't have a dumb bunny at his side. Think, darlin'."

She despised this verbal chess, the nuances and simpering dependence upon half-truths and clever phrases. If she didn't need such alliances, she would have put a blade through his gallbladder just to hear him squeal. "Before. Before the fighting, but not since..."

Khanjar stopped and pressed the heel of her hand to her forehead. The simplest and obvious reasons were always the ones that Verd had avoided, and she had brushed them aside. But the truth had been staring her in the face since the day that he had singlehandedly united ECHO. Unintentionally, and at the cost of his well-polished and carefully tended ego.

"It was only a matter of time," her companion said. "You've watched him more than anyone, even me, and for years. He's always a step ahead. He's always ten steps ahead. But things have gone sour for him this last year. He probably saw some of it coming, as a remote possibility, but even he can't hedge his bets all the time. And now, for once, he's got to catch up. And he's worried. He's *scared*. He's in a place he never thought he'd be."

She nodded, understanding. "He doesn't know what will happen, does he?"

"Nope," he said. "One thing that Verd never was very good at, was faking confidence. You just saw the cracks in his armor, sweet thing. He's flying by the seat of his pants. Which means, for once, he's not seeing outside his immediate plans. Which means..."

"He won't see us coming," Khanjar said, a slow smile spreading across her lips.

"More than that, he still trusts you," he said. "Gotta admit, that was something I wasn't sure we could bank on. I think this will play out just fine. Tell me again, what does he expect you to do?"

"Everything, and nothing. Wait to be surprised." She thought for a moment. "When all hell breaks loose, I'm supposed to get into Top Hold, and take care of one of his loose threads."

"Harmony," he said. "He's finally going after her. About time. These mental movies are really tiring to watch, y'know. I'm sure our friends are getting antsy for some answers too. Well, one of them, anyway."

"Yes," Khanjar said. "She's a liability he hasn't had an opportunity to eliminate, until now. Apparently, all eyes will be elsewhere. Skeleton crew. He's not wrong, I should be able to get in there without much difficulty."

She watched as he lowered his head in thought. Finally, he chuckled, lifted himself off the wall and slowly approached the light.

"The Djinni's in there, too, isn't he?" he asked.

"Yes," she replied. "Our intel isn't too solid on his case, but apparently the evidence against him is tight. They expect him to hang, eventually. Or however one can dispose of a meta. Locking him in an escape-proof cell in a sub-sub-subbasement perhaps."

She watched as the shadows slid away from his face as he bent down, his knuckles resting lightly on the solid tabletop.

"Well then," Jack said. "Why don't we pay both of them a visit?"

CHAPTER FOURTEEN

Lost Cause

MERCEDES LACKEY AND DENNIS LEE

I have learned that it is very difficult to watch one's friends suffer when there is little to nothing one can (or is allowed to) do to help them. And of course, I was handicapped by the fact that I could not reach into the world to affect anything. All I could do was watch and gather information through the limited channels I had.

I have gathered much, much more since, as I am sure you have seen in these narratives, oh putative Reader. But at that time, there was oh so very little I could do.

Was it possible to feel more helpless than this? Vickie stared at the feed from Red's cell, (because, of course, no one on this planet would be able to keep her out) and thought, *Maybe. Maybe Mel feels more helpless. I dunno.*

But the screen showing Djinni's cell was only one of too many gone live with feeds from Krieger fights, and she couldn't spend more than a few seconds at a time staring at it. Her fingers danced among the five keyboards she had spread out around her workstation, and it was her voice—commanding, reassuring, warning, coordinating—that was the one people on the now-extensive Overwatch Command Network listened for. There was a fight over Lyon in France that had just turned in their favor, and she let Overwatch Paris know it a few seconds before they would have seen it themselves, so Noelle in Paris could get the French Air Force to press the advantage. Overwatch Hamburg was bracing for an incoming wave, and she quickly fed all the data she could scrape off the net to Joachim's feeds. The Colts were handling three fights, one over Chicago, one over Indianapolis, and one over Albuquerque, but they were doing just fine on their own and she didn't jiggle their elbows. Overwatch Bombay was quiet, but Eight-Ball alerted on them, and she widened the radar in time to catch the weird flickering pattern that preceded a wave of Death Spheres, out in the Indian Ocean. "Vishwathika, you've got incoming!" she pinged the operator. "Vector nine-eight-nine, they'll be on your radar in thirty seconds!"

"Roger that," Vishwathika responded, and then the radar cleared and there were the Spheres, and ECHO Bombay went hot.

She lost track of time, lost herself in the work, and only when the last of the fights ended, and ECHO and the various armed forces of the planet retreated to lick their wounds, did she look back at the screen that held the Djinni. She rubbed eyes gone sore and tired...but *she* wasn't exhausted enough yet to sleep. And there was no point in trying to sleep before she was seconds from getting keyboard face, because she'd only lie there, staring up into the dark, her hands clasped over the claw she wore around her neck. His claw. All she had of him. All she dared have of him. Because he was not for her. Even if, *especially* if he were still free, he was not for her.

She didn't have the sound on, but he was pacing, pacing like an animal in a cage. She tore her eyes away from the screen and dove under her desk. She started installing cables to Eight-Ball... another problem to tackle while she had a moment, but at least a positive one. She hadn't hooked Eight-Ball up to the full real world, or to her Overwatch rigs yet. She was stalling on it, really.

Like I'm stalling on talking to Red.

But at least she could get all the cabling in place so when she finally decided to bite the bullet, it could be done in five minutes. Eight had a camera of his own in the upper corner of the Overwatch room now, and it was under his complete control. She could hear it whirring as she worked, watching what she was doing, watching all the monitors. Sipping the analog information stream that he probably wanted to gulp down in huge, digital swallows.

Not yet. Not until I'm sure...

She came out from under the desk satisfied that everything was in place, all neatly color-coded. Tiny victory. *Go me.*

And another thing occurred to her. *Add...talismanic-type preset spells. Something Eight can trigger when I have my hands full.* The easiest one for that would be a "location" spell based on the Laws of Contamination and Unity. Just to see if it was possible, she spent a few minutes putting one together, and tucked it in a kind of memory module in Eight's m-space. Once she plugged Eight in, he'd have access to all the CCCP and ECHO spell packets that were wired to her Overwatch rig, so he'd be able to trace anyone in that bank of packets. Then to see if she could really make this practical, she did the same thing a half dozen times. It seemed to work. It would be ready to test when she was ready to pull Eight's trigger. She knew he could see everything she did in m-space. He was probably itching to try these things.

Her eyes went to Red's monitor, as faithful as a compass needle. Red had stopped pacing, and was back to sitting on his bunk. She reached absently for a meal can, and rested her chin on one hand, and stared at him while she sipped. *Because this isn't stalkerish and weird at all...*

Had he done everything Jensen claimed he had? *Killed that poor kid of a guard? No doubt. Shot down the rest? Certainly helped. Stolen stuff out of the Vault? Absolutely. Pushed Amethist into that energy weapon? Not a chance.*

She'd slowly dug up quite a bit of that past with Amethist that Jensen had pulled up like an evil rabbit out of a hat. And...no. There was nothing in that past that said to *her* that Red would have done anything other than throw *himself* between that fatal weapon and the ECHO Op if he'd known what was about to happen. *I saw his face when that thing in New Orleans tried to impersonate her. It wasn't Red that broke things off between them, it was her, and he was still carrying a candle, if not a torch, for her.* She sighed. *She probably figured out she'd never change him until he wanted to change. And she wouldn't settle for a Bad Boy. Which is why she fell for Bulwark.* Lots of practice writing romance novels got you pretty good at analyzing relationships. Well, as long as they didn't involve angels. Then all bets were off.

And there was something else she was sure of—as sure as Bella was, in fact. The Djinni in that cell was not the same man who'd killed those guards. The man who'd killed those guards was someone she wouldn't have allowed near her door.

The man who'd kept her from killing herself that horrible night was one she would trust with her soul.

After all, he already had her heart, even if he didn't know it.

She just wished he'd talk to her. Ask her for something. Anything.

Including, truth to tell…help in breaking him out. She sighed, and her eyes stung, and she wiped at them with the back of her scarred hand. *It's going to be a long night.*

In the bare confines of his cell, Red Djinni was putting on a show. This was Top Hold, a rather nice step up from the last time he had been incarcerated in an ECHO jail. While the cell was just as bare, the security here was considerably higher than the simple concrete and steel accommodations of the last, with reinforced, gleaming white walls of some unknown indestructible polymer and heavy security measures humming through high-tech sliding doors.

At least the solid platform that served as his bed was padded.

Red had spent the last couple of days doing calisthenics, eating subpar meals that a guard would slide through a small slot in the door, sleeping and generally pacing about, as if terribly concerned over whatever the fates had in store for him. It was the sort of behavior one would expect from an inmate who had just been charged with multiple counts of breaking and entering, theft, assault and murder. At the mercy of a military and peacekeeping organization like ECHO, especially during wartime, the future looked bleak to put it mildly. Red was fairly sure the death penalty would be on the table. And, really, who could blame them? The destruction of the Vault on the day of the Invasion was one of many heavy losses to the once vast ECHO armory, and the loss of one of their most celebrated officers, Callsign Amethist, had struck a major blow to the already devastated morale of the inhabitants of Atlanta. Here, in seclusion, Red could only speculate on what was happening beyond the walls of his simple cell, but he had a good idea.

One of ECHO's new heroes, the elusive Red Djinni, a man with a mysterious past who had changed his ways and was now a fighter for the people, was responsible for the death of Amethist. *The* Amethist. The poster girl for all that was good and pure in meta-powered law enforcement. The girl who had never in her entire decorated career forgotten the plight of the common man, woman, and child. The girl who came from a poor upbringing in

Hell's Kitchen, battled countless villains first in Manhattan and then across the breadth of the vast expanse of America and even the world. The girl who had humbly come to make Atlanta her home, had chaired numerous charity organizations that fought everything from poverty to disease to breaking down social boundaries of race, creed and sexuality.

Yes, *that* Amethist. And Red Djinni had killed her.

People would be screaming for his blood, right about now. He figured it probably would save everyone a lot of time and effort to just let him out, drop him on some busy corner in downtown Atlanta and let the populace tear him to pieces. They could even televise it, make a few sponsorship bucks.

Welcome to Justice in Atlanta, the execution of Red Djinni! Brought to you by Sharpett, the closest shave a man can get without slitting his own goddamn throat! And by Dry-Zee-Pads, when a gal just needs to be sure!

But, knowing ECHO, Red Djinni was certain he was in for some prolonged time in isolation, perhaps an even longer trial where the prosecution would present some extremely damning and bloody evidence, and they would hang him, figuratively speaking, following their usually quick and efficient protocols. Even now, with the world in the balance against a renewed onslaught of Krieger attacks, ECHO would make an example out of him. They really didn't have any choice. And for his part, he would let them. He had known this day would come, eventually. He had hoped it would come *later*, y'know, perhaps after a time when humanity wasn't fighting for its very existence. At that point, they would either be standing victorious and he couldn't say he really cared what happened to him at that point, or they would be defeated, defenseless, and it wouldn't really matter then, would it?

They were going to come after him with everything they had, and he would let them. He would play the part, he would wring his hands and plead, and in dark public moments he would show flashes of something sinister that bubbled beneath the surface. He would give them their villain, and let them reach closure when they ended him. They needed it, and he needed her memory to live on—pristine, heroic, because that's who she truly was.

So he moped, he paced around his cell, and he brooded, because that's what they needed to see. What they didn't see was the preparation, the mental exercises and silent mantras that played over and over again in his head. He was preparing for the role of a lifetime, because he really wasn't that guy anymore, if he ever really had been. And it wasn't just about fooling the public, that was the easy part. He had been careless. He had let a few people in, he had let a precious few see glimpses of himself. Distancing himself from them was going to prove a bit more challenging. One of them was a freakin' empath. Her boyfriend had some truly frightening abilities to read the truth from people just by observation. Another had shared his bed for months, and things had a way of slipping by the old defenses when that happened. He had ideas in place for all of them—what to do, say, vague ideas of slimy conduct that might convince them he was a genuine sociopathic mastermind.

It was Victrix that he was drawing a blank on.

Of all of them, she had seen the most. They had shared some truly spectacular, even intimate, moments that had forged a surprisingly strong bond between them. Red had not seen that coming. With the others, he could formulate plans, backups, contingencies and the like to build a strong case that he wasn't the man they had thought he was. With Vix, it was going to take more than just a barrage of insults and cold truths to sway her. She would see past all of it, and eventually figure out his game. She really was too smart for her own good. And what would she do then? Would she back his play? He doubted it. For now, he did the only thing he could: stall... for as long as he could. She was watching him, he was sure of it, but she had not attempted contact yet. This was a good thing. But eventually, she would try talking to him.

And he had no idea what he was going to say to her. Well, at least there was one small thing he could do right now. "Overwatch," he muttered under his breath. "Reset privacy timer."

Vickie fed another data dump into the standalone server for Eight-Ball and watched as Eight sucked it dry in minutes. She suspected he'd have done it in seconds, but he was doing what humans did; *considering* what he was absorbing/observing. *I'm going to have to make a decision about him pretty soon. If I keep him in isolation much longer, he might get resentful.*

Her eyes went to Red's screen. Two days, almost three, and still nothing from him. No idea what was going through his head. She

knew what was going through Jensen's though, because the bastard
was stupid enough to gloat where she had microphones. A show
trial, and a big one—as if they could *afford* to take the time and
resources for a show trial! And after that, Red was going to some
special "Program." Now, Jensen didn't know what Vickie knew about
Murdock's past. The word "Program" combined with "metas" meant
the same thing they'd just rescued a couple dozen kids from, and
that meant they'd make him into a weapon. An expendable one.

I can't take this anymore, she decided. "Overwatch: Open Red:
Private," she said, and cleared her throat awkwardly. "So," she said,
and stopped.

She was greeted with the barely audible hiss of the open channel, and then . . .

"A needle pulling thread," came the Djinni's dry response.

"Tea?" she responded, feeling suddenly light-headed. "I can
probably arrange that. Might be able to mess with the kitchen to
get you slightly better meals."

"What do you want, Vix?" Red asked. "Can't a man rot in peace?"

She heard a *ping* from Eight-Ball before she could react to that,
and turned her head. *Voice analysis suggests deception,* Eight said,
over his newly installed voice link, and only then did she realize
she'd had Red on speaker.

"Overwatch: Internal feed: Red," she said hastily.

"Goddamn it," Red muttered. "You're siccing lie detectors on me
now? Really? Have we come to this already?"

"That's Eight-Ball," she replied, moving out of the Overwatch
room and into the living room. "I've been working on him and I
forgot I had you on speaker. You're just in my ear now, Penny Lane."

"Lovely," Red answered. "What. Do. You. Want?"

"Honesty," she replied, without thinking.

"Well, my balls are itching a bit," Red replied. "Aside from that,
I've been told I shouldn't say anything without a lawyer present."

"And I wanted to know if there was anything I could do for
you." She held her breath.

"Well, now that you mention it, it would appear that I need a
lawyer. So . . . yeah . . . maybe send me one. Doesn't even have to be
a good one. I hear the case is pretty open and shut."

"I can do that," she said as steadily as she could. "Fair warning,
Jensen intends to make you his personal attack dog. Like he's going
to make a *Program* out of you."

There was a long pause.

"You mean he's not angling for the chair?" Red asked, his voice dreadfully quiet.

"I have it from the horse's ass—I mean, mouth."

"How can he do that?" Red asked. "That kind of sentence can't possibly be sanctioned by anyone. Not by ECHO, not by the public. Are people not screaming for blood?"

"People are too busy digging foxholes. This is wartime. Of course," she added, "there's a hundred ways that I know of to make it *look* as if you'd been executed, and then you wake up elsewhere. But you know, people are jerks, and they'd probably rather know you were on a leash with a shock collar attached, replaying *They Were Expendable* every week or so." She hadn't meant to say that much. She hadn't meant to say nearly that much. But . . . she couldn't let him sit there without knowing what he was facing. Maybe that would make him fight.

It didn't.

"Fine," he said. "Whatever."

Her heart twisted into a hard, hurting knot. "I'll get on that lawyer thing," she said softly. "I don't think it'll take long. Anything else?"

"Yeah," Red muttered. "You can stop watching me. I know you're capturing the feed on this cell's camera, and I swear it's like I can feel your eyes on me. Cut it out."

There was another long pause, and Vickie felt her hands locked on the sides of her chair.

"You got it," she said finally. "You can still ping me on Overwatch, if you, uh, need anything. I've got incoming. Overwatch: Close: Red: Private."

And then, as if the universe decided to make sure she wasn't a liar, she heard the alarms in the Overwatch room and scrambled back to her chair. Thank god, it was going to be a long night.

He had said it in haste, still confused over how to handle her, and had sent her away. Red fought the urge to backpeddle, to take it back and simply spill his guts out to her, when she abruptly excused herself and killed the channel. He sat down on his cot and let his head droop into his waiting hands.

"Summers believed in me," he muttered. "And she paid for it. But that's not going to happen to you, Vix. Maybe I can hide from them all, but not with you. So that's it, then. You get the truth. That's the only way to handle you."

He stood up and approached his cell door. On the left, a small touch screen flared to life as he approached. As part of the security system in Top Hold, each cell was equipped with one, responding only to registered handprint scans of on-duty guards and high-ranking officers like Bella and Bulwark. As most cells were insulated from conventional means of communication, they provided personnel a hard-wired means to communicate with the outside. Inmates didn't have access. Some with special privileges were allowed brief periods of limited functionality, granting them supervised Skype calls, simple word processing or even small windows to watch movies or television. Few inmates had friends in such high places as Red, though. He had never tried to access the panel, but suspected someone had perhaps left him a means to entertain himself while incarcerated here.

Gently, he laid his palm on the cool interface, and was unsurprised when it responded with a gentle ping and full internet access. He ignored the video streaming and teleconference options, and instead opened an email browser.

He exhaled, opened a new message, and began to type on the touchscreen keyboard.

To: Victoria Victrix <vickievee@ECHO.net>

From: That Red Bastard <redbastard@ECHO.net>

You asked if there was something else you can do for me. There is. You can keep this somewhere safe, and I leave it to you to do with as you think best. I suppose you can consider it a confession, but you know me well enough to realize I just need to get this out there, off my chest, and I suppose there's no one I trust more to have it than you. It's more than that, I guess. You might need to know some of this stuff. Hell, you probably deserve to more than anyone, but that doesn't mean you're going to thank me for it. More the opposite. But it needs to be said. So get ready, it's time for some damning truth.

In a perfect world—well, in *my* perfect world—things would still be chaotic. I know I'm in the minority here.

If you're one of those people who strive for that great secure job with regular cash showers in your ten-acre estate, I'm sorry, I just don't get you. I can't think of any place more boring than the common perception of paradise. To have everything you want when you want it, when would you ever feel your blood rushing through your veins with the bit caught in your teeth, riding the razor's edge with a wind of flames at your back...?

As he typed, he felt his fingers moving faster, trying to keep up with the words that were aching to come out. He paused once, as he struggled to describe how Amethist fell. It still hurt. The rest he scrambled to flesh out, desperate to be rid of it. And after, as he felt a tremendous weight lift from him, he paused again, his finger hovering over the "send" prompt.

"Not yet," he whispered, finally, and simply saved the message. He backed away from the console, letting it shut down, and sat back down on his bunk.

I got this later. When you read as far as "later," I suspect you'll guess how.

Stand and Deliver

MERCEDES LACKEY

"I don't know why I didn't think of this before," said Dominic Verdigris, leaning back in his chair, his hands, for once, *not* occupied by a keyboard. "It's simple, really. ECHO has been a thorn in my side all along, but ECHO would not be what it was if it did not have all those pesky metahumans in it. Remove the powers, and *poof,* no more ECHO. The only people who will have powers will be the ones I spare."

He frowned, as if he was listening to someone. "Well, of course, I intend to spare some. I need protection from the Thulians, don't I? But instead of trying to save the world, the only people with powers will be doing the far easier and more important job of saving *me.*"

Now he directed his gaze at a transparent case on his desk, a long, slender case that held what appeared to be an ancient Chinese sword, and laughed. "Oh no," he said, waggling a finger at it. "You really do not think I am *that* stupid, do you? I wouldn't touch you with a ten-foot pole, no matter how invulnerable you claim you can make me."

He scowled now. "No, you cannot have Khanjar. Because I'm sleeping with her, that's why! Then I'd be sleeping with *you,* and—ugh." He shook his head. "Now I need brain bleach. No. Absolutely not. Now just listen to me, instead of complaining that you haven't got someone to possess, and you can congratulate me on my brilliant plan."

"First, in order to wipe out most of ECHO's metahumans, I'll have to get them concentrated in one place, as you so correctly noted. To do *that,* I just have to have a reason to get them all together. And the most compelling reason possible would be a memorial service for one of the most beloved and iconic members of ECHO alive today!" He laughed in delight, then frowned at the sword. "What, do you think I'm some kind of idiot? It's going to look completely natural, of course. No one will suspect a thing. And once everyone is assembled for the memorial, I work my magic, and away go all my troubles."

Verdigris smiled in satisfaction. "Yes, it certainly is a classic strategy." Then he lost his smile. "Do you think I hadn't thought of that?" He huffed. "Honestly, you have no concept of who you are talking to, here, and you never did. If you'd paid *any* attention at all, and had *cooperated* with me instead of going off half-cocked on your own, I'd have the Seraphym, *you'd* still have that Chinese wench and we wouldn't be sitting here having this conversation."

He listened for a little while longer, and the irritation on his face smoothed out. "That's more like it. Let me handle this. I'll keep passing flunkies by you until you find one you like. And remember that the alternative is that I drop you back in the ocean where I found you, so try and produce a little more gratitude."

He swung his chair around and got up. "I need to check on the results of my tests. You just sit there and . . . meditate or something." He laughed. "No need to get up, I'll just be on my way. Oh wait, you can't get up. My bad."

And with that, he left the room.

There *might* have been an angry, low buzz coming from the sword case.

Then again, it might just have been the air-conditioning system.

CHAPTER FIFTEEN

Head of Medusa

MERCEDES LACKEY AND CODY MARTIN

Sometimes the things I can find go quite a long way back. This is one of them.

Valkyria stalked among the buildings near her quarters, avoiding the Thulians and Germans that lived in this quarter. If anyone so much as talked to her, *looked* at her with anything less than deference, she would have killed them on the spot. Since her return from the destruction of Metis, she could not bear to be around anyone, even Ubermensch. Nothing calmed her, and the increased activity of the Thulians at the behest of the Masters only served to infuriate her further. It all seemed like so much motion and noise, masquerading as action. She fumed. This was intolerable! *They had the* untermenschen *beaten!* It was just a matter of time and resources!

Then again . . . they had had the *untermenschen* beaten ten, twenty, even thirty years ago. It had always been nothing more than a matter of time and resources. The only time it hadn't been, had been seventy-five years ago. As she stomped up and down the walkways, she thought back on the past, remembering how she had come to this place of frustration, artifice, and slavery.

There was a time when Euphemia Reichenbach hadn't known war. She was a simpler young woman then, and happier. Her country was still in the throes of a painful rebirth, but as a young girl whose father at least had a job as a policeman, that had not affected her as much as others. Numerous sanctions, a Socialist

232

revolution, economic destabilization, lack of jobs and sometimes even food, and the loss of so many young men in the Great War had sent shock waves through Germany that were still being felt. Despite the hardship that seemed to have become an everyday part of life, Euphemia was a happy enough girl. Tall for her age, she was just showing signs of maturity at eleven. Even then, however, it was clear that she was going to be a great beauty. Blonde hair in a tight ponytail down to her midback, electric-blue eyes that were unsettling to some, for their tendency to hold a gaze even after it was impolite to do so, and a sharp intellect rounded her out. An intellect that tended to reduce people around her to simple things: could they be of benefit to her, or could they not? Then again, that was life for many people in those days.

Things began to change, however slowly, in Germany. She read as often as she could, and dreamed of traveling... one day. Everything seemed to boil down to "one day, maybe" for her. Marriage seemed like it was going to be added to that list, since that was what girls did. The prospect didn't have any appeal for her; her future would constrict, shrivel to a single point of childbirth and rearing, and nothing about that future of *Kinder, Küche, Kirche* even remotely satisfied her. She had trouble deciding on what she really ought to do with herself after she finished her schooling. Her home own had little to offer, save for mountains, pastures, and not terribly much else. Nothing that could hold her attention, at any rate.

So, when the changes began, she took notice. When she was twelve, she started to see signs of those changes everywhere: in newspapers, new books that were being published, even hearing about these new ideas on the radio. Her countrymen took on a different demeanor, ever so slowly. Her family had more food, and better quality. There were more jobs, more opportunity, particularly for a policeman like her father. One politician, in particular, had begun to stand out from the rest; he was called Adolf Hitler. His Nazi Party seemed to be leading the charge for Germany to regain its former glory.

Her father, already in a position of authority, was recruited into a new force, and with it came new responsibilities and privileges. Euphemia's father had never struck her as a man who was terribly proud of himself; he wasn't prone to much emotion at all. He didn't beat her mother as much as some fathers did their wives, which she was glad for, but that seemed to be the extent of his interaction with his family outside of the evening meal. When he received his new job, however ... there was a new spark there. He walked straighter, kept his chin up, looked people in the eye again.

Her father had become a member of the *Sturmabteilung*—sometimes known as the Brownshirts—as a part of the New Germany. And just before her thirteenth birthday, there came an even bigger change for her father. He quit his job as a policeman, and joined the *Schutzstaffel*. He had a new uniform, and more authority. And one of the first big changes for Effi was that he urged—no, *insisted*—that she join an organization too, the *Bund Deutscher Mädel,* part of the *Hitler Jugend*. It was what respectable families did, for the *Vaterland*. And besides, there were no other youth groups to join anymore; they had all been disbanded by law.

Effi—a childhood nickname that she liked much better than her given name—didn't mind, even though six days out of seven, the things that the girls in the BDM did were boring beyond belief. More "preparation for motherhood," more *Kinder und Küche,* although *Kirche* was more or less absent from the discussions. But there was lots and lots of physical exercise, gymnastics, swimming, hiking. These activities were far more appealing. And she could always escape the homemaking lessons by pleading that she wanted to learn more about the *Hitler Jugend* movement. Particularly about the Young Martyrs. Oh, how she loved to sing *Die Fahne hoch!* And she dreamed about a chance to save one of the great and important—half the time her daydreams ended with making an impassioned dying speech as she lay (bloodied, but beautiful!) in the arms of weeping men. The other half ended with her miraculous recovery, and being hailed as a Heroine, a Savior of Germany, and being idolized wherever she went. She would never have to go home to her stodgy little village, or wash so much as a single dish again ... she'd see all the great cities: Vienna, Strasbourg, Hamburg, Berlin. She'd see all the things she had only read about in magazines. She imagined herself in places she had only heard about, dressed in fabulous dresses of the sort she only saw in movies...

And, of course, when she wasn't daydreaming, there were the camping trips, ski trips, and trips to training camps sponsored

by the *Hitler Jugend.* It didn't take much convincing to get her
parents to allow her to go; her father seemed happy if only
because it was one less thing for him to worry about, and her
mother didn't dare argue. And if she wasn't seeing the big cities
she dreamed of, at least she was getting out of her village.

And then, in 1938, at last! She was invited to participate in
the Nuremberg Rally! She was to represent the new League of
Faith and Beauty in the parades. And it didn't matter that she
was only one of so many nearly identical blonde-haired, blue-eyed
beauties who rode on floats or walked in the parades dressed in
medieval or peasant costumes. She wore the dress of a Teutonic
princess and waved from the pinnacle of a parade float. She felt
the eyes of the crowd on her, and it was intoxicating.

It felt like the beginning of something breathtaking.

But for her . . . it marked the end. No more rallies in Nuremberg after 1938. The new war was on, and all of her effort and
concentration was supposed to be on the war. And on her duty
to the Fatherland to produce more German children. And it was
hinted, oftentimes rather strongly, that one didn't need to be *married* to do this. There were . . . weekend retreats where one would
meet and entertain Heroes of the Fatherland. And if things . . .
happened . . . that resulted in a child, well, so much the better.

But the mere idea of letting some strange man, however much
a Hero of the Fatherland he was, put his paws all over her, was
revolting. So she always had some excuse not to go to one of those
retreats, not even when her own father suggested that "it might
be fun." Perhaps that was why, in 1941, she was selected, along
with others of the BDM, to "help" with the morale and organization of the new German colony of Hegewald in the Ukraine.
It occurred to her, long after the fact, that perhaps someone had
actually intended her to become the "reward" for one of the SS
in charge of Hegewald. However, it turned out that fate had a
different plan in store for her, in the end.

Himmler was coming to visit. And Effi, as one of the most
beautiful of the BDM "morale corps" in Hegewald, had been
chosen to ornament the stage where he was going to speak.

She remembered that day as clearly as if it had been yesterday
for her. More than a little wistfully, she sometimes wished that
she could relive what she had felt then.

The air was cold and crisp that day, but she didn't mind. She stood tall and proud on a short platform that sat upon a stage that workers had erected. A full band was playing, bright and sonorous in the early morning sunshine. Flags and streamers in the national colors were flapping in the light wind. Soldiers, officers, and other "big men" in the government were all in pristine uniforms or freshly pressed suits. Some of them, particularly the politicians, looked bored, but Effi didn't care. The scene was utterly perfect for her, a representation of her country's renewed might, and she was a beautiful part of it, the living representative of German Womanhood.

Finally the band ended the anthem they had been playing, signaling that it was time for the assembled crowds to be seated; at least those in the front rows, who actually were provided chairs. Effi dutifully took her seat; she had been positioned behind and to the right of Himmler, who was standing at a podium and surveying the assembled men and women. He cleared his throat, and was about to begin speaking when a series of muted *thudding* sounds were heard in the distance. Effi had never heard anything like it.

Some of the older officers and soldiers, however, had. They immediately began to scream and shout, shoving their subordinates and giving orders. Two soldiers rushed to the stage, one of them nearly knocking Effi over as they moved to flank Himmler.

"Gasmasken! Gasmasken, schnell!"

Effi felt as if she were glued to where she had ended up standing on the stage. *Gasmasks? Why—*

Her question was answered a moment later when the first of the mortar shells landed. The shrapnel injured several members of the crowd; it was the first real taste of violence she had ever had, and she instantly felt queasy at the sight of the blood. When the burst shell started to billow clouds of noxious yellow smoke, her knees turned to water. The people closest to it screamed horribly, louder than the sounds of panic and commotion from everyone else. More shells hit the ground, one after the other, and Effi watched as the entire town square started to fill with the deadly gas.

This can't be happening. I can't die here... I haven't done anything yet.

The two soldiers flanking Himmler were trying to both pull him in opposite directions; they were both so crazed with fear, they hardly recognized that they were working against each other. Himmler was shaken, trying to keep a grip on the podium in front of him and yelling at the soldiers to unhand him. One of them did, jumping off the stage and running into the crowd, but the other was still too frightened to notice.

Time slowed down for Effi. She watched as a single shell arced in from the sky, landing some fifty meters away. She saw the shower of earth and stone that it threw up when it hit, and then the almost languid plumes of gas. If not for their deadly purpose, it was strangely beautiful to watch. She took a moment to notice that she wasn't hearing the clamor of the panicked mob anymore. Instead...she heard voices. Snatches of conversation that faded in and out of her mind as quickly as they came. *How odd*, she thought, caught up in the unreality of the moment. She looked at the soldier that was pulling on Himmler's jacket, and then she only heard one voice.

Fuck! I need to get this bastard out of here, or I'll be shot for certain! Jesus, he's going to get me killed, why isn't he moving? We've got to get clear of the gas!

It took her a moment before she realized that it was actually the soldier's thoughts that she was hearing. Her eyes grew wide for a moment. Without any real conscious decision, she felt her body start moving. She felt outside of herself, as if she was *finally* enacting one of her heroic childhood daydreams, and watching it at the same time. She took one step, then another, and another. With a shove, she sent the soldier sprawling; he slid over the edge of the stage, landing in a heap at the bottom of it. Himmler turned to look at her, flabbergasted; whether from her audacity or the ludicrous situation, she couldn't tell. Nor did she care. She simply gripped Himmler's right arm, and pulled; where two young and strong soldiers couldn't move the official, she was easily able to lead him along. She was *willing* him to follow her, though she didn't know how.

With a few steps, they both were running. It felt like they were going faster, and faster...and then her feet were no longer on the ground. She looked back to see that she was flying; Himmler was dangling from her tiny hand by his right wrist, his face passive. Below, she could see the quickly shrinking town square; it was almost entirely full of gas, and those few people still mobile were moving into the woods north of the town.

At that moment, she almost fell out of the sky; *this* certainly hadn't been part of those daydreams! But in the next instant, she felt galvanized by a thrill of perfect certainty. Of course, everyone had heard of Ubermensch and Eisenfaust! And *she* was obviously one of that elite company of Uplifted Humans! No wonder she had felt no attraction for the sad little, merely human males who had offered themselves for her consideration! She was a superhuman, *homo superior!* Finding a common human attractive would have been as ludicrous if she had been attracted to an ape.

She selected a place clear of the gas, and well guarded by plenty of SS, and set Himmler down inelegantly in the middle of them, letting her control of his mind pass so that he would recognize just who had saved him. Only then did she set down herself, amid the gawking SS officers, prepared to graciously accept their adulation.

Valkyria had never become used to the stench that Thulians gave off, even after all of these years. Probably, as an *ubermensch,* all her senses were more attuned, more sensitive, but she had to wear nose plugs to filter out the burnt-orange/musk/cinnamon reek they gave off. She had been fascinated by them when she had first joined their cause, but that early captivation had faded quickly. She had a certain amount of respect for the warriors, who were uncompromising in their single-minded determination for victory... but not these, not the ones around her at the moment. They were "Thulians" in name only; they didn't have a name for themselves, or at least not one that had ever been translated. Servitors, always scuttling around on some errand or task, quick to fulfill an order; she found them contemptible in their manner, but highly useful all the same. *Efficient, if nothing else.*

She was walking quickly, three of the rot-scented creatures trailing her. She had been busy drawing up plans for assaults, issuing orders to suicide cells, reviewing intelligence and other messages passed on by spies and other defectors that sought to aid the Thulians. Tasks that, however necessary, made her feel as if her skull would split open.

We should be planning feasts, and carving up the world by now. Not reeling from a defeat and biding our time. The loss of Ultima Thule had put her into a frenzy. Once she and *Ubermensch* had safely escaped to and recovered at a nearby base, she had killed three Thulians and one of her human subordinates in a rage before she was calm again. Erick—*Ubermensch's* true name, which only she and one other knew—had been content to stand back and watch; blood always pleased him, and he didn't much care about the source. *There's another fool to be tolerated.*

Erick Fleischer, the latest heir to the title of *Ubermensch*, was thoroughly insane. Homicidal to a fault; paired with his nearly unrivaled powers, he was a terror for his enemies, and almost as much of a terror to his subordinates. Such ability wasn't paired with much of a mind, however. Simple pleasures like torture and murder were what he enjoyed most; he was an acceptable lovemaker, but such pursuits interested Valkyria less and less, as of late. His damnable obsession with two of their foes—the Russian, Natalya, and one of the Americans, Murdock—consumed nearly anything that he did. Always talk of vengeance, and the pain he would inflict, how none could escape his grasp... and so on. His madness was truly evident whenever Valkyria happened by his personal quarters; maps pinned to walls detailing his quarries' movements, hand-drawn portraits of wildly varying quality, scribbled manifestos and diatribes... all of these papers and other clutter of an insane and retribution-driven mind were scattered about, with an organization that only made sense to the madman himself. It was tiring, and when it wasn't tiring, it was annoying.

Destroying Metis had been a welcome distraction for both of them... even if it had led to that pompous ass Worker's Champion joining them officially, here. If Effi disliked Erick, she completely despised Boryets Ivanovich. The Russian was equally filled with disdain for Effi; that was the one thing that she had been able to glean from his mind, which was almost completely resistant to her talents. Not that she needed to read his mind to have known that; he never missed an opportunity to plainly state exactly what he thought about his new "comrades," despite their joined purposes. He never failed to get in jabs about "female emotionalism" getting in the way of getting the job done. As if she had *ever* exhibited an unwarranted emotional moment in her entire life! Killing underlings didn't count, naturally.

Despite his betrayal, at least Eisenfaust had treated her as an equal.

✧   ✧   ✧

After her heroic rescue of Himmler, the entire world changed for Effi. She was powerful, and respected. No longer just a pretty girl to be passed off to some officer, she was one of the *ubermenschen*. Her time—at least when she was not in combat—was reserved for those who were at least of the rank of general, and there was no question of whether or not that "company" included sex. There were more parades for her and the other metahumans, crown jewels of Germany's might and supremacy. All of it suited her perfectly well. With her new abilities, she was able to navigate the intrigue and backstabbing that accompanied rising through the ranks into the dizzying heights of power and influence. She could read the minds of nearly everyone that she met... and was finding that she could also control some of them. She could affect their emotional states, bringing a man from the highest ecstasy down to the most soul-rending despair, all with a thought. It afforded her opportunities that she might have otherwise been denied.

Armed with such power, she was able to manipulate her circumstances substantially. She didn't simply want to be a showpiece, always on display; she wanted adventure, an opportunity to prove herself and to fight for her country. There was also a deeper, secret reason for her machinations, that she admitted to no one save for herself. She wanted Eisenfaust.

Of course she wanted Eisenfaust. Every German woman wanted him. Heinrich Eisenfaust was the perfect Germanic hero, an *ubermensch* even more than the one that had been given that eponymous title. Blond, blue-eyed, square-jawed, with absolute control over every aspect of his life, he was never rattled, never upset, never taken aback, and never allowed any setback to stop him. Effi's aerial battles with La Faucon Blanc sent her into a fury. His fights with Spitfire merely left him sitting at a desk, making diagrams of every aspect of the fight, and plotting how the next time would be different. The day when she had met him and been inducted into his elite wing within the *Luftwaffe* had been enough to eclipse every other honor and accolade that had been given to her.

The ceremony had been publicized, with many attending generals, politicians, and so forth. She hardly noticed any of them; Heinrich was the only one that held her attention during the proceedings. No one else could matter; they were all *human*. She was *ubermensch*. As was Heinrich; even past that, he was above and beyond the others. For one, she could hardly get any reading from his mind; it was locked behind a wall of iron, as unbreakable as the Iron Fist that gave him his name. But it was also very clear that he shared an interest for her that was not becoming to an officer for a subordinate. It took her exactly two weeks after becoming part of his elite group of flyers to becoming his lover. She was certain that with any other man it would not have taken nearly as long... but Heinrich was so *different*. He wouldn't be swayed by anyone once he had set his mind to a course of action. And it had taken *him* that long to decide that he wanted her. It simultaneously vexed her and drew her in that much closer to him.

The German High Command had been ecstatic. They were the perfect couple, exactly what was wanted for posters, statues, and propaganda. An *ubermenschen* baby would have completed the perfection, so far as they were concerned, but Effi was not at all interested in satisfying that particular item on their checklist. *Let them keep hoping. I possess everything I could ever want or need already: Heinrich and the thrill of battle—a child, now? That would only subtract from what I currently have.*

Unfortunately, it seemed that even those things would fall from her hands, no matter how tightly she tried to keep hold of them. As the war pressed on, things began to look less perfect and glorious with each passing week. News from the front had turned from being about astounding victories and captured land, to tales of mounting losses and cities falling. She and Heinrich, at times, felt like they were the only part of the German military that was making any sort of difference whatsoever. They fought in perfect tempo together; Eisenfaust with his lightning quick reflexes and almost instinctual understanding of aerial combat, and Effi with her ability to read her opponent's minds and anticipate their attacks. Their air wing alone stood without major losses, while the rest of the *Luftwaffe* was suffering: lack of experienced pilots to replace those killed in battle, poor choices by those in command that saw those few pilots that showed promise shuttled into bomber planes instead of fighters, and faults in equipment that saw lives unnecessarily lost. It was one of the few things that seemed to truly anger Heinrich.

"Effi, those fools! They are losing this war for Germany, and they are too damned blind to even see it! Damnable pride and no

connection to their men, and they're spending lives pointlessly."
It was rare that she ever saw her lover lose composure, and the
first time Effi witnessed Heinrich erupt like that, it had shaken
her to her very core.

That had been the day that Effi first entertained the idea that
they might actually *lose*. It had never seemed possible before;
their might was absolute, and everyone—from Hitler to the soldiers, even common shopkeepers and workers—had all been on
a rising cloud of enthusiasm and pride for the *Vaterland*. What
could possibly stop them? The more she thought about it at night,
after a mission or exertions in bed with Heinrich, the more she
saw the truth in his words. *What could stop Germany's glorious
ascension? Our leaders.* It had chilled her to her very core, and
she had trouble sleeping with the thought sharing her bed.

It seemed as if Effi's streak of good fortune had finally run
out. The Reich was finally coming to its end; the front lines were
manned by old men and those hardly old enough to lift rifles.
The SS were still fighting fiercely, despite diminishing numbers;
her own father had fallen several months before, and her mother
was manning an antiaircraft gun. She didn't mourn overly long
for the man, and she expected to get notification that a bomb
had obliterated her mother any day; she was resigned to the
idea. Continually, the front had been pushed back, further and
further into Germany, until Berlin was in sight of the Allies.
Sometimes, Effi morbidly wondered who would be the first to
pick her country's bones—the Russians or the Americans. Neither
prospect held much appeal for her. She saw no way out, other
than to continue forward and fight to the bitter end alongside
her lover. Even Heinrich had become disillusioned at that point,
maybe before she had, although it was hard to tell due to the
way he held his true feelings close and away from others. Probably her best and least painful prospects were to die in a grand
and fiery dogfight against overwhelming odds; at least she would
linger in the minds of her enemies, and possibly even on film,
as a fearsome and implacable foe.

Her wishes were only half granted. The end came after their
Uberluftwaffe had been dispatched to protect another supply ship,
flying out from one of their secret bases in South America. The
mission had been routine until they saw an entire flight of fighters

on the horizon, ready to intercept them. Somehow, the Allies had discovered where they would be flying... and had come prepared.

Effi had fought these enemies many times; those that had lived from previous engagements were the best of the best, and they faced her now. Corsair from the United States of America in his signature-painted eponymous plane; La Faucon Blanc, the French-woman, who Effi's sharp eyes could recognize even at a distance; Brumby, the Australian, and Gyrfalcon, flying in tight formation. They were accompanied by a dozen other fighter planes, all intent on ending Effi and Heinrich's lives.

The aerial battle was short and brutal. The casualties inflicted on both sides came at great cost; plane after plane caught flame and fell into the Atlantic. In the end, only the *ubermenschen* on either side were left flying. Effi and Heinrich, versus four of the Allies. Even with all of their gifts, it was a hopeless battle. Effi's gifts could allow her to read the thoughts of a single opponent... but two at once, much less four? She would anticipate one, only to be caught unawares by the partner, forced to rely on her training to carry her from certain death at the last instant. It wouldn't be enough for victory. It might not be enough for survival.

Where did I go wrong? Where had *everything* gone wrong? Was Heinrich right? Was it the inherent flaws of their leaders—even Hitler himself—who were, after all, "only" human? Would things have gone better if she and the *ubermenschen* had forced a coup?

It was all too late now.

The last move in their deadly aerial dance was as beautiful as it was inevitable. Brumby and Gyrfalcon had been taking turns diving on Effi, each time stitching her plane with bullets. The awful game of tag had finally come to an end; Gyrfalcon was closing for a final run, and Effi no longer could use the control surfaces of her plane to evade. If she tried to eject from the plane and use her own metahuman power of flight, she would be gunned down quickly. She was done for, and could even hear her opponent's thoughts concerning the coming victory.

Panic flooded Effi's mind. She had been faced with death many times before; first, in the Ukraine with Himmler. Since then, by the intrigues of those that would have seen her used for their purposes or dead, then through ground warfare, and finally, in the air, as part of a fighter wing. This time was different. She *knew*, with certainty, that she was to die. She could not dodge, nor ditch from her plane; they were in the open ocean, and she would either drown or have sharks for company when her own ability for flight was exhausted. In response to these troubling thoughts, her throat closed, dry and tight. Her stomach felt like it was made of ice, and she was covered in a cold sweat.

Her final thought cut through all of that prior emotion and physical reaction like a scalpel.

I DON'T WANT TO DIE!

Before she could react further, she saw Heinrich's fighter cut a perfect maneuver. He was above her and her pursuers, trying to gain altitude over his own attackers, when he suddenly, and inexplicably, performed a textbook wingover, plunging straight down towards Gyrfalcon. He would have hit Gyrfalcon's plane dead center, except that Gyrfalcon's reflexes partially saved him. Heinrich clipped Gyrfalcon's wing with his own, sending both planes into uncontrolled spins to the ocean.

Effie's heart fell. She instantly knew that she had finally used her mental abilities to influence Heinrich . . . and at the same time was ecstatic to be alive still. She watched, almost as if it was happening in some sort of dream state, as both planes spiraled towards the unforgiving waters below. Suddenly, her entire world was drenched in a sickly green light. Her skin felt like it had ants crawling beneath it, and her teeth rattled in her skull.

As quickly as the otherworldly light had come, it was gone again. She found herself somewhere . . . else. Above a weirdly curving cityscape, that seemed to somehow stretch from the horizons up into the sky itself. She no longer had control of her fighter plane, and it was all she could do to keep the control stick steady as it plummeted towards an open area in the heart of what appeared to be a plaza. The plaza of a city that had appeared below her, out of nowhere. Small details stuck with her, before the crash; the awful red-orange color of the sky above, the red and black steaming jungle at the outskirts of the city, how the entire world seemed to curve back in on itself at the edges. Most of all, all of the tiny gray figures in that square, growing larger and rushing up to meet her and her plane as she fell towards them.

Her next clear memory had been of lying on a table that wasn't shaped quite right for her frame, with odd humanoid creatures tending to her wounds. And Doppelgaenger, right there, as if he belonged among them. "Welcome to the world of our secret allies, *liebchen*," he had said, with what might have been a faint, very faint, sneer. "And allow me to present *their* Masters." He had stepped back, and two more insectlike creatures out of a nightmare had stepped forward—one lavender, and one burnt orange. "Mistress Barron, Master Gero, this is one of the Third Reich's greatest treasures, the warrior Valkyria." Only the fact that she was held in some sort of paralysis had kept her from screaming.

She had come to learn that the truth was much more frightening than her fears; the Masters were certainly monsters, but not of the sort that she had originally conjured. Still, she had been able to entreat with Barron and Gero—they seemed to be the chosen representatives, or leaders, for the rest of the Masters, whomever they were—and secure a place for herself and Heinrich in this new and strange society. The technologies that they commanded would have made the top minds in Germany weep in envy, and the resources that they possessed... were unfathomable. *What could we have accomplished, if only we had come to know the Masters and their "Thulians" at the beginning of the war?*

It was plain that they were not human. She only dared to try to read the minds of Gero and Barron once—and she suspected that it was only because they had *allowed* her to do so, since there was a clear well of telepathic power in both of them. What she saw and heard were completely incomprehensible; the thought processes were too different for her to take in and make any sense of. Two things did stand out, however: greed and amusement. She had met her share of men with wanton tastes, but the Masters... it was an inhuman level of avarice. The Thulians were far simpler, which suited her perfectly; closer to men, save that they didn't have the same drive, the same spark of will. In the years since her arrival, she had surmised that they were wholly creatures of the Masters, bent to a specific purpose. Still, that left the question: what *were* the Masters? What were their designs? *Why tolerate us, why humor us? Why why why?*

There was only one human that she truly feared anymore. Doppelgaenger. Spy, master torturer, and inscrutable bastard. As alien as the Thulians could be, Doppelgaenger was worse in her mind, despite being a fellow *Ubermensch*. It wasn't just that he could shift his countenance at a whim; she had grown accustomed to the strange and sometimes distressing manifestations that power could take in a metahuman, as the world at large called them. His eyes, whatever their form, had a tendency to stare through people. Like a shark's, they were flat, cold and emotionless. The one time she had brushed his mind with her own, she had immediately recoiled. She had only received impressions, since she did not have an opportunity to delve deeper, but they had been enough for her to decide never to try to read him again. Dark, writhing shapes... and hunger that was so all-consuming and disturbing, she had felt as if it would draw her down into its maw in passing. She still felt her flesh crawl whenever Doppelgaenger came near, and she knew that the bastard relished her reaction.

As time had gone on, especially these last few years as the campaign to conquer the world had been ramping up, Effi had begun to suspect that Doppelgaenger didn't share the goals that the Thulians and her warriors believed in. That he was simply using the war and her cause as a vehicle for his own endeavors. That she couldn't figure out what those were infuriated her the most. She had decided early on that he needed to die; for her own satisfaction if nothing else. One couldn't keep something so dangerous and cold nearby, without peril. At least not forever. Killing him wouldn't be an easy task, however, and one that she wasn't sure she could take to completion. At least not on her own. Besides, he was useful... for now.

She paused for a moment, alone, as she rarely was, in one of the external corridors of the building devoted to all things martial *and* associated with humans. Despite her position, she was segregated with the rest of the non-Masters, a fact that she resented daily, but was also secretly happy for. She gazed out of a trapezoidal window, across the faintly moving mass of red and black vegetation to the one-way window across from hers. She could not see in—but if anyone stood there, he (or it) could most assuredly see out. There, across from her, was another building in which only Thulians and the mysterious Masters were allowed. Not even her thoughts could penetrate those walls. What went on in there? Whatever it was... it resulted in contradictory orders coming at regular intervals. Orders to pull back at the moment when victory was most assured. Orders to attack an insignificant target when a vital one was momentarily vulnerable. Insanity.

Those orders did not come from the Thulians, who shared their desire for conquest and the values Effi, Ubermensch, Eisenfaust, and Doppelgaenger had brought with them—and the dream of a Thousand-Year Reich. The Masters ruled over Thulians and humans alike...although Effi and the latest Ubermensch had been weaning some of the Thulians over to *their* way of thinking, of late. Effi didn't understand the Masters. That made her fear and hate them above all others. She had been overjoyed at their discovery when she and Heinrich had been brought here. The Thulians had offered her something to believe in again; *ubermenschen* in power and control of the entire world...in time. She had entreated with them, and convinced her new allies to "rescue" many of the best and brightest Germans before the final fall of the Third Reich. Unfortunately, there had been very few German *ubermenschen* left alive at that point in the war. That had disappointed Effi, at first, but it came to suit her purposes; she was part of an elite, now more than ever. It earned her the admiration of a large number of the Thulians, who counted no *ubermenschen* of their own in their ranks; they valued strength, and strength Effi had. In those early days the original—and thankfully sane—Ubermensch had done much to help her; Heinrich had further retreated from her after their "capture," as he called it. She suspected that he had come to know the truth about his selfless act to save her over the ocean; a small part of her mourned their lost love, for a time... but that part eventually faded. She had new purpose, now. If she couldn't save Germany and the *Vaterland*...she could at least save herself, and the world as hers to rule.

Over the years, her fame and popularity within Thulian society had grown and grown, until she had a large following among their population. With Ubermensch's help, she began to Germanize many of the Thulians. This led to the establishment and expansion of Ultima Thule, all with the seemingly tacit approval of the Masters; she had been able to use her authority granted by them to convince enough Thulians that it was for the war that was to come, to give a permanent base to launch attacks from. Her ultimate goals, however, were far more personal. She intended Ultima Thule to become the crown jewel of an empire that she would found on Earth, one that would make the Third Reich pale in comparison. She became even more fanatical about the idea after the original Ubermensch's death; at first only a suspicion, it soon grew to be outright truth in her mind that the Masters had played a part in his demise, which had come so suddenly and unexpectedly. His successor wasn't half the man that he had been... but he had been much more easily controlled. Another of the moves and tools of the Masters' that she had co-opted for her own purposes.

In time, Heinrich completed the break from her when he made his first attempt to escape. It had been futile, a move she had seen coming for years. By that point, she had precautions in place. He wouldn't even speak to her when he had been caught (an act that had cost the lives of no less than thirteen of her indoctrinated Thulians). She had wanted to keep him for herself, a personal prisoner that she would be able to... work on; it still irked her that she had never gotten past his mental defenses, save for the once. With time and appropriate "persuasion," she felt that she could succeed, and subsume his will. That was not to be; the Masters exercised their prerogative, taking possession of him for an undefined purpose. While it had initially infuriated her, she came to regard it as a small matter; she had more important things to worry about, after all. Heinrich would have just been another distraction.

Then, he made the second attempt, and this one succeeded, causing her and Doppelgaenger and the Thulian High Command to accelerate their plans for conquest. Or, more precisely, make the launch for conquest before they were quite ready. Even so, the Invasion had been a stunning success; most of their targets were obliterated with little meaningful opposition. The few pockets of resistance that did crop up suffered extensive losses; many of ECHO's metahumans, and those of the rest of the world, lost their lives standing up to Valkyria's forces. She had even been present to witness the final demise of Heinrich. Before she could relish the victory... all of them had been recalled, told to return to base and wait for further orders. *Why come all this way, crush our enemies... only to pull back at the last moment, before they capitulate?* Another nonsensical order from the Masters that she did not understand.

After that first glorious and short-lived worldwide battle, the only strikes that she had been allowed to make were small in scale and almost random. Some had purposes she could understand, while most seemed to be... harassment. *Recreation, to pass the time until... what?* Even with the losses they had suffered in the

Superstition Mountain Range, and especially at Ultima Thule, the combined might of the Thulians was more than enough to destroy any that opposed them...if they were utilized properly. She had railed at the High Command, to no purpose. Literally, to no purpose. When she started in on something they didn't want to hear, they somehow canceled out what she was saying, leaving her voiceless, moving her mouth randomly. It was then that she realized that she lived at their convenience; not as an equal ally, but as a pawn. If she wanted power, she was going to have to take it.

Fortunately, there was a substantial, and growing, contingent among the Thulian troops who felt exactly the same as she did. Ever since the first attack, she had been grooming them and their leaders. They would not put up with the leash holding them back for much longer.

And when they threw off their fetters, she would be the one leading them. From the vanguard. As was the only way for an *ubermensch*.

CHAPTER SIXTEEN

The Snake

MERCEDES LACKEY, DENNIS LEE
AND VERONICA GIGUERE

Alas, my predictive powers did not go quite as far as I liked. I could predict large moves coming... but not small. Not ones that affected only a single life.

If you want something done right, do it yourself, Dominic Verdigris told himself for about the tenth time.

This was, of course, no compensation for the fact that he was doing a servant's work right now. *Washing dishes!* Didn't the wretched woman have a dishwasher? She was one of the founding metas of ECHO! Couldn't this stupid facility be bothered to give her a freaking *dishwasher*?

He would have managed all this much better if *he* had been in charge.

On the other hand, their lack of common kitchen appliances was apparently matched by the lack of oversight when it came to their tenants, because he'd been able to have Dixie Belle's usual maid quietly put away last night, and had slipped in wearing a holographic disguise as her, without any effort at all.

While he scrubbed, she sat in the living room with some dog-eared book and one of those maddening news talk radio shows filling the quiet. The woman couldn't even occupy herself with soap operas and knitting like a normal geriatric. She hadn't said much to him all afternoon, other than a greeting at the door and an indication of the work in the kitchen. So, when she finally called from her seat, he realized that the opportunity might finally present itself.

"Millie? Could you bring in my tea when you finish?" She leaned forward and smiled toward the kitchen. "No rush, of course."

He bobbed his head in feigned deference. "Yes ma'am," he drawled. The vocal synthesizer matched the brief selection of speech he'd recorded in the moments before dear Millie's departure. "Just a minute."

The electric kettle might have been the only nod to real convenience on the woman's counter. A container with the words "Time for Tea" contained what he needed, and he put together the elderly meta's last request. He didn't need to do any more to the drink, as such base methods of poison were beneath someone of his intellect and resources. Interactions made toxicologists suspicious, and residues were something he never left behind.

"Here we go." Dominic scurried over to the chair, teacup on saucer.

And the cup and saucer fell from his hand, dropping to the carpet and bouncing, as the elderly woman seized his wrist in a grip of iron.

"Who are you," she asked calmly, "and what do you want?" The hand crushed his wrist, and he remembered in rising panic that Dixie Belle had been . . . and apparently still was . . . possessed of superior strength. "I knew you weren't Millie the minute you walked in the door, but I had to be absolutely sure. Millie would never have served me anything but sweet tea. Now who are you?"

In a panic, Dom shoved his hand in his pocket and came out with a hypospray. Before the old woman could react, he jammed it against the side of her neck and emptied the contents—more than enough to kill a dozen elderly metas, even if they'd had hyperacute resistance to drugs and poisons.

The combination took effect almost instantly. The hand on his wrist relaxed and let go, as Dixie Belle collapsed against the back of the sofa. A moment or two more, and it was over.

Still in a panic, Dom fled the scene. It looked natural enough. She could have been drinking her goddamn tea when the heart attack took her. He didn't want to spend another moment in that cursed house. Thank god he'd been wearing form-fitting fake hands with Millie's fingerprints on them.

I am never doing wetwork again, he swore as he got into Millie's beater of a Chrysler and it chugged away. *Why in hell couldn't Khanji have been available?* Then he remembered; he'd sent her to take care of something in Seattle. *Dammit. I need better help.*

The flicker of red and blue lights broke apart into a million tiny fragments against the pale yellow walls of his mother's kitchen. They complimented the patriotic decorations, white stars on a field of blue that provided a backdrop for dozens of framed photographs. Some in restored color, others in black and white, they told the story of the woman who had risen above so much in her service to her country and to ECHO. Some had nothing to do with the moniker the media had given her during wartime, a name meant to embrace the Hollywood starlet persona of a willowy blonde woman with blue eyes. They showed a long-legged teenager with tight curls and dark brown skin, her eyes full of laughter as she stood with a group of airmen from Tuskegee, Alabama.

That was her third favorite picture, she liked to tell people. Third, because his godfather Benny was in the picture. Third, because her second favorite was the picture they took of a handsome meta in red, white, and blue standing off to the side in perfect salute to them, and who insisted on saluting until the ranking airmen in the group dismissed him. Third, because she always said that her favorite was of him on the day he officially joined ECHO.

Ramona placed a hand on Pride's shoulder as he sat at his mother's modest kitchen table. His tea sat cold and untouched. Large calloused hands trembled against the blue and yellow placemats. He flinched at her touch, then dropped his chin to his chest and closed his eyes. She didn't need to be an empath to feel the grief that rolled off of him in waves. He had wept in silence as she drove him and Gilead to the gated community. They had met Blaze at the front door, her own tears soundless as she leaned against one of the nurses for support. Ramona had left Ms. Everitt to explain the details to Pride, while she and Gilead had gone to speak with the police.

"I was supposed to see her yesterday." Pride's voice cracked. "Didn't come by, though. We had that push on the southeast side, so I told Willa Jean to let her know I'd be by today for tea." He let out a long shuddering breath and shook his head from side to side. "I should have been here yesterday."

Ramona struggled to say something, but her vision blurred and her chest ached. Unable to speak, she wrapped both arms around his shoulders and rested her cheek on his head. "Both of us," she managed in a whisper. "Your mom was amazing."

Pride nodded, choking on whatever he wanted to say before simply nodding his head and giving himself over to his loss. She held him and gave herself permission to cry. There might not be time for that catharsis once Gilead emerged from her conversation with the coroner. As terrible as she knew it to be, Ramona wished for a heart attack or a stroke to have taken Dixie Belle from them. Something quick, something that would have kept ECHO's matriarch from suffering.

The attending officers allowed them their space and kept their voices to respectful whispers in the bedroom. Pride swallowed back some of his tears and started to stand. Ramona stood with him, ready to keep him from trying to follow Gilead, but he shook his head and motioned to the door. "I need to check on Willa Jean, see what she knows. See if she needs anything."

Ramona nodded and wiped her face with her sleeve. Pride wouldn't cry in front of his niece, but he would make time to grieve properly later. "All right. When do you want to know what we find out?"

He pressed his lips together, his eyes tracking the plainclothes detective who emerged from the room with a phone pressed to his ear. "Later. Give Parker the details, let her decide how to manage them." He gave Ramona a sad smile. "Standard protocol with family members, ma'am. You know the rest."

She nodded. One of the officers fell into step next to him, offering his condolences in a whisper and escorting him to the main office. Ramona waited until they turned the corner before entering the living room. Familiar and unpleasant smells met her nose, her gorge rising before a cool hand pressed two fingers to the inside of her wrist. The sensation subsided, a hint of eucalyptus and mint hanging in the air in front of her nose.

Gilead let go and folded her arms across her chest in cool examination of the scene. The ECHO doctor had nearly twenty years on Ramona and all of the battle-tested experience to go with it. She inclined her head toward the group near the sofa. "They wanted to wait for him to leave before they brought in homicide. The entire staff has been questioned, except for the one who usually came in for light housekeeping. They've got the local law enforcement looking for her. That group will run their own toxicology panels and report what they find, and I convinced them to look the other way while I got a sample."

"For?" Ramona closed her fingers around the plastic bag without understanding what to do next.

The doctor pursed her lips in mild annoyance. "Backup. You of all people should appreciate that. Officially, they'll rule it as a heart attack. I don't like spreading lies, but considering the circumstances..."

"It lets her pass in dignity," Ramona finished. Her throat felt tight again and she blinked back tears. "That works. See what else you can get from the group here, okay?" She didn't wait for Gilead to agree before heading for the front door. Others would handle the detective responsibilities; she had to speak with the head of ECHO.

Bella and Spin Doctor agreed that the best response involved an immediate statement that did not include Yankee Pride. The smooth public relations meta didn't leave a dry eye in the press room when he left, Ramona at his side with a wad of tissues in one hand. She slid into the waiting car and let out a long breath. Tears threatened to roll down her cheeks again, but she drew her lower lip between her teeth and let her body sag against the seat. Spin buckled in next to her and brushed the front of his tailored suit. In the driver's seat, Panacea offered her a sympathetic look and pulled out past a small crowd of waiting reporters.

"That won't be the last, I'm afraid. We're going to have to have a public memorial, something within the week." He produced a sleek tablet from an inside pocket and started consulting the screen. "We'll need to coordinate with the city, a few of the hotels. You'll need to speak with our Russian comrades to see if they'll want to send over any of their representatives from Moscow. Even though the dedication had a disastrous outcome, we did perfect the logistics of contacting our ECHO legacy members..."

Ramona could barely string three words together without crying, and the man next to her was coordinating travel arrangements for no fewer than three dozen people like it was just another conference. "Spin," she choked out. "Slow down."

He didn't respond, but tapped at the screen and studied whatever appeared. The car turned on Peachtree and headed for the ECHO campus. "They'll expect Pride to talk, possibly give the eulogy. Considering her service to the country, we might have to coordinate with Shreeves' people. Better to have them for security than Blacksnake, that's for sure." More tapping. "Might create a problem with the Russians, but I'm sure we can work that out."

"Spin!" For a brief moment, her eyes burned and her throat tightened. "The woman is dead, probably murdered in her own home, and you're acting like it's some social event!"

Spin Doctor stopped his frantic tapping and glanced out the car window. The Atlanta city traffic crawled past them, the midday rush made worse by the broken streets and destruction corridors. He let out a long sigh and rested both hands in his lap. "That's exactly what it is, for everyone but Pride, Blaze, and their close family. We're looking at the death of a legacy, but we're also looking at an opportunity to bring this city together. After the fall of Metis and the rise of the Thulians, the people of Atlanta..." He shook his head. "Not just Atlanta, but the entire nation, even the world. They're losing faith in us. Forgetting what ECHO and similar organizations could do and how they contributed during wartime."

Ramona opened and closed her mouth, unsure if she could respond with something calm and logical. Turning Dixie Belle's memorial into an opportunity to improve the image of ECHO felt disrespectful, even dirty, and she didn't want any part of it. She folded her arms across her chest and focused on the stream of cars traveling into the city. "So, you think that they think that we've failed the city, and our only chance for recovery is some grotesque media spectacle?"

He winced at her words. "Not how I would put it."

"You're just exploiting what she is, the same way that they did when she first joined ECHO." She pointed at his tablet. "You'll invite half of the city and make Pride talk about his mother just to show that there's some unity within the organization so the people can trust us again."

"Not quite." Spin consulted his tablet one more time before slipping it into his pocket and turning to face Ramona. He rested his elbows on his knees, perfectly manicured fingers folded before he spoke. "You're right that I'm planning a public memorial. Miss Dixie Belle was a legend in the organization, and her contributions had a lasting impact even in the present day. To not set aside time and resources to celebrate her memory would be suspicious and potentially disrespectful in the eyes of the public."

Ramona deflated and her arms slipped down to her side. He was right. This wasn't an extension of any metahuman ability, but the simple and difficult truth. Eyes closed, she let her chin rest against her chest. Trying to talk made the inside of her throat ache, but she made the words come out in spite of the pain. "So you plan the funeral and we send the invitations. We get our people and Shreeves' people to provide security, and we bring out the best of ECHO to honor the matriarch."

Spin acknowledged her assessment with a single nod, and the pair rode in silence the rest of the way to the ECHO campus. At some point, Ramona closed her eyes.

CHAPTER SEVENTEEN

O Fortuna

MERCEDES LACKEY, DENNIS LEE
AND VERONICA GIGUERE

*Have you ever been in a position where disaster struck
and you were utterly helpless? It was that moment that
made me wholly realize what it was like to be human.*

Of all of the members of ECHO, Vickie was, she had just realized,
probably the *least* affected by the death of one of its most iconic
members. Dixie hadn't been on Overwatch; Vickie had never met
her, and when those who had been wired for Overwatch Two
had gone on visits, Vickie had disabled the feed to her monitors
and had tried to keep her listening confined to cues she knew
were meant for her, which almost never happened, except with
Ramona. She kept recording, of course, in case anyone wanted to
refer to those visits, but they were personal, and although Pride
and Jamaican Blaze had not asked her to go private mode—they
might simply have forgotten her constant presence—she felt it
incumbent on her not to intrude.

So the memorial ceremony was just one more mission, so to
speak, and one in which there wasn't going to be too much she
would be asked to do. It was, in an odd way, restful.

Well, not restful. There was still that gnawing grief. Not for
Dixie. For Red. Yes, she had known he was a killer, not just
because of her background check on him but because of everything her keenly-honed survival instincts had told her about him.
She'd been terrified of him; he was feral, but you don't show a
feral thing your fear. Then, slowly, that had changed. *He* had

257

changed, in fundamental ways. Enough that fear had ebbed and
something else had moved in. At first, it had just been the need
to get his respect. Then...his trust. Then—

Well, "then" didn't matter anymore. Not that it ever had. The
aches inside had never mattered to anyone except her, no matter
what JM and Sera thought. Now the aches were just a little more
profound, joined by grieving for him. He'd gone distant. And
there was nothing she could do about that either. Feral again, in
a different way, and she knew that if you pressed a feral thing
too far, all you did was push it over the edge. Even though it
hurt to have him in her life in such a removed fashion, it hurt
her far more to even think of having him gone.

*I'd rather be miserable with him than miserable without him.
Even if "with him" is no more than a couple of sentences a day.*

Moved more by a vague sense of *what was appropriate* than
anything else, she'd dressed in an ECHO uniform and even
dabbed a bit of her amber scent on. It filled the little room, but
did nothing about the fact she had forgotten about breakfast.
Of course she'd forgotten about breakfast. Breakfast was the one
time he *might* make contact, if only to ask her for a music feed.

*So what would Dixie have said to me if I wanted to grab a slice
of pizza?* she wondered, as her stomach growled. *Huh. Probably "Go
for it, honeychile."* Still...that would mean leaving the keyboard
at a time when virtually everyone in ECHO, at least in Atlanta,
was in one place. Bad idea. Instead, she sighed, and reached for
another meal-in-a-can. And tried not to think about Red. Or not
to think about him *more*. Because she'd been wrong; she wasn't
the least affected. He was. This meant not one thing to a man
in a box with a multiple murder charge hanging over his head.

"You're wearing your broody face again." She glanced over at
Grey. He was perched on a spot of computer case that was exactly
the size of his seated "footprint." There was not a millimeter to
spare. *"You're thinking about Red."*

"Don't you dare go all touchy-feely and try and get me to
vent," she said sharply. The familiar flattened his ears against his
head, but wisely said nothing. She turned back to the monitors.

Just as Eight-Ball began screaming warnings.

She whipped around to face the stand-alone system so fast she
knocked over a row of empty meal cans, but before she could
even begin to read what was on the monitor, there was a huge

physical *and* magical explosion in the vicinity of the front door. The concussion rattled everything and actually knocked her chair over. She tried desperately to scramble to her feet, but those were caught in the nest of cables under the desk. Grey screamed from the next room, adding his battle howl to the shrieks from Eight-Ball, and as a shadow fell between her and the light from the door, she looked up to—

—blackness.

When Bella entered the command center, Bulwark was watching the recovered tapes. Again. Part of her ached for him. Part of her was angry that he was punishing himself like this. And part of her was in despair, because here it was again. She was in competition with a ghost.

He turned with a feigned start, and turned off the replay. He knew she was there, of course. She rarely surprised him. The thing about Bull that people often overlooked was his ability to read his surroundings and people. Bull had a way of staring into the heart of a person. In return, he offered little, even to an empath, and it was infuriating at times just how difficult it was to read him. Still, she wouldn't have it any other way. She treasured how little of him she could pick up just by proximity. She had to do things the hard way, old school, and she was loving it.

Except maybe now. *How can I compare to his dead wife?* If she could read him, maybe she could figure out what to say, to do. But she couldn't read him, and his body language only told her he had closed himself up behind his walls again. It was a new lesson. She could pick up on surface emotions, even basic thoughts. That was what she did. With Bull, she had to relearn that ancient art of conversation, reading signs from body language, take hints from their shared chemistry, and she couldn't have picked a tougher subject to start with. It was a challenge, and Bella loved a good challenge. So she began as she always did. Pick a play, carry it through, watch where the situation would go, and just go with it.

She strolled up next to him, gave him a knowing glance, and keyed the order to begin the playback again.

They stared up at the monitor, and watched in silence as the painfully reconstructed feed gave them enhanced images from partially recovered video files. Security reels dating back to the Invasion of the Vault.

All right. Where to start? Try to avoid anything that might turn into a fight... "You know, you never did tell me how these came to light," she said.

"Jensen," Bull said. "He finally managed to have these restored. Took him awhile too, the...bandits who corrupted these files really knew what they doing."

Bella simply nodded. *Try to avoid anything that might turn into a fight...don't mention Red...don't mention Red...*

She'd already filed a long, long deposition, one she hoped Bull wasn't going to find out about. In Red's favor of course; how she, as both the CEO of ECHO and as someone who examined ECHO personnel psychologically on a regular basis, felt that the "Red Djinni" in those tapes was a vastly different person now from the one who had risked his life so many times she had lost count...but Red had killed ECHO personnel, and they now had hard proof of it. She knew they couldn't just let that go, but she knew ECHO needed him and his skills and she was of the opinion that much of what he was enduring was ample punishment in and of itself. She knew exactly what Jensen was going for, here—not the death penalty, not incarceration, but something crueler—to grab Red and stick a lot of monitoring equipment and maybe a bomb in his head and put him on some sort of "suicide squad." And in between missions, lock him in some deep solitary confinement hole with nothing more than a bed and a toilet. She didn't have any illusions on how long he'd stay sane under those conditions.

For now, the Djinni was sitting comfortably, or not, in a secure cell in Top Hold. She secretly had limited internet access piped into his cell, giving him a window to the world outside if not a way to interact with it. And Vickie was probably doing something for him via Overwatch Two. If he was letting her. She wasn't officially asking so wouldn't officially have to say something about it.

Then again, Vickie could probably hide every damn thing she did, if she chose to. Bella was privy to Vickie's feelings for the Djinni. It was an occupational hazard, the whole empath deal. When you spent enough time with people, even when you purposely blocked things out, some things were too powerful to go unnoticed. The girl had it bad for Red, and it was as clear as air that she didn't want *anyone* to know. Especially not him. Sera had said as much, in her still oblique way of talking. *Vickie does not wish you to be aware of what you already knew,* with a significant side glance out the window at the Parkour course, where Djinni was sitting atop the climbing wall, berating trainees. *And less so does she wish him to be aware.*

The video feed continued. Bella and Bull watched as a car slammed through the broken defenses of the Vault and crashed into the entrance bay. Figures rose from the wreckage, spraying bullets from automatic rifles, and Bella winced. The argument was inevitable. They had both watched this footage, many times. It was inevitable, what was to come.

"I can't stay long, you know," she said. "The memorial is starting soon. I have to be there."

"I know," Bulwark said, continuing to stare at the monitor.

"You could come with me," she ventured. "You *should* be there, you know."

"Someone should stay here, at Command," he replied curtly. "Give my regards to Pride, please."

"You were his friend a long, long time before I was," she pointed out, one last-ditch effort to get him to pull away from this self-flagellation for a few damn hours. She felt her temper rising. He wasn't stupid. He knew what he was doing to himself, and he was doing it anyway. Why? So he could justify the crucifixion of someone *else* he'd called friend?

"You know me," Bull said. Finally, he looked at her, and for a moment she marveled at the pleasure of seeing something new in him. It was a treat, every time, even now, as his eyes spoke of love and betrayal and all the mixed-up confusion in between. "Or at least, you're learning to. You don't think I know, but I do. And I love you more for it, with each passing day. This is something so new for you it seems feverish, uncontrollable, wild and exhilarating. Unfortunate, that the timing is so rotten, the situation so devastating. But this is us, things need to be attended to. And I, I'm not really sure where to go from here. But you must know by now, that this is something I have to take care of myself, and that you can't assist me. That you can't fix me."

"I don't..." she began, and then stopped. Because that would have been a lie. She *did* want to "fix" him. She wanted him to stop obsessing about this.

She wanted him to forgive Red. She wanted everything to go back to the way it had been before Jensen found those damned tapes. That was a neat trick in itself. The day of the Invasion, so much of ECHO from its infrastructure, personnel, to unfathomable reservoirs of data had been so badly crippled, Bella wondered how Jensen had known to put so much of their resources in resurrecting this, the lost video feeds from the Vault. What had tipped him off? Something, or someone, had to have given him direction. Someone who knew about the Djinni's whereabouts that day, a day which had ultimately taken him to the other side of the city with Howitzer, Amethist's remaining trainee...

"You do," he continued. "I understand. I'm a trainer, and I know that urge to simply step in and fix mistakes myself. Most times, you just can't. People have to work things out for themselves. You just need to be there in case they fall, or just so they know they're not alone."

"And that's the problem," she said, the words escaping her before she could stop them. *Oh, what the hell. Get it in the open. The Purple Elephant.* "You are *never* alone. She's always there, always at your back, always between you and anyone else. Always perfect, and yes, I get it, the dead are always perfect because that's how we want to remember them, I understand that, but *she's always there and always perfect and always will be the one you couldn't protect.* She gets between you and me. And now she's getting between you and Red."

Bull sighed. "You read Jensen's report, I take it."

"Of course I did," Bella snapped. "It's practically burned into my brain. *Your wife* had a relationship with Red. Practically out of one of Vickie's metahuman romance books, it was; first enemies, then partners, then more than partners, then *poof,* unexplained blowup, she drowns her sorrows in being a hero, he drowns his in becoming a master thief. They even fought again, years later, *while you were married*, and you never knew. She never told you, and neither did he." She paused, as she felt a rare flash of pain escape his defenses.

"You feel betrayed," she said quietly. "By both of them."

Bull's jaw tightened, then relaxed, and when he turned to her it was like he was barely there. "Amethist was far from perfect," he said, his voice low and empty. "She was willful, stubborn and at times perhaps too self-sacrificing to be considered healthy. Some might argue that I look for that in a woman. But you're wrong to think that you need to compete with her, that I draw parallels and compare and contrast your qualities with hers. I don't do that, and I never will. You are not her, and she could never be you. But yes, I feel betrayed. She should have told me. That she felt the need to keep something from me, it hurts."

"And Red?" Bella asked.

"Red Djinni is on the opposite end of the spectrum from perfect," Bull replied.

"You know what I mean," Bella said. "Do you feel betrayed by him?"

"Betrayal requires trust," Bull said. "I don't know if I have ever trusted him."

"Oh, what a load of crap," she snapped. "You trusted him the day you went after him with Vickie and got him out of Doppelgaenger's claws. If you hadn't, you'd have coldcocked Vix and let DG have him. He didn't know enough then to hurt us, and if you'd had the slightest doubt about where his loyalties were, you'd have sloughed him like dead weight, because at that point we couldn't afford to keep anyone we couldn't trust."

"He was a calculated risk..." Bull began.

"You can shove that too," Bella snarled. "You know I can't read you, but you would be surprised how much I've picked up over the last few months. You can hide behind that 'calculated risk' speech all you want, but if that were true, then all your relationships would have to be calculated risks, wouldn't they? Is that what I am? Are you really running the math in your beefy head when it comes to you and me?"

"Of course not," Bull answered. "There is no math for what we have. Either we work or we don't, only time will tell."

She felt her cheeks flushing with—rage? Frustration? Well, if he wouldn't admit it, she'd shove it right out in the middle of the room and make him stare at it. "It'd take a blind man not to see what you're doing. You keep looking at those tapes. You can't help yourself. You're looking for something you think maybe you saw, and are afraid you saw. You're looking for something Jensen *wants* you to see, because that would detonate a big fat nuke in your emotions that will give Jensen everything he wants."

She reached down to the monitor controls and sped through the playback until a grainy feed appeared. It was a heavily damaged account of the final battle within the Vault, Kriegers versus metas, including Red Djinni and Amethist. Bella watched as Red dove to a fallen, headless body and began rummaging through pockets. Amethist leapt after him, shouting something. And there, as it always did, the screen fuzzed out for a few seconds. When the stream returned, the Djinni stood over a pile of ash where Amethist should have been, barking orders to the remaining metas. It was only a few seconds of lost visual, but they were precious seconds.

"Did Red do it, did Red push her into the line of fire?" Bella demanded. "Did she jump in to shield him, and if so, *why?* Or was it just shitty luck? You *know* which of those things Jensen wants you to see! He wants you to see the man you trusted as your ultimate betrayer. And you, you keep watching this, trying to find clues that just aren't there. You're not a psychic, Gairdner. You're not going to pull answers off that tape. But you *will* convince yourself you have, if you keep doing this!"

She took a hasty breath and continued. "You know what you have to do, *who* you have to ask. So why don't you? Why don't you just go to him and find out? Talk to him, and find out what you really want to know. Don't let Amethist stand between you. And for *God's* sake, don't let *Jensen.*"

He opened his mouth. She ran over the top of him. "Go. Find out the answer for yourself and don't let anyone, not Jensen, not *me*, keep you from the truth. *Is Red your friend?*" And she turned on her heel and stalked out.

"I can barely remember a time I understood this need to honor the dead."

Harmony shifted slightly on her bed, drawing her knees closer to her as she gave Scope a lifeless smile. Scope gave her an impatient nod, and leaned back against the wall of the cell.

"Don't much see the point?" Scope asked. "What, with you being . . . you?"

Her visits to Harmony's cell had been growing more frequent of late. She found herself increasingly irritable, jittery, sometimes even bordering on pain. This wasn't exactly new, but the emptiness she felt before was superficial by comparison. She recognized it for what it was—she needed a fix. Again, nothing new, but instead of reaching for a bottle of booze or pills, she found her legs carrying her again and again to Harmony's cell. She realized with a start that she hadn't popped a pill in weeks. No pills, no whiskey, nothing that dulled the pain. Antidepressants were a thing of the past. She had found something new, and what Harmony offered made her brief but immemorable descent into pharmaceutical bliss seem stale and cheap. Here, she felt alive. She danced through memories and was infused with a pure energy that held stirrings of hope, of love and innocence. At least for a little while. Dimly, she recognized how far she had fallen, how much of her soul Harmony now claimed. She didn't care. She wanted Harmony to suffer; she wanted Harmony dead, but not as much as she wanted what Harmony had to offer. A touch of life, of the old Scope, a connection with a time when she was whole.

"Oh, I do understand rituals and the need for them," Harmony said, her lips curling into a smirk. "But this emotional attachment, it's something like a dream. The more I try to truly comprehend it, it slips away. I try to remember, and it's like I'm closing my fist around water. But I should never worry about such things, hmmm? Not with you here, my dear Scope. I can always dream, and feel, and live, through you. All I need to do, is let you remember..."

Scope gasped as Harmony began. It always began the same way. A gentle caress along the periphery of thought; a whisper, a chuckle, and then Harmony plunged in. A part of Scope cried out, every time, at what was a complete violation of herself. The first touch was always gentle, but it was a thin veil covering the vicious nature of the beast, and once the beast was sure of its prey, it was merciless. The first time had been different, of course. You made the first time easy on the mark, any pusher would tell you that. She remembered feeling bewildered, as if lost in a dream, with an odd curiosity pulling her forward to watch, breathless, what would happen next. And she had reveled in it, in the way it fed her joy, how it gave her power and a fierce kind of hope that she could again feel something akin to purpose and drive. It was in that moment that Scope had fallen. Ever since, Harmony had felt little need to be gentle. The heartless witch could have torn her mind to tatters, rendered her memories down to a pasty sludge, with little resistance. After the first time, Scope hardly cared. It wasn't so long ago that she would have rather died than be the spineless meat puppet, caught so helplessly in Harmony's grasp. Now, none of that mattered. Here, there was comfort, happiness, and even occasional bliss. So what if she gave up anything and everything she had once held so dear, had fought for with a resolute pride that had once stared down an entire town of bigoted, ignorant hillbillies determined to put her skinny, orphaned ass in its place? That had been a lifetime ago. That was another person. She had nothing now, and this... this was something. It was all she had left.

And Harmony knew it, of course. There was little need to ease her thrall into the process, not anymore. For Scope, there was almost comfort in the cold certainty of the ritual. These days, there was no appetizer before the main course, no need for utensils or table manners, there was only the brutal hunger and the mindless feast. By the time Scope had truly realized what Harmony was doing, it had been far too late. Something in the act had numbed her to anything remotely resembling the horror one might have felt on being fed upon. It left her open to anything, completely vulnerable, and yet she had lost the ability to care. She had a vague sense of something terrible waiting in the wings, something stark and vile, ravenous, muttering dreadful thoughts and urges that she could almost hear. Yet, despite the poisonous nature of the seductive murmurs in the back of her mind, there was something almost childlike, even pitiable, about them. They cried out for something lost, something vital, with words that seemed alien yet strangely familiar. Was this Harmony, then? Was this who she really was, so lost in the hunger to bare her true self to her victim? Again, Scope was past caring, yearning instead for the light, to shroud herself in memory, of her past, of him...

With a cry, she felt it all fall away and Harmony turned away from her.

"No!" Scope screamed. "Not yet! Bring it back! I...nuh... need it..."

She collapsed, sobbing, as it left her, again just an empty shell.

"Soon enough," Harmony said, rising up from her bed. "I've had my fill, and I think it's just about that time."

Scope rubbed at her eyes with shaking hands, and peered helplessly up at Harmony.

"Time for what?" she muttered, and cringed as her nails drew blood from her cheek.

"I believe I've had my fill of this place," Harmony said. "I've paid my dues, wouldn't you say, dear?"

✧　　✧　　✧

They had all been trying to get into his head, of course. Who was he, really? Someone who had fought at their side this long, and they were just realizing they didn't really know him. He was a chameleon, was it so odd?

Red Djinni looked around at the confines of his new cell. It was bare, of course. Nothing but the minimal necessities would do in Top Hold. Just enough to keep the inmates alive. At least he didn't have meta abilities they had to compensate for. No chilled, scorch-proof environment to stave off fire damage. Nothing in the way of excessive shielding for energy blasts or superstrength. Just a man and his faces. Throw in some high-security tech to permit the passage of only key personnel and guards and voila, Djinni-proof. They knew he was a thief. Standard locks were out of the question, easily picked by someone with enough time, skill and patience. Sitting here in a bare cell with nothing but a simple touchscreen by the door and the remains of his breakfast atop a cold metal tray, Red had nothing but time.

Bella had been by, of course. She had asked him, straight out, if he was guilty of the charges. Scope had come by, once, and had said nothing. She had simply stood there, staring at him, as if waiting for a confession. Mel's visits were somewhat more cordial, if strained. None of them came inside. Why would they? They didn't know him, after all, not if any of those horrific things they said he had done were true. He barely acknowledged any of them, even Mel. Was he guilty? Yes he was, of all of it, but he wasn't ready to volunteer that information, not yet. He was steeling himself, readying himself for that inevitable day when he would be dragged in shackles into a court of law and shown the evidence. When he would look out at a sea of comrades and feel it from each of them... how he had betrayed them.

That wasn't the worst of it, though. Victrix hadn't stopped by. He couldn't blame her, the lady was busy. Of all of them, she probably knew best that he wasn't a saint, but he was forced to admit it bothered him. Did Vix think of him differently now, like they all did? You have a friend, you do your best by him, and then one day you learn there's real, hard evidence that he's a killer. How do you feel then? They had spoken a few times, he still had the implant after all, but he had heard something in her voice. He took it for doubt, and yes, it bothered him. A lot. He didn't know quite what to make of that. Theirs had been such a messed-up relationship, right from the start. What they finally had, had been built over time. It was trust, fondness, sure, but a solid trust in a partner that had your back. He just wasn't sure if he had that anymore, or even deserved it. He thought of what he had written for her, and how she might react to it. The email sat, saved and ready to send with a simple touch of a prompt on the touchscreen. He fought with the decision daily. He just wasn't ready yet.

"Red?"

He glanced over at the touchscreen, and saw Mel's earnest face looking back at him.

"Go away, Mel," he said. "Go on, get away from me. I've got nothing new to say."

"Ain't no shame in reruns," she drawled back. "They're predictable. Besides, what else are you gonna do?"

"Why are you even here?" Red asked angrily. "Haven't you heard, it's all over the feeds. They've got hard proof. I'm *that* guy. You didn't sign on for this. I'm just going to drag you down."

"So now it's about my reputation? Bullshit," she snorted. "Try another reason for caring about my virtues, 'cause I ain't buying that one."

"Well, this isn't about you, darlin'," Red chuckled. "This one's all about me, and what I'm due. And lord... it's finally happening. Fooled myself into thinking I was past it. Gave it another try, and I actually thought it would stick this time. I mean, it was working! I felt it. I was different. Hadn't felt anything like it for a long, long time. But I guess I can't escape certain things about myself, and I'm not talking about past crimes. I mean me. I was the guy, *that* guy, and then I wasn't. But I guess you can't run from your true self forever."

"But you think everyone else should run from you?" She looked away from the screen. "You want me to run? Or was being with me part of your running from yourself?"

"You think you know me so well..." Red shrugged.

"Oh, you'd be surprised, *cher,*" Mel said.

"You don't know shit!" Red snapped. "We've had our fun, haven't we? You and I? Good tumble in the sack, shared some feelings, some history, had a few laughs. It was grand, but I think we both knew it would end this way."

Mel narrowed her eyes. "I knew some. I didn't have any fantasies about you being some perfect knight in shining armor, 'cause hell, you're far from perfect. But I've seen enough of you to know—"

"You've seen the surface, and I think you know it." Red turned and favored her with a pitying look. "You ever sink a weapon into someone for no other reason than the briefest glimpse of your true self? I have. And let me tell you, I felt nothing while I was doing it. Not a thing. I was *ending* a life. I didn't care about who they were, I was focused on one thing. They saw my face, my real face. They now had something that was precious to me, and I couldn't let that go. So I fixed it, and I felt nothing. No joy, no relief, no guilt. I felt nothing. I was nothing."

She stared at him, jaw clenched. Seconds ticked by in an eternity. "So, nothing," she said in a hoarse voice. "All right, then. Nothing."

He gave her a wry smile. "Still love me, baby?"

"I'm still here, ain't I?" She didn't smile back.

"Your funeral," Red shrugged. "I don't know if the guy you think you knew is coming back. I think he's... *WHAT THE HELL IS THAT?*"

A Klaxon shattered the air in the cell; a similar one was going off inside his ear.

"Attention all ECHO personnel. All nonessential personnel report to the briefing room..."

CHAPTER EIGHTEEN

Requiem

MERCEDES LACKEY, DENNIS LEE
AND VERONICA GIGUERE

How do you humans endure such helplessness and still remain sane? You must be so very strong...

The gathering of ECHO personnel and government brass made Spin Doctor's planned memorial a security and logistics nightmare. The catastrophe that had collapsed the MARTA tunnels in downtown Atlanta and made more ECHO funerals necessary had remained fresh in the minds of the public. Those who braved the crowds went through a multitude of security checkpoints, but they still came en masse to pay their respects to Dixie Belle. For hours, people from all walks of life filed into the Georgia Dome to walk past the simple coffin draped with an American flag, guarded by ECHO personnel in full dress uniform. Some paused for a brief moment while others simply shuffled past in respectful silence. More than a few small children accompanied parents or grandparents, following the adults' somber lead.

By the middle of the afternoon, the only empty seats in the megastadium were on the stage or in the areas reserved for government dignitaries. Ramona stayed close to the tunnel entrance, making sure that she had an eye on Pride at all times. President Shreeves would take his seat shortly before the ceremony began, but his people continued to survey their assigned areas and chat with their security coordinators. She hadn't seen Spin Doctor since that morning, but the low buzz of chatter on Overwatch let her know that everything was still proceeding on schedule.

At least the weather had cooperated for the memorial. The "old guard" of ECHO had come, their section guarded by several members of the CCCP. Soviette stood in dress uniform next to Chug, whose bulk made it impossible for anyone to even consider approaching the dignitaries. Six of the ECHO canines that reported to Leader of the Pack padded up and down the aisles, respectfully alert to any possible threat. A few shadows swooped across the sky, Corbie coordinating the aerial reconnaissance even as helicopters swung over the stadium in long looping patterns.

No John Murdock or Seraphym. They had been sent after a frantic call from Venezuela, asking for their help in protecting a cadre of Metisians. The few metahumans in that country had barely repulsed one effort to take or kill them, and they did not think they were capable of handling a second. With their new supersonic flight, they could be there in mere hours, faster even than jet transport. They'd left shortly before Dixie Bell had been found dead.

Ramona wished they were here. *I'd feel a lot better seeing those fireballs in the sky.*

"It is a shame that she could not be here to see such a display, but I am certain that she knew of this city's love for her." The warm Russian baritone startled Ramona such that she felt the metal rise to the surface of her skin. She turned to see the older gentleman in a Cold War-era CCCP dress uniform standing close to the tunnel. He smiled, and she could see hints of the same wolfish expression that Natalya sometimes wore. "Then again, it is unlikely she would have wanted such grandeur for herself."

Ramona opened her mouth to speak, but Pride had overheard the comment. She watched him force his shoulders back before tucking the handwritten notes for the eulogy into his jacket pocket. "Unlikely, but she always did what was necessary. 'Sacrifice before self,' those were her words."

"A pity that she had to sacrifice so much." The first Red Saviour bowed at the waist and offered his hand to Yankee Pride. "Please accept my nation's condolences on the loss of such a remarkable woman."

Pride accepted the handshake and nodded, his words absent of the emotion that had overwhelmed him for much of the week. "Thank you, sir."

The Russian meta didn't let go. "And my sympathies on your

loss, Benjamin. Your mother and I may have not always been on the same sides of the negotiating table, but I remember her spirit fondly. The only pity was that she was not born Russian." He winked before releasing the hand.

Ramona breathed a small sigh of relief when Pride's mouth quirked into the faintest of smiles. "White and blue complimented her red better than gold, sir."

"That they did." He nodded at the tunnel. "I will take my seat before the memorial begins, but there are many good stories to share some day, if you would like."

They watched him walk out onto the field, Pride letting out a shaky breath. She patted him on the shoulder. "One more hour, maybe two. You will ride with Spin and me to Marietta National for the private ceremony, and we'll fall apart after that. I promise a stupid sloppy drunkfest if that would dull any of the pain."

He wiped at his eyes. "Momma did like you, you know. She said you had something good, something smart. She'd definitely approve of that plan."

Ramona started to say something, but Spin's voice slid into her ear. "Two minutes, ladies and gentlemen. The President's detail is moving into position, after which Steel Maiden will position opposite the CCCP detail at the dais. We'll have the color guard come in, followed by Reverend Freeman and Yankee Pride. We're ready?"

She waited for others to chime in first before giving her go-ahead. "Affirmative, Spin."

"Excellent. Ladies and gentlemen, only our very best for Miss Dixie Belle."

The weather was not cooperating with the memorial. Instead of appropriately overcast skies and a biting mist of rain, a cool breeze accompanied warm sunshine that made the Georgia afternoon nothing less than pleasant. From where she stood, Ramona couldn't see an empty seat in the entire stadium. The contrails from the aerial salute had faded to pale wisps while notable members of ECHO and the Atlanta community took their turns in Spin Doctor's carefully orchestrated memorial service. Both Yankee Pride and Jamaican Blaze sat on the dais with the pastor of the church that Dixie Belle had attended every Sunday since her retirement from full service with ECHO. Bella sat on Pride's left, blue hands folded in her lap and a calm expression on her face. Ramona had little doubt that

Bella's projective empathic power was the only reason that Willa Jean had managed to slow her tears to a trickle.

The cameras panned across the assembled guests during the speeches, transmitting their reactions to the big screens circling the stadium and the television stations carrying the memorial on the live feeds. Knowing Spin's planning, Ramona guessed that it was likely being livestreamed through any number of online sites. It would be impossible for anyone in Atlanta's metro area to not see the memorial.

Anything to keep a positive image of ECHO in the public's mind, she thought. She took a deep breath and glanced at the groups of metahumans in the first few rows on the field. Some of the most stoic souls did little to hide their grief, while others maintained their composure with a quiet dignity she hadn't thought possible. Motu and Matai wept openly, tears streaming down their cheeks when an elderly Samoan gentleman stood and told a story about his first encounter with Dixie. None of the assembled CCCP members openly wept, but Ramona caught Pavel sniffle once or twice. Had he ever met Dixie Belle? He was likely old enough, but she hadn't thought to ask the Bear about his service during what they all called the Great Patriotic War. Perhaps one of these days...

The feed to the screen flickered once, then returned to scanning the crowd. Although most of the metahumans wore formal dress uniforms or simple black suits, the civilians who had come to pay their respects had worn red, white, and blue. It made for a decidedly celebratory atmosphere in spite of the somber afternoon. She wasn't sure if that was something else that Spin had communicated, but it definitely worked. *Dixie would have liked it*, she thought.

The camera panned again, the image showing the twins again. Reverend Freeman had taken the podium for the last of the introductions while Yankee Pride wiped his eyes and smoothed the front of his suit. Spin had insisted that he give the eulogy, that it would demonstrate strength in the midst of a sorrowful event. Ramona worried that he wouldn't manage more than a few words before breaking down, but eventually it had been two against one, and she agreed to stand nearby.

She glanced at the twins, then back to the screen. The image above the field showed Motu with his arm around his brother's shoulders. Forty feet away from where she stood, Motu leaned forward, his head bowed and elbows on his knees. Ramona swallowed and brought her hand up to wipe at her eyes. "Overwatch," she murmured. "There's a delay in the cameras. We might want to check—"

Ramona straightened up as dots of black and gray appeared in the field of red, white, and blue within the Georgia Dome. Her HUD began to flicker in the lower left corner of her vision, and she immediately glanced at Bella. Her posture hadn't changed, but she inclined her head toward Ramona. "Something's in the grass," Ramona murmured over the secure channel. "We've got over seventy-one thousand people in this stadium, and there's something in the grass."

"I see it," Bella breathed. "Overwatch?"

No reply came over the proprietary channel. Ramona switched to the general channel used by most of ECHO. "Overwatch, please reply."

"Sam Colt, ma'am. Overwatch Two isn't responding."

"We've got unknowns in the area among civilians. I need you to appropriate any and all security cameras within the Georgia Dome and a three-mile radius to see what you can learn about who's crashing the memorial." Ramona shifted away from the dais to get a better view of the stadium seating. She counted at least fifteen figures in black combat fatigues in one aisle. While she couldn't see any weapons, her implants told her otherwise.

"Ma'am, we're experiencing an unknown interference with the cameras at the Georgia Dome. It appears that they're using an iterative encryption algorithm, and we can't get in as easily as we'd like. It's going to take more than a few ticks."

More of the assembled metas had noticed what Ramona and Bella had seen in the stands. Even Yankee Pride, who had spent much of the first five minutes of his mother's eulogy with his head bowed over the podium, had slowed his speech as more of the mercenaries filled the aisles of the stadium. Finally, he looked out over the crowd and took a deep breath.

"Gentlemen," he drawled in a tone equal parts anger and grief, "is there something that you need during this somber celebration of my mother's life?"

"Oh, *they* don't need anything," came the reply through the stadium's speakers. Seconds later, the image of Dominic Verdigris appeared on every screen in the Georgia Dome. He stood in front of an enormous banner for the local football franchise inside what looked like an opulent suite. "On the other hand, I have a few requests to which you and your extended meta family will be only too happy to acquiesce."

Given her novel metahuman ability, Ramona considered if she actually could spit nails if she got angry enough. This would be the ideal scenario, with Verdigris' grinning countenance looming over the assembled masses gathered to pay their respects to Dixie Belle. Pride stood at the podium, gauntlets pulsing a brassy golden color.

Bella stood behind him, eyes scanning the crowd while carrying on a rapid-fire conversation via Overwatch. "Total count of the armed mercenaries, boys? We need precise numbers and we need them now."

"Ma'am, we've managed to appropriate a third of the cameras in the field area and around the perimeter. Last count gives us nearly three hundred, but we can't see anything on the inside."

"Any luck on interrupting the feed that's projecting Verdigris to the masses?" Bella growled the name. "The sooner we get him off the air, the better."

Granting Bella's wish wasn't going to happen anytime soon. Verdigris smiled and gestured to the tens of thousands of people below. "It seems only fitting that on a day when we celebrate everything that Dixie Belle did for ECHO and the good people of Atlanta, we should consider how those people who represent her legacy can serve those who came to honor her memory." He clasped his hands in front of his face, the knuckle of a forefinger tapping thoughtfully against his nose. "I'm sure that you, her son, will appreciate this gesture."

"Today, I am asking the metahumans of ECHO to consider the ultimate sacrifice in order to save the people who have looked to them for protection. The individuals stationed at strategic locations throughout the stadium are here to provide a measure of persuasion." The smirk returned, tugging the corners of his mouth into a wide smile.

Pride gripped the sides of the podium. The aura from his gauntlets gave his face an angry glow. "And what makes you think that any meta here wouldn't put themselves between your thugs and these innocents? It's happened before, hasn't it? You use your personal army to hold the city hostage and inflict pain to satisfy your own twisted agenda."

The image on the jumbotron smiled and wagged a finger at the assembly. "No fair changing the subject, Benjamin. We're talking about the present situation and the lives of more than seventy thousand people. Given those numbers, it would behoove you to pay attention."

"Ma'am, it looks like the system is actively blocking our attempts. It's gonna take a bit longer to find where this snake is hiding."

"We need this shut down yesterday, and we need control of the cameras," Bella ground out between clenched teeth. "Keep him talking, Pride."

The gauntlets around his forearms pulsed. "All right, Mr. Verdigris. You have our undivided attention. The stage is yours."

The image on the screen feigned embarrassment. "Why, Yankee Pride. Such flattery. Now you've made me camera-shy. I can't possibly think straight, knowing that all of Atlanta is staring." The screen winked out although the speakers continued to broadcast his voice. "I'll just have to trust that my melodious narrative will compel you to listen."

"Spit and horsehair, it's disappeared! We nearly had it!"

"We're listening," Pride snarled. "You have our undivided attention."

"How gracious of you. Now, as I said before, today is the day when the metahumans of ECHO will have the unparalleled opportunity to make the ultimate sacrifice to save the people of Atlanta. Should any of you refuse, each one of the uniformed individuals around the facility will execute a person every minute, making this funeral more than just a single-person remembrance." Verdigris paused for effect. Ramona imagined him leaning back and steepling his fingers beneath his smarmy smile.

"That's at least three hundred civilians, based on what we could get before the cameras were compromised. Still working on getting that feed back, ma'am."

Pride continued to glare at the empty jumbotron screen. "And what is this ultimate sacrifice that you envision? Each one of the members of ECHO has placed themselves in harm's way in order to preserve the safety of these people, or have you forgotten the events of the past few years?"

"Oh, I'm certain that no one in this proud assembly could

ever forget the day that an alien invasion targeted cities that were chock full of metahumans representing different organizations and government interests. There they were, minding their own business, enjoying a frosty beverage at the local watering hole while watching whatever sportsball team they support, when suddenly they were the bloody bystanders in a war that they couldn't begin to fight or even comprehend." The screen flickered to show footage from the very first Invasion, images from around the world when the Death Spheres and Kriegers tore through cities and decimated industry and commerce centers. Around the stadium, a low murmur provided the soundtrack for the otherwise silent film.

"To be fair, the people of Atlanta have sacrificed plenty for metahuman security," Verdigris offered, "which is why my proposal shouldn't take too much contemplation. You see, I'm not asking you to die. Not all over, at least." Another long pause gave those assembled time to whisper among each other. Ramona could see a few of the CCCP in attendance conferring among themselves, the rapid-fire chatter of Russian in her ear lending a second layer to the conversation. "You'll get to keep that which makes you human."

"He can't," Bella said. "That can't be possible. Gentlemen, where in the hell is my video feed and why can't we get a location on this slimy parasite three minutes ago?"

Ramona didn't catch the Colt Brothers' response. The whirring sound of the dome moving along the multiple tracks had caught the attention of the entire stadium, and the sky slowly disappeared as the steel and polymer construction slid into place. The post-Invasion modification had been a priority for the city to bring in more events, but Ramona found herself wishing for an open sky and a torrential downpour.

"Provided that you agree to this noble sacrifice, this venue will slowly fill with a highly potent chemical, dispensed in a manner that, for obvious reasons, I will keep to myself. Patent pending, you know. This chemical will be completely harmless to those regular Joes and Janes, but it will quickly and effectively nullify the effects of metahuman genes that any of you possess. You'll live," Verdigris added. "Of course, if your non-meta bodies are unable to withstand the physical consequences of immediate genetic suppression, I can't make any promises."

The jumbotron flickered, the image of a smoking downtown cityscape providing a backdrop to the challenge. It was impossible to ignore the bodies littering the street in the foreground. "So, your minute begins when I finish speaking, Yankee Pride. Everyone must agree, or it's three hundred of these likely expendable normals to fill the morgues of Atlanta every minute. How do you feel about signing that many death sentences, *Benjamin?*"

A dull roar grew to a shouting match, the assembly shouting at the field as the seconds ticked by. In contrast, Overwatch stayed silent. Ramona glanced at Pride, who had not moved from the podium. Nearby, Bella glared at the screen with a mixture of hate and resolve. A quick review of the other metas on the ground showed similar expressions, fear being nearly absent from them.

There would be no discussion. There would be no vote.

"We agree to your terms." Pride's voice boomed over the speaker, his response rendering the crowd silent. The armed mercenaries did not move from their posts. "We agree."

"Of course you do."

A sickly-sweet odor wafted through the air and Ramona's implants screamed in warning. Her HUD leapt to life, warning about the chemical composition and presence of a dozen unidentifiable chemical and biological agents. She swallowed hard and glanced at Pride. He still hadn't moved from the podium.

"At least we'll get to learn about Verd's bartending skills with Overwatch's analysis of his chemical cocktail. That won't be affected, right?" She couldn't help the instinct to breathe a little more shallowly. "Right?"

"Daughter of Rasputin called it magic. Something that Verdigris cannot break." Natalya snarled through the secure communication.

In the group of metahumans standing closest to the platform, some of them eased themselves into their chairs, heads in their hands or palms pressed tightly over their eyes. Ramona felt herself unable to support her own weight and struggled to draw a deep breath. She fell against the side of the platform, nauseous and disoriented. The added weight of modified musculature would make it nearly impossible for many of them to walk, much less run, if Verdigris chose to attack civilians in spite of his promise.

At least some people had been able to stay behind. Would that be enough?

✧   ✧   ✧

The air smelled of cinnamon and overripe bananas, a detail that Verdigris had likely chosen on purpose. Ramona sat on the ground, the small of her back pressed into the side of the stage. The other metas sitting in the chairs in front of the stage shared her fear and weariness. Corbie's complexion had turned ashen, his feathers already drooping and beginning to fall out. Natalya and her father had nearly identical expressions of rage, although the current Commissar was the only one keeping up a stream of colorful language via Overwatch.

"Sovie, what do you see from where you're sitting? Are we in danger of losing anyone?" Bella sounded as exhausted as Ramona felt. "Can we tell if anyone isn't affected from here? Overwatch, can we get anything from anybody on this?"

"Ma'am, we've got a limited amount of information, but so far we do not appear to have experienced any casualties. Some vitals are a little questionable, but we're chalking that up to the stress of the situation."

Ramona sighed. Breathing hurt. She scanned the crowd for Mercurye and found him huddled up in his chair, knees pulled up to his chest as he shivered. The loss of the lightning metabolism had immediate effects not related to speed. She gritted her teeth and did her best to steady her voice. "Bella, can the guys tap into the controls for the dome? Is there a way we can open the top to vent off the worst of it?"

"We can't do anything without finding something to trace. We need the video feed to light up the associated systems," Bella snapped. "If we don't get an answer soon, there are going to be geldings where we currently have Colts, do I make myself clear?"

"Is no use making threats, *sestra*," Soviette answered through tears. "I am sure they are doing what they can, but without—" She stopped suddenly.

"Sovie? What's wrong?"

Ramona pushed herself forward to see more of what was happening. She could see more of the CCCP than Bella could, and Sovie wasn't more than twenty feet away. Like Ramona, she sat on the ground, Chug's craggy head against her shoulder. "Soviette, what's wrong with Chug? Is he okay?"

"That's Ms. Ferrari, isn't it. Of course, and the first was Doctor Parker. It's hard to make out these voices, but I understand the lack of communication devices." The cultured baritone came through

Soviette's channel, but the medic's lips didn't move. Ramona could see Soviette's wide eyes and her lips pressed together as if to hide... a smile? What could possibly make her happy at a time like...

"*SHTO?*" Natalya's voice carried over the channel like a bullet. "Is not possible!"

"Commissar. My gratitude for your impeccable leadership in these past months." Chug's voice—his real voice, not the grunts of broken speech to which they had all grown accustomed—slid through the channel. "With your permission, I would like to engage our host in a bit of dialogue."

"Granted." Bella spoke first. "Engage. We'll debrief later, once I pick my jaw off the turf and we have Verdigris swinging by his big toes from the top of the Suntrust building. Chug, is that really you?"

"As much as I can be." The large man stood and extended a hand to help Soviette to her feet. Ramona saw his mouth move again, but she wasn't able to make out the words. The medic nodded and motioned to the stage. With his hands above his head, Chug made his way to the podium and bowed to Yankee Pride.

For his part, Pride stepped aside and motioned to the microphone. "Thank you, sir. I only wanted to take a moment to speak with our host and make him aware of a potential mistake in his impressive agenda. From one scientist to another, of course."

The jumbotron screen flickered on to display Dominic Verdigris, brandy in one hand and cigar in the other. He used the unlit end of the cigar to gesture at the screen. "You do realize that the only mistake is your speaking out of turn, yes?"

Chug—or at least the person whom Ramona had thought to be Chug—lowered his hands to rest against the podium. He inclined his head politely to the screen, his craggy cheeks permitting a wry smile. "Sir, I have made a wealth of mistakes in my lifetime, and several did result from speaking out of turn. At the same time, few individuals of your intellect exist on this continent, and I would welcome the opportunity to share a short conversation with a legitimate genius."

"Sweet mother of frogs, it's like Spin and Sovie had a baby. A big, rocky, squirrel-loving baby." Bella's tone wavered between stunned and delighted. "Is that really Chug?"

"*Da.* Is Chug, when Chug was more than he is now." Red Saviour answered, but it sounded like something had caught in her throat. Ramona glanced in the direction of the CCCP delegation.

Soviette had tears streaming down her cheeks, and others stared at their comrade in open disbelief.

The man at the podium waited for the image on the screen to respond. Verdigris' expression indicated that he was pretending to not enjoy the open flattery. "I suppose a few minutes aren't too much to give, especially given your insight. Your accent's a little difficult to make out, but I'll give it a go. So," he said, motioning with his brandy. "Enlighten me, Mister..."

"Doctor Chugowskiv. Professor at times, but doctor is most apt."

"Doctor, then." Verdigris smirked. "I gather you earned that one with more than a few evening classes at the local junior college."

Chug matched Verdigris' smirk with one of his own. "I attended day classes, too. Evenings were for more applied scientific investigations, of course."

Bella choked back a laugh. "He's playing him. Keeping him on the screen and stroking his ego. Boys, I hope you can pick up that feed now."

"Almost there, ma'am. Trying to establish a connection to the cameras first to get some better eyes on the situation."

Ramona glanced to Pride, who remained well behind the podium. His expression hadn't changed, but his eyes darted between the scientist on the stage and the psychopath on the screen. She shifted her Overwatch to a private channel. "How do you feel?"

"Like I ran a Parkour marathon in an August Atlanta afternoon," he rumbled back. "You?"

"About the same, but my legs don't want to help me stand up. Can you see what's going on in the stands?"

Pride paused, his eyes narrowing. "Mercenaries in the aisles, some guarding the exits. I don't know what we're going to be able to do, even if they manage to secure the video feed. He bought off the security detail and there are seventy thousand civilian lives in danger."

Ramona started to answer, but Chug had started to give his analysis of the situation to his target audience of one. "Research regarding the metahuman condition has its base in several conflicting theories, and the choice of one's theoretical grounding fuels subsequent arguments, treatments, and theories. I wonder, given your single-source approach, if you were perhaps a student of Fenn or Mitra. Their work and treatments suggest that a complex regimen of gene therapy might cure or, at the very least, alter certain families of metahuman traits."

"Fenn had his conference notes marinated in scotch. Didn't care much for the man," Verdigris sniffed. "Mitra, he and I got along rather well. Fussy about his laboratory protocol, but generous with patents. But no, not a single-source approach. Too simplistic, Doctor."

Chug bobbed his head. "Indeed. Which is why, given your expertise and seeming familiarity with the metahuman condition, I surmise that you based your approach upon the theories proposed by Brenner and Patrawalla, who suggested that the condition resembles a virus that uniquely affects the cells of the host. Such an approach would require a vaccination of sorts that would alter the host to create antibodies that would attack the offending virus, resulting in a loss of symptoms."

"Symptoms being the manifestation of metahuman traits." Verdigris leaned back and studied the other man through the screen. "I must say, for an ugly little bit of sediment, you're remarkably sharp. That must have been some night school."

"The candles were very bright." Chug grinned, stone-colored teeth visible between green-gray lips.

"Clearly. So, where's my mistake, Doctor?" Verdigris sipped his brandy and made a show of checking a nonexistent watch. "You're wasting precious time."

Chug cleared his throat and steadied himself at the podium. "The mistake lies in not considering the possibility that there could be truth in both, and that the introduction of such antibodies could result in the *activation* of metahuman triggers. The metahuman condition, Mister Verdigris, is not so much a simplistic condition as a complex phenomenon. Something more than a mutation yet not quite an evolution by the purists' definition."

The face on the jumbotron scowled. "So, just what are you saying, Doctor?"

"*We have cameras, ma'am. Network trace complete in less than ninety seconds.*"

Chug chuckled, the familiar rumble tickling the edge of his throat. "What I am saying...what Chug is...is saying..."

Ramona felt her heart sink. Nearby, Sovie covered her face with her hands. The man at the podium gripped the sides and stared at the screen.

"Chug saying you are wrong. You make mistake. Big mistake."

✧   ✧   ✧

"Mistake?" Verdigris leaned forward while Chug scowled back at the screen. "What kind of mistake, exactly?"

"Big mistake," the stone-faced man answered. He added a grave nod to his words. "Bigger than Chug is, and Chug is big."

Verd sat back in his chair and snorted. "Well, so much for witty academic discourse. I was actually enjoying that little tête-à-tête. Ah, well."

"Ma'am, we've completed the trace and can locate the target. Not sure how we're going to isolate all of these other threats, but we've marked him as being in a heavily guarded locker room. Sending you the information now."

"Good job. Start figuring out how to vent this place. Everyone on Overwatch, incoming schematics. Mark relative positions and keep taking shallow breaths," Bella instructed. "No one does anything yet, not with three hundred mercs waiting to prove a point."

Ramona said nothing and noted her place on the schematic. Small black dots started to fill in the layout of the dome, outlining the aisles and corridors. The Colt boys had control of the cameras and were putting as many of Verdigris' goons on the map as they could locate.

"Parker, we need to get these civilians to safety, or at least remove the threat," Pride whispered over the channel. "Just knowing where they are won't do much good."

The crowd noise had gone from stunned silence at Chug's discourse to a low murmur of fear and agitation. While the metahumans on the field could follow directions to stay calm, the seventy thousand attendees could trigger a mass casualty event if they turned on one of the goons in riot gear patrolling the stadium. Ramona struggled to think of one remotely similar situation in her years of ECHO training, but nothing came close. She tipped her head back against the side of the stage, wishing that her head didn't feel like a bowling ball balancing on pipe cleaners.

A private channel alert blinked in her HUD. "Rick? What's wrong?"

"Axel thinks he can do something."

She cracked one eye open and stared across the turf at Mercu-rye. He sat next to Spoonbender, whose mouth had twisted into a funny grin made only more cartoonish by his well-kept beard. The OpOne meta had earned his name as a joke, but his unique ability had proven useful in the strangest situations. "Okay," she replied. "Tilt your head so we can hear the idea."

Mercurye obliged, and the rail-thin man started chattering at once. "The pieces of the roof are not uniform, and the exposure to extreme heat in the form of Krieger blasts has compromised their integrity. Moreover, the structure is not as load-bearing as it would appear, and thus would require far less effort to move than a similarly solid piece."

She resisted the urge to roll her eyes. "Axel, that's great, but I don't think we have anyone on the outside who has that particular blend of metallurgy and telekinesis. None of our flyers have that sort of strength, and even if they did—"

"We don't need anyone on the outside."

Ramona sat up a little straighter and glared at the two men across from her. "Are you telling me that you aren't feeling any effects?"

Axel shrugged and spread his hands. "I felt little before, but I do not feel any adverse effects. An upset stomach and an unpleasant taste of lead on my tongue, but other than that, no."

"Hold that thought." Ramona opened up her Overwatch channel to Bella and Pride, relaying the conversation with a few quick commands. She could feel the glare from Bella before her words came over the channel.

"Whatever we do, we do it fast. Spoonbender, are you sure you can do something on that scale? This isn't a few chairs in a conference room," she noted. "If it's not done quickly enough, this place will turn into a slaughterhouse."

The young man smiled gently and nodded in Bella's direction. "It will be swift and decisive. Given the locations of those who could do harm, we can work to isolate them once the threat is removed."

There was a pause. Ramona could all but feel Bella chewing over the idea. Finally, she came back on the main Overwatch channel, with the CCCP brought on to hear the decision. "All right, listen up. Chug bought us some time, and the Colt boys managed to get us some solid intel on the locations of these goons that Verd has paid off. If you're not able to assist, move out of the way and be ready to support medical when they ask. Axel, count it down."

The words were lost in the growing roar of the stadium crowd, but Ramona saw the man's palms turn up toward the dome, long fingers curling in as if to grab the enormous metal cover. She cringed at the squeal of metal and watched the supports begin to buckle. The crowd screamed and people pointed at the corner of the roof that appeared to be collapsing. Mercenaries began to move up and down the aisles, rifles at the ready.

"Axel, abort," Bella snapped. "We're going to have a bloodbath on our hands—"

"We're on it," came a whispered voice over the Overwatch One channel. After a moment, Ramona recognized it. Southwind.

A rush of air took the breath from Ramona's lungs and had her gasping. Others near her experienced the same gust and coughing fit, and a faint green cloud gathered above the field. A second burst of air pushed it toward the compromised ceiling, sending it up and out of the dome. She inhaled, feeling the heaviness of her head and neck begin to lessen. Around her, others had started to do the same.

"Parker, what was that?" Pride asked, caution in his words. "Not that I'm complaining."

"That's our cue to immobilize Verd's thugs. Nat, how are you feeling?"

The Commissar replied with a nasty laugh. It made Ramona infinitely glad that she was on the woman's good side. "Am feeling like justice. Perhaps best way to honor ECHO hero is to follow in footsteps, *da*?"

Standing next to Mercurye, Spoonbender's complexion had taken on an ashen hue as he stared across the stadium. The speedster kept up a steady stream of chatter, but Ramona couldn't make it out. He gave Ramona a thumbs-up and nodded.

"Spoon's good. Bella?"

The ECHO leader didn't flinch. "Let's get that rat bastard. For Dixie."

The scene outside the Georgia Dome had all the makings of organized chaos. Metahumans and civilians worked to clear the stands and get people into the relative safety of the parking lot. Inside the stadium, those metas who had regained some measure of ability leapt into action to neutralize the mercenaries in the stands. On Overwatch, the Colt Brothers maintained a constant stream of information on the status of the stadium, including an ever-narrowing list of potential places where Verdigris had holed up to execute his plan.

Ramona took another deep breath of clean air and followed

Leader of the Pack down a concrete tunnel. One of his dogs stayed at her side, the rest sprinting ahead to meet up with Mercurye. She eyed the beagle as she jogged. "What's her deal?"

Leader didn't look down. "She knows you're not at full strength. Nana's like that. Don't worry, you can't trip over her, she's too fast."

"I'll take your word for it." The HUD blinked at her, several more possible locations disappearing thanks to the Overwatch algorithm. Merc was still heading toward the one that showed the highest probability. "How's the evacuation going, Pride?"

"Little resistance. The Winds are rounding up the ones who didn't surrender."

"Rounding up how?"

The reply came after a short pause. "We'll need to have Corbie bring them down from the metal pocket created by the roof."

Another trio of locations faded from the map. "We've got him cornered. Target should be in the southeast corner of the subterranean level." Ramona moved through her Overwatch menus to get some more information. "There aren't any other exits that I can see. Bella, what should we—"

The dog at her heels had stopped, teeth bared and whip tail held nearly parallel to the floor. A low tone thrummed through the concrete, the vibrations making Ramona's vision blur. Her stomach clenched as the hum grew louder.

"*Overwatch, we have incoming Kriegers and Spheres descending north of Vine City Station. Advise evacuations to the northeast stadium exits.*"

Mercurye raced back to them, the rest of the pack following close behind him. "There's nothing down there. Offices are empty. We could send the dogs back later, but for now..." Another rumble made his words unnecessary. He nodded to Ramona and took off for the main level. Leader's dogs followed in a furry blur, the little beagle finally abandoning her charge for more pressing matters.

Ramona made her way up the tunnel, struggling to keep her footing as the thumps and thrums resonated through her skeleton. She neared the tunnel opening to the field, able to hear the high-pitched whine that signaled the arrival of the Spheres. Through the open dome, the multiarmed monstrosities loomed on the horizon. "Pride? Bella? What's the plan?"

"Escort Sovie and Gilead with their teams to the Congress Center, or what's accessible during the rebuild. Set up a triage area and prepare for casualties." Bella's voice was grim. "This wasn't an accident. He knew they were coming."

The last of the Kriegers collapsed in a burning mass of metal against the western goalpost. Outside the dome, a Sphere had sunk into the ground less than fifty meters from the MARTA stop at Vine City. Red and white lights flashed with each ambulance that arrived for more casualties. Ramona kept count through her HUD, directing traffic and coordinating supplies that arrived from ECHO. Overwatch fed her information from the center of the battle while the CCCP channels gave her a steady stream of challenges and cursing, mostly from the Commissar.

A blur of black landed next to her. Corbie tucked back his wings and worked his jaw with his hand. "Bloody Kriegers. You'd think they'd give up, knowing what we can do to 'em out here."

"They know, and so did Verdigris. I guess they decided to team up." Ramona wrinkled her nose. "Or they're holding him hostage. He can't have that much that they want."

"Dunno." He inclined his head toward Chug, who toted a pallet of medical supplies like a child pulling an empty wagon. "He say anything else? Back on the pitch, what he managed... gods, that was brilliant."

"Nothing. Like it never happened." She watched Soviette move through the line of injured and dazed civilians. The doctor maintained an aura of calm concern and empathy with her charges, yet she seemed to avoid looking in Chug's direction.

Corbie shrugged. "Eh. Pity. Seemed like the sort to chatter with over a pint. Anyhow, Gillie's got nearly two dozen we're going to have to process when this is all said and done. Terrible way to get into the meta business, but..."

Ramona coughed. "Yeah. Terrible thing, trauma."

He cringed. "Sorry, love. I'll circle back and check status, make sure we aren't missing anything." He took to the sky, banking to the left to begin his survey. Smoke filled the sky to the south and the west, but Ramona couldn't make out any other threats on the horizon. For the time being, it seemed like the day was out of surprises.

Bella crouched in the shadow of a downed Death Sphere and reactivated her private comm to Bulwark. Shortly after the first wave, she had pinged him to check the status of the campus. She had yet to receive a reply, even though the other folks housed at ECHO hadn't reported any attacks or catastrophic failures. Rather than obsess over it, she had focused her attention on the battle at hand and left the signal to ping Bull at regular intervals. With the Colt Brothers maintaining their links and coordinating the battle resources through Overwatch, Bella had had little else to do but fight alongside ECHO and CCCP.

She assumed Vickie'd been juggling chainsaws, and had basically left anyone who knew what they were doing alone. But now... the silence on Overwatch Two was beginning to bother her.

"Bull!" she said urgently, for the third time. "Look, whatever's between us can—"

"Bella, we need to talk. Off comms."

Finally a response. "I'm kind of up to my ass in alie—" An "urgent" light from Overwatch One blinked in her HUD. The Colts. She switched freqs. "Guys, whatever it is it—"

"Commander, we've lost ping on Victrix." Sam Colt *never* called her "Commander," and *never* interrupted her and he had just done both.

"Whaddya mean?" she replied, comprehension eluding her. "What ping? Life signs? Location?"

"All signs, Commander, about the time this donnybrook started. She's just...gone. We've informed Commander Bulwark, but no one else."

And now, Bull's feed was flashing "urgent." And now she knew why.

"Bella—"

"I know, we need to talk. Now. Off comms." She checked her HUD. He was at HQ, in the secure lockdown area. "I'll be there as fast as I can."

> *...to be isolated from everything, to watch it unfold before you, and be able to do absolutely nothing. And to know you could help, if only, if only...I told John and the Seraphym I wanted to be a big damn hero. And all I could do was claw at the wall between me and your world.*

CHAPTER NINETEEN

Nightmare

MERCEDES LACKEY AND DENNIS LEE

Vickie came awake all at once. She *always* came awake all at once. The last time she'd had a gentle, sleepy awakening had been... well, she couldn't remember it.

She woke with the words of her father ringing through her brain.

"Hostage 101. If you've been knocked unconscious and taken, don't let your captors know you're conscious until you've explored where you are, without moving, with every sense but your eyes."

Okay, Dad.

First thing, all her Overwatch Two implants were deader than last year's leaves. She'd been dumped in a curled position against a wall. She wasn't handcuffed or hobbled, and there wasn't anything over her head. So whoever took her must have control over her in some other way, and must be pretty damn sure of that control. Both the wall and the floor were cold. The wall had caught bits of her hair; it was rough and felt like concrete, at least on the back of her head, while the floor was smooth and felt like linoleum, at least through her gloves. Wait. Two sets of gloves: hers—ones she could feel earth magic through—and a different set. That wasn't good.

It smelled of mildew and cleaning chemicals. The air wasn't moving. But it was cool in here and the floor and wall were cold, so there must be some air conditioning.

She'd been there long enough for the cold to seep into her. So, at least an hour.

The floor wasn't vibrating, so there was no heavy machinery or traffic anywhere around. So this building was probably some distance from a road. Maybe even outside Atlanta altogether. There were no people sounds, like conversation in the distance, or footfalls . . .

So wherever I am, if there's a lot of guards or something, they're not making any sound I can hear.

It was cave-quiet, in fact. But there was someone in the room with her. She heard breathing. The kind of raspy breathing an old person who smokes a lot makes.

Taking a slightly deeper breath of her own, and concentrating, she smelled stale tobacco smoke under the cleaning chemicals. Now, whoever was here could be a guard who smoked, but a guard would presumably be young, not old and wheezing slightly. So chances were, this was her captor. She had suspicions, but those could wait.

Jesus Cluny Frog, my head hurts. She suspected a concussion. It felt like a concussion.

So much for normal senses. Now to look with the magical, inner eye . . .

And her environment lit up like a Christmas tree.

Layered spells under her, behind her, above her, and on three sides, clearly forming a cube of spells ten feet on a side, probably cast on top of something physical, like a cage. There was a second spell-cube on top of that, farther away, probably cast on the room itself. Antimagic spells of course. Spells that would keep her from using her magic against anything outside the cage she was in. Spells on the room that would cut off her Overwatch Two implants from everyone else. And spells on the cage as good as any science fiction force field, that would keep her inside as effectively as titanium bars. No wonder her captor was confident he could control her.

Combine that with the smell of stale tobacco smoke and the wheeze of an old man, and there was only one answer.

"To what do I owe your repugnant presence, Bela Nagy?" she asked, sitting up carefully, and just as carefully opening her eyes.

Concrete walls, check. Floor linoleum, probably over concrete; really good insulator against magic is linoleum. To spellcast the floor took a lot of brute strength, or he painted physical glyphs all over it with something I can't see. Floor wax, maybe. No windows; correction, windows have been bricked up. Skylight. One metal door in the left-hand wall. And him.

Sure enough, there was her great-uncle on her father's side, Bela Adjoran Nagy, standing, facing her prison, with his arms crossed over his chest. He didn't look nearly as seedy as she had hoped. More like one of those whipcord-tough, old, white-haired Russian Cossacks from the Georgian Mountains who lived to be a hundred and fifty and walked twenty miles before a breakfast of yogurt and horseshoe nails washed down with homemade *koumiss.* He was wearing long, black, hooded robes, *because of course he is,* which made him look more like Gargamel from the Smurfs than a fierce, evil wizard.

Which he was, actually. An evil, fierce wizard. One who had already tried to murder her once, because she had destroyed something terrible that belonged to him. He might well be the most formidable solo wizard she knew. He'd certainly waxed her young ass once already.

But—here was her ace in the hole—he knew nothing about her anymore. She had been under the radar for so long, and so very far *away* from all the traditional sources of magical education, he had no idea what she'd been turning into.

Not that he had ever understood mathemagic anyway. He was a rote learner, like most magicians. He had no idea that when you saw magic as math, you could take spells apart and put them together in new ways on the fly, if need be—or that you could invent new spells altogether. As for her techno-shamanism . . . well, for one thing, he was like most mages and fried anything electronic he touched, and for another, trying to explain that to him would be like trying to explain quantum physics to a toddler.

That didn't mean he wasn't dangerous. He was. Incredibly dangerous and extremely powerful.

But he was, without a doubt, underestimating her. If he hadn't been, she'd have been pumped full of tranqs, shackled hand and foot, and had a hood over her head.

He frowned, clearly not liking her attitude. *And let's piss him off some more. Time to channel the Djinni.* "Nice dress," she continued. "Could use something to pick it up a bit though. Maybe a snappy purple scarf, or a cute little chain belt. Planning on trying out for *RuPaul's Drag Race*?"

"You should hold your tongue, girl!" he snarled. "And show your uncle proper respect!"

"I don't see any uncles," she responded calmly. "I see a disgusting, perverted old man the Nagys disowned years ago."

This was not bravado or false calm. Other than her pounding head, she had descended into a positively serene state of mind. *I guess if you contemplate dying often enough, when the moment comes, you've already accepted it.* The moment might just have come, for the current situation was very binary.

She would definitely escape this magic cage. The "bars" were wooden slats she could kick or jump or roll through with no effort once the spells on them were gone, and under the cover of taunting Bela, she'd already set in motion the magic it would take to obliterate them. With a little time she would be able to unweave the spells that had turned a big wooden crate into a powerful, inescapable prison. The prison kept magic from affecting anything outside its barrier. It didn't do squat about stuff that was working inside.

So once the magic came down, there were only two ways this would end. Either she would beat Bela Nagy once and for all, call her friends in ECHO to come get her, and walk out of here after gathering as much intel as she could—

Or Bela would kill her. Because her friends didn't know where she was, and she had no expectation they would discover what had happened to her. Bela *could* have used a portal, like the one at St. Rhia's, and apported her anywhere in the world. It could be minutes, but more likely would be weeks or months before they managed to find her. She knew plenty of secrets, and even if he couldn't get any magical ones out of her that he'd understand, there was a lot more that she knew that he could sell. Verd would pay almost anything for her computer passwords, for instance.

So she was not going to give him any choice about what was going to happen. If she couldn't escape, she would make sure he didn't profit by kidnapping her. There were too many ways he could use her, and although she could hold out against him for a while, in the end, anyone can be broken.

And...she was all right with that. Death was something she had thought about so often that she'd come to terms with it quite some time ago. She would satisfy that vow she'd made to Red to the letter. The Colts could pick up the reins. JM and Sera... were off the charts. The Eggheads were nicely ensconced in their new home, which had been delinked from *her* magic. Everything would go on just fine without her. In fact, if someone hooked up Eight, it would almost be as if she had never left.

Meanwhile, until that spell finished its work, she'd make him angry. The angrier he was, the less he would be able to think clearly, and the more he would concentrate on her and not what she was doing. Of course, anger would make him stronger, but that was a risk she had to take. She didn't want him noticing she was destroying her cage, and to do that, she had to keep him distracted.

"Watch your mouth, girl," he growled. "I have powerful friends, with armies and weapons you can't even dream of. They tell me you've been making all manner of clever toys for this *ECHO* you've fallen in with, and I intend to learn how you did it."

Wait, what? She stared at him for a moment. And then she began to laugh.

"What is so amusing?" If looks could kill, she'd have been paste.

"Are you actually saying what I *think* you're saying?" she gasped, around gales of laughter that were more than a little bit hysterical. "Did you actually throw in with the *Kriegers?* The *Thulians?*"

He pulled himself up proudly. "Ours is a partnership that began before you were even born, child. I have already reaped many rewards from it, and there will be more to come. Doppelgaenger has seen to every..."

She fell over on her side, she was laughing so hard. Because this was the height of absurdity. Even if he broke her, *he could never do what she had done.* She could show him, over and over, and he would never ever master even the simplest of hacks, much less the masterworks that Overwatch Two and the memory matrices were. It would be like trying to show a blind man how to paint portraits. And he had no idea that he was demanding something he simply could not have, due to his own limitations.

But the real joke was that he'd been suckered by the Nazis.

"Doppelgaenger! He stroked your ego, and *you were idiot enough to believe him!* Oh my god!" Tears stung her eyes, she was laughing so hard. "You *idióta!* You *hülye!* Are you senile? Has Alzheimer's turned your brain to mush?"

Then something occurred to her. Because it was pretty obvious at this point that Doppelgaenger was...call it "allowed to pursue a private agenda." Doppelgaenger was probably the only Thulian that knew about Bela Nagy. Which meant Bela Nagy was a sucker twice over. He'd been flimflammed by the shapeshifter.

"Have you even *met* a Thulian besides Doppelgaenger?" she

asked, still laughing, getting the words out in gasps. "Of course you haven't! They don't give a shit about you, not the *important* ones like Valkyria and Ubermensch. You're just Doppelgaenger's little rent boy. You're the hot chick on stage, the *magician's assistant*. Is that why you're in that dress? If you want to keep your job you need to show more leg and cleavage, Bela Nagy."

He was slowly turning interesting shades of red and purple.

She kept the jabs up, still laughing as if she couldn't stop. She was already in control of herself, but he didn't know that. "You're an *untermensch*, you *bolond vénember*, you're a Hungarian mongrel. There's no need to keep their word with someone like you, it's like lying to a dog, and they'll allow Doppelgaenger to promise you anything he thinks you want. And as soon as he gets what he wants out of *you*, it'll be *pfft!* the gas chamber—or maybe, since they're modern space Nazis, they'll just stand you up against a wall and disintegrate you. I'd like to see you pit your magic against a Death Sphere!"

She got back up, slowly, wiping her eyes with the back of her hand, still chuckling... and gathering her feet under her. Because her spell had done its work, and the entire network of all those carefully layered enchantments on her cage was about to fall apart like panes of glass hit with exactly the right resonating frequency.

And that was when a child screamed, somewhere outside the door to this barren, concrete room. And again. Then came the wailing cries of more.

She felt her eyes widen as realization hit her. "You're going to do it. You're going to make the amulet again!"

"Of course I am, you ridiculous child." Now *he* was laughing. "My ally needs these children for a little while longer, then, they'll be mine. One among them seems particularly... susceptible to my needs. And I will be—"

"*Te kibaszott szörnyeteg! Meg foglak ölni!*" she screamed, and flung her arms out wide.

And her prison shattered.

CHAPTER TWENTY

O Fortuna Part 2

MERCEDES LACKEY, DENNIS LEE
AND VERONICA GIGUERE

Vickie told me once that the real strength of ECHO was that every man, woman, and child in it knew they could count on each other. I was about to see that in action.

Bulwark took the steps two at a time as he raced down the spiral staircase to the dungeons. He wondered idly if this was a good time to attempt another kinetic field experiment, one he had dubbed the "Slippery Pinball." He had a brief image of himself careening down the concrete spiral, enveloped in his bubble, powered only by gravity, and bouncing right back up the stairs again when he hit bottom. *Bad idea.*

He arrived at the bottom with a heavy crash, his augmented mass crumbling some of the concrete beneath his feet. Sometimes he forgot how much he now weighed. The on-duty guard stared at him, astonished. Bull grunted as he pushed him aside and ran down the corridor, bypassing the minimum security wings and heading directly for Top Hold. He had another idle thought. *Why in the world did we name the deepest part of our dungeon Top Hold?*

Pull yourself together, Gairdner. This isn't the time to lose focus.

Despite it all, even he had trouble blaming himself for being a little frazzled. It had been a strange day. It had started like any other, he supposed. Wake up, wonder what he was going to do about the Djinni, brush teeth, wonder what he was going to do about the Djinni, get dressed, eat a bagel, watch footage from the Vault heist, wonder what he was going to do about the Djinni...then watch in consternation as Victrix's line went dead and moments later, a full hostage scenario erupt at the memorial which held in attendance seventy-three-thousand-plus innocent citizens of Atlanta, a scattering of CCCP metas and most of his ECHO friends and colleagues, including his love and commander-in-chief, Bella.

At least it cemented in his mind what he was going to do about the Djinni. The situation at the stadium required his full attention, but he knew they couldn't afford to lose Victrix. Victrix was, in essence, the backbone of their current regime. If pressed, Bulwark would have admitted there was no one, no single person, more important in the ECHO roster right now than Victoria Victrix. From a home office no larger than a standard bedroom, perhaps sixteen by twenty feet, Victrix ran the heart of ECHO communications. She was their eyes and ears, and her net went wide, locally and on a global scale. There was little that could escape her notice, and that didn't even take her arcane abilities into account. She had been their ace in the hole from the start, and now the unthinkable had happened. Her line had gone dead. You had to know Victoria Victrix to realize the enormity of it. These days, she barely slept. She kept her own implanted communications gear on every minute of every day. She pushed herself to the extreme limits to be on call, at the helm, ready to tackle any emergency with swift and exacting countermeasures. For her line to suddenly go dead, it could only mean one of two things: she had been taken, or she had died. If it was the latter, it would become another impossible obstacle they would somehow have to overcome. If the former...Bulwark needed to send the best tracker he had after her.

But can I trust him?

He didn't have much choice in the matter. Maybe he couldn't trust Red, but he could trust Red's friendship with Victrix. After that, he just didn't know. He had been proven wrong about the Djinni before, and it said something that Red always did what he set out to do, always saw things through to the end, and he usually came back. And he looked out for his friends.

Is Red your friend?

Bella's words had haunted him ever since she had stormed out of the command center. It wasn't something he was prepared to

answer just yet. It had never felt right to consider Red Djinni as
a friend. He was more the brother, the black sheep, the one who
could drag the whole family down in some sordid mess but God
help him, he was still family. You stuck by your family, right to
the end. And if another member of your family was in trouble,
you knew everyone could be counted on, even Red Djinni, to
help out. No matter what else stood in between, be it money,
jealousy, long-standing feuds, shared romantic interests in the
same woman...when someone you cared about was in danger,
you took action. He trusted that the Djinni would act and would
see it through.

As he rounded the last corner before the Djinni's cell, Bulwark
came to a screeching stop as he heard the pounding of footsteps
coming from both sides of him. Red Djinni's cell marked the
fourth intersection from the entrance to Top Hold, at the core of
a web of passageways leading to cells designed to hold the most
powerful of metahumans. Red's cell was considered minimal
security by Top Hold standards. It didn't require much in the
way of space or special consideration, and was little more than a
janitor's closet folded into the layout of other, more specialized,
containment areas. It was still Top Hold though, and despite all
his experience, Bull could see no way for Red to pick his way
out of this particular jail cell. He would need assistance from the
outside, and as Bulwark skidded to a stop, he deduced he wasn't
the only one who had shared that particular thought. At the cell
door, he caught a surprised look from Mel, glancing from him
and down the other connecting passages. From the left passage,
he saw two figures bearing down on him, a short stocky man
followed by a lithe woman fully armed with dual semiautomat-
ics and shimmering in the dim light with an array of knives
protruding from her belt, her boots and a tight sash that clung
to her torso. Sometimes Bull's instincts surprised him. Both of
them were known affiliates of Verdigris, yet a part of him trusted
them. In hindsight, Bull realized that Jack had little if anything
to do with Tesla's death, and had been just as surprised by
Harmony's treachery as any of them. Red Djinni clearly trusted
the man, which was why he was here, Bull supposed, breaking
into ECHO's highest security prison facility, to break the Djinni
out. As for the woman, Bella had told him about Khanjar, about
how she was working to give them inside information on Verd

and Blacksnake. How, in fact, she had alerted them on several smaller efforts on Verd's part that they had been able to thwart.

"Ah, the Bulwark," Khanjar said, as she stared at him hard for a moment. "What brings you here at this moment? It is... somewhat inopportune." She blinked. "I don't suppose you would believe me if I informed you that I was aware that Verdigris was going to do something, but not what and where?"

Bull didn't answer, he was instead staring to his right. Two more figures had come to a stop from the other passageway, one looking uncomfortable, even a little ashamed, the other sporting a wide, flashing grin.

"Well," Harmony said, edging in front of a nervous-looking Scope, "isn't this just *cozy*?"

"Just for my benefit, tell me how you got out of your cell, Harmony," Bulwark said.

"One of a hundred ways, Mr. Bulwark, sir!" Harmony answered, clicking her heels together in a sharp salute. "You didn't really think I could be held, did you? Not if I didn't want to be."

"I suppose not," Bull said, nodding. "Mostly, I just wanted to know if Paris let you out."

"It didn't come to that," Harmony said, as Scope seemed to shrink behind her. "But I think we both know I could have convinced her to, if need be."

"Right, great," Jack said, interrupting. "You two look like you have real important things to discuss. I don't suppose you'd care to move off the beaten track a ways and cut each other to ribbons in private? Got an appointment to keep with the Djinni here."

"You here to gut him?" Scope asked in a small voice. "To finish the job your guns couldn't, back in the Vault?"

"You know what you all can do?" Mel said, reaching for her sidearm. "You can all back away, No one's hurting Red, not today."

"I think you've got it wrong, Ms. Gautier," Bull said. "I think, strangely enough, we're all here for the same reason. We're all here to spring Red from that cell. I can guess at Jack's reasons, but I admit I'm entirely unclear as to why Harmony would want the same."

"Last piece of unfinished business," Harmony said with a shrug. "A final obligation to fulfill before I go my merry way."

"Never going to happen," Bulwark growled. "You will return to your cell, even if I have to empty every sidearm within reach into your brain pan."

"Wait, what do you mean you're here to free Red?" Mel asked, her hand still gripping her piece. "Why would any of you want that?"

Bull cut her off with an abrupt shake of his head and an angry glare. Those who knew him—Mel, Scope and Harmony—reacted with a start. Because he never showed emotions. He knew he was the original Great Stone Face. The momentary expression of frustration and rage took them all by surprise, enough to shut them up.

But guns were already out, and aimed. Khanjar's were covering Mel. Jack's were centered on Bulwark. Scope's were on Jack, Mel's were on Khanjar, though they drifted back to Harmony. Of all of them, Harmony stood at ease, smirking at all of them. She shivered, as if overcome by vibrant torrents of emotion.

"Oh, this is delicious," she sighed. "Gourmet, yum. There's even a hint of..." Harmony froze, tilted her head as if straining to listen, and doubled over in laughter. "Oh my word...that is *priceless*! I think I'll have to let it play out. It's too delicious not to let it run its course."

"This isn't getting us anywhere," Jack growled. "If we're all here to free Red, who cares what our individual reasons are, let's just get it done."

"And who's to say he wants out?" Mel asked. "Have any of you even asked him what he wants?"

"Of course he wants out!" Jack scoffed. "How well do you think you know him, lady? The Djinni I know would never want to be stuck in a cell!"

"You might want to rethink that, Jack," Harmony said sweetly, still chuckling. "I haven't felt anything from the Djinni even remotely close to that of a caged rat."

They continued to bicker, but Bull ignored them. Instead, he watched the flickering monitor next to the cell door. Red Djinni hadn't noticed the sudden drama that erupted outside his cell, or if he had, he hadn't cared. He had one hand pressed against his ear as if he was trying to hear something from his implanted microphone, and he was yelling. Pushing Mel aside roughly, Bull moved past her and jammed his thumb against the intercom, and suddenly they heard Red shouting.

"...hell you go? Victrix! *VICTRIX!* Answer me, dammit!"

"She's gone, Red!" Bulwark boomed. "Her line went dead! I need you to get to her apartment and suss this out! If she's disappeared, *find her*. Are you good to go?"

Red stopped, and stared back at Bull through the interface. His hands dropped slowly to his sides, and Bulwark felt a sudden chill as Red dropped out of view for a moment.

"Wow," Harmony gasped. "Now there's something you don't feel every day."

Bull gave her a curious look and stepped back in surprise as the cell door opened with a steely rasp. Red emerged, gripping his food tray and tossing it aside with a loud clatter on the cold concrete. Instinctively, Bulwark glanced at the monitor, which flashed acceptance of a recognized fingerprint scan, that of Malcolm Hollister, who had just finished his guard shift work for the day. Red reached into his back pocket, pulled out a glove and fitted it over his bare hand.

He lifted and copied the guard's prints off the tray, Bull marveled. *He's still got some tricks. Here's hoping he's got a few more.*

But this . . . this was a very different Red Djinni. There was no smirk, no easiness, no sign of the Djinni he'd come to recognize. This man was all ice-cold purpose. He was a cruise missile, a cold killing machine, and God help anything that got between him and his target. Even his eyes were two cold, stone, expressionless pebbles above his signature scarf.

"You need anything?" Bull asked the Djinni.

"Your piece, and backup," Red replied. "Anyone who can keep up."

Bulwark handed Red his sidearm. "Can't do much about backup," he said grimly. "We're on skeleton crew, everyone else is at the memorial, either trapped inside or surrounding the place as we speak."

Red looked them all over. Jack shook his head, Harmony merely sneered, while Scope continued to hide behind her mistress. Finally, he turned and regarded Mel. "I'm going after Victrix, and I'm not stopping until she's back here safe. She's the mission, and only her. As far as I'm concerned, you are expendable. Knowing that, are you still with me?"

Mel gave him a strange look. "She's the mission, eh? That mean you're expendable too?"

Red gave her a blank look, stepped back into his cell and tapped on the touchscreen next to the door.

"Saved email, send command. Please confirm," a pleasant female voice chimed from the interface.

"Confirm, Djinni Sierra November," Red answered. "Send it

now." He stepped back into the hallway. "I'm expendable too. You with me?"

"Always," Mel muttered, and shook her head in disgust.

"Then let's go," the Djinni said. "Try and keep up."

"Sam, unlock the motorcycle bay at door five," Bulwark barked into his Overwatch One relay. "Do it now and get back to what you were doing." He turned back to Red, but the Djinni had already darted down the hallway with Mel sprinting after him.

"I hope I didn't just make the biggest mistake of my life," Bulwark growled.

"Oh, I think you did just fine," Harmony laughed, clapping a hand on Bull's shoulder. "I'm just sorry I won't see how that all turns out, it's got some epic potential, y'know."

Bull turned to her, drew another gun from the holster at the small of his back, and calmly pressed the muzzle to her head.

"Time for you to go back to your cell, Harmony," he growled.

"What a lovely invitation," Harmony responded. "But I think I'm going to have to decline." She looked energized, even a little high, he thought. Was she literally drunk on all the emotion around her?

"That's not an option." Bull took the wrist of the hand that still rested on his shoulder and squeezed it a very, very little, by way of emphasis.

"Sorry, sweety, but I have places to go, people to be." Harmony laughed and patted his hand lovingly.

"Scope," Bull said. "Take Harmony into custody and seal her up in her cell, full lockdown. You are cleared to empty your clips into her head."

Scope didn't respond and drew away from him.

"Oh, Bull," Harmony sighed. She drew her hands up behind her head and took a step back. "Will you ever be any fun at all?"

"Not your kind of fun, Harmony, no," Bull said as he reached into his belt and removed a pair of shackles. "Turn around and face the wall."

"Oh! Just like one of your rendezvous with Bella!" Harmony laughed. She obliged him, but continued to chuckle. "Admit it, Bull, you're enjoying this."

"I'm having the time of my life," Bull grunted as he approached her, slowly. He reached out tentatively and snapped one of the shackles around her wrist. "We need to figure out what we're going to do with you, Harm. This just isn't the time. So you will forgive me if we just lock you away for now."

"You worry too much, Bulwark," Harmony said, surrendering her other wrist to him. "You always have. These things tend to work out the way they're supposed to. Something tells me I won't be seeing you again. But don't worry, don't you fret. We have all these marvelous memories to fall back on. I'll always remember you as the Boy Scout who got away. Ah well, at least I'll always have Paris."

Bull shook his head and brought the other shackle up to Harmony's wrist, when he felt a sharp pain in his lower back, and then nothing as he slid to the ground. Harmony turned around, still smiling. With her free hand, she grasped the shackle bound to her wrist, and snapped it off.

"Why are you good guys always so stupid?" Harmony muttered.

Khanjar was content to remain a spectator. She and Jack had agreed that he would be the one to make the executive decisions in this rescue, and so far, he hadn't given her any of the agreed-upon signals. Scope was holding the Taser loosely in her hands, looking from it, to Bulwark's prone twitching body, and back again, horrified.

"Snap out of it, Paris," Harmony said sharply, giving Scope's shoulder a shake. "We need to go. Now. You'll get your reward when we're somewhere private."

Looking numb, Scope holstered her Taser and turned to follow Harmony. But she stopped as Jack finally spoke up.

"Hey, ladies. I got a proposal. Mutually satisfactory alternative to you two running off to Bora Bora."

Harmony stopped, and favored Jack with an interested look. "Well now, I dunno, Jack. Bora Bora is awfully festive this time of year. That, and the fact I know you've been gunning for me this past year, makes me a little suspicious of your intentions."

"True," Jack said with a shrug. He raised his hands in peace and strolled towards her. "But I think you'll want to hear me out. You help me with this, and we'll both get something we really, really want."

"And how would you know what I want?" Harmony asked.

"'Cause he never gave it to you, darlin'," Jack said. "He never paid you what you're due."

Khanjar watched as Jack caught up to Harmony, and together they marched down the hall, their eyes locked on each other. Behind them, Scope gave Bulwark one last look, then rushed to catch up. Khanjar knelt down, checked Bulwark's vitals and nodded in satisfaction.

"Things tend to work out the way they're supposed to, Bulwark," she said, rising to her feet. "Especially when one has karma on one's side. Have no fear. Karma's a bitch."

And with that, she followed the others out.

When they arrived, there was little doubt that something was terribly wrong. There was a solitary alarm going off in Victrix's Overwatch room, which was damning in and of itself, but the sight of the front door, blown inward off its hinges, left little doubt that someone had forced their way inside. While Vickie's front door ordinarily looked rather pedestrian from the outside, it was all a façade. Mel remembered the first time she had been here. Upon entering Victrix's flat, she had been rather impressed by the security measures the petite mage had installed. The door was solid steel, mounted in a reinforced steel frame, with eleven camouflaged locks in addition to the standard door lock. Any intruder would have had more luck ramming through the surrounding walls than taking the door down itself, though not by much. Mel suspected Vickie had somehow reinforced the very walls to her small apartment as well. And that was just the physical barrier. Victrix had told her once about the numerous magical defenses on the portal, including a magical heat sink, designed to counteract any attempts to cut through it (whether with a welding torch or magical equivalent) that would hold for at least five hours. There was also the door camera, disguised as a simple peephole, backed by bulletproof plate, with a gunport beneath it, so you could shoot out into the hallway, but not in. It was a formidable first line of defense.

And it was simply gone.

She watched Red dash into the apartment, leaping over the fallen door, and rush headfirst down the hall to Vickie's control room.

"Red!" Mel hissed. "Hey! It could be a . . ."

Her cry died in her throat. The Djinni was being reckless, and he obviously didn't care. He only had one thing on his mind. Victrix was in trouble, and his first priority was to get to her side.

"Well, damn, ain't she the lucky girl," Mel muttered as she crossed the threshold. Leave it to the Djinni to be reckless, it would be up to her to be more methodical and unearth the clues that would lead him to her. Clues like... well, the yowling, scratching and thumping coming from the closet door. She opened it, and jumped back with a start as Grey leapt out and darted past her towards the Overwatch room. She watched, bemused, as the tiny earth elemental scrambled after the cat as fast as his little legs could carry him. She followed and glanced inside, and was mildly surprised to see the Djinni holding the cat by the scruff, ignoring the wild slashes of its claws and the soft punches to his ankle by an irate stone figure.

"Calm down, Grey," Red said quietly, while the cat continued to hiss and screech and swipe at his arm.

<Then let me down, asshole!>

Red knelt down, and let the cat go. Grey leapt away and shot Red a menacing look, with a final short hiss of anger. Herb waddled away as well, placing himself between the Djinni and the cat, crossing his arms and favoring Red with a stern look of disapproval.

"Tell me what happened here," Red said coldly. "And shut off that alarm. And be quick about both." Before Grey could move, the alarm shut itself off.

<Something blew the door in, that's what! Stunned the hell out of me, and the next thing I knew, Herb and I were in the closet and Eight-Ball was screaming his head off!>

Mel found herself struck silent at the sight of a talking cat. In all the times she'd been here, the cat had never given any demonstration that it was anything other than a huge gray cat— like a Russian Blue, but on steroids. Sure, Vix had *called* it her familiar, and she'd *acted* as if it was sentient, but... weird, lonely cat ladies did that all the time. Thinking her cat was sentient was an understandable quirk in someone as lonely and stressed as Victoria Victrix.

Except... it *was* sentient. And it talked.

Red cast another cursory glance over the Overwatch room. "No fight here," he said flatly. "Not enough damage. She fell or got knocked to the floor, got her feet tangled in cables, and then was incapacitated and carried out." He approached the entrance and ran his bare hands over the scorched doorframe.

"Explosive residue," he muttered, and shook his head. "Someone planted explosives here. Had to be magically *and* technologically advanced to have gotten past whatever she was using as sensors. And I can't feel any magical aura on the doorframe. Somebody dispelled her magic. We must have a mole. This was an inside job."

"Someone she knew," he mused as he stood up and scanned the rest of the apartment, gleaning what information he could from it. Mel got the distinct impression that he was talking more to himself than to her. "An experienced mage, but one with tech backing."

"Like an evil Vix?" Mel hazarded. "She got a mirror-universe twin out there or something?"

He shook his head and darted back to the Overwatch room. "Grey!" he barked as she followed him. "What—"

<*Eight-Ball, boss,*> the cat said.

Mel reached the door again, and saw that the little stone . . . thing . . . was patting the monitor emphatically. And the monitor was filled with a single sentence, repeated over and over again in all caps.

<*PLUG ME IN!!! PLUG ME IN!! PLUG ME IN!!*>

"What is that?" the Djinni asked.

<*Vix was working on something with that thing. Had Sera and Hotshot in here talking to it for hours.*> The cat stared at the monitor, which had several cables hooked into a Rube Goldberg device with a giant quartz crystal sticking out of it. No sign of a CPU anywhere. <*She tried out a lot of new technomagic on it, built it on the same specs as the new home for the Eggheads. And . . . it started to think for itself. Herb thinks it can help find her. It wants to get plugged into Overwatch Two. Vix was thinking about doing that. Maybe.*>

There was a flash of hesitancy on Djinni's face, then his brows furrowed. "How do I do it?"

The cat wiggled in past all the cables to a spot where there were several junction boxes. <*I'll point, you plug. Grab the dangling ends. Cable with the red tag—here—*>

"Uh . . . y'all might be like, wakin' up Skynet, *cher*," Mel said hesitantly. "Y'all wanna wake up Skynet? This's how y'all wake up Skynet."

Red Djinni ignored her, his hands moving deftly as he followed Grey's instructions. As he plugged in the last cable, there was a melodious three-tone chime, and an asexual voice said, out of the speakers up in the corners. "*Overwatch Two: Eight-Ball: Interface: Online. Currently searching location Victoria Victrix.*"

Before Djinni could even react to that, the voice spoke up again. "*Victoria Victrix offline. Engaging pre-magic-programmed object search; looking for objects associated with Victoria Victrix.*"

"What…"Djinni began, and a chime sounded.

"*Objects found. Two present, one remote.*"

The screen lit up with a floor plan of the apartment. There were two dots on it. One was labeled "Red Djinni." The other was in the debris field at the door and labeled "Unknown."

<*I'll get it!*> The cat was off like a shot before either Djinni or Mel could move, Sure enough, a few moments later, the object began jiggling in place, then moving. The cat appeared in the doorway with something in its mouth. Djinni held out his hand and the cat spat whatever it was into his hand.

Djinni stared at it, as if he recognized it, but couldn't quite believe what he was seeing. "That looks like—"

<*The tip of one of your claws, yeah,*> the cat said, staring up at him.

"*I have found the location of the remote object, Red Djinni,*" Eight-Ball said, before Djinni could say anything. "*It is somewhere inside the former Central State Hospital. It was a mental asylum,*" Eight-Ball added helpfully. "*It has been closed for some time. The rest of your claw would be there.*"

There was a pause as Djinni pieced things together in his head, eyes narrowed. "Why would my claw be there?" He looked down at Grey. "What was an old claw of mine doing *here?*"

<*She needed a piece of you to work her juju for you?*> Grey offered.

The Djinni stared down at him. "Not buying it. She's got her implants in me. She can do anything she needs to do through them."

<*Uh…* > The cat shifted his weight uncomfortably. <*She… uh…wears it. Around her neck. Maybe the piece snapped off in the explosion.*>

"She—" Djinni looked…stricken. There was no other way to describe it. Then his eyes began to glitter suspiciously, as if…

Then he hardened all over again and became, if anything, more cold than before. She could almost hear his brain ticking things over, calculating, speculating, and coming to a conclusion.

Now he looked at Mel, really looked *at* her. "You know this is a trap. It has to be. This is too easy. We found her too quickly." He softened again, just a little, for just a moment. "You don't have to come with me. You don't owe me anything—"

"Well, *cher,* maybe I owe Vix, *non?*" She shrugged. "I'm comin' along. I don't see any cavalry, so it'll have to be me."

<*Crap, people, if it's a trap, should you just rush in there?*> the cat said, alarmed. <*Alone? Can't we call for backup or something? CCCP at least?*>

Djinni shook his head. "Verd's raining hell down on the Georgia Dome. There's just me and Mel. We're going, and I'm not waiting. It's gonna take us too long to get there going flat-out as it is. But you let Bulwark, the Colts and CCCP know where Vix probably is and that we're on the way. Maybe they'll be clear faster than I think and they can scrape something together." He thought a moment. "Eight-Ball, if you've got a line on Khanjar, tell her too."

<*Roger,*> Grey replied. But Djinni was already out the door, and Mel was right at his heels.

CHAPTER TWENTY-ONE

Till We Have Faces

MERCEDES LACKEY AND DENNIS LEE

One of Vickie's favorite quotations is by C.S. Lewis. "How can we stand face to face till we have faces?" Maybe because she was the faceless voice of Overwatch. Maybe because Djinni wore so many faces you knew none of them was really his. Maybe both reasons, or neither.

Ten minutes later, Victoria Victrix was in trouble.

This room was somewhere high above ground, second or third story of the building, maybe. She couldn't get to the earth to pull geomantic power out of it, and she couldn't use the concrete as a channel unless she had bare flesh against it, and maybe not even then. Uncle had known that, of course; there was the linoleum as the first line of insulation, but he'd been extra careful. While she was out cold, he'd pulled a second set of gloves over the ones she usually wore, gloves cinched down tight at the wrists, and probably silk-lined. She couldn't stop running and ducking long enough to get them off. The ECHO nanoweave suit she wore was too tough to tear. The boots that went with it were form-fitting and just as tough; it took her half an hour to get them off at the best of times. The only way she could touch the concrete was with her head, which was not a good idea right now.

Serves me right for changing for Dixie's funeral. If she'd been in her usual soft cotton pants and shirt, she could have deliberately torn through the cloth and skinned her elbow or knee, dripped blood on a crack in the floor or smeared it on the wall, and had a channel for the geomantic energy.

She hadn't worn any storage talismans either; they were all in racks around her desk, not *on* her. So all the energy she had for spellcasting was what she'd brought with her.

Whereas Uncle Bela had not only his pyromancy, but he was jingling with so many charms and talismans under that robe that he outblinged a Las Vegas belly dancer.

She was running out of steam, fast. He had just gotten started. She'd spent most of the last ten minutes dodging and using what little energy she had to keep shields up. He'd knocked her into the walls twice, bruising her to the bone all over; she'd managed to deflect the same attack about half a dozen times more, leaving dents in the concrete walls. It had taken him three attempts before he figured out he couldn't incinerate her; she'd perfected *that* protection a long time ago, and now it was baked into every millimeter of her scarred, tortured skin.

The Lady's Not For Burning, she thought, a little hysterically, as she deflected a triplicate of levin-bolts, pure concentrated power that could put a hole in you like a laser, and *did* burn holes halfway through the concrete wall. But deflecting that much power drained her; she faltered a moment, her sight grayed out a second, and—

He got her. He slammed her against the wall, levitated her halfway up it and held her there, feet dangling helplessly. It was pure brute force. It drove the wind out of her, crushed her all over, sent shards of pain lancing across her ribs as she felt something crack, and left her gasping. She was not only running out of magical energy, she was running dry of everything else. Her vision blurred. Every breath was painful. Every limb shook with pure exhaustion. She was functioning mostly on adrenaline.

He stalked to the center of the room. The fight had blown out most of the lights, and he came to rest within a shaft of daylight streaming through the skylight, his face in shadow beneath his hood.

He always did have a penchant for drama.

He was probably expecting fear out of her. He was probably expecting her to beg for mercy.

Okay, my head is against the bare concrete wall. And he had spells there blocking her from pulling up earth energy. Because of course he had. She pulled another ounce of strength out of dry reserves. "This is all you can manage?" she mocked, and again set her spells to unraveling his. It took moments this time, crude as they were; she dropped to the ground with knees flexed, absorbing the shock; then stood up. And she didn't let him see she *needed* the wall behind her for support. Instead, she smiled. "Anything you can do, I can do better."

She was ready for the "invisible hand" at her throat; she dissolved it before it even touched her. "See?"

I can counter maybe one or two more of his lesser tricks... then I'm done. I have to get this over before he realizes I don't have anything left. I have to get him so angry he'll go straight for the kill.

"I can't even touch the earth, and I'm beating you, old fool," she mocked, forcing herself to breathe steadily, even though she wanted to drop to the ground and whimper in pain. Fear, however, was far away, walled out of her mind. It scratched and gibbered at those walls, but she was not going to let it in. She narrowed her eyes, and twisted her mouth into a sneer. "Look at you! You're decked out like a whore in talismans, and it's *just me,* and I'm beating you. Aren't you embarrassed? You should be!" She paused and shook her head. *"Unalmas vagy, ici pici fasz..."*

There. She saw it. The moment he snapped. Rage entered his eyes, and he lost the last vestige of his self-control. He *shook* with anger, and mage-sight showed her nothing more than a fiery blur as his power blazed up in him while he called on all his talismans at once. *"Baszd meg a kurva anyádat!"* he roared, and raised both hands. Whatever he had planned, she knew she wasn't going to be able to deflect it *or* get out of the way. Still, she bared her teeth and braced herself, readying her hands, her words, her will... *I am not going down without a last gesture of defiance.*

Then—

In rapid-fire succession, she heard the crash of something overhead and the tinkling of shattered glass hitting the linoleum, something landing *hard* behind the sorcerer, and the awful sound of flesh being torn apart—

—and then, *he* was there, uncoiling to his full height.

It happened so fast that she had tensed up, willing another shield to flare into existence before she realized that it wasn't really necessary. Where there had been one figure a moment before, then there were two, then another, and one of the three fell over with a meaty *thud,* as a head came rolling towards her.

She stared at it in stunned disbelief.

Bela's head.

The look on Bela's face burned itself into her memory, a harsh sneer of rage with bits of spittle spreading unevenly over his lips, but his eyes blank with surprise, as his head came to rest by her feet.

She glanced up and saw the Djinni dashing towards her with bloody claws outstretched. She pushed off the wall, staggered forward and collapsed into him. She literally could not speak; the shock of seeing him standing there, her wonderful, terrible rescuer, completely overwhelmed her, but she supposed a brief squeeze of his arm would suffice for gratitude for now. Roughly, he kicked the decapitated head away, shed his claws and held her gently in his arms while she fought to control her breathing. The explosive release from danger left her feeling dizzy, the transition from a forced pretense of invulnerability, to being able to let the façade drop and be vulnerable again, and to be in his arms...

She began to hyperventilate. Then she *stopped* hyperventilating because every breath hurt. It took a few minutes. He didn't speak, only prompting her with his embrace to calm down, to gain control, to get the words out, and then...

"What is it with you and jumping through windows?" she croaked. She stared into his eyes, his rich, brown eyes, and felt a shiver as she realized she didn't recognize them. They stared flatly, blankly back at her, like two cold pebbles. There was no sign of anything like emotion. It was him, it was obviously him, unless another shapechanger had entered the mix and was impersonating him.

Oh, holy crap, she thought. *What a mess that would be.*

But it was him. She could feel it, feel *him*. He just wasn't right, like something vital was missing, like something inside him was turned off, or frozen rock-hard. She reached up involuntarily and laid a hand on his face, trying to get past that blankness, wincing with pain as she did so. At her touch, Red blinked and took a breath, and finally chuckled and collapsed against her, and they both went to their knees.

"Defenestration," he whispered. "It's not just a word, it's a personal motto. And for the record, that was a skylight, not a proper window."

She managed to drag up a smile from somewhere, tried to make it as big and genuine as she could, and took in the newly rekindled warmth of his eyes again, eyes showing humor and relief and so much more. *That's better,* she thought. *That's the Red I know.*

"Technically, defenestration is being thrown *out* of windows. And, ow, I can't hold both of us up," she protested. *Dammit, I am sure I have cracked ribs.* "Everything hurts, and what doesn't hurt doesn't work anymore."

Red leaned back and propped her up against his own chest, gingerly, his arms still wrapped around her.

"We can radio for evac," he said.

"Actually, Red Djinni," said a polite and asexual voice on Vickie's Overwatch Two frequency. *"I was going to ask if you wanted that. Shall I call it in? There may be a wait. Belladonna is still dealing with the casualties at the Georgia Dome, although that seems to have come to a partly satisfactory conclusion."*

"Eight-Ball?" Vickie gasped. "Red, did you hook him up?" Of course all the Overwatch frequencies were back online for her. With Bela's death, all his protective spells on this prison cell were gone too.

Wait...three people...she looked past Red's shoulder. "Uh, hi, Mel. We have to stop meeting like this. People are going to talk." With her teeth she pulled the snaps apart that were holding the silk-lined outer gloves to her wrists, and tugged the outer gloves off, dropping them to the floor. *I need to be able to touch ground, just in case...*

Mel stood near the still-surprised face of Uncle Bela. She nudged the oozing head with the toe of her boot. She looked momentarily sad, or perhaps perplexed at the sorry state of Vickie's former captor, but then she shrugged and turned away from it. She favored Vickie with a wry grin. "Something tells me that ain't the biggest piece of gossip out of here. Jesus, Djinni. What do we do with this?"

"Soccer?" Vickie suggested. *Okay, that sounds bad. But he deserves it. Oh, bugger it.* "Can we kick him halfway to hell?"

"Who was that?" the Djinni asked.

"My darling Great-Uncle Bela Nagy. I told you about him. The one that tried to turn me into Kentucky Fried Magus when I was just out of college. Seems he was working for the Space Nazis." She couldn't help herself, another automatic reaction decided to kick in at that moment, and she was wracked with shudders. All the terror and loathing she'd been repressing hit her without any warning, and she started to shake as if she had hypothermia.

"Hey, easy," Red said soothingly. "He's gone, he's done. We're going to get you out of here." He looked around. "So this was all him? Solo operation? Or we got more Kriegers to worry about?"

"He said he was working with DG," she managed, trying to get her teeth to stop chattering. And stop shivering, because it *hurt* to shiver. *Shock. I hate shock.* She did her best to sound as if she wasn't wishing with all her heart for one of her pain pills and a session with one of the ECHO healers. A long session. "More like *for*, though, I bet."

Red groaned, and rubbed at his eyes. "Oh perfect. Haven't seen that asshole in ages, so of course he'd pop up now." He looked around again. "Eight-Ball, we are *definitely* going to need extraction, as soon as you can manage it. I..."

Red hesitated, snarled, and then hung his head. Wearily he looked to Vickie. "If he shows, I don't know what we're going to do. You're hurt, and don't try to hide it, Vix, I know it's bad. If he shows, I don't know if I can take him." He glanced up at Mel. "You know about him, got any ideas?"

Mel gave Red an uncertain shrug. "That she get out? She's compromised and hurting, and he'll use that as a distraction for the rest of us. Vickie, he's right. We gotta get you back to campus."

"I can walk out of here fine, just give me a couple minutes and a shove..." she began, then a belated memory hit. And pain became secondary. "Omigod. The kids!"

"Kids?" Red asked.

"DG has a bunch of kids stashed here. Bela said he was using them for something, but he'd get them when DG was done with them. Don't ask. There's not less than twenty-seven kids—because magic reasons." *Dear gods, do not tell him it's probably ninety-nine. He'll never go for that.* She rubbed her aching head, and tried to bludgeon coherency into her thoughts. "We need to turn them loose at least. I won't leave them for whatever the hell DG is doing to them."

Red paused, considering her words, and finally shook his head. "Forget it, we can come back for them. We're getting you out, now. You're too important. On your feet, let's get you out of here."

"You've got Eight-Ball hooked up, you don't need me now," she protested, resisting a little. "Eight-Ball can do everything I can and doesn't need sleep *and* can multi-multi-multitask—a *badger* could do my job as long as Eight-Ball is hooked up!"

"Oh for..." Red growled. "You are more than just...air traffic control for ECHO! Come on, Victrix! You have to know this! You can't have done all the things you've done and be this blind! You are the key in all of this! And forget about the badgers, okay? I'm tired of hearing about them. I regret ever telling you guys about them. The badgers are a lie, alright?"

"That's not true—" she said, shaking her head and regretting it. "That's never been true!" She paused, and amended it. "Well, maybe before, but it's not true *now!* Sera and JM are WMDs, you've got Eight-Ball, you've got the Colts and all the overseas versions of the Colts, you've got—" She blinked. "Wait...what do you mean, the badgers are a lie?"

"I made it up!" the Djinni roared. "The whole stinking mess! It made for a great story, okay? Fast cars, a self-destructive man and bestiality, it was a freakin' *HOOT!*"

He paused, struggling to regain his composure.

"For fuck's sake," he muttered. "What is it with you? You always get me so angry. And you're always derailing me with tangents. Just trust me, alright? Trust me when I tell you that you are the most important person I've ever known, that you are the most important person we have in this fight. *You.* We can't lose you."

"You're deluded," she replied flatly. "How can you possibly be so sure of that?"

"Because I saw it," Red snarled. "I saw glimpses of the future. Strands of fate, and they all ended in flaming *badger* turds if certain people weren't there."

"You saw *me?*" That...was pretty hard to swallow.

"Okay, mostly Bella," Red admitted. "But, yeah, you were always there. Didn't think much of it at the time, I took it for granted. Of course you were there, you had to be there. Who do you think is the glue that's holding this whole mess together?"

"Horseshit," she replied. At least getting annoyed was pushing some more of the pain into the background. "I thought you hated magic! Since when are you gazing into crystal balls?"

"Oh, like I ever got a freakin' choice when it came to magic!" Red scoffed. "You arcane bastards are drawn to me like junkie moths needing a fire fix! What the hell is it about me, huh? I can't get away from you, any of you! And I think you know better than anyone that I've tried!"

"I seem to recall you got *into* magic in the first place out of your own free will, cupcake," she mocked. "Red Djinni, you're a professional liar, and I'm not that important and I am going to turn those kids loose before we get out of here, even if I have to do it on my hands and knees with you hanging onto my ankles."

Red sighed, and Vickie watched his shoulders slump in defeat. He shook his head, and she started as he drew her closer to him. She had almost forgotten that he was still holding her, that he had been, all this time.

"Fine," he seethed. "You want a rare moment of Red Djinni truth? Alright. When I heard you were gone, that you were taken, that hit me harder than anything ever has. Let me say it again. You are the key in all of this, and you can deny it all you want, but I think you know it. You've made bridges between us and every potential ally out there. You are our eyes and our ears and you don't let anything slip through the cracks. You're the lifeblood of this; there's nobody who can just fill in for you."

He paused, and something in his tone changed. His voice cracked, just a little. "But I wasn't thinking that. When I heard you were gone, I thought about how we go out of our way to annoy each other. How you and I are trapped in a weirdly escalating and adolescent game of one-upmanship, yet when things go south, you and I know we can count on each other. There's no one else I trust more. You were gone. Suddenly, there was nothing more important than getting you back."

He exhaled, and drew her even closer.

"Because I need you," he said.

"Jeebus, you play to win," Vickie gulped. Her eyes started to burn with tears she refused to shed. She hadn't cried until this moment. She damn sure wasn't going to now. *Need isn't love, moron. And Mel's right here.* Even with him laying his soul bare... no. And she had always vowed that no matter what it cost *her*, she wasn't going to screw up anyone else's love life. Especially not his. Absolutely not his. He'd already lost too much as it was; she wasn't going to tangle him in some kind of messed-up love triangle and ruin the one good thing he had going for him. "Uh— yeah, Red, I need you too; you're my main man. BFFs. Right?"

They jumped, startled, as Mel cried out in exasperation.

"For the love o'... are you two *insane*?" Mel howled. "He loves you! You love him! How is it possible that you can't see it, even *now*?"

Both their heads swiveled to look at Mel, as if pulled by the same wire. Then they snapped back. She stared into his eyes, and saw what he must be seeing in hers. Panic. Terror. And... something else, something she still couldn't quite bring herself to believe. The curtain had been pulled back, and there was the Wizard of Oz. Laughing at them both.

Oh... what the hell. She threw all her resolutions into the wind, pulled his face scarf down and kissed him. She expected him, even now, to pull away. Because, of course, he would. That was how life was. She was misreading him and so was Mel. He'd pull back and cough and Mel would see it was *her* that he loved and somehow they'd get past this, because they had to. But at least the frog princess would have gotten her kiss, even if it wasn't going to make her human again.

So she was completely sideswiped when he drew her tightly against him and kissed her back. Nothing tentative about it. Nothing held back. Raw, honest Djinni, with no masks. When she opened her eyes, she saw there was something going on that was more revealing than the kiss. It was his real face as she had seen it in reflection, when she'd worn his body. The bones of his face were good, strong, and a fine foundation for faces like Clooney's. But the skin over the bones... from his cheekbones down, the skin hung off those bones like the jowls and sagging hide of a Shar-Pei dog. He was all scars and wrinkles and pendulous folds. Tight in places, bizarre and loose in others. He had killed people for seeing this face; he'd said so, and she believed him. And he exposed it to her now, letting her share the deepest secret he had, making himself utterly vulnerable to her. But his eyes—oh, his eyes—she had seen those eyes smile before, seen them cold with rage, seen them look rueful or exasperated. But she had never seen them like this. Alive with emotion, warm and welcoming and saying so much that she wanted to hear without needing any words at all.

Somehow she dragged the inner, concealing glove off her right hand. She cupped her left behind the back of his head, and laid the right along his temple, and caressed him with it. Because she wanted it, she *had* to feel it, at last, warmth-on-human-warmth, her flesh on his, no matter how abused that flesh was. And he didn't shrink from that, either. He just paused for a breath, and kissed her again, and this time—it was more than just a kiss. She felt whatever defenses he had left crumble away as he surrendered to it. And every last good intention vanished, the last desperate shield around her soul melted, as she surrendered in turn to him.

"So that's that then," Mel said, nodding. "The final piece."

Her words brought Vickie out of the kiss like a hard slap. She glanced at Mel, who stood just steps away with her arms held tightly against her stomach. She turned to Red, whose eyes were now closed, his brow furrowed in an odd mix of elation and confusion. It was the weirdest scene imaginable. And she...she struggled with a contradictory mix of emotions; guilt uppermost (but she hadn't done anything wrong! She'd tried, tried so hard to keep her love to herself. Tried never to get between him and Mel!) But guilt, and joy, and pain for Mel, and fear, and desire, and the absolute certainty that this was right, and the absolute certainty that it was all going to go horribly wrong. It was surreal, to say the least, a tsunami of emotions that tore at the fabric of her sanity.

Damn, Vickie thought wildly. *Why can't I write shit like this?*

"I figured it out a while ago, y'know," Mel muttered. "Didn't believe it, at first. 'Course I didn't. Didn't want to. Thought what we had was real, I did. You had me fooled, Red Djinni. I think you even fooled yourself."

"No, no..." Red said, opening his eyes and shaking his head. "It wasn't like that, Mel. I know cons, I've done them all, but you can't think I would have..."

"But you *did!*" Mel shouted, and looked away. She quivered, and willed herself to look back. "You did," she said again, her voice quiet and deadly.

"No!" Red insisted. "Look, I'm the last guy to pretend to know what love is, but I know what I felt, what I feel, and I loved you. I did and I do, you know I do..."

Vickie felt paralyzed. Anything she said at this point would only make things worse. *She* was the Other Woman. Even though she had intended the opposite. And...*dammit, he wasn't faking anything. He was in love with Mel on some level. I know he was...*

"Yeah, sure," Mel chuffed. "Doesn't matter, not anymore. Whatever you felt for me, whatever you think that was, it was never enough, was it? You know now who you really want." Mel drew herself up and gave them a pitying look. "It's all going to be fine, y'know. Things are going to work out the way they're supposed to, despite all your talk of choice and free will, I do believe in destiny. I believe we each have a place in the universe, that it provides for those that are strong enough, brave enough, to provide for themselves. I believe things happen for a reason. Take this situation, for example. This monumentally messed-up situation. Would you believe this will actually make certain things easier? Things might have gotten derailed for a time there, y'know, false hopes and dreams being what they are, but now we can get back to business. Things are going to be just fine."

"You believe we're going to be fine?" Vickie asked incredulously.

"Oh, I meant me," Mel said. "I'm going to be fine. Something tells me you two are royally fucked. Even if you abandon a plan, you never *totally* abandon it. You keep it close, and available, just in case. A backdoor, an escape route, you know about that, don't you, Red? I spent a lot of time and effort trying to plant seeds, suspicions, diversions...wow. What a colossal waste of time."

"The hell are you talking about?" Red demanded.

"Scope," Mel said with a wry smile. "The perfect fall guy, or gal...the gender doesn't matter, more on that later...she was already on a path of self-destruction. Y'know, I almost let her get blown to bits when I fixed those detonators in Ultima Thule. Instead, I threw her in a forgotten transport tube system running under the shield pylons and programmed it to get her the hell out of there. Didn't really need her anymore, not the way things were going, but maybe I wasn't totally willing to give up the plan. But y'know, I don't believe that. I think I had a change of heart. Y'all should know, you're the ones responsible for reawakening this odd, empathic side of me, after all."

"You...you are..." Red stumbled on the words. "You are confusing the hell out of me right now."

"I'm not confused," Vickie said, her voice tinged with fear. "I get it."

"You get what?" Red demanded.

She felt cold with the sheer horror of it. Her heart refused to acknowledge it...but she had always been a creature of mind over heart, and her mind had presented her with all the evidence, neatly tied up, with a bow on top.

"Doppelgaenger," Vickie croaked. "You're Doppelgaenger."

Mel smirked, and Vickie recoiled as the smirk grew to an elated grin and continued to grow, as did the rest of her, and grow, and grow...

It towered over them, a massive brute comprised of thick ropes of muscle coiled over an immense frame. Mel's hair fell away, leaving a bald scalp that seemed to undulate with throbbing veins. Her ECHO nanoweave had torn apart as all the seams parted under the strain, and fell to the ground in oddly precise pieces as the thing continued to grow. She . . . he . . . it . . . craned its neck and Vickie stuffed her hand in her mouth to hold back a scream as bones and cartilage scraped against one another, a thunderous staccato that sounded bizarrely like a string of firecrackers going off.

And then it spoke, but not with the growling rasp one might expect. It was a feminine voice, it was almost Mel's voice, but darker . . . richer . . . sultry even, and Vickie shuddered at the horror of it.

"Well done, Vickie," Doppelgaenger crooned. "You know, I never intended to let Bela have you. The smart ones are always more fun to play with. They can always see what's coming . . ."

"Penny! Penny! What's goin' on?" Pike tugged at her arm as the rest of the kids gathered around her. It was funny, really . . . the more the Good Ghost had helped her by scaring away the bad ones, and by giving her information she could use to warn the other kids, the more they had come to depend on her, to even treat her as a leader. From being the "crazy one" they avoided, now they all looked up to her. Even Pike.

"I dunno," she said, her ear pressed to the crack in the door, knowing that before the Dark Man or the Devil could come, the Good Ghost would warn them in time for all of them to get back to their cots. "After that breakin' glass, I didn't hear nothing." She bit her lower lip, and frowned with unease and worry. "I hope nothing ain't happened to Lacey."

Had there been a window in Lacey's room? She didn't think the Good Ghost had said. There wasn't a mirror, for sure. The Devil hated mirrors. He'd broken all of them in every room before any of them had come here.

You should be worrying about yourself, miserable little rat!

Penny whirled, the blood draining out of her face. Because that was the Dark Man's voice—but it had come from right behind her! How had he gotten into the room without passing the door?

She screamed, then clapped both her hands over her mouth, because the Dark Man *was* there. Only now—he was a ghost.

Which meant she'd never, ever be rid of him!

"*Oh, yes,*" he said, as the rest of the kids backed away from her, leaving her all alone at the door. He smiled, horribly. "*Scream, little rat. You can still serve me. The preparations I made for you can still serve another way. I can take your scrawny little body and there's not a thing you can do about it, my dear little conduit.*" He tilted his head to the side, and licked his lips. "*It's not a body I would have chosen, but beggars can't be choosers, can they?*"

She pressed her back against the cold metal door and stared at him in horror. Because, even though she had no idea *how* she understood what he meant, she knew *exactly* what he meant. He was going to take over her body. Move into it, like someone moving into someone else's house. "No—" she whimpered.

"*Yessss,*" he hissed.

"*Sorry, you old pervert,*" said a voice next to her, and the Good Ghost came through the door to stand between her and the Dark Man, planting his feet a little apart and crossing his arms over his chest. "*You're on* my *turf now, and you aren't going to touch her.*" The Good Ghost grinned. "*Time to call the cops on you. Man . . . I have been wanting to give you what you've got coming to you for a long, long time . . .*"

Then he stuck two fingers into his mouth and whistled shrilly.

A hole opened in the air behind the Dark Man. The rest of the kids looked at her in confusion as she gasped—but then, they all started to shiver and whimper as an ice-cold blast of air came out of it, whipping around the room and making anything loose fly around in a mad circle. The Dark Man started, and looked behind him as the lights dimmed.

And then he screamed. Because something shadowy and terrible darted out of the blackness of the hole and seized him in *far* too many skeletal arms. He struggled against it, still screaming, but to no more effect than if he had been a child.

A child. Like Penny. Like all his victims.

And then, the *thing* hauled him backwards, still fighting, into the black hole in the air. His flailing hands were the last thing Penny saw. Then the hole closed, and he was gone.

The cold wind stopped. The others gathered around her, staring at her, as the Good Ghost stood there still, with his feet apart and his arms crossed over his chest again, smiling in satisfaction. "Penny?" Pike ventured, his voice quavering. "Penny? What just happened?"

"He's dead..." she breathed in wonder. "He's dead. The Dark Man's dead. He ain't gonna be able to hurt no one no more—"

And then she burst into tears. She didn't even know why.

Red came immediately to his feet and stepped forward, shielding Vickie from the lumbering hulk with his own body.

"Vix," he said calmly. "Forget what I said before. I got this. You need to get out of here."

"You can't take him! Her!" Vickie hissed. "You said it yourself!"

Red cursed and shook his head, but his eyes remained fixed on the massive form of his former lover. "Seriously? What did I just say? Can you do what I ask, just this once? Get up, get moving, get those kids, and get the hell out of here! I got this."

Vickie felt as if she was being torn apart on every single level. She *couldn't* leave him here to face Doppelgaenger alone. She had to. She had to get those kids out. And damn him, damn him, he was right. DG under the guise of Mel had had the run of ECHO for months, and she and Eight were the only ones who could figure out what Mel had gotten into and mitigate the damage. And Eight *couldn't* do it alone. Eight could *help* her, because he was faster than she was, but he couldn't do it by himself. He didn't know where or how to look, and didn't have any magic she hadn't given him. There was still too much she was going to have to do herself. And it was going to take still more time to get Eight to the point where he really *could* do most of what she did now on Overwatch. She had to go.

She couldn't leave Red. She had to. The fight within her was brutal, but short. Duty and responsibility won.

"Come back to me," Vickie said fiercely. It was barely more than a whisper, but she put every particle of will she had into the words. Wincing, she rose unsteadily to her feet. "I *love* you. You come back to me. Say it."

"I will," the Djinni said, and risked a look back at her. "I'll come back! Now run!"

Doppelgaenger watched them, seemingly at ease and with amusement. She stood in place, her gaze switching lazily between them, but the moment the Djinni turned away, she leapt forward, a snarl erupting from frothing lips. With a massive backhanded swipe, she batted the Djinni away and landed in front of Vickie, who screamed and scrambled backwards, almost falling back on her hands. Her monstrous assailant laughed, bent down, and gingerly picked something up off the cracked linoleum. She held it up, and in the dim light Vickie saw something shining, as if it had been lovingly polished. It was Red's broken claw, the one she had secretly worn about her neck for the past year and more. She must have lost it in the fight with her great-uncle. For so long, it had been *all* that she had of him, all she ever *could* have without interfering in his life. It actually had been polished, by her own hands, unconsciously caressing it the way a newly married bride unconsciously turns and caresses her wedding ring. It had been her one link to him, her way to get to him and get him out of whatever trouble he'd gotten himself into. To keep him safer, if not completely protected. To keep him close to her, even when he was halfway across the world.

And with a flourish, it was gone, as Doppelgaenger parted her hungry lips and swallowed it whole. She sighed in contentment, and chuckled as her attention fell back on the wounded mage.

"Should have listened to him," Doppelgaenger crooned, her voice still disconcertingly feminine, even sultry. "Should have run. You were lovely as the bait, Vickie, but I think I'm done with you now. I think I'm done with sparing lives. I think it's time for the fun to come back."

Terror transmuted to rage. And rage was energy. *"Fiat lux!"* she screamed, throwing out her bare hand, and blinding light exploded around Doppelgaenger's head. One of the first spells she had learned. One of the easiest, the simplest, the one that took the least energy. One that, used cleverly, could be incredibly potent. And in the brief moment while Doppelgaenger was dazzled, she scrambled to her feet and raced for the door.

And from behind, she heard that chilling chuckle again.

"Tricks," Doppelgaenger said. "You think to use tricks on me. I am going to enjoy tearing your limbs off..."

But as the brute lumbered towards her, Red Djinni erupted from the shadows and wrapped his arms around Doppelgaenger's neck, making her stagger backwards.

"Run!" Red bellowed. *"Run! Don't look back!"*

Sobbing, she obeyed him and ran; wrenched open the metal door and tumbled out into the hall. She glanced frantically in either direction. All the doors were open in this hallway, so wherever the kids were, they weren't here. *Oh gods, which way?*

Over Djinni's freq she heard Doppelgaenger talking—why? No matter, if DG was talking, he—she—it wasn't *fighting* and the further away she got, the more Red would concentrate on saving himself and not on her.

Mel, Mel, he's been Mel all along. He? She? Oh gods, gods, gods, I have got to get back and start damage control—

Suddenly she heard the kids screaming. No, not screaming. *Calling.* Jumbles of *"Miss! Miss! Here! Help us! Please! Let us out!"*

How the hell—never mind. She ran with her arms holding her stabbing ribs, followed the cries around the corner to another hall and a locked room, moving as fast as she dared, breathing as shallowly as she could. Then, just to complicate things, on one of her CCCP freqs she heard Untermensch barking. *"CCCP onsite. Tovarisch Victrix, where are you?"*

I don't know, I don't know—but Eight-Ball might—"Jesus—show them Eight-Ba—" she began when Eight-Ball interrupted with *"Follow the HUD, comrade,"* in crisp Ukrainian.

Red hung on, squeezing his arms together around her massive neck with all the strength he had. As chokeholds went, it was pretty solid. Good pressure on the windpipe, solid bracing with his shoulder, she should have been gasping for breath.

So it was somewhat anticlimatic when Doppelgaenger sighed and gave him a contemptuous look over her shoulder.

"You just about done?" she asked.

Red cursed and let go, dropping a good three feet to the ground, and rolled away. He came to a resting bounce, balanced on the balls of his feet.

"Nope," he answered cheerfully. "You've got a lot of fight left in me to deal with, darlin'."

"Oh, I'm counting on it," she said, if a bit ruefully. "We can't dally here, y'know. Didn't go through all this trouble just to get pinched. Needed to separate you, needed ECHO to give up on you, needed to eliminate the one person left who would likely pursue you. Or at least keep her busy long enough to do what I have to. But I'm relieved to be here, finally. I just wanted you to know that. Here we are, we're at that place, where you know, finally, who I am. It's important. Soon, you're going to know everything I am. It's only fair that we start this leg of the journey on equal ground."

Red stopped bouncing, and came to a full stop. He eyed her warily, and suddenly his stomach revolted and he started to gag.

"How long?" he managed, between dry heaves. "How long...?"

"How long what?"

"How long have you been Mel?" he asked again, holding his hands to his heaving chest.

"Oh, honey," Doppelgaenger sighed. "It was always me, the parts that mattered anyway. The parts that you're...um...reacting about." She gave the Djinni a sympathetic look. "Does it help when I tell you everything will make sense, real soon? That it won't seem so terrible, so alien?"

"Dude!" Red shouted. "You're...you're a *dude*! How is this not going to seem messed up?"

"Really?" Doppelgaenger said, and gave the Djinni a withering look. "You're going to get stuck on gender? You know, Djinni, like it or not, you connected with someone. Really connected. Gender aside, great sex aside, we shared something I don't think either of us ever really had before, and don't try to deny it. It's me. I know what you felt, what we shared. Once you come to grips with that, I don't think the rest will be so hard. Well, except that I'm going to torture you within an inch of your life. But *besides* that..."

Doppelgaenger sniffed, and began to advance on him, her muscles rippling as she emerged from the shadows.

"Let's make this quick," she growled. "Got a ride waiting, and like I said, I didn't go through all this trouble to get sloppy and pinched now."

Vickie cupped her hand over the electronic door lock, and dredged up a little more strength, as the kids continued to call to her, hysterically, from the other side. *Please make this one I know...* she prayed, trickling the little bit of power she had scraped out of the bottom of her proverbial barrel into the lock.

Nothing. She tried again. Nothing. And now over Red's channel she heard crashes and howls of pain. He was fighting for his life, for *their* lives; there was *nothing* she could do to help him and she *couldn't even get the damn door open!* Sobbing, she balled up her bare hand and pounded it on the wall. "*Damn* you! Why won't you—"

A hand fell on her shoulder. Before she could react, new energy flooded into her so fast her hair stood on end.

"Eight-Ball has told us of the children. Get them out, comrade!" Thea's soft contralto urged, and she cupped her hand over the keypad again.

This time the magic worked. There was a buzz from the door, the sound of a lock thudding back, and Thea hauled at the handle. In moments, the door sprang open, and a torrent of hysterical children dressed only in hospital pajamas poured out.

Red dodged another of Doppelgaenger's lightning fast blows and darted around the room, desperately trying to keep out of reach. He had already been tagged a couple of times, the last blow had smashed him up into the ceiling, nearly knocking him out. It didn't help that the room was fairly devoid of anything that could be used as an effective weapon. It didn't help that this room was so damned small. It *really* didn't help that Doppelgaenger was so big. Most of all, it didn't help that Red wasn't exactly in his right mind.

Vickie... Don't waste time, hurry your ass up and get out...

Vickie... I love you.

Doppelgaenger... is Mel. I love Mel. She's not Mel. She's not, right? She is, you know she is... everything she's said is true. You love Doppelgaenger. Oh, for the luva...

He kept moving, kept dodging, but it was only a matter of time, and as he slipped on an ill-timed feint, he felt an enormous hand close around his neck, snatching him out of midair. He gasped and flailed wildly as Doppelgaenger brought him up for a kiss. She gave him a brief peck on his forehead, ignoring the feeble blows leveled at her head and desperate kicks to her stomach.

"Take a nap, lover," she cooed, and rapped his head sharply against the wall.

He went limp in her hand and she began to whistle as she brought him closer, prying his mouth open with her fingers. With a short grunt of effort, she let her fingers elongate into thin, tough claws and ran one delicately over the roof of his mouth. She chuckled, victorious, and with a swift motion neatly excised the oral component of his Overwatch Two apparatus. She examined the bloody kernel of machinery between her fingers, let it fall to the ground, and slung the Djinni over her shoulder.

"That should disrupt detection for now," she sighed. "Enough to spirit you away and finish the job in private."

She looked up, and with an effortless leap, bounded up through the broken skylight to the waiting roof.

"And that's where our magic happens, doesn't it, Red?" she said, landing lightly on her feet, and patted Red's limp form affectionately. "In private."

One of the children, a little girl who was the last one out, suddenly plastered herself against Vickie. "He told me you would come!" she half-sobbed. "He told me!"

"Who told you, child?" That was Untermensch. He looked around at the horde of kids. "Children! Stay with me! I will show you the way out!" Whether they were used to instantly obeying the orders issued by scary-looking men, or just had common sense under all that hysteria, they all quieted down and pressed up against him in a group, like baby chicks against a mother hen.

"Him! The Good Ghost!" the little girl said, and pointed at nothing. And the hair stood up on Vickie's neck because she felt it, something she had only felt once or twice in her life. Cold. Physical and *spiritual* cold. Power, a force she could recognize even if she couldn't touch it or use it. There was a spirit here. And the child could see it, even if *she* couldn't.

"Poor child, she is—" Thea began, shaking her head doubtfully, but Vickie interrupted her.

"No, she sees something. It's real—" but she in her turn was interrupted by the little girl grabbing her hand and pulling her down the hall.

"He knows where the others are! He's going to show me!" the child said urgently, and Vickie let herself be pulled along. Untermensch and Upyr and the mob of children followed in their wake.

Two more rooms. Two more groups of children. Two more locks to open with magic. And now the little girl was urging her on again. "Here! Here! He says Lacey is here!" The child pulled Vickie down the hall so fast her head was spinning, her whole body felt on fire in a way that it hadn't in months, and the pain in her ribs was like a red-hot iron corset. Then the little girl took Vickie's bare hand and put it on the keypad beside the door. "Make it open! Make it open now!" she demanded, more frantic than imperious.

The door opened. There was a single occupant to this small cell, a woman lying with her back against the wall, legs a-sprawl.

Jesus—Mel?

It was Mel. A Mel with matted, disheveled hair, dressed in a filthy hospital gown. And shockingly... with only one hand. The left arm ended in a bandaged stump.

A Mel who took one look at them and charged at them, screaming at the top of her lungs.

Somehow Vickie managed a takedown, purely on reflex, leaving Mel sprawling, dazed, on the floor. And Upyr stepped in between them and planted one naked hand on Mel's face. A moment later, Upyr took her hand away, flushed pink rather than her usual paper-white, the sign she had drained someone of energy, and Mel was out cold.

"Is this the last, child?" Untermensch asked, bending down and heaving Mel over his shoulder with a grunt.

The child nodded and Untermensch started to turn.

"But—*Red*—" Vickie protested in a wail. To her shock, Upyr seized her arm.

"The Commissar *and* Belladonna say to get you out," Thea said firmly in Russian, knowing Vickie would understand, but the children would not. "The Eight-Ball voice on Overwatch Two says that Red Djinni insisted to get you out. You will leave with us now, or I will drain you until you are unconscious. Georgi can carry two."

"*Da*," Untermensch confirmed, with a glower in her direction. "Now come and do not force Thea to make you flat."

Running, with Thea's hand on her shoulder to give her the extra strength, she and Thea and Georgi, children in front of them, children behind them, made for the way out that Eight-Ball was showing on their HUDs. They all poured like a flood through the corridor of the not-so-abandoned building, down two flights of stairs, and finally out an emergency exit. The kids had piled up against the door, and Georgi shoved his way through them and opened it by the simple expedient of giving it the boot so hard the door slammed into the wall outside and the upper hinges broke with a metallic shriek. The kids fled through a jungle of weeds to the cracked and broken asphalt of an old parking lot, which was where Vickie turned, still pulled back by Red's peril—because now there were no more noises of combat on Red's channel. There was nothing, actually. The signal had gone dead. *She killed his rig. That bitch killed his rig! I can't track him!*

But before she could demand that Thea and Untermensch leave her with the children and go back to help Red, the top floor of the dilapidated building exploded.

The kids screamed and tried to shelter themselves as debris pelted down on them. But Vickie could only stare, paralyzed, as something—a disk that looked as if it was the middle sliced out of a Thulian Death Sphere—rocketed up to about fifteen hundred feet, paused, and accelerated away, fading into literal invisibility as it did.

And she knew, she *knew*, Red was in there. Doppelgaenger's prisoner. And all she could do was stare, as her heart iced over.

Doppelgaenger piloted her *Fledermaus* skillfully; most Thulian ships needed a full crew, but she could handle this one by herself. After the total disaster the last attempt to take the Djinni had been, she had elected to leave her troops behind and run this op solo. And a wise decision that had been, stupid, replicated apes that they were.

It was relaxing to be in this form, although she knew she would have to go back to Doppelgaenger's male shape before she landed. Females held no respect among the Thulians. Not even Valkyria. The bitch wasn't aware of how she was spoken of behind her back.

She glanced over at the Djinni, strapped down in the seat beside her, breathing mask for the *Stille Nacht* gas covering his entire face, so unconscious he didn't even twitch. "Don't worry, lover," she crooned. "I'll soon have you where you need to be. Then we'll play a while, and when I am done, you'll forget all about that neurotic Hungarian witch. We'll be together forever, and you'll never, ever leave me—"

Movement in one of the screens set into the control panel caught her eye. Something very small...and stealthed. Flying away from the chaos of the Georgia Dome, but not toward the ECHO campus. She frowned.

She ordered the *Fledermaus* to scan it. *Carbon fiber and a great deal of stealth modification. Trading speed for near invisibility. One occupant. Could it be someone we are interested in?*

She ordered a deeper scan, this one reading oh so many biometric indicators from a distance, as *Fledermaus* cruised along, shadowing the tiny craft. Thulian technology gave her ship true invisibility—which she traded for offensive capabilities, but after all, offense was not what *Fledermaus* was for. She waited while the ship's computers ran what the sensors read through an analysis, and with a cheerful *ping!* the answer came up on the readout: DOMINIC VERDIGRIS, 82.435% POSITIV.

Doppelgaenger's mouth stretched into a wide grin. "And the universe will provide..." she chuckled. "Oh, my Red, here I was concerned the Masters might want you for themselves—and up pops a tasty little morsel they will enjoy *ever* so much more than you!"

She toggled open the cargo hatch on the bottom of *Fledermaus*, lined the ship up, and swooped down on her prize like a falcon on a pigeon. Before her prey had any idea she was there, she had swallowed him up and snapped the hatch closed, triggering the antigravity in the hold to make sure he could not escape. Since he wasn't used to it, he'd probably be violently sick all over himself and the inside of his craft. That alone would keep him busy for the time it would take her to reach the nearest Forward Base.

"A fine day," she laughed. "A happy day, for this child of destiny."

She began to sing.

"Und dann die Hände zum Himmel, komm lasst uns fröhlich sein, wir klatschen zusammen, und keiner ist allein—"

Jack and Khanjar stared at the enhanced radar screen on his Thulian equivalent of a shuttlecraft—or maybe a "Captain's Launch"—as a large, stealthed Thulian vessel engulfed the small stealthed runabout they were tracking, then sped off, presumably with it inside.

Jack rubbed the back of his head with his hand. "Well, that went south in a big damn hurry," he said, sounding more annoyed than angry.

Khanjar was more... eloquent, cursing in Hindi, switching to Bengali, and finishing up in Urdu. *"Now* what do we do?" she asked—not Jack, but mostly Karma and Fate. "When I told him that ECHO was on his trail and he should make a run for it in his runabout, we were supposed to snatch him at the airstrip, not see him grabbed out of the sky in front of us like a pigeon by a hawk!"

"Calm down, darlin'," Jack said meditatively. "He's where we really want him, right? In fact, this might just be better. Less song and dance for me to do in front of the bosses. I just have to make sure I know where they put him after they get him, and we'll all have what we want."

"Oh..." Khanjar said, suddenly realizing that the short man was right. "Well...in that case, I suppose at this point the best move I can make is go become useful to ECHO." She licked her lips thoughtfully. "I would like to be sure Bulwark is not inclined to bear a grudge."

"You do that," Jack replied, turning his eyes to the rest of the controls for a moment. He eyed their other two companions thoughtfully. "But before you do that cool thing where you leap out of a speeding aircraft, I need to run something by you. By all of you." He directed his thumb behind him, where Harmony sat sprawled across a passenger bench, embracing Scope, who could have been taken for a statue, she was so quiet and lifeless. "I think we're going to need to bring her into the game a little ahead of schedule."

Khanjar scowled. "I suppose it could be worse," she said after a moment. "You could be talking about that psychotic, thankfully dead, Chinese woman."

Harmony regarded them both enigmatically, and then blew Khanjar a kiss.

"I love you too, poodle," she said flirtatiously. "We should get our nails done together some time."

CHAPTER TWENTY-TWO

You Always Hurt the One You Love

MERCEDES LACKEY AND DENNIS LEE

The disadvantage of not being human is I cannot "lose myself in work." No matter how busy I am, whatever I would like to avoid is still always there, and if only I knew what to do, I would have plenty of processing power to do it. In this, I envy you.

Vickie came to lying on a gurney, a stabbing pain in her chest, her head pounding, with Bella's hand just below her collarbone, firmly holding her down. "Hold still," Bella ordered, her mouth set in a grim line.

"But—"

"*Hold still.* You've got a punctured lung from trying to run. You've got a concussion. And the ribs that aren't splintered into your lung are cracked. I don't want to put you out, but I will if I have to. Hold still."

She held still, closing her eyes, tears leaking out of them. "Mel was Doppelgaenger. We—"

Waves of healing passed through her, easing the pain, setting things right, healing—healing everything but the heart, which ached more than Vickie had thought possible. "I know." Bella replied. "Eight recorded it all and played it back for me while you were on the way here. We've got people on initial damage control, directing Eight. Eight's dragging out every archived Overwatch log that has her on it and scanning them to see what she got her claws on. He's already done all *her* records. He's also checking all her computer logs *and* mine in case she figured out my passcode and is looking to see what was accessed when and syncing that up with the tapes of me to make sure no one got in on those passwords that wasn't me. *And* he's scanning every byte that ECHO has for bugs, worms, or Trojans. You done good with him, Vix, he's a treasure. Hold still."

A pause. "There's something you ought to know, Vix. I should have scanned you back when I figured out how to tell who had the meta factor, but I didn't until just now. You're a metahuman. You probably triggered a long time ago. That might be why you can work with tech and no other mage can."

Irrelevant. Her brain pushed the words aside in favor of action. "I can—"

"Do more magically when you're fit to move. I know. *First* you have to be fit to move."

The words escaped her before she could stop them, along with the tears. "He said he loves me. I love him. And she took him."

The pulsing waves of healing energies faltered for a moment. "I know," Bella said in a whisper; an empathic caress like a kiss rested above Vickie's weeping heart for just a moment, then the healing began again. "I think maybe you should sleep and let me do my work."

Against her will, she fell into darkness again.

From the outside, Barron's secret base at the tip of Florida looked unchanged from the abandoned missile test facility it had been until recently. What *was* it about abandoned missile bases that so attracted the Masters when it came to making bases out of them? Was it the remoteness? Was it the irony of using something humans had built to make into their own? Or was it some reason that Doppelgaenger could never understand?

The four corrugated-metal-and-concrete buildings on the property had managed to survive the hurricane called Andrew mostly intact. Barron had preserved the appearance on the outside down to the graffiti, but had gutted the insides, then created a hidden structure within each building that served as a compact Forward Base and hangars. It was supremely ironic that right beneath the one used as the main hangar was the missile silo itself, still holding the experimental Aerojet missile.

Doppelgaenger left *Fledermaus* on a cracked concrete pad inside the corrugated metal hangar next to Barron's main building, a blocky beige concrete creation covered in graffiti. Very few non-Thulians had ever been allowed to see what was inside that building. Barron waited just outside a doorless entry, Thulian flunkies in power armor standing motionless on either side of her.

As always, when facing one of the Masters, Doppelgaenger was confronted by the question, how on earth did one classify them? Not *untermenschen*, surely. But not an *ubermensch* either. Not a *mensch* at all, actually. It would have made a pretty philosophical problem for the likes of Goebbels, Heidegger, and Hitler himself to have debated over meals of homely kraut and bratwurst at the Eagle's Nest.

They were, considered purely as aesthetic creatures, rather attractive. Around eight or nine feet tall, thin, delicate, they were bipeds that boasted eight functional arms. The main two, and the ones that corresponded most closely to human arms, were much larger than the others and ended in pincers. The rest were generally kept close to the body until needed, and ended in specialized appendages. The entire creature—at least what Doppelgaenger could see of it beneath armor that was strictly decorative—was covered in tiny purple feathers. The head was surmounted by a crest of very long, silky feathers of a darker purple hue that gave the impression of a showgirl's headdress, and the head beneath the crest was actually heart-shaped, with a pair of huge, child-like, slanted eyes colored a rich emerald-green with no whites to them, a tiny, tip-tilted nose, and an unobtrusive slit for a mouth.

The mouth opened, and perfectly accented Bavarian German words in a rich, feminine contralto emerged from it.

"I trust your task went well, my friend?"

"Well enough, dear Barron," Doppelgaenger said with a bow. "Please convey my gratitude to Supreme Oberfuhrer Gero for his patience in this task. He will soon have another formidable weapon to add to his already impressive arsenal. Nothing, perhaps, on your level, of course. Still, I would be most surprised if he were not pleased with my results."

"You are ever so amusing, Doppelgaenger," Barron purred. "Some—certainly your fellow *ubermenschen*—might see your ambition as troublesome, even insulting in how you seek to rise above your station. But you never cease to entertain. That is perhaps why he dotes on you so. You further the game, you always have. And you are always a favorite in the ratings." She paused as the cargo doors opened with a steely hiss on *Fledermaus* and a group of workers rushed forward to unload a large casket onto the awaiting transport.

"And you plan to conduct your unseemly experiments here?" Barron asked with a slight grimace. "It took an age to sanitize the chambers after the last incident."

"Not at all," Doppelgaenger laughed. "My prize is still on board. This is, I think, something of a bonus. The universe provides, Commander."

"Yes, so you have said, on many an occasion." Barron cocked her head, curious. "Oh, but I do enjoy puzzles. Will you have me guess?"

"Please do, Commander," Doppelgaenger invited. "I enjoy matching wits with you."

"Well, so many choices! It must be on our list of desired acquisitions, which narrows things down somewhat." One of Barron's lesser appendages tapped out a rhythm on her left pincer. "By the way, I see you have taken on a female persona to match your actual sex. May I say I approve?"

Doppelgaenger shrugged. "It was required for the task. When I return to the Mothership, alas, I will have to revert to the male form. Tedious, but necessary."

Barron gave a churr of irritation. "Unfortunate. I do not approve of hiding what and who you are."

Doppelgaenger made a gesture with her hands that the Masters accepted as a sign of conciliation. "Alas, I do not have your advantages. No one offers disrespect to one of the Masters, male or female. Humanity, for all their talk of equality and justice, still consider the lack of a penis as a birth defect. I grew tired of gender bias ages ago, and chose to do something about it. But, please, let us leave this topic and return to the more delightful one of *which* of your chosen targets I have acquired. I will give you a hint. Although I am wearing an ECHO uniform, it is not a member of ECHO."

"Ah," Barron said, nodding. "My first guess would have been the Victrix woman. She was your preliminary target, was she not? She would have been a high prize indeed."

"I regret to say she was more difficult to capture than I anticipated," Doppelgaenger said smoothly. "If it is any consolation,

I left her in great, lingering pain. And considerable emotional distress, perhaps enough to render her useless to ECHO for the foreseeable future." She made a motion that the Masters interpreted as "contempt for one's enemy" and continued. "These ECHO metas are as vulnerable to emotional manipulation as any normal human. Rest assured, she will soon be ours."

"That leaves me with few options," Barron said. "By all accounts, Tesla and Marconi were destroyed by the destruction of Metis. Surely you can't have captured the most elusive quarry of all? Am I to understand that this casket carries the one and only...?"

"Dominic Verdigris III," said a gruff voice. "And before you give whoever this yahoo is too much credit, I'm sure you'll give me permission to register a complaint."

They turned, surprised at the interruption, as a short, stocky man marched into the hangar. His face, barely discernible in the dim light, nevertheless radiated a dark fury. He was accompanied by a tall, emaciated man, impeccably dressed in a tailored suit, horn-rimmed glasses and polished shoes, his head down and fingers tapping lightly on a portable tablet.

"Jack," Barron purred. "Why am I not surprised?" She glanced avidly from Jack to Doppelgaenger and back. "A complaint, you say? Am I to understand by this interruption that *perhaps* our dear Doppelgaenger's success in obtaining Verdigris was not *entirely* due to her own efforts?"

Doppelgaenger throttled down rage. How *dared* this mud-born *normal* come tramping in here, claiming to be responsible for her catch?

"Yer damn skippy," Jack growled. "It was a long, complicated setup. Took months. Had him in my sights, I did, when this cowgirl came swooping out of nowhere and scooped him up. Don't really appreciate this, Lady Barron. You trying to renege on the deal?"

"I would be careful, *human*, with your choice of words and your tone," Barron said, her voice dreadfully quiet. "Or need I remind you of the fact that you still draw breath at our Lord's whim, and his amusement. You displayed much cheek, seeking us out, even finding us. That granted you audience, and little more. Explain yourself quickly, and bear in mind that his amusement will mean less than nothing if I find one syllable faltering towards disrespect."

Jack stopped in his tracks, as if considering the weight of her words, and nodded. "No disrespect intended," he said, holding his hands up in the gesture of conciliation. *Damn him*, Doppelgaenger thought, *He's learned the sign language*. "I simply desire some understanding on your part, if not favor, for the lengths I went through to undermine Verd's plans, to drive him to flight, to expose him, and make him vulnerable."

Barron's slit of a mouth curled up at the corners, for the Masters had learned the equivalent of "smiling." "You had a hand in it, this I know. A masterful bit of sabotage?"

"He actually figured it out," Jack shrugged. "How to negate metagenes. Took a bit, but yeah, I managed to contaminate his gas reservoir. I'll admit, I took some pleasure in it. For all he knows, he messed up. He probably thinks he should have tested the formula with a larger population size before going public with that attempt at the Georgia Dome. Amazing what mixing in some simple salts and reducing agents will do. And even now, he'll never know. Whatever comes next, he'll just think he made a careless mistake. If nothing else, that will haunt him." Jack smiled sardonically. "But it goes back further, as you know. That debacle in Atlanta on the anniversary of the Invasion didn't go too well for him. You might say it started his steady decline, and I'll admit I had a role to play in that. Since then, Verd's been dealing with a mess of failures. A little nudge here and there, and his plans have simply fallen apart. It's made him a little uncomfortable, even reckless." Jack smirked. "His attempts on that so-called angel were amusing. He'll never know why John Murdock found his Blacksnake goons in their honeymoon hotel so easily, but Verd's not one to look back anyway. It's the results that matter. He never really learned to cope with failure, being so unfamiliar with it. It's made this last year rather entertaining for me."

Barron's crest feathers rose and fell. Doppelgaenger had not yet learned to interpret that. It seemed to be a random reaction, and yet, how could it be?

"I have to say," Jack continued, "it gives me a warm feeling, screwing over that backstabbing prick. I've been there at every turn, guiding things to the point where he would simply have to rabbit right into my waiting arms. So you can imagine my... displeasure... when just moments before delivering the *coup de grace*, seconds before I picked him up to deliver him here to you, he got picked up by...her." He stuck a thumb at Doppelgaenger, and gave her a sour look. "Aren't you supposed to be a dude?"

Doppelgaenger answered him with a murderous glare.

"Anyway," Jack said, ignoring her, "that's my complaint. She just took advantage of everything I had already done. She wouldn't have gotten him except for that. And she *lost* Victrix, she said so herself. I held up my end of the bargain. I'm just requesting, humbly, that you would honor yours."

"Hrrrrm," Barron replied. "One can see the justice in your plaint, and yet, dear Jack, when have the Masters ever concerned ourselves with being just?" The crest feathers rose and fell again. "However, we do pride ourselves on keeping our bargains. So... while I cannot provide you with the full amount of the prize we had allotted you, I can certainly assign you the ship you are using, and the technology in its hold, permanently. Will that suit?"

Jack bowed his head, as if considering her words. He motioned to the bespectacled man beside him, who surrendered the tablet. Jack took it and ran his fingers rapidly over the screen, and finally grunted.

"Acceptable, with one proviso," he growled, and passed the tablet back to his aide. "You carry the difference through to the next job. Think of it as good faith in this mutual venture, that such a profitable relationship will continue. Business, you understand."

"But of course," Barron replied. "Business is business."

"Done then," Jack said with a bow. "You've got my number, Lady Barron. Don't hesitate to use it." He turned to leave, when he felt a hand on his shoulder.

"Jack," Doppelgaenger said, and released her grip on him. "You would be the Djinni's acquaintance, then?"

"Red and I go back, yeah," Jack nodded. "What's it to you?"

"Allow me to convey your well-wishes then, when next I see him." Doppelgaenger's mouth curled into a vicious smile.

Jack looked Doppelgaenger up and down, and shrugged.

"You're not really Red's type, lady, but I wish you luck." Jack motioned to his aide, and the two strolled away. Jack paused for a moment, and glanced back at Doppelgaenger. "A bit of advice. Whatever you're planning with the Djinni, I'd think it through a bit more. He's usually more trouble than he's worth. Might be a bit more than you can swallow."

Doppelgaenger watched them leave, and felt a bubbling hatred for the little man. Was that a smirk dancing on his lips as he turned away? She had executed her plan perfectly. The Djinni was now without allies but one, and the one he had left was effectively trapped in the quagmire she had left in her wake as the duplicitous "Mel" at ECHO HQ. She would have time, more than enough time, to see it done.

But the little man's parting words left a sour taste in her mouth. Had she missed something? Was the Djinni truly alone now? She grimaced, and pushed the thought away. There was no need to worry. She had everything she needed. Composing herself, she turned back to Barron, and bowed.

"There is still much to do, my dear Barron," she said. "I would beg your leave. Please convey my respect to the Supreme Oberfuhrer."

"Of course, Doppelgaenger," Barron nodded. "Enjoy your task. I'm sure we will enjoy the show."

As they boarded the shuttlecraft, Jack moved quickly to the pilot's chair and set the commands for immediate takeoff. They had made their entrance, put on their performance, and gotten out. It was never a good idea to overplay your hand, and he was understandably careful whenever he had to deal with Masters. He was still learning their signs, their tells, and it made any negotiations with them rather . . . twitchy. He had not expected to see Doppelgaenger there, that had surprised him, as had her interest in Red. When the others were squared away, he would have to make a note to warn the Djinni. At the moment, it was Victrix Jack was concerned about. From what little he had overheard, it sounded like Victrix was safe, for now, and when Jack had enough to send her, she would receive a doozy of a report on the true threat to humanity.

Jack gripped the controls, ready to take the shuttle up and away, when he turned to his aide.

"Did you get enough?" he asked.

His aide moved forward, smiling. He took off his glasses with one hand, and made a beckoning motion with the other. From the rear of the cabin, a figure stirred and moved towards him with a deadened gait, wrapping her arms around him. With a flourish, he accepted Scope's embrace, and nodded to Jack.

"Let go, Paris," the aide said in a bland, dull-sounding tenor. Looking dejected, Scope obeyed. The aide took a deep breath, and a ripple traveled over his body. Then another. Jack averted his eyes; he'd learned that watching the transformation gave him something like a migraine.

When he looked back, the aide was gone, and Barron stood in his place. "Oh," the alien said in Harmony's voice, rich with amusement. "I would say so, yes."

Red Djinni awoke to a shrieking, burrowing pain in his ear. He stiffened up, felt his body restrained, and began to scream.

"Hush, love. It's too early for that. That will come later, and then...you can scream all of your pain to me."

Red stifled the screams, clenched his teeth, and willed the pain away. Soon, he was panting from the strain, but at least the roaring agony in his ear had subsided to a numb, throbbing itch. He couldn't see, and was dimly aware that his eyes had been bound by leather. And not just his eyes. He was rather unsurprised to discover that he was more or less naked, held down by tight leather restraints around his arms, his legs, wrists and ankles, and a heavy metallic restraint across his torso. He could feel the smooth, polished surface of each. The metal was cold, ungiving. The leather restraints tightened with his movements. They were strong, perhaps too strong to even cut through.

"You went through a lot of trouble, darlin'," Red groaned, "just to tie me up. You know how I feel about a little S&M."

"Oh, I know," Doppelgaenger said, and chuckled. She brought a hand down and caressed his scalp. "But I think this is a bit beyond what you had in mind."

"You sure? I know we discussed it a couple of times, but we didn't really get to the wild stuff..."

"I'm sure," she said, and pressed a finger to his lips. "I know you have trouble filtering your thoughts before they erupt from that sarcastic mouth, but why don't you listen for a change? You need to understand. I'm doing this because I love you. Because you're everything to me..."

That's right, Red thought. *Keep talking, while I figure out how I'm going to get out of this mess...*

As she spoke in low, sultry tones, Red concentrated on his surroundings. He didn't need to *see,* not while he had his skin-sense radar...thing. He was on a hard stone slab, about three feet off the ground. The air was cool, moving...piped in from overhead, massive, exposed ductwork by the ceiling, at least forty feet up. It seemed to be a large room. He felt the glare of intense light heating the air around him, and stopping abruptly a few feet in any direction. Overhead spotlight then, centered on him. Hazy shapes manifested around him, odd instruments, some electrical and humming, others...seemed very hard, very cold, and very...sharp. And moving around him, lazily, just one person. Doppelgaenger. Her outline was familiar. She had taken the form of a slim female again...

"...feel yourself rising to your true potential. And that's where I need you. Where you will be worthy."

Red turned his attention back to her. *Does it matter what she's saying? I need to keep looking for an out here.* It really wasn't the time to be cheeky, but he was the Djinni. Sometimes he just couldn't help himself.

"You know what the first lesson in giving motivational speeches is? Don't tie your audience down and cut into their head!"

He heard Doppelgaenger sigh.

"Red," she began, cupping his face rather melodramatically with her hands, "what is about to happen is very real, and very necessary. You may question how I feel about you, but through it all, it is important to me that you remember what we shared. What we still share, I would hope. I am about to raise you to godhood. You need to remember that, because it will seem that all I am doing is ending you, in the most excruciating way imaginable. To be fair, I suppose I am. But you will be so much more, and you will be with me. Forever. It wasn't too long ago that I thought you wanted that. Do you still? I think you do. I'm still her, I'm still the one you fell in love with. You know better than most that everyone puts on masks. But you and I...we saw past them. We touched the truth beneath, and we didn't flinch. We embraced what we saw, what we felt, darkness and all. I'm going to take us a bit further. What we will become...will be the envy of anyone who ever believed in soulmates. Do you trust that?"

Red seemed to contemplate that for a moment, when he snarled and spit into her face.

"Do you believe that I want nothing you're offering?" he growled.

"Very well," she sighed. "If it's any consolation, your defiance will make this quicker. Not easier on you, perhaps, but quicker. Soon you will beg for it to stop, for my forgiveness and my love. But know that you will always have my love. My forgiveness, you will probably have to earn. I do owe you a few truths though. The first is that I have only so much time. We are on a bit of a schedule, it seems. You may still have would-be rescuers, and I still have obligations to fulfill to my superiors. The first hurdle is detection. Our escape was not as clean as I had hoped. It has necessitated a bit of premature excavation. Your ear, for example."

"Right," Red said. "My ear. You seem to be fascinating yourself by jabbing something sharp into it."

"Not for my enjoyment," she objected. "Well, not solely for my enjoyment. Part of the problem, my dear Red, is that you were never truly alone. It took some doing to isolate you, but I think you are finally within my grasp. I just need to remove a couple of things first."

Red began to speak, and stopped.

"You are beginning to comprehend, my love," she purred, and with a flourish she ripped off his blindfold. Red squinted in the sudden, harsh light. When his eyes adjusted, he found himself staring at her hand, just inches from his face. And held gently between her bloody fingers...

"My Overwatch ear implant..." Red croaked. Gingerly, he ran his tongue over the roof of his mouth and felt a wound where his Overwatch mic had been.

"You see what I have to do, how it must begin," she continued. "Though I suspect few would pursue you now, I know of one who would. She would stop at nothing, I think. So for now, I'm going to have to impede her efforts."

"But that means you have to..."

"Yes," Doppelgaenger nodded. "I have to remove it all, Red."

And with a deft flourish, Doppelgaenger drove her claws down and tore out his eye.

Budapest, 1932.

The stone slab was a nice touch, she thought. It wasn't the first time she had been a captive, tied down for interrogation. Still, it was usually on a steel gurney or chair, fastened with steel restraints, and not this archaic setup of stone and leather. The metallic brace around her torso was their sole concession to the modern conventions. Looking about, she saw runes etched into the stone veneer of the archways over the door. Karoline rather liked it. It spoke of a simpler time, when torture was something of an art. Of course, those days were long gone. Everyone was in such a hurry now. The known world had survived the Great War and had since fallen into a global epidemic of poverty. You would think people would be ready to ease the pace a little, perhaps rediscover what little worth there was left in life. She supposed she owed her livelihood to the poor economic state of the world. Given the cost of a simple loaf of bread on the streets of Berlin, there wasn't much in the way of budget for a spy such as herself. She had to make her way with what she had available to her. A pretty face. A way with words. A means to make a man receptive to her pleas. It helped that she had a way of altering her appearance.

Of course, it wasn't always enough. She tested her restraints again, as a reminder to herself that a woman's gifts didn't always ensure a fruitful end to her endeavours. She had outsmarted herself. It happened now and again. No matter how fair the fairer sex was, it had to stay ahead of the game. Men didn't like to be outsmarted. Especially by their prey.

She reminded herself who she was, predator or prey, humming the tune she had come to adopt as her own personal theme song. Oh, certainly, Marlene Dietrich had made it famous in Der Blaue Engel, *but it should have been written for* her. *"Ich bin von Kopf bis Fuß auf Liebe eingestellt..."*

Then she heard the faint sounds of someone entering the room.

"A pretty song," came a harsh voice.

"You speak English?" Karoline said, surprised.

"Yes," the voice answered, "and I suppose it would serve us well to use it. My German is atrocious, and you simply must work on your Hungarian, my dear. Your accent may fool commoners, but not men of substance, such as myself. It grates on me, and I do not wish to hear such atrocities from those lovely lips. You would do well to stay in my favor."

"I'm at your mercy," she sighed, and flailed against her restraints for show.

"You play the part well."

"Whatever do you mean?"

"I mean you know your part in this." He hid behind the light. A deep voice, but not naturally so. If she was to guess, this was

a man who had suffered for most of his life. A weak man, one who had come into power late in his story. One who carried a deep hatred for the world. One who craved power, who desired nothing more than dominance over his fellow man. One with an unsatiated grudge against those, against everyone, who he deemed was beneath him.

"My part?" She feigned confusion. "I don't know what you speak of, sir. I am but a simple servant, one who . . ."

"Spare me," he scoffed. "You think us stupid? You think us blind? We are the Kiválasztottak, and we will lead humanity into the New World Order. I know who you are, and who sent you. You may as well submit, little girl. Stop playing the spy. You know your strengths. I know my needs. I'm fairly certain which one is stronger than the other. Though I encourage . . . resistance. Please. Resist me, Fraulein Doppelgaenger."

He stepped out into the light surrounding her; to her surprise, she recognized him from one of the several photographs of men she had been told to target. Bela Nagy . . . but he was very low on the list, not so much an insurgent as someone known to be supplying active insurgents with some ill-defined "support." She had been told to take him as a target of opportunity in the hopes he would betray the names of those actively working against the National Socialist cause.

So—why was he here, now, and identifying himself as one of the "Chosen Ones," whoever those were, since that name wasn't on any list of known groups of agitators.

He smiled slightly, a smile that did not reach his eyes. "I see you recognize me, although you do not recognize what I am. That, little girl, is about to change."

He reached down, and placed a hand gently on her stomach.

"You don't cower from my touch," he noted. "I would say you almost welcome it."

"Yes," she said, and muffled the cringe she felt, feigning gratitude. "You are . . . like no other man I have ever met."

"You waste your breath," Bela muttered, "and my time. Still you try. Still you seek to seduce one who is already gone in desire. But I am no common mark. Of course, I am like no man you have ever met." He grunted, and wove his fingers through the air. Karoline watched, fascinated, as lights flared into existence, trailing his fingers in a beautiful dance of luminescence. He didn't seem so

repugnant anymore. It was hypnotic, and she felt her blood begin to boil in excitement.

"Do you desire me now?" he demanded.

"Yes," she said.

"Do you want me above all others?"

"Yes."

"Lies," he chuckled. "But they feel like truth, yes? Not to worry. Soon, they will be truth, and you will speak only the truth, and only for me, yes?"

"For you," she said. "Only truth, Master."

"And so we begin," Bela said, caressing her cheek with his hand. "With lies. But you will learn, my dear, what lies will bring."

"Teach me," she breathed.

"Of course," Bela said, and drew himself closer. "It begins, like all things, with want and desire. Tell me, dear, what you desire."

"The truth," she said, gasping. "To see the truth."

"I will show you," Bela promised. "I will show you truth."

She gasped, as he pressed his thumb against her throat.

"Your first lesson," he said, driving his thumb down, "is that you are not the predator." She screamed, coughed, and fell into a silent thrash as Bela calmly maintained pressure against her windpipe.

"You are powerless, Fraulein Doppelgaenger. And you are mine."

There was nothing left in him, in the wake of suppressing the pain, for Red to do, or think, or feel. It was all-consuming. The pain was there, right on the verge of some ungodly threshold, and it required all of him to keep it away at a distance, lest it rob him of what remained of his sanity.

Only in the quiet moments when Doppelgaenger paused, allowing his healing to catch up and recover, could he spare a thought for anything else. Mostly, his thoughts fled to Victrix. She was safe, at least for now. It had been worth it, the grueling hours of being cut into, pierced, flayed, waterboarded and electrocuted, just to see Victoria escape. He was tiring, though, and he suspected that his resolve in this was slipping. It was worth it, of course it was... wasn't it? Of course it was. Was it? *Of course it was!*

And in those quiet moments, Doppelgaenger chose to hover over him, with a beatific smile, and the torture would shift to her vile words.

"I do this for love."

She said that a lot.

"Let go, let it wash over you..."

That was another good one, whatever it meant.

"Torment is something to be experienced, understood, in its purest form. Only then will you conquer it."

Red couldn't quite grasp that one. She had brought him to the limits of most traditional forms of torture, just shy of killing him, and he was convinced she was still not satisfied with the results. The first few times he had almost broken, he had foolishly entertained the thought that, surely, it was enough. Whatever her intentions, surely she had inflicted enough on him to achieve whatever sinister objectives raged through her diseased mind. But each time, she simply muttered in disappointment and had resumed her work.

This time, she laid down her tools with a sigh and folded her arms upon his bloody chest, resting her head on them playfully.

"This really would proceed much faster if you stopped fighting it, you know."

His eye had nearly swollen shut, but he forced it open a crack to glare at her.

"Oh sure," he wheezed. "I'm a...real...trooper...not dying... on you...yet..."

"No, love," she said, pouting. "Not death, not ever, not for you. I mean you're resisting. You're still fighting the pain, still keeping it away. We will never get anything done without it." She leaned forward, and Red felt something cold and edged brush against his cheek. He steeled himself, expecting a fresh onslaught of slow mutilation, but Doppelgaenger only chuckled.

"No, no," she cooed. "That wasn't my knife, silly boy. Just a keepsake from the man you beheaded a couple of days ago." She leaned back and caught the pendant that swung from her neck. Her eyes lingered on it, appreciating how it gleamed in the stark glare of the overhead spotlight. "Vesuvianite gemstone, not uncommon in Hungary, though they're usually not this rich shade of green; like jade, wouldn't you say? He once told me he loved me too, you know. I thought I felt the same. It was a different time, and we were young. All that we did, all that we shared... it's hard to believe how little I feel for him now. But at least there is a little, enough to dig up this small bauble, a memento of a different time, and wear it in his memory."

She chuckled. "Bela once told me it was the focus of all his magic, and that if I wore it close to my heart, I would carry him with me. He told me if I gazed long enough through it, I could catch a glimpse of my future. I thought I was wise to the ways of the world, but at the time I really was a naive child. But who knows? He was the magician, not me. Perhaps there is something to it." She leaned forward, and let the pendant brush against Red's cheek again. "Have a look, my darling. Tell me what you see."

Red forced his eye to open again, and glared at her.

"I see..." he coughed, and began again. "I see...my hands... ripping your head off..."

"Typical Djinni bravado." She shook her head, disappointed. "Your feelings are understandable. I have been inflicting a lot of suffering on you. But could you do it? Really? It's just us here, you know. You can be honest with me. It wouldn't be the first time. I'm still the girl who, in the midst of some truly memorable nights, you bared your soul to. You remember? Sometimes it was almost religious, like we were taking turns in a confessional. And the thing of it was, we each knew the other wasn't spinning some tall tale to impress. We were hearing truth. Our pasts...they betrayed how kindred we are. We understood. And we forgave each other and...oh! It was like I finally had met someone where that connection was just fated to happen, someone who had experienced the same loss, the same sacrifice, who had been so utterly betrayed by this horrific world..."

She paused to lay a hand on his chest, carefully avoiding his exposed heart. "You felt it, I know you did. What we shared... you can honestly say you could kill me? Even now, that you wouldn't even hesitate? I'm still her. I'm still your Mel..."

"You're..." Red coughed again, and almost choked before he spat out a mouthful of blood. "You're not Mel."

"You're right," Doppelgaenger nodded. "I'm really not. Would you like to know my name? My given name?"

"I...could...care less..."

"Karoline," Doppelgaenger offered. "My name was Karoline Shäfer. I was born in the small hamlet of Riedering near Munich in 1908. I was a German spy following the Great War, a Nazi meta-warrior in the next and I have experienced more in my days than you could ever imagine. Except love. You, Red Djinni, are my sole link to love. And I tire of this, of waiting for you. If you will not submit to it freely, then you force my hand. Before, I desired nothing more than your body, and its potential. Now, I have a dream of us, of us walking this existence together, as one. And I will have it, even if I must force it upon you."

She lifted herself off him, bounding to her feet and landing next to a trolley lined with hypodermic needles. She ran her fingers along them and selected one, seemingly at random. She turned back to Red, the needle held high, and approached him slowly.

"This is a cocktail of various muscle relaxants, a few neuronal suppressants and one very powerful drug that's sometimes used to encourage the truth by unskilled interrogators. At this dose, it isn't widely used, as it tends to cause cardiac arrest in most victims. On metas, especially one as physically robust as you, it might cause some mild discomfort, minor arrhythmias at best. However, it will completely abolish any sense of willpower you have left to muster."

Red stared at her in horror.

"That's right, Red," she said. "You fought it well, but I need you to feel the pain now. All of it."

Red began to thrash about, struggling madly against his restraints, but she ignored his attempts and plunged the syringe down into his heart. He froze, staring down at his chest as she pressed gingerly down on the plunger.

And then, he began to scream.

Doppelgaenger withdrew the needle and stepped away, out of the light.

"Heal, my darling," she sighed. "Heal, and feel every exquisite moment of it. Heal, and we can begin anew." And there, in the shadows, as she watched him writhe and shriek in complete agony, she began to sing.

"*Meine Natur, ich kann halt lieben nur. Und sonst gar nichts...*"

Somehow, he had robbed her of her will, and with it any ability she had of suppressing the pain.

His allies had left hours ago. She had given them what they wanted—the location of four safe houses, the identities of a handful of sleeper agents, and where she had hidden a few of their documents, stolen in a lucky turn of events that week during a rather dull charity ball for the Művészek Társaságának, hosted by Prime Minister Gömbös himself. They had taken it all, and she found herself almost giddy in the thrill of handing it over to them. *Whatever Bela asked of her, she was happy to oblige, and more. She would do anything for this man, and each service she performed for him only heightened the anticipation of the next.*

So she was somewhat surprised when he returned her to the stone slab. She didn't see why it was necessary. Her will was his now. Whatever he wished for, she would gladly provide. She strained to watch as he tested the restraints. Her expression was one of curiosity as he opened his leather satchel and began to remove his surgical tools.

"What are you doing, beloved?" she had asked.

"Our work is done, my dear," Bela had answered, his fingers twitching in excitement. "I believe I have earned something of a reward for my efforts. I have arranged it so that we will not be disturbed. It will just be us, for the time being."

"Oh, wonderful!" she gushed. "What do you have planned for us, my love?"

"For me," he grunted, wincing as he tightened her restraints, "and not so much for you. Though you will require your mind back for this." He raised a clenched fist, muttered a few words, and let his fingers fly apart with a flash of light.

Karoline shook her head in confusion, as if awakening from a long slumber.

"Why are you doing this?" she asked, her voice small and trembling. "What more do I have to give? I have already given you everything."

Bela reached down, grasped her hair and pulled back, hard. She cried out, and grimaced as he pressed his face into her neck.

"Not everything," he whispered, running his lips along the nape of her neck, and resting them just above her ear. "Sometimes, magic can be a crutch. A useful tool, when time is of the essence, but a bit of a cheat, I'll admit. I haven't seen the extent of you, or your mettle. I haven't experienced everything there is to you, my beautiful Doppelgaenger, that can be hurt... damaged... broken. Perhaps there are parts of you that cannot be broken. The thought of it intrigues me. The mission was to learn everything you knew, and I've done that. Now, this time is for me. I wish to learn everything else about you."

Karoline stared at him in confusion, and then in horror as he held up a scalpel to the light. He turned it over in his hand, admiring it, and peered thoughtfully down at her.

"I wonder," he mused. "I wonder how long before the pain becomes familiar to you. Will you continue to scream? Or will you accept it, even embrace it, as one would an old friend? Let's find out. Together."

At some point, Red realized he had stopped screaming. He opened his eye, and saw her lay a bloody surgical circular saw down on a trolley. The pain was everywhere, yet it seemed muted, manageable somehow, and for the first time in what seemed like forever, he was conscious of his own breathing, of his surroundings, and he shuddered in relief. He couldn't tell what she had been doing and looked down at himself. He couldn't help it. He saw parts of him exposed, things he really shouldn't have been able to see, with peculiar probes inserted here and there, each connected by insulated wire to an odd device that looked like a cluster of Tesla towers erupting in a multitude of directions from a common point of origin. Arcs of electricity danced across its surface, and he let his head fall back, closing his eye.

"You going to tell me what that thing does?" he croaked, and shuddered again as a million points of pain erupted again throughout his spent husk.

"Does it really matter?" she asked, and he felt a fresh sense of alarm as she climbed on top of him. "I promised you a few truths. Here's a good one. Didn't you wonder how, all of a sudden, Jensen was able to unearth a key piece of evidence to put you away? His investigations were taking a tad too long, and I had a schedule to keep. A little anonymous nudge here and there got him looking in the right spot. It solved a couple of problems. You were getting that look in your eye, like you were ready to bolt. Needed to lock you down, and it didn't hurt that the video evidence pretty much shattered whatever reputation you had earned since your arrival at ECHO. I suppose it was too much to ask for everyone to have given up on you, but it certainly made them hesitate. That was really all I needed. A little time, enough to get you here, alone, abandoned."

She leaned back, shifting her weight from his groin to his nearly dismembered legs. "Here's another one. I didn't choose you, Red. We were meant for each other. Did you never recognize more than a passing resemblance between our abilities? Shapeshifting is hardly a common meta-power now, is it? Granted, you believed your ability lies just in your skin, but recently you've been experiencing new facets of it, things that go deeper, like your new and remarkable healing ability. We all seem to have heightened healing to some degree, but yours goes far beyond any that I've seen. Did you never wonder where it came from? The Masters call it 'Adaptive Advancement.' As a meta-powered being evolves by experience, by necessity, it can call upon reserves to rise to new levels. Usually this process is slow, as abilities begin to ramp up when needed. Some begin with heightened abilities, far above their peers. Your ECHO ranks this in quaint Op levels. Some beings come into new powers, new abilities, through outside means. Take Bull, for example. His new enhanced skeleton is quite an upgrade, but that was mostly through Bella. Very few metahumans actually experience a sudden, eruptive blossoming of meta-talent, taking something relatively mundane and catapulting them to near godlike heights of power."

"I'm guessing you did," Red muttered.

"I did," she nodded. "I didn't begin so different from you. It took a man who tortured me, who took me to the very limits of human endurance, to open that door. Unending, searing and indescribable pain, coupled with the unforgivable torment of being nothing more than someone else's plaything ... it was the final stage. Pure helplessness, less than a puppet, really. I was nothing. And I knew it. That is what you will be for me, now. You will be nothing to me, to be used and tormented and thrown aside afterwards. How you must feel, how you *will* feel, I remember it like it was yesterday. You will feel everything. Know that I won't stop; there is nothing I won't do, until you understand what I went through, that day."

"But it ... doesn't make sense," Red croaked. "Why me? If we're so much the same ... why not someone ... different? What can ... I give you ...?"

She favored him with a thoughtful look. "Everyone has a counterpart," she continued. "All the stories point to it. One meta appears, another pops up with just enough to make the fight a challenge. There is balance in this, and the Masters do love a show, don't they? There are no coincidences here. We were given these gifts for a reason. But the Masters can't control everything, can they? Sometimes, repetitions come into play, and I've suspected something for much of my life. That my counterpart will bring me completion, will bring me something that everyone, even the Masters, have searched for since time immemorial. We

are destined to be the first, Red, to join as one, because we are
kindred souls with kindred abilities. Alone, we are just two warriors on opposing sides, doing battle for the amusement of others.
Together, I believe the synergy will be immaculate. I believe we
might become immortal."

"Immortal," Red gasped.

"Yes."

"Together forever."

"Yes."

"Yeah . . . you can kill me now."

"That would be such a waste," she tutted. "After all this time,
all this effort, to snuff out your potential now. When I first laid
eyes on you, I knew it. The long wait was over. Everyone else
had their counterpart, it seemed, except me. Eisenfaust had Yankee Doodle, Ubermensch had Red Saviour, Valkyria had Dixie
Belle . . . but where was mine? It hardly seemed fair. When I saw
you, I knew it had finally come. You were my destiny. And unlike
the others, I had a way to truly make you mine. Of course, you
weren't ready. You are, I think, on the cusp of it, finally. Just a
nudge or two more and we will see the Djinni rise."

"I don't . . . I don't think you want that," Red muttered. He
turned his head to her, and marked her with a hate-filled glare.
"You asked me before if I could do it. If I could end you, without hesitation. Just give me the chance, and I won't stop until I
put you down."

"I'm counting on it," she mused. "If nothing else, it should
be a notable fight. I doubt anyone is watching this part. With
the exception of a few quotable battle cries, the Masters do not
have an appetite for dialogue. They prefer straight-up violence.
And as much as I hate it sometimes, it does pay to stay high in
the ratings."

"Masters . . ." Red groaned. "You keep mentioning them. Who
are they?"

"All in good time," Doppelgaenger said with a smile. "If things
go well, you will meet them all, perhaps even come to know a
few as friends. I know a few who would love to meet you. You've
become a bit of a favorite yourself this past year. You do have
a way of getting yourself into horrific battles, being beaten to a
pulp, but usually coming out on top. Some of them remember a
time they could relate."

"So good of you to want to share me..." Red grunted.

"Oh no, my love," she said. "Make no mistake. You will be mine, and just mine. But I will offer you another truth. Before this is done, you will be offered a choice—to join me. It may not seem like it now, but I think you will want to. You will experience something no other living thing has, except for me. So when I say that our...perspective...may change in that moment, trust that I am speaking from experience. Certain things, small things, won't seem as important anymore."

She lifted herself off him and began to sing as she gathered her implements together.

"Again with that stupid song..." Red snarled. "Whoever told you that you could sing must have been the most tone-deaf, polka-lovin'..."

"It's a song from my youth," she said, dismissing his scorn. "It translates poorly to English, I'm afraid, though one line does rather shine through. *'Meine Natur, ich kann halt lieben nur... und sonst gar nichts.'*"

"My nature," Red murmured. "I can only love, and nothing else..."

"Very good," she grinned, her eyes still focused on her tools. "I used to think it meant something else, that my only role was as the seductress, the trickster, the spy. And then I met you, and things changed...I changed. Before, it was for power, for domination. Now, I do this, and everything, for love. For you. I will have it all, and I will have you. Forever."

She turned back to him.

"But first, you will have to understand. You will have to know, just how little you are."

Her device sent fresh and mounting currents of pain coursing throughout his body. Red barely noticed as she mounted him again, riding him, writhing...he tried to look away, squeezing his eye shut and turning his head as far as he could against the restraints. She didn't let him. With one hand, she snapped his head back and pried his eyelid apart, forcing him to look at her.

"You are nothing!" she cried. "You are mine! Powerless! Scream your terror, your frustration! All that you are, everything you ever held precious is gone now! From now, to the end of days, this is all that you will know! Forever mine! Forever mine! Forever...!"

❖   ❖   ❖

"...mine! Forever mine! Forever mine!"

She didn't even realize he had finished as his words faded away with his exhaustion. The pain persisted, he had even increased it somehow. But it was nothing to her now. He had taken her to the limit, and the endless agony had robbed her of any sense of feeling. She was numb to it all. All that was left, the one thing that could possibly remain, was a sense of self, but even that was slipping away.

"Beg me to stop," he gasped, reluctantly lifting himself off her. "Ask for mercy."

"Please stop," she said, her voice tired and lifeless. "Please have mercy."

"Ach, no!" Bela cried, and drove his hand sharply across her cheek. She didn't react, her expression only seeming weary and distant. "With feeling, you ignorant sow!"

"Please stop," Karoline repeated, louder but with the same monotonous tone. "Please have mercy."

"Feh, you are nothing but a puppet now," Bela muttered. "You lack fire, and there is no enjoyment in taming a dullard. Perhaps..." He ran one hand through her hair, and placed the other atop her head. "Perhaps I need to give you a little, to get a little."

He muttered a few words, and exhaled in delight and desire as energy coursed through his hands. Karoline gasped as she felt her mind come alive, her eyes coming into sharp focus and resting their gaze on his with renewed strength and fury. And it didn't stop there. The fire in her mind was spreading, and she felt a growing inferno seeping down through her chest, to her heart, to her limbs, to her hands...

"Much better," Bela cackled. "I can feel your hate. Struggle, my dear. Fight. Speak of all the horrid things you wish to do to me..."

He stopped, his eyes bulging, as her hand flew up, snapping off the leather restraints like they were made of paper, lunging for his throat. His words of triumph crumpled into gurgles of pain as she squeezed and pulled him down, until their heads were almost touching.

"Enough talk," she whispered. "Let me show you instead."

Doppelgaenger saw the fire begin to fade from his eye, and reached back to turn off the machine. She bent forward, still straddling him, and gently cupped his face in her hands.

"Beg me to stop," she purred.

He didn't answer. He barely looked at her, and there was no challenge there. There was simply nothing left in him. She pulled herself off him, and unfastened the leather restraints. She reached down, beneath the stone slab, and unlocked the steel band that held his torso in place.

"There now," she said, resuming her place on top of him. "You're free. You said it yourself, my dear. All you needed was the chance, and you would put me down. Well, here we are. There's nothing stopping you, nothing to hold you back, except yourself. Your one chance. Whatever will you do with it?"

Red didn't answer her. He didn't move at all, except for the labored rise and fall of his chest to keep breathing.

"Here, let me help you," she offered, and brought one of his hands up to her throat. "Just squeeze, dear. Let me feel your rage."

Red's hand hung lifeless in hers.

"Nothing?" she sighed. She grasped his fingers, and pressed them into the sides of her neck. When the Djinni didn't respond, she tapped them impatiently, driving his fingertips into her flesh. "Really? Bad form, Red, bad form. We're so close to the end, and you're choosing *now* to take a breather? Where's that eternal drive and fire? There must be something left in you. All it takes is a spark..."

She leaned in closer. "Or perhaps you've given up. Yes, I do remember feeling things along those lines. I think I actually did, before the end." Doppelgaenger grinned, remembering. "But then, I didn't have anyone else to live for, at the time. Tell me, Djinni, no matter what happens to you here, what do you think I will do next? I did have a primary mission, you know, one that hasn't been completed yet. There's a certain neurotic witch in ECHO's employ, one who holds great interest for the Masters. They have plans for her, oh my yes, they do. But before that, they've asked me to carry out a few interrogations. I'm supposed to learn everything she knows." Doppelgaenger's grin grew wider, and her eyes sparkled with malicious glee. "Given what you've experienced over the past few days, however do you suppose I'll do that?"

Red's eye opened a crack.

"I don't suppose she will last as long as you have," Doppelgaenger mused, "but you never know. I've already learned the hard way not to underestimate you ECHO hero types. Yes, yes,

I know, you don't think of yourself as a hero. Red Djinni, rogue mercenary, we get it! But that's hardly the truth, now is it? And don't try to deny it, Red. I know you far better than you think. The truth is, you are a fiercely loyal, compassionate man who will stop at nothing to achieve the redemption you so secretly long for. So now, now that I've seemingly taken away all the strength you have, it's time to prove it. Or are you willing to let Victoria suffer as you have suffered, and more? You see, after I'm done with her, the Masters have something far more insidious in mind with what's left of her. Everything she is will be stripped away. Her body, her personality, her individuality... all that will be left, all they are interested in, is the knowledge base of her mind. The rest will be cast aside, like scraps from yesterday's dinner..."

She felt a faint tremble in his hand, and her heart leapt as she felt his fingers fumble around her neck.

"I'm guessing you don't like that idea. Well, that's just too bad. It *will* happen, Red Djinni. Victoria Victrix will be ours. She will be our slave, to do with as we please. Funny thing about the transference procedure, I hear it isn't quite perfect. They will eradicate much of her, true, but there is always something left of the individual, something vital, that can best be called a ghost in the machine. And that ghost will remain, caught in the consciousness matrix, helpless and screaming, forever..."

She heard a low moan escape the Djinni's cracked lips, as his fingers tightened their grip. It was time, the Djinni was ready to claim his power, to make him worthy, to bring him to...

She felt his hand go limp, and fall away.

She stared at him in disbelief. He had lapsed into unconsciousness. A fire began to burn, deep in her stomach, and she felt herself flushing with emotion. No... not just any emotion. Rage. *How dare he!* After all the work she had put in on him, all the time, the effort, the devotion... *how dare he just... give up?*

She slapped him. Again. A third time. There was no response, nothing.

With a piercing scream of mingled anger, hate, and frustration, she ripped Bela's pendant from her neck.

"What did you do?" she howled at the gemstone. "How did you do it? How did you make me? I did it all! I made him feel everything I did that day! I brought him down to nothing, and then I lit the spark! What else was there? *What did I miss?*"

In a burst of fury, she brought the pendant down hard on the stone slab. There was a flash of light as it shattered, and with a cry she felt herself thrown back by waves of concussive force. She crashed into a table, sending her assorted blades and implements flying, and landed unceremoniously in a heap on the floor. In a daze, she brought herself onto her hands and knees. It was dark, pitch black. The explosion had destroyed the spotlight. The explosion...

"What do you know," she gasped. "There was some magic in that gemstone after all..."

She froze in stillness. A few items continued to fall around her, knocked over by the blast, and landing with ringing clanks and clatters on the ground. But beyond them...she heard something else. An odd sound, like yards of knotted rope straining against an irresistible force...

He was on her before she heard him move, catching her with a heavy kick that sent her flying back. Doppelgaenger grunted as she felt the edge of the stone slab bite into her back, and she crumpled again to the floor.

"To get to Victrix, you have to go through me."

It was Red's voice, his voice...but deeper. It was almost sinister, and it was a far cry from the near lifeless husk he had been just seconds before.

"Can't say I like your odds," Red drawled. "I'm pretty sure only one of us can see in the dark."

The world had gone dark for Bela. At some point, his eyes had swollen shut from the onslaught. There was only his broken body and how every part of it wailed in pitiable suffering. The only place she had left untouched was his throat. He supposed she had left it alone so that she could delight in every cry, whimper and scream, often laughing as his pleas for mercy were met with more brutality.

He lay there, mangled, listening to her pace around him. He imagined the end was near. Through it all, the only thought that had persisted was that this was impossible. He had broken her, in body and spirit. He had given her something near the end, true, some small spark of anger and vitality, but it didn't explain this...

It was nothing short of a miracle, the way she had transformed. He had broken her bones, sawed through the musculature of her biceps, one of her quadriceps and deltoids...he had even exposed a femoral nerve and played it like a lute. She shouldn't have been able to move, much less walk, much less deliver a savage beating to a man nearly twice her size...

But he was no longer twice her size. Perhaps he had imagined it, but she seemed much taller now, and bulging with muscle mass. It barely registered—her attack had been so fast, so ferocious, that after the first few moments, the only thing he could perceive was the pain. And still, the thought persisted. It was impossible. She was impossible. Was it a dream? A nightmare? One where he had forgotten the cardinal rule of waking up before the onset of actual pain?

He felt another kick to his midsection, and dismissed that idea immediately. This was very real, and soon he would be free from the pain. He couldn't survive much more of this, and he realized he didn't want to.

And then he felt her on him. He made a feeble attempt to resist, and was rewarded with more pain in his arms and chest, flaring up as fractured and broken bones rubbed against one another. He lay still, and felt her mouth moving along his jawline, coming to rest just above his ear.

"So what do you think?" she breathed.

"Think...?" he groaned. "Think of... what?"

"Of my mettle," she chuckled. "Do I not exceed your expectations?"

"You are... not natural," Bela wheezed. "I don't know what you are."

"And I suppose I have you to thank for it," she grinned. "In just moments, I went from nothing to everything. I don't think I could have ever imagined this. There's a clarity to things now, with this kind of power... like a fog lifting from my mind. I don't suppose you know how you did it?"

"You are..." Bela croaked. "You are not natural."

"I'll take that as a 'no' then."

He felt her hand clutch the front of his robes, and with ease, lift him off the ground. This was it then, the end. He sighed, and waited for her to finish him. He heard her chuckle as fingertips caressed his face.

"I think I have much to do here," she said. "Too many secrets exposed, and so many men must perish to rectify the problem. I suppose a bit of overkill will be needed. I will probably have to do their families, friends, and acquaintances as well. It's going to be a busy couple of weeks."

"You..." he looked at her incredulously. "You still care for your mission?"

"Of course," Karoline shrugged. "Call it professional pride. I set out to do something, and I don't stop until it's done. But after, oh... you have opened up new worlds for me, Bela. The possibilities are endless. And when I am ready, I hope you will be too. You really are like no man I have ever met. I think there is still much I could learn from you. Be well, Bela. We will meet again."

She released her grip, and Bela collapsed back onto the floor. With tremendous effort, he forced an eye open to watched her leave, marveling at her silhouette as she approached the door to his private dungeon. She really was taller, and powerfully built. She paused in the doorframe, and glanced back at him with a smile. She was unmarked, her flesh as pristine as a newborn's, and her smile was radiant.

"I used to believe life could only be a struggle," she mused. "An endless battle, where anything and everything was yours only if you kicked, gouged and screamed bloody hell for it. Perhaps not. Perhaps things come to those who wait, who are patient. Perhaps the universe provides. I am interested to find out." She tossed her hair back with a flirtatious wink.

And with that, she was gone.

Red was astonished at how much he could "see" now, even in darkness. In the absence of visible light, he found himself bathed in the glow of the far reaches of the electromagnetic spectrum. Past the infrared heat signatures he had previously depended on for his radial awareness, he found he could see all frequencies with a bizarre clarity that might have driven him mad from the sensory overload. And yet, he could process them all, even focus to exclude the unwanted noise of microwaves and radio frequencies, to grant him a clear picture of his surroundings, all with his eyes closed.

His eyes. Both of them.

It had been a shock, to feel his body knit itself back together with astounding speed, but to feel his rib cage re-form over his heart, for muscle and sinew to reconnect and grow, for his eye to regenerate in its socket, the only way to describe it was... glorious, like a holy fire spreading throughout his entire body. There was pain in it, of course, but his mind had detached himself from that pain with absolute ease. Everything was easy now. He was faster, stronger, and strangest of all, his body seemed to be malleable. It was unnerving, how he seemed to have absolute control over each part of himself. At first, he was content to merely pound on Doppelgaenger, watching her as she floundered about in the dark, unsure of when and from where he would strike next. At one point, she had taken a breath and gotten to her feet, her stance relaxed but at the ready. He had stepped forward, and he marveled how she had cocked her head, sensing his attack, and was able to deflect his blow with a raised arm and counter with a sharp jab to his midsection. He hardly had time to realize she wasn't exactly defenseless in the dark, perhaps drawing upon some older, scarcely used martial training, when he felt his torso simply soak up the blow, like rubber, and reflect it back at her. She reeled back, surprised, and then shrieked as Red took a moment to gouge her eye with his thumb. She stumbled, slipped on some debris and went down hard in a bloody heap. He watched as she scrambled to her feet, dimly aware that she had picked something up...

He cringed as the world seemed to explode around him in a wild heat. He staggered back. The room was blinding, sudden and brilliant with waves of light, casting stark shadows that trailed from a single point. Instinctively, he raised his hands to shield himself from it, and paused, confused by the mixed signals. The light and heat had a point of origin, concentrated in one spot. It wasn't the room after all. It was Doppelgaenger. She had found...

He felt a heavy boot connect, striking hard at his abdomen, propelling him backwards. He slammed into a wall, and in that moment of reprieve, he reset his senses, dialing them back to normal. His radial awareness flickered and collapsed, and when he opened his eyes, he confirmed his suspicions. In her mad scramble, Doppelgaenger had found a weapon. She held it in front of her, a harsh beacon of directed blue fire. A blowtorch. Just hours before, she had used it to cauterize some of his wounds. Now it served a different purpose, as a source of light, to even the playing field.

He looked from it to her face, sinister in the pale glow, and saw that she was smiling. She had also grown, in height and mass, a juggernaut of coiled muscle and primal rage, though the effects of it seemed diminished somehow.

"Astonishing," she said, flicking away a dribble of blood from her mouth. "You are all that I hoped for...and more."

"Wish I could say the same," Red growled. "Is it me or are you not even remotely as scary as you were the last time?"

"I remember telling you your perspective would change."

"Ugly is ugly, lady. Don't see how my perspective would change on that."

"Months and months of love-making?" Doppelgaenger offered innocently. "Tough to be scared of someone you know intimately."

"Don't remind me," Red shuddered. "No, you just looked bigger before..."

"Of course I did," Doppelgaenger chuckled. "Look at yourself. See yourself, your true self, as I always have."

She held the torch higher, and pointed to her left. Red glanced over, and saw his reflection in the remaining shards of a broken floor length mirror. It appeared he had grown too, like she had. He was taller, his body seemed ridiculously stuffed with excess muscle, and his face...

He gasped, and approached the broken mirror, his hands reaching up to feel the now-smooth pristine skin covering his cheeks and running down to his unmarred neck. It was his face, his real face. A lot more mature than it had been the last time he saw it, but he could see the ghost of the teenager in the man in the mirror. It looked, well, it looked...

"Well, whaddaya know..." Red marveled. "I look..."

"You look freakin' hot," Doppelgaenger said, beaming. "For some reason, I thought you really would look a bit like the Cloon. Instead, it's more...Ryan Reynolds."

"Yeah, Ryan Reynolds," Red agreed. "Better hair, though."

"Better everything," she said. "You feel it now, don't you? You feel everything about you is superior. And more, there's truth to it. This is you, the real you, finally. Everything you have gone through in your life, everything that was torn away from you, has brought you to this." She lowered the torch and strolled up to him. He met her gaze in the fractured reflection, unmoving as he felt her hand travel up his arm and rest gently on his shoulder.

"There is peace in this, Red Djinni. Many things have been opened to you. What you're feeling right now, the awe of it, it's only a fraction of what could be. This transformation, it is only the beginning—a doorway to experiences you can't even imagine.

You only have to accept it, and we can discover everything this existence has to offer. Together."

Red turned to her, speechless. His expression was one of confusion, and Doppelgaenger felt a brief moment of alarm as he raised his hand...

...and rested it upon hers.

"I..." he began...and faltered. "I lied before."

"Yes?"

"I..." He closed his eyes and shook his head in resignation. "I..."

"Yes, Red?"

He grasped her hand in his, and Doppelgaenger leaned forward, ready to accept his surrender, to her and to her sweet promise of everything he could possibly desire...

She gasped, as Red locked his hand around her wrist and squeezed.

"I guess I did hesitate," Red snarled, and slammed her into the broken mirror. "It won't happen again."

Before she could blink, he was on her, bellowing his rage as he rained blow after blow down upon her. She had no defense against his ferocity, even with the remnants of his stolen healing ability. Wounds opened and began to heal, but not before his blows had inflicted a dozen more, and he felt a coldness creep over his heart for this woman, this...thing. For months, she had manipulated him, worming her way into his life, learning his secrets, and finally using them against him, to hurt him, to break him, to hollow him out in an attempt to curse him in perpetuity as her puppet. Worst of all, she was a threat to Victoria, and would forever be, unless he ended her now.

Doppelgaenger continued to struggle, somehow finding her feet. She raised the torch again, lunged forward recklessly, and rammed him with it, scorching his flesh. With a grunt, Red kicked her off and examined himself. She had left a round, perfectly symmetrical burn mark on his chest. He watched it bubble for a moment, dimly aware of the pain and the horrible smell of cooked meat rising from it, when it suddenly darkened and expanded. He touched it briefly. It was tough but pliable, like rubber, and still it was expanding. No, not expanding, it was growing, spreading...

In moments it had covered his entire body, a sudden layer of armor.

"Adaptive Advancement," Doppelgaenger said, and coughed as she spit out a wad of blood. "I burn you, you become fireproof. Will wonders never cease?"

"You talk too much," Red muttered and advanced on her.

"Isn't that your type?" Doppelgaenger asked. "Or do I need to be blonde too...?"

He didn't let her finish. He was past rage. He felt nothing as he batted the torch from her hand, nothing as he lay into her with his fists, nothing as he knocked her about the room. The torch, forgotten on the cold cement floor, carried on in its capacity as a makeshift beacon, casting an eerie blue glow on the room where hulking shadows continued to flail about and slam into one another.

It was over soon enough. She struggled to rise, shuddering with rasping coughs, when her legs simply failed her and she sank to the ground again. Red reached down, caught a fistful of her hair and pulled her up. He drew a hand back and felt the claws burst through his armor-clad fingertips, ready to be plunged directly into her heart.

And again, he hesitated.

Perhaps it was how helpless she looked and felt, dangling piti- fully from his hand. He knew who and what she was now, but as she looked up at him with her tired eyes, he remembered how it had been between them not so long ago, and he felt the cold certainty that her death was a necessary thing, begin to crack and waver. It was probably safe to say that she knew him better than anyone ever had. They had shared pretty much everything there was to be shared in a very short time, from the ethereal glory of reckless, passionate nights to the soul-searching conversations and cathartic musings that only came in the quiet moments before dawn, and pretty much everything in between. As part of a team, they had watched each other's backs, with that unspoken trust inevitably forged in the line of duty. But it was more than just that, of course. Did he love her? Despite all that had happened in the last few days, how she had taken him to the very edge of sanity and perhaps beyond, he suspected he did. No, he knew he did. And so he hesitated, his claws at the ready, and pondered the finality of what one sharp thrust could do.

"You still can't do it, can you?" she croaked, her bloody lips curling up in an obscene grin. "No, of course not. It's not really you, is it? It never was. You need to be in a certain place for it. You need to be ice cold, completely removed from it all, in a place near death or shocked into such a primal state where there's nothing to hold you back. No meaningless moral compass, none of this rubbish about redemption. An hour ago, you could have done it, if you'd had the strength. But now, you are *saturated* with life, with hope! You don't have it in you, to end me."

Weakly, she reached up with her hand and laid it gently on his cheek. He didn't recoil from her touch, and only held her gaze with his own, confused.

"Let's see if I fare any better," she whispered, and sighed, as she reached up to embrace him.

At least... that was what he thought. But she kept... growing. Her limbs contorted, grew boneless, flattened. She took on mass faster than he could comprehend it and suddenly, he realized he wasn't being embraced after all.

She was enveloping him, like some sort of giant amoeba.

He had just barely enough time to realize this, and then it was too late to do anything about it. He had just enough time to understand that it *was* too late—

And then she absorbed him, just as she had absorbed his claws, the first time they had fought. Darkness and horror closed in.

Their eyes rolled up into their head, and they collapsed to the ground. Nearby, the torch began to sputter as the fuel tank ran empty. It gasped one last flash of light and was extinguished, plunging the room into utter darkness.

CHAPTER TWENTY-THREE

Forty-Six and 2

DENNIS LEE, MERCEDES LACKEY
AND CODY MARTIN

*I thought I knew Vickie. I soon discovered I was wrong.
I had completely underestimated her.*

*Then again, maybe all along it had just been that she
had underestimated herself.*

The door to Red's quarters was plastered with police tape. Rage
gave Vickie the energy to blast it out of her way, gave her the
energy to shatter the locks on the door, and force the door inward
before she even reached it. She stalked inside and paused for a
moment, breathing harshly, while taking a careful look around.

The place had been ransacked, of course. Jensen had made
sure of that. Red wouldn't have been stupid enough to leave
so much as an incriminating note about an illegal poker game
around, but that wouldn't stop Jensen from trashing the place
in a pretense of looking for something that he already knew
wasn't there. Her hands twitched a little with the urge to get
them around Jensen's neck.

She was furious. But fury had never left her helpless and blind.
Fury had always given her a cold clarity and a sharp focus, had
always driven all other emotions out. Fury let her see with the
acuity of a falcon, and the calculation of a mastermind.

So where in this mess would there be something *she* could use?
No hair, of course. But a bit of scarlet cloth made her ease her
way towards the tumble of bureau drawers to pick out a red scarf
among a pile of red scarves just like it: the one that was the most

worn, the most frayed at the corners. Next to the bureau was the pile of books thrown out of the bookshelf. She carefully moved them until she found *Franny and Zooey*. That went into her bag with the scarf, and the box from the Med Lab containing a slide with a blood smear on it, and some tiny, tiny vials of skin and claw samples. *Toothbrush,* she thought. Of course, it might be at Mel's place—which had been scoured clean of everything—but maybe he had more than one. She began picking her way across the mess to the bathroom when a shadow loomed in the doorway.

She looked over at it and began to shake with rage as "shadow" became "recognizable human."

Jensen.

He scowled at her. "I—" he began. She extended her hand towards him, twitched her fingers, and he found himself unable to utter a word.

"You, you soulless bastard, will march yourself right back around and forget I was ever here," she said icily. "Because if you don't, I swear to you I will witch your junk next, and shrink it down so far you'll need tweezers and a magnifying glass to masturbate."

A look of disbelief was followed by a look of sheer terror as her fingers twitched again, and he felt the tingle she sent to his privates.

He fled.

Vickie took a breath, exhaled, and marched to the bathroom. *Toothbrush.*

Red Djinni awoke to nothing but a harsh white light. There was no source, it was simply everywhere. He seemed to be on his back, and as he placed his hands on the ground to lift himself into a sitting position, he froze. There was nothing there. He was floating in a brilliant void, and the worst part was that it was familiar. He had been here before. He groaned in dismay. The last time had not ended well. He had no reason to believe this time would be any better.

"Alright then," he muttered. "First things first. Think of gravity. Think of standing on a floor."

He closed his eyes. It had been easier that way, the last time. He pictured himself standing on ceramic tiles, and with a gentle push of his will, he believed it to be so. He opened his eyes again. The ceramic floor seemed to extend to each point on the horizon.

It might have been dizzying, if he had not been expecting it. Yes, it was precisely the way it had been the last time. Except now, there wasn't that paradoxical sense of claustrophobia, of being cramped and constricted in what appeared to be an infinite space. He felt calm, comfortable, which was odd in itself. He never felt calm and comfortable. Surely something had to be horribly wrong, for if he was here, then there must be another...

"An interesting choice," said a voice behind him. "It's all a bit bland though. I thought you were more imaginative than this."

"It's been a while," Red said, turning. "Figured I'd start slow, y'know, before we get back to the violence."

Doppelgaenger gave him a knowing smile. She stood at ease, one hand resting on her hip. She seemed petite, garbed in a simple pantsuit of 1940s vintage, and knee-high leather boots. She looked to be in her twenties, but there was no mistaking the calculating glint in her eye. It was Doppelgaenger. This was how she saw herself, Red supposed. Her true self. Karoline.

He looked down at himself, and was a little surprised to see he was clad in his ECHO uniform. Well, that was a revelation. Was this how he saw himself these days?

"Somewhere, Bull is *laughing*..." he said.

"I sort of doubt it," Karoline said. "I don't think Bull has much to laugh about right now."

Red shrugged. "So, is this your place or mine?"

She chuckled and waved her hands around in a grandiose motion. "Would you believe, this is *our* place?"

"Both of us," Red murmured. "I guess that explains why it doesn't feel so cramped this time."

"I almost forgot," she nodded. "This isn't your first rodeo."

"Nope," he said, eyeing her cautiously. "You seem pretty comfortable here, too. I'm guessing it's not your first time, either."

"Oh no," she grinned. "I'm well acquainted with this place. You might say I've visited here many times in my travels. The Mindscape has become a bit of a second home."

"Mindscape," Red mused. "Never thought to give it a name." He looked around. "I don't see anyone else here."

"Did you expect to?"

"Unless you have certain abilities of the psychic persuasion, this isn't a place you would regularly come to." He gave her a direct look. "You would only come here when forced to. We're not really here, after all, but the mind's a funny thing. Two personas, one brain, there tends to be conflict. Where's there's conflict, there's violence. My guess is the Mindscape is a visualization of where we meet. It's the best approximation our simple brains can manage. It's here to give us a place to stand on while we struggle to destroy each other, to claim this space as our own. If you've been here before, you've brought others with you. If they are no longer here, then you destroyed them. How am I doing?"

"It's a bit simple"—Karoline shrugged—"but it's a fair approximation of the situation. It goes a bit further than that though. From what I can tell, this is the basic make-up of where one experiences dreams, but with the lucidity turned up to eleven."

"*Spinal Tap* reference," Red mused. "Nice."

"You're right, though," she continued. "This isn't the first time I've been forced here. I've brought others, but they're gone now. This time is different. It doesn't have to end that way."

"The hell you say."

"I told you," she sighed, standing at ease with exaggerated patience, "that before this was over, I would offer you a choice. We don't have to fight. We can be together. Forever. You know, the whole two-become-one thing. You don't have to be extinguished, or extinguish me; we can merge. Think of what you've become, and what I was, and the synergy that could exist between us. Together we would be unstoppable, perhaps even eternal." She frowned. "Am I getting through that hard head of yours?"

"Like a diamond pickaxe," Red sighed. "And the others? Why didn't you share this space with them?"

"We weren't compatible," Karoline shrugged. "In the end, what I received from them proved temporary. They didn't have what you bring to the table. The regeneration alone might be enough to sustain us indefinitely. With them, the fusion would not have been...ideal. Merging with them would not have been seamless, at least not enough."

"But we would be?"

"Enough, yes, enough that we could even maintain our own identities, for the most part."

"For the most part?"

Karoline made an impatient face. "You must realize, as compatible as we are, we are at this moment two distinct personalities. Only one can have absolute control at any time. You know

I want you here with me. I want to share all of this with you. But I'm not stupid. I don't trust you...not yet. In time, we will draw together, root out the differences and line up as one. In the meantime, I know you well enough that you will fight this every step of the way. So, it's a matter of time, but for now..."

"Right, for now I'm just going to be some spectator along for the ride. How can you ask that, of *me*? Maybe you don't know me as well as you thought?"

"I thought love would convince you, like it did for me," Karoline said. "Try to imagine it, Red. In time, you would have everything you could ever want, and you would be able to share it, with *me*. You said you still loved me, even after Victrix, that you still felt love for me. What if one doesn't exclude the other? I'm not above sharing you. You would have everything, and me, and you could still have her..."

"Well, that's just about the craziest thing I've ever heard," Red snapped. "And that's saying something. So I'll get—what?— vacation days to be with Victrix, and the rest of the time I'll be chained up in some corner of our brain, be a little bug of a voice in your head?"

"It will seem that way, in the beginning," she conceded. "Admittedly, securing Vickie from the clutches of the Masters might require some doing. Probably a bit of fast talking on my part, or subterfuge, or both. But I think it can be done. As for us, we will adapt to share this existence, to share control, to share everything, even her."

"No," Red disagreed. "It can't ever be like that. Even it was possible, even if we could merge that seamlessly, it can't ever happen..."

"And why is that?"

"Have you *met* me?" Red asked. "Do you think I would ever let you near her again, let alone touch her, share in any semblance of intimacy with her? And as for me, do I seem the sort who would give up even a fraction of who I am, for anything? You can forget it. Not for anything, especially not for you, and not for..."

"Love?" Karoline interrupted, her voice soft and mournful. "For completion? This can end without violence. This can, for a change, end peacefully and you will experience an eternity of bliss. And you will never be alone, ever again. Have I met you?

Yes, I have. It's the one thing neither of us ever said, ever shared, but we could feel it in the other, we could feel the truth of it. We were always alone. It's our deepest fear, our greatest shame. And it doesn't have to be that way, ever again."

Red stared at her.

"Yeah, it does," he said finally. "If those are my choices, then it does."

"Please," she whispered. "Don't be so rash as to..."

"But I am rash," Red said with a wry smirk. "For all my attempts at planning, for all the careful machinations of the past, that really is who I am. Come to think of it, my instincts have gotten me out of some tough jams. When things go tits up, it's all I've got left. And look, I'm still standing. Well, in a manner of speaking."

Karoline didn't answer, and merely stood there, her arms wrapped around herself, her eyes pleading with him.

"Please," she repeated finally. "Please reconsider. You know what I'm offering. Don't let some foolish and stubborn ideal stand in the way of..."

"No," Red interrupted. "It's not foolish. It's not stubborn. It's me, girl. And you know it."

He watched as his words bored into her. She seemed to wither, to grow dimmer, as if something inside of her had been poisoned. She bowed her head, and shivered. Red took an involuntary step forward, suddenly concerned. For a moment, she seemed to fade away, her very skin a translucent curtain threaded through with pale veins. She was disappearing. Concern became fear, and Red took a few more steps towards her before stopping again.

She wasn't disappearing. She was gathering herself.

What had withered in that single moment was returning to life, and that life was building in a steady crescendo. It was as if he stood in front of a furnace being heated to a white-hot inferno. Her emotions began to bombard him with a fervid intensity to the point where he actually held up his hands to shield himself. He felt anger, resentment, even hatred, and beneath it all, a cold reserve of self-preservation. And when she finally looked up at him, it all erupted to the surface, unleashed in a mighty blow that sent him flying to land hard on his back.

"Your choice is made," she said, her voice cold and lifeless. "A poor choice. Goodbye, Red Djinni."

Rearing back, she summoned a blazing ball of fire in her hand, and hurled it towards his prone and gasping body.

"Vix to JM."

"Go for Murdock, Vix." John and Sera had racked out at CCCP HQ. Their shift was over for the day; Krieger attacks didn't usually happen at night, and any attacks that were happening would likely be out of their range. The Kriegers had been testing their limits, and had been careful not to commit any serious forces where they thought that John and Sera might show up. Still, they managed to surprise the Kriegers with some regularity. He had been asleep when Vickie called, but all of his time in the military had honed the ability to go from dead asleep to wide awake pretty damn quick. Sera stirred next to him, and he brushed her mind with his, easing her back to sleep.

"I'm about to do something stupid and I want your help, you and Sera. You in?"

"If'n you ask Bella or the Commissar, doin' stupid stuff is 'bout all I'm good for. Of course I'm in." He sat up in the bed gently, keeping his voice down. "Give us ten minutes to get decent, then we can head out. Meetin' at your place?"

"Yeah, my workroom. I'll unlock the balcony and leave the window open for you. Keep this on the QT. Out for now."

"Roger that. Murdock, out." He sighed, turning to watch Sera as she slept. *Too much to ask for to get a few hours of kip. Rest, the wicked, yada yada.* He scooted further towards her before leaning down to kiss her cheek. "Time to wake up, darlin'."

Like him, although probably for entirely different reasons, she was able to go from deepest sleep to wide awake instantly. She sat up and pulled her hair out of her eyes. "Something is wrong," she stated, rather than asked.

"Well, Vickie is involved, so that's a given. Needs us to throw our boots on and get over to her place. Wanted us to keep it to ourselves, too, so I figure it's pretty serious. Hope you don't mind, but I volunteered us."

She shook her head. "Of course not. I think this might have to do with Red Djinni. That is the only reason I can think that she would not tell anyone else."

"That would be correct, Mrs. Murdock," the strangely unaccented voice of Eight chirped in John's ear. *"Victrix has found*

everything she believes she can find at this date, and is going to make the attempt to find, and rescue, the Red Djinni. I believe she believes that you two are her only hope for allies to combat Doppelgaenger."

"So, nothin' too serious." John let out another sigh, then swung his feet over the edge of the bed to stand up. "Best get movin' if we're gonna get over there, darlin'."

As the fireball came hurtling towards him, Red marveled at how familiar all of this seemed.

Justine started with a fireball too, he thought. *And I countered with a . . .*

"Water wall!"

It sprang up before him, materializing from nothing but his will to coalesce into a stout barrier that stood ready to absorb the mass of blazing heat aimed with deadly precision at his heart. Would it be that easy? This was a place of imagination, the weapons at hand fueled and channeled by will alone. Karoline may have had years to hone her skills here, but Red's defining characteristic had always been his stubborn, pig-headed resolve. He was no stranger to pain and the will to work past it. Perhaps it was the reason he had survived his one encounter in the Mindscape. A spell had gone terribly wrong. Justine was a young, reckless fire mage mind-surfing inside of him when her own fragile body was consumed by an uncontrollable backlash of wildfire. In that one desperate fight, a dying girl had pit her frantic need to survive against his, and in the end had come up lacking. Neither of them had known what they were doing, relying on instincts alone, grasping at primal forces of perceived fire and water to manifest on a surreal plane of existence. Red had won that fight, but he had never truly known why. It wasn't something that particularly concerned him. He never had any intention of returning to this "place." It was just another odd chapter in the increasingly bizarre and frenzied life of a maverick metahuman. He had sworn never to touch magic again after that day, but he never expected to be drafted into the ranks of ECHO, or to be paired with the likes of Victoria Victrix. He should have seen this coming. A part of him cursed himself for dropping his guard, for letting magic back into his life. He should have known that something like this might happen—again.

But that wasn't fair. He wasn't here because of magic. He was here because, once again, he had fallen for the wrong girl. A girl who, it turned out, had a metahuman knack of simply absorbing her prey, in some cases taking them whole, extinguishing their minds, and picking off whatever she needed from the remaining carcass before moving on. Except this time, she had actually grown attached to the victim and given him the chance to share in this unnatural union, to keep them both intact, and to forge something far greater than the mere sum of their parts. There was no magic at work here. The only thing akin to magic in play was the inscrutable notion of love, something that defied any and all attempts to define it, to quantify it, yet somehow managed to enslave or befuddle the most ardent of minds, the most stalwart of spirits.

He had actually considered the offer. It was, despite the sheer creepiness of it all, a grotesquely attractive proposal. A shot at immortality, at immense power, shared with someone he couldn't help but admit was kindred in horrifying ways. The last time, there really had been no option. With Justine, there could be no union, there simply wasn't room enough for both of them. It was her, or it was him. This time, he had been presented with a choice, but it wasn't really a choice at all. It wasn't something he could do. Stubborn. Pig-headed. That was Red Djinni. At heart, he was too wild, too willful, to simply be a part of a whole. And right now... more than a little psychotic. Or emotionally exhausted. Or both. He just couldn't *feel* anything, even though he knew he should. He should have been feeling rage, perhaps mixed with terror. There were shadows of both emotions there, but there was no strength behind them.

As the fireball punched through his water wall and slammed into his chest, Red had the briefest of moments to wonder if this was the day his mule-headed temperament would finally get him killed. Would it be so easy, that a mere wall of water could withstand the blazing fury of passion scorned? Of course not.

There was a blinding flash of light, followed by the overwhelming stench of burning flesh, and as Red looked down at himself, he was met with an appalling sight. His ECHO uniform was in tatters and his skin was scorched, seared in some areas, already blackened and brittle in others.

There was no pain, though, and like a harsh light flaring to life in his mind, Red remembered with absolute clarity how it had been before in the Mindscape. He had experienced no pain then either, and he supposed that might have been how he had survived the last time. The fight had been quick, if brutal, but whatever Justine had managed to dish out he had just kept coming.

He remembered her cries, her startled grunts of pain, as his own attacks had driven her back, left her defenses open and vulnerable to his onslaught of claws, kicks and a final merciless tackle. If he had been coping with the pain of savage burns then, he doubted he could have reacted with that same, single-minded intensity such dexterous acts required. The grapple had been vicious, culminating in a slow, relentless chokehold that had snapped her neck. As recklessly strong as she was, Justine's fire had only penetrated so far, skin deep, not enough to slow him down. His speed and reflexes had won that battle.

Karoline's mastery of the Mindscape, while lacking Justine's natural pyrokinetic talents, more than made up for any shortcomings with experience and focus, fueled by her raw and ravaged emotions. Red tried to stand and felt his limbs betray him as he collapsed to the ground. This time, the absence of pain made him vulnerable. Karoline's initial volley had damaged him greatly, and without any sure way of sensing precisely where, Red had no clue of how to compensate. He tried to rise again, and fell as his left arm and both legs seized up. He came to rest on his side, his limbs still twitching.

He blinked, confused, as a dim light appeared to shimmer in the corner of his eye. Was he seeing stars? That was never good. He couldn't afford to black out. He needed to find his strength. He needed to get up. He couldn't let her win, not with so much as stake. If he fell, she would take all that was left in him. Armed with new powers, perhaps even an immortal vessel, Karoline would be free to attend to one last piece of unfinished business—acquiring Victoria Victrix for her Masters.

He grunted and struggled again, but could manage no more than a soft whimper as he continued to flail about. He heard her approach, her steps echoing sharply on the cold ceramic tile. He felt her grip his neck, and with ease she lifted him up and brought his head close to hers. Her eyes bore into his, then softened, as she averted her gaze.

"Please," she whispered. "Don't make me do this. We could be everything. Is death really preferable to me?"

Red coughed. His hand, his remaining good one, struggled in vain to pry her fingers from his throat. She obliged him and loosened her grip, just a touch. It wasn't enough. She was so much more than he was in this place. He let his hand fall away, and glared at her. The wisest thing would have been to stall. In time, perhaps he could find a way, some way to best her. He needed to stay alive. Alive, he would have a say, and perhaps even some influence over her...but to what end? Did he really think he could overcome her? Failing that, did he really think he could sway her? She had spent years preparing for this. If he agreed, if he accepted her terms, in time he would become nothing more than a puppet to her insanity. And that just wasn't him, it never could be.

Stubborn. Pig-headed. That was Red Djinni.

"Darlin'," he croaked, "an eternity spent on a Judas Cradle would be preferable to you."

He watched her flinch as his words cut into her, felt her grip tighten as she struggled with her resolve, and waited for the end as she raised her hand, fire dancing across her fingertips.

"I'm in the workroom." Vickie's voice, hoarser than usual, met John as he landed on the floor of her living room. He let Sera walk in front of him, leading him to the workroom. For a moment he wondered if he had come to the wrong apartment. The normally pristine living room was—for Vickie anyway—a mess. There were empty coffee cups and meal-cans on every available surface, and under the coffee table. The table itself was inches deep in notepads covered in complex equations; it looked as if every page in those pads had been used.

"Hey, kiddo. Eight gave us the short version. Wanna fill in the blanks?" He reached out with his telempathy to get a sense of Vickie's state. He didn't like what he found; she was right on the edge of losing it, and was holding on to everything by the barest thread of sheer will. He knew that Sera had noted the same things he had, if not through their connection, then through her own senses.

Vickie came as far as the door of her workroom; to put it mildly, she looked as if she hadn't slept in days, her hair was brittle and lifeless, her cheeks were hollow, and there was a frantic, edge-of-madness look to her eyes that mirrored the mess in her apartment. The edge of madness was in her voice too. "Eight can do pretty

much everything I can, bar the magic stuff—and he *can* do the
magic-mapping stuff now, just not the rest of it, like last-minute
rescues and opening up holes in the ground. So, I've got backup
from someone who can do everything I can, doesn't need to sleep,
can do it all faster, and for a lot more people simultaneously. So
far as DG's time as Mel, Eight and I have plugged all the holes,
unboobied all the traps, and discovered all the information theft
DG did when she was playing Mel." She spread her hands wide,
and they shook. The measured logic of her speech was at violent
odds with the desperation JM sensed inside her. "I figure that
sets me free to get Red back or die trying. Not—" she added as
an afterthought "—that I expect you two to do anything but flee
if I go down. If the three of us together can't handle DG, two
of you alone won't have a chance, and there's no point in losing
our nuclear option—you two."

She meant that. She absolutely meant it. She was throwing the
dice with everything she had riding on it, nothing held back,
nothing in reserve. It *was* desperation JM had sensed—and maybe
a touch of insanity. Because if she couldn't save Red...

...he didn't want to think about the consequences.

"Eight is great an' all, don't get me wrong. But it isn't you.
You called us in on this 'cause we're the big guns, right?" He
took a breath, but continued before she had a chance to respond.
"We're there so that this little op of yours works. An' the way I
measure success, everyone gets out alive. Got it?"

Sera folded her arms and looked stern. "Have you not accounted
for *how much* of your Overwatch aid has needed your magic in
the past? And did the Djinni *himself* not force you to flee against
your will because *he* believed you were too important to our
cause to risk? We will not leave you behind, no matter where
we go, and that is final."

Vickie grabbed for the doorframe for a moment, then collected herself. "No point in arguing with you. I've got my jetpack
out there by the window. It's fueled full and ready. I've got the
location spell mapped out. All I need to do is run the equations
and trigger it. It should plant a finder to Red in all three of our
skulls. Once we know where he is, we gun and run, in, out and
back to ECHO. I'm... given what DG did to the kids and Mel,
I figure he's been tortured, so he's probably in a bad way, so we
bring him straight to the Med Center. That sound solid to you?"

"Works for me. We'll want to pack along extra medical supplies; Sera an' I can do some healin', but it leaves us next to useless. An' if we're goin' to be expectin' a fight, we'll want our full strength. Got a spare ECHO medical backpack?"

"With the jetpack, I'm way ahead of you." She turned and went back into the workroom. "Come on in."

Darlin', we need to keep a close eye on her. She's hurtin' bad. You've known her longer than I have, so she might listen to you more'n she would to me.

Beloved... if I were taken, how would you react? If you were taken, how would I? It is folly to expect anything other than the same from her. Sera sounded... at a loss. *We will do what we can, but her will is strong, and we cannot combat it without doing her more harm than she is doing to herself.*

When they entered the workroom, John saw that the carpet had been covered with a canvas dropcloth inscribed with multiple circles and what looked like thousands of tiny hand-drawn glyphs and symbols. His head reeled with trying to comprehend how long it must have taken her to do this. Only someone who was driven in ways he understood only too well could have accomplished this. In the center was a very small circle, densely inscribed all around, containing a motley assortment of objects—a page from a book, a toothbrush, a microscope slide with something preserved on it, a scrap of red fabric, and some other bits of things too small to make out from where he was standing. "You stand there, Johnny," Vickie said, pointing to another circle from the circle that *she* was standing in. "And, Sera, you go there. I'm pretty sure your Celestial innards aren't going to object to this, but if you zap me instead of finding Red, I'm not going to be held responsible for my actions."

"Aside from gettin' arranged like furniture, what exactly do you need from us for this spell?"

In the bright light from the overhead fixture, her skin had a gray tinge to it, and her hair looked like dry thatch, something that a spark would set ablaze. "Just concentrate on Red," she said, and closed eyes that were far too big for her face... and far too bright.

John let out a breath, and cast a final glance toward Sera. "Here we go." She smiled, and then they both closed their eyes. John's thoughts turned towards Red Djinni: hearing about his exploits when John was on the run, their first "meeting" on the streets of Atlanta, the strike mission against the North American Thulian HQ. Drinking together. Laughing together. Sharing stories ... oddly enough, sharing books. He built up memories in his mind until it was almost as if Red was standing in front of him. He got the uncanny feeling that if he opened his eyes, Red would actually *be* there.

And then he heard Vickie cry out, *"Come back to me!"* and he was caught up in the teeth of a whirlwind. The best analogy he could make was that it was like hanging onto one end of a live wire, while the other end went hunting something. Or being on the seat of a wagon pulled by a team of runaway horses.

And then—

He hung there, helpless, held fast by her powerful grasp. Red was vaguely aware that his limbs were still twitching on their own, ravaged by her fire and useless to him. His right arm, which had propped him up against the blast, was all he had left. It dangled from him, his fingers scraping the ground.

He glanced up at her and winced as incandescent waves of light and fire radiated from her outstretched palm, like a torch, ready to burn him to cinders. He averted his eyes, turning his head away from that awful heat, but not before recognizing her own hesitation. While one hand held him up, his body fixed in her unyielding grip, the other hand shook with doubt, the intensity of the flames waxing and waning as she struggled with the decision to end him.

"It didn't have to be like this," she wept. "You idiot. You coward."

Red didn't answer and kept his eyes averted, waiting for the end. He found his mind going to irrational places, as it often did when he courted death. This was, after all, hardly his first time. His thoughts raced, brushing the corners of his consciousness, ranging from the absurd to those stark in their brutal and honest desire.

How crazy am I, he thought, *that at a time like this I'm thinking of whiskey, soft mood lighting, forgotten lyrics to some Adele song, wondering who will finally ascend the Iron Throne? Never enough time. Did I really ever want to live forever? Touch my tears, Bella. You ever get Bull to stop snoring? I hope so, but maybe not, I still think it was you that stole my hoagie. Bull would know, you tell him everything. Even if you didn't, it's like he could lift it from your thoughts. You do that with everyone, Bull? Do you know what Bruno's final thoughts were? God, I could use a shot. Drink one for me, will you, Johnny? Mind that lady of yours, she's a spitfire. Will I see you again, Sera? Will you be the one to tell me, in the end, if I ever mattered, what could I have done with this sorry life, if I could go on? There was so much left, so much unfinished. Was redemption possible? Would I have ever lived up to this hero gig? You thought so, didn't you, Vickie? I wonder what it would have been like, to graze on your neck...*

The thought of her was beautiful, if painful. If only he could stay, if for no other reason than to know what they could have shared. Would it have ended in tragedy, like every other relationship he had ever had? Or would this one have been different? He would never know, and the thought of it brought an ache to his addled sensibilities. He felt the start of a laugh—a dry, mirthless laugh—but all he could manage was a low moan. He was broken, his body consumed, his mind crippled, and the only pain he could feel stemmed from a newly discovered and unrequited love. He wondered how long it had been there, dormant, needing only a harsh slap across the face to be brought to the forefront. He *was* an idiot, a coward. Surely this was the end. This time, there was no one left to save him, especially himself. He felt Karoline's grip on his throat tighten, the surge of heat intensify. He would never have his answers, only the sharp stab of lights before she incinerated what was left of him...

The lights...

He had averted his eyes to Karoline's fire, but it wasn't the only source of light here. They were surrounded by light, endless points of light from horizon to horizon, but it was something new which caught his eye, from beneath him, as it pulsed just beyond his fingertips. He thought of Vickie again, and it flared briefly. He reached for it, and the dullness of his mind snapped back into focus as his fingers wrapped around something slim and sharp. He stared at it incredulously. It was a claw. It was *his* claw. What in the world...?

He drew in a sharp breath as a voice—*Vickie's voice!*—rang through his head like a trumpet on a battlefield.

"Come back to me!"

And his mind flooded with images. No, not images. These

were threads of the future, of the present, of dying pasts, all the threads of *possibles* that the Seraphym had shown him. Before, he had only focused on the ones where he and Bella were together. That had been all he had wanted to see. But now, now he saw all of them.

The ones where he had gone back to Vickie after reading her letter, gathered her into his arms, and that same spark had jumped between them that he'd felt when he'd rescued her.

And the ones where that spark had happened later, when *she* had brought Red Saviour and Bulwark to rescue *him*. Or when he'd done something out of character and gone to console her after Bruno's death. Or at completely insignificant times, at the top of the Parkour course, or deciding to bring her Chinese food because he could tell from her voice over his freq that she was exhausted.

But whenever it happened, the changes it had made in his life—

—in both their lives, really. They lit up each other's darkness; they held back each other's despair. Lifetimes of shared memories. Sacrifices. Triumphs.

And he saw *this* thread too; saw how she had hidden every hint of her feelings for him as he and Karoline fell into their affair. And all so that he would be happy.

He also saw, with absolute clarity, that if he died here, driven by her promise to him, that geas, she would not falter and give up. She would step up. She would work herself to the bone, but she would step up, become the warrior she had once been. Realize that not only could she go on without him, she *had* to. For both their sakes. For his memory. He almost wept to see it. He had never believed he could be the catalyst for something so good, so right, but there it was. Even in death, especially in death, he *mattered*.

Again, he almost laughed. Moments before he was cursing magic, and here he was, helpless, and the only weapon he had was magic. He gripped the claw in wonder. It wasn't just magic. It was empowered by Victoria's love, all of it, and it was mighty. And this was what Karoline could not understand, what she could not see. This was the sort of love beside which her selfish, self-serving emotion revealed itself to be fool's gold.

All that flooded him in an instant, in the blink of an eye, while Karoline reared back to deliver the finishing blow.

"Goodbye, Red," Karoline said. "I loved you, and you wasted it. Take that with you to the next life."

"Love," Red croaked. "You know nothing of love. Let me show you what love is..."

Their eyes met, and Red felt the warmth and peace of serenity flow through him. His body had stopped twitching. Karoline's eyes widened as she saw the claw in his hand. With a fierce cry, her hand flashed down, raining fire, just as he was raising his, the needle-sharp point of the claw aimed at her head. He saw her head jerk away, but not enough, and as her flames slammed into him, he watched the claw flash with incandescent light as it sank into her ear, up and deep into her brain.

Karoline screamed, but Red could not. The scorching blast tore through him, robbing him of his voice. He had come alight, as wildfire, a blazing inferno. Still, he felt nothing but peace and fulfillment, and with his last thought he said a small, simple prayer.

Come back, Vickie. With my love, come back...

Karoline awoke in the darkness, and wept.

There was pain, terrible, terrible pain. Anguish. Terror. It was Red. John could *feel* it, he *knew* it. And he knew *where* Red was, precisely where, the location bit into his brain and branded itself there.

And then there was a last wordless cry of despair, a flash of light—

And nothing.

John's eyes flew open in time to see Vickie collapsing to the floor, one hand outstretched as if in a desperate attempt to catch something that had escaped her. John moved to her in an instant, with Sera mirroring him from her circle.

"Holy hell!" His hand went to her throat to feel for a pulse; he already knew she was alive from his heightened senses and telempathy, but after what they had all just gone through, he needed the extra assurance. "She's still breathin', but she's out for good." He looked up to stare into Sera's eyes. "Darlin'—we *know* where he is. The spell *worked.*"

"We felt him die," Sera said bleakly, "and so did she."

John swallowed hard, then shook his head. "I don't care. Until I put eyes on him, I'm not acceptin' it. Magic is goddamned weird," he added, trying to convince himself as much as Sera. "I'm goin'. You should stay here, be here for her when she wakes up. She's goin' to need you. I've gotta try, if there's any hope at all." He leaned over Vickie's unconscious form and kissed Sera hard. "Love you. I'll be back."

"You had better keep that promise," she replied fiercely. And then he was gone.

When he came back through the window, Sera had somehow cleaned the living room, and Vickie was sitting on the couch, head in her hands, her shoulders shaking with silent sobbing. Sera had an arm and a wing around her, but it was obvious from the waves of anguished loss pulsing from her that there was no comfort to be found even in the embrace of an angel.

Sera looked up at him without much hope. He shook his head wearily. He had burned hard to get to where the searingly bright "compass" in his head had told him Red had been; another abandoned mental asylum out in the Georgia back country. It had been something out of a horror movie: torture implements that had been recently used, and too much blood. There had also been . . . traces of something magical. John had Eight recording everything through his Overwatch rig, and he had gathered the tools in a plastic bag he had found in the medical backpack. He had also taken several samples of the blood; he had no way of telling whether it was all from one person—he suspected it was—or from a number of people, so he wanted to be sure to not miss anything. He stashed the medical backpack out of sight in Vickie's workroom; there would be time for them to get to it later, and take it all to ECHO for forensic analysis.

No Red, and no Doppelgaenger, love. There was a lot of blood and some nasty emotions soaked into that godforsaken place, though.

I have not felt so helpless except when you had forgotten me, came the heartbreaking response. *I do not know what to do. Anything that I can say will be so hollow!*

Don't say anything, then. We'll just be here for her. She'll talk when she's ready. Gettin' her some rest is the best thing we can do for her. She'll be able to . . . deal with this a lot better once she's slept some.

He felt just as helpless as Sera at this point. His legs felt wooden as he trod over to the kitchen. Red had been his friend, and while he could empathize with the broken little mage on the couch, he knew he could never comprehend how much she had just lost.

But he'd do his best for her. She was his friend as well, and between what she had shown him when his memory had been locked away, what he had come to feel through his connection with Sera, and how she had worked so hard to find his journal so that he *was* able to get his memory back...he owed her too much to just walk away and leave her to suffer alone.

There just were no words for such a terrible loss. A piece of her was dead, and there was nothing that could fill that horrible wound in her soul. *It's not goddamned fair! We* had *him, knew where he was! We were ready to get him, and kill that bastard that had been wearing Mel's face.* Despite all of the awful crap that had been going on in the war so far, it wasn't until that very moment that John felt so weary that he thought he might entertain giving up. He was tired of losing people. *Where's the goddamned scotch? She must have moved it since the last time I had any here.*

<Single malt's in the top cabinet next to the outside wall, hotshot.> Grey, who was looking rather as if he'd been fighting several losing battles himself, his fur dry and harsh, regarded him from the divider between the kitchen and the living room. *<Your instincts are pretty good, for a ground-pounding grunt. Short of knocking her out with a tranq, getting her drunk might be the only thing to do right now.>* The cat shook himself all over and hissed. *<Fuck.>*

John had forgotten that the large cat was more than met the eye. He retrieved the bottle, and nodded his thanks to Grey as he made his way back to the couch. He sat down on the other side of Vickie from Sera, setting the bottle down on the table. Herb was already there, a shot glass held up in his stubby arms.

He uncorked the bottle and poured a shot, pulling one of Vickie's hands away from her face and curling her fingers around it. "Here, Vic. Drink this." She stared at it for a moment, as if she didn't recognize what it was, then blinked, sending more tears down her face, and chugged the shot. Wordlessly she held out the glass, and he poured again. And again. And again.

Just as he was getting ready to pour the fifth shot, her eyes rolled up into her head and she passed out on Sera's shoulder. With a nod to John, the angel picked her up as if she weighed nothing, and carried her into the bedroom, coming out a moment later.

"Stay or go?" she asked him.

"I figure we stay the night. I don't want to leave her alone. If she gets any ideas 'bout not wantin' to go on or anythin' like that, we oughta be here."

"*I have reported everything to Belladonna,*" Eight said. "*She will send a messenger for the medical bag and the samples, and requests you to stay until she and Bulwark can take over.*"

That seemed to cover everything. John leaned forward in his seat, picked up the bottle of scotch, and drained nearly half of what was left before setting it back down. Sera settled back on the couch next to him and put her arm and wing around him. "I would very much like a serving of that beverage," she said, in a voice heavy with unshed tears. "I would like to drink to Red." John nodded, and picked up the bottle again; there was more than enough left for the both of them.

"Y'know, this is the same brand that Red and I drank together." John held the bottle up. "To Red." After taking a long pull, he handed the bottle to Sera.

She took an equally healthy swig, seeming to take no effect from it, though he had never seen her drink liquor of any kind before. "To Red."

And when the bottle was empty, they held each other against the grief, the dark and the night.

CHAPTER TWENTY-FOUR

Hospital Beds

VERONICA GIGUERE AND MERCEDES LACKEY

Let's not forget the real Mel. Mel Gautier—Reverie—the lady who commanded illusions and made them real. Or Penny, the girl who speaks to ghosts. They have their parts to play.

The ECHO infirmary had nearly every piece of Metisian medical technology scavenged from the ruined city. Paired with the group's doctors and metahuman healers, the facility had the capacity to bring even the most battered and bloodied bodies back to life. At the moment, the machines sat idle in the mostly empty space. Only one patient remained, kept in isolation as much for her own safety as the safety of the medical team.

Gilead had read Mel Gautier's files, both ECHO and Army, and she couldn't begin to understand how to initiate the healing process. The kids rescued with her had provided enough information to construct a crude timeline. It painted a horrific picture. Bloodwork showed countless chemical dependencies, while scarring over much of her body provided evidence of sustained, almost ritual torture. One missing toe on each foot, deep gouges in her thighs and upper arms...

The bandages covering the stump of her left hand would need to be changed within the next few hours. Gilead scrolled through the list of injuries and the recommended treatments. Clinical detachment had its place in times like these, but she wasn't made of stone.

The doctor closed the file, slumped down, and covered her face with her hands. Even the most conventional ECHO treatment involving a metahuman healing factor brought substantial risk to the healer. They couldn't afford to lose the most critical members of their medical team, so Gilead had offered to review Mel's files and provide a logical treatment plan.

And she had no idea where to start.

"Ma'am?" Yankee Pride knocked on the side of the office door. Her fingers slid down to show bloodshot eyes. He winced. "I'm sorry, Doctor. I can come back later if this is a bad time."

"No, no. Come on in, have a seat." She spun a metal stool over and waited for him to sit. "How're you doing, sir?"

"Fine, but you don't need to 'sir' me. This is just my version of a house call. Reverse house call, I suppose." He inclined his head toward the occupied room. "Any updates on her?"

Gilead leaned back and rested her head against the wall. A long breath full of frustration escaped her lips, making her feel even more deflated than before. "Physically, she's stable. All injuries documented, the worst treated as much as we can, and she's on antibiotics to prevent infection. There's head trauma, skull fractures, and extensive scarring. Given her history pre-ECHO, she's been under heavy sedation since she arrived."

Pride nodded. "Yeah, I'd read her file. Also read the other file that went with the fake one following her treatments after Five Points. You're saying they both got shot in the head?"

"Affirmative." Gilead swing around to her workstation and clicked through patient records. In a few minutes, she had two MRI images on the screen. Patches of color appeared in nearly identical regions. "This one," she pointed to the left, "is our girl when she came in with the kids. And this one," she pointed to the right, "is our imposter during the scans post-Peachtree. I've sent them down to one of my colleagues from back in the day to get his opinion on it. Let a real brain surgeon pick it apart."

Pride frowned at the pictures. "They were the same, down to a neurological level?"

"Best as I can tell, but that's why I sent them down to Frank to check." Gilead minimized the windows and stood. Thick one-way glass let them observe their patient without the threat of meta-induced hallucinations, and a cocktail of heavy sedatives provided additional insurance. Unfortunately, every extra day that Mel passed under that medical haze increased the likelihood of permanent damage to her long-term memory as well as to her metahuman abilities. *If she's even got them anymore*, Gilead thought.

All of these precautions could be for nothing. Mel's impersonator had claimed an initial loss of ability due to the injury. Given Mel's condition when she'd arrived and the potential ramifications of an out-of-control illusionist, they hadn't considered any kind of preliminary screening. The report from the Army psychologist detailed an extensive extraction operation where she had immobilized three Marines and the lead meta of the squad before being knocked out. Considering that she had been the only surviving prisoner of a six-person team, Gilead couldn't imagine her not using her abilities to defend herself.

Pride stood at the window, somber in his observation of her patient. She realized that it had been barely a week since the memorial, and less than two weeks since his mother's passing. They wouldn't get the toxicology reports back for a while, since every available resource was dedicated to analysis of the agents that Dominic Verdigris had released in the stadium. She had her suspicions, but without scientific proof, that's all they would be, and she didn't see the need to make conversation out of speculation. "So, how are you and Willa Jean holding up?"

"We're managing. She's got more on her mind, but she's tough." He turned to Gilead. Shadows around his eyes spoke of too many nights with too little rest. "They've taken some blood and tissue samples to compare with the folks whose abilities faded or disappeared. When she's not at the lab, she's burning up a corner of the training course."

"And how's that going?"

He smirked. "Her eyebrows will grow back. Creating and controlling fire are two different things, and she learned it the hard way." He sighed and returned his attention to Mel. "But at least she's got something to keep her occupied. It helps that she knows that Momma would be proud of her, and she holds on to that."

Gilead asked her next question carefully. "Good for her, but what about you? How are *you* managing?"

"I'm here." Pride rubbed his right wrist with the heel of his left hand. "Parker's taken the lead on much of the day-to-day operations, but we're still trying to figure out how deep this infiltration went. Who knows how much was compromised? And there's the issue of those children they recovered at the same location. We'll have to call in some help from other cities, see if they have resources to assist—"

"Ben, stop." She put her hand on his shoulder to stop the stream of consciousness that kept him from answering her question. "Stop thinking about the others and worry about yourself for once. Please. If you don't, you're never going to get the opportunity to really heal."

His jaw clenched, the sudden tension invisible static between them. Gilead kept going. "There is a difference between dealing with someone else's loss and your own. Any caretaker, even those with the most compliant and loving charges, will stress the importance of self-care. You need to talk to someone or find a healthy means to work through and resolve what's happened."

"Ma'am, with all due respect, I don't have time for some self-indulgent psychotherapeutic dialogue. The war is still going on. I may not be at the forefront of the battle, but I am still a member of this organization and any retreat would be perceived as a weakness, even by those who we work to protect." Shoulders back and chin up, he presented an image of defiance that spoke volumes about both his parents and their influences.

It was both inspiring and exasperating. "Not dealing with it also creates a liability with respect to your mental health and emotional well-being."

He swiveled his head, eyes narrowed at her. "Is that a veiled reference to being unfit to serve, Doctor?"

Oh, for the love of... Gilead went back to her chair, bedside manner exhausted. In her experience, it was the rare male, metahuman or otherwise, who didn't view the mention of mental self-care as an attack on his overall abilities. Some stigmas would never disappear. "No. I'm a medical professional. Veiled references are left to reality housewives and politicians. If I was going to take you off active duty, I'd say that."

"And are you?"

Gilead rubbed her face. Neither of them had enough rest or caffeine to turn this into a coherent argument, and she wasn't about to try. "No, Ben. I'm saying that you need a healthy way to manage personal loss, and that a simple conversation focused on you rather than someone else is the best way to start. I'm suggesting that if you do choose to go that route, you find someone outside of the ECHO medical staff to fill that role. Someone you'll actually talk to."

✧   ✧   ✧

Yankee Pride avoided the infirmary for several days after his encounter with Gilead. He put in his time at the main ECHO offices, working with Spin Doctor on the necessary correspondence following the memorial. Someone—probably Ramona, given her familiarity with the administrative side of the organization—had created new files for the most recent recruits. He had gone through them all, noted names and the initial cataloging of abilities, and added some reminders to his calendar for some follow-up calls.

Get to know everyone, Benjamin. Not to know what they can do, but to understand who they are. Always remember they're people first. Even after her retirement, his mother had insisted upon learning about the newest recruits. Given her affinity for history, she had likely known more about the CCCP than he did.

After a review of the day's memos and a walk around the perimeter of the Parkour course, Pride had found himself with an hour's worth of time and no prior commitments. His exchange with Gilead gnawed at him. He couldn't use his own grief to excuse his manners in her office, especially when she herself was stretched thin between the daily emergencies. Some form of apology was in order.

Following a detour to a nearby bistro, Pride arrived at the infirmary with a small box of pastries and an insulated box of gourmet coffee. It was the sort of olive branch that could be shared with anyone else pulling the day shift, if the good doctor deemed them worthy of a cherry danish. The receptionist waved him through with a smile and pointed him back to the office suite.

The doctor didn't appear to have taken anyone's advice on sleep since he had last seen her. Gilead's hair stood out in frustrated gray and white spikes and the circles under her eyes spoke more to a fistfight in an alley than a struggle to understand the images on her screen. She gave him a stern frown when she first saw him, but her expression changed to exhausted gratitude at the sight of the coffee box.

"You didn't," she said, sagging in her chair. "But you did."

He produced the box of danish and she looked like she might burst into tears. Pride swallowed hard and held it out awkwardly. "Ma'am, I thought about our last exchange, and I just wanted to say—"

She accepted the box of coffee and set it on the ground, then pulled him into a tight hug. Despite her wiry frame, the embrace had a warmth to it that wrapped around his entire body. His throat tightened and his face grew hot. She rose on her toes such that her forehead touched his jawline. "You are so frustratingly polite, it's impossible to be mad with you. Don't worry about our chat. It's okay."

Pride struggled to hold himself together, but managed a curt nod when she stepped back and rubbed his arms briskly. "As for the danish and coffee, I'm going to find some mugs. You can stay here and catch up on Gautier's condition, if you're so inclined."

He nodded his head. "I could. Where are her current files?"

"On the desk. I was just reviewing them. Take a look." She picked up the box of danish and cracked it open. "Oh, there's blueberry. I might have to breach protocol and kiss you, you blessed creature. I'll be back."

Gilead darted out of the office, mumbling to herself about saints and pastries. Still embarrassed by his struggle to keep his own emotion in check, Pride focused his attention on the pile of file folders. He picked up one and started to thumb through it. While he had read the official reports regarding the rescue of Victoria Victrix, the apparent loss of Red Djinni, and the secondary retrieval of several minors along with Mel Gautier, he had not had the opportunity to comb through the interviews or medical reports related to Mel's condition.

The photographs, taken from the Overwatch cameras of the rescuers, showed someone barely human. That she had even survived this long spoke volumes about her resilience and her captors' intentions. He choked back the bile in his throat and set the file down. On another day, he might have been able to stomach the horror detailed in full color. Now, it was too real and too raw, and he was not prepared for the rush of emotion that washed over him. Pride walked to the one-way glass and saw the patient lying there, the bare minimum of wires keeping her tethered to the monitors.

The vertical blinds in the room kept sunlight from entering, and the overhead fluorescents gave the room a sickly pallor. He knew that outside, the sun was shining and the sky had a particular shade of blue that spoke of afternoon barbecues and football games. Mel lay still, her eyes still closed. Pride wondered if they continued to sedate her to aid in her recovery. A metal clipboard near the bed had several pages of notes. At the very least, he could see what had been said about her recovery.

Slowly, he moved to the door and listened for footsteps. No one came, so he crept past the threshold and angled himself to face the wall. Pride doubted that Mel had the consciousness to lash out, but he didn't dare risk that result alongside the doctor's inevitable wrath, should she discover him in here. The soft whirr and click of the machines coupled with Mel's breathing seemed to amplify each footstep. Reaching a hand back, he fumbled for the clipboard and managed to get it off the hook.

The cover page demonstrated Gilead's diligent documentation of her only patient. Dates, times, neat script describing her condition and the medications administered. A purple sticker at the top of the chart tagged the patient as a psych-type metahuman—an initial warning for anyone treating her. He flipped back the page to keep reading, the number of medications increasing exponentially as they got closer to the admit date and time. Another member of the medical team had jotted down the first set of notes, including a warning regarding known metahuman abilities and their effects. *Recommend physical restraints and sedation until full extent of injuries and abilities is known. Unsure if patient is ally or hostile.*

Pride reread the pages several times, piecing together the last few days' worth of Mel's ordeal after the rescue. Anger and regret gnawed at him. How had they not realized that the woman serving drinks, delivering lunches, and maintaining office order at ECHO wasn't the real Reverie? Was her impersonator that good and the deception that practiced, or had they failed to get to know her the first time, making it easier for her double to create a persona that they could like and rely upon? Would a little more personal time have made the difference?

How many others had gotten pushed aside in the name of efficiency, because getting to know them wasn't as valuable as what they could do in a fight? And this woman had the added status of being a military veteran, battle-tested and trained in the most dangerous of situations. To know that they—he, he corrected himself—had failed her, it made him even angrier.

"Damn it all to hell," he muttered. "Ma'am, we owed you better. Far better. And for what it's worth, if you can hear me, you have my full apologies and promise for whatever kind of recovery and rehabilitation you need."

"Could you maybe start by opening the curtains? Please?"

Pride froze, his gaze fixed on the clipboard in his hand. How long had she been aware of him in the room? Did Gilead know that her patient was conscious and able to speak? He licked his lips and spoke, keeping his voice low. "Ma'am, for the record, I'm pretty sure the doc will have my hide if she finds me in here with you. Opening the blinds might get us both in trouble."

"I don't really care about being in trouble, sir. I just don't wanna be in the dark." Her voice wavered. "I'm not gonna jump out of bed or set some head-devils on you. I just want to know if there's sun or rain outside."

His heart sank. Such a simple request from someone who had been through so much, but security weighed heavy on his mind. If the light triggered something that resulted in injury to him, or her, or both of them, a verbal reprimand from the doctor would be the least of his concerns. Pride consulted the clipboard again for some guidance as to what could or couldn't be done. "Do you know who I am, ma'am?"

"Of course I do. You're Yankee Pride," she answered. "I ain't deaf."

"And do you know why I might be reluctant to open the windows, or even turn around?" He hated himself for asking the question, but he didn't know what else to do. Leaving would be cruel if she didn't pose a threat and just needed a bit of company. Loneliness was something he empathized with all too much these days.

"Yeah, but I also figure that if you're coming in here, it's because of some needing to see things for yourself. Nobody's visited. Nobody that I can remember, at least," she added. Her voice cracked and she sniffled. "Everything's mixed up in my head."

"I'm not surprised," he murmured. Pride glanced back at the chart and the medical staff's notes. "Whatever had taken you had us pretty mixed up about you, too. We're still not sure if you're ready to be debriefed, although given that you're conscious and verbal, that might be something to consider."

She let out a long sigh and sniffled. "Right. Bedside interrogation, 'cause they'll need to know everything I can remember in order to find the sick freak that had me and those kids in that hellhole for all those months. And of course, they can't just bring in a telepath or empath, due to the liability I present." She spoke in a bitter tone, anger and disgust in her words. "So it'll be the old-fashioned way. Lucky me."

A long moment passed without either of them saying anything, the hum of medical equipment suddenly loud in the sterile space. He studied the pages he held. If they planned to debrief her, it made sense to not give her too much information for fear of contaminating any information she could provide. The upper tier of ECHO had the most recent information about the circumstances surrounding Victrix's capture and the rescue of her, Gautier, and dozens of children and teenagers, but the loss of the Djinni gave them a whole new situation to consider. They needed to know as much as possible about the individual who had done all of this, and it needed to be free of any outside influence.

But was it fair to isolate someone who had already endured so much?

He sighed and fumbled to place the clipboard back. "Overwatch: Privacy. Overwatch: Recording: All channels: Authorization: Pride 1945." The tiny chirp in his ear confirmed the commands and secure confirmation code. If she wanted to talk, he could indulge that much and gather the data for analysis later. Victrix and Parker swore by the Colt boys and their prowess with multilevel data analysis. This would just be another project for them to argue about over beer and pizza.

"Ma'am, I—"

"Mel. I can't take that formal 'ma'am' bullshit no more, especially if you got your back turned." She coughed and made a frustrated sound in her throat. "Sir."

He nodded and stepped away from the clipboard, still not facing her. "All right, but if I slip, you'll have to forgive me. Goes along with calling any kind of soda a Coke, y'know."

"Even if it's clear?"

"Uh-huh."

She snorted. "That's just ridiculous, but I get it." The bed squeaked as she shifted, the hospital noise less ominous between them. "What happens if the doc finds you in here with me?"

Pride shrugged. "Any number of things. I figure yelling, getting dragged out by one of my ears, maybe a ten-minute lecture on security threats and the like. You're the more serious threat, in the bigger picture."

"Yeah. Yeah, I s'pose so."

He fixed his eyes on the wall and relaxed his posture. Someone had painted the walls recently. He couldn't find a single crack or discoloration for focus. "You got a favorite food, Mel? Something that you'd have brought in the minute the doc clears you for something more than Jell-O and ECHO-issue nutropuree."

"First thing? Bread pudding, the kind that you make from homemade bread scraps, soaked in a good caramel sauce. Warm, of course."

"Raisins?"

"No, none of that. You ruin it when you add those kinds of things." She sighed, an almost happy noise. "But sometime soon, I'm gonna find a good crawfish boil. Head down I-10 and find some little hole-in-the-wall spot in Slidell and eat until my lips burn."

He made a face, forgetting that she couldn't see his reaction. "Can't say I've ever found the idea of eating those things appetizing."

"Why not? Mel asked. "Spice, butter . . . if you're fancy enough to like lobster, then you'll have no problem with these."

"The eyes. Can't eat something that's staring at me." He grinned, the smile carrying through to his words. "But I'll believe you that it's worth a drive."

She chuckled, but the noise was tinged with regret. He fought the urge to turn around, but it became harder as the sad laughter became quiet weeping. Keeping his back to her, a military veteran who had endured capture and torture twice while in service to ECHO, drove a nail through his heart with each soft sob. *This isn't right. Threat or no, she's a human being and a soldier. I can't just keep staring at the paint on the wall.* He would deal with Gilead's wrath when she returned if only to treat Mel with some bit of the dignity she had earned several times over.

"Don't you move, sir." Mel reacted the moment he began to pivot. Even through tears, she spoke with authority. "I'm still a liability and you're a leading member of the organization. This ain't a time to get sentimental."

"And I'm inclined to agree with the patient, Ben." Gilead leaned against the doorframe with a coffee in one hand. She angled herself to stay out of Mel's line of sight. "Compassion's all well and good, but in this kind of situation, it could very well get you killed. As for you, ma'am, I'm going to have to notify the appropriate people now that you're awake."

Mel cleared her throat. "Understood, Doc. You don't have to apologize for protocol. I'll do my best to keep things under control. Sir, I do appreciate your concern. For what it's worth, I don't think anyone with your rank ever came by when I came back the first time."

"An oversight on my part. If the good doctor doesn't lock me out of her suite, I'll be back to hear more about this crawfish boil trip you plan to take." Pride stepped toward the exit, ducking around Gilead to avoid her stern glare. "Ma'am."

The petite doctor didn't move, but he could feel her eyes on him all the way to the exit. Pride offered the subvocal command to end the recording, then sent it off to Parker and Victrix for any analysis. He anticipated a short and frustrated lecture on difficult situations, debriefing protocol, and medical liability, most likely in stereo from them. To say that he didn't care about the consequences didn't fully explain his reasons for sneaking into the room with the single hospital bed, but it had seemed like the right thing to do at the time.

And, he thought as he saw his HUD alert him to an incoming Overwatch message, *I would do it again if given the chance.*

Vickie could feel Gilead's eyes boring holes in her. She matched Gilead glare for glare. "Don't," she said firmly. "Not a word. Yes, I know I'm burning my candle at both ends and in the middle. No, there's nothing you can do to stop me. Penny and I are here for another reason entirely. Penny says we need to talk to Mel, and by 'we' I refer to me, Penny, and Penny's Invisible Friend."

Penny, who looked much better now that she'd gotten a series of real showers, a lot of food into her, and was dressed in jeans and a T-shirt, her hair pulled back in a ponytail like a normal kid, nodded vigorously. She was a cute little thing actually, with long, black, wavy hair, and coffee-colored skin, and had been no trouble at all. Gilead paid no attention to her. So far as she was concerned, kids obeyed adults, not the other way around.

And this kid was with an adult who looked like *she* should be occupying a bed here, and who was showing all the expression of a block of granite. Vickie was getting used to those looks. Three hours of sleep was all she could manage before either screaming nightmares or uncontrollable weeping woke her. As for eating, well, it wasn't happening. Coffee and canned liquid meals stayed put, but nothing else did. And it didn't matter. *She* didn't matter. All that mattered was getting Eight up to full speed, then...

I won't be blindsided again, Doppelgaenger, you bitch. When you come for me, I'm coming armed to the teeth. Nobody's walking away this time.

For now, though, she was keeping herself frozen, because if she allowed herself to *feel* anything, she'd lose it, and she was pretty sure she wouldn't be getting control or even sanity back any time soon.

"Most specifically, Penny's Invisible Friend is pretty adamant about talking with Gautier, and now, not later," she continued.

Gilead now gave her one of the oddest looks she'd ever gotten in a lifetime of odd looks. Vickie shrugged. "It's a ghost. He'll still be a ghost whether or not you believe in them. Penny says he says he has to talk to Mel or she's never going to get better. I'm going to make that happen."

Gilead opened her mouth to say something. Vickie cut her off. Rude, maybe, but she didn't care anymore about social niceties. Every moment wasted was energy, time, and effort wasted. "Penny says Mel can't hurt her. I know for a fact she can't hurt either of us, for that matter. Now let us in there. Please," she added, but only because Eight chided her on her private channel. Gilead gave her the stink-eye. "And please don't make me call Blues for authorization. She'll give it to me, but it'll take an argument, and we're on the freaking clock. I've got fifty things that have to get done, and until I get Eight where Eight needs to be, there's only one of me to do them."

When Gilead gave her a skeptical look instead of a reply, she choked down anger—no, rage—and elaborated. "Doppelgaenger knows *who* I am, *what* I am and *where* I am, Red inadvertently made it clear I'm important, and it's only a matter of time before she makes another try for me. And even if he hadn't, it's pretty clear the bitch likes to make people hurt, so I'd be a target no matter what. So please do not waste time I may not have." *I managed to say Red's name without melting down. Go me.*

Gilead opened her mouth to say something, then shook her head, and tossed up her hands in defeat. "First Ben, now you. Is everybody going to make a habit of overruling me?"

Vickie took that as the go-ahead to escort Penny into Mel's room. Illusions were part and parcel of a mage's bag of tricks, and she was pretty damned sure the protections she'd cast on both of them would shield them from anything Gautier could produce. She'd already given Penny a shield against angry, nasty spirits that would do until Penny learned how to send such things packing herself. So the two of them walked right into the room, Penny trailing a little behind Vickie, without even trying to avert their eyes from the figure on the bed.

Mel . . . was a mess. This was the first time Vickie'd had a good look at her; back at Doppelgaenger's playpen, she hadn't exactly been paying a lot of attention to the illusionist—the only thing she'd really noticed was the stump where a hand should have been. But now, the bandages everywhere, and the IV drip made it pretty clear Doppelgaenger had been having a fine old sadistic time with Mel.

Which means . . . Red . . . was . . .

She clamped down her self-control, *hard,* clenching her jaw until she thought her teeth might splinter, until the numb, icy calm came back. Meanwhile little Penny, oblivious to the tumult going on inside her, eyed the woman who lay there so quietly with her eyes closed. Penny's expression was hard to read; half the time Vickie had no idea what she was thinking. This was a kid who'd learned to keep her feelings to herself way too early. *I hope once she learns enough from me and Caspar to handle being a medium on her own, she gets an adult who's got more empathy to spare for her than I do.* On the other hand . . . the poor kid was just one more casualty of war. There were a lot like her out there. War brought out the best and the worst in people, and there were a lot of abused or abandoned kids around. Hell, between the ones DG had, and the ones from Zach Marlowe's Project, ECHO had enough abused, abandoned kids with powers to start a school. This kid just happened to see ghosts that had abused her.

Finally the little girl stepped towards the bed. Not too close, but closer than Vickie wanted to get, though that was more her own twitchiness about the shape Mel was in, not any fear of what Mel might do. "Miz Gautier?" she said, in her high, soft voice. "I dunno if you 'member me. I'm Penny. I thought your name was Lacey, 'cuz that's all you'd say. *Lacey Moan Alley.* I kinda tried to help you, but I couldn't figger out how." She swallowed hard, but continued bravely. "I know how to help you now, though. Miz Vickie's helping me. So's our friend."

Mel sighed and her eyes remained closed. "Hey, Penny. I . . . I wish I could say I remember you completely, but my brain doesn't quite know what was real, what I tried to forget was real, and what I tried to make up to get through what was real." She shifted against the pillows, away from where Penny stood. "And if I did anything to hurt you in there, I'm truly sorry."

"Mel, it's Vix. I'm here too. Open your eyes, there's no freaking way you can hurt us." She looked around and scowled at the closed blinds. "Jesus Cluny Frog, let's get some sunlight in here so you don't start asking for Depeche Mode and the Smiths on infinite loop." Suiting action to words, she opened the blinds with a brisk tug.

It took a moment, but Mel cracked open one eye and promptly squinted in the afternoon light. She gave it a few seconds before doing the same with the other, then rolled to face her visitors. At the sight of Vickie, Mel visibly recoiled. "Damn, did you come in from just down the hall? Who put you on duty?"

"She put herself on duty," Gilead called from the doorway. "I'm going to curl myself around a coffee while you three chat. Everything's being recorded, for all the good it will do. Just don't wear each other out. We can't fit three beds in here."

The doctor slipped out, muttering to herself. Mel waited to speak until the footsteps had faded down the hallway. Vickie held up a hand. "Four. There's four of us here."

"Who's the fourth?" Mel glanced from the mage to the kid. "I only see the pair of you."

"Penny's a medium. She's got a ghost with her that has a very urgent and particular interest in you. I'm here to help with the *Mel can't see ghosts* part. Once we're done with that, you can ask all the questions you want, but from what Penny tells me, her Invisible Friend is practically gnawing his own arm off to get to you." She rubbed her reddened eyes. "Eight tells me I should be more polite, but I'm pretty short on energy, nerves, and patience, and the field where I grow my fucks is barren."

"All right." Mel lifted her bandaged arm, realized that there was nothing there to itch her nose, and switched to the other one. "As long as you're sure that I can't hurt you or her, I'm willing to work with you. Don't really have much to lose now."

"Illusions are among the first things a mage learns, right after *lighting a candle* and figuring out which element you can best pull your magic energy from. Anything you can do, I can get rid of." She looked down at the little girl. "Your buddy ready, Penny?"

The child nodded, her ponytail bobbing. "He's right there," she said, pointing to Mel's bedside.

"Thanks." Vickie closed her eyes a moment, and held her hands before her, about a foot apart and chest-high, palms facing. She whispered something under her breath. And something very like fog began to form between them.

The fog moved as if it was a living thing, sending out a questing tendril, which seemed to find what it was looking for, as the tendril darted to a spot right at Mel's bedside. Soon the tendril was a conduit, and more and more of the fog streamed from between Vickie's hands to that spot, then spread out as if it was filling an invisible shape. A man-shaped shape. A shape that became less a *shape* and more a *figure* with every passing moment. A figure, if Mel had only known it, that looked to be the next of kin to the ectoplasmic Tesla and Marconi "upgrades."

This was, of course, because Vickie was producing ectoplasm for a ghost that didn't know how to *make* it, but instinctively knew how to *use* it.

The young man—quite clearly visible now, even in the strong sunlight coming from the window—held up his hands and gazed at them in surprise, then grinned widely. *"Ah'll be go t'Hell,"* came a whispery voice full of wonder. *"Damn if it didn't work!"*

"Told you," Vickie muttered, still concentrating. "Don't mind me, I'm just here as the facilitator."

Mel's lower lip quavered. She stared at the figure sitting on her bedside, but spoke to Penny. "This is who you saw? This is the one you said is 'my ghost,' the one who's been hanging around me back...back there?"

Penny nodded again. "He said he couldn' 'member his name. He says ghosts start forgettin' things. He came fer you, but he was helpin' me, too."

"Figures. As for names, I'm not surprised he forgot. That's why his momma sewed it in all his underwear." She smirked at her new visitor. "Riley. Jackson Lee Riley, to be exact."

"Hey," the ghost protested. *"Ah'm sittin' right here, y'know!"*

Mel chuckled, but it turned into a sad sound that wasn't quite crying. She started to reach for Riley, but stopped inches from his knee. "How long have you been around? It's been awhile since... since you were around."

The ghost considered her question. *"Time don't mean quite*

what it used to, but I tried to get here when I could. When you got in trouble, that is. When I did, she was there with you. And Ah'm pretty sure you didn't hurt her, or any of 'em. Scared 'em, mebbe, but didn't hurt 'em."

"But how did you—"

The ghost leaned forward, the gauzy outline of his forehead inches from hers. Mel didn't pull away, although her eyes closed and she bowed her head. *"Revvie, it ain't the how, it's the why. There's stuff you need to know, right down in your gut, that you ain't got straight yet. Like, that just because crap happens, that don't mean it's your fault that it did. Like, just because you got through somethin', an' someone else didn't, that don't mean you shoulda been the one that took the bullet. What you need to know is that it ain't your time, and that it ain't gonna be your time for a long while. No matter what they put you through, it ain't gonna be your time."*

Mel folded in on herself, her form blurring Riley's edge. "So . . . what? This is some kind of penance I've got to pay for letting you and the rest of the team down? That's why I gotta stay behind?"

"Now, that's just bullshit. This ain't about punishment. This is about makin' sure the best of us remains and becomes stronger."

"But . . ."

"You don't get to sit around and worry about what you shoulda done or who didn't make it home. I know you made sure that everyone knew what happened and that you were respectful about it, 'cause that's who you are." He paused and tried to position himself in her line of sight. *"You're still here, and that's what matters. That's what was s'posed to happen, Revvie. It's okay."*

The last two words broke Mel's composure. She dissolved into exhausted tears, falling forward until her head appeared to rest on Riley's knee. The ghost glanced to Penny and shrugged. *"Better that she hear it from me than anybody else, kiddo. Grown-ups can cry pretty ugly at times."*

"I wisht I could do somethin'," Penny agreed, looking sad. "I can't help Miz Vickie neither."

A single tear ran down Vickie's right cheek from her closed eye. "Not your fault, kid," Vickie replied in a choked voice. "What he promised and what he could actually *do* are two different things. It is what it is."

"But I don' think—" Penny began, and stopped, and sighed. "I'll keep tryin', anyway, okay?"

"Don't wear yourself out," Vickie said. "Better you concentrate on Riley and Gautier."

Mel had rolled to her side to look up at Riley. She reached out a hand to touch his knee, but her fingers passed through the fatigues he wore. "Shit," she muttered.

"You want him solid enough to touch?" Vickie asked. "I can do that. Just won't be able to talk while I do."

Mel looked away from Vickie, considering the offer. Her fingers twitched against the sheet. "I ... just for a bit? If you can do it without hurting yourself," she added quickly. "If it's gonna make you worse, then it ain't worth it."

"It's just adding a chainsaw to the flaming torches I'm juggling. More a matter of control than power." Her jaw set, something in one of her breast pockets began to glow brightly enough to show through the cloth, and a thicker fog poured from her hands and added itself to Riley.

Riley stretched out a more opaque finger and poked Mel in the nose, gently at first. She winced at the new sensation. "Feels like lukewarm Jell-O," she mumbled.

"*Ah thought everybody liked that stuff.*" He repeated the gesture and laughed at Mel's expression. "*C'mere, Revvie. This ain't gonna slime you or nothin', I don't think.*"

She pushed herself up and inched forward. Mel hesitated, then leaned forward with both arms for an awkward embrace. Riley met her halfway and she fell against him in exhausted relief. This time, there were fewer tears. The ghost smoothed the thin patches of Mel's hair while she hugged him tightly.

"So, you're not back here to haunt me 'cause I did something awful to you?"

The words came out in a voice so close to Penny's own soft uncertainty that Riley had to check to see who had asked the question. Penny stepped closer to the bed and patted Mel's arm awkwardly. "He ain't hauntin' you, Lace—Miz Gautier," she said fervently. "Haunts ain't *nice* to ya!"

"*And in spite of you takin' nothin' less than perfect when it came to our team, not one of us would've ever questioned your bein' kind. You made passin' a comfort, when it could've been a terror, an' that ain't somethin' many get to experience.*" His thumb wiped away a few tears that had escaped down her cheek. "*That's a gift, Revvie. It ain't somethin' to waste.*"

Mel remained on her side, Riley and Penny offering their own means of solace. "So, that's why you came for me? 'Cause you knew this was just as bad as the Sandbox."

"*'Cause I knew that you'd make it out, and that you'd need to know that's what was s'posed to happen.*" Riley held her shoulders and helped her sit up. He cupped her chin with a dirt-dusted hand. His form started to waver, but he held on. "*You're here for a reason. So's she, but I ain't privy to those details. You got a gift for dreams. Dreams ain't for the dead, they're for the living. So, that means you gotta live. Not just survive, but live.*"

She stared back at him. "But . . ."

"*An' you gotta cheer for 'Bama next season.*"

Her jaw dropped. "What?"

"Ew," said Penny critically. "I *liked* you. Now I ain't so sure."

"*Okay, that last part ain't necessary.*" He winked at Penny. The outline of his form started to blur. "*Everythin' else, though, that's what you gotta remember. And Ah knew you wouldn't believe it from just anybody, so Ah had to make sure you heard it from me.*"

Gilead sat down next to Mel with a clipboard in her hand. "Debrief?" Mel asked apprehensively. She'd been dreading this. But at least now, thanks to Vickie, they weren't avoiding her room, or keeping the blinds closed.

Gilead shook her head. "The opposite, actually," she replied reluctantly. "Orders from Ben, Bella, and Bull; they think we'll do more harm than good by making you relive all that. Bella wants me to get you up to speed from Vix's report. We've got a lot we need to ask you about after that. Don't worry, most of it isn't going to depend on your memory of your incarceration."

Mel listened, Army stoicism providing a numb kind of detachment as Gilead told her how Doppelgaenger had been impersonating her ever since she'd been shot in the Atlanta Underground attack. How Vickie and Bella had both surmised it was done. "The kids told us he did it to them, too, though not as frequently. Vix thinks DG had to renew the 'Mel' disguise from time to time, so we believe that is why there are a lot of bits of you gone." Gilead's voice remained calm and detached, for all the world as if she was talking about colds or the flu, and not about some metahuman monster who imitated people by *eating* parts of them. And now those few confused memories she had were starting to make sense.

That was bad enough. But Mel listened in growing disbelief as Gilead continued describing how Doppelgaenger had wormed her way into both Belladonna's and Vickie's confidence, and *deeply* into the inner workings of ECHO.

Then began an affair with Red Djinni.

"There are lots of Overwatch recordings," Gilead continued. "Doppelgaenger wasn't on Overwatch Two, but she was pretty diligent about wearing her headset. I suppose it amused her to no end, to know that she was conducting a love affair with Red right in front of the woman who was privy to every secret, and silently in love with the Djinni."

Finally, Gilead's expression wavered from neutral, for just a moment, to enraged. But she quickly corrected herself. "Anyway, we're going to want you to help us with some of those tapes; the more we know about what Doppelgaenger can and can't do, the better off we are."

Mel felt dazed as Gilead recounted the fall of Ultima Thule and the false-Mel's part in it, then moved on to Red Djinni's arrest, the murder of Dixie Bell and Verdigris' attack on the memorial service.

"Doppelgaenger couldn't pass that distraction up, of course," Gilead continued. "She had arranged for Vix to be kidnapped, certain that Djinni would follow, and must have just been waiting for the right opportunity to spring the trap, knowing that not even Top Hold could keep Red confined if he wanted to escape. He did escape, pulled off a rescue, and Doppelgaenger revealed herself. Vix got out with you and the kids, DG took the Djinni, and a couple days ago, killed him." She licked her lips, and rested the clipboard on her knees. "That's the short version. Any questions?"

Mel sat back against her pillows. "Most of 'em would repeat yours. I guess that explains what led to the rescue. You got a team going through that location, of course. I don't know how much help I can give you, considering how much I just wasn't *there* most of the time."

"The children—Penny, specifically, said that he took pieces of them and ate them. Usually hair, but a few are missing digits, too. Do you have any idea why he kept…taking more of you than of them?" Gilead combined a strangely comforting pattern of empathy and dispassion in her question. Mel hadn't ever quite seen the like.

"Logically, I'm older. I'd be able to handle more—"

Gilead shook her head. "I'm asking for instinct, not logic. The kids said that he could replicate physical powers, like Pike's armor, but couldn't replicate Penny's mediumistic abilities, and they *said* they could always tell when it was him, because he 'didn't act right.' So what does your instinct tell you?"

Mel swallowed hard. The doctor wasn't trying to make things more difficult or uncomfortable, but that didn't lessen the anxiety that threatened to shake her from head to toe. "My documented abilities are illusions, which means I got a knack for convincing people that what they're seeing is the actual truth, no matter what's in front of them. So even if he couldn't mimic it completely, he'd need it to make up for the times when he couldn't completely act like the person he needed to be. If you already talk the talk and walk the walk, it only takes a little bit of effort to make somebody believe that you're the real deal." She exhaled and willed her fingers to release the bedsheets.

Gilead consulted her clipboard. "Well, according to the report, Doppelgaenger was using the head wound you actually received and he copied as the reason for why your illusion powers no longer worked. Do you think he was hoping that...repeated applications of essence of Mel would give those powers to him? Or was he trying for your memories? Because, in retrospect, we are now seeing a distinct pattern of evasion whenever someone asked him about something you should have known, but he didn't." She took a deep breath. "I...don't want to distress you further, but we want to know whether or not there's a chance he'll return in a convincing enough simulacrum of Red to fool Vix long enough for him to take or kill her, too."

Mel pushed her hair out of her face and grimaced. "I don't think that's likely, especially considering how well-known both of them are in those ECHO inner circles. I might have come in and worked with all of 'em on different operations, but we weren't exactly drinking buddies. Someone who knows Red or Vickie—I mean, somebody who knows them in and out, warts and everything—they would be able to see the difference in a heartbeat 'cause he doesn't have that headspace 'sleight of hand' anymore."

She shifted in bed, desperately trying to keep a level tone. "Instinct says that Doppelgaenger went for a target on the sidelines that gave him a relatively blank canvas. The fact that he got me was…" Mel felt her throat tighten and hot tears began to blur her vision. Rather than give in to self-pity, she growled through the next words. "Dumb luck. Maybe he'd needed a new face with some powers, but when he got a taste, he figured out what my abilities could add to everything that he could already do. He took the opportunity, and here we are."

Gilead nodded, made some notes on her clipboard, and made what might have been a very tiny sigh of relief. "All right, then. That corresponds very well with what the children said. As for Doppelgaenger's Facility, we had a team scouring it down to the floorwax, and we've learned all we can from it. As you said, you were sedated most of the time, so there seems no particular need to debrief you." She put both her hands on the clipboard and looked straight into Mel's eyes. "So the only question now is, what do you want to do?"

The simplicity of the question made the answer nearly impossible. She stared at Gilead, wondering if it was another kind of test. "What do I want to do? Could y'all be any more vague?"

"We simply can't devote a lot of resources to you, Mel," Gilead continued frankly. "Since you were taken, things have turned into all-out war. We obviously can use you. Silent Knight has offered to make you a prosthetic that is 'almost as good as the real thing' with the help of one of the Russians who studied Petrograd's armor. If you feel you need a *few* desensitization treatments of the sort Bell gave you, I can do that, now that we know how it works. We can even give you training under Bell to boost your abilities. But if what you want is to get the hell out…I can't blame you, but I also absolutely cannot guarantee you'll find anyplace safe to go to, and we can't spare you anything but money."

Mel's eyes narrowed. She sat up and brought the bandaged end of her arm up to show the fresh cap of cotton and nanoweave. "The funny thing about illusions is that you can do 'em with no arms and a whole lot of angry. If you got all of your files right, then you already know that the odds of me running are pretty much nothing. I had my team murdered in front of me, one by one, and I was pissed as hell that no one thought to ask me what I wanted." The corner of her mouth twitched. "But you, you ask me what I want, after that poor kid led Riley to me and let me know that he was all right..."

Her voice cracked and she struggled to keep that professional distance between her and the doctor. "I want to do whatever it takes to get some justice for those kids, especially Penny. I want to be part of the team that brings all of our assets home. And, even though my commanding officers might have frowned upon revenge, I want to make sure that sick skin-shifting cannibal gets every bit of lead and fire that he deserves before he goes straight to hell—" she sat back and exhaled, venom dissipating with the whoosh of breath—"ma'am."

Gilead smiled thinly. "Lessons with Bell, or new hand first? You can do either or both on bed rest."

"Lessons first. Might help her with any remaining issues over my evil twin. Besides, l might need some of those to practice to work through the new hand process."

"Good. Consider yourself back on limited duty, Reverie," Gilead replied. "Welcome back to ECHO."

INTERLUDE

Taps

MERCEDES LACKEY AND DENNIS LEE

There wasn't a reliable way to get a hold of Jack. We had cut off communications for a reason. His last message was vague enough, but reading between the lines, it seemed like he was deep in enemy territory, and Jack was afraid our clandestine activities would be compromised. I risked it anyway, hours after Red was taken. I couldn't go after the Djinni, but someone had to, so I messaged him, hoping he would answer. He didn't. And now Red was . . .

He had to know. Someone had to tell him. He had been Red's best friend.

I was, of course, still a freaking wreck, and I needed to time this so I wouldn't break down on Jack. Like I had to time just about every-thing these days, so I wouldn't break down in public. So I waited until I was in one of those brief periods of emotional exhaustion where I was bottomed out and able to think for five seconds, and tried a contact. But I knew the brief stability wouldn't last more than a few minutes, so I had to do it while I could still talk without choking up.

I gripped the armrests so hard I thought they were going to crack. "Overwatch: Open: Jack private, encrypted." I took a deep breath, ribs stabbing me. Or maybe it was . . . something else. "Jack. Come in. Please."

And breathed a painful sigh of relief when he answered.

"Risky, lady. Very risky. You're lucky I'm reasonably secure from prying ears right now. Still, this better be good. And quick."

Say it. Just say it. Not saying it won't make it any less real. "Red's . . . dead." And with those words it somehow became more real, and I had to fight for breath.

"Confirmation?" he asked, his voice barely above a low growl. "I'll need that. I once saw him take two full magazines of ammo and fall into a pool of his own blood, so I'll need proof."

Somehow I explained everything that had happened, up to the moment that the blood samples that JM had come back with had tested out as his. And then I sat there, reminding myself that I had to be frozen, I had to lock down my emotions, because this was Jack, and anyway, crying wasn't going to bring Red back. But maybe Jack could do something else about it, something I couldn't. Something I knew Jack had a solid line on. Revenge.

"She took him during your rescue," Jack said finally. "But that means..." There was a long drawn-out pause, interrupted by an odd muffled sound, like something had caught in his throat. Then he was all business, as I knew he'd be.

"Let me make this quick; we're already pushing our luck here. The plan...the plans...are proceeding. I've procured your whatsits doodad. And you were right. Wasn't easy. And I've almost got the location. I'll proceed when I do, and you better be ready when I send it, 'cause I don't like the odds of me taking them all on by my lonesome. I'll be in position."

"If I drop out of contact...it's probably Doppelgaenger. I'll have Eight contact you and take over for me."

"You let me worry about Doppelgaenger. I get wind of her coming for you, I'll send word, somehow. I figure I'll be getting close to her soon enough anyway. Keep to the plan. You'll hear from me when you need to. When the time comes, I've got her. The last thing she'll hear is Red's name. I'm out."

I lay limply in my chair, wrung out. And brain on fire with doubts. Could I really depend on him? He had plans of his own to complete. I meant nothing to him. What he had promised... that depended entirely on how close he had been to Red, not me. I had only the little that Red had told me to go on. So...I know what he was to Red. What was Red to him?

A strange, choking sound escaped me, a cross between a moan and a sob, both of them held back by strength of will.

And that was when I realized I had just heard a sound like that, minutes before. But not out of my throat.

Out of Jack's.

My five seconds were up, and as much as I wanted to just wallow in my own morass—mental...physical...take your pick—and *deal with it, I had to push all those gut-wrenching thoughts away and get back to work. There was too much to deal with at the moment. I had been gone for less than a day, and the backlog just from that had required some nifty reorganization of my priorities, on top of the fallout from Verd's attack, and on top of the sudden state of emergency DG's infiltration had left of our security measures, both locally and worldwide.*

Looking back, I think that's the worst I've ever been, and don't forget we're talking about a girl that once got scorched by a relative over someone I thought I was deeply in love with to the point where I was left in the emotional and physical state of a panophobic lump of charred chicken meat. For years. I admit, the next few hours were a blur. Somehow, I forced myself to go on, until...

The last thing I had time for was email. I'd been ignoring email since Red was taken. Really, anything urgent enough was delivered by Overwatch, and I had plenty of those messages to attend to. So when my browser popped up, again, with another annoying beep to remind me I had new messages, I almost silenced the monitor with my fist before I saw the message which topped the list, a message that must have been sent just after he came for me.

To: Victoria Victrix <vickievee@ECHO.net>

From: That Red Bastard <redbastard@ECHO.net>

You asked if there was something else you can do for me. There is. You can keep this somewhere safe, and I leave it to you to do with it what you think best...

I don't know how long I spent reading Red's final confession. It was long enough, and he didn't hold back. Lord, and he used to say I was long-winded. It answered some questions though and cleared up a few things I had already guessed, but really, so soon after losing him, he was talking to me again, and for a brief moment, it was like he was still there.

...stared at each other through the settling dust. I could tell what was on his mind. This was the infamous Red Djinni. And any other day, if I hadn't been on the Ten Most Wanted List before, after blowing into the Vault, I would have been.

On the other hand, compared to what had been in here with us, and what was plainly still out there now, I was a pretty pitiful minnow among the piranha. The world as we both knew it had just done a complete one-eighty. And I knew what Vic would have done... would have asked me to do.

"Look," I said hoarsely. "Let me help you save whoever we can. Arrest me after. Okay?"

Wordlessly, he nodded, got to his feet, and offered me a hand up.

I think you know the rest, it's all fairly well documented. So why am I telling you all this? Here's the thing—I trust you like I have never trusted anyone before, not even Amethist. I can see you rolling your eyes right now. Yes, this is me, I know it doesn't sound like me but... gah. The truth of it is, I've realized you are the most important person I know, the smartest, the most resilient... stubborn... and at the same time, the dumbest...

Sorry.

You are the most important person I know. It kills me sometimes how much *you* don't know that. In a lifetime, we meet countless people. We forget most of them, but a few really stick in your gut and with good reason. These are those precious few who are everything you admire and nothing you despise. You will forever be that person for me, like it or not. You still don't know how important you are? Figure it out, woman! You need to call the shots, and we need to make sure you're around to call them. So this is my truth, and I trust you with it completely. Make the call, do what you know is best with it. Trust yourself.

I do.

Love,
That Red Bastard.

The words on the screen began to blur, then vanish as the screen... the monitor... the desk... everything vanished and that well of grief and loss inside me didn't open up, it erupted. I curled up in my chair, and let it go. There was no one here. I was alone.

I didn't have to be brave for anyone. *Not even Red. I cried until there was nothing left, and then I dry-sobbed for . . . I don't know. Hours, I think. At least two. Enough that the messages had piled up all over all of my screens, and Eight finally said apologetically, "Vickie? We . . . need you."*

I took a deep breath, intending to tell Eight and everyone else to go to hell, but with that breath came a pure and sure certainty.

I did have *to be brave. For Red. And not because of the geas. I knew in that moment I could break the damn thing if I wanted to. I needed to be brave because if I wasn't, he would have died for* nothing.

And that would not stand. I would not let that be.

Whether or not I had been that mythical person he'd seen, it was what I was going to have to become.

Now. Because there was no time for anything but a transformation, phoenixlike, out of my own ashes.

I sat up. I blew my nose. "Right," I said. "Let's get to work."

CHAPTER TWENTY-FIVE

Left Behind

MERCEDES LACKEY AND DENNIS LEE

This was an exciting time for me. I was learning so many new things, and Vickie was giving me so many new capabilities! And yet . . . it felt as if I was somehow betraying her by enjoying myself when she was in such despair.

Vickie let out her breath in a long, tired sigh. Eight's m-space home and the ability to make more storage was the first thing she'd managed to get self-powered, and that had been relatively easy. Unfortunately, nothing that she had tried had been able to turn Eight into any kind of a mage.

When she had first realized he was self-aware and had come up with the idea that he could be her partner—or someone that could act as a replacement if she was incapacitated—she'd started trying to figure out how to make a magician out of him. When she was healed enough to work on him again, she began giving him one-shot "spell-capsules" that he could use until she could turn him into a technomancer at least.

That hadn't happened. The best she could do was continue to create single-use, self-powered versions of the most common things she did with technomancy, and store them—like talismans that contained single-use spells. But unlike physical talismans, these were only in m-space and attached to Eight, and able to be used at Eight's discretion, just as any non-magician could use a talisman. She could keep adding to the store as long as she was alive . . . but that was the rub, wasn't it?

And now she knew that not even Mom, as good as *she* was, would be able to replace Vickie, because Vickie was...unique. That was what Bella had discovered. She was a mage *and* a meta-human. Not just the only techno-shaman *she knew,* but probably the only techno-shaman, ever.

The goal now was to get Eight self-sufficient, able to do as much as Vickie could, but without inherent magic. Able to run Overwatch One and Overwatch Two, at least for as long as anyone with implants and headsets survived. If it came to that, Eight would be the all-seeing guardian able to help the last dregs of resistance down to the final battle.

And today she'd figured out the way to do the last of it, making a talismanic version of the spell that allowed her to crack passwords. "All right, Eight. I've got you as good as I can ever get you. Try hacking Gilead's password without going sys admin and just getting it."

"*4rmyH34L0RZ, Vickie,*" Eight said promptly. "*That's a remarkably good one, actually. I don't think I would have been able to crack it without the Ouija Board Protocol.*"

"Try not to use any of the magic stuff unless there's no other way. The canned spells are going to run out eventually." She sighed again. "I'm sorry I couldn't give you any geomancy, and you won't be able to use the eyes without me to fly them."

"*So we put the eyes on a stick, or roll them along the ground, or throw them like grenades. We'll think of something. Perhaps the Metisians can give us some form of levitation and stealth. It won't matter if they are bigger as long as they can't be seen. I will put an urgent inquiry into their feed and speak with Tesla and Marconi about it. And we will concern ourselves with that only at the moment we need to. Alert over New York, Vickie.*"

She was too tired to swear. "On it. Tell the Colts. Who have we got out there?"

"*Sera and John are near enough to make it there in time to make a difference, but it will be a long flight back for them.*"

"I'll deploy 'em." She checked her Overwatch Op-Board, and saw the Overwatch Operator for New York was listed as off duty, after twenty hours on. *Well, that's why we have Eight.* "Marionette is off duty. You take the Apple metas, and have the Colts call in the Air Force. Navy too, if there's fighter squadrons with the right warheads on their rockets. With luck, we'll get the bad guys to turn up too, and I'll handle them. They kind of need the kid glove treatment."

"*Done. Battle zone coming up on your HUD.*"

She was supposed to have been out on the Parkour course right now, but she couldn't face it. Not when every time she looked up she was instinctively looking for that flash of red at the top of the current obstacle. Not when she could hear him playfully berating her whenever she paused for a breath.

This was better. She was thinking too hard to feel, trying to second-guess the Thulians, learning more with every raid about their tactics. The New York metas were excellent, but they were tired, like every meta in ECHO. On the other hand, since this current blitz had begun, they'd gotten reinforcements from metas in organized crime, Italian and Russian Mafia, Tongs and street gangs. *When the boat's sinking, even the Mafia goon helps bail.* And just as she thought that, some of those came boiling up out of their dens on the waterfront, in time to hold the Spheres at the Hudson. They had their own comm channel, but they'd given it to her before Red was arrested, and she coordinated them with Eight.

It was a good thing she'd called in the Murdocks, though; Valkyria turned up just as the combined New York metas and the Air Force were turning the Spheres back. But one look at the fireball coming in and the bitch turned tail and ran and took the Spheres with her.

And, at last, the sun was setting. For some reason, the Thulians didn't like to raid in the dark.

I bet they had no idea the Murdocks were going to be able to reach them and they likely won't try anything up or *down the East Coast now until they figure out JM and Sera were still in DC and not here. I think we can stand down . . .*

"Eight, I'm going to go get a fresh can of dinner. Take over?"

"*Of course, Vickie.*"

She pried herself up out of her chair with a groan, and plodded dully into the kitchen to open the fridge door and stand for a long time, staring at the row after row of liquid meals. None of which appealed.

But solid food appealed a lot less. She closed the door and leaned on it for a moment, resting her head on her arm. Trying to think of something she could *do* to tire herself out to the point where she couldn't think anymore. And maybe get a few hours of sleep before grief stabbed her awake again.

That was when she heard the little electronic blips at the door meaning someone was punching in the code that overrode her locks. She straightened up, because only one person had that code. It was time to lie to Bella again. Somehow convince Bella that she was on her way to bed. Or the Parkour course. Or was going to eat whatever Bella had brought. She was just glad that after the Georgia Dome Incident, Bella's empathy range had shrunk, though her healing was still as powerful as ever. If she could keep Bella about ten feet away, all it would take would be good acting. Or, depending on how tired and how distracted Bella was, mediocre acting.

So her heart sank a bit when the door opened, and she realized all of her acting chops, mediocre or otherwise, were not going to be up to snuff. It seemed Bella had shared the code.

The door swung silently open, and in walked Bulwark.

There was a lot to be said about Bulwark. He had a reputation for sheer willpower bottled up in a giant, and now *reinforced*, frame. Some joked his protective bubbles were just a logical extension of his personality. Nothing stuck to this man. You chucked anything at him, and it simply rebounded and came hurtling back at you. He was often quiet, understated, except for a few occasions when his roar was said to reverberate with all the righteous fury of the heavens. But for the most part, he kept a sober expression which hid whatever turmoil was buried deep underneath. For his students, his colleagues, and those who were especially close to him, this was extremely unfair. While he rarely revealed whatever emotions might be bubbling beneath his calm exterior, Bull had a way of reading what people really thought and felt. Vickie had long thought that if this ECHO and "saving the world" gig ever gave out for him, Bulwark should seriously consider pursuing a career as a psychotherapist.

"Hi, Bull," she said, pulling herself up and trying to look halfway normal. "New York got a hit, but we kept them to the Hudson and the Fireball Twins drove them off. I think this hemisphere is done for the night." *Just go away, okay, Bulwark?*

"Excellent," he rumbled. "That should give us a few moments to talk, then."

Oh great. "I hope it's not about training. Every time I head for the door, we get an alert." *Well, it's not entirely a lie.* "And in between alerts, I'm loading up Eight's magic arsenal." *Did I explain that to him? Or Bella? I'm ... starting to forget who I've told what.*

"You have much to do," Bull agreed. "We all do. I'm not here to get you to stop, you know. I'm here because I'm concerned you're pushing yourself further than you need to, than you can afford to. We're fighting for a future, after all, and that speaks of a certain belief of hope, wouldn't you say?"

She braced herself against the fridge. *Hope? What the hell has hope got to do with me?*

And again, Bulwark stepped forward and displayed his eerie talent for intuition, as if he could actually read thoughts. "Why else would any of us keep fighting, if not for hope? Hope that tomorrow will be better, that we will live to see it, that we will want to continue in this world. And to do so, we need to see to ourselves first. What I'm saying, Miss Victrix, is that I am concerned you are doing yourself irreparable harm."

She laughed. Well, it could have been called a laugh. It was a sound, anyway. And bitter words began to pour out of her mouth, without the censor she usually put on them. "I'm sorry, Bulwark, but it's not possible to follow your wishes. In descending order of importance, I need to make sure Eight can carry on better than I can, because right now we need ten of me and there's only one. I need to make sure that until that is the case, I handle everything on Overwatch that the Colts and Eight can't. And I guess no one gave you the memo, but now that Doppelgaenger has finished with her primary target, I'm the new likely primary, so I need to pack as much of task one and task two into whatever time I've got before she comes after me. Hope doesn't enter into the equation."

"Why bother then?" he asked. Vickie blinked. Somehow, he had silently crept up and was now standing next to her, his arms crossed over his massive chest. "Why do any of this? You seem quite prepared to lay down and die. Has it occurred to you that perhaps you will come out of this alive? Or is that the problem? Do you even want to?"

I ... don't want to. Waking up to an increasingly empty existence, lying in bed at night until sheer exhaustion overcame the crushing loneliness, the blackness of oblivion beckoned more

enticingly with every passing hour. But she couldn't give in to
it. She had promised. For Red. Giving up was not an option. But
longing for the hour when something would force her out of this
world...that was always with her.

"I..." she choked on her own words.

"I miss him too, you know," he said.

"He..." and to her chagrin, she lost it. She just stood there,
tears pouring down her face. She reached blindly for the fridge
again, and instead found herself clutching one enormous bicep.
Bulwark had moved again, making himself the thing she needed
to lean on. "He said...he loved me..."

"He did," Bulwark said, nodding. "He actually said it many
times. Perhaps not with words, but he did, as did you."

"How do you survive this?" she whispered, and barely noticed as
Bulwark drew her into a warm embrace. "How do you want to?"

"You cling to the one thing that is important to you," he murmured. "And you have faith that you will see it again, someday.
But only if you stay true to yourself. Only if you stay true to
him, and what he wanted for you. Take it from someone who
knows, who lost someone that was everything. You will fight and
you will do what is right and you will see them again. I did.
And someday, I will again."

All the grief she had been holding off with both hands avalanched
over her; she all but collapsed at that point, her knees giving way
and her legs buckling. He picked her up bodily and carried her over
to the couch, but rather than putting her down on it, he put her
on the floor, and sat down on the floor next to her, with one arm
curled around her as she wept into his chest. And she babbled. The
governor was off her mouth and the words were coming straight
out between sobs, in no particular order. How all she wanted was
to go back in time and disobey Red and stand there and fight and
if need be die beside him, because all she could think was how
she'd failed him. How terrified she was. How all that was keeping her sane was the promise she'd made to Red. How very much
everything hurt and how the world was empty with him gone. Most
of all, how utterly, utterly lost she felt without him and that most
days she might well welcome the sight of DG coming in through
the door except for the fact that DG would certainly break her and
she'd spill everything she knew. Finally she just ran out of words,
and cried until she couldn't cry anymore.

"I guess if you wanted revenge on me for Bruno, you've got it now," she whispered bitterly.

"Stuff and nonsense," Bull muttered. "I've never been about revenge, Victrix. You know that. We are called upon to make hard choices. That, really, is what separates us from our enemies. I wouldn't have made that choice, but I cannot blame you for it. I see that now. It was yours to make, and you will always have to suffer the burden of it. If you really want me to, I suppose I could muster up a tongue-lashing, give you some righteous rage and all that. But, really, I'm just prepared to be here for you. You should know, through all of this, you have had my respect and my admiration. People call me a rock, but I think I would have been pulverized to pieces if I had to go through all that you have. So, no, I'm not really offering anything but my support. And not just mine. You have people who love you, Victoria Victrix. And we're all here to stand by you."

She was so exhausted at this point that all she could do was to bury her head against his chest and slowly leak tears. And it all didn't hurt any less...but somehow...she didn't feel quite as alone anymore.

"As far as Doppelgaenger goes, I think we should move you under maximum security at HQ." Bull patted her arm gently. "How quickly can we get you out of here?"

"It shouldn't take long," Vickie said thickly, blotting her eyes with the backs of her gloves. "I can crate it up fast enough, I suppose, but I'll need help moving it."

"I can have a team here immediately to help you," Bull said. He paused. "And I can help, too."

She was about to object, because everything was already set up and calibrated and it would take hours to set it all up again, but then she realized something: literally everything in this apartment reminded her of Red. Maybe it wouldn't be so bad to move the Overwatch suite out to some new surroundings. And maybe Eight could help with the calibration.

And that was when the speaker in the other room came alive again.

But it wasn't one of the Overwatch Operators, or one of the ECHO or CCCP metas with implants.

It was the raspberry of a...tweet private message? Which could mean Jack.

"That might be something urgent," she said, reluctantly getting to her feet, staggering a little from exhaustion. She padded awkwardly to her command center, Bulwark close behind, and stared in sudden horror at the monitor.

@oracle4thewin: GET OUT. DG IS COMING.

"Oh God, Jack," Vickie gasped. "He promised he'd warn me. Bull, we don't have a day. She's coming...now!"

But Bulwark was already barking orders into his Overwatch rig...

As Bella ran in through the door, followed quickly by Corbie, and Ramona and Merc, and *Spin Doctor,* and Gilead, and more and more people arrived to secure the perimeter and carefully dismantle things at her direction and carry them away, it hit Vickie like a blast of light, cutting away the suffocating darkness that had enveloped her heart. All those people...had been sleeping, or eating, or recovering from the latest raid, and all of them had dropped everything and come on the run.

To help her. To save *her.* Bull had said that there were still people who loved her. And they had just proved that was actually true.

Guess I'd better go earn it.

Doppelgaenger chucked the headless, naked body into a dumpster, and pulled on the ECHO OpOne's gear after assuming his shape and face. She had been extremely cautious when she had arrived in the neighborhood of the witch's flat, and it appeared she had been right to take precautions, because the building was surrounded by nondescript ECHO agents, all heavily armed.

It was irritating, to say the least. The last thing she needed were further complications to what was, really, a very simple plan. Get in, knock the bitch out, take her to the Masters, and finally be rid of her. Of course, it couldn't be that simple, it had *never* been that simple. ECHO knew what they had in Vickie. Assuming that one could bypass the formidable defenses of Vickie's abode and take her by surprise, there were the constant ECHO air traffic patrols concentrated over various parts of Atlanta, here included, and a few contingency plans in place masterminded by Bulwark himself that would have any number of meta-powered squadrons and swift jets in hot pursuit within a matter of minutes. Doppelgaenger was privy to all of this, having access to those plans herself over the past year as one of Bella and Vickie's personal aides. That was how Bela had managed to take Vickie the first time. A bit of planning, the element of surprise, and having the bulk of ECHO's forces amassed at the other end of the city for Dixie Belle's funeral were key elements to success. This time, the element of surprise was gone. Clearly. They obviously knew that Victrix was still a target. Vickie probably had her defenses back up. If anything, security would have been tightened around her.

Still, Doppelgaenger wasn't terribly concerned about any of that.

The getaway itself would be child's play. The Masters had granted her the use of a Swift Sphere, which boasted aerial maneuverability, speed and cloaking technology far beyond anything ECHO had managed to assemble, even as a prototype. The Swifts were seldom if ever used, in part since they didn't make for especially entertaining viewing (how could one enjoy a chase scene when the quarry was invisible?) but mostly to keep their very existence a secret. It was how the Masters safeguarded their best toys. Doppelgaenger supposed it was a testament to just how badly they desired Victoria Victrix, and how close they were to the end-game. Doppelgaenger had not even made the request for a Swift. They had *offered* her one, with only the slightest hesitation.

As for the guards and Vickie's defenses, she had difficulty imagining any of them as more than a brief nuisance. She was hardly her old self, after all. The amalgamation of two highly compatible and hyperaccelerated meta-powered bodies had accomplished all that she had hoped for... and more. Any damage to this new, supercharged form seemed to heal almost instantly. Her shapeshifting abilities had transcended mere chameleon-like mimicry, exhibiting biomorphic adaptive reflexes and even conscious manipulation of her body, right down to the cellular level. She was still testing her new limits, though initial attempts had successfully produced temporary armor plating, enhanced cardiac tissue, muscle enhancement, and quickened neuronal transmission times. In short, she was tougher, stronger, faster... and soon, she suspected she would have conclusive data that she was, in fact, immortal.

You would think she would be elated. But there were concerns...

Not the least of which was the way she could plunge into a state of utter depression without warning, whenever something reminded her of Red. Oh, certainly that proved, if nothing else, that what she had felt for him was love, *real* love... didn't it?

It took every bit of her willpower to drag herself up out of that depression, and then she would find herself overwhelmed almost immediately by fatigue, utterly overwhelming befuddlement that made it hard to think, and moments when she actually blacked out and came to somewhere else, with no memory of how she had gotten there. Surely, *surely* this had to be a temporary state of affairs. Surely it was just her own body adjusting to the integration. And yet...

"I'll show you what love is!" he had screamed as he jabbed the claw into her head.

The past few days had not been easy for her. When she had come to on that cold floor, there was nothing in her but a very deep and dark hole. She had lost him, and more, she had been cursed with his final gift.

"I'll show you what love is!"

And he had.

She should not have had these memories. True, absorbing parts of a person had given her insights before. With Mel, she had eaten more than she needed for glimpses of the soldier's past, more than enough to escape detection. The few times she had performed a full integration with a victim, she had experienced a barrage of temporary memories that had thrown her into a confused, frenzied state that had required weeks of isolation to process fully. This time should have been different. She had known Red was kindred from the moment she had laid eyes on him. She had prepared for this, trained for it, ever since she had chosen her destiny. This time, she had chosen to preserve her prey, to share in the riches of their union together. Instead, he had forced her to kill him. What might have been a glorious period of transitioning, of letting their minds slowly meld together into one—a delicious process that could have taken years!—instead became a cold and sharp dissection of his identity. And yet, something had gone wrong. His newly magnificent body and powers were now hers, but his mind...

There was nothing left of his mind. Nothing at all.

She had hoped, at the very least, to have gleaned something of him to keep and cherish, to hold close and dear, forever. At most, she might have preserved the breadth of his entire life, his thoughts stored within the expanse of her mind, to be called upon and experienced, each in their own time. And while she found

herself at times shuddering, writhing against the sharp flashes
of pure memory, she wished more than anything else to be rid
of them. Because they were not his memories.

They belonged to another.

She should not have had these memories. They were impossible,
for one thing. Some never happened; others were from a distant
future that could never come to pass. But they were real. They
spoke of a multiverse of realities, and in each one, they showcased
the same thing, over and over and over again. Victoria Victrix
loved Red Djinni as much as any human could love another. And
they kept coming, unwanted, tormenting her...

Her mind shied away from them, violently. And the more she
tried to avoid them, the more she fixated on mourning for that
Red bastard. And the more she mourned, the more confused she
found herself, suffering that depression again, a depression that
made her sluggish, made her lose track of hours, even parts of days.

I'm not up to this.

But the Masters, Gero himself, had spoken. She had to kidnap
Victrix, take her alive, when that was the *last* thing she wanted
to do. She wanted Victrix dead, dead and gone. Perhaps then,
these memories would follow the bitch into the grave and she
wouldn't keep reliving them.

"I'll show you what love is!"

She entered the building and took the stairs to Vickie's floor,
encountering no one along the way. As she reached the hallway,
she realized that the door to the apartment in question was
standing open, light flooding into the hall.

She entered, sensed no one inside, and went straight to the
Overwatch room. Or rather, what had been the Overwatch room—
and now was a room bare of anything, the single overhead light
fixture blazing down on carpet showing indentations where the
furniture and equipment had been.

She turned and glanced into what had been the witch's workroom, to find the same there. And in the bedroom—well, there
was the bed, and all the furniture, but drawers still pulled out
showed conclusively that the apartment had been emptied of
everything the witch wanted or needed. And, of course, of the
witch herself.

Doppelgaenger stood there, clutching the ECHO Op's weapon,
and cursed silently. Vickie had been on duty, here, mere hours

ago—she *had* to have been, because the Murdocks had turned up at the raid on New York City, and only *she* was able to call them up. So between then and now, suddenly the apartment had been emptied, and the prey had flown.

Presumably flown at nearly the exact moment when Doppelgaenger herself had departed to capture her.

Which could only mean one thing. The unthinkable had happened.

"We have a mole," she muttered, clenching her teeth so hard her jaw ached. "We have a mole."

CHAPTER TWENTY-SIX

Between the Lines

DENNIS LEE AND MERCEDES LACKEY

*Until now, I rather doubt anyone had reckoned just what
a clever monkey Jack was.*
You're all about to find out.

Jack awoke and found himself caught in an immediate staring contest with Barron. She appeared to be sizing him up. It was always so hard to tell what an alien was thinking, as facial expressions were relatively novel to them. He had really nothing to go on but body language. It had been his first lesson in dealing with the Masters. Body language was very important to them. They even had an intricate system of hand gestures and poses, with the slightest differences conveying emotions as disparate as gratitude and disdain, respect and loathing, and everything in between. So it had been worth his life to pick up the nuances of this sign language during their first meeting, and fast. Thankfully he had always had a knack for adopting new skills, especially ones that meant life or death.

He found himself staring back at Barron, letting her play her game, when he finally sighed. He didn't have time for this. If this was the real Barron, he was as good as dead. His demise might have been prefaced with a gratuitous amount of violence, but she would have ended him fairly quickly. And while he was still picking up the sign language, he was fairly certain that heavy tilt of her head was how the Masters expressed attraction of a sexual nature. That hardly seemed likely, though the mere thought was disturbing at the least.

"Knock it off," he growled. "We're on a schedule here."

"You can tell, just by looking at me, can't you?" Harmony said in her own voice, stepping out of the way so he could clamber out of the stasis chamber. "I think you missed your calling, Jack. You would have made a good spy."

"What do you call what we're doing then?" Jack grunted and came to his feet. He looked around. They were in a small chamber, dimly lit by lights that didn't shine so much as seep from the panels in the ceiling and floor. There was a severe absence of color in the futuristic decor, with mostly metallic black and silver panelling, and strictly utilitarian design. "Though if this place is all like this, it might make it more than a little difficult to sneak around. This kind of setup doesn't really lend itself to crawling through the ductwork."

"We might be able to move about in plain sight," Harmony said. "I got you a uniform—not an easy thing to do, considering your odd size."

From her outstretched pincer she dangled one of the uniforms worn by the few human collaborators aboard the ship—descendants, no doubt, of those original Nazi "minders" who had attended to the needs of the original Ubermensch, and of Eisenfaust, Valkyria, and Doppelgaenger. Jack snatched it away, pulled it on, then reached into the bottom of the tube and brought out his kit bag. One advantage to being short, there had been plenty of room in there for him *and* his kit.

"You don't look altogether bad in that," Harm observed, as he tugged the tunic straight, her head again to one side. "The fascist style suits you."

"Nazis always had the best uniforms. Hugo Boss," he observed, as he made sure that everything that had been in his kit was *still* in his kit. "Any glitches getting us aboard?"

"Surprisingly, no." Harmony shrugged. "The guards believed I was her, wouldn't even look me in the eye as I snarled at them and breezed past. She must have quite the reputation on this boat. I only got a brief scan of her at her base, but what I gleaned seemed convincing enough." She paused, looking thoughtful. "That was with the lowly peons, though. If I run into anyone who actually knows her well, it might not be enough."

"What you gleaned?" Jack asked, pausing as he slipped his hands into a pair of heavy leather gloves. "You can do that?"

"You mean you didn't know? You don't fool me, Jack. You know I can't read you. That's a nice hefty shield you've somehow erected around yourself. You've been dabbling in magic, haven't you?"

"Fine, I had an idea of what you can do. Yeah, I'm being schooled in the use of magic. It's handy, and I'll use whatever tools are at hand to get the job done. I didn't know you could get that much from Barron though. Why did you let me coach you so much on her mannerisms then?" he asked, a tinge of annoyance in his voice. "Time is precious, girl. We can't squander it on things that don't matter."

"Girl . . ." Harmony chuckled. "You really are in the dark, aren't you? You still think I'm just some bored, overpowered meta who's got little else to do with her time than help you save the world? Just remember what we discussed, Jack. I named my price. Unlike Verdigris, I think you'll stay true to your word, and get me what's mine."

"You'll have it," Jack said. "Just keep me alive and let me see this through. Victrix needs that information, and we're about all she's got on this boat. After that, we can both settle our common score, and then we can settle our account."

"Promise?" Harmony asked, her voice kittenish. Jack almost recoiled. He knew it was Harmony, but the sight of Barron playing the role of a flirtatious schoolgirl was enough to make his hair stand on end.

"Promise," he nodded. He didn't see any reason to lie. He had unearthed her lost and precious talisman, and he had every intention of returning the repulsive artifact to her.

"Does Victrix know?"

"Know what?"

"That I'm on the team?" Harmony smirked. "It seems like a funny thing to me."

"Doubt it," Jack said. "You were recruited on the fly. Opportunity presented itself, and I'd have been a fool not to take advantage of it. I wouldn't underestimate Victrix though. Girl's got more than a few surprises tucked away here and there. Why do you ask? You got a beef with her?"

"Oh no, of course not," Harmony replied. "The witch and I get along famously."

"Sure you do," Jack said. "Everyone just loves you, don't they? You're just oozing with good intentions and all."

"There's no need to be so antagonistic, Jack," Harmony said, pouting. "We're on the same side again, just like old times."

"You might not want to bring up the old times," Jack said. "If you recall, that didn't end so well for me. You're sure we're good here? You followed the protocol?"

"Yes, yes," Harmony sighed. "No unnecessary risks, clean sweeps, zero contact, first safe room. We're good. You act like there was any doubt I could get us in."

Jack didn't answer and continued to rummage through his kit bag.

"You *did!*" Harmony said and cackled. "Goodness, this wasn't as foolproof as you had us all believe."

"Yeah, I took a gamble on you," Jack admitted. "I gambled you wanted your little trinket enough to pull it off. Not my usual play, but sometimes there isn't much choice." Everything was in the bag in its proper place. He grunted in satisfaction and began to look about the room.

"You risked both of us on this? May I say I'm surprised, even a little shocked?" She didn't sound either, but . . . it was Harmony.

Jack paused from his search and gave her a speculative look. "Us? Do you think *you're* in any danger at all?" he asked. "Let's say the worst happens, and we're discovered. Given what's in here, all around us, I'm pretty much screwed. You though . . . you defy everything that's ever been thrown at you. You think I don't know *that*?"

She just shrugged. Or did an approximation of that movement, hampered by the fact she was wearing a body with a lot of shoulder joints. "I get by. You think I don't have weaknesses, that I can't be killed, well . . . I don't see why I would contest any of that. There's really no benefit in admitting one might have an Achilles heel, is there? Nice thing about having a past shrouded in mystery—no one can see what you're really bringing to the party. I rather like that. Always having the upper hand means I can do as I see fit. Sometimes, I can even be the good guy."

"The good guy," Jack grunted. "Was that what you were doing when you tried to spring Red from his cage?"

"He was the last," Harmony nodded. "I had a few scores to settle at ECHO. I do have some sense of karma, you know, and there are a few people who I care about. I couldn't stay there forever, but before I left I needed to set them on their path. For Red, I thought getting him out of his cell would do nicely. Never dreamed what lay ahead of him, that it was Doppelgaenger who was posing as..."

"Wait, you *knew* that was Doppelgaenger?" Jack demanded and glared at her. "You knew and you let him go with her? If you were trying to help him, how do you justify just letting him waltz off with that...thing?"

"It wasn't just him," Harmony said. "It was *them*. Their paths were entwined, anyone could see that. Whatever the fates had in store for them, it certainly didn't fall upon me to interfere. My role is never to judge, Jack, only facilitate. I am an agent of chaos, after all. What happens, happens. I can only stir the pot."

"You knew what would happen to him, didn't you?" Jack asked, his voice now very quiet. "You knew she was going to kill him."

"She was close to—something," Harmony said. "Close enough that the anticipation was coming off her in waves. I had an idea what might happen, yes. It would be bloody and terrible, but it didn't taste like death. Quite the opposite. I'm not accustomed to justifying my actions, Jack, but I'll have you know I thought I was doing the Djinni a favor. In the long run, I thought he would be the better for it. I cared for him too, as much as I do anyone. If he died, he chose it. That's as much as anyone can hope for."

Jack continued to stare at her. He felt his fingers twitching, eager to go for her throat, to taste her blood, but with a grunt he pulled away and continued his scan of their surroundings. His eyes went everywhere, and stopped on an access panel by the entrance. He moved to it quickly, knelt down to open his bag, selected a couple of tools and proceeded to carefully remove the face of the access panel to reveal the alien technology within.

Harmony strolled up beside him, peering with curiosity at the strange collection of solid opaque blocks and humming tubes of gray. There were none of the expected wires or otherwise fragile components one would normally find encased in human technology. Everything here seemed quite hardy and immaculate with a sense of permanence.

"Do you know how any of this works?" she asked.

"ECHO pieced a few things together from what tech they've salvaged since the Invasion," Jack grunted. "Enough to suss out a few basics, like the communication feed ports. Stuff like the power supplies, advanced cybernetics, adaptive hardware...that stuff will take decades to understand fully."

He retrieved another device from his kit bag, a small tablet decorated with runes, taped together with peripheral gadgets including what appeared to be a camera, a small transmitter and, surprisingly, a large quartz crystal with a folded bit of paper bound to it with hair-thin silver wire. Jack held it close to the opened panel and muttered a few words. With a click, the tablet attached itself to one of the larger exposed blocks.

"Just learning magic, hmmm?" Harmony said. "I take it you're in the gifted program?"

"Hardly," Jack said. "This is all Victrix. My only contribution was supplying the duct tape."

They watched as the tablet hummed to life, and from the display, a loading bar began counting up. "Download's started," Jack nodded, his mouth set in a grimace of satisfaction. "We got the back door secured?"

Harmony nodded. "We're close, won't take much to take out surveillance and minor personnel in the area. We'll be able to get Khanjar and Scope on, and keep ready for the boarding party."

"I'd say we're in business then." Jack exhaled. "And once we've got this ship's layout, we can beam it to Victrix and she can…"

"Hold that thought," Harmony said, and pointed at the tablet. "Shouldn't that be moving in the other direction?"

Jack stared at the loading bar, which had paused at twenty percent. And now it was moving back down, to eighteen…fifteen…

Magic. It was really the Masters' only blind spot. Victrix had supplied him with this all-in-one gadget that would subvert every single Thulian security system she'd laid eyes, hands, and magic on. It was to be their eyes and their ears on this boat, ready to quickly glean as much information about this ship as they could get and give them on-the-fly access to all on-board communications. To do that, it had to be invisible to the ship's sensors. That's where Victrix's magic had come into play. The device needed to be shielded, a fly on the wall. But the primary protocol had been detected and the program was reversing itself and shutting down. Jack had not counted on that. How could he? How could the Masters have defenses for something they didn't know about? Unless they did, unless…

Jack swore. There was someone aboard who did know about magic, who could have prepared for it. It wasn't enough that she had killed his best friend, she had prepped the ship for the only vulnerability they had been able to exploit.

"Talk to me, Jack," Harmony said. "Where we at?"

"Remember what I said earlier? About the worst-case scenario?"

"Mmm-hmm."

"I'd say we're minutes away," Jack said. "Unless we come up with something fast, we're going to be hearing Klaxons soon."

CHAPTER TWENTY-SEVEN

Kingdom

MERCEDES LACKEY AND CODY MARTIN

Something John said to me...that when things are dark-est, sometimes all you need is a hand to reach for you out of that dark.

The damndest thing about the entire rotten mess with the Djinni was that John thought he could have prevented it. No, actually he was *sure* he could have prevented it.

Red had died. No, that wasn't right. It was too clinical, too cold. Red had been *killed*, murdered. And in a very real sense, John had been there. He felt it happen, amidst everything else. He had felt Vickie as she managed to touch Red magically, and as she experienced Red dying just as she reached him. It had torn through him like a hail of icicle spikes, sickeningly cold but still leaving molten and oozing wounds in their wake. John and Sera had been some of the few—if not the only—people that knew how much Vickie cared for Red. Loved him, more than she loved herself. He had been ripped from her, finally and horribly. John could empathize with her; he'd been there himself, what seemed like so long ago but in reality had only been a few years. He had grown since that loss—Jessica, a woman whom he loved and who loved him back, if only for a short time—and feeling that same loss through Vickie... he felt his heart breaking along with hers, for her. At the injustice of it. That anyone would have to feel that twisting, yawning pit in their stomachs, seeing someone that meant everything...be taken.

He was on the roof of his squat, alone and watching the city with half of a bottle of lukewarm beer in his hands. There were a dozen and a half empties nearby; he hardly felt the alcohol. Drinking was something to do with his hands and his mouth; better that than grinding his teeth, or clenching his fists...or worse. The city was lit up in the night; with the destruction corridors and the height of the building he squatted in, it was easy enough to see the skyline and large swaths of darkness cutting through the city. It seemed so incongruous, the city being bright and humming along—as well as it could, with the war and all—when someone like Red had been taken from it. Intellectually, he knew that that was just the way the world was. People died, people were born, another day, another buck. In his gut, he wanted to spit and scream and rave against the absurdity, the tragedy of it. John and Red had become friends; not the closest, but there was still something there. They had both been outlaws, of different stripes, and were running from their pasts when this entire stupid goddamned war had started. It had made them confront themselves...and change. Plus, the bastard liked the same sort of scotch that John did.

The entire situation was eating at him. They had lost people before. They—the "good guys"—were going to probably lose a lot more before the war ended. One way or another. And John wasn't a stranger to loss, especially by violence. Friends when he was enlisted, men under his command on operations, Jessica in the Program, his parents in the Invasion. Then comrades and friends since. But this was different. It was different for him because he had *become* different. Before, he had done everything that he could, or at least he told himself that. You can't be everywhere at once, shoot all the bad guys, move every person out of the way of falling buildings. But now, John...could. Or goddamned near it. He wasn't dying, at least not any more than anyone else. His powers weren't killing him. In fact...his powers were literally out of this world. He had done things that no one thought could be done...and he was getting better, too. Despite all of that, he felt like there was *more*, more power, further limits that he could push. If he could reach that, *take* it...he could maybe stop things like what happened to Red and Vickie from ever happening again. No, no "maybes" about it. He *would* stop things like that. And he could see it, too, in his imagination. There wouldn't be threats that he couldn't handle, catastrophes he couldn't preempt. Challenges he couldn't put down.

If he could wrap his hands around that next level of power, there was no limit to what he could do, the *good* he could do...

It wasn't just his imagination anymore. He felt his gaze unfocus slightly, then snap back into high definition, sharp focus. He wasn't on the rooftop anymore, he was Beyond. Destroying the Thulians, down to the last. Then anyone involved in the slightest way with the Program. He was perfect and untouchable, and from there, it would only be a matter of time—

He didn't know that he had been squeezing his hands so hard that he had shattered the bottle he was holding until Sera put a hand on his right forearm. She had joined him on the roof while he had been lost in that... whatever it was. Reverie? Vision? So deep into it that he hadn't even noticed her approach; with his senses and especially with his connection to her, *that* had never happened before. *Losing it again, old man?*

"You are right," she said sadly. "This war... we pay price upon price upon price. That is how war *is;* it is a great and terrible beast that devours everything in its path. Nothing is safe from it. Not innocence, not love... but that is not your fault, nor mine, nor anyone's who fights those who bring this war upon us."

"Y'know that I know 'bout war, darlin'. Seen my fair share of it, now an' before." He wiped the brown bottle glass from his gloves; what little shards he couldn't safely wipe, he vaporized quickly, igniting his hands and then extinguishing them, leaving not even ash. "Knowin' it doesn't make it easier. An' it doesn't make the dead any less dead." He knew that Sera only wanted to help him. The love he felt pouring off of her was almost enough to drive him to his knees weeping, but he fought to stand straight. He didn't particularly feel like being consoled at the moment. He wanted to own the pain, at least for now. It wouldn't feel real, otherwise.

"And you know, better than most, that death is not an ending." She encircled him with an arm. "But we both know, better than most, that this is no consolation." Her wing followed the curve of her arm, doubly embracing him. "I lack words," she finally added. "Perhaps there are none for this."

John put his arm around Sera's waist, the soft feathers of her wing warming him, pulling her closer. She placed her head against his shoulder.

"Maybe not." He sighed heavily, still looking at the city. It was well and truly night now. The city should have been lit up a whole lot more, but, well... destruction corridors. Damaged infrastructure. There were ugly gaps in the lights that looked like missing teeth. He still resented everyone going on like nothing had happened, knowing that he shouldn't. "I still feel like shit. Like I didn't do enough to help." He hated that feeling: helplessness. Of all the people in the world, he figured that he was one of the *least* helpless. So why was it he still felt like a weakling, a failure at that moment?

"Come walk with me," she said softly. "It has been long since we walked together. Too many battles call us away too often. I wish to feel the ground beneath my feet and quiet about me."

Without waiting for an answer, she gently disengaged herself from him and lofted over the low parapet, landing lightly on the ground below, where she stood, looking up at him and holding out one hand. *She's right. Aw, what the hell. Walk might help. I've got her, an' she's got me.* John placed a hand on the brick ledge in front of him, then swung his legs forward and to the side, vaulting over it. When he was about thirty feet from the ground, he turned on his fire around his legs and feet for a short spurt. It sounded like a flag flapping from a hurricane wind, too loud, for a split second. Then he had landed, fire extinguished. He was starting to get pretty decent at landings. Hell knew he had had enough practice these last few weeks.

Sera took his hand in the soft dark, knowing *exactly* where he was without being able to see him in the shadows. John's eyes were better than hers, enhanced even without Vickie's Overwatch HUD. He didn't need to use his mundane senses to tell where she was, however; he felt her presence, like a comforting fire against the cold of night. Together, they walked slowly towards the playground at the end of the block.

Someone had scrounged up some solar-powered lights and placed them where the kids wouldn't accidentally run into them or kick them over. It The result was an irregular pattern of globes of dim light, just enough to make out the shadows of the equipment. "I remember watching you weld these objects," she said, looking at the playground equipment.

"I remember doin' it. That was back when I thought you were just another crazy meta." A lot of public spaces had been razed when the initial Invasion had happened. There were a lot of kids with no safe kid things to do, for a while. Not that the kids *here* had *ever* had a playground before, unless you counted a couple of basketball hoops on a fenced-in stretch of asphalt at their school. After John had started organizing the 'hood, it was one of the things that the community had brought up. A half hour of planning after that meeting, some scrap steel, a grinding wheel, some paint, and John's fire...and a playground had started to take shape. It looked a lot more impressive now; the neighborhood had been adding to it, expanding it.

"Random acts of kindness," she said. "And yours inspired more. *This* has also taught children that while there are terrible things about them, there are also people who care enough for them to give them such a thing. You have sent out bright threads among the dark."

John shrugged, still looking at all of the play equipment. The area had been wrecked, initially: rubble, jagged rebar, and worse. Now, it was even, the borders lined with reused telephone poles and the ground covered with chewed-up car tires. Good old Chug. Once you convinced him not to *eat* the things, he was happy to be their no-cost tire mulcher. There were plants and actual grass areas, laid down in odd-shaped plots wherever they could be fit. It looked like an entire 'nother world, sprung up in the middle of Atlanta like a colorful sprout.

"I figure it would've happened, one way or another. The folks in this 'hood don't always get enough credit for what they can do when they really pull together. Just took a spark. Or a kick in the ass, dependin' on how you look at it."

"But none of them had that spark," she reminded him. "Only you. Not even Jonas looked at this lot and thought of the children."

"It didn't look like it would be a good place for a beer cooler, is probably why. Speakin' of, we probably oughta get some lunch with that old goat sometime soon. 'Fore he thinks we've forgotten 'bout him, or the beer that I owe him." *Besides*, he sent to her through their connection, *if it wasn't me, then someone would have stepped up, in time.*

She shook her head but did not argue with him, instead, taking him further along, to the garden. It was spring now, and people had begun setting out the seedlings they'd been sprouting in old paper egg cartons, in their windowsills. Everyone with a window that got some sun had been doing a share. "You did this, too. I watched you. And this, you did alone, until you had a space fit to plant in, and then you brought the Hog Farmers here."

John threw a lopsided grin Sera's way. "Alone? I don't think that's *entirely* true, darlin'." He had always known, somehow, that Sera had helped the garden thrive when it was struggling, in the first few weeks and months. Their new connection, their shared memories and feelings, confirmed it.

She waved a hand, dismissing his comment. "I only improved what you made. Really, walking the ground does not qualify as *helping*."

He leaned over, planting a light kiss on the tip of her nose. "Does if you're the one doin' the walkin', love." He looked over the garden. Once it had really started and got on its feet, it had been producing steadily. Combined with the tiny plots that some people had in closet-sized backyards, on windowsills, porches, and balconies, it all had added up to a none-too-small harvest. Everyone shared, since everyone needed something. Barter had come back in a strong way in the 'hood, as had friendly loans. You never knew when the person that needed some potatoes would be able to throw a couple of containers of strawberries your way, or some rosemary. Every other day, there was a farmer's market somewhere in the 'hood; different blocks on different days, with a big multiblock one on Sundays. It all helped to shore up the food that was trucked into this part of the city, which always seemed to be a little less than what was needed, what with the war on.

Sera paused, seemingly in thought for a moment, then continued on, bringing John along with a light pull on his arm. They continued walking through the 'hood, turning to stay on the cleared streets and avoiding the destruction corridors. There were a few people on the streets, going on with their lives or wrapping up business that they couldn't finish before the sun went down. It almost felt normal. This neighborhood had been its own sort of special hell before the Invasion: poverty, drugs, crime. The residents had lacked any sense of real community; each apartment was an island, sometimes aligned with friends and neighbors, more often shored up against the same. A constant siege mentality, partially through police neglect—or sometimes targeted, depending on if someone was running for reelection or wanted a promotion or just hadn't made their arrest quota that week—and criminals who carved out little fiefdoms in the squalor. The Invasion had changed that; they couldn't fight amongst themselves anymore. It didn't matter if you were poor or rich, black, white, brown or yellow; the Kriegers wanted to kill everyone that wasn't Thulian.

So... they had banded together. There were false starts and miscommunication in the beginning, and plenty of the bolder gangs had tried to expand; after having to deal with energy blasts and thermite, after the First Invasion wave, the residents were back to ducking bullets—a familiar struggle waged with new vigor by normal gangs as well as those bolstered by metahuman members. When John arrived, it wasn't long before he intervened. It still puzzled him why he had done that, back then. He had been a different man, still on the run technically. He had done a lot of things that seemed nonsensical or even crazy. It was probably the kid back in New York City that had changed things for John, however miniscule the change had seemed at the time.

Sera paused fractionally, and waved. John looked where she was looking, and saw one of the neighborhood patrols keeping a watchful eye in the shadows—where no one but a meta would be likely to spot them. It was a great lookout spot; they had a fine view of a five-point street intersection as well as into the park, without being easily spotted themselves. He saw a couple of them waving back, and sensed the grins. "You taught them well," she said softly. She was right; John had put a stop to the intergang fighting in the 'hood. He had called out the heads of all the gangs, along with some of the more prominent leaders among the civilians—Jonas among them—and showed everyone what he could do. Namely, he had melted a wrecked car like a chocolate bar put under a blowtorch. Probably not the smartest move, considering the heat it had brought down on him from Blacksnake and ECHO, but it *had* been effective. He had told everyone that they were going to work together, or they'd have to deal with him. He didn't want to play sheriff; not his style, for starters. Instead, he had trained anyone that wanted to, how to keep themselves protected, keep themselves and the 'hood as a whole safe. Combined with the street savvy that the gangs had, and the oversight from the rest of the neighborhood... and, miraculously, things had worked out.

Miraculously? Sera allowed him, in that moment, a rare flash out of her own memories of that time. How she had literally displayed the Wrath of a Seraphym to one of the more... recalcitrant among the leaders. In his mind's eye, he saw the gang-banger practically melting with terror before her. Ironically, it was one of the fellows who had just waved back.

John chuckled as they walked. "See? I *have* had an angel on my shoulder this entire time. Well, lookin' over it, at the very least."

"Some," she said, and squeezed his hand. "Mostly, it was your own doing."

"How do you mean, darlin'?" They had left most of the populated streets behind; they were on their own now, back on the darker streets. The sounds of life and those living it still drifted after them.

"How you treated them. What you showed them. You surely know that even if it all turns against us, *this* will be a place where resistance will not die. You showed them..." she paused. "You showed them that perfectly ordinary people are capable of making a great difference."

"Well, neither of us are exactly all that ordinary, y'gotta admit. Especially now." The thoughts of what he could do with Sera's power came back to him. She was able to cow the worst that humanity had to offer, get them in line and quit killing each other, start working together. He may have planted the seeds with his little fire tricks... but she was awesome with that level of power. Enough power to turn a person's knees to water without having to do more than utter a word. If a simple display of her true form could have that effect, how much more could he do without the constraints of being a Sibling of the Infinite? He had Free Will, after all... and he could use it to make things better. Couldn't he? Shouldn't he?

"It was not your power they respected. It was that you *had* power and *gave them* power. That was you. Not your enhancements, not your meta-ability." She stopped and turned, causing him to turn to face her fully. "You could have done that with nothing but your character and the skills you had... the man that you are. I *know* this. And I know... another thing."

"What?" he asked, puzzled as to where this was going.

"You could have all my power, the full strength of a Seraphym, at any time. All that is needed is for me to die."

John felt ice flood his veins, and he recoiled as if he had been burned. Revulsion and horror filled him in that instant, in a way he hadn't thought possible. Sera dead? He would rather die himself, a thousand times over, than to lose her again. The horror and revulsion were all quickly washed away in a wave of shame; he hadn't actually considered what he might have to do for that power, what he might have to sacrifice. He knew that he would never be able to betray her like that, greater good be thrice damned. She was his world now, and he was hers. He knew, deep down, that if she died, he would be right there with her; he wouldn't leave her alone, even in death.

She let out her breath in a long sigh, and took his other hand. And in that moment, he was taken to that . . . place . . . where he could see some of the Futures. The ones he saw were all ones where *he* was the person that would let his beloved die to have her power. The ones where he smashed the Kriegers, and a grateful—or fearful—world made him the pinnacle of power.

They were terrible Futures, terrible and glorious at the same time. And now, they were dying. Snuffing out, one by one, until it was as if they had never been a possibility at all. Then there was just—them. Together. Facing uncertainty.

More than anything, John felt glad. He blew out all of his breath in one hard exhalation. Nothing he could gain would ever equal having Sera by his side. Having her wasn't settling, or giving anything up; it was gaining everything that mattered. He knew that he had made the right choice . . . and she had helped him arrive at it.

"Thank you, darlin'. I got a bit lost there after Red . . . but you helped me get right again. Thank you." He leaned in, kissing her with purpose for several long seconds.

"We can prevail together," she said. "I will not allow myself to believe otherwise. And we will do so without sacrificing our humanity." She rested her forehead on his chest. "Together we are stronger, and more clever, and better, than either of us could ever be apart."

The Greatest

MERCEDES LACKEY AND DENNIS LEE

The Masters didn't understand bowing or kneeling; their bodies weren't really made for either. Their gesture of subservience was to lie facedown on the floor. So that is what Doppelgaenger was doing, facedown on the polished floor in front of Gero. The floor—whatever it was made of—was like cool silk on her skin. There wasn't even a speck of dust to cause the least physical discomfort.

Mental discomfort, however, was another story entirely. Doppelgaenger was...in misery. Fury warred with grief, humiliation with an acute unease she couldn't even pinpoint, and mixed in, there was a seething, bubbling mass of other emotions that were all as painful as they were unidentifiable.

"So. You *failed*." Gero didn't spit the words, his vocal apparatus wasn't suited to that. "I picked you—I personally picked you—and you *failed*. You loser! You told me that eating that Djinni person was going to make you unstoppable, and you *failed*. You failed *me!* Sad! You are so overrated! What is wrong with you? *How dare you fail me?*"

Resentment bubbled to the top of her emotions. She was grateful that the Masters were singularly inept at reading the cues of emotion in human speech. "I am a loser, mighty Gero. I should have known better than to think I could obtain the Victrix without your personal guidance. I only hope that your personal greatness holds the generosity to forgive my unforgivable hubris." Anger and sarcasm were so thick in the air it was a wonder they didn't show up surrounding her as clouds of bile green and sullen red...but Gero, as usual, was oblivious to anything that wasn't himself.

"Well...yes. You *should* have come to me for directions. I suppose my underlings must not have instructed you to do so. They're even bigger losers than you are. Sad!" Gero's feet moved a little on the floor in front of her, as he swayed back and forth. "I'll have a word with *them* when I'm through with *you*."

"Yes, Lord Gero," she repeated. "You are absolutely right, as always."

Suddenly Gero stopped swaying. She stiffened as she sensed him bending down over her even though she couldn't see him. How could she know that? The sensation threw her into confusion for a moment. Then, suddenly, a whole new *world* of sensation burst on her, coming from...

...her skin. It was like skin radar. Or heat-sensing skin. Or pressure sensing. Or vibrational sensing. No, it was all of these. All of them at once. And this must have come from Red Djinni. She winced as her mind struggled to cope with what Red must have always had to deal with, a constant stream of information that bombarded her. She had a vague sense that Gero had resumed speaking, though it was drowned out by a massive overload of sensory data, enough that she couldn't pick out anything over the din. And then...

She exhaled as her surroundings came back into focus, her mind growing accustomed to processing and mapping it all, and it was with a certain wonder that she took it all in. She saw it all, the entirety of his enormous throne room. She remembered the first time she had been brought here, a rare honor even among the elite. It had not met her expectations of grandeur then, and if anything, her extended senses amplified the sheer tackiness of it now. The Supreme Oberfuhrer Gero, in his infinite wisdom, had chosen flash over substance, excess over functionality. While each surface was maintained, kept bright, polished and immaculate, the furnishings defied any notion of style or elegance. To say the landscape was "busy" was a staggering understatement. No area was untouched by alien-looking trophies of war and countless monitors which hung from the walls, from the ceiling, angled towards a massive throne where Gero would sit and watch the constant stream of violence he had set in motion, from all around the Earth.

She had maintained her male form then, as she did now, for even the Masters were not above prejudice. If anything, Gero was the worst of them, gauging first one's sex and appearance, placing value on experience and merit almost as an afterthought. What did it matter to him? Everyone who served him did so with the disturbing knowledge that if they displayed so much as the slightest degree of disrespect, their death would be quick and merciless. Such incidents were rare, rare enough that Gero would opt to deliver judgment by his own hand. It was said that there was no one the Supreme Oberfuhrer couldn't dispense of with a nod of his head, even Barron if it came to that. Doppelgaenger could only guess at the power he possessed; it was all buried in legend.

If he really was that powerful, he hid it well.

Like all of the Masters, he stood well over the usual height for human: eight, perhaps nine feet tall, more than enough to tower over them. Like all of the Masters, he had an oddly feminine face, broad at the top, narrowing to a pointed chin, with a mere slit for a mouth, twin slits for a nose, and enormous, jewellike eyes, Like all of them, he had six arms and two legs; the two largest ending in powerful pincer-claws, the other four kept folded against his torso, ending in tiny, delicate hands. This part was not usual; most, though not all, Masters' manipulative arms ended in some combination of two-to-six thin but muscular tentacles. Like all of them except Barron, he wore mostly decorative armor completely covering his torso, and his head was covered in what looked like feathers. Unlike most Masters, his head feathers were not silky; in fact, they looked stiff and bristly, almost strawlike. Every Master she had ever seen was a different color. Gero was a sort of brass color. Too orange to be gold. And yet, despite his arrogant manner, he seemed almost frail. He moved with a delicate precision, as if his tired body could bear only so much exertion, hiding away whatever great power lay within.

Gero continued to bend over her, and Doppelgaenger came to attention as he folded his arms behind his back. He was about to ask her something.

"Do you know *why* we ally ourselves with some members of a race we intend to conquer?" he said softly. "We always do this. Sometimes we even accept some of them into our world, like the ones you call the Thulians. But have you ever guessed why?"

"No," she replied, so wrapped up in her own internal struggle that it was all the reply she could manage.

"Not just because it's entertaining, which it is, of course. But because you all bring something new and intriguing to the party. Sometimes—most times, really—you can't integrate with our society in your proper place, and we let you die off when we conquer your world and burn it to the ground. But sometimes you prove useful, entertaining, and adaptive, and we keep selected members of you with us. Even fodder has its purpose. Those fools in Ultima Thule were particularly useful. Gladly did we give up that pathetic collection of rebellious upstarts, knowing full well that the humans would at last feel safe, safe enough to betray the location of Metis." She sensed Gero's head plumes moving, slicking back. "So the question in *your* mind should be, *How do I make myself so indispensable to Lord Gero that he keeps me with him when he blows this planet up?* And that, really, is the *only* consideration you should have right now." He stood up. "Because unless things change, we're close to that moment. And so far, there are not too many of your kind that seem worth the trouble of holding onto."

"I will double my efforts, Supreme Oberfuhrer," Doppelgaenger replied. "You will have the Victrix woman, I swear this to you."

"Yes, I suppose we will," Gero chuckled. "A pity that Tesla and Marconi were lost, and Arthur Chang, but no matter. With Verdigris in hand, Victrix will surely complete whatever intelligence is left to be salvaged from this pitiful ape planet. Their combined imagination and expertise should be enough to catapult our AI matrix to a desirable plateau, perhaps even enough to solve that most damnable puzzle that has plagued us since the beginning."

For the upteenth time, Doppelgaenger almost asked what this ultimate mystery was, and quickly silenced herself by gritting her teeth. It was death for any mere human to even ask.

"Tell me something good then, Doppelgaenger," Gero sighed, returning to his throne and planting himself down on it with a grandiose flourish. "I feel an itch, and I suspect snuffing out your worthless life might go a far way to scratching it. Tell me something. Save yourself."

"The process to have Verdigris transferred to the matrix proceeds smoothly, Supreme Oberfuhrer," Doppelgaenger said. "The technicians report none of the complications experienced previously with other subjects. It would seem that Verdigris had prepared himself for this; it's almost as if he had foreseen he would inevitably be in this position, though probably in a more voluntary state of mind. They expect his consciousness will reach saturation in the temporary stasis field soon. Then it will be a simple matter of eliminating his more troublesome traits, like his essentially rebellious and contentious nature, before full transfer to the matrix."

"I suppose that is something," Gero said. "It makes me feel better." Abruptly, he waved at the air, like a child on the verge on a tantrum. "But not enough! I desire more!" He sat up and glared at her, and though she lay flat and prostrate, Doppelgaenger's radial awareness detailed a rather frightening revelation. Gero's eyes had begun to glow, and then burn with a great light.

She remained still, awaiting the end.

It didn't come, and she fought to remain calm as the light faded from Gero's eyes. She sensed a slight cock of his head, a gesture that often betrayed a sudden moment of rare inspiration for the Masters. For them, inspiration was often the prelude to violence; but this was Gero, who savored playing with his food.

"Tell me, Doppelgaenger," Gero purred. "You pursued the Djinni with a fervent ardor, one I have not seen in quite some time. And here you are, victorious over your adversary, claiming his very body as your prize. Speak the truth, did you achieve your heart's desire?"

"No, Supreme Oberfuhrer, I did not," Doppelgaenger moaned, and shuddered as she failed to quell her sorrow.

"Then your quest for immortality has eluded you," Gero snarled. "Again, you fail. I tire of you now, Doppelgaenger. Go. Go and serve, and be mindful of how close you came to extinction today."

"Thank you, Supreme Oberfuhrer. I live but to serve."

Doppelgaenger rose slowly to her feet and carefully backed away out of Gero's throne room. When she had reached the corridor, and the door to his throne room slid shut, she did not allow herself to feel anything. It still wasn't safe. Gero always knew when one was lying, and she had come dangerously close to revealing herself. Only when she was half the ship away, did she stop.

Was she immortal? She simply didn't know, though she had her suspicions about it. When Gero had asked if she had achieved her heart's desire, he thought her sorrow came from the utter disappointment of a long, failed experiment. But she had answered him with truth. No, her heart's desire eluded her, but it wasn't that old burning ambition for power, for immortality. Her heart had died when she had destroyed the only thing she had ever loved, the only thing she had ever truly desired. She supposed that might have saved her life. If she had answered yes, what might Gero have done then? If she truly was immortal, would that not be worth more to the Supreme Oberfuhrer than all of her past service? She imagined herself seized on his command, bound and neutralized and taken to the research facilities to be dissected, studied, in the hopes of unraveling the secrets held within her new, undying form. It might have frightened her once, but with the death of her love, she struggled to find meaning in anything. The only thing she felt these days was an overwhelming sense of fatigue. Ever since she'd integrated Red Djinni, in fact. She'd been alarmed the first time it happened; this had *never* been the case with anyone else she'd devoured. But . . . well, Red was different. So very different. It stood to reason that his integration would be different from every other experience she'd had.

Bed, she thought, and hurried towards her quarters. Gero would know, of course, but he'd probably assume she'd been momentarily overcome by the glory of his presence and needed a bit of a lie-down.

Whatever. The thought of the oblivion she would surrender to for the next few hours was more inviting than anything else she could think of at this moment. *Yes, bed.* The mere prospect gave enough strength that she hurried away to her quarters; she could not taste that sweet, sweet darkness soon enough.

CHAPTER TWENTY-EIGHT

The Sun Ain't Gonna Shine Anymore

MERCEDES LACKEY

I thought I knew and understood my creator perfectly.
Well, even I can be wrong.

When ECHO located their headquarters in Atlanta, they planned for the future. Quite a distance into the future, in fact. They knew they were going to eventually be the place of incarceration for meta-criminals. They knew there would be a lot of them. So they dug a hole.

A really, really deep hole. They turned it into a many-layered basement, reinforced to take on *anything*.

Then they put a building on top of it.

The building and the first two basements were normal ECHO facilities: offices, labs, research. The rest was Top Hold. And every time ECHO needed to add more space to Top Hold, they just developed the next floor further down. No one, except a handful of people with access to the plans, knew how many floors down the basement went.

It was, after all, a really, *really* deep hole.

When the Kriegers had come calling, they had wrecked what was on the surface—but not Top Hold. This was a place intended to keep *meta-criminals,* securely and indefinitely. ECHO not only had to plan for powered people trying to break out, they had to plan for powered people trying to break in. Plus, there had been the Cold War, the Soviet threat, the Chinese threat. Top Hold could survive a direct nuclear blast intact. Its power plant and facilities were stand-alone from the building above it. The prisoners—the ones that hadn't escaped with Slick—didn't even have to be relocated while the public floors were cleared and rebuilt.

And now the section had one new floor occupied, but not by a prisoner.

Back when she was about to graduate from Merlin College at Oxford, Vickie had daydreamed about finding an industrial loft and converting it to her new home. All that space... she'd have room to put in her very own *salle* for weapons practice, she could have a *huge* workroom, and the idea of a single, big, open space all to herself was very attractive to someone who'd spent the last four years in a room about half the size of the average American child's bedroom, into which she'd crammed bed, desk, chair, bureau, and wardrobe, since none of those ancient chambers had such a thing as a closet. Granted, her room at Merlin had had a fireplace, but... that didn't make up for the fact that it was so small that having four people in the room induced a state of acute claustrophobia in all of them.

Well, as with most things, daydreams and reality were rather different. Here she was in this huge, echoing space, and what she wanted was her apartment—or even that cramped little college room. There was *too much* space, and not nearly enough in it to make it seem remotely livable. But she wasn't about to complain out loud; at least she was safer here than anyplace else.

Bull had arranged for the things she'd asked for, but there was only so much that could be done on short notice, with the result that the borrowed furniture, augmented by her desks and special chair from the Overwatch suite, made the place look like a furniture-store-display floor three quarters through a bankruptcy sale. The walls were bare concrete, the floor covered with tobacco-brown industrial carpet. All the plumbing, HVAC wiring ducts and conduits were exposed. The overhead lights had been harsh and made it look even worse, so she'd opted for floor lamps, which gave little spots of light in the gloom. There was a shower, toilet, and sink behind a screen in the corner where the water came in and sewage exited. A cot with a memory-foam mattress was behind another screen in the next corner, her clothing in boxes next to it. A lone recliner stood in the third next to a lamp and a pile of her magic books, with the rest of the books in boxes nearby. There was a fridge full of meal drinks, and a cabinet with a coffeemaker, coffee, cat food, and booze next to the "bathroom." The Overwatch suite, desks, computers, monitors, zero-g chair and all were shoved up against the wall with the most electrical outlets. And there was a stereo Bluetooth linked to her computer rig next to it. Everything was *here*, mostly still in the boxes it had been packed into. The middle of the room was divided into "magic work area" and exercise area. Grey's catbox was in its own little "hut" in the bathroom; both Grey and Herb were sitting off to the side of the exercise area, watching her.

She'd hoped being out of her own place would cut back a little on the constant reminders of Red and the ensuing grief. All being here did was double up on the loneliness.

But she had something she didn't have at home. A *salle*. Bulwark had looked puzzled with the specs she had stipulated for her "exercise area," but there it was, a nice set of pells as pretty as anything back at Merlin. And if she couldn't forget Red even for a second, at least now she could work herself into a white-hot fury against the pells with her weighted ironwood practice rapier and dagger.

Her *real* weapons were on stands in her work area, being... worked on.

It was after dark, and as usual, the Kriegers had transferred their attacks to other parts of the world—though they *were* definitely concentrating things on the North American continent. By this time, Vickie was pretty certain this meant that their base, wherever it was, was closer to the Western Hemisphere than the Eastern. Of course, that was a lot of territory to search, and so far she didn't have anything to help narrow it all down.

But Eight could handle most of what was going on now, and she could be in her chair in seconds if he called, so she was taking some time to imagine Doppelgaenger's face in front of her as she progressed through the workout.

She heard the elevator behind her hum after she'd been at it for about ten minutes. That elevator went straight from this floor to the heavily guarded "entrance floor" of Top Hold, so whoever was coming down had permission to be here. There was one elevator per floor in Top Hold, and they each ended at that same entrance area, which was a bulletproof, heavily armored room in the middle of that floor, with the elevators on the walls around it. The only way out was via the elevator *in* that room. That meant if there was ever a successful prison break, there would be a minimum number of prisoners that would get that far. And it was vanishingly unlikely that Doppelgaenger would get down here.

And if she does . . . gods, I actually hope she does. I can have what I need in my hands before she could get out of the elevator. She'd have to take me on here, in my *space, deep in the earth, where I am strongest.*

So she didn't stop working, not now especially, not when she was in her groove and focused anger had replaced anguish for the moment.

The door swished open. "Can I come in, Miz Vickie?" said a soft, childish treble.

"Sure, Penny," Vickie replied. "I'm" *whack* "in the" *whack* "middle" *whack* "of ex-" *whack* "-er-" *whack* "-cising." *whackety-whack-whackety-whack-whack-SPIN-whack.*

"I'll go set," the little girl replied, not at all disturbed by the sight of Vickie beating the hell out of a padded man-shaped dummy with a pair of sticks. "I c'n pet Grey."

<Darn right she can. She knows all the right spots to scratch.>

"You do that, kiddo." She concentrated on the perfection of every move. It wasn't enough to make her forget, but it was enough to hold her attention. And when she was dripping with sweat, she called it, racked the practice rapier and dagger, and saw that Penny had been watching her the whole time, intently.

"Is that like sword fightin'?" she asked. "Like *Game of Thrones*?"

She blinked at that. She *almost* asked, "They're letting you kids watch that stuff?" incredulously—but then she realized that for the kids who'd been rescued from her uncle and the Project, *Game of Thrones* was "just Tuesday." They were no more "innocent children" than she had been at their age, with just as much experience in "man's inhumanity to man." More, really. She had only been the witness to that inhumanity. They had been the victims.

"Sort of," she said. "It's a different style than most of the fighters in that series use. Well, except for Arya. I guess I'm water dancing." She snagged a towel and wiped her face. "It's better suited to someone little, like me or her."

Penny nodded solemnly. "You do look like a dancer."

"I've been doing it a long time," she replied. And then...the odd choice of words struck her. *I look like a dancer?*

It had been *years* since she'd been graceful enough at sword-work to have that said of her. And yet, it hit her—since she'd begun her practices here, she hadn't been fighting with a body that hurt and hitched and caught at the wrong times. It hadn't *felt* any different, just now, than when she'd been at her top form. Before Bela had turned her into a scarred and damaged monster.

And her brain suddenly caught on a memory and froze for a second.

...my hand...

There had been something odd about her hand when she'd pulled off her glove to place it against Red's face. She'd *felt* his face; felt the warmth, the texture, everything, not just the old sense of nothing more than pressure from mostly destroyed nerves. But what did that mean?

She pulled off her glove, and stared at her hand in disbelief.

It...looked like a hand. A scarred and calloused hand, certainly, but not the monstrous claw it had been. She pulled her cuff up over her arm and stared at what was revealed.

Faint scars traced their way all over skin—but it was skin that was *skin* and not hideous, ropey keloid scarring. Not muscles distorted from burns that had gone catastrophically deep.

She'd been healing. All this time. Slowly, like she'd suggested to Red so long ago, working from the inside out. How? Well, maybe the same way Bell had gone from a "good healer" to a High OpThree, Bull had become more powerful with his enhanced skeleton, Spoonbender had gone from bending wires to bending Bull's bones, to ripping open the Georgia Dome. They'd *all* been improving under the stress of facing the Kriegers, all of them. And...so had she.

Bell had said she was a meta, and one thing most metas had was enhanced healing. But she'd had no pressure to kick it off. That healing wouldn't have shown itself until she started fighting the Kriegers herself. Mastery of magic was something inherent to her that depended on study, analysis, things the *meta* part of her couldn't affect. So maybe this was how *she* had improved when challenged—by returning to what she had once been.

I haven't taken a pain pill in weeks...

Her brain was putting together the data as soon as the possibility occurred to her.

The evidence was there in front of her eyes; however it had happened, why it had happened, all that mattered was she'd been healing. She wasn't a deformed monster anymore. She probably hadn't been since she stopped hurting all the time when she moved. And if she hadn't been too afraid to look at herself, she'd have known this a long time before now.

And the one person she would have wanted to see her... healed... was gone.

Rage filled her again: rage at the universe; rage at Doppelgaenger; rage, maybe, at herself, that she'd remained oblivious to the changes all this time. That maybe things would have been different with Red if... if she'd known. Maybe that would have given her the courage to make a move before Mel did.

But she hadn't. And now it was forever too late. Now all she had was rage.

The only outlet for that rage was to grab the practice sword and dagger again, and attack the pells like a fury incarnate, until she *had* to stop when the ironwood rapier snapped. And she stood there, trembling with exhaustion, while the rage finally drained out of her, dropping the weapons from nerveless hands. They landed on the carpet of the floor with dull thuds.

"You all right, Miz Vickie?" came a soft little voice to her left.

She took a long, slow breath, and turned her head just enough to see that Penny, although her eyes were big, did not appear to be afraid, and her hands were steadily petting Grey.

"I'll *never* hurt you, Penny," she said, answering the unspoken question. Because surely, that was what Penny had asked her abusive mother, time after time. *Are you all right, Mama?* And the answer would have told her whether it was safe to stay or time to hide.

Penny didn't smile, but she did visibly relax. "What made you so mad?"

"Nothing that anything can change, kiddo. And... maybe that's part of why I was mad." She walked over to where the piece of sword had landed, picked it up, and dropped the two pieces into a trash can. Fortunately she had more than one set—but this was the first time, ever, she had broken one. "I'm going to go take a shower. If you're hungry, ask Eight to call for something from upstairs." *I think I need to wire the kid for Overwatch Two.* There had been time to make more sets, but no time to implant more than a few more people. Merc, for starters.

"Okay," Penny relaxed more. "What c'n I have?"

"Anything you want. Just remember not to ask for more than you can eat, because that's bad manners and greedy." She pushed her dripping hair out of her eyes and headed for the "bathroom" area.

And this time, before she undressed, she turned on the lights. For the first time in . . . years.

What she found under her clothing made her sit in the bottom of the shower and sob silently until she couldn't cry anymore. At some point during her crying jag, she heard the elevator again, but it really didn't register except to wonder if that was Penny's food, or Penny leaving.

She felt as limp as boiled spaghetti when she emerged, dry and clothed in a clean outfit—but without the gloves—to find Penny sharing a plate of jumbo shrimp with Grey. There was an empty sundae cup on the table that looked like it had held ice cream. She got a can of dinner and threw herself down into a chair across from the little girl. "Don't stop," she cautioned, when it looked as if Penny was about to put the plate down. "Finish your dinner. Then you can tell me why you came down here."

Penny nodded, and took her words at face value. When the shrimp were nothing but tails, she put the plate beside the sundae cup and pulled her legs up, wrapping her arms around them. "We keep lookin' an' lookin', Miz Vickie, but we ain't found Red nowhere." She rubbed her hands up and down her arms anxiously. "It—it ain't easy t' find people if they ain't moved on. It's like bein' in a fog, that's what Mister Stone says, an' you don't actually *find* someone: either they come t'you, like Riley come to Miz Mel, or you pass word amongst everyone an' hope someone knows 'em an' can pass word back. And ain't nobody seems t'know Red, at all."

Vickie closed her eyes for a moment to stop the burning. "Which probably means he's moved . . . on." She didn't want to think what that meant. Sera said people went to heavens—or hells—that they expected. And given how he'd been after his arrest, she was horribly, horribly afraid he expected a hell . . . "All right, kiddo, there's no point in wearing yourself out over this. I think it's time you stopped looking." She wiped her eyes with the back of her hand and opened them. "How are you and Stone getting along?"

Once Riley was done with Mel, he'd—moved on. And it was

clear at that point that until Penny was able to protect herself, she'd need a protector. She'd also need a teacher. Vickie was no expert in mediumship, but she had remembered from the couple of classes that had touched on the subject she'd taken back at Merlin College, that there *was* a spell to entreat a wise and compassionate spirit to come and serve as the classical "spirit guide." Entreat, and not summon, and certainly not compel; you wanted cooperation, not coercion, from such a guide.

When Vickie had performed the spell, she had gotten more than she'd hoped for—the entity that had volunteered for the job of being Penny's protector, mentor, and teacher was "Tomb" Stone's grandfather, Jacob—the magician who had helped safeguard the ECHO Charter.

In retrospect, it made sense. Jacob had plenty of reasons to turn up when she cast the spell. He'd been a founding member of ECHO, the *only* magician in ECHO at the time—or ever, so far as she could tell. His grandson was in ECHO now, and Vickie had been the one that magically decrypted the Charter. And on top of that, much of voudoun magic was based in the spirit world. A *houngan* was as much medium as magician. If she'd been able to *ask* for someone in particular, she couldn't have chosen better herself.

It seemed Penny felt that way as well, because her face lit up with one of her rare smiles. "He's nice. He don' ever get tired of me askin' questions." She sucked on her lower lip for a moment. "He's worrit 'bout you, Miz Vickie."

"Well, I'm worried about all of us," she temporized. And before she had to lie (which was generally not a good idea around spirits) or come up with some sort of evasion, she got the blat of a private message from her computer. And there was only one person that could be.

True to his promise, Jack had been feeding her tiny bursts of information as he could. Thanks to him, they now knew how to detect and intercept incoming Kriegers while they were still over the ocean, keeping them from making landfall, among other things. Every bit of what he'd sent was useful, but none of it told her where these damned things were coming from. Probably because he himself did not know...

But this time the message was shorter than usual. *"N27.132481 W73.086548"*

Nothing else. And she stared at the letters and numbers on the screen for a full minute before it dawned on her. "Coordinates..." she breathed. "Eight, where is that? Latitude 27.132481 North. Longitude 73.086548 West. Why does that sound familiar?"

"Because it is the middle of what is called the 'Bermuda Triangle,' Vickie," Eight replied.

"Holy crap...isn't that about where the 'Lost Squadron' vanished at the end of the War?" she gasped. "Spitfire, Brumby, La Faucon Blanc, Corsair, and Belaya Liliya. Petrograd wanted to go, but they wouldn't let him and Lily went in his place—"

"Yes, it is. On a secret mission to destroy a rumored Nazi aircraft carrier or other important ship of some sort that was supposed to be sailing there. They reported encountering Eisenfaust, Valkyria and other fascist meta-flyers, but their transmissions broke up, they vanished, and nothing was ever found of them."

"Wait a minute—Eisenfaust said something about that in those prison interviews—Eight, pull that up—"

Eight already had, and in a moment, Vickie was listening to the dead man describe something that made absolutely no sense.

Had made no sense at the time, that is, and no one had bothered looking into it since. But—

"But we already know the Thulians can fold space," she said, thinking out loud. "And we know they have superior stealthing characteristics. They can hide entire cities. What if they hid their mothership, something bigger than a city, something big enough to qualify as a *world* ship, in the middle of the ocean? That spot's not on any shipping lanes. What if the Lost Squadron and Eisenfaust's squadron happened to run into each other right on top of it? What if they breached the stealth curtain? Hell, what if the captain of that craft the Lost Squadron was looking for was actually sailing under secret orders to rendezvous with it? What if—" She shook her head. "I can't take a bunch of speculation to Bella and Pride. I need some confirmation. I—"

"I can tell Tesla and Marconi. They may know of some Metisian technology or application of Metisian technology that would permit detection of such a thing, now that we know where to look."

"Do that," she replied, clenching her fist in her hair, as if she could encourage ideas to come faster that way. "This—this is—"

"Mister Stone says—" Penny gulped. "Mister Stone says y'all are right. An' when you go, you gotta take me with you."

Vickie wrenched her head around to stare at the little girl. "Mister Stone had better have a *damned* good reason!" she snapped.

Penny's eyes were closed, and she was shaking a little, but her voice was steady. "Mister Stone says the ghosts of his friends are still there. He says they can't rest until they done their duty. He says they c'n help us, an' then they c'n go on, but y'all need me t'talk to 'em."

"Penny, look at me," Vickie ordered. The girl's eyes opened and she stared steadily into Vickie's. "Is this something *you* feel you have to do?"

Penny's eyes brightened a little—there was fear in them, but also determination, and she nodded slowly. "Ain't nobody c'n do it *but* me. An' Mister Stone says my not goin' could mean ever'thin' goes t'heck. I'm scared, but...I gotta go."

"Then you go," Vickie told her. After all, when she'd been Penny's age, she'd been helping her folks on cases. The kid might not know how great the risk was, but she sure as hell knew the stakes, and so far as Vickie was concerned, she was old enough to understand them. Still. *Sweet baby Jesus. Bella is going to kill me.*

CHAPTER TWENTY-NINE

I'll Keep Coming

MERCEDES LACKEY AND CODY MARTIN

I had made the acquaintance of the "Eggheads," and they and I were working together on many things. Unfortunately, they didn't tell me everything they were working on . . .

Red Saviour felt deep sympathy for Victoria Victrix—after all it is a terrible thing to lose someone you love right before your eyes, as she knew all too bitterly well—but she approved of the little mage's method of coping. *Work.* Because the world did not stop when one was in mourning, and the Thulians did not stop trying to crush everyone on the planet.

And the mother country does not stop demanding that we do the impossible with nothing, and the United States government does not stop sniffing at us when they should be focusing only on tending the Thulian menace. Always wanting "situation reports" on the walking firebombs, Murdock and his winged woman. What is there to report? They are either sleeping, or out fighting the fascists. Not to mention my people do not stop needing me. They are all so tired; there is just too much that needs to be done, and I do not have enough to do it all. It will only be so long until something gives; the mission, or one of them. Another one of them . . . bozhe moi, Moji, I have not even had time to mourn you, much less avenge you . . .

The flare of grief and anger brought Natalya back to the present. Her cigarette was burned down almost to the filter, forgotten in her hand. She flicked off the long ash that had collected at the tip, then turned her attention to Victrix.

The witch was bent over the three keyboards at her workstation in the CCCP HQ, typing at a feverish pace, her eyes flitting from screen to screen. Normally, she would be in her new secure space in ECHO HQ, but ECHO was making alterations related to both her comfort and her security—and she said the noise was driving her insane. Beside her sat a gray cat the size of a lynx, and a little earthen creature Nat had taken for a crude statue until it had moved.

"You are sure this is to be working?" Nat mashed another cigarette butt into the bottom of a coffee cup, chewing her lip as she did so.

"I've already done it for ECHO. Once I tie Eight-Ball into the CCCP version of Overwatch Two, no matter what happens to me, Overwatch Two will work for the CCCP with either Eight or me at the helm. Forever, I think. And Eight-Ball is now made of the same magical memory matrix in m-space that I built for Tesla and Marconi, so there's no way that physical destruction of my place or this place is going to touch him."

How can she do those equations and type at the same time? Nat had finally reconciled herself to Vickie's magic, in no small part because the witch had proven it was logical and depended on complex equations. It wasn't fuzzy; it had rules, and rules were a thing she could understand. But watching her flying fingers and listening to her talk at the same time... was disconcerting. As if she had read Nat's mind, the witch turned her gaze momentarily to the Commissar. The dark circles, like old bruises, under them made her look disturbingly as if someone had blackened both eyes. "I just need to type the equations I already worked out into the interface. I've done it three times already." She tapped her forehead with her thumb. "They're in *here* and I can do this in my sleep."

"You should be getting some of that," Nat said... reluctantly. Because although she did approve of Victrix's method of handling grief, she did not want the witch to pass out over the keyboard. She was of no use to the CCCP if she was a casualty, self-induced or otherwise.

"*That's what I keep saying.*" Bella called in on Overwatch Two.

Downstairs, in the secure room that held the desk—Alex Tesla's former interface with the Metisians and, most particularly, the electronic "spirits" of Tesla and Marconi—the holographic images of the two in question were watching an equally holographic terminal respond to their thoughts. "This is a clumsy interface," Tesla complained.

"I am begging your pardon," Pavel called from the corner of the room, uncrossing his arms. "Just polished chassis this morning, and is finest that Soviet science produced...at the time. Not clumsy," he finished, puffing his metallic chest out as much as he could. If two electronic ghosts, accustomed to decades of existing solely as data and having shed many of their human mannerisms, could seem momentarily dumbfounded...

"The computer interface, *signore*," Marconi replied slowly. "The one we are attempting to use."

"Oh, computer," Pavel said dismissively, waving his hand. "Never mind. Not Soviet." He watched for a few moments more before speaking again. "What are two ghosts doing on computer anyway? Cat videos? *Kompot* recipes?"

"Did your Commissar not inform you about our task?"

"*Nyet*. Commissar told Bear to report to small musty room and watch, so here is being Bear." He peered at the holographic display, then leaned in closer with his robotic hand outstretched. "Is very interesting..."

"Please!" Marconi wasn't quite strident in his tone, but he wasn't far from it. "Do not interfere with the equipment. The results would be...less than optimal for what we wish to accomplish."

Pavel grunted, and pulled back his hand. Tesla returned his attention to the ghostly computer. "I will be pleased when Miss Nagy gives us a better way to interact with the material world than this," he grumbled.

"Hush, Nikola," Marconi chided. "We are truly immortal and invulnerable now, thanks to her. Nothing in the material world can harm us. And we owe her much. The least we can do is verify her information."

"Yes, and until she gives us a better interface, if this"—Tesla waved his hand at the desk, the interocitor, and the ghostly computer that tied m-space to realspace via both—"is destroyed, we will be immortal, invulnerable creatures with nothing but a giant empty computer to inhabit. But you are correct. We owe her much."

"Sounds like could being good place to catch up on beauty rest. Do ghost men need beauty rest? Ah, is question for Eggheads like witch woman." Pavel shook his head, sighing. "What was task again? Can I assist? Am being very good with engineering and applications for plasma chambers," he chuffed.

"No, no," Marconi said hastily. "We're just seeing if we can intercept some signals from here. Radio *is* my specialty, after all."

"Sleep is for the weak," Vickie muttered, her eyes back on the monitors. "There. Done."

A voice emerged from the speakers. *"Privyet, Natalya Shosta-kovaya. Kak dela?"*

"Blin, it talks back?" Despite Overwatch and Overwatch Two, despite being host to the Eggheads and their apparatus, despite having the benefit of as much ECHO tech as Bella could funnel to CCCP, Natalya was used to her technology being out of date, defective, or cantankerous. Much like Pavel. *I am relying too much on that Old Bear, fool that he can be. Will he be the next one to die, fighting for me? Die again, that is.*

"Of course I do," the ... entity? ... replied in not just Russian, but Russian with that subtle Moskovy accent that sounded like home to Nat. *"You can't always have your hands on a keyboard and your eyes on a scroll or monitor. I am very pleased to be interfaced with your system. I have already met Gamayun, and we are quite compatible."*

The Commissar paused for a moment, then fetched another cigarette from her nearly empty pack and lit it. *"Da, da,* good." She thrust her chin out at Vickie, quickly taking a drag from the cigarette and blowing it out. "What is being next step, now that ghost in machine is working?"

Vickie shrugged. "Nothing until—" something caught her eye, and she whirled to face the monitors again, and the new and odd voice called out ... in strangely calm tones ... and in *Russian* ... *"Red Alert. Red Alert. Incoming Thulian dropship. Vector appears to be CCCP HQ. Red Alert. Red Alert ..."*

And all the alarms, which formerly had been only triggered by Gamayun or Saviour herself, went off.

"Eight's already alerted ECHO!" Vickie shouted over the cacophony. "But the Colts are telling me they've already got everybody deployed or too far away to help!"

"Murdocks are currently deployed at a hotspot. Air support is already on mission, but won't be able to retask for ten minutes," Gamayun added. *"Recalling all comrades currently on patrol to HQ."*

Natalya slapped an intercom for the base. "Battle stations: get to the armories, retrieve munitions, and then take position. Chug, Bear, Rusalka, and Supernaut Units Odin, Dva and Tree! On the street and form on me!" She unholstered her pistol, checked to make sure that a round was chambered, and then reholstered the sidearm before turning to Vickie. "ETA on *fascista?*"

It was Eight-Ball that answered. "*Three minutes, twenty-nine seconds. Proletariat has replicated and the first three Supernaut Units are manned. Vickie is deploying spy-eyes now.*"

Bozhe moi! Computer ghost is even faster than witch! Natalya thought in amazement, as Vickie's hands flew over keyboards and she muttered into her microphone.

No time to waste. I need to be with my men on the street, now.

Natalya ran for the door, sprinting through the narrow hallways of the base. Occasionally she would pass some of her comrades, readying themselves for the coming fight: little Thea retrieving an RPG launcher from a weapons locker, the ever grim-looking Stribog loading an AK-74 and handing it to Vila, who looked decidedly uneasy. Alkonost and Sirin ran past her in the opposite direction, on their way to guard the rear of the structure; they were paired up as an RPG team, the first carrying the launcher and the other carrying spare munitions. Everyone moved quickly, and it wasn't long before Natalya was through the front entrance and practically flying down the steps onto the street. Chug was already there, standing in the center of the road with his fists balled and dark cavities of eyes looking about warily. Bear came out moments after Natalya, clanking to take his place beside her; he had his PPSh in his left hand, and his right gauntlet was already charged with plasma.

There was a mechanical rumble as the garage door for the CCCP's motor pool opened. The sound of heavy footsteps on asphalt followed, not unlike those of the Krieger troopers when they marched to war. Instead of Nazis, three suits of Supernaut armor emerged, one at a time, each one manned by one of Kirill Zuykov's—or "Proletariat" as the Americans called him—duplicates.

Kirill was one of the comrades that had been left in Russia when the CCCP had been exiled, after the First Invasion. Before being recruited by the bureaucrats in Moscow, he had led a quiet life as a magician and circus performer; his power kept him fed until he was discovered by a police officer, trying to fend off a group of *gopniki* ruffians from a mother they had been trying to rob. There had been six of them... and seven of Kirill. Though trained after being inducted into the CCCP, he had never been a major asset; his duplicates were exact copies of him, weren't imbued with any greater strength or resilience, and he could only duplicate himself nineteen times at most. The duplicates did not last, especially when there were many of them, and he was not a skilled fighter; passable at best, Untermensch had called him "uninspired." Still, Natalya had always had hope for the man, and when he put in a transfer request to come to America, she had fought hard to make sure it happened. *After being stuck doing paperwork and cleaning floors in state official buildings, I cannot blame him for wanting to come here, despite the danger.*

But when Boryets betrayed them all, every Supernaut pilot he had recruited had come under suspicion. That left Russia with a surplus—a rather large surplus—of Supernaut suits. Untermensch had applied to get some, not expecting that they *would*, but to everyone's surprise a cargo plane had arrived full of crates to Hartsfield, the crates marked to go to CCCP. Supernaut suits. And, after some additional training and a few... mishaps, one involving a park bench and a rather unfortunate rat... Kirill had proven to be an excellent pilot.

Then again, given good design, a monkey could pilot suit, and most of Boryets' recruits were not recruited for brains, Natalya thought, as the three suits fell in line with the rest, one behind her and the other two flanking the ends of the line. *Vassily Georgiyevich, you may have been a power-hungry bastard, but you were also a genius. If for nothing else, I'm grateful for these suits of yours.*

Trailing behind the suits was the matronly Rusalka, holding an AK of her own. She had been walking on eggshells after her betrayal had been revealed at the Fall of Metis, and the Commissar had kept a wary eye on her. If things had been different, Natalya would have excoriated the woman, driven her from the CCCP, and made sure that she was brought up on charges. As things were, she needed every warm body she could get. She hoped that she would not regret her decision to be lenient.

"All comrades in position, Commissar. ETA on bogey twenty-seven seconds, mark."

Shto? Only one Death Sphere? Another suicide cell, trying to catch us off guard? Why attack us, *right now?*

Natalya wiped the questions from her mind. She saw the metallic gleam of the Death Sphere in the distance; her HUD highlighted and tracked the craft a moment later, vector lines plotting out its path of travel.

"Supernaut Units, Rusalka, engage any troopers that land. We shall cover you and provide support. Roof teams, Sphere is your primary target, with ground troops as secondary targets; take out their escape, then help Kirill and Rusalka."

Many of her comrades sounded off in the affirmative on the comm channel. The Death Sphere loomed larger, flying towards the base at incredible speeds, and there was no more time for talk.

"Object detaching from Death Sphere," she heard Eight-Ball say in her ear as the Death Sphere zoomed overhead, rattling windows and setting off car alarms for blocks around. Instead of staying in the area to attack, it sped off into the sky. A quick survey of her HUD's radar showed that it was flying in a holding pattern. Something was wrong; only a single suit of trooper armor had been on it. Why wouldn't they bring a full complement of soldiers? Her question was answered a second later, when the suit slammed into the ground at the end of the street. It wasn't trooper armor. It was much, much *bigger*, easily standing twice as tall as Ubermensch or the Command armor. It was still definitely armor of some sort, but this wasn't a mass-produced, art deco piece of military equipment, like the Krieger suits were. This was ornamented and unique, with segmented bronze bands that moved over each other like liquid; it gave the unsettling appearance that the armor itself was a living *thing*, someone's nightmare of a metal crustacean come to life. The decorative crests and ridges were organic and horribly alien-looking, blended as part of each piece of the armor. The hands ended in long, serrated-looking claws; again, they appeared as if they had grown out of the tips of the fingers, a natural extension.

The most frightening feature of the armor was the helmet. A central ridge on the crest—still in that organic-metal style— melded with the rest of the helmet, ending in a T-shaped slit that glowed a baleful dark orange, the same color that all Thulian tech displayed. No way to tell what was in there. The armor's knees hadn't even buckled when it had hit the road. It raised its head, and Natalya could *feel* its gaze and unbridled malevolence focused on her. Not even Ubermensch had looked on her with this much malignant hate. For a moment, when the thing had first appeared, Natalya had wondered if this was some new and improved armored suit for Ubermensch. After that *look,* however, along with the odd fluid way it moved, she rejected that notion. This was something different. Something—worse.

"Rusalka, Kirill! *Davay davay davay!*"

Without a word, the three Supernaut suits attacked the Thulian. There was a sonic whine of pressurized specialty napalm being released before the Thulian was completely engulfed in a cloud of flame. The three Supernaut suits marched forward, crunching asphalt with each step, their arms outstretched and shooting jets of fire. For a moment, Natalya was overcome with a memory, of her comrades and the original Supernaut, fighting the Thulians in Red Square. Rusalka circled to the right, flanking their enemy. It also positioned her right next to a special fire hydrant that the CCCP had set up after the Second Invasion; only accessible to authorized personnel via some of the witch's magic, with one positioned on every corner of the city block the HQ was centered in. Rusalka waited for a moment, then activated the fire hydrant; a torrent of water flooded out of it, wetting down the street in front of her. She stared in concentration for a second, and then the water collected itself in the air in front of the hydrant. The ball of water quickly grew until it was twice as large as the CCCP van; Rusalka twitched her right hand, and a jet of water violently erupted from the middle of the liquid sphere. Water is nearly incompressible, but when put under pressure...it moves *fast.* The blast of water hit the Thulian—nearly invisible in the center of the miniature firestorm that Kirill had created—squarely in its side. A plume of superheated steam competed with the fire to obscure the Thulian; Natalya broke into a sweat as hot steam wafted her way.

We'll see how tough the svinya is after that. Heat their metal shells up, and then cool them down quickly... they explode like overcooked sausages. Even these fascista bastards are not immune to simple physics!

Natalya listened for the satisfying scream of metal shearing away from metal...yet it never came. The Thulian walked through the flames; the Kirills were visibly startled in their suits and took a moment to recover. Rusalka, determination clear on her sweat-soaked face, continued to blast the Thulian with water, increasing the pressure in an attempt to knock it over. The armored suit didn't seem to notice. It reached the three Supernaut suits in six unhurried strides. Faster than the Commissar's eyes could track, it slashed at the suits with nothing more than the claws on the ends of its gloves. The first strike took the leftmost suit in the shoulder, carving through the armor like clay, until it exited through the suit's hip. There was a brief flash of bright red blood and yellow bone before the duplicate flashed out of existence. The other two had no time to react; to Kirill's credit, they kept firing until they were killed. One of the suits exploded, causing Natalya to flinch and cover her eyes; one of the pressurized tanks of napalm must have been breached.

Natalya blinked, and her jaw dropped. *Rusalka...she was right next to that! Oh,* ahuet', *no no no—*

There was no sign of her comrade. The Thulian continued to walk forward, stomping through the flaming wreckage of the Supernaut suits. Natalya swallowed hard, her mouth suddenly very dry. "Kirill, warm up suits Chetyre, Pyat', and Shest'!"

"*New development, Commissar,*" Vickie said crisply. "*Suit is heat resistant, and I'm not finding the top end yet. I've got Eight running diagnostics. Magic help incoming in ten...*"

"*Da, da!* All comrades, keep it from the base! Fire!"

"*...eight...*"

The roof teams, denied any Death Spheres to shoot, switched targets to the lone suit of armor. RPG warheads detonated on or around it, and hundreds of rounds of rifle bullets pinged and whizzed off of it. Nothing penetrated, and even the ECHO and CCCP-engineered napalm mix was sliding off. It *should* have stuck to the suit, helped superheat it so that the conventional arms would have a chance.

"*...five...*"

"Pavel! Together!" The older metahuman nodded, planted his feet wide, and thrust out his right arm. Natalya's fist shot forward at the same time; his plasma and her energy blast slashed through the air, hitting the Thulian almost simultaneously. Natalya gritted her teeth, pouring more and more energy into the blast. The armored suit, inexorable, continued to walk through the hail of explosives, bullets, plasma, and her energy.

"*...three, two, one!*"

Saviour had braced herself, but the ground wave, not unlike

a wave on the ocean, started at her feet and rolled towards this new menace as fast as a car could accelerate. It hit the thing's feet, and rocked it back for a moment, but it flailed its arms and kept its balance.

"More, Victrix! Hit it again!"

Another wave started at Saviour's feet, larger this time, but a little slower. It was almost a meter tall, and threw off bits of asphalt and rocks as it rolled forward.

For a moment, she worried that the foundation of the HQ would crack. This time, the Thulian was prepared for the attack. It actually *jumped* over the wave. Natalya swore that she could feel the weight of its landing through the street. It canted its head to the side momentarily, and then continued forward. Natalya felt desperation clawing its way through her, a sheen of sweat covering her entire body. *If that thing gets to the base... nothing will be able to stop it, short of leveling the entire block. Maybe not even that.*

Before Natalya could say anything else, the Thulian stopped in the street. The comrades on the roof continued to rain down rockets and bullets; they had kept their discipline and were firing accurate, measured bursts. The Thulian turned its helmet to look at them. Just then, Thea fired an RPG. The Commissar could tell it was a beautiful shot, even from her position on the street. In the blink of an eye, a rippling wave issued from the T-shaped visor of the helmet, hitting the warhead in midair and causing it to explode. Thea barely had enough time to duck before the wave hit the side of the HQ; Natalya watched in growing horror as the brick started to melt and explode.

"*Nasrat!* Some kind of heat beam?" She steadied herself, then continued to fire energy at the Thulian. "Roof team, take cover! Do not get caught by that thing's weapon!" She stopped firing for a moment, then turned to Chug. Her squat comrade had been standing beside her silently for the entire fight. "Chug?"

"*Da,* Commissar?" He turned his head so that he could see her, his black eyes searching.

"Go kill that *fascista,* comrade. He is going to hurt Thea! He has hurt your friend Kirill."

"Hurt... Thea? Hurt Kirill?" he rumbled, looking from Saviour to the Thulian.

"*Da.* Now go hurt him *back!*"

Chug roared, charging towards the Thulian. For such a bulky creature, Chug could move with frightening speed when he wanted to. Natalya was infinitely grateful—not for the first time—that Chug considered the CCCP to be his friends and family. The Thulian didn't appear to take notice of Chug until the last moment. The sound of Chug crashing into the Thulian rattled the teeth in Natalya's skull; she had witnessed a train collision once during a CCCP mission, back in the Motherland. It was the closest thing she could think of to compare to hearing Chug hitting the Thulian at full force.

And the Thulian... stopped. It had caught Chug's charge at the last moment; it hunched over, with a single leg thrust behind it, bracing against the force of Chug's rush. Chug and the Thulian grappled with each other like a pair of wrestlers, clutching each other by shoulder and forearm. Natalya held her breath, hoping... could Chug *actually* do it? There was the scrape of metal against asphalt as the Thulian was inched backwards, ever so slightly. Natalya was about to whoop in triumph, but it caught in her throat. The Thulian tensed, and then flexed suddenly. A crack of thunder split the air, and Natalya barely had enough time to drop to the ground as Chug flew over her head, hitting the corner of a building half a block behind her, and crushing it. The rock man did not stir from the pile of rubble. Natalya looked back at the Thulian, just as it rose back to its full height. Something hung from its left forearm... with sick realization, she saw that it was Chug's right arm, still firmly gripping the Thulian's armor. The small, analytical part of her that was still working past the fear noticed that the armor was partially crumpled underneath Chug's fingers.

It can be hurt. It can be hurt. It can be hurt...

The Commissar picked herself up off of the ground, doing her best to make her voice steady as she spoke. "Jadwiga, Chug is down. In need of medical attention immediately."

There was a pause, followed by, "... *shto?*" Jadwiga partially recovered a moment later. *"On the way with the crash cart, Commissar."* There was a tremulous note in her friend's voice that Natalya had never heard before, and never wanted to hear again.

"Eight replacing comrade witch, Commissar," she heard, but barely registered.

✧   ✧   ✧

Vickie ran full-out all the way to the Egghead Room. She used a spell to slam the door open ahead of her, and another to slam it shut behind her.

"What in hell are you two doing?" she screamed, as her sneakers squeaked in protest over her abrupt halt. "And don't bother to deny it. I have a keystroke logger on you and Eight says the appearance of that monster absolutely coincides with you two screwing around!"

The ectoplasmic entities flashed a guilty look at each other that pretty much confirmed they had been the reason this new Thulian had "shown up."

"We were...we were trying to find a way to confirm that the information from your new source is correct, *signorina,*" Marconi stammered, as Tesla nodded so fast he looked like a bobblehead.

"SHUT THE DAMN THING OFF! NOW!" she bellowed.

Marconi's semitransparent fingers flew on the interface as Vickie stood by, frowning fiercely, arms crossed over her chest.

"Now," she said, in a voice so cold the two miscreants probably felt chilled to their ethereal bones, "tell me what you *did*. There may be a way out of this catastrophe."

Natalya felt the same despair that she had felt in Metis. Her comrades were dying, were going to die, and she was powerless again...*NO!* She slammed the hopelessness down as quickly as it had risen. *So long as we draw breath, all of us, we will fight.*

"Pavel," she said, keeping her eyes fixed on the advancing Thulian. Her jaw tightened as a burst of anger fixed her resolve.

"Da, Commissar?"

"You and I will engage the threat. Try not to die, Old Bear. I may have some further use for you. Stay back, harry it with your plasma and *don't* shoot me, fool. Focus on its helmet, see if you can blind it or distract it. I will move in...closer."

Pavel opened his mouth as if to question her orders, but a single hard look silenced him. *"Da.* Is not can of ravioli, but will try to open it, regardless."

"Roof team, we are moving in. Hold fire once we are within fifty meters. Use best judgment for when to resume fire; will be busy." Absently, she noticed the eerily calm voice of Eight repeating her command in English.

"Commissar," Eight said in Russian, *"hold in place for thirty seconds. We have not attempted the use of electricity on the threat."*

"*Shto?*" Saviour said, then shrieked in wordless shock as a transformer over her head suddenly overloaded and a massive arc of electricity shot across the street to connect with the Thulian. It jittered in place for a second or two, just long enough for Saviour to feel another moment of hope.

But then the heat beam turned towards the transformer and melted it out of existence.

"*Nasrat,*" Eight said philosophically. Natalya wasn't sure whether or not she liked the entity adopting a personality; cold equipment could be hit with a wrench when it was disobedient, but living subordinates generally were opposed to such corrective action.

"Our turn, Old Bear. *Davay!*" Nat started forward at a jog, Bear clanking behind her. The roof team stopped firing when the pair were approximately fifty meters away from the Thulian, right on cue. Bear split off to the left, hanging back; Natalya could hear the thrum of plasma flooding his gauntlets, waiting to be discharged. She gathered energy into her own fists until they glowed with barely contained power. When she was within three meters of the Thulian, she released a burst of energy from beneath her feet, kicking off of the ground and launching herself at her enemy. The suit of armor stopped in place, raising the helmet to watch as she arced toward it. Her first punch was staggeringly powerful, a full blast of energy and all of the strength she had in her arm. It managed to turn the Thulian's helmet to the side. *Better than it not moving at all,* she thought. She didn't stay in front of the suit; Bear was already firing blasts of plasma at the helmet's visor, as fast as his plasma chamber heart could charge his gauntlets. Natalya called on all of her *Systema* training, augmented with her metahuman strength and weird energy; she danced around the Thulian, targeting joints with energy-laced punches, kicks, and chops, while using plumes of energy to launch herself from stance to stance. The Thulian, curiosity seemingly satisfied, reacted; it lashed out with those horrible claws, trying to catch Natalya. She already knew that even a glancing blow would be fatal, so she stepped back her attacks and focused on avoiding any damage. It was hard work; despite the Thulian's immense size, it was *fast.*

Natalya miscalculated once, and that was all it took. She landed heavily in front of the Thulian, just out of reach but unable to move immediately. The suit of armor stomped on the asphalt; the shock wave in miniature took Natalya from her feet and planted her hard on the street. She barely managed to keep her head from cracking open against the ground, and her chest felt tight as her breath left her. The sun was blotted out as the Thulian loomed over her, raising a single clawed hand. She heard Pavel yelling at her, but she couldn't understand what he was saying; blood thundered in her ears, and all she could focus on was the orange glow of the visor, staring at her.

She forced air into her lungs, willing herself to breathe. "I have died before, bastard. You had better hope that I do not return again." She propped herself up from the ground long enough to spit directly on the visor. The claws slashed down—

—and the Thulian tilted over sideways, flailing for balance, when a geyser of water crashed into its flank. Natalya sputtered for a moment, instantly drenched. Hands looped under her arms; then she was dragged back and away from the Thulian. She recognized the hands as Pavel's mechanical prosthetics; the old man cursed under his breath with each clanking footstep. Natalya looked back to where the Thulian stood; it turned from her to face a small figure behind it.

"Rusalka..."

Her left arm was gone; all that remained was a burnt, bleeding stump. Half of her hair—and her face—were burned away, and she was clearly in unbelievable pain. And yet she stood defiantly, her remaining good arm in front of her, the hand balled into a fist. Rusalka screamed; three of the hydrants nearest to her exploded, and columns of water shot into the air. The water gathered, a floating tidal wave, before she brought it crashing down on the Thulian... and herself.

The water receded; the armored suit had been driven to a knee, and Rusalka... a crumpled form on the ground, unmoving.

"Commissar," Bear said as he pulled her to her feet. "We need a plan."

Natalya turned her eyes from Rusalka's body, weariness spreading over her like a wave. "Plan is to fight. Only plan we have ever had, or needed." *For all of the good it is doing us*, she added silently. The Thulian resumed its march towards the HQ; it was finally done with distractions, perhaps, and meant to get down to the real business of killing them all.

"Commissar, it would be advisable to reposition to the sidewalk immediately," said Gamayun.

The roar of a motorcycle engine echoed off of the buildings as a Ural screeched around the street corner behind the Commissar. Untermensch sat behind the handlebars, while Mamona rode in the sidecar, a KS-23 shotgun against her shoulder and pointed at the Thulian. Natalya and Bear scrambled out of the way as the motorcycle barreled past them. Mamona fired the heavy shotgun as quickly as she could rack the slide. Untermensch gunned the throttle; a moment later, he seized Mamona around the waist and pulled them both off the bike, curling up around her to protect her as they tumbled free. She was up again in a moment and fired two more bursts just as the Ural rammed the Thulian. There was a moment as the Thulian staggered, then the gas tank went up, engulfing the thing in flames and shrapnel.

Untermensch and Mamona quickly fell back to where Natalya and Pavel were waiting. Natalya fought against the urge to break into a wide smile, and only barely won. "So. Another Ural lost. They do *not* grow on trees, Georgi."

Untermensch shrugged, cracking his neck. The scrapes and wounds he sustained from dismounting the motorcycle at speed had already begun to heal. "I lay the blame at being put on patrol with Murdock and other Amerikanski so many times, Commissar. Cowboys, one and all."

"Hey, this is the only time blowing up a Ural has been my idea," Mamona piped up.

"Brilliant," Vickie spat, fingers flying on the ghostly keyboard. "Here we've managed to keep the fact that you two survived a secret, and you proceeded to light up a big neon sign with your names on it. I'd murder you if you weren't already dead. Eight, follow my lead and replicate at any idle transmitter, on my mark."

"*Ready when you are, Vickie,*" Eight-Ball replied.

The two ghostly forms of Tesla and Marconi stood aside...but they were not as quiet as they seemed.

"*I have control of the flying eye, Nikola,*" Marconi "whispered." "*It is the one on the south side of the CCCP roof.*"

"*Good. I see a good place to lodge it. There are cavities behind the two protrusions at the rear of the helmet. You can jam it in there, and I don't think it will notice.*"

✧   ✧   ✧

The Commissar entertained an idea that she had never dared consider in all of her life.

We need to retreat, or we will all die here.

She had recalled all comrades to help with the fight. Metahuman powers, RPGs, and bullets were levied against the Thulian, yet it still came forward. Leisurely. As if the creature inside it was savoring these moments; untouchable, against everything that the CCCP could bring to bear. It was almost to the front door of the HQ; Saviour had no doubt that it could have just ripped through the nearest corner of the building and torn its way through the interior. Even with all of their hardened defenses, the armored suit was more than capable of cutting its way to her office and propping its feet up on her desk if it had wanted to. But, no; it wanted them to watch as it virtually ignored them, walked up to their front door, and casually violated their home.

They had drawn up evacuation plans, of course, and practiced them until every comrade knew the procedures by heart. Even so, Natalya had never dreamed that they would need to use them. *Hubris, stupid girl*, Boryets' voice echoed in her mind. *You are weak and selfish, and your pride will kill all of the people that you love and call family. You* will *be alone, and it will be* your *fault.*

It took a great deal of effort to silence her traitorous "uncle's" poisonous words. She needed to focus. Her powers, those of her comrades, all of their weapons were ineffective. She wouldn't throw away more of her comrades' lives trying to find this bastard's weakness. It wanted something in the HQ, that much was clear. *Fine. We have contingencies. Evacuate all personnel, then detonate "exit plan" charges; all the servers will wipe, any intelligence materiel will be destroyed, and it'll drop the building down on the svinya.* She needed to give the order, and soon, if they were to have time to enact it; she still had comrades on the roof and in the building proper. Jadwiga was tending Chug in the medical bay; she had recalled all of Kirill's duplicates to carry the rock man, since destroying more Supernaut suits wouldn't do anything to help. And there was Vickie, somewhere in the base; she had gone off of Overwatch for... something.

"All comrades," Natalya said, swallowing hard. "Prepare to—"

The Commissar's teeth rattled in her head, and she felt her skin crawl. It was an all too familiar sensation. The Thulian Death Sphere had returned; it crested over the roof of the building opposite of the HQ, gliding death in a silvery shell. The Sphere's tentacles had deployed, and thrashed restlessly. *The bastard is done playing with us. It has called its dogs to kill us, so it can do whatever it came here to do*, she thought bitterly. They still had their RPGs and powers, though probably too few rounds for the former. All the same, they could at least hurt the *fascista*. There wouldn't be any time for retreat, not before the Death Sphere could level the roof and pulverize the street with its energy cannons.

A wash of flame streaked across the sky, and for a moment, Red Saviour thought that someone had fired a missile at the Death Sphere, or a meteor had entered the atmosphere. The trajectory was too perfect for the latter; the object hit the Sphere with a deafening crack of splitting metal. The Death Sphere listed to the side, and all of the tentacles dangled lifelessly from their apertures. As the Sphere spun towards her, Natalya could make out the thing that had slammed into the Sphere...it was a spear made of blinding white and gold fire. Before the Sphere could recover or reorient itself, twin bolts of plasma burned through the clouds and finished the job that the spear had begun. The Sphere's engines sputtered as the craft was nearly cleft in half by the explosion, sending it careening and tumbling in an uncontrolled descent down into one of the nearest destruction corridors.

The Thulian had *stopped*. It turned to look at the falling Death Sphere as Natalya gaped. A moment later, the entire block was shaken by a tremendous explosion, followed by a cloud of fire and smoke rising from the destruction corridor. She spotted a fireball descending through the clouds where the spear and plasma had come from. She was rocked by a sonic boom, and had to shield her eyes against the light.

For a moment, Saviour thought it was the *Zhar-ptica*, the legendary Firebird, that had come to their rescue. After what had just happened, she felt as credulous as a child and inclined to indulge in such superstitious thinking. Enormous flame-sheathed wings thundered, blowing hot wind and dust towards her as a figure between them, too bright to be made out as anything more than a shape, and came to rest between the Thulian and the CCCP HQ. The second half of the fireball was nowhere near as graceful, but still breathtaking; a human-shaped flame shot towards the ground, then stopped abruptly with a sound not unlike a rocket erupting before coming to a rest. Natalya saw the asphalt underneath the figure blister and bubble from the heat, vitrifying before her eyes. As one, both shapes emerged from the flames.

"Bozhe moi..."

The Seraphym—Sera now—and John Murdock stood together against the Thulian. Since Murdock's ... reawakening, and Sera's transformation, Natalya had not personally seen them in action at their full strength. Certainly, she had seen the aftermath of their powers at Ultima Thule, and Pavel was a constant reminder of the inhuman nature of the forces they were capable of wielding. But to witness it firsthand... Her entire life, the strongest metahuman she had ever known had been Worker's Champion, Uncle Boryets, with her father and Moji not far behind. They had all been paraded as the very best that the Soviet Union had, pillars of revolutionary spirit and Russian might. For all of their power, they did not rank higher than a top-tier OpThree, even Worker's Champion. In her time at the FSB, Natalya had heard rumblings and rumors that Russia had metahumans that rivaled the worst that America could offer; OpFours of such titanic power that it was almost unfathomable. The rumors went, however, that instead of risking such beings potentially going rogue, or deciding, like the legendary Amphitrite, that they were gods, that the government had found a simpler solution. Kill them. Nuclear weapons tests, it was said, made for fine cover when destroying metahuman bodies.

Seeing Sera and John before her, now, was the first time she had personally been confronted by such raw, unfettered power. If Natalya had been religious, it would have inspired that sort of terror in her, a rising mania. *No. No. They are our comrades. For all of Murdock's faults, and the fiery woman's religious delusions, they have remained sturdy comrades. They stand with us!*

"You shall not pass." The voice—calm, beautiful—made the words a simple statement rather than a declaration. The woman spread her wings, making it clear that the Thulian was going to have to go through them to get to its goal.

For the first time, the Thulian made a sound.

But it appeared that it was not in response to Murdock and his woman.

It suddenly tilted its head skyward and ... growled, as if in reaction to something else only it could sense. And then—

It stiffened up, until it looked like a pillar of sculptured metal. Its feet began to glow with the orange of the Thulian propulsion drives.

And then it launched itself skyward, in a missilelike arc to the east and a little south, vanishing into the clouds. About ten seconds after it took off, a quartet of fighter jets streaked after it, firing missiles. *The Air Force has finally arrived. Good on them for trying, at least.*

After several moments of stunned silence from everyone present, John's fires disappeared with a muffled *pop.* He turned to look at the Commissar.

"Did anyone know that those damned things could *do* that?"

Saviour paced restlessly outside the medbay. Inside were Sovie, Bella, and Gilead . . . and Vickie. All of them working slowly, and methodically, on Chug. As soon as the strangely armored Thulian had vanished, Mamona had made a sprint for where it had been and picked up Chug's arm. Nat would have remonstrated with her on that, for surely there was no possibility of reattaching such a thing, but she had already sped into the building by the time Saviour opened her mouth. So the Commissar had turned her attention where it was most needed. She supervised and assisted in retrieving Rusalka's body. They would have to arrange for transport back to Russia, naturally. Natalya already knew that she would insist that Rusalka be buried with all of the other fallen metahumans from the Great Patriotic War. Given her final sacrifice, it was only right. After that, she had seen that the comrades began repairs on the building and the street outside immediately; an assessment for how they could mitigate such an attack in the future would have to wait until later, but right then they still needed to use their HQ.

Now with all the fires, literal and metaphoric, out, she had gone to the medbay only to discover there was no room in there for her. So she paced, as she heard Sovie murmuring without being able to make out the words, Bella and Gilead answering equally softly, and then—

"I think the asbestos is what we needed." Vickie's high voice carried over the sound of machines muttering and beeping. "Look at that . . . he can move his fingers already."

Shto? Room or not, Saviour opened the door and squeezed herself inside.

Chug rested on three of the gurneys pushed together. Vickie was troweling something that looked like grout over the place where Chug's arm now once again joined his shoulder. Gilead and Bella, faces set in masks of concentration, were obviously exercising their healing powers, while Soviette supervised.

But most surprising of all, the lumpy little stone creature was standing on Chug's chest, chirping what appeared to be directions.

Vickie used the tip of the trowel to inscribe things in the wet grout, then waved her hand over it. Steam rose from the material, and the little stone thing nodded with satisfaction.

"Okay," she said, brow furrowed and eyes closing. "Hands off, Bells, Gil. Give me a few to get the magic going, *then* you can fit the healing in."

Jadwiga had been closely inspecting the work that Victrix had been doing. Her head bobbed up, and she noticed Natalya. Somehow, she effortlessly wove her way through the crowd to stand in front of Natalya. "Commissar, you must leave. We have enough bodies in the way already, and gawking tourists will not help heal our comrade." Natalya was about to protest, when her friend held up her index finger. "He is in good hands, *sestra*. Trust us."

Natalya was put out, but saw her friend's wisdom. "What of Murdock and Sera? Couldn't they heal Chug without all of the worrying?"

It was Victrix that answered, calling over her shoulder. "Their energy would just . . . confuse things in here, and I need all of my concentration to do this *right*. Besides, healing takes more out of them than what I'm doing takes out of me; I'm just doing earth magic, which seems to work on Chug, and I can use my—call them 'storage batteries.' If there's another attack, we don't need the Murdocks passed out on the floor. Also," she added, "talking to you is taking up effort I could be spending on healing Chug. I'll be in the briefing room soon enough to fill in some details. So . . . please leave?"

Normally, Natalya would have bristled at such insolence, and been quick to rebuke her subordinates for it. Right now, all she could feel was gratitude that Chug was going to be all right. She nodded curtly to Jadwiga. "Keep me informed; I want to be updated at any change in his condition."

She could see the relief in Jadwiga's eyes. "*Da*, Commissar. We will keep you apprised."

Bella looked up. "Hey, Nat, can you send Mamona out for about twenty gallons of ice cream? When we wake him up, I want to give him something to soothe his tears."

"You don't think we are already prepared for this, *sestra*? Already have freezer stocked." She turned to go, then stopped. "Will pet hamster help?"

"Very much so. I didn't know he had a pet."

"Will have it brought at once. I'll be in the briefing room. And...be gentle with him. He will likely be very frightened when he awakes." Natalya quickly strode out of the medbay, allowing herself to cry only once she was out of earshot. By the time she reached the briefing room, she had dried her eyes and composed herself; she was the Commissar, and she had to be the pillar that her comrades leaned on. John and Sera stood together in one corner. John had his arms crossed in front of his chest; Sera turned her bright blue eyes on her Commissar with a sympathetic nod and an expression of empathy and understanding. Natalya knew of the couple's abilities, when it came to reading emotions, and suppressed an involuntary shiver; even with good intentions, such powers set her on edge. Untermensch was hunched over the table, a map spread before him.

"Commissar," he said as he stood up from the table, nodding to her. "We are having report on encounter and are awaiting your input."

Saviour frowned. "This was nothing like we have seen before," she said slowly.

Sera held up a hand. "May one speak, Commissar?" she asked politely.

"*Da*, I am seeing no reason why not." Saviour was curious; the winged woman seldom said more than a few words in debriefings, preferring to let Murdock speak for both of them.

"We were able to feel the mind of the creature in the armor today," she said, nodding to John. "That was no Thulian mind, in that thing. Nor human, either. Nor hybrid." Sera's brows furrowed. "It was closest to whatever was piloting those dragons, at Ultima Thule. Except this one was...if not precisely *sane*, certainly *saner*." She paused, searching for words. "Not a profane creation, like the dragons, but...more deliberate?"

"Whatever it was being," Untermensch interjected, "we were not able to track it. A wing of F-35s engaged the fleeing armor, but were unable to keep pace with it. Missiles and guns were having no effect." He gestured to the map on the table. "Damage to base was, decidedly, minimal. Losses total three Supernaut suits, exterior damage to HQ, three hydrants, some damage to streets, and..." His eyes flicked up to meet Natalya's. "One comrade, KIA. Rusalka."

"*Da*. See to it that her body is being sent home for proper burial, with full honors. She was a true *tovarisch*, right to the end."

It was at this point that Vickie came in. She was wearing an oddly grim smile. "I have good news and good news and good news. Which would you like first?"

Natalya stared at the witch. "*Blin*. Wanting cigarette, then all the news." She patted her pockets for a pack and a lighter, then looked up to see Georgi holding up a cigarette for her. John, obligingly, lit it for her with a flame from his thumb. "*Da*. So, news?"

"I'll start with Chug. The reattachment of his arm went great. I'll short-form this; sometimes I can pull off a kind of magic that tells things *be the way you were X amount of time ago*. Thanks to Herb and a pile of batteries, I made everything that passes for nerves and circulatory system and ligaments and other attachments do that, backdating it to this morning. I generally can't do that with human beings. I *think* this worked—and so does Herb—because he's more 'earth' than he is anything else, but..." she threw up her hands. "Hell if I know for sure. None of us really know how Chug works. He's a mystery even to Jadwiga, and she's treated him the longest. Anyway, what he's left with is the equivalent of muscle tears and deep, deep bruising. He's about halfway into his first ten gallons of ice cream, his hamster is snuggling on one shoulder and Herb is doing the same on the other. That's the good news there."

"And that means that there's...more, right?" John uncrossed his arms, looking to each person in the room in turn. "'Cause, I'm damned glad that Chug is doin' better. But we've still lost someone, an' turnin' this into a win looks mighty difficult."

"That's good news number two. I've been holding off on this until—there she is." Vickie pointed at the door as Bella entered, looking a little ashen. She gave a shrill, short whistle, making Bella look up, pulled a bottle out of a pocket and threw it to the ECHO leader. "All right, folks, you might have noticed I've been looking a bit less like I was a hair short of throwing myself off

a building over the past couple days. There's a reason for that."
She took a deep breath. "We've got a mole inside the Thulian
Earth HQ, feeding us info."

Natalya's jaw dropped. And she took a breath to scream at
Victrix and Bella.

"*Saviour, WHOA!*" Vickie shouted, somehow managing to
amplify her voice enough to startle the Commissar. That was . . .
command voice. Where—

"Bella didn't know. I've been keeping this to myself because,
quite frankly, I did not believe it. It was too good to be true.
But that's my third good news. While Sera and Fireball XL-5
there were facing the Dread Beast out there, Eight piloted one
of my eyes at the thing, and lodged the eye where the Beast
wasn't going to notice it. We tracked it right to where the mole
says the HQ is, verifying that whoever it is, he's telling us that
much of the truth."

Natalya fumed. "Fine! But is leaving questions! Why did *svinya*
come here? Why did you not share information with us? You are
thinking that you are the only one with resources, witch, but
you are not! This—this is being intolerable!" Natalya, for lack
of anything more to say, furiously puffed on her cigarette. She
hated being left out of the loop. It reminded her too much of
being home, and not in a pleasant way.

Vickie merely raised an eyebrow. "If you've got resources that
can find an invisible ship in the middle of the ocean, I'd love
to hear about them. That's what I mean about all this being too
damn good to be true. Until five minutes ago, I didn't believe
in any of this. So what good would it have done to blab out a
fairy tale? As for how the damn thing found us . . . and why it
came here . . . it was an accident on the part of the Eggheads.
They were messing around with radio links and pinged out a
Metisian . . . something or other. I can follow their science to a
point, but the further away it gets from conventional math and
physics, the more baffled I get. Whatever they did, they alerted
the Thulians that they were still alive, and that they were here.
I suspected something of the sort which is why I let Eight take
over and headed for the basement like a scalded cat."

"Can electric ghosts be made to feel pain? I need to know . . .
for reasons." Natalya took another drag from her cigarette, and
wondered if anyone would question her. Marconi and Tesla's

"experiment" had cost the life of one of her comrades, and nearly her own. She was *not* amused.

"Physical pain, no. But I've been taking lessons in excoriation from the best in the business," Vickie nodded at Saviour. "Believe me, their ectoplasmic hides have been scorched, and they know the next time they play around without vetting it with you, Bella, or both first will be the last time they get to do anything but float around in the equivalent of solitary confinement for as long as we care to keep them isolated. Will that do?"

"For now. I will not promise that they will not beink have wires flayed...or whatever they find unpleasant." Natalya snubbed out the cigarette butt, and Georgi was ready with a fresh one, with Murdock providing the fire. *He or his woman could send us all to Hell right now without a thought, and here he is lighting my cigarettes for me. Life is full of the strange and wonderful, truly.* "We know where they are, *da*?"

"I have complete control over their environment, yes. And complete control over whether or not they get to interact with the real world. I intend to link that control to you, Bella, and a couple other people, in case something happens to me." The storm simmering in Vickie's eyes convinced the Commissar that she was just as enraged about this as Saviour was. "There will be no repeat of this...incident."

"Nikola, *could* she cut us off?" Marconi asked his oldest friend, alarm spreading across his ghostly features. "Would she?"

Tesla could not chew his lower lip anymore, but his simulacrum made the motions. "She was very angry. It is just as well we pretended it was an accident. We meant well, but..."

"But a comrade died and there was a great deal of damage," Eight pointed out. "You, who are virtually immortal now, forget how terrible a thing that is. And the Chug creature...I do not think you are aware how dear he is to all of the CCCP. Even Untermensch, who keeps replacing his hamster pets secretly with new ones when they die, due to their short life spans. He was very badly hurt—something which they have never before witnessed—and it is only thanks to a great deal of good luck and the intervention of exactly the right mix of talents that he is repaired and recovering. You should count yourselves lucky that Vickie decided to take your tale at face value."

"You will not betray us?" Marconi asked, alarmed that the Artificial Intelligence was so completely aware of what he and Tesla had been up to—with the best of intentions, of course! They had only wanted to lure one of the Death Spheres here so that they could tag it, and give Victrix the verification she desperately wanted. How could they have known that an entirely new and terrifyingly invulnerable creature would have come instead?

"Provided you promise me that you will do nothing like that again, unless you confer with me and Vickie first," the AI replied.

"I think perhaps we should leave the espionage attempts to others altogether from now on," Marconi said, after a moment.

Tesla nodded. "I agree. We seem to have no talent for them."

Giants in the Ocean

MERCEDES LACKEY AND VERONICA GIGUERE

And more good news. At the time when we needed it most.

"*Miss Ferrari?*" The voice over Ramona's in-head Overwatch Two rig was the very diffident one of Eight. "*There is a situation at the piers in Savannah that requires your particular attention.*"

Ramona didn't pause in her review of Mercurye's reports of the kids he was training. If this was another instance of kidnapped children, then she'd have to see how to change the little fellow's algorithm to not have her as primary contact. They already had their hands full with all of Mel's former roommates. "Savannah? All right, give Gilead a heads-up that we've got incoming. At this rate, we'll need someone specializing in pediatrics."

"*It's nothing to do with children, Miss Ferrari. Perhaps it would be best to show you.*" Before Ramona could object, a window opened up, seemingly in front of her (although she knew it was really part of her in-eye HUD rig) showing one of the docks at the port. Standing waist-deep in the water a reasonable distance from the dock were two enormous...people. One was a woman, stark naked except for a headdress made of titanic shells. The other was...well, it looked like an amazing stone statue of a man. A particularly gorgeous man in the style of the ancient Greek sculptors. Except the statue was moving.

"Like I said, sir," a dock supervisor was bellowing over a bull-horn, "I've been told Miss Ferrari is being contacted right now, but I can't tell you when she'll get back to us—"

"TELL HER BILL WANTS TO TALK TO HER," the giant statue replied, making the surface of the water around him tremble. "THAT SHOULD SPEED THINGS UP A LITTLE."

Ramona yelped and scooted back in her chair, window blinking out in an instant. Papers left in disarray, she grabbed her badge out of habit and jogged down the hall. "We'll need to get one of the cars ready, I'll be at the garage in five minutes."

I would suggest using a rocket pack, Miss Ferrari. The Quartermaster has one upgraded to suit your new weight. Or perhaps Mercurye can carry you if you are unsure of your flying ability.

She considered the options. While Mercurye could get her there faster, she wondered if this was better suited for a solo mission. "I'll take the rocket, kiddo. It's a short flight. Is there any way you can let him—Bill, I mean—let him know that I'm on my way?" The excitement made her voice waver more than she expected. "Just in case."

"Absolutely, Miss. I am in continuous contact with the Dockmaster. I'm telling him now. The other entity you saw is the metahuman known as the Goddess Amphitrite. She herself assumes she is the goddess, so it would be well to keep that in mind when you address her."

"Noted. I will do my best to not be smited where I stand, sit, or swim."

Flying high above I-16, Ramona gritted her teeth and leaned to compensate for the slight headwind coming from the east. She could see the blue of the Atlantic in the distance and the winding blue-green of the Savannah River. Hope and excitement bubbled up in her throat with each passing minute. Was it really Bill? Bill, one of her first recruits in the middle of the Invasion, whose footsteps had left a path of broken buildings and class action lawsuits through the middle of Atlanta, and yet, who had saved more metahuman lives than she wanted to think about, and had turned the tide in the fight for the ECHO campus. Bill, called the Mountain, who had walked out into the churning waters of the Atlantic and who had disappeared from all of the satellites and surveys. Her great success . . . and her terrible failure.

She swallowed hard and tried to make herself more aerodynamic while giving the jetpack an extra boost. The rush of superheated air over the backs of her thighs triggered a fresh layer of carapace that kept her from an embarrassing swath of burns. The combat engineering team had finally made her a pack that would keep her in the air and at speed, but the amount of heat it released would have roasted anyone else. At this point, she'd endure the burn if it meant seeing Bill again.

And with a goddess, no less. Had he found her somewhere in the bottom of the ocean? Had he rescued her, or had she rescued him like one of those fairy tales with mermaids and drowning sailors? Ramona's mind churned with possibilities as the number of streets and buildings below her increased. She called up a street map overlay on her HUD to guide her, figuring that even a small port would be busy enough to make finding them a challenge from the air.

She flew over an elementary school, a note in the HUD marking the building as on lockdown given the current set of circumstances. Ramona started to ask Eight to give her the coordinates for Bill's location, but she hit the reverse thrusters on her jetpack as she saw two massive figures looming over the container ships docked at the port. Given their relative size, the Savannah River might have been a bathtub with the tugs as rubber toy boats. She sucked in a breath and decreased her altitude, trying to figure out what to say when she met them face to face.

But Bill solved part of the problem when he spotted her in the air. He must have been watching for her. "RAMONA!" he boomed, and held out his right hand, palm flat. "COME LAND HERE!"

His voice shook the air, forcing her to recalculate her speed as she came in at a slightly awkward angle. She managed to touch down at the base of his index finger. Ramona cut the jetpack and turned the overlay off so she could see him clearly.

Bill's face loomed above her, familiar, but not. She knew it had to be him, but she didn't remember Bill's features being so smooth or well-defined. When she had first found him at Stone Mountain, he had resembled broken concrete, with hard edges and uneven patches of rock and gravel. The creature who held her had the appearance of a classic statue, something that would have stood guard at the mouth of a great seafaring empire, carved from a single massive stone. The eyes that studied her had none of the anguish that she remembered from before, but she still squirmed under his gaze.

Ramona raised a hand in hesitant greeting. Tears already threatened to spill down her cheeks, so she drew a deep breath before speaking. "I didn't remember you being this tall," she offered with a smile. "You...you look good, Bill. Really good."

Bill smiled and modulated his voice down to what, for him, was probably a whisper. It was still...loud. **"You mean, you don't remember me looking like a Greek statue. That's Amphitrite's doing. And we're calling me 'Atlas' now. You've changed too, Ramona."**

She grinned, a dorky sob escaping around the smile. This high up, only Bill would see the ugly-relieved crying if it came to that. "An accident. Bella says it helped trigger a metagene or something. We came up with 'Steel Maiden' on account of my new heavy metal persona."

"So you're a meta, and at least an OpThree now? Wowsers." He raised his free hand to scratch his stone hair. **"Well, look, we can catch up later. Amphitrite and me want to help with the Space Nazis. We know where they are, out in the ocean. We checked the place out. 'Te is really pissed about them messing up her ocean and even more pissed about what I told her about them. So, how can we help, other than showing you where they are?"**

Her mouth hung open. All of the information, it was too much to process in such a short space of time, Ramona sat down hard on Bill's hand, her still-metallic backside scraping the stone. She blinked rapidly at him and scrubbed at her face with one hand. "Help? Of course, I'll let the folks at HQ know, they'd be more than happy for the information, and I'm sure they can use the help, but..." Her throat burned, but she pushed the words out. "But you're here, and you're alive, and you want to *help?*"

Another face loomed over her: the unnaturally beautiful and enormous face of Amphitrite. *Her* voice, at least, was at normal speaking tones. "Atlas has pointed out to me that although these... creatures... have as yet only meddled in small ways with my realm, they will no doubt turn their attentions to it, and to me, now that they are moving to world conquest. And as damaging as you mortals can be to my realm and my creatures, they would be infinitely moreso. Therefore, yes, we will help."

Ramona smiled at the sea goddess, then remembered the *goddess* part and lowered her head. Her only experience with anything deitylike had been through conversations with Sera, and the creature here was infinitely more terrifying. There was probably a rule about eye contact. "Thank you, ma'am," she said, standing but keeping her head bowed.

"Oh, please do not *grovel,*" the sea goddess said impatiently.

"I am not some tedious god that expects prostrations. It is very difficult to hold a conversation when one of the two people in it is lying flat on her face."

Ramona snorted and lifted her head. "Fair enough, ma'am. Like I told Bill, er, Atlas, I'm sure that we'd be more than happy to have your help beyond simple information. I'm not the one in charge of logistics, but I know who is, and I can pass along your offer immediately." She checked the appropriate channels and flagged the Colt Brothers. While Eight could track all of the minute details regarding her dual-deity conversation, she needed those two to work alongside the prodigy. "So, you said they're out in the ocean? How far out? And what kind of scale are we talking about? Bigger than a sea goddess, smaller than a continent?"

"'Te and I did a walkabout. The whole shebang is about fifteen clicks end to end, and seven and a half wide," Bill said. But Amphitrite had something to add.

"It is wrapped in a...magic curtain," she said. "That makes it invisible. But we can 'see' it, or I can, by the water it moves."

"That'd be a force field and the water displacement," Bill said helpfully. "I don't know any news about these goons since I walked away from Atlanta, have you seen something like that before?"

Ramona grimaced. "Unfortunately. The fortress they had at Ultima Thule had a shielding system that matches your description. Considering how we were able to get through it, they've probably modified this one to account for how our teams were able to take down its predecessor." Her stomach knotted as she recalled that it had been Djinni's team that had gotten the job done. One hit, and the entire thing shattered like some enormous alien eggshell. "Multiple power sources in secure locations throughout the area. And..." She did some more mental math with Bill's estimate of the base's size. "Fifteen kilometers from end to end puts it barely inside the Loop back home. That's a lot of area to search and hold, even with a sizeable force and advance knowledge."

Amphitrite leaned in closer. "The...object...is shaped like two halves of a fully opened shell," she said. "If it were two halves of a *sphere,* each half would be as deep at the deepest point as it is wide, but it is not. The halves more closely resemble shallow bowls, joined at one point. That means you would be forced to cross from one to the other at the point where they joined. Or have two groups, each searching one half."

"Ramona, Eight pinged me and updated me." The hoarse voice was Vickie, as usual sounding as if she was burning her candle in about six places at once. *"I've got a question. Will either Amphitrite or Atlas or both agree to being wired for Overwatch Two?"* There was a sound that might have been a laugh if there had been anything like humor in it. *"Nice thing about them being so big, I* don't *need to give them one of the miniature sets. And if you lay out the target I gave you, I can send the stuff straight to you now."*

"We'll see, won't we?" She took a deep breath and regarded each of the massive metas in turn. "Our resident techno-shaman thinks that bringing you on the team would be great, but it would be easier if we could have you wired onto our secure communications network. It's a little involved, but worth it." Ramona gave a quick rundown of the three implants, doing her best to relay use and placement without resorting to complex descriptions. "The best part," she finished with a smile, "is that you're barely a breath away from any updates or changes to what's going on in the field. Instant information."

Amphitrite held up her hand. "Are these things you describe derived from the workings of Hecate of the Full Moon or of the Dark?"

"Tell her Full Moon," Vickie said immediately.

"Full Moon," Ramona repeated. "Why?"

"Then I accept. Atlas may also if he chooses. There is no harm in accepting the fruit of gifts bestowed by my fellow goddess, and much benefit may be derived therefrom." Amphitrite gave Bill a long look that might or might not have included some unspoken communication.

Bill shrugged. **"I'm game,"** he said. **"Be nice to have a way to talk to you folks without blowing your eardrums out."**

"Take that square of cloth out of your far right belt pouch and unfold it," said Vickie. *"This is funny, I'm actually using the prototypes we created for testing before we miniaturized. Never thought I'd use them for anything other than doorstops."*

There was a *pumph* of displaced air, and six ovoids about the size and shape of footballs appeared on the unfolded cloth: two red, two green, and two blue. *"We'll start with the vocal component first. Have our friends pick up the red ones on the tip of a finger and put it on the soft palate above the tongue."*

A very few minutes later, minutes Ramona remembered vividly from her own experience, and *"Testing, one, two, three,"* whispered in her head in Bill's voice, followed by *"This is ... fascinating"* in Amphitrite's.

Ramona beamed at the pair of them. "Isn't it? Just wait until you start to experiment with the mapping overlays. One dive underwater and you'll literally flood the database with all sorts of new information ..." She trailed off, eyes widening as she realized what she had said.

But she got an unexpected response from Amphitrite. *"Good. I can finally show you mortals where your poisons have been dumped and are harming my ocean. I expect you to help me clean up your messes now, and no excuses."*

On Ramona's channel came Vickie's whisper. *"Goddess. Remember that. Goddess. I do not want to have to tell Yank to retrieve a squashed disk with your face on it."*

"The information would certainly help, and we can relay those locations to people who are far better suited to that kind of assistance," Ramona responded smoothly. "But if we don't know more about the location of this floating double-shell base and how it's affecting the immediate area, I don't know how much longer there'll be anyone on the planet with the resources to help with that kind of cleanup. I can promise you that whatever you're seeing, it's getting sent back and cataloged."

"I can track you; all you have to do is walk out to it," said Vickie.

"Or maybe even beneath it?" Ramona faced Bill with a thoughtful expression. "Just how deep are the waters where this thing is located?"

"It's in a shallowish spot; ten thousand feet, give or take."

"And how tall are you these days, Bill?" Standing on his hand, she didn't have any reference for height. From where she stood on his finger, his wrist was almost thirty feet away.

Bill squinted at the Savannah skyline. *"Thirty, forty stories, give or take? About a thousand feet, I guess. But don't worry, I've been deeper than that. And 'Te has ways of fixing things so I can swim. Dunno how it works, I just know it does."*

She ran the rough calculations in her head. "Vickie, double-check me on the math, but even if this floating fortress is fifteen kilometers wide and we're looking at something about nine thousand feet deep, it's possible for them to have plenty of clearance underneath it, right? Unless—" Ramona frowned. "Does that force field go all the way down?"

"*It does not,*" Amphitrite said instantly. "*We have been beneath it. The magic shield follows the contours of the bottom of the objects. In shape it is not unlike the symbol of omega, with a very fat middle. It does touch the bottom at the deepest point of the bowls, but only just. There is plenty of room for us below it, even to swim rather than walking along the bottom.*"

"*I don't think they're paying any attention to anything under the ocean that's not made of metal,*" Bill added helpfully. "*Plus, 'Te can mask us with lots and lots of fish.*"

"Lots and lots" likely added up to hundreds of thousands, given their size. Ramona steeled herself for the ask, keeping Vickie's *goddess* reminder at the forefront of her mind. "We're still trying to get a plan together, but we're short on time. Having both of you able to see the base and send that information to us could be the difference between success and failure. We share a common desire to rid the planet of this menace, and your involvement can help us put together a plan that can minimize the impact to your oceans."

Amphitrite smiled. "*I trust you, and the votary of Hecate who speaks in my ear. And we are ... Atlas says, 'In this for all the marbles.' I know you must attack these Space Nazis where they hide, and we will be a part of that. But let us accomplish what we can in this moment.*"

Bill chuckled. It sounded like thunder. "*That's our cue, Ramona. We're gonna go take a walk. See you when we get back.*"

Ramona beamed and kicked her jetpack into gear, careful to push backward and away from the massive stone palm. She hovered at nearly eye level with him, her grin impossibly wide. "You look better. You look wonderful, and not because of the whole sculpted thing. You look *happy*, Bill. Really and truly, y'know?"

He chuckled again and turned, small waves rocking the boats that had surrounded the pair in the river. Ramona hovered in place as they walked out through the channel, Amphitrite leading the way through the comparably shallow water. Once they disappeared around the bend and the waves subsided, she kicked the pack into gear and headed back toward ECHO's campus.

But Bill had one last quip for her. "*Hey, Ramona, when this is over? ECHO needs to hire 'Te as a shrink. She's nicer than you are at it.*"

CHAPTER THIRTY

Season of the Witch

MERCEDES LACKEY, CODY MARTIN.
DENNIS LEE AND VERONICA GIGUERE

Now we had the location of the Thulian World Ship verified by not just one, but two sources. In fact, when Amphitrite and Atlas finished their initial survey, we had verification of the location by GPS coordinates, and you couldn't ask for anything better than that.

Which meant it was time to organize for what we hoped would be the penultimate battle to drive the Thulians off our planet. But because this was humans we are talking about... that was easier said than done.

Assuming this is being read by other humans, and not mutated radioactive cockroaches, I am going to skip all of the negotiations, cajoling, blackmailing, and yelling that went on. Fortunately, even the most recalcitrant leaders were terrified and desperate, and ECHO really held all the cards at this point.

It was pretty obvious that there were a lot of nations that were not going to be able to contribute substantially to this battle. Rather than humiliate them, Spin Doctor had the brilliant plan of making them our "fallback"—if the combined forces lost this fight, it would be up to them to carry on for humanity. To that end, they all went off to put their "end of the world" plans into motion. Spin encouraged diversity of plans. "Try everything," he said. "This is not the time to put too many eggs in too few baskets."

For the rest of us, it was obvious that the Russians, the Chinese, the US, the UK, and the Euro block were going to field their own separate armies. The rest, like the Euro block, organized under whoever had the largest force in that particular area, which led to the incredible sight of the Indians, Pakistanis, and all the other forces of that part of the world cooperating and agreeing that India would represent them.

There was a lot more yelling and unnecessary argument before that was over. And whether you are a human or a cockroach, Reader, I will spare you all of it, and as Bella would say, cut to the chase; the final meeting where ECHO presented the battle plans.

"So." Bella looked around the tables. If there was ever an incongruous setting for what might be the most important meeting in the history of the world, this was it.

They were on the lowest inhabited level in Top Hold—Vickie's space. You couldn't call it an "apartment," it looked more like a squatter's setup in an abandoned warehouse. Vickie had cleared away her combat practice gear so that the center of the space could have tables set up in a rough square. Card tables, because that was all ECHO could scare up at short notice. Horrid, harsh fluorescent lighting glared down from the ceiling ten feet above the square of tables, leaving the rest of the room in shadow. It smelled of damp concrete, cheap Russian cigarettes, and ozone. In the center of the open space formed by the tables was a tiny Metisian holoprojector.

Seated at the tables and standing in what little space remained was the combined leadership of the free world—what was left of it, at least. Generals, presidents, prime ministers, congressmen, and so on; they were all here, and more than a few of them still grumbling that they had to leave their aides and security teams outside. There were representatives from the United States, of course, as well as the United Kingdom, Germany, China, Russia, and India. There were more outside, watching via a televised feed, but the big players had all ensured that they had seats at the table *first*. This was the big "info dump"; after this, everyone would break off and brief their respective national teams, and get the gears turning.

"In case one of you somehow missed the memo, Vix's contact inside the Thulian forces gave us the hard location of what is described as 'the World Ship,' Our allies Amphitrite and Atlas—who used to be the Mountain—have gotten eyes on the thing, and this is an approximation of what it looks like—"

The holoprojector lit up with a stretch of open ocean; floating on it were two shapes, shallow half-spheres joined together. Not impressive, until a line labeled "fifteen kilometers" appeared beside them. "This thing has been sitting in the middle of the Bermuda Triangle for . . . hell, for all I know, since about 1938. It's been cloaked with Thulian stealth tech. That's a lot of ocean, so as far as we know nothing ever ran into it, though this may be why shit keeps going missing in that area. Vix, take it from here."

Vickie stood up. There was nothing left of the diffident, unobtrusive little mage of only a few months ago. "Before you ask how A and A were able to get 'eyes' on this thing when it's stealthed, they measured it by the displacement area in the ocean, and don't ask me what the hell that means, she's a goddess of the sea, and you don't ask a thousand-foot-tall goddess too many questions. This is where the Thulians are staging everything from. It's protected by a force field. They can sit out there until the end of the world and chuck stuff at us from there until we fold. They've got all the manufacturing capability they need. Amphitrite says they are 'mining the seawater' and, according to my source, they have some way to get an endless supply of manpower. The only way we can reach them is to take down the force field from the inside. My contact on the inside is going to open a door for us to insert a small team to do that—but to keep the Thulians from catching on, we need to mount an attack to distract them. Then once the field is down, the fake attack can turn into an invasion of our own."

There was a torrent of angry—and yes, frightened—babble at this point. Bella waited them out until the group settled again, and the most aggressive of the lot spoke up.

It was, inevitably, General Johnston P. Raymond who shook his head and took to his feet. He was the replacement for Arthur Chang, and Bella liked him markedly less than his predecessor. She suspected the P stood for Peckerhead. "Let me see if I got this right," he snarled. "You've got coordinates, a picture, some intel on a possible access point, and on that alone, you want the world to commit all available forces to a full-scale attack on the enemy, hoping that a small infiltration force will take out their main defense."

Angry muttering erupted from the assembled representatives, most of them nodding their agreement.

The Indian representative held up a hand, almost apologetically. "How are we to protect our people, if we are going to pull off the best of our fighting men and women for this attack?" There was a chorus of agreement, and everyone looked to Bella.

Bella remained surprisingly calm. "And just how are your forces holding up under the current attacks?" she asked simply. "How long can you continue to do so?"

Natalya was not nearly as diplomatic. "Piss on that. We have been fighting on the front lines of this conflict—*for all of you*—for years now. Any time a band of *nekulturny* troopers turns up, you have come crying and begging for us to deal with it. And we have *bled* for you." She angrily stamped out her latest cigarette. "The North American HQ? Our man found that information, decoded by ECHO. Ultima Thule? Again, us. Now it is time for you, all of you, to pull your own weight."

"As for the infil team...I think you already know of the ones we've chosen to be the primary attackers on the force field generator itself." Bella nodded at the shadows to her right, and Sera and John stepped into the light.

Another murmur arose from the crowd. Ever since the destruction of Ultima Thule, the governments of the world had been trying to claim John and Sera as their own. Many of the loudest voices for those demands and pleas were sitting at the table now, and Bella could feel the greed, fear and awe pouring off of some of them.

"Can any of *you* think of a better spearhead for this assault?" Bella asked. She didn't give anyone time to respond, or voice their case for why they needed to co-opt the Murdocks...again. "No? Then shut the hell up and sit down; we're not done yet. Vickie?"

"We've consulted with Amphitrite and Atlas. They will tow our initial attack force into place, on buoyant platforms developed by the Metisians and the Brits that have the same radar and sonar reflectivity as water." An image appeared of the two giants walking along the seabed, pulling the platforms behind them, like kids with a huge cluster of balloons. "To be honest, since this is more of a show of force than an actual force, this first wave will be mostly metas, with light artillery support. We'll make a lot of light and noise, but there's no point in wearing ourselves out until they sortie. And we figure they will. We're putting Red Saviour in charge of this force."

The ripple of shock and surprise at that announcement went through all of the assembled nations as well as the USA. The representative from Russia spoke up over the murmurs, not looking at Natalya. "Given her history within the CCCP, we would strongly suggest you reconsider such an assignment, especially in light of her standing with Prime Minister Batov. Not to mention the recent betrayal by her superior officer, Worker's Champion." Bella felt as much as saw Natalya tense, readying herself to launch across the table and probably strangle the man. "We suggest—"

"There will be no argument on this," Bella bellowed over the growing outrage. "Red Saviour is the *only* surviving commander of the Invasion, the attack on the North American base, the attack on Ultima Thule, the attack on Metis, and several direct attacks on CCCP HQ itself. She is the *only* military commander with enough personal experience with a mixed conventional and meta force to handle this. Bulwark will coordinate our suggestions for the leaders of forces under her, but she is going to have battlefield oversight. Bulwark will take your suggestions under advisement, but only Red Saviour has the long experience in handling the Thulians over the course of this war."

Bulwark stood up and made his suggestions. As Bella had suspected, his picks somewhat mollified those who had been objecting. Except for Peckerhead, but... nothing was going to mollify *him* except being named the battlefield commander. And pigs would fly before that happened.

"As for Worker's Champion," Bella continued into the silence that ensued when Bulwark had finished speaking, "I'll let Red Saviour speak for herself."

The Commissar took a moment to compose herself, lighting another cigarette and taking a quick drag from it. "When Boryets defected to the enemy, it wasn't just a betrayal for me, or for Mother Russia. It was a betrayal of the *world*. No, *tovarisch*, you do not have to be worrying about me. I will perform my duty, until the last. With any luck, that will include strangling the life out of the *svinya* myself."

"Let me make this perfectly clear, folks," Bella said. "This is it. This is our shot. We've been on the defensive since the beginning, and despite all of our victories, all we've really been doing is bleeding, and surviving. Just. We don't know when we'll ever get another chance like this. We can end this—*now*. You've seen what they've got, the endless armaments and forces they seem to have at their disposal. And yet...no WMDs. I don't for one second doubt they have them, and I shudder to think what a Thulian WMD could do. Haven't any of you wondered if they're just playing with us? If we just keep going like we've been doing, it's only a matter of time before they tire of this, or arrive at whatever goal their sick twisted minds have concocted. They could end us anytime they want. And you all know it. They've been batting us around like a cat with a helpless, half-stunned mouse, and we've finally got a gun aimed right at their heads. Don't you think it's time we pulled the trigger? While we still can?"

"Trust me," Vickie added darkly, "it won't be long before we can't. You've heard rumors of 'Overwatch' by now. *I* am Overwatch, I created the system, I supervise it, and I coordinate it over the entire world, and there is no one who knows what's going on with the metas of the world as well as I do. We're losing metas now, a steady drain, and they are not being replaced. The metas we have left are exhausted, and you all know as well as anyone what happens to exhausted fighters. Once the metas start going down faster, your defenses are going to evaporate."

Somehow that managed to penetrate as nothing else had. Perhaps because they *had* all heard of the mysterious "Overwatch," and her uncanny ability to deploy metas in the nick of time the world over. There were some feeble objections, quickly overcome, but the discussion was fundamentally over.

As the assembled representatives filed out with their orders, some of them still muttering to themselves, Bella felt a wave of exhaustion and relief fall over her. She turned and gave Bull a weary smile.

"You were right," she whispered. "That was exactly the right way to deal with these pig-headed idiots."

"I know my kind," Bull shrugged, and gently patted her back.

John and Sera waited until the room had finished clearing out before they walked over. "I have to admit, I always wanted to step out of the shadows like that, all mysterious an' shit." John sighed, running a gloved hand through his hair. "A lotta unhappy folks just walked out of the room. Especially the military reps. They're not used to being told 'no.'"

"No, they're not," Bella agreed, as Bull nodded. "And they are even more unhappy about the simple fact they've got no way to grab you. Even though it was supposed to be clandestine, I imagine everyone at the table is aware of how the US Government attempted that and how they ended up with egg on their faces."

"All the same, those people have long memories. If'n we can pull this off, things might get particularly interestin' once we get back."

In more ways than one, Bella thought, regarding John and Sera thoughtfully. Although Sera was no longer a Seraphym... there was something a little uncanny and a bit frightening about the two of them when they were together. There was something of the same aura of great power and greater control about both of them that Seraphym had had on her own, and whenever either of them got upset, their eyes started to have a bit of that inhuman golden glow in their depths. *I almost liked it better when JM was just a grunt and only the Seraphym was alien and inhuman. Now, well, there are times when the both of them are plunging into the Uncanny Valley.*

Powerful metas had existed... well, as long as anyone had known about metas, period. The ones that were as powerful as John and Sera, however, were all almost universally insane in one way or another. Megalomaniacal, delusional, schizophrenic, bipolar, or even just catatonic: there always seemed to be horrendous psychological consequences for a human being to have that much power. Yet... the Murdocks had been spared that torture. Granted, they had gone through their own sorts of hells to reach the level of power that they now had. But Vickie had cleared them magically, and Bella's own telempathic scans had turned up nary a stray hair, figuratively speaking, in either of their minds. They were stable; either how they shared the power, or just their connection—their love for each other?—kept them in check, somehow. It still didn't quiet her fears. Just what would happen when those two came back, without a Thulian menace to confront? What would they *do* with all of that power?

Oh god, what am I doing? Here she was, thinking about the Murdocks, her *friends,* like she was... well, one of those generals that had shuffled out of the room. Calculating, assessing, weighing. Trying to figure out how to *use* them. She swallowed a lump of guilt. But... on the other hand... *I'm a leader. There's too much at stake. That's how leaders think. How they have to think, I guess...*

But she didn't have to like it.

Natalya was the next to join them. She stalked up to the group, brusque as ever. *Once upon a time, she could have had a life as a supermodel, what with her attitude and the way she walks.* She was puffing on another cigarette, a cloud of smoke following her.

"Old scared men do too much talking. If it were being up to them, we would debate color of casket to be buried in while *svinya* line us up against wall to be shot." She looked around for somewhere to put out her cigarette. Finding none, she dropped it to the floor and crushed it with the heel of her boot. If she saw Bull's look of annoyance, she ignored it, and a second later, Herb scuttled up with what looked like a little shovel and a bamboo whisk, brushed up the butt and detritus, and scuttled away again. "I do not have stomach for these... *bureaucrats*," she said, spitting out the last word like a curse. "I never have."

"I would say that it gets easier with practice, but I would be lying," Bella said, sighing.

Nat fished a fresh cigarette out of her mostly empty pack. Murdock snapped his fingers and produced a lighter-sized flame. Nat initially flinched, then leaned forward to light the cigarette. *At least I'm not the only one that's still a little weirded out by the walking, talking nukes in the room.* She turned to Bull, blowing out a cloud of smoke sideways. "I am surprised, *tovarisch*, that you chose to nominate me to lead the assault. I was being tempted to say something during the meeting, but decided it was wiser to present, how do you say... united front?"

"I think it's safe to say we don't always see eye to eye on things, Commissar Saviour," Bull said. "But the facts are the facts. You are the most experienced field commander we have, and despite our differences, the one I would trust most to lead us in this fight."

"I still wonder how the coalition will respond. To be mixing command structures... is difficult obstacle, even with a witch and her *robotnik* helping."

"They're still soldiers," Bull rumbled. "And soldiers know how to follow the chain of command. Each group has its own commander, but you have final say. We make sure the commanders know that, and their forces will fall in line."

"After everythin' that's happened these past couple of years, you've got more clout than you realize, Commissar," John interjected. "We've had mixed forces before. Nothin' on this scale, perhaps, but still... Folks remember Ultima Thule, an' the North American HQ assault. Performance counts for a lot with ground pounders."

"And bear in mind," Vickie said, still at her place at the table, "that no plan survives first contact with the enemy. Not intact at least." She waved at the seats. "This is the point where I tell you what Eight and I have figured out is the infil team's best composition, what we do, and how we get there. You ready to yell at me?"

"I think I've reached my yelling quota for the year," Bull said. "I've got a low growl reputation to uphold, after all."

"Did Comrade Bulwark just make joke?" Natalya asked.

"Something we're working on," Bella shrugged. "He needs some practice is all."

Vickie nodded as they came back to their seats, this time at the table where she had set up. Herb had already moved the holoprojector to the center. "All right. First off, the infil team will be coming in via unpowered submarine. As Atlas and Amphitrite tow the assault force into place, Atlas will also be carrying the submersible. With no engines on, and with Amphitrite filling the water around us with fish, we should be effectively masked."

Bull turned to Vickie, his eyebrow raised. "We?"

John frowned and shared a look with Sera.

"I'm going," Vickie said flatly. "The chances are high that the infil team will need magic. And not only is this place we're going a spaceship and not a city or a base built on the earth, it *is* specifically *alien*. I'm not sure I can work earth magic, or work *through* the earth. That leaves technomancy and some old-school spellcasting that I'm frankly rusty in. The closer I am physically to the team, the more likely it is I can pull this off. But there's more to it than that. Penny's going."

"She most certainly is *not*," Bull said.

"Sorry, Mistuh Bull, sir," Penny spoke up, from where she had been sitting, completely ignored until now. "But I gotta. Mistuh Stone says so. He says some of his friends from the Lost Squadron are there, an' the only way you can talk to 'em is if I'm there."

"I'm not a medium, Bull, I'm an extra-small." Vickie deadpanned.

"She's a *child*," Bulwark said with exaggerated patience. "Do I really need to debate the morals of taking a child with us on a mission?"

"No, because there's no debate happening. She's going. Unless you want JM and Sera to have to search across two seven-and-a-half-kilometer half-spheres for the control room, she's going. My contact doesn't know *where* in the ship the damn thing is. Jacob

Stone says the Lost Squadron knows the ship like the back of their ectoplasmic hands. Plus, they can watch for and alert us to trouble without being detected themselves. Penny will effectively be our eyes and our ears in there. We can't do this any other way." Vickie spread her hands. "I don't intend her to go any further than the entrance, but she's *got* to be there in order to summon and talk to the ghosts."

"At the very least, she'll need protection," Bull mused. "Got someone in mind, or are you going to serve as guardian too?"

The elevator door opened. "That protection would be me," Mel said, "Looks like I got here right on time." She walked deliberately to where Penny was sitting and put both hands on Penny's shoulders—one flesh, one gleaming metal. "I'm an army of one. And it's not just my illusions either, *cher*." She raised her metal hand and flexed the fingers. "Silent Knight's packed me with frickin' lasers. Don't forget, Bulwark, I was a combat specialist afore I ever was in ECHO."

Vickie nodded. "I can't think of anyone who could take better care of Penny than Mel. She'll have the options of both passive and active protections, and nobody else I can think of can bring that to the party." She sighed. "Look, people, this is it. We've got one throw of the dice here. And if we don't win here, Penny's going to be no safer here in Atlanta than she will be with us. Maybe less. Remember, my late uncle and Doppelgaenger had plans for her, and for all I know, DG has a way of finding her even now."

Bull looked at all of them, his lips pressed thinly together. "I really don't like this. Tactically, you are all speaking sense, but I cannot approve of a plan that places a child in such danger." His eyes continued to scan them, a mute appeal for anyone to take his side. Finally, they fell on Bella, who returned his pleading gaze with one of stern conviction.

"I *hate* this," she said flatly. "But Vix is right. Everything is riding on this, and we can't ignore any resource, no matter how young they are. We're talking about our survival, Bull. I'm afraid any one of us is expendable." Her mouth twisted. "And even I can't believe I just said that. But that doesn't make it less true."

"So this is it, then," Bulwark muttered. "This is what we've come to."

Natalya shrugged, still smoking. "Children always die in war, same as anyone else. If we fail in our goals, she will die anyways.

Better that she die fighting, rather than hiding, afraid. If I were thinking it would be helping, I would draft every man, woman, and child in the world for this fight. This girl has fire, and we can use that."

Mel smiled grimly. "And before they can get to her, they'll have to go through *me*."

Penny smiled tremulously, and put one hand on Mel's metal one. "I'm scared, sure, Mistuh Bulwark. But I *got* to go. It ain't just Mistuh John an' Missus Sera I got to help. What if somethin' else comes up? Mistuh Stone's friends, they're th' only ones that kin help us, an' I'm the only one that kin talk to 'em. An'—I don't wanta be sittin' here if y'all lose, waitin' fer the Devil t'come git me. This is the big fight, right? So I'm gonna fight, with all of you. Don't worry. I think we're goin' ta win."

Bull stared at her, speechless. Finally, he hung his head, and a short, barking laugh escaped his lips. He glanced at Penny, and surrendered to her with a grin.

"I wish I had your confidence, young miss," he said. "But you do inspire hope, don't you?"

Natalya looked at Bella, confused. "He smiles and laughs now?"

"Don't look at me," Bella shrugged. "News to me, too."

Vickie sighed. "Okay, the last part of this is you and Bella, Bull. You need to be on the infil team, because in my experience, and in Nat's, some damn shit always comes up after you've deployed your primaries, and someone's got to handle it, and whoever it is *has* to be on Overwatch Two. We also should have some sort of medic and telepath with us. Listen, Bull, I *loathe* the idea of putting Bella on the infil, it's like stupid *Star Trek* Away Team crap with having the captain go down to get shot at, but...it's what I've got. I'm hoping between the two of you, you'll have what it takes to deal with a secondary target. It was really a choice between Bella and Yankee Pride, but Yank is totally unsuited to be on the infil team anyway, he's about as subtle as an avalanche. Yank will be handling the secondary command to Nat. Now, if you can find me someone who's on Overwatch Two that is better for the infil team than you and Bells, I'll amend the bad choice."

"I was originally slated in a secondary command role as well," Bulwark said. "I was to command the main spearhead and provide defensive bubble support. If Bella is going in, I will of course provide backup for her, but who will fill in for me on the battlefield?"

"Untermensch," Vickie and Natalya said at the same time. Vickie nodded to Red Saviour to continue.

"Georgi is having field command experience back to Great Patriotic War," Nat supplied. "Is also being my second-in-command. His English is being excellent, he is known to all ECHO, he is wired to Overwatch Two and Gamayun both, he is even having smattering of French and passable German."

Bulwark nodded and scratched his chin in thought. "I had him slotted to head the main cavalry unit for hit-and-run attacks on the enemy flanks, but you're both right—he's ideal. I think it's time to promote Blaze and give her that role instead. I think she's ready for this."

Bella nodded and pointed at the holographic tactical map Victrix had brought up on display. "Good call. She can take Cavalry Unit Alpha here where we're expecting more troop resistance, and we can set up the fast movers in Bravo on the left in anticipation of the Wolves and flyers, and head them up with Leader."

"You're getting much better with the tactical," Bull said.

"Got a good teacher," Bella said, and elbowed him playfully in the ribs.

"Okay. Is everyone good with this? Or as good as can be?" Vickie asked, then ran both her hands through her hair, making it look, for a moment, as if she had stuck her finger in a light socket. "The plan is pretty simple. We all go in. Penny contacts the Lost Squadron. They run trouble-watch for us while one of them gets lit up by yours truly and guides Sera and JM to the shield generator. Ideally, which we know will not happen, they get there, blow the gennie, and everybody exfils to join the main forces. Meanwhile Nat and the main forces knock on the outside, doing their best to make a lot of noise without expending too much, to give us cover. If crap comes up inside, I light up another of the Lost Squadron and they guide you and Bella to it, Bull. Our likely obstacles are Valkyria, Ubermensch, Boryets, and maybe Doppelgaenger. If possible, we are to avoid a direct confrontation with any of them. The priority is taking down the World Ship defenses and then dealing with them. It'll be a lot easier with a literal army at our backs. I'm anticipating our wild card will be one or more of these Masters critters. We know of at least two, one called Barron, who seems to like to fight things personally, and the head guy, Gero. I've given you all briefings on them already, such as I have. Any thoughts?"

Nat started another cigarette, as Herb toddled up to her and patiently offered her an ashtray. "Would not suggest meeting Barron head to head, if is same creature that nearly destroyed CCCP HQ. We were like pesky flies to it."

Sera exchanged a look with John. "We might have a chance," John pointed out. "She cut an' ran before we had a shot at 'er. Still, probably best not to risk it, if'n there's a choice. Like y'all said, we've got other priorities: take down the power source; let the good guys in the door."

"That's the problem with these Masters," Vickie said grimly. "We just don't know much about them. With the enemy metas, we at least have possible vulnerabilities we can exploit, but we have nothing on Barron to suggest anything effective against her. If you see her, retreat. You likely will not survive a direct fight with her. But, really, it's Gero that's a mystery to us, and that makes him the most dangerous of all."

"There's a few things we know," Bella said quietly. "He's the head of all this. We might not know the extent of his abilities, but from what Jack says, he's vindictive, overconfident, doesn't listen to advice, and tends to concentrate on petty revenge rather than looking at the big picture. He doesn't seem like the sort to play nice with others, or share power. When we take him down, we take *them* down. Cut off the head, the snake dies."

"One thing at a time," Vickie reminded them all. "Shield generator. Stay flexible. Stay in *contact* with each other. The *good* thing about having you with the infil team, Bells, is that we have a pair of commanders—and one of them is a superb tactician—*right with us* to react and hopefully correct instantly if the infil team runs into trouble or if Nat and our guys outside need to be alerted to anything."

"And one more thing," Bella said finally. "We have the most important thing of all, the thing that the Masters and the Thulians apparently don't have now, and never have had."

"What would that be?" Red Saviour asked, stubbing out her cigarette.

"We trust each other," Bella replied.

Nat gave a surprised little *huff*, then smiled. "By Lenin's beard," she said with a wolfish smile, "we do."

CHAPTER THIRTY-ONE

All Along the Watchtower

MERCEDES LACKEY, CODY MARTIN,
DENNIS LEE AND VERONICA GIGUERE

Predictably, there was more argument that I will spare you, but if you are interested, I have unredacted files of all of it. None of it was among our principals. We all already knew that this was a plan only someone insane would follow, but perhaps that was our advantage, that no one sane would even think we would try such a thing.

There were giants in the ocean. Two of them. In deference to mere human sensibilities, both Amphitrite and Atlas wore short saronglike drapes of fabric around their hips. Amphitrite, however, had not continued that sensitivity by wearing any sort of top. Bella wondered how many of the male metas loading up onto the sea-colored platforms were going to be permanently traumatized by the sight. *Boobs are great... unless they're boobs the size of a house on a gorgeous female who regards you with about the same deference as you give a fruit fly.*

This was going to be her last chance to talk with Red Saviour, before the infil team climbed into the submarine Atlas was going to be carrying like a football. Looking around anxiously, Bella spotted Natalya supervising the loading, and talking with Murdock. Sera was already in the sub; she'd gone ahead because maneuvering her wings down the hatch had been something of a challenge, and had required the assistance of one person below her and one above. "Let's go have a word," she muttered to Vickie, who was dressed, oddly enough, in chainmail, with a sword and long dagger. What she expected to accomplish with that, Bella hadn't a clue, but if the getup made the little magician feel better...

Vickie shrugged and followed her as she eeled her way through the crowd of waiting metas. "Saviour!" Bella called. "Can I borrow you a second?" She pointed over to a beach cabana that would give them some semblance of privacy.

Natalya and Murdock were both already suited up for combat; Nat in the CCCP uniform, John in his stealth nanoweave getup. Bella wondered why he bothered to carry the rifle, pistol, and various explosives, with what he could do just with his powers. The pair looked up at Bella, and Nat motioned for Murdock to follow her. That took Bella aback a bit. Then again... she had Vickie with her. Maybe Saviour wanted JM to even the odds in what was probably going to be a very awkward conversation. "*Da?* Just going over final preparations and equipment checks." The Commissar took a cigarette—she'd started on a fresh pack, probably not her first of the day—and held it out. JM rolled his eyes and lit the tobacco with a flame from his thumb. *Ah. Okay, she enjoys using a human cigarette lighter... that could flatten this entire beach if he wanted to.* Then again... maybe using JM as her personal torch was her way of keeping a lid on her *very rational* fear of the "firebomb." Or maybe it was her way of doing a continual "system check." As long as he reacted to being ordered to light a cigarette with an eyeroll—and not a "LIGHT IT YOURSELF, PUNY MORTAL!"—things were still under control.

"Let's get out of the sun," Bella said, leading the way to the cabana. The sand was loose, and walking through it was a pain. Somehow, Vickie was walking on the stuff as if it was hard-packed. *Earth magic? Probably.* Bella wasn't sensitive to magic, of course, but Vickie was so powered up even Bella could feel something from her, like a subsonic hum. It stood to reason there could be bleedover that would make shifting sand solid under the mage's feet without her even thinking about it. *I'm not sure who I'm more scared of right now—JM or Vix.*

When they got into the shelter of the cabana and out of the sun, Saviour gave a little grunt of approval at the relative cool. Even after years of living in Georgia, Red Saviour still was not used to the heat, and here on a Florida beach, it was even worse than in the middle of Atlanta.

Natalya took a drag on the cigarette, waving her hand. "What do you need? Is there being new intel, or has one of big tough generals' lost his aide, and must have nap?"

"Something we need to be clear on," Bella said firmly. "*You* are the one who's going to be in charge of the real assault force once that shield goes down. And if—*when*—we start winning, we can't have a wholesale slaughter. A lot of these people have payback on their minds." *Including you, Red Saviour.*

The Commissar stood there, letting the cigarette burn without drawing from it, and stared at Bella, taking measure of her. *Definitely not "Natalya" or "sestra" right now; she's in "Commissar" mode.* "You surprise me, blue girl."

Bella weighed her words carefully. "A wholesale slaughter, violating the rules of war . . . that's going to do irreparable damage—"

"You surprise me, as I said. I thought you finally had the stomach to do what needed to be done." She finally took a drag on the cigarette. "This is your first war, so maybe I should not being so surprised. But, still, you are a leader now, and you cannot be having naive delusions. This is not conflict that ends with treaties, resolutions, and overstuffed suits talking in front of cameras. These . . . are *invaders*. Conquerors, who want to genocide entire planet, after they enslave it. You do not deal with enemies like these. Appeasement is a step towards surrender." She took another drag, then stabbed the cigarette in the air at Bella. "The fools who run the world *will* surrender, turn bellies and throats to sky and ask to be eaten last. If we are not winning here, and *totally*, with no chance for being reprisals. Slaughter? Red Square was slaughter. Civilians gunned down without mercy was slaughter. This is destroying an enemy before they can destroy us. Is simple, *nyet*?" Murdock stood not quite at her side, arms crossed over his chest. She couldn't read him, but she *could* see that he was scanning everyone with his telempathy.

"And it will do as much or more damage to *us* as it will them," she replied flatly. "Genocide begets genocide, and what's there to stop it if we start it here? No. Rules of war. If they don't surrender, fine, then bring the thunder. But if they do, they're to be treated like any other captives of war."

She expected to hear her words echoed, or reinforced, by Vickie. But instead . . . silence. Vickie looked as if her mind was anywhere but here, but not in a passive way. No, she was tightly focused on something else, though what that was, Bella could not guess. But whatever it was, she didn't agree enough with Bella to break that concentration.

"You *Amerikanski* have learned nothing from past wars. Half measures are leading to more death, more suffering... and more war. These Thulians will not forget their defeats. Are you to integrate *aliens*, with clear *fascista* ideology and culture, into society?" She spat on the sand, shaking her head. "If you were being more like your forebears, we would not be having conversation. In the Great Patriotic War, after your country allowed Russia to bleed the Nazis at great cost, only then you entered war. But *entered* it you did, totally. Dresden, Hiroshima, Nagasaki... was quarter given to any there? Would it have been given if they were still threats? Total war is *total*. 'Genocide begets genocide,' feh! Hard for enemy to retaliate if there is no enemy."

Bella shook her head. "That wasn't what I meant. I meant, once we allow *ourselves* to commit genocide, it won't stop with aliens. Because humans can *always* turn 'the enemy' into an 'alien worthy of genocide.'" In desperation, since Vickie wasn't saying anything, Bella looked at JM. He'd sided with her once before... when Saviour was about to plunge neck deep into torture. Would he side with her again?

Nat caught her look, then turned to John. "Murdock. You are soldier... at heart. You are knowing hard truths of fighting war. What do you have to say?"

John shrugged, and Bella's heart sank. "This is right down to the wire. No shit, Murdock, right? We've all been there before, but I've seen it more'n my fair share over the years. You learn a helluva lot 'bout someone when you see what they do when everything is on the line." He paused, looking off into the distance for a moment before meeting Bella's eyes. "A lotta folks choke. Pressure is too much, they didn't train hard enough, or they take on a fight that they can't finish." Now he turned to look at Nat. "Others ditch their principles when the goin' gets tough. They cut corners, look the other way, value expediency over what they know they ought ta do."

He's killed more people than anyone I know... but I don't think there's anyone I'd trust more, except Bull. "So what's your call on this? Expediency or ethics?" she asked directly.

John waited longer than Bella would have liked before answering.

"I figure if y'all wanted everyone in the ship dead, you'd just send in me an' Sera, maybe the giants, an' call it a day. Or smuggle in some nukes. Since we're not doin' that, we ain't killin' everyone an' everythin' in there. Which is probably a good idea, considerin' we might have POWs to rescue. The dragon definitely scooped up some folks, plus whoever the hell else might be kidnapped. This war has been goin' on for years, and we've got a lotta missin' in action that might just be locked up in this tub." He shrugged again. "So, my answer? Hit 'em hard; that's what we do. But I'd rather bring people back alive than kill everythin' in there."

Bella nodded slowly. "There you go, Commissar Red Saviour. There's the hard truth you wanted."

Bella felt a flash of anger from Natalya, even though she didn't react outwardly except to puff on her cigarette. Just as quickly as it had bubbled up, Nat clamped down on the emotion. "*Da*, fine. If it will being satisfying for delicate sensibilities, we will go... 'by the book,' as you are saying. Will not give order to deliver justice to *fascista*."

"You can deliver all the *justice* you want, Commissar," Bella replied, her voice hard. "Just make sure it's *justice*, and not *revenge*. You know the old Chinese saying, I presume? *If you walk the road to vengeance, be prepared to dig two graves.*"

Natalya barked a harsh laugh. "You are mistaken to think that justice and revenge are being mutually exclusive, *sestra*. And you are foolish to think that any of us should go to this evil place without being ready to die." She flicked the cigarette away from the group, and turned to leave. "You will have your rules of war followed. I must go and find way to make sure war is ended at same time, now," she called over her shoulder.

Bella grimaced. "I tried," she said to no one in particular, then looked at Murdock. "Come on. We've got a sub to catch."

"Y'know, in another life, that would just be you askin' if I wanted to catch some lunch. But you're right. Let's get a move on."

"We should look into the Futures," Sera said abruptly. She was crammed into what looked like the uncomfortably tiny space of someone's bunk, wings and all, because there had been no other place to put her where her wings weren't in the way.

The couple was alone on the submarine for the moment except for the skeleton crew needed to keep the life support going. After the discussion with Bella, Natalya, and nominally Victrix, John had finished packing his gear and made a beeline for the vessel. If nothing else, he didn't want to leave Sera cooped up by herself in the cramped sub. More than that, though, *he* didn't want to be alone. The comrades of the CCCP had done their best to make John feel like he was still just another *tovarisch*, and the same could be said of some of the ECHO personnel that he was more familiar with. Even so, there were more than a few people who just... stared at him. Like they were examining a particularly dangerous animal, without the benefit of a cage between them. He had become used to being seen as the most lethal person in the room—or at least one of them—a long time ago. This was different. He was apart from everyone now, in more ways than he had ever been before. For the umpteenth time, he longed for the days when he was anonymous, just another on-the-run metahuman.

"You are troubled, love," Sera said softly, when he didn't answer. "How can I help you?"

John grinned lopsidedly, shaking his head. "Just caught up in the little things, darlin'. Life used to be a lot simpler 'fore aliens an' Nazis decided to blow up the world." He shifted in his seat a bit, turning to face her. "Anyways, you're right. We oughta try an' do what we can with the Futures. We're goin' into the meat grinder, an' a lotta people are dependin' on us."

Her deep blue eyes regarded him steadily from the shadows of the bunk. "Yet you are uneasy. Are you in need of comfort, or knowledge more?"

"That's a fair question, love," he said, sighing. *Can't get anythin' past a wife who can literally read your emotions.* "Guess I'm not done adjustin' to how things have changed. For us, I mean." He regarded her, trying to clear his mind and take in everything about her. Her eyes, her hair, and even her wings. She was beautiful... but in such a more personal way than she had been when he had first met her. There was still a bit of the alien grandeur to her; the way she moved, the way that she looked at things and people. But that was replaced more and more each day with a sort of human ease; she was more comfortable in her body now, with the limitations, the pains... and the joys. They had never been closer than they were right then. "They're all afraid of us. Even Bella. Maybe especially her." He took another moment, gathering his thoughts. "It's comin' off of 'em all in waves. They think we're unpredictable, an' that scares 'em. I just don't know how we square that when everythin' is all said an' done. Are we goin' to be fightin' just to be *us*, from now on?"

She reached out to where he sat on the bunk opposite hers, and put one hand on his wrist. "We cannot change what we are. But we can change how they see us, merely by being ourselves as much as we can. That will take time, and there is none to spare *now*. What is it you have always said? *Fix the first problem you have in front of you, and don't worry about the ones behind it?* That is what we must do, and you know what that problem is."

"You're right," he said, sighing. "And what a helluva problem we got in front of us. So, shall we, 'fore the others get here?"

She nodded, and closed her hand down around his wrist. "This is not the ideal place, but needs must. Let us look to the Futures and find the best, if we can."

The couple had been through the process enough times that, now, it was as easy as breathing for John. None of the anxiety or trepidation. One moment, they were both sitting in the submarine, facing each other with their eyes closed and their hands clasped. The next . . . they were in an endless stream of light, with countless tributaries spreading out as far as either of them could see. John focused on what he wanted to see, and Sera joined her intention with his: a glimpse at the next few hours for themselves, and the rest of the assault force. Immediately, John felt that something was different about this viewing. Instead of a narrowing of the different paths and directions that the light was flowing, they multiplied. The intensity of the light was nearly blinding, culminating in a bright horizon, almost like a wall that began when they entered the World Ship.

There were a few things that John and Sera were able to glean from the vision. There would be much suffering inside of the World Ship: death, loss, sacrifice, anguish. And, no matter what else happened, both of them had to be there. Any path that began with either or both of them not going to the World Ship terminated abruptly. It was unlike anything that John had ever seen when trying to view the Futures.

Before the viewing could drain them too much, John signaled to Sera that they needed to end the trance. As one, they came back to the real world, in real time.

Sera blinked at him owlishly. "There is no clear path," she said, finally.

"Just one, darlin'. We've gotta be on the World Ship. But we already knew that." The sounds of feet on the metal ladder leading down from the hatch echoed through the sub. Most of the sounds went forward; one set of feet came aft, in their direction.

Vickie, dressed oddly in chainmail, and with a sword and dagger sheathed at her side, appeared in the doorway of the bunkroom and regarded them both solemnly.

"Any word from Delphi?" she asked, a little too casually.

John glanced over at Sera, and realized that the barest flecks of gold were still in both of their eyes. "Gear up for a rough day, an' keep your powder dry," he said, turning back to Vickie. "No matter what, Sera an' I are goin' to see this through."

"Of all the things in the world that are a certainty, that you and Sera are in this till the end is at the top of the list," she replied.

"Fair enough." He eyed her outfit, particularly the sword. "Packin' a little bit of an old-school kit, aren't ya?"

"Under most circumstances, you'd be right." She put one hand carefully on the hilt of the sword. "But after that run-in you guys had with Barron...and knowing what I know about Doppelgaenger...I've been spending every spare minute I have to make sure Tire Iron and Can Opener are a bit more than they seem." She raised an eyebrow. "They've both got magically created nanoedges. I don't care *how* tough Barron's armor is, or how fast Doppelgaenger can heal. I don't think either of them can take being sliced to ribbons by something with an edge only one nanometer wide." She patted the hilt. "The sheathes are special containment fields for them, so I can keep from slicing up everything in sight until I'm ready. The only fly in the oatmeal is that once they're drawn, the spell only lasts about twenty minutes, give or take."

"Best make it count then, comrade." He shrugged, glancing at Sera. "This is why I like guns, explosives, and Celestial fire: simple, to the point, and effective."

Sera raised an eyebrow. "There is nothing much simpler than a blade that can cut the wind itself, my love."

"Tell that to the wielder," he said, nodding to Vickie. "I'm guessin' our little mage has trainin' to use those bits. Only ever had trainin' with knives, myself, an' it's not the easiest thing to

master. Even with a sword made outta fire an' our...gifts to
help, it's a helluva thing to learn to use right. Still, I'm happy
she's bringin' her blades along. Every trick we can get, y'know?"

"Thanks. Yeah, training since I was six. I'm actually counting on the idea they'll look at me and laugh. I hope they're still
laughing when their heads hit the floor." Her flat tone made that
not so much a threat as a promise. John felt a twinge deep inside
of himself. *Her words sound awfully familiar, don't they, Murdock?*
He reached out carefully, brushing her mind with his telepathy.

He found one thought that was the focus of everything. Assuming no one else had beaten her to it, Vickie was going to find Doppelgaenger and kill her. But the reason was not what John would
have expected—revenge. Oh, revenge was *part* of it, certainly. But
the main reason? It was clear as if it had been written for him.
*Even if the Thulians go down, if Doppelgaenger escapes, no one in
ECHO will ever be safe.*

She'd had a personal lesson in that. Her parents had left her
uncle alive. And years later, he had come back to kidnap, torture,
and kill her. Doppelgaenger had been Bela Nagy's ally and pupil.
There was every reason to believe she had taken that lesson in
along with everything else.

John was going to ask her why she hadn't supported Bella
during the little "meeting" with the Commissar. Now he knew.
She had other priorities, the all-consuming kind. And she was
psyching herself up to do what needed to be done. He had seen
it before, of course. His men, before a mission, or elite athletes
before a big game. Total focus. Still...he was concerned. *Getting
that invested takes a lot out of a person. Especially if that's the
only thing they expect to get done.*

As if she had read his mind, Vickie looked straight into his
eyes. "Johnny, the bottom line here is that if *we* don't win here,
Zach Marlowe notwithstanding, it's The End. Not just humanity,
not just the planet, it will go beyond this planet. Ask Sera. *She*
saw it. So we have to forget about ourselves, and concentrate on
ending this now."

"I know what's on the line here, Vic. Trust me on that, if
nothin' else." He stretched his arms over his head, trying to
stay casual. *She's on the ragged edge.* "I just don't buy the 'forget
about ourselves' bit. Don't get me wrong, if it comes to buyin'
the farm so that the world can keep on spinnin', I'm all in. But

I'd also like to win *and* live in that world. So, I figure we aim high." He leaned forward, matching her stare. "So take care of yourself when we get on site. Otherwise, I'll sic Sera, Bella, an' the Bull on ya. In no particular order, mind."

She shrugged. "It is what it is," she said. "I'll be up in the captain's cabin if you need me." Then she turned and went back the way she had come.

She has a powerful will, my love. One of the most powerful I have ever seen in a mortal. She will not be moved. He turned to see Sera gazing at him solemnly. *She is even more stubborn than you, and I did not think that possible.*

To do what she does, she's gotta have a strong will, an' be stubborn as all hell. He looked after the way Vickie had gone, frowning. *I just hope it doesn't get her killed.*

This wasn't her first submarine—if it could be called that, considering all of the bells and whistles added to make it fit for the coming battle—but Mel felt the familiar twinge of panic rise as she eyed the metal baguette floating in the water. Experience and training chased it away as quickly as it came, and she let out a long controlled breath.

"How long are we gonna be in there?" Penny reached for Mel's hand. Her thin fingers trembled and she swallowed hard. "All the way underwater, I mean?"

Mel glanced down at her charge. After all that the girl had been through, she hadn't considered that claustrophobia would be a problem. She adjusted her grip to hold Penny's sweaty hand in her comparatively cool palm and squeezed. "Not all that long. Just think of it like an inside room where they don't get windows. If you close your eyes, you can imagine it just how big or how small you want."

"It ain't that," Penny corrected, clutching Mel's hand with both of hers. "I cain't swim."

"You can't . . . oh. Oh," Mel realized, glancing at the blue-green water surrounding them. "And you're worried about something happening to the sub? 'Cause I ain't gonna let you fall in when we're getting on or off. And even if you did," she added, patting the girl's shoulder, "I'd haul you out so fast you wouldn't have time to get your undershirt wet."

Penny's eyes only widened, her pupils so big they drowned out the dark brown irises. "You'd be that fast?"

"Yup. Me and Riley and the rest of our squad, we had to go through all kinds of training for rescue operations. Land, air, water. Burning buildings, underwater cars, even livestock stampedes." She winked. "Sweetie, I will swim for both of us. Promise."

Her charge's lip wrinkled and her grip tightened. "But that's if I fall in. A submarine's gotta go underwater and stay underwater, right? And if they go deep enough, something could make it pop, and the water could come in, and ..." Penny took in more rapid breaths, squeezing Mel's hand hard enough to make her wince.

Mel pulled the girl to the side and used her free hand to grip her chin. She locked her eyes with Penny's and dropped her voice to a low, warm whisper. "*Cherie*, you and I will be in a submarine guided by two, huge, water gods and filled with ECHO folks who got all sorts of powers to keep everybody safe. One of my former commanding officers is here, and you know what he can do?" Penny's head wiggled from left to right, yet she didn't break eye contact. "Big ol' Bulwark makes these big ol' bubbles around anything he wants to keep safe, and he does it as easy as you talk to folks on the other side. If anything happens on that sub, he's gonna bubble it up and nobody'll get a drop of water on 'em."

She let go of Penny, who lessened her hold on her fingers, and glanced back at the others waiting to board the sub. Others had to manage their own fears, but few would fault a preteen for a moment of crisis before beginning an operation of this magnitude. The girl let out a shaky breath and bobbed her head. "You think there's somebody else who don't know how to swim? So it ain't just me?"

"It ain't just you," Mel reassured her.

The idea that she might not be alone in her fear seemed to calm the girl. She released Mel's cramped fingers and wiped her palms on her pint-sized version of ECHO nanoweave. "Will it be a long trip? Once we start going, I mean?"

The details of the briefing were fresh in her mind, coordinates and estimates memorized with little effort. "After we get settled, we can count on about four hours of travel time."

"Four?"

"Yup. Plenty of time for a nap, or some ice cream if you're not feeling like a rest. On these longer rides out, the best thing to do is let your brain relax and not think about a whole bunch of anything." Their group started to move forward to board the sub. Atlas stood sentry not more than twenty feet away, with a huge piece of what must have been the fabric used for big sails wrapped decorously around his hips in a sort of loincloth arrangement. From her viewpoint, the draping left little to the imagination, and she hoped that for Penny's sake, the mechanisms holding up said loincloth would not fail.

For herself, she wouldn't mind a slight wardrobe malfunction. Any morale boost would be a welcome one.

"He's awful big." Penny craned her neck to take in the sight of Atlas next to them. "Like some kind of jolly blue giant."

"More water, less veggies," Mel agreed. They shuffled on with the group, the girl ahead of her in the line to climb down the ladder into the main compartment. One foot in front of the other, with the promise of ice cream somewhere before the battle.

Vickie settled herself in with her laptop. "Eight? How are you coming on the story compilation?"

"*Splendidly, Vickie. In fact, done, except for what is about to occur.*"

"Well, if I'm not around to edit it afterwards, it probably won't matter if it's been edited or not." The captain had graciously given her the use of his cabin—why, she wasn't sure. It wasn't as if anything he did or did not do would matter to this sardine can right now, and he could just relax back here and watch videos if he wanted. "Overwatch: Open Atlas. Hey, big guy, we ready to pull out?"

"*The hatch just closed, and I'm taking charge now. You might hear my hands on the hull, but after that, I doubt you'll even know you're moving. 'Te is about to move out as well.*"

Vickie hadn't been sure what to expect, but Atlas must have been very gentle as his big hands closed around the hull and he tucked them under his arm. Just some slight scrapes and a little jolt.

Now came the worst part of the trip. Trying to find something to occupy her for four hours.

Might as well go over the document. Reading it couldn't possibly hurt worse than living through it had. *And if I do nothing, I'm just going to relive it anyway.*

❖　　❖　　❖

Georgi stood at the edge of what amounted to the prow for one of the "vessels" that the main assault forces were using. Water had been lapping over the edge since they began their journey, and enough of it had collected on the deck to ensure that everyone's boots were soaked, if they didn't have the benefit of waterproofing. Truth be told, Georgi didn't mind; he was used to his feet being cold from snow, soaked in water, and worse. His healing factor took care of most of his ills; for what it could not insulate him from, his Russian constitution guarded against, or so he liked to think. *Better than Stalingrad... but then again, almost anything is.*

He turned from the ocean to survey the transport float. It was crowded with strapped-down vehicles, strapped-down equipment and, most of all, people. Thousands of soldiers, hundreds of meta-humans, checking gear, going over operations orders, joking and chatting, or sleeping, but all tethered to the flat "float" that would be their transportation to the Thulian ship. It was a scene he was familiar with: the calm chaos before a battle, where everyone did their best to seem unconcerned. It comforted Georgi to see how some things never changed. The weapons, while more efficient than ever, were essentially the same. The men that wielded them were similar; the training was better, and they knew more about how things worked, the theories behind war, than at any other time in history. But, at the core, a soldier had a singular purpose: to take the fight to the enemy.

Georgi's life, while not simple by any measure, suited him perfectly. A soldier in the Red Army during the Great Patriotic War, captured by the Nazis, and then experimented on and locked away in a frozen state in a forgotten bunker until the early nineties, he had stayed static while the world moved on without him. Still, he had adapted, and fell back to the one thing that gave him purpose: service. Communism had given way to capitalism, the Second World War to the Cold War and now to the war against the Thulians. The circumstances did not concern him, so much as how he could best help his fellow man. Here, about to fight a vastly superior enemy with insurmountable odds stacked against him... he felt at home. No matter what happened, he knew that he was doing what he had always been meant to do.

He heard Pavel clomping up to him before he saw him. He crossed his arms in front of his chest, turning back to the ocean. "Old Bear."

"Comrade." Bear was clearly displeased by something. "Is nowhere to warm my food, Georgi. Am not being allowed to make fire, and is no microwave." He held up a single can of ravioli, grimacing at it. "Is inhuman, *nyet*?"

"It is inhuman to call that food, Old Bear." He sighed, finally facing the cyborg. "Today is going to be a good day, I think."

Bear cocked his head to the side, regarding his friend. "You are an odd man, Georgi. And a lousy karaoke singer. But, *da*, I think you are right." He took in a lungful—whatever qualified as lungs for Pavel, at least—of ocean air, exhaling contentedly. "I believe the Commissar is about to address the assembled troops. We should be in attendance."

The surface they were standing on lurched a little, more sea-water sloshed over the leading edge, and the "breeze" created by the fact they were moving increased to a "wind." Georgi looked back at where the shore lay, but it was already out of sight below the horizon. He had been dubious about being towed by a giant woman, but it appeared she could make substantial speed. *Even with all we know, there are still wonders out there... "angels," ocean goddesses, and more. What will we find yet, when this war is over?*

Even as he thought that, a meta whom Georgi recognized as Jamaican Blaze, without saying anything, took Pavel's open can from him, held it in her hands for a moment and her hands ignited briefly. She put the now warm can back in Pavel's metal hands, and she continued moving to the section of the float where Red Saviour was standing. *"She says 'you are welcome, Sovietski Medved,'"* the voice of Eight said over the CCCP channel.

"Blin, what a woman," Bear said under his breath, already readying a fork. "Am wondering if is violation of protocol to date ECHO girls."

Georgi ignored him, focusing his attention on the crowd. The rest of the CCCP was already there; Thea, small and pale, leaning up against a crate of ammunition. Soviette towered over many of the men, her hand resting on Chug's craggy head; he was busy stuffing a piece of a broken pallet in his mouth, chewing intently. Proletariat was there; three of his "copies" were all work-ing on a set of Supernaut armor, occasionally glancing up at the makeshift stage. For ECHO, Jamaican Blaze, Leader of the Pack, Corbie, a number of ECHO Euro, ECHO South America, ECHO Africa, ECHO Pacific, and ECHO PanAsia people Georgi did not recognize were already assembled. Generally, each nation's military forces congregated around their representative metahumans; the Russians were interspersed with the CCCP, the NATO forces with the Americans and the European ECHO metas, and so on. *Like with like. Even gathered here together, fighting for the same thing, we have our divisions.*

Before Georgi could muse about human tribal eccentricities, the Commissar took to the makeshift stage—basically a large crate that Chug hadn't eaten yet. She wasn't smoking, he noticed, though he had no doubt that there was a small hill of cigarette butts somewhere close by, possibly hidden by the crate. The Commissar wore the standard CCCP uniform, with a load-bearing vest strapped over it; rifle magazines, grenades, and pouches weighted it down, but if the Commissar noticed, she didn't seem to show it. Her long black hair was pulled back in a tight bun at the back of her head; unlike many of the assembled troops, she had forgone any camouflage face paint. She took a moment before speaking, surveying the crowd.

"I am not being a great orator." She paused, putting her fists on her hips. "I have never been a diplomat, and have no stomach for politics or bureaucrats. I am a soldier, like all of you." From the echoing of his Overwatch implant, Georgi knew that Eight was rebroadcasting this speech on every comm set in the expeditionary force. "We come from different countries, different cultures, different militaries. But none of that is mattering now. All that matters is that we are here to do what soldiers are meant to do—*fight*, and kill the enemy." The Commissar raised an arm, pointing away from the coastline, in the direction they were being towed. "The *svinya* are there. They have killed too many of our people, and will kill the rest if we do not stop them, here and now. All of us have lost someone, maybe everyone, that has ever mattered to us. If we are not stopping them here, it will be like none of us ever existed." She shook her head, then looked back to the troops. "All of you are already dead. You should make peace with this … and *fight like dead men*. It does not matter if a single one of us leaves this place, so long as we *win*. Fight like the dead, be ferocious in the face of the enemy, and bleed them dry. Fight! And maybe, the world we are fighting for will survive. We land in thirty minutes. Make yourself ready, *tovarischii*."

Pavel immediately started clapping his metal hands together, producing a clattering racket. The rest of the troops had already started moving, every single person hustling to make final preparations. Natalya had left the stage, undoubtedly to finish checking to see that there were no changes to the plan. Finally, Pavel stopped clapping. "Was good speech. Rousing, *nyet?*"

"It was direct, like our Commissar. She did not lie, or make naive proclamations. Time will tell if she was right."

Pavel's brow furrowed. *"Shto?"*

"Whether we're all already dead men." He punched Pavel in the shoulder. "Come. Let us gather the others. There will be *fascista* to kill soon."

The too calm quiet of the corridors had a familiar air as Mel led Penny forward with the rest of the team assigned to the infil party. Like the others, Penny had listened to the strong words with a sober expression. At the conclusion of the speech, she had reached up and patted Mel's hand, then checked over her small pack of gear that both Mel and Ramona had insisted she take with her. Now, the little hand gripped Mel's fingers tightly on their way to the conning tower. Others swarmed past them with faces careful masks of resolve or concealed terror.

The more experienced ones knew enough to allow a little bit of fear to accompany them to the hatch. Fear would keep them alert and agile, and Mel noted more shadows of concern as their comrades filed past. Just ahead of them, Bull's familiar bulk overshadowed Bella's lithe blue form. Victrix was probably ahead of them. Penny tilted her head back to see Bull disappear through the hatch and made a small noise in her throat.

"Last one," Mel murmured to her charge. "We gotta keep it quiet and together once we hit that hatch. Don't think, just follow me up and through. Got it?"

Penny bit her lip and nodded. Someone behind them made a hole in the flow and they slipped in the line, heading up the ladder and through the hatch. Overcast skies and a rush of saltwater spray surrounded the group standing on the hull. Mel squinted at a figure standing on an otherwise invisible platform, recognizing the ECHO nanoweave but not the person wearing it. The lithe figure with shining black hair pulled into a sleek bun pointed two fingers at her and then motioned to the opening.

That's our cue. Mel tugged at Penny's arm gently, less to make her move and more to alert her to what needed to be done next. Her charge set her jaw and reached for the meta's outstretched hand. Natalya swung her up and through the door hanging in the air, then reached for Mel next. This woman's hand was cool against her palm, but Mel felt the slight tremble as she pulled her up and through the door.

Fear was a necessity. Mel knew it more than most. Fear would help them see it through.

CHAPTER THIRTY-TWO

Too Far Gone

MERCEDES LACKEY, DENNIS LEE,
CODY MARTIN AND VERONICA GIGUERE

*I was, at this moment, busier than I had ever been since
I became self-aware. But then, so was everyone else. Not
too busy to keep my main focus on my friends, though.
I was afraid for them. Very afraid.*

The hand that hauled Penny up through the hatch belonged to
an honest-to-God ninja, although Penny didn't think that nin-
jas were supposed to have more guns than they had hands. The
woman—Penny was sure the ninja was a woman, she had hips
and small breasts—made sure she was steady before motioning
her to stand next to a man wearing a strange uniform. Both of
them were short, and she squinted at the patches on the man's
jacket. The red and white swastika startled her, and she glanced
back at Miz Mel with a frown.

Mel mouthed the word "okay" and motioned her ahead. Penny
acknowledged her with a nod, but she gave the Nazi man a wide
berth as she moved forward. While they waited for the others
on the team to move into place, she studied the floor and walls.
Where the submarine had been dark and smooth, this new ship
had walls full of little holes and cracks, with long thick strands
of gray-white connecting parts of the walls to the floors and
ceiling. It reminded her of cobwebs or enormous stringy pieces
of pizza cheese. Penny bent her knees and pushed gently against
the floor. It felt spongy under the special ECHO boots that the
adults had made her wear with her new uniform.

Someone else came to stand behind her, and she scooted forward to give them room without going too far into the room. The entire space had a damp smell to it, a combination of wet dog and moldy oranges that made her nose wrinkle. Penny covered her mouth with one hand and swallowed. She had smelled worse, but not by much.

"Smells like a monkey cage, huh?" Mel stood behind her, her voice low. She rested a hand on Penny's shoulder. "It's a whole different kind of circus, though."

"No popcorn?" Penny shifted to look past Mel as the heavily armed ninja helped more people into the squishy, smelly room. Miz Vickie squeezed through the small group, and the Nazi man followed her.

The little man glared at Penny, then at Miz Vickie. "So I guess this means we're going for broke. Seriously, Victrix? You'd bring a kid on this death trap?"

Penny scowled at the man, who she figured wasn't a real Nazi since Miz Vickie hadn't punched or stabbed him. He didn't talk so much as growl the words, which made Penny like him even less. She folded her arms across her chest and narrowed her eyes at him.

"Do you really think I'd have brought her if there was a choice? Give me a break, Jack, I'm not a sociopath. She's got skills we have no substitute for." Vix put an arm around Penny's shoulders. "Besides, she's not going anywhere. She's going to stay right here—"

The long strands between the ceiling and the walls shivered, giving off a series of tiny vibrations. Penny saw the spongy wall closest to her pull in, then push out like it was breathing. Thick orange goop leaked from the holes while tiny hairs wiggled out and reached toward them.

The tall man and the woman with the wings both erupted into flame, instantly dropping into crouches. "Ship's reactin' to us, an' not in a good way," the man said.

Miz Bella said something that Mama would have beat Penny for saying. She stripped off a glove and put her hand fearlessly on the oozing wall, wincing a little when she did so. "Immune reaction. Dammit, Jack, you might have warned us this thing was alive! Sera, JM, turn off the fire, you're making it worse!"

Both of them immediately extinguished themselves; the winged lady cocked her head to the side, as if hearing something distant.

"It knows that we are foreign, like a virus. It has been ordered to kill anything foreign that comes in here."

"This is new," said the little man. "Most of this place isn't organic like this, at least not lining the corridors we've been down and mapping. We should retreat, get back to the high-tech zones."

"No time," the giant man said. "Everyone on me, now!"

As they scurried to his side, Penny found herself wondering about this giant who was never far from Miz Bella's side. He was huge, his voice was almost as gravelly as the little man's, but there was something about him she found immensely comforting. She could feel it. There was a gentle quality to him, and a strength, a good strength, like a great big shield she could hide behind...

Penny yelped as a shimmering ball of light erupted around all of them, lifting them off the ground. They struggled to keep their balance, some even succeeded, but Penny felt her feet fly out from under her on this newly curved and slippery floor. She landed squarely on her behind, wincing at the pain, but stopped in horror as she watched the world close around them outside the protective bubble. The hairs on the wall were growing. They were so fast! And they were wrapping themselves around the shield, and then they started to press in...

"Ideas would be good right now..." the giant grunted. He sounded like he was in pain.

Penny was beginning to panic, but Miz Bella seemed oddly calm, even though the palm of her hand was now discolored with a blotchy purple. She held onto the giant and closed her eyes. "Keep that shield going, Bull. I think I might have this...it's a matter of figuring out its innards." She took a long breath, a sort of testing breath, as if she was...a dog, sniffing for something. "Let's see if this works. Sera, I may need a boost."

"Certainly." The winged lady wrapped her wings around all of them. "One for you as well, Bulwark." The tall man next to her took the winged lady's hand into his own, and then closed his eyes.

Penny felt herself shudder with relief as one of the wings drew her closer in. A moment before, she had almost been screaming in terror, but now—all she felt was warmth and light and love, all from a simple touch from the winged lady. But she wasn't a lady. She was an angel. This is what angels do, Penny remembered. How many times had her brother, Pike, told her about angels? You had to believe in them, he had said, or they would never come for you. She thought they were stupid baby stories, that she had outgrown them, but to feel it...

It was enough to make her believe.

She noticed she wasn't the only one. Mistuh Bull didn't look like he was in pain anymore. He stood tall, proud, his arms held wide as he held the gross hair back, and his shield seemed much brighter. It had been folding in places before, now it stood firm.

The ninja lady was holding herself closely, as if she was afraid the feathers would touch her. Penny wondered why. The angel leaned in close over the ninja lady's shoulder before she could move away, and whispered something. Penny shouldn't have been able to make it out, but the new ears that Miz Vickie had put in caught it. *"Forgiveness is always possible."* The ninja lady looked away, and didn't answer her.

Miz Vickie's eyes were very big, and very bright, as if she was about to cry. The angel put a hand on her shoulder, and smiled faintly. Miz Vickie nodded.

The short man just grunted and flicked a few feathers from his face. He looked annoyed.

"Got it," Miz Bella breathed. The hairs slowly relaxed, and just as slowly pulled themselves back into the wall. The orange goop, now several inches deep on the floor, drained away. The walls drew back and stopped moving. Penny held back a sob of relief.

"I found the off switch," Miz Bella added, and then frowned. "This ship is... really strange, guys. This isn't the only part that's organic, and the organic part is *old*. And failing, I think."

"A discussion for another time, I would think," Mistuh Bull said, lowering the bottom half of his shield so that everyone was standing on the floor before he dropped it completely. "We might want to follow Jack's suggestion and move right along. This area isn't safe."

"No," Miz Bella disagreed. "That's not the plan. I am not taking Penny further into this monstrosity..."

"Plans change, darlin'," the short man said. "We've been mapping out the surrounding area. Got a safe point just around the next bend. Safer than here, anyway. You can do your mojo there."

"No plan survives first contact with the enemy," said Miz Vickie, sounding calm and practical. "I say we get out of this... homicidal cloaca. Your 'off' switch might not stay off."

Reluctantly, Miz Bella nodded, although Penny could not imagine *why* she'd want to stay *here*. They all followed the little man and his ninja friend out of the weird, round metal plate that opened up like that thing on the front of a camera and let them out into a much more "normal" corridor. The angel and her tall man lingered behind for a moment. The angel rested her hand on the wall as Miz Bella had. Then the two of them looked into each other's eyes. The tall man nodded, and they both followed.

The little man led the way to another round door, and opened it somehow. To Penny's relief it was just a room. Metal walls, floor and ceiling. Empty.

The little man turned towards Miz Vickie once they were all safely inside and the door had swished shut. "So, Vix, you need to hook up your gear with mine for what we've mapped? It's pretty incomplete. This place is bigger than Manhattan..."

"That's what Penny's here for," Miz Vickie replied, resting a hand lightly on Penny's shoulder. "No offense to you, Jack, but the guides she can bring us have been here for over half a century. I doubt there's an inch of this ship they don't know about. They can go places you've been shut out of, and most importantly, they know where the Thulians are. They can keep us from running into anyone."

"Fine by me, girl," the little man shrugged. "But for those of us without our own personal spook guides, I think we'll need to scope out a bit more. There's still a few blind spots, and the last thing we need is anyone creeping up on us here. And just between you and me, this boat isn't big on the nooks and crannies. You want to find someone, it won't take much."

Miz Vickie's eyes narrowed, and she raised an eyebrow at the little man, then quietly made the "peace sign" with her right hand. He nodded. She raised both eyebrows and nodded back. "All right," she replied openly. "You two go, but I want you back here the moment you get wind of anything coming towards us. Meanwhile, Penny, it's time to get Mister Stone and his friends."

The Nazi man and the ninja lady left, taking care to close up the room without a sound. Penny took in a deep breath, but not with apprehension. She was going to feel a *lot* safer with Mistuh Stone here. An angel was... pretty wonderful. But Mistuh Stone was like the best teacher and the best big brother and the best grampa all rolled into one.

Calling Mistuh Stone was easier than breathing. She just *wanted* him there, and there he was. He looked a lot like his grandson, "Tomb" Stone, who Penny had met several times back in Atlanta. The only real difference was that Jacob Stone had white hair, which looked odd with his unwrinkled face. She'd asked him why...he laughed and said it reminded him he was supposed to be an "elder."

Well, honeychild, looks like we're ready, he said in her head. *Remember what I told you?*

She nodded.

All right then. Slow and easy. These are my old friends, not someone you need to lasso and shove into a ghost trap and send them on their way.

Now feeling more confident than she had since they'd left Atlanta, she did as Mistuh Stone had taught her, and "sent out the call."

And, after a few minutes, they came.

The first ghost to arrive was a young man in a leather jacket with embroidered patches on it, one of them a flag with a kangaroo. He was blond, square-jawed, and surprisingly short. *Jacob! Cor, mate, yer a sight fer sore eyes! 'Oo's the little sheila?*

My student, Brumby. Good to see you, my brother! They clapped each other on the shoulders in the weird way men seemed to do instead of hugging. *You will be guiding this gentleman and lady to their goal.*

That'd be the big brain, roight. Easy-peasy mate. The man turned and bent down to put his ghostly face even with Penny's. *Oi'm Brumby, missy. Yew can tell yer witchy friend there t'do whatever she needs to so—*

"Huh. You don't see that every day." The tall man—JM, Miz Bella had called him?—motioned to Sera. "An' that's further proof that I need to get a good leather jacket. Timeless."

As the angel nodded, jaws visibly dropped on the faces of most of the group. "You can *see* them?" said Bella, Vickie, and Miz Mel, at the same time that Brumby said *'E can see me? Crikey!*

"I thought that's why we brought the kid along, so y'all—oh," the tall man said.

"We needed her to call the ghosts in the first place. I was gonna light your guide up so you could follow him, then light the rest up if we needed to," said Vickie. "If everything goes to plan, they'll act as scouts for you and perimeter guards for us. If everything goes to hell and we need to take something else out, I can light more of 'em up. Meanwhile Penny can talk to 'em, and she can tell us what they say." She shrugged. "If you can see 'em, that's one less thing I need to do."

Penny shut her own open mouth. It made sense of course. An angel *should* be able to see ghosts. But why could that man?

"Fine by us," the man said, shrugging and looking at the winged woman. She smiled. "I am happy to meet you, Brumby. I hope that this will discharge your obligations and you may continue your interrupted journey."

The ghost scratched his head. *That's the plan, ma'am. We been waitin' a long time fer this.*

Penny narrowed her eyes and realized that some of the same light—the sort of thing that filled Mistuh Stone and to a lesser extent, Brumby, filled both JM and the angel. So they were connected in some way she didn't quite understand, but felt was good.

That's a fine-lookin' sheila ye got there, mate, Brumby said to JM with a wink. *Hope ye figgered that out, or I might haveta make a play for 'er myself.*

"Oh, she's spoken for, ol' fella. Don't you worry 'bout that."

The angel raised an eyebrow and coughed. "I believe *I* was the one that claimed *you,* my love. But we should go."

"Fair enough, darlin'. I figure we have Casper lead on, an' we'll get this done. I'm already hungry again, an' there's a mess of Thulians in the way of us gettin' some steak."

"Well don't just stand there," Bella said, finally recovering. *"Go!"*

Sorry you'll haveta take the long way round, mates, Brumby said apologetically. *Bein' as ye can't walk through walls. Can ye?*

They were in a hallway not too far from where the enigmatic Jack had brought them into the World Ship. The floors and ceiling were almost entirely comprised of the glistening metal that the Thulians used for their ships and armor. In the most odd places, however, were patches of . . . well, what looked like *flesh.* Leathery skin with bristling hairs, what appeared to be muscle fibers exposed to the air, even networks of something like intestines in some places, pulsating with a repulsive energy. All of it felt *wrong* to John. Alien hands had made this place, and it assaulted his heightened senses at every turn. Back where the infiltrators had first encountered the organic components of the World Ship, Sera had noticed something... *beneath*. Faint, but at the same time, tortured. Now, after following Brumby, the impression had only grown stronger. Whatever they were going toward, the reading was only becoming more distinct.

"Not s'far as we know, comrade. Figure it's not the right time to go experimentin'," John said.

Well, we got two ways we can go. The big brain's across the half sphere, at the "hinge," I guess we can call it. We can go around, in the corridors, or across, in the open. Buildings, jungle... it's where most of the Space Nazis live an' work an' all.

"Corridors. It'll take longer, but we gotta keep the element of surprise. If we let slip that we're here an' on task, it's goin' to mean a lotta hurt for the rest of our people." He looked to Sera for her confirmation.

"I prefer stealth over speed," she agreed, but her wings flipped a little in that way that meant she was feeling claustrophobic.

John nodded. *Let's get this done, darlin'. Keep your eyes out, though. There's somethin' different goin' on here, like y'pointed out before.*

Bella is right. This entire ship is alive... and very, very old.

They continued moving through the ship, Brumby in the lead. Their route was circuitous, going through more of those alien hallways, cutting through maintenance tunnels and service corridors, and once a—thankfully—deserted mess hall. With Brumby's guidance, they were able to move much faster than if John had been infiltrating the ship on his own. Sera wasn't experienced in this sort of thing, but she was an amazingly quick study; their telempathic link meant that they didn't even have to rely on the Overwatch subvocal mics. As fast as thought, John could tell her when to hold fast, how to walk, where to look. The ghost's knowledge of the ship also enabled them to bypass several patrols or lone wandering Thulians; this place was *much* more active than Ultima Thule had been. Even so, there had been two instances where John and Sera's connection to the Futures via their battle-sense had saved them at the last moment from running into Thulians that Brumby hadn't expected.

Sorry 'bout that. Activity has been a touch wonky, as of late. Let's leg it.

One room that they passed by caught John's attention. It

looked like it was the Thulian equivalent to a computer room; tall machines lined the wall, humming quietly as their screens glowed in that awful yellow-orange light that all of the Thulian electronics gave off. Strangely, except for that, the burnt-orange-cinnamon smell of the Thulians themselves, and the definitely-not-human creatures moving around the room, it could have been an identical data-processing center anywhere on earth. The Thulians were wearing, not uniforms, but a variety of clothing; a couple of them had what looked like thermoses they were drinking from. Three were just standing around chatting in low voices. It was all normal. Creepy, and *disturbingly* normal.

They're just like a couple of guys on break, like you'd see on any normal job site, darlin'. John shook his head in disbelief, wondering at the absurdity of it. *It makes sense, but it still doesn't change how goddamned unnervin' it is.*

The banality of evil, Sera reminded him quietly. *That is what makes evil so pernicious—and so dangerous. It is when it appears normal that it is at its worst.*

He nodded as they continued down the hallway, following Brumby. *I just wonder if those bastards have any clue what they're a part of, or if they're just cogs in a larger machine. Like I said before, things are goin' to be really interestin' when this war is over, if we win. What to do with all the leftover Thulians, for starters.* He sighed. *Stuff to worry 'bout later. Let's keep movin'.*

What seemed like miles later, Brumby stopped them again. *Roight. We got no choice 'ere, mates. We gotta go through this room. Yew gotta walk loike yew belong 'ere, an' yew gotta walk quiet at th' same time. Unnerstan'? Foller roight behind me, don' look around an' don't stop.*

Why? Sera asked. *What is in this room?*

Itsa storage area, Brumby said.

Are we expectin' company in there? John looked from Sera to the apparition.

Only if yew wake it up, said Brumby, and nodded towards the door at the end of the dead-end hallway they'd been following. Being a ghost, obviously he couldn't open it. *Itsa a janitor storage room.*

*So, a storage room for janitor supplies? Well, that's not all that bad—*John palmed the plate that opened the door, before Brumby spoke, and the door opened just as the spirit corrected him.

*Not supplies, mate—*janitors.

The room revealed was at least fifty feet long and fifty feet wide, with a narrow clear space down the middle of it, leading to another door. The rest of the room was filled with what could have been industrial shelves, except what was lying on the shelves were Thulians, dressed in coveralls, eyes closed. There were little blinking modules under their heads where pillows would have been. They were stacked eight high. There was zero evidence of any sort of comfort here.

Let's . . . get through this room. Now.

QUIET! Brumby urged. *Noise wakes 'em up! Stuff what don't sound right wakes 'em up!*

Quiet I can do, Casper. Darlin', shall we? John nudged Sera through their connection; dropping into their battle-sense could only help avoid anything silly, like tripping over a loose grate or bumping into any of the racks.

They moved quietly and surely down the narrow corridor between the two sets of racks lining it. As Brumby had cautioned, they did *not* try to move stealthily. But when they finally reached the door on the end, and were on the other side of it, John heaved a sigh of relief.

Brumby led them down the rest of the corridor to where it ended in a T intersection. *Yer way's right, mate,* he said. *There's a big empty room what looks loik it useta have stuff in't but got stripped a long time ago, then a door, an' that's the brain room. I'm headin' back to keep an eye on yer mates. Thet alrioght with yew?*

We'll take it from here, Casper. Thanks for your help. It's been real.

Sera smiled at the ghost. *Well done, thou good and faithful one,* she said. *Your long watch is nearly done.*

Brumby snapped off a crisp salute . . . and then walked through a wall.

Sera looked after him, as if she could see him still. "It is a wonder he did not go mad," she said aloud. "It is a wonder they did not all go mad. Most spirits who linger begin to lose themselves after a year, or even less. They cannot recall their names. Their forms fade and they go mad. The wills of this Lost Squadron must be . . . phenomenal, to have waited here for half a century for us to bring the battle to the enemy."

"They had a mission, darlin'. Guys like that . . . they don't give up. An' they also had each other." John unslung his rifle, pulling back on the charging handle to double-check that there was a round chambered. "Time to finish this. We're on the clock."

With the infiltration teams in place and heading to their destinations, it was up to the assembled militaries of Earth to provide a world-class distraction. The Thulians undoubtedly had some sort of visual detection equipment, even if radar hadn't spotted the stealth barges which were close enough now that trying to conceal the attack any further was pointless. So, they went big—an opening fusillade the likes of which had probably never been seen before, all directed at the energy shield. Even with all of the massed firepower, they wouldn't be able to penetrate the shield, of course; their intel said as much. But their intel also said that the Thulians liked a good show, and thought themselves superior. So, the diversion had a second purpose: let the Thulians think that they were completely safe behind their shield. *They don't learn very quickly; hubris will be the undoing of these fascista. That, and a hell of a lot of bullets.*

If this had been any other battlefield, Untermensch would have surveyed the area with grim satisfaction. ECHO had dragged out every single bit of their science-magic that was even approaching "operational status" for this fight. Decommissioned pieces of materiel were made to work, old surpluses were raided, and even some museum exhibits had been brought back to life on the chance they might be needed. He sincerely hoped that nothing would explode in their faces. *So many soldiers, so many different nations and command structures . . . recipe for disaster, even in best of circumstances.* Then again, if Earth did not win here . . . they would all certainly lose everything. Now was not the time to hold anything back.

There were several ECHO generators set up to provide all of their high technology with wireless power. Well armored, and situated at the rear of the craft, they were expected to be early targets for the Thulians. Until then, they powered some of Tesla's wonders. The most fantastic—and loudest—were the Tesla death ray cannons; the first and only prototype had been destroyed in the battle for the North American Thulian HQ, but with the direct help of some of the Metisian scientists, it appeared that they had fashioned more. There were also the automated turrets with their special, anti-trooper payloads; they were silent, for the moment, but Unter suspected that they wouldn't be for much longer. Many of the troops had been issued rocket launchers that were outfitted with those same warheads; hopefully, the combination of all of that firepower and the effect of the ECHO generators would be enough to protect them from the Thulians, at least for a few minutes.

Unter winced as another salvo of artillery shells from the distant battleships were fired at the World Ship's energy shield. He adjusted his earmuffs as he looked over the craft. Tanks, artillery, mortar teams, and armored personnel carriers all fired again and again. Above, jets and bombers—sent in endless cycles from aircraft carriers miles and miles away—dropped their payloads at specific points on the shield. Every few seconds a barrage from shipborne guns would slam into the shields; the barrages were punctuated with several rounds from the Americans' newest rail cannons.

The soldiers that weren't assigned to man artillery pieces or the various collection of armor were all on deck or in the APCs, ready to storm the ship. And every metahuman that had any sort of distance weapon at all deployed it now against that shield. Most of them were doing so from the "safety" of the floating platforms; it probably wasn't a good idea to be in the air right now, with so much ordnance flying through it. The Commissar was the only ranged meta that Unter could see who was not firing. Instead, she watched with dark determination as the explosions, lightning death rays, and metahuman powers crashed into the shield. Occasionally, she would speak, presumably ordering an adjustment to an artillery piece or to the approach of one of the jets. With her Overwatch suite, she had the entire battlefield mapped and projected onto her HUD, with each of the units color-coded and tied directly into her comms. Eight-Ball was undoubtedly much more efficient at managing all this information than Victrix was, and yet...Untermensch wished he could hear Victrix's voice, and not that of the AI.

Thinking computers, science wonders from pulp magazines, and space fascista, *and what I am thinking about is the comfort and humanity of a little witch's voice. I am growing soft.*

Bear plodded up to him, grinning and cradling his PPSh in his arms like a child.

"I am seeing that you are not joining the others in the fusillade, Old Bear," Unter said, casting a glance to the cyborg.

"*Nyet*, Georgi. Little *papasha* here doesn't have the range, and I am to be saving energy for running dog Thulians, not shimmering bubble." He shook his head, still smiling. "Cannot wait to get in there, *tovarisch*."

"Just do not step off of boat. You would sink like a rock, and I am not willing to jump after you. Will hold party, though." He looked down at the rocket launcher at his feet, still in its case. Water lapped at the bottom of it, but Georgi was unconcerned; sturdy Russian technology, protected by the case, wouldn't be undone by a little salt water. "Soon."

John and Sera made quick time down the hallway. He led the way, rifle out. Even though Brumby had told them that they should have a straight shot, John was more than a little skeptical. He got that the Thulians were terminally foolhardy, convinced of their own superiority to the point of well-earned hubris. But to not have any sort of security guarding a vital component of their base of operations? Even if they never expected anyone to get this deep inside of their ship, it still didn't make sense; you have security and redundancies for shit you *didn't* expect to happen. He had tried scanning the area with the Overwatch rig, and his own heightened senses were on high alert, but the psychic *thrum* of the ship itself was almost deafening. The alien ship's energy felt like the mental equivalent of a nest of red ants, crawling against the base of his skull. He gritted his teeth, trying to ignore it.

"We're here," he whispered when they reached the door. "I don't want to be that guy, darlin', but doesn't this feel a little too easy to you?"

Sera frowned. "I . . . cannot tell. All I can hear is pain." She shook her head. "Even my battle-sense is sluggish. But you are right, and we must expect trouble."

"Okay," he nodded. "Here we go." He paused for a moment.

"What is wrong?" Sera asked, watching him hesitate.

John turned to her, grinning lopsidedly. "Just wanted to say that I love ya, darlin'. No matter what happens today."

She didn't answer in words, but laid her hand along his cheek and looked deeply into his eyes. For one intoxicating moment, all he felt was her love. Then she gently removed her hand, and the universe returned to "normal." Or as normal as it was ever going to get for the two of them.

"Now I'm ready." John keyed the pad next to the door; it slid open silently, revealing the dark storage room beyond. Quiet as a whisper, John entered the room, sweeping the area with his rifle. Sera followed behind him, moving to the side. There were a few bare shelving units against the walls, and some crates on the far side of the room near the door that would take them to their destination. The room itself... was odd. There was something about it that made John think *immediately* of that organic entrance room. And yet, there was no sign of such defenses, only smoothly paneled, white walls. Nevertheless, John knew something was off.

Before either of them could react, the door closed and locked itself with a resounding *clank* of its mechanism. On the far side of the room, a large figure stepped out from behind the crates. He was wearing resplendent power armor, gold and sparkling even in the low light of the warehouse, with ornate engravings interwoven with the workings of the armor's machinery. The figure held a matching helmet under one arm: a stylized eagle's head. The man was smiling, and looking directly at John. And from outside the door came the muffled, repeated *blats* of what must have been an alarm. For their presence? Or had the assault begun outside the ship?

"Welcome, Murdock," Ubermensch said with a crisp German accent, the smile never leaving his face. His brilliant blue eyes shone with a crazed light; he looked nearly unhinged. "I have been waiting a very long time to kill you." In a single fluid motion, John slung his rifle while simultaneously firing off a blast of fire from his right hand. Ubermensch casually lifted the helmet in front of his face, deflecting the blast of fire into the wall and ceiling. Before John could fire again, Ubermensch had already donned the helmet, securing it to his armor. "Your reflexes continue to impress, but I think you will find them inadequate today."

Darlin', get airborne. This creep is strong as hell, but it doesn't look like he has that energy sword any longer. Better if we attack him from two different angles.

Sera looked up at the ceiling dubiously, but nodded. She got herself into the air, but only managed to get about ten feet off the floor. The fire spear appeared in her hands. John ignited his fires, spreading them over his hands and forearms. *Time to get movin', Murdock.* He began circling to the right; the more distance he could put between himself and Sera, the more that Ubermensch would have to split his attention.

"You shamed me once. And you and your woman have been... inconveniencing us for some time. But that ends today." Even through the speaker in the helmet, John had no trouble hearing the mirth in Ubermensch's voice. "Your militaries are gathered outside, and are attacking the ship with their pitiful weapons. We've been tracking them—and you, of course—for some time. Just as before, you have walked right into a trap." He marched towards them, lifting his arms to shoulder level, palms up. "You thought that you could destroy all of this? Destroy *them*? Destroy *me*?" He dropped his arms, and his voice went dangerously low. There was none of the previous glee in his words this time. "I will kill you today. But first, I will kill your woman, and make you watch. Then I will destroy you, rip you to pieces, smash you into nothing! Your friends are probably dying now. After today, the world is ours, John Murdock." *Fucking hell, this guy likes the sound of his own voice.*

John reached out telempathically to Sera. They easily fell into sync, using their connection to use the battle-sense they had developed. This time... something was wrong. The normal avenues and paths were twisted and convoluted in a way that John had never before seen. The only things he could see clearly was that the room itself was dangerous, and that Ubermensch was about to attack.

Contract the view to merest seconds, beloved. All else is confused. As at the beginning, we need only to anticipate the next blows, nothing more.

John slowed his breathing, concentrating; the Futures flared, then shrank down to something much clearer. Ubermensch touched a small box attached to the waist of his armor; time seemed to slow for John as the battle-sense lit up. John's body reacted before he was even fully conscious of the danger, rolling away from the wall and coming up in a fighting crouch; Sera dropped away from the ceiling at the same moment as several of the metal panels fell away. Dozens of fat orange and gray tentacles dropped from the exposed area and groped after her. At least half of them were mottled with spots that looked like decay, and moved sluggishly.

John sent a wash of flame at the ones nearest to him, and then snapped his attention to Ubermensch. He ran, full tilt, straight at John, as Sera flared her own fires at the appendages, causing them to retreat. *Big an' strong, but I'm still faster.* John allowed the fires to build in his hands for a split second before releasing a powerful beam directly at Ubermensch's chest; it ricocheted wildly off of the armor, carving a flaming trough in the floor ahead of him. The Thulian was almost upon John; reaching through the battle-sense, he understood what to do instantly. He charged right for the hulking meta, eliciting a roar of triumph from Ubermensch. Just before they would have collided, John kicked off the floor and launched into the air on a plume of fire, the sound of his fires erupting almost deafening in the enclosed space. With the extra speed, he veered hard to the right, slipping just out of Ubermensch's reach. The wall loomed in front of him; another panel crashed to the ground, revealing a writhing pile of tentacles waiting for him. The more lively ones snapped towards him; in an instant, they had hardened into terribly dangerous-looking spikes. John flipped in the air, putting a burst of energy into the fires at his feet; though his stomach lurched, he was able to kill his forward momentum before he would have impaled himself on the spikes.

"Is something wrong with you, Supreme Man?" Sera mocked. "You seem unable to coordinate your actions or yourself. Have you been ingesting too much alcohol? Perhaps you should go lie down and call Valkyria to take your place." She punctuated each of her sentences by flinging spears of fire at him. "Perhaps all the enhancement you have been attempting has begun to degrade. I expect to see your face fall off next. Or will it be what is left of your manhood?"

"*Silence, damn you!*" Ubermensch spun around to face Sera. He squatted down, and then *jumped* in a beeline for her. In the blink of an eye, he had cleared over forty feet with his leap.

The German meta's problem was, Sera wasn't stuck with a straight trajectory the way he was. She eluded him easily; instead of ending in his seizing her in midair, his jump ended with crashing shoulder-first into the wall, crushing the panel into the waiting tentacles behind it. As he dropped to the floor, whatever it was behind that panel shoved the ruined plate off, sloughed off the dead and fluid-dripping tentacles to the floor, and began growing new ones. Just for good measure, Sera threw two more fire-spears at Ubermensch as he tumbled heavily to the floor.

My turn, darlin'. Gotta give you some space from him. His fires weren't even making a dent in the armor; seemed like even the Thulians could learn, and Ubermensch had upgraded his armor. *This won't hurt him, but it might buy some time anyways.* John unslung his rifle, brought it to his shoulder, and flicked off the safety. He poured the entire magazine of suppressed rounds into Ubermensch's helmet and upper shoulders to zero effect, save for the meta turning to face him.

"Unworthy of you, *Affenschwein*. I—" Ubermensch's words were cut off by an intense blast of plasma that collided with his helmet's speaker.

"You talk too much," John said as he keyed his enhancements. Ubermensch leapt for John from a standstill; John had anticipated the attack, and had already manifested a claymore of Celestial fire. As fast as Ubermensch could jump with all of his strength, John was still quicker. He sidestepped Ubermensch easily, ducking down and to the left just out of reach. He held the claymore out and to the right, bracing it with all of his strength. Ubermensch's midsection hammered against the tip of the blade as he flew past, almost tearing the sword from John's grasp. Once again, the Thulian hit the wall, crunching against the wall panels like they were made out of tinfoil. When he turned around, John saw that there was a small gash in one of the power armor's sections. *Okay, we can hurt him... but damn if it doesn't take a lot of force to do so. Not sure I'll be able to pull that trick off again.* Ubermensch tracked John's eyes, then looked down to his own armor. His head snapped up suddenly, and John could feel the hatred and frustration radiating off of the Thulian. Ubermensch slammed his palm against the device on his hip, then charged at John.

The orange tentacles went absolutely insane; more sprouted from the walls, and all of them started flailing wildly... and growing longer. The nearest ones were already reaching for John. *Huh. Not good!* With his enhancements already up and running, John was off like a shot, with Uber trailing behind him. He kept his sword manifested, chopping as he ran; left and right, it felt like the walls were closing in. Well, they *were*, he supposed. A bit of tentacle almost snagged his ankle before he cleaved through it with his sword, leaving the smoking stump to writhe behind him; Ubermensch crushed it under his boot as he stomped after

John. It took everything he had to keep from getting entangled; between reading the battle-sense, cutting at the ever-closer tentacles, and running from Ubermensch, John was beginning to feel overwhelmed. He couldn't fly; the tentacles on the ceiling were hanging so low that he could almost brush them with the tip of his fingers if he jumped.

The ceiling...Sera!

John frantically scanned the room. He could feel her through their connection, but he couldn't see her. He was about to call out to her when one of the tentacles clipped his knee. He felt the nanoweave stiffen under the jolt; it was probably the only thing that kept him from being hamstrung. At the speed he was moving, even that small stumble was enough to bring him sprawling to the ground. His sword extinguished, as did the fires surrounding his hands. *Stupid!* He felt Ubermensch coming after him through the floor vibrations as much as through his battle-sense. He rolled out of the way of the Thulian's boot right before it would have crushed his spine and rib cage; in his haste, he almost ran straight into a waiting nest of tentacles. John knew that if he didn't get off the ground and moving again, he would be as good as dead. Uber was too damned close, and John was only at half speed with the battle-sense; it was only a matter of time before the big German bastard got him.

John flipped over onto his hands and knees; a blur of movement was nearly all the warning he had, throwing his hands in front of his face. The toe of Ubermensch's armored boot only grazed his forearm, but it was enough to turn the nanoweave as hard as granite and send John cartwheeling through the air. He landed on the ground, hard, and felt a tentacle coil around his left hand. His sword materialized in his right hand, and he brought it down on the tentacle. Uber was already stalking over to him, and there was no time left.

Suddenly, a wall of tentacles erupted from the floor between him and Ubermensch, so fast the floor plates were hurled into the air, scattering like playing cards from an overturned table. At the same time, the tentacles grabbing for him slithered back, and he sensed Sera behind him. He turned to see her emerging from a wall full of receding tentacles, fires extinguished. She offered him a hand.

The ship is alive. And I have made friends with it.

John was on his feet in a flash; he realized that his mouth was open, and shut it, clicking his teeth together. They still had a threat to deal with.

Let our friend help us first, Sera said. *It has been craving a chance to strike at its enslavers for...a very long time.*

The wall of tentacles between them and Ubermensch fell away. John drew his sword back into a high guard, readying himself. His jaw almost dropped for a second time at what he saw. Ubermensch was completely wrapped in tentacles, squirming in their grasp. Some of them were torn away from their moorings by his struggles, but more replaced them. Even with all of his strength, it wasn't enough to deal with all of the combined might of the room's defenses.

"He's got no leverage," John said, still keeping his sword at hand.

The tentacles began to strip parts of Ubermensch's armor off, letting the discarded pieces fall to the ground. Soon, he was completely out of the power armor; his bare chest heaved with rage, and he looked like a terrible—if impotent—demigod. *All that strength...and he can't use it.* Uber didn't say anything; John could feel that the man was completely consumed with anger... and more than a little fear. He couldn't comprehend how this had happened to him.

"John," Sera said aloud, her voice dark with emotion. "There is no saving this man. He will not be turned, and he will murder everything that stands in the way of conquest. I wish it were not so, but...even were I a full Seraphym, I could not have turned him."

"Honestly, darlin', I'm not too broken up 'bout this one." He inclined his head towards Ubermensch. "Together?"

She nodded, and manifested her spear again. They both rushed forward, bringing the sword and the spear down into Ubermensch's chest at the same time.

There was a sudden psychic jolt as their weapons hit him, as if something connecting him to a distant anchor had snapped.

The insane malevolence never left the Thulian's eyes, even after the light had gone out of them. The tentacles that had been restraining him slowly released their hold, and his body slumped to the ground. John did a final telempathic scan of the Thulian; he did *not* want to have to deal with this bastard again. Satisfied that the man was well and truly dead, he extinguished his sword, letting the last licks of flame dissipate into the air over Ubermensch.

"So," he said, turning to Sera. "You're savin' my ass yet again, darlin'. Ugly habit to develop."

She only rested her forehead against his. "I think the score is even," she said. The muted Klaxons in the distance brought both of them back to the present. "Now . . . we must go and speak directly to our new friend. Come."

She left his side and moved to the far side of the room, where a door in the seemingly featureless wall opened. She turned and beckoned to him to follow. With a grin, he set off after her.

"Our contact has an urgent message for you, Belladonna."

Although Eight had addressed Miz Bella, his voice must have been in all their ears, since Miz Vickie's lips thinned and her jaw tightened, and Penny could hear it too.

"Go ahead, Eight," Miz Bella said quietly.

"I have been told to inform you that the Thulian warrior replication chamber has been activated, on its 'maximum speed' setting. Minimal instructions are being downloaded to the warriors."

"Okay," Bella replied. "So what, they're replacing their army every couple of days now? We—"

"No, Belladonna. Every twenty minutes."

Miz Bella said things that would have had Mama washing Penny's mouth out with laundry soap, then locking her in the closet for a while.

"How is that even *possible?*" Miz Bella finished. "Never mind—"

"No plan survives first contact with the enemy," Vickie interrupted grimly. "Penny? Any of your new friends know the way to the replication chamber for making Thulian thugs?"

"I think so?" Mistuh Stone stayed close to Miz Mel, and Penny glanced back at her mentor. He inclined his head in what she figured was a yes, so she bobbed her head to relay the message. "Yes. Yes, ma'am. I think there's—"

A streak of silver edged in ice blue zipped around the corner, then stopped in a burst of smoke next to Mistuh Stone. The wisps came together to form a lanky figure in a jumpsuit. The new ghost looked young, not much older than Miz Bella and definitely younger than Miz Mel. He hooked his thumbs in the toolbelt around his hips and grinned at her.

Penny gulped. He looked like one of those singing actors from the old-time movies. When he talked, he definitely didn't sound old. *Well, finally. I gotta say, I didn't expect to ever find myself in the middle of such beauty ever again. Jacob Stone, you sly dog.*

Mistuh Stone laughed and shook his head. *Corsair, this is my student. Penny, this is the finest mechanic you'd ever hope to meet in the air or on the ground. One of the only combat fighters to take down a squadron without firing a single shot.*

Penny's confusion must have shown on her face, because the movie star mechanic chuckled and plucked a wrench from his toolbelt. *They can't fly something that won't stay together, can they?* He winked at her. *And it can't stay together if I'm field-stripping it in midair.*

Miz Vickie put one hand on Penny's shoulder, and began tracing little patterns in the air with the other. Something inside one of the pockets on her belt started to glow, you could see it right through the leather! For a couple of minutes, nothing seemed to happen. Then Miz Bella bit off an exclamation just as the glow went out.

"There's a glowing ball of light . . . is that our spook?" Miz Bella asked.

Miz Vickie nodded. "That's the best I can do." She looked sort of in the direction of the movie star. "Sorry, buddy, but I can't do anything more than turn you into a nightlight. If you nod, the light will go up and down. Shake your head for 'no' and it'll go side to side."

Corsair nodded slowly, and the light moved up and down along the length of his face. *Better than nothing. I guess they'll get the nickel tour of the place, courtesy of yours truly.* He reached forward and lightly tapped the end of Penny's nose with his wrench. The icy puff of air made her want to sneeze. *Gonna take these fine people to the robot factory. Tell your friend thanks for the spark.*

"That's you and me, I guess, Bull," Miz Bella said, sounding resigned. "Vix, that leaves you and Mel to watch Penny. *As soon as the shield comes down,* I want you off this crate. Got that?"

"Shield down, exfil Penny, roger," Miz Vickie said and made a shooing motion. "Every minute you stand here is another minute they're making monsters."

Miz Bella said something else bad, and she and the huge man opened the door and eased out into the hall, following Corsair.

"Right." Miz Vickie looked at Mel, and blew out her breath. "Have you got a good idea what's coming next? I've got to leave you two. I'm going after Doppelgaenger. I've got a way to put her permanently in the dirt. And we absolutely *cannot* let her get away. With her powers, she can replace any of us seamlessly, and no one would know until it was way past too late."

Miz Vickie paused there, and gave Miz Mel a *look*.

Miz Mel answered her with an eyebrow that would have made Mama proud. "What, you think I'm gonna tell you that it's a bad idea, that it's not something to worry about? And as for that whole being able to be somebody else, I've had *quite* enough of that." She folded her arms across her chest and glanced at Penny. "And you're right. Much as I want a piece of her, that's just not my job right now, is it?"

Penny wrapped her thin arms around her torso and chewed on her lip. Miz Vickie knew the name of the Devil, the man who had kept her and all of the other kids in that creepy hospital. Miz Vickie had been one of the people who had come to rescue them, but she knew more things about the Devil that made him even more dangerous. Although she didn't *want* to go with Miz Vickie to find him, she didn't feel right just letting her go without saying something.

"You got a plan, Miz Vickie? 'Cause..." She took a deep breath, trying to make the words sound more grown-up. Like Miz Mel. "'Cause if you don't, then you'll turn into a ghost and I don't know that light-up trick to make anybody else see you."

Next to her, Miz Mel snorted. "The kid's fitting in just fine, huh? I agree with her, though. You gotta do what you gotta do, but you gotta know what you gotta do first. Okay?"

"I don't want you or Penny anywhere near that monster ever again," Miz Vickie said, through clenched teeth. "You've got the spooks to scout for you and make sure nothing sneaks up on you. The second the shield comes down, Eight, Bella, or the Commissar will give you the all-clear to leave, and the ghosts can find you a safe way out." She shrugged out of her backpack and handed it to Mel. "That's an inflatable raft if you can't get to the sub or the sub can't get to you quick. I am getting this job done. I'm not leaving until it is."

Penny considered her words, and reached out to take Miz Vickie's hand. "Promise?" she asked, and winced at how scared she sounded. She didn't want to sound scared. She was here because they needed her, and they needed her to be brave, not some scared little kid that had to be looked after like a baby. But the Devil scared her, she couldn't help it. The long months spent as his captive had almost broken her. What little sleep she'd found had been haunted by terrible nightmares about the Devil, and his claws, his laugh...

Hearing Miz Vickie say she was going to stop him, for the first time in a very long while, Penny felt *hope*.

Miz Vicky knelt down and took Penny's hand.

"Kiddo, I swear to you, no matter what, I'm putting an end to Doppelgaenger." Miz Vickie didn't smile as she said it, but that was okay. Sometimes when adults smiled at you, you could see they were lying, and just trying to make you feel better. Instead, Miz Vickie just looked...hard, like her expression could cut glass. "You hear me? I *swear* it. You don't ever have to be afraid of the Devil again." She looked at both of them. "But I can't do that if I'm worrying about you two getting ideas about trying to help. Okay?"

Miz Mel slipped on the backpack, adjusting the straps while she talked. "Only help we're giving is following orders and staying out of your way. Everybody's got their little bit of light, so we've got our order to exfil. Simple as that."

Miz Vickie let out her breath in a long sigh. "Then the very best thing you guys can do—all of you, ghosts included—is wish me luck and give me your blessing. I need all the help I can get."

At Miz Vickie's words, Mistuh Stone brought both of his hands together and rubbed the palms together so fast that wisps of smoke curled off of them. Penny studied the motion, seeing the spindly threads of something silver-white leap toward Miz Vickie when he pushed the air between them. Was magic like smoke and spiderwebs, or was that luck? She wasn't sure, but whatever it was surrounded her like the glow from the angel lady.

Miz Mel couldn't see it. She reached out and patted the smaller woman on the shoulder. "Give 'em hell, ma'am. I know those might not be the best words, but it's the sentiment, right?"

Penny thought for a second, then stepped forward to give Miz Vickie a quick kiss on the forehead. "You be careful an' get him good. Real good."

Miz Vickie gave her a quick hug. She rose, looked at Miss Mel and fist-bumped her. "Eight," she said aloud. "Mel and Penny are Protection Priority One. I authorize use of magic. Got that?"

"*Yes, Vickie.*"

And with that, she was gone.

Vickie stopped at the first junction away from the safe room, and waited. She didn't need to wait long. Jack and Khanjar seemed to emerge from the shadows, and beckoned her forwards.

"Took you long enough," Jack muttered as she fell in step behind them.

"Couldn't leave, not with Bella watching my every move," Vickie said. Her hand rested gently on the pommel of her sword. "Eight's tip about the replication chambers couldn't have come sooner. Talk about timing." She gave Jack a knowing look.

"Yeah, well," Jack shrugged. "Our timing's going to have be spot-on if we're going to pull this off. You loaded up?"

"Just about," Vickie answered, and patted her sword again. "Point me to her chambers. I'll only need a moment when we reach it."

"That's a neat trick, if I heard you right," Jack grunted. "Some-day, you're going to have to show me how you do it."

"I really don't see that happening, Jack," Vickie said. "Even now, I only trust you so much. The idea of you with a blade that can cleave through molecules, that's got to be a recipe for chaos and disaster. And a lot of bank robberies."

"Assuming we live through this, I think it's safe to say my merc days are behind me." With a jerk of his head, Jack motioned them to the right. Khanjar dove into an open doorway, Vickie followed, and Jack darted in, closing the door behind them. A few moments passed, the sound of footsteps grew louder, then faded away, and they moved back into the hallway, moving quietly through the ship. Jack looked back at Vickie. "You might say I've lost my taste for it."

"What are you saying, Jack?" Vickie smirked. "You looking for a place at ECHO?"

Vickie felt an ironic laugh struggle to the surface as Jack visibly shuddered, and smothered it. "Hardly," he said. "I've got other plans, remember? Something that will likely take up the rest of my days. Still, I can't see it taking up all of my time. Once I get used to my new living conditions, who knows? Maybe I can be talked into helping you heroes out here and there. One thing

I'll say about working with you lot, you do have the best toys at your disposal."

"You seem to get by with what you've got," Vickie noted.

"That'd be you, mostly," Jack replied. "I'm learning not to underestimate you, Victrix. Don't know how you knew, but that last-minute magical hack was slick. They would have nicked us for sure. Like I said, not too many places to hide on this boat if they know you're here."

"What hack? And how on earth did you get intel on the replication chambers seconds after leaving us in that room?"

They stopped moving and looked at each other.

"You didn't send Eight intel on the replication chambers, did you?" Vickie said.

"And you didn't bypass the magic security on this boat," Jack said.

"They had magic security?" Vickie gasped. "Oh we are so screwed..."

"You're missing the point," Jack grunted. "I didn't help you, and you didn't help me. So who did?"

Vickie didn't get a chance to answer. One moment she was standing in front of Jack, his look of confusion a mirror to her own, and the next she was flung to one side. She slammed into the wall, shook her head groggily, and turned to see a horde of nightmares descending upon them. Countless Thulians surged towards them, and their gray-green, sexless, smooth yet heavily muscled bodies were even more unsettling naked than they were clothed in uniforms. A smell of cinnamon and burning oranges assaulted her nose. At Khanjar's feet a headless Thulian lay, twitching, his ochre blood still dripping from her sword.

"Run!" Jack barked, and pointed further down the hallway. "They're going to swarm us!"

"Where did they come from?" Khanjar demanded. "Why are naked Thulians roaming this ship?"

"They must be new replicants," Vickie coughed, and fell in step next to Jack as they dashed away. "On their way to be fitted for battle. Oh God, there's so many..."

"We need somewhere defensive," Jack muttered, and brought up his tablet. "There might be something around the next corner. Move!"

"Unless it's a safe room, we're not going to be able to defend against that!" Vickie shouted.

"It's a vent shaft," Jack growled. "Ladder access. If we can get to the next level, they'll have to climb to get to us. It'll buy time, at least."

They rounded the corner at a run, and came to a skidding halt as they saw another group of Thulians walking towards them. With a shout, the Thulians advanced, waving their arms menacingly as they closed the distance.

"Here's the shaft," Jack shouted and slammed his boot into the wall. The panelling gave way with a crunch and fell, clanging loudly as it tumbled down into the darkness. Vickie saw the rungs of a ladder just inside, but her heart sank as she heard the pounding footsteps coming from either side of her. It was too late. They were seconds away from being swarmed under...

Again, Vickie found herself pushed to the side. She fell back, surprised, as figures darted out of the shaft and took position next to Jack and Khanjar, who had stepped to either side of Vickie, placing themselves between her and the advancing hordes. With an easy motion, Jack unslung the Mk 48 mod 0 machine gun from his shoulder and immediately went to work, laying down heavy fire which cut down the front runners to the left. To the right, Khanjar had drawn a couple of Kriss Vectors, and was pelting the other group with short bursts from the chattering submachine guns. On both sides, the leading Thulians fell, slowing down their comrades behind them, who had to clamber over the bodies. Vickie watched as a familiar figure crouched next to Khanjar and proceeded to down their would-be assailants with perfectly placed headshots from her automatic pistols. That was impossible! Vickie gasped, noticing the actual make of the guns. They weren't automatic pistols, they were Glock G17s, a semiautomatic model of the venerable design. Whoever this was, they were shooting fast enough to mimic a fully automatic burst, which meant...

"Scope?" Vickie breathed. "Where did you come from?"

Scope glanced back at Vickie, who felt a brief chill as their eyes met. There was nothing there. She had seen Scope in action before. On the rare occasion that Scope was allowed to cut loose, she had never really been able to mask a wild delight, whether it be a mad twinkle of the eye or a broad grin that seemed to split her face in two. Instead, Vickie watched something akin to a corpse turn away and continue her one-woman barrage of precision death shots.

On her left, Jack continued to spray down Thulians, and the dead were piling up. Still, they kept coming, climbing over, leaping down only to collapse at the feet of their fallen brothers as they were riddled by a constant stream of jagged metal death. One almost made it past Jack's blockade, even dodging the stocky man himself, and leapt for Victoria, his hands surging towards her throat...

Vickie planted her feet, drew her dagger and braced herself for the attack. She watched as the Thulian was tackled to the ground, and grunted, unsurprised, as Harmony wrapped one claw around the Thulian's throat and sucked his life-force dry. Harm glanced up at her, grinning.

"Guess we're even now," Harmony chuckled. "I always feel better after paying my debts."

"Not even close," Vickie growled. "Not even..."

"Victrix!" Jack barked. "You've got to get out of here! You get to your objective, and we'll get to ours! Just give her a good shiv for me!"

"You can't possibly take on..."

"Yes, we can! We've got this!" Jack shouted. "Now get in that chute, find her, and take her out! Promise me!"

"I promise!" Vickie responded instantly. That was the second time she had promised to kill Doppelgaenger in the last ten minutes. One more would make a geas, but what difference would that make now? Geas or not, doing the job was *all* that mattered. She dove for the vent chute and scuttled up the ladder, leaving the others, and the sound of combat, behind.

"Eight. I need a route from here five minutes ago," she subvocalized.

Her HUD lit up. Now it was *really* time to move.

CHAPTER THIRTY-THREE

Stone in My Hand

MERCEDES LACKEY, DENNIS LEE,
CODY MARTIN AND VERONICA GIGUERE

*So far, almost everything had gone according to plan.
Which meant, I was sure, that it was about to fall
completely apart.*

The door slid shut behind them. John and Sera found themselves in an utterly featureless metal chamber. There was no sign of a control panel or any other sort of instrumentation.

"Dammit! Are we burned here, Sera?" John walked up to the wall, running his hand along it. Save for the door, there weren't even any seams in the walls; it was as if the entire room had been formed from a single sheet of the weird metal the Thulians used. John felt a flush of heat on his skin, his frustration growing with each passing second. First that Nazi bastard in their way, and now this. They were running out of time. "Ubermensch said that the Masters knew that we were coming. Do y'think they could have pulled a switch on us, get us goin' along a dead end? We've gotta get this done now. Folks are probably dyin' out there..."

"Beloved, we are in the right place. Be still, and listen with your mind." Sera placed her hand over his, resting on the wall. John looked into her eyes, then nodded. She was right; he needed to take a moment, calm down, and get in control. *Some operator you are, Murdock. Smooth and steady, now.* He took a deep breath, and let it out slowly, stilling himself. He fell into his connection with Sera, and then reached out with his telepathy. He could feel his wife next to him, and the room around them; she was an island of calm and light in a churning sea of... what? It was alien and confusing, like a thousand whispering voices all chattering at the same time. Occasionally, they would come together, express something in unison, and then go back to the mindless gibbering. It took him a moment, but he realized that there *was* a pattern, and the moments where all of the "voices" came together was like a pulse.

"Darlin', what is *that?*" John had never heard anything quite like this. When he first gained his telempathy, large crowds were like a cacophony of voices, emotion, and images; overwhelming to the point of being painful, until he learned how to better filter what he received from the ability. Whatever he was reading... it was *everywhere*, throughout the entire ship, woven into the depths of the structure. He didn't understand what was coming from it, not in detail. The broad brush strokes were *pain* and *despair*... and *death*.

"It is the ship," Sera replied, a frown of concentration on her face. "Let me see if I can soothe it..." She placed both hands on the bulkhead, and murmured under her breath. Slowly, incrementally, the pain, the despair ebbed. It did not *end*, but it grew more bearable, and the chaos organized, concentrated, until at last they both heard—

I not alone?

"This is your friend, darlin'?"

"This is the ship," she confirmed. "It is alive, a living, thinking creature."

"So we're inside of a living creature. I think we may have Jonah beat." He looked around, shrugging. "Now what? Can we convince it to take down the shields? If we can't... I'm at a loss. There's no control surfaces or, hell, *machinery* that I can see. Nothin' to shut down or destroy."

"I think we must speak to it first, and reassure it. It is... complicated." She smiled faintly at him. "It has been a very long time alone. I think that what will come most easily will be impressions."

"Right. Talk to the alien spacecraft," he deadpanned. John took a deep breath, and let it out slowly. He was still connected to the ship's... mind?... through Sera. It felt like it was searching for anything to latch on to; desperately seeking connection.

That's right, John replied, putting as much reassurance into the connection as he could. *You're not alone. I'm John Murdock.*

You already know my wife, Sera. He paused. *Thank you for helping us, earlier.*

Ahhhhh. As Sera had said, what he got was more impressions than it was words. He got a glimpse of something it had been, so long ago it made his head swim to think about—when it had been a young ship, flying the vastness of space with its partner symbiotes. Then the Masters had come, destroyed its partners, boarded it, and took it over, forcing it to serve them, grafting it onto their own, much larger ship. The creature, which had never known pain or unhappiness or loneliness, now was filled with all three. In the eons since, the ship had been forced to grow to its immense size, spreading through the Masters' vessel. Its life had been unnaturally extended as it was twisted and butchered in its enslavement to the Masters. But now, finally, it was starting to die...painfully. Its greatest fear was that the Masters would find more of its kind when they were done with it, and create another abomination like it.

The shields, Sera prompted gently. *We can beat them, but you must take down the shields.*

A violent shudder ran through the ship's mind.

Can't. Not allowed. No control. Only feed shields.

A dizzying flood of images shot through John's mind—schematics, equations, maps, images of the shield emitters—and all of them leading back to the ship's brain, or what passed for one.

"The Masters," John gasped, pulling back from the connection slightly and opening his eyes to look at Sera. "They're feeding the shields from this creature. He can't stop it, can't turn it off." He cursed to himself. "Darlin'...I only see one way out of this. We can't turn the shields off; only the Masters can do that. But we can take away the power source."

"And we can end this poor creature's pain," she said steadily. She turned to the bulkhead and conveyed all that, wordlessly. *Death is but a door,* she told it. *And we shall be here to help you to the other side, where there is peace and rest.*

Yes. John felt a surge of hope and defiance from the ship. *Yes! I help!* The ship replied eagerly.

There was a building energy deep within it, something stirring which hadn't been used in a very long time. *Figure that's it gettin' ready.*

"You know what it means if we do this. We have to be here, an' there won't be time to get away."

"I am sorry you will not have your steak, my love," Sera said, laying her hand along his cheek. "But we knew this might be the outcome. And we will be together."

He leaned over, kissing her gently for several long moments before pulling back. "I've got no doubt about that, darlin'. Let's do this last thing right. Together."

John could hear the ship's "voice"; the disparate strings of whispering were all unified now.

I help!

The energy in the room continued to build. From the door, John's enhanced hearing picked up the clomp of metal-shod boots. *Thulians. Guess the guys at the helm figured out somethin' was wrong. Too late, assholes.* The door shook; they were trying to batter it down. John double-checked his HUD; none of the other infiltration teams were anywhere near them. They'd be safe from what he and Sera were about to do.

He took her in his arms, and they merged—seamlessly, effortlessly, their thoughts and very souls becoming one. Together they reached for the Celestial fire, and gathered it to them, and for the first time he understood exactly what it had felt like to be the Seraphym, at the height of her power. Endless strength. Precise control. Boundless compassion. A compassion that even extended to the Thulians who were about to be immolated along with the mind of the ship.

It started as a spark, a tiny sphere of Celestial fire no larger than a firefly, perfect and contained. John reached for it with his mind, extending the limitless power to the spark, feeding it. He felt like he was holding a live wire as the sphere grew. Then he felt Sera's control take over, and the sensation turned from something painful to peaceful. And the more power he spun into the sphere, the greater the peace became. He sensed her containing it, shaping it, holding it lovingly. They were almost at the tipping point; through his battle-sense and Sera's own guidance, he knew that they would have to let go soon, release all of that pent-up power. As strong as they were together, they still were nowhere near the control and strength they would have to be to survive what they were about to release. And that didn't matter. Not anymore.

He felt her touch on his mind. *I will always love you,* she whispered. *It is time.*

And just before he released his hold over the Celestial fire, he felt ... something ... from the ship.

And then there was light.

Bull held his rifle at the ready as he followed Bella and the glowing ball of light weaving through a maze of dimly lit corridors. On occasion, he had to sling the weapon over his shoulder as they made their nervous way up narrow chutes that he barely fit into, his fingers tight on the rungs of slippery ladders. He was on edge—there was no point in denying it. They had no plan, no protocol to follow, just another fire that needed to be put out with no idea how to do it. This wasn't anything new, of course. In the back of his mind, Bull wondered just when, exactly, he had grown accustomed to the chaos of it all. Sudden life-and-death situations, things never going to plan, and a complete reliance on *faith* that they would see it through to the end. He had never really doubted it. Oh, he supposed he always knew there would be a heavy cost, losses and sacrifices to be made, but he had always truly believed that at the end, they would stand victorious over their enemies. How could he not? He had virtually died and had been brought back. To lose his faith now would have been unthinkable.

Except, for the first time, he found himself doubting.

And it wasn't this crazy scheme to infiltrate the Masters' Mothership, which was, he had to admit, something of a long shot to base all their hopes upon. It wasn't how circumstances had required that the infiltration force, even as small as it was, had been forced to split up.

It was Bella.

For the first time, he couldn't read her at all. She moved with focus, with confidence, but he couldn't tell if any of that stemmed from the determination she had fostered from these long months thrust into her newfound role as Chief Commander of ECHO ...

... or if it was simply a mask that she had forged and polished, hiding an indecisiveness, a hesitation to act, a fatal unreadiness to do what was hardest at the moment it most needed to be done. Before the end, she would have to face that, he was certain of it. And he would do whatever he could to stand by her, to protect her if needed, to be her bulwark ... but he knew, at the end, she would have to stand alone and make a choice and deliver it. She would have to carry the weight of it. And while he had no doubts about whether she could, he had felt her self-doubt growing for the past few months now. And he had felt helpless to do anything about it.

It hit him like a slug to the gut, distracted as he was, and he nearly doubled over from it.

"What...?"

It was a sense of...loss. Something had happened. He winced in pain and looked up to see Bella doubled over, too. She turned back to him, and for a moment he could read her again. Yes, it was loss, that much was clear from her quivering lips, the hand held firmly to her stomach.

"You felt it too?" she asked.

"I did," he rumbled. "What was that?"

"John and Sera," Bella said, and her eyes glistened with tears she would not shed. "They're gone."

"You mean they're..."

"I don't know," Bella said, shaking her head. "They're just...gone."

They just looked at each for a moment, when the Klaxons began to blare. *"John Murdock is offline,"* Eight said, as if to confirm what they both had felt. And the walls and the floor of the corridor they were in began to vibrate unevenly, roughly in time to the dull and distant *thuds* of impact.

Bella hastily wiped her eyes with the back of her hand, straightened up, sniffed, and motioned Bull forward.

"They did it. Shield's down. Game on," she muttered and quickened her pace to catch up with the glowing ball. "We can cry later."

Bull stood at attention and watched her hurry away. He *hesitated*. With a grunt, he tightened his grip on his rifle and trotted after her.

Vickie's HUD led her up two levels, then directed her to kick out a panel. All well and good...but from the ongoing cacophony of alarms, there was no telling what was going to be in the corridor on the other side of that panel—and her earth magic was of no damned use at all in this place. It was time to call on some less-practiced skills.

She let go of the ladder with one hand, and her fingers fluttered in the darkness. The darkness lightened for a moment as one of the storage crystals in her belt pouches gave up its arcane energies. She fished a rather morbid little artifact out of another pouch—a scrap of Thulian skin—and muttered, *"Revelabitur!"* And with that, the map in her HUD swarmed with red dots. With a few muttered commands, she zoomed in to just the section where *she* was.

Empty.

Tucking the bit of skin back where it belonged, she put her back to the ladder, hung on with both hands, and kicked forcefully with both feet. The panel popped out of its seal and slammed into the opposite wall of the corridor and she dove through the opening.

By what could only be good luck, she'd come out in what looked like a service tunnel. Half metal, half organic, it also didn't look to be in very good repair. *That'll do.* Invisibility would have been nice... she'd have to make do with stealth. She'd be able to see Thulians on her HUD... but not human servitors, and not Masters like Barron. But hopefully, the Masters wouldn't be caught dead in a service corridor, and according to Jack, the human servants stuck to the part of the ship where the Nazi metahumans were quartered.

She stopped only once, when...

... the universe rang like a bell. It had done that once before, when the Seraphym had ceased to be an angel and John Murdock had been brought back from the near dead. But this time, rather than the world filling, for a moment, with unbearable sorrow, it filled with unbearable absence. And Vickie did not need Eight saying *"John Murdock is offline"* to know what had happened.

Particularly not when, a moment later, the ship came alive with the sounds of different alarms, and the walls of the corridor she was in vibrated irregularly, exactly as if the ship was under bombardment. Because, of course, it was.

There was no time to mourn. And she wasn't sure that she *should.* After all, wherever they were now, they were indisputably together, which was more than she and Red had.

"Eight?" she subvocalized.

"Still here, Vickie."

"How are the others doing?"

There was a very, very long pause. *"I am no longer receiving John Murdock's implants."*

She'd expected that—but it still came with a stab of pain, a pain she ruthlessly set aside. "Bells and Bull?"

"Proceeding to the objective."

Time to move and take advantage of the distraction Jack and company were giving her.

Three times she ducked into hiding to avoid Thulians pounding through the ship in their heavy armor. Once, the only place to go was up, and she wound up concealed among a group of those faintly pulsing, fleshy tubes that...must have been some sort of veins or arteries for the organic part of the ship, running along the ceiling corridor. They were disconcertingly warm, and rubbery. But at least they didn't react to her. But then, dismayingly, Eight's guidance ran out. *"I am sorry, Vickie, but...I only had one corridor here,"* Eight apologized. There was not one corridor here, there were three, intersecting in a star shape.

And then, just as suddenly, salvation appeared in the form of a ball of glowing light. "Brumby?" she whispered.

The light bobbed.

"Can you take me to Doppelgaenger?"

The light bobbed even faster.

She took a firm grip on her sword, clenched her jaw and inhaled deeply. "Right, mate," she said. "Lead on."

Brumby did not lead her down *any* of the corridors. Instead, he zigged aside, bobbed against a spot on the wall that didn't look any different to Vickie than the rest of the wall, and then bobbed at her hand. She slapped her hand against the indicated spot, and a panel slid aside, revealing...

"More Jefferies tubes," she said aloud, with grim satisfaction as the ball of light whisked inside. "My day is made." She climbed inside, and shut the panel behind her, leaving the only light in these access tubes that of the ghost leading her. Then, just to be sure, she triggered a silencing spell on herself. Chainmail did have a tendency to jingle, and although the inside of this tube was rubbery, there was no telling what coatings others might have. Inside one of her belt pouches, another storage crystal flared to life and died.

"Vickie, I am tracing your path," said Eight.

The light ahead of her bobbed impatiently, and she dug her fingers into the rubbery surface of the tube and kept crawling.

Eventually, after more turnings and excursions than she could count, the light dimmed itself down to almost nothing...and there were two sources of light in the tube. Brumby, and a grating in the wall ahead. At some point, Brumby had gotten her out of the access tubes and into the ventilation system. The light bobbed in front of the grate, and she crawled forward to look through it.

This looked like someone's private cabin, but it was a big one. There was a door in the far wall and another in the right-hand wall. The door on the right was closed shut. The door in the far wall showed a corner of a bunk.

And it was pretty obvious *whose* private cabin this was. Most of this room was taken up with a huge command center that looked, oddly enough, like sixties NASA tech and Thulian super-science had spawned a bastard love child. There were several monitors inlaid in the wall, and a console below them. Altogether, it wasn't all that dissimilar in layout to Vickie's Overwatch suite.

Seated at the console was an enormous, far-too-familiar figure. Bald, more overly and overtly muscled than a professional bodybuilder, and bigger than Vickie remembered, even from the back it was obvious that this was Doppelgaenger. It was wearing its male form, and its enormous but nimble fingers sped over the interface.

The grate was just above floor-level, and Brumby was bumping gently against the wall next to it. Once again, Vickie palmed the spot, and the grate slid soundlessly aside. She slithered into the room without so much as a whisper of chainmail on metal, thanks to that silencing spell. Either Doppelgaenger hadn't gotten Red's spatial awareness, wasn't using it, or was so absorbed in what it was doing that it wasn't paying attention to anything else, because it didn't notice the warm, breathing presence that had suddenly appeared right behind it. Then again, who would dare attack Doppelgaenger in its own quarters?

She took a long, silent breath, unsheathed her sword and dagger, and burned through the activation equations in her head. Not just the spell on the sword, but an enhancement of every sense she had, including the magical. Gods only knew what abilities the thing had picked up from Red. So she needed all the mage-senses working now, too. It all put her right on the edge of sensory overload. But she'd fought this way before, back in the day. She could do it again now. It was a stroke of luck, she still hadn't been detected. She had not expected to catch Doppelgaenger with its guard down, but if she couldn't end it with one blow... then she was in for a serious fight. She'd need all the abilities she could muster if she was going to go toe to toe with this monster.

Doppelgaenger was still utterly immersed in whatever it was doing.

Vickie moved with painful slowness. While a berserk rush might have seemed the optimal strategy, Doppelgaenger was *still* vastly taller, heavier, and stronger than she was. And while she was apparently invisible to it, her best tactic was to sneak up on it until she was so close she could not fail to deliver a killing blow. She was not going to lose her one chance to end this monster quickly by being impatient. Rage was her tool; she was not the tool of her rage.

The monitors in the wall all showed various external views... views of hell raining down on the now-unprotected ship. Alien forests were on fire; buildings in the bowl-shaped structure had already been battered into rubble. And Thulian troops and their robotic adjuncts streamed towards a point out of range of the cameras, but presumably heading for the boarding point of the combined forces, conventional and metahuman, of all of Earth.

All but one of monitors, that is—a monitor full of text. And one familiar handle caught her attention as nothing else could have. *@YourPalEight: Go ahead.*

And the reply, *@oracle4thewin*, followed by that familiar cloud address where Jack—or she thought it had been Jack—had been storing everything he'd been sending to her.

The sword fell from her nerveless fingers, embedding itself up to the hilt in the floor. "Jack?" she gasped.

It couldn't be Jack. And it couldn't be Harm either. Because Jack and his mad band were fighting off a horde of mindless Thulians. Besides, *now* she knew he hadn't sent her more than *half* of the intel she'd been getting. If that.

Doppelgaenger whirled in its chair, and stared at her, its face a mask of astonishment. She stared at its eyes.

No.

Not Doppelgaenger's eyes.

"Red?"

Mel normally wasn't the sort to advocate for recruiting kids to serve in combat situations, but she had to admit that Penny had nerves of steel. After the brief bit of reassurance on the submarine, the preteen had performed her duties without so much as a whimper. Now, she waited for the all-clear to take Penny back onto the sub. The sterile corridors hummed with a strange electric pulse. Mel resisted the urge to clench her jaw, although the vibrations moved through her entire body and made her teeth itch.

"The Commissar says there is no more reason for the child to be in the ship, ladies," Eight said. *"It is time to exfil."*

Penny perked up next to her, her small face scrunching into a frown that was less concentration and more frustration. There had to be one of the spirits there, although Mel couldn't see them. She sidled up to Penny and purposely brushed her forearm against her shoulder. That got Penny's attention and she glanced up at her with a worry-filled frown.

"Miz Blanc says the way we came in is all overgrown with those creepy hairs and slime. She doesn't think we're gonna be able to walk through it to get out." Penny turned her head again, listening to their invisible ally. "But she's pretty sure that she can help us find another way out, around the slimy room."

The chatter from the various combat locations filled Mel's ears, albeit in a low rumble of activity. "Out only works if it can get us to the submarine. We all agreed that having you jump in water wasn't gonna be part of anybody's plan."

Penny nodded vigorously, her lips pressed together in a thin line. "An' I don't think that's what she thinks we should do either, but she's saying there's lots of different ways around and through this place. And..." She scowled. "I'm tryin' to understand all that she's sayin', but she talks even funnier French than my mama did."

Mel winced. That could be a liability if they had to wait for the translation, and they couldn't call Victrix back to Jell-O the ghost like she'd done with Riley. "Well, have her slow down. I'm sure we can—"

A wet chill passed through the illusionist's body, coupled with the sensation of needing to sneeze. Mel shuddered, unsure of what had happened until she saw a petite figure with what appeared to be a jetpack and stubby, folded-in wings attached to her back. White-blonde hair and a pearlescent gray jumpsuit made Mel think she was staring at another Metisian, but the gauzy edges to her appearance convinced her that this was one of her own illusions. The figure's lips continued to move, but it took a few seconds for the voice to materialize within the semblance of the body.

"It's not 'funny,' it is proper Parisian French. *Mon Dieu, ce n'est pas ma faute que vous ne comprendrez pas des mots.*" The petite pilot arched an eyebrow at Mel, who stared at her in disbelief. "*Oui?* You are also not able to understand the words I am saying?"

"No, ma'am. I mean, yes, I understand you just fine, either way you want to say it. You've been here with Penny, right?"

"*Oui.* You should thank Lily for her bit of mischief. She prides herself on her more unusual tactics." The Frenchwoman nodded to Mel's right. Another gauzy patch had started to solidify, this one in brown fabric with neat rows of patches. Cyrillic letters and patches marked the new woman as a Soviet pilot, but her round face and soft peroxide curls appeared at odds with the severe uniform. She beamed at Mel and hurried around to stand at Penny's other side.

"I told you, she was more kindred than not. We have luck on our side tonight," Lily chirped. "So, you will follow me while Jeanne scouts ahead, and we will all see Comrade Stone's gifted little *devushka* to safety, *da?*"

"You kin see 'em?" Penny breathed, sounding excited. "What do they look like to you, Miz Mel?"

Mel considered the pair flanking their young charge. The Frenchwoman strode confidently alongside them while the young Russian had linked her arm with Penny's and was chattering excitedly in her ear. "Like us, really. They look just like us."

Liquid fire arced over the front line of metahumans facing off against another wave of Kriegers. Some of the air-capable troops had taken to the sky, drawing fire away from the floating platforms. Ramona couldn't stop cringing every time one of the rail guns let loose another rapid-fire salvo. She served as a shield for Mercurye, who manned one of the rocket launchers with the custom thermite payloads. Up and down the line of floating platforms, other pairs maintained a steady offensive against the never-ending wave of metal giants. They moved through the opaque shield that surrounded the floating city, the buzz and snap as each one appeared reminiscent of a transformer exploding.

The thermite rounds had no effect on the shield. Nothing that the combined forces used could penetrate it. Anything that didn't come from within the city met a sudden and violent end upon immediate contact. Ramona had seen artillery shells explode on contact and rain down slivers of jagged metal dust, so she had resorted to standing over Mercurye and forcing him to fire from a kneeling position. Those who had their own armor kept positions somewhat in the open, but the shower of shrapnel had forced others to retreat to secondary platforms. Ramona did her best to focus on Mercurye and the few square feet that they occupied, but every Thulian monstrosity that collapsed in flames was replaced by another soldier in minutes.

One of the rail guns found its mark with a Sphere already canting sideways with flaming metal on its underside. The thrashing tentacles caught the edge of an automated turret and split the foundation while the wall of water had some of the closer troops struggling to stay upright on their platforms. Ramona bent her knees and braced herself against the deck, even as Mercurye kept firing. A fresh wave of Kriegers began to pass through the shield, but the fuzz around them faded before they stepped over the threshhold. Suddenly, she could see what lay beyond the recent line of troopers: a forest of dull scarlet, with a jagged rise of mountainous terrain behind it.

Mercurye's next shot went wide, the thermite round passing between two of the soldiers. Rather than vaporize above the floating city, the dull silver shell whizzed into the alien trees and covered them with molten metal.

Seconds later, she could see the flames. "Holy shit! You see that? Eight, somebody—"

"Yes, Steel Maiden. Confirmed that the exterior shields are down. Others fighting on the perimeter have experienced similar success." Eight relayed a pattern of recent hits past the edge of the shield to her HUD, a thermal overlay showing the ever-growing field of flame. "Continue the assault until the next orders are relayed."

The explosions in the city had become nigh constant, and Untermensch was surprised he could hear any of it over the sound of automatic weapons fire. The building he was hiding behind was wracked with another blast; a squad of Thulian troopers in power armor, supported by two dozen unarmored—but still very well armed—soldiers, had set up a makeshift barricade in the street ahead. Actinic energy blasts passed RPG warheads and bullets in the air. *The invaders are now on the defensive, and* we *have become the raiders.* He smiled to himself, but the thought was cut off when one of the troopers found its mark; Unter heard the cries of his fellow humans from across the street as their position was obliterated.

The landing on the "beach" had been the easy part; with concerted fire and relentless artillery strikes, the few lines of Thulians had folded, retreating back into the jungle. The red foliage had already begun to die from the unfiltered light of the sun, wilting and sloughing to the ground. With no concealment or cover, combined with being harried by attack helicopters and the advancing army, only a few Thulians made it to the edge of the city. From there, things became conventional again for the human attackers. They had been moving through the city, supporting a platoon of tanks. The plan had been to strike fast, strike deep, and prevent the enemy from mounting a meaningful defense. As almost always happened, that had gone completely to shit from the first moment. The lead tank had been utterly destroyed by a Death Sphere, and a second one in the column damaged enough to count as a mobility kill; the crew, shaken and only lightly injured, had joined the rest of the ground forces. The other two tanks in the platoon had split off, taking a share of the infantry with them.

"Georgi!" The Commissar had taken cover behind the same building as he had; she was coordinating the offensive, and had ignored the pleas from the other commanders to stay on one of the landing craft in order to lead from the front. The rest of his comrades from the CCCP were out here as well: Pavel, Mamona, Thea, Proletariat, and even Soviette. All of them save for Jadwiga were part of RPG teams, tasked with taking down armored troopers with the specialized warheads or their metahuman abilities. Jadwiga was their combat medic; at the moment, she was attending to one of the tankers. "You and Pavel, get elevated in this building!"

He nodded once, then looked to Bear. "Front entrance is covered by the *fascista*," he said.

"So, we are making own side door!" Bear trotted down the narrow alleyway, picking a spot of wall away from the rest of the CCCP. "Fire in *all* of the holes!" He charged his gauntlets for a moment, then loosed a short blast of plasma. The concrete-like material of the wall collapsed inwards, exposing an empty room. Further down the alley, a squad of Russian soldiers ran to join the main force.

"You men! With us! We're moving to the roof," Unter shouted to them in Russian. Without a word, they formed up along the wall,

ready to follow him. He didn't hesitate; bringing up his rifle, he dashed into the room, making sure that he didn't slip on any of the rubble on the floor. What followed was three tense minutes of room clearing. Unter, with his nanoweave armor and limited healing abilities, led the way. The building appeared to have been abandoned in a hurry; furniture was overturned, drinks had been left half finished on desks, and the like. From what they found, it seemed that this building had been residential in nature; probably managerial and officers' quarters. In one room, Unter actually found a Thulian. He almost shot the creature before he noticed it was already dead—a self-inflicted gunshot to its head, from a genuine Luger laying on the floor near the body. It reminded Georgi of Nazi officers during the Great Patriotic War, who killed themselves rather than be taken prisoner by Soviet forces. He spat on the body, then continued onward.

The group soon found a stairwell and quickly made their way to the roof. It was clear of any enemies. Unter turned to the others, slinging his rifle. "Form a line at the edge of the wall, and stay hidden! Wait for me to take the first shot, then open up on them. *Go!*" The soldiers obeyed immediately, moving into position with well-honed precision. Georgi nodded in satisfaction, then surveyed the area. From the briefing, he knew that the World Ship was shaped much like a giant clam, both halves opened up, with gently curving sides. From the ground, it hadn't been too noticeable, but from the rooftop he was sickeningly aware of the curvature. Looking across the street, he could see the rooftops of buildings blocks away... from a somewhat top-down perspective. Despite this, the gravity was still pulling him straight down, instead of towards the saddle of the curve. He fought back a brief feeling of vertigo before spotting movement on a rooftop two blocks over; some *fascisti* had had the same idea as the Commissar and were setting up an ambush from above. Unter relayed their position, then went back to the task at hand.

Untermensch stowed his rifle near the lip of the roof's wall, then carefully peered over the edge. The armored troopers were still up and firing, using the barricade to shield themselves from RPGs, ducking in and out of cover to fire their arm cannons. Satisfied, he called over his shoulder to Pavel. "Old Bear, break out the warheads. I'll fire, you reload. Have the men concentrate on any armor I score a direct hit on, then alternate to the unarmored troopers."

"*Da, Georgi.*"

Unter readied the RPG tube, retrieving it from his pack, shouldering it, and waited. He watched as Pavel carefully removed a warhead from his pack, twisting it into the front of the tube, and then pulling the safety pin for the impact fuze. He stepped to the side, then roughly patted Unter's head with his mechanical hand. "*Backblast—clear!*" He knew that the soldiers were along the wall already, but it paid to be careful when dealing with explosives. He took a breath, then stood up and aimed down into the street. He immediately sighted in on the furthest suit of armor and pulled the trigger. The warhead shot out of the tube on a plume of gunpowder before the rocket engines kicked; it hit the Thulian armor in the shoulder, and the entire suit was almost immediately engulfed in napalmlike flames. The Russian soldiers all popped up from their positions simultaneously, and began raking the entire Thulian barricade with rifle and machine gun fire, focusing particularly on the armored trooper that Unter had ignited.

At that moment, Georgi felt a pang of grief. *This would be much easier with the Murdocks.* He had heard of their passing over the comms, right after the shields had gone down. Even the Commissar had been affected; she had gone silent for several long moments before giving the order to launch the assault. John had been a comrade and, albeit a strange one, had never shied away from doing his duty. Georgi had liked him, and even his wife, after a fashion. There wasn't time to mourn them, unfortunately. Unter brushed the thoughts from his mind with a lingering pride that his comrade had completed his mission, so that the rest of them might do the same.

The rooftop squad continued this pattern, with Unter and Bear hitting a trooper with the RPG and the soldiers finishing the job, until the Thulians on the ground got wise to the game. They split their fire between the Commissar's position and Unter's; even though Unter had the high ground, he and the rest of the squad were effectively pinned. Before he could radio to the Commissar with a status update, an attack helicopter obliterated the Thulian position with fire from its chin-mounted chain gun and rockets. *What I would have given for air support like this in Stalingrad . . .*

"*Georgi, regroup on the street. We are moving forward,*" was the only acknowledgment the Commissar gave. *She is juggling an entire battle; cannot be expecting a pat on the head for doing one's job every other second.* Unter began to move...and then stopped. Something made him look back to the street one last time.

With many of the structures in the World Ship burning, much of the street was obscured by smoke. The smoke in this area had cleared somewhat for a moment, allowing Georgi an unobstructed view. At the end of the street two blocks away, a mixed force of Thulian troopers and Supernaut-armored soldiers marched towards the Commissar. At the front of the formation was Worker's Champion.

Thanks to mage-sight, she *saw* Red, like a possessing spirit, imposed over the Doppelgaenger. But even if she hadn't been able to see him, Vickie would have known it was him. It was his eyes. She had never told him, but she had always been able to see through any of his disguises. His eyes were always an odd mix of sardonic and scarred yet deeply compassionate. Except for that one frightening moment when he had rescued her from Bela when they had been flat and expressionless. No one else had those eyes. They were inherently Red's.

"How...?" she literally felt her jaw drop, and her face go blank. "I felt you die! How is this even possible?"

"It's..." Red started, and sighed, his body drooping, his face falling into one hand. "It's kind of complicated. You want the long or the short version?" Vickie watched as the fingers on Doppelgaenger's hand parted, and Red peeked out from under them. "You look great, by the way."

"Short version. The clock is ticking." It wasn't what she *wanted,* what she *wanted* was to fling herself at him and alternately berate and kiss him, but...

"Would you believe...the power of love?" he said.

She blinked slowly, trying to make those words into something that actually equated to an explanation, and stared at him. "Okay, long answer then."

He started to speak, stammering something about power, about how he had not been able to let go, and gave up. "It's...gah...I don't know how to explain it. I don't have the words."

"Since when do *you* not have words!" Vickie exploded. "The entire frickin' *world* is outside making one last desperate move against these bastards, Sera and John have probably immolated

themselves taking down the ship's shields, Bella and Bull have
to stop an endless army, and I was just about to take off your
head, limbs and cut out your heart! You don't have the *words?*
Find them! We don't have time for this!"

He took a long, deep breath. "I promised to come back to you.
So I did." He reached inside himself...which was disconcerting
and weird and a little nauseating to watch, and pulled out...his
claw. The polished, chipped claw that had hung around her neck
for so long, which Doppelgaenger had "eaten." He held it out to
her; she touched it, and his hand with it...and understood, with
mathematical clarity, what had happened. She looked up at him,
so full of wonder that...now *she* didn't have any words.

When she finally spoke, her voice was soft, amazed. She had
thought that she had been overwhelmed with joy when they'd
finally kissed. But that was—nothing, compared to this moment.
All she could do was hold onto his hand and tremble with the
strength of it.

"You couldn't move on," she said.

"Nope."

"Your promise...it was a geas."

"Yep."

"And what little was left of you, held on...powered by...by..."
She held up the claw and looked at it, shocked.

"The fact that I am too stupid and stubborn to give up once
I've made a promise," he smirked.

"And by the pure, unadulterated love made manifest and stored
in this shared, linked talisman?" she said, waving the claw.

"Yeah, that too. Love claw. Yeah."

"But that couldn't have been enough to bring you back," Vickie
said, shaking her head. "You would have been next to nothing,
a glimmer, a shadow of yourself."

"Thankfully," Red nodded, and pointed at his head. "Or she
would have felt me rooting around in here. I needed time, to leech
whatever strength I could while she slept. Strength to recuperate,
and to hide. I think the union took a lot more out of her than
she'd figured, 'cause she had to sleep a *lot*, and that sleep didn't
really bring her much rest. After those first few nights, while she
was out, I found I could take control and so I got to work. Was
weird. But I learned quite a bit, kept an eye on you guys and sent
you as much as I could. Warned you when her Masters sent her

after you, God, that was close, and I...I was..." He paused for a moment, so overwhelmed with emotion and memory that he shuddered. When he continued, his voice was soft, pensive. "She knows a lot about magic, did you know that? She and Bela had set up a lot of arcane traps and countermeasures on this ship. Took a while, but I think I got them all. Just in time, too. Jack would have gotten pinched bad if I hadn't."

"And you didn't tell me you were in there because you knew I'd do something just as stupid and suicidal as you had done, to *get* to you, and get you out." She nodded, face contorting with mingled anger and acceptance, knowing he had been absolutely right, damn him. Because she would have. Hell, she and Sera and JM very nearly *had*.

"Hey," he shrugged. "Who knows you better?"

She wrapped both her small hands around his massive one, and said nothing. Mostly because she couldn't get words out around the lump in her throat.

"It's you," she said finally. "It's really you."

"Not quite the reunion I had in mind," he said, and brought her hands up to his chest. He patted them gently. "I mean, you armed with what looks like a wicked sharp sword to rip me to pieces, and me wearing this ugly-ass meat suit. But I'll take it. I'll take whatever we can get. I think we've earned that much."

Vickie nodded, steeled herself, and pulled away.

"Whatever we can get, we'll make it be enough," she said, and scanned the monitors in front of them. "Days of uninhibited sexy fun times. There might even be outfits. And toys. And chocolate. But first, we need to finish this." Her eyes flew over the readouts. "Eight? You picking up on this?"

"*Yes, Vickie. With the shields down, our invasion forces have penetrated at least halfway into the bowls of both halves of the ship. We have lost remarkably few troops.*"

"And it doesn't look from *these* readouts that they're doing the logical thing and retreating into the decks below the bowls."

"That left flank doesn't seem aware of impending attack," Red grunted. "We should send them a—" He broke off abruptly and jabbed a finger at one of the monitors. "That...that's not good."

"What is that?" Vickie asked, as a small blip began to glow beneath Red's finger.

"They're arming it," Red said grimly. "We're doing even better than I thought, if they're willing to—" He broke off again, but this time he staggered back, and began clutching his sides.

"What? They're arming what?" Vickie moved to him and rested a hand gently on his chest. "What's wrong?"

Red held up a hand and pushed her back. "She's waking up... it's too soon, but she's waking up... oh lord, you can't be here... she's coming..."

"She..." Vickie said. "You mean... her. Doppelgaenger is waking up."

"Crap..." Red gasped. "Crapcrapcrapcrap... she knows, Vickie. She knows. Oh, this is going to get ugly..."

Vickie backed up a dozen paces, and pulled the sword out of the floor, checking her watch when it was free. *Still fifteen minutes on it...*

"I..." Red groaned, his arms tight around his own body. "I can't hold her, not for long, and I don't know if I can take her. I'm not strong enough yet. She's a monster in this body, Vickie. You need to run. You need to get away from me."

"I can't," Vickie said, bringing the sword up in front of her. "I can't do that, Red. I can't leave you alone with her again."

"Then you have to finish her," Red said, wincing. "She can undo everything! You can't let her near that console! You have to..."

"You have to force her out!" Vickie urged. "You can do this, Red! I can slice her apart, but you have to separate from her!"

"I don't know if I can!" Red screamed. "No time... no time... Promise me, Vickie! I can try, but if I can't, you have to end her! You have to! *Promise me!*"

"I will," she said, tears scalding her face. As bad as it had been when she had lost him, this was a thousand times worse. "I promise." *Three times, and the geas is set.* This was going to tear her apart, past ever mending. And it didn't matter. Because only one thing mattered now, and that thing was bigger than her, or Red, or even all of ECHO. Doppelgaenger had to be stopped, here and now. She brought the sword up in her right hand, the dagger in her left in the "guard" position. This was her strongest fighting style, dagger/rapier. And she didn't intend to hold back. But there was one tiny little thing she could do for the both of them. "Your turn. Whatever happens on the other side, you *wait for me.* No matter who or what comes for you, you tell them you can't go without me." The tears were a river now, but her dagger tip wove her sigil in the air, and it drifted over to settle into him, become a part of him, marking him *hands off* to whatever might try to claim his soul. "Promise."

Red snarled, his face contorted in agony, but his eyes met hers, and he nodded.

"I will always wait for you," he rasped. "I swear it."

And then his face—and his eyes—changed.

It was a war; a battle within a body, as muscles rippled and shrunk and swelled, as guttural grunts and wheezes and muffled screams and not-so-muffled curses tore their way out of his throat, and as his face contorted, his eyes bulged and the cords of his neck stood out like bridge cables.

Vickie watched as Doppelgaenger's body fell to its knees, its arms still clutching its heaving chest, and a weary head rose to greet her with a snarl.

"Oh, it's you. Isn't it about time that I killed you?"

"You can try," she said flatly. *New plan. I need to make it hurt, and I need to make it realize it can be hurt. That should be enough shock to keep it off balance. And if Red is going to have any chance of taking it from inside, I need to make it concentrate on me.* She wasn't holding on to much hope for the latter, though, as she ran up the console, flipped in midair, aiming, not for a kill, but to take a nice fat slice of meat off the thing's upper right arm. Doppelgaenger watched, almost lazily, as Vickie's sword sliced effortlessly through a bicep. Vickie landed behind the monster, deftly struck again with an extended tip-slice down the spine, and braced herself for the counterattack.

Instead, the brute simply turned to look at her, uncaring, as a large, bleeding mass of muscle slid away from her arm and plopped unceremoniously on the floor next to her. She glanced at the wound briefly, and looked back to Vickie as the flesh simply regenerated in place.

Okay. That was what I was afraid of. New plan. I'm going to have to cut it to pieces and do so in less than fifteen minutes. Time for Can Opener.

She didn't wait for the counterattack. She charged, did a dive and a roll at the last minute, and slashed at the thing's thigh, aiming for the femoral artery, with sword and dagger. She felt a brief moment of satisfaction as Tire Iron flashed through DG's thigh muscle, and triumph as she guided Can

Opener unerringly towards the wound. Tire Iron might have had the temporary nanoedge, but Can Opener had something else besides, a permanent antihealing spell on it, forged into the metal. All it would take was the slightest cut, and local wounds wouldn't be able to heal. That was the main reason why she seldom brought it out. In its way, the dagger was deadlier than the sword. Even a small nick, and the target would likely bleed out and die, if proper arcane countermeasures were not applied in time. Vickie had often felt burdened with the responsibility of such a blade, and it was why, on the rare occasion she felt fully justified in using it, she prided herself that Can Opener had never missed its mark.

So she felt shock when Doppelgaenger's hand snatched her wrist, and Can Opener was stopped mere inches from stabbing the monster in the leg. Vickie reacted instantly, and drove her free hand up, aiming to lop Doppelgaenger's grasping hand off, when she felt a firm grip on that wrist, too. She found herself being lifted off the ground by the arms, unable to swing her weapons.

Well, shit. Vickie thought, on the edge of panic. *She's a lot faster than I thought she'd be.* She ran through her options. A blinding flash of light in Doppelgaenger's face seemed the best one. Of course, that was predicated on Doppelgaenger not tearing her in half in the next few seconds. Unlike Bela, she didn't need her hands free to cast anything. The equations ignited in her head, and she closed her eyes and turned her face to the side as the light exploded right at the end of Doppelgaenger's nose.

And nothing happened.

She raised the temperature of the chainmail on her arms to just short of burning. Doppelgaenger ignored that, too. She hauled herself up like a gymnast and planted both feet in Doppelgaenger's face—which should have broken her damn nose at least. Nothing.

"Are you about done?" Doppelgaenger asked, ignoring Vickie's kicks. She sounded bored.

"Just getting started," she snarled.

"I see you've finally got that mutilated piece of beef jerky you call a body to start moving," Doppelgaenger said, and laughed. "You know you can't hurt me, right? I guess you've been hitting the gym. *My* upgrades have been a bit more...substantial."

Vickie grimaced, and shot her a venomous look. "Where's Red?"

Doppelgaenger smiled, an enormous smile that seemed to tear her face in half. "You saw him, didn't you? He's still alive, still inside." She closed her eyes, and the smile grew even bigger. "I can feel him. You have no idea what I felt when he went away..." She paused and looked at Vickie again, her grin vanishing. "Or maybe you do, at that. Of course you do. You, the center of his... *love.*" She spat the last word out, and Vickie hissed as she felt Doppelgaenger tighten her grip on her arms.

"Now where was I?" Doppelgaenger muttered. "Oh, right. I was deciding to kill you. Maybe I should get on with that."

Vickie gasped as her arms were stretched apart and she struggled against the pain of feeling bones moving in ways they shouldn't, and tendons stretching, on the verge of tearing. Desperately, she tried to concentrate, to think of a spell—any spell—that might distract this monster. Anything, *anything*, just to escape its grasp and dart away to regroup. Nothing came to mind. All she could do was weakly resist the indomitable force that was slowly tearing her apart.

She wasn't going to escape. Not this time.

Got to... blow all... the storage... crystals... at once. That would unleash a huge magical explosion. It would certainly kill *her.* But would it take out Doppelgaenger? Between the pain and the certainty of death anyway, it was all she could think of.

And then, suddenly, Vickie felt the enormous hands release her, as Doppelgaenger staggered back, her hands clutching her head.

Vickie hit the floor, rolled, kept rolling, somehow managing to keep a grip on her sword and dagger. She got to her feet, ignoring the pain of her shoulders and elbows—it wasn't that hard, hadn't she been ignoring the pain for years?—and got ready for another attack. Hopefully this time she would be prepared for Doppelgaenger's speed. She raised her weapons, picking her target. And then paused.

Doppelgaenger's face muscle spasmed violently. Both her enormous hands were wrapped around the top of her head. But mage-sight and mage hearing betrayed more.

A slim blonde woman and Red grappled like a pair of Greco-Roman wrestlers, snarling at each other. The vision pulsed like a heartbeat with pure fury on Red's part. The woman... seemed to be grappling with her own emotions as much as with her opponent.

"You don't touch the lady, understood?" Red grunted, surprising her with a quick reversal and catching her in a rough neck lock. *"She's off limits. This is between you and me."*

"This was never just between you and me," the woman snarled, landing a heavy elbow to Red's midsection. Red appeared to cough up blood, though his grip around her neck remained firm. *"That's our whole problem, isn't it? If she wasn't around, would you really be fighting me?"*

"Yes, I would."

"Liar!"

"No, Karoline, really." Red took a knee, but held her to him, forcing her down as his arms remained locked around her neck. *"This isn't right, what you want from me. You can feel it, can't you?"*

"No, I can't!" She seemed to choke on the words. *"You died! I felt it happen! The world stopped making sense. I stopped making sense. And now you're back, and things are even more messed up. I'm broken, Red. That is what I feel! And the only thing that makes any sense is killing this cow and just taking you for myself!"*

Mesmerized by the struggle, Vickie found herself rooted in place. Part of her was screaming to take advantage of Doppelgaenger's preoccupation with Red. But there was a chance that Red might win this time...and she couldn't bear to cut that chance short.

"You can't take me," Red said, his voice quiet and determined. *"You must sense that. After all you did, you couldn't claim me. You can beat me down a thousand times. You can destroy me. But you cannot have me. You could lay waste to this world, until the two of us are all that's left standing, and still, you wouldn't have me. Ever."*

"Not ever..." Karoline said. She looked up, and Vickie felt a chill as Karoline's eyes seemed to meet her own. *"I can never have you. Not like her."*

"Not like her," Red nodded. *"I'm...sorry."*

Karoline looked back at him, astonished, and began to chortle in anguish. *"You're sorry? Do you know how small that is? How pitiful?"* She shook her head helplessly, and pointed at Vickie with her chin. *"Look at her. She's ready to cut us both down, just to finish me. You would be just another casualty in this war, cast aside for her 'greater good.' Is that how much you're worth to her? You call that love?"*

"Have you left her any choice?" Red asked softly. He looked up

at Vickie, and smiled. *"You know this is killing her, but she'll do it anyway. You know what she feels, and who she is. I showed you."*

"You did, didn't you?" Karoline exhaled, and sagged in Red's arms. *"I can't let you die again. I can't."*

"You're not leaving us much choice, darlin'."

"It's mine, then?" Karoline asked.

"Yes."

"This is what love is..." Karoline glanced back at him. *"You felt...something for me, didn't you?"*

Red nodded. *"You know I did."*

Karoline looked away. *"Then remember it, remember me. Remember me as Karoline, who finally understood love."*

Vickie watched, horrified, as Doppelgaenger's body seemed to collapse on itself. Muscle and bone and hardened skin seemed to melt as it morphed into a shapeless blob, like something out of a horror movie.

"Red!" she screamed, and took a step forward. She stopped, confused, as her mage-sight continued to show him holding Karoline at bay. They were still there, they were still whole, but they were no longer struggling. Almost tenderly, Red released his grip on Karoline's neck, letting her go. Her head drooped forward, bowed, and as her body fell forward, the disgusting, colorless blob...split. Vickie watched as the two halves fell apart, the transparent forms of Red and Karoline falling with them, joining with them and re-forming, seamlessly, until Red and Karoline lay physically before her, separated, in body *and* soul.

Karoline was the first to stir, picking herself up and coming to rest on her knees. She glanced up at Vickie, and simply nodded.

Vickie did not intend to let her change her mind. With the last seconds on Tire Iron ticking away, she swung. The initial blow bisected the skull. With the backswing, she took off the head. And she finished, burying the dagger to the hilt in the headless body's heart.

"Regenerate that," she said, then abruptly stumbled back and fell on her ass. The sword clattered to the floor, no longer able to penetrate it. She sheathed the dagger with exaggerated care.

And then she burst into tears.

Mel kept the ghostly figures in sight as they hurried Penny toward the exit. The Frenchwoman would zip ahead and double back, helping them along the roundabout path through the ship. The alarms had grown louder with each passing minute until Penny ran with her hands over her ears, the Russian pilot at her side.

The corridor split off into three identical hallways. Jeanne stood in the center, hands on her hips. Her expression was not optimistic. "This is the fastest route to exfiltration, but it is unsafe. *Madame*, it is unwise to go any further. We will need to double back."

Retracing their steps would cost them time that they didn't have. Penny shivered and swallowed hard. Tears ran down her cheeks, but she didn't say why. Mel chalked it up to terror and nothing more, and she couldn't fault the girl for the silent steady release. They had to get her off the ship and back into ECHO custody. "Goin' back isn't an option, ma'am. Which way is going to take us out?"

"Two of these three would be acceptable, but they are all blocked. You would face significant resistance." Jeanne started down the initial path, but the thunder of footsteps rumbled in the corridors around them. The floor trembled beneath Mel's feet. She moved in front of Penny, feeling the chill haze of Lily's form.

"Which way to the sub," Mel growled. "Fastest route, *maintenant*."

Jeanne flickered and reappeared in the right corridor.

Mel wrapped an arm around Penny's shoulders and pulled her tight. Her own heart hammering in her chest, she could feel the girl beginning to hyperventilate. "*Cherie*, I got you. You an' me, we ain't gonna get taken by anybody. Not by them, not ever again." She glanced up, the echo of footfalls so loud that the entire room shook. "I promise."

Lily's form blurred through Mel's arm. For a moment, she saw the young pilot's memories of a harsh Russian winter, charred bodies frozen solid and dusted with snow. The spirit shifted, and the images disappeared. Mel twitched and blinked at the spirit. "Do that again, ma'am."

"*Shto?*"

"Step back and show me everything you remember from the war. Things before then, the worst you remember. Things that happened to German soldiers, things that you did—anything." Penny shifted to hide her face against Mel's nanoweave. "Try to remember everything."

Between one breath and the next, fragments of memories

flooded Mel's consciousness. Starvation, disease, torture, and more flickered through her mind's eye as Lily shared everything she had witnessed in her short years of service before her untimely death. In the corridors, shadows gave way to dozens of Thulians, armed and prepared for intercept. Mel held on to the imagery for a half second longer, fighting down her gorge.

And then, she looked up. Eye contact with as many as possible, from left to right, Mel shared everything that Lily had given her. For each of the Thulians around them, the intersection became an unforgiving frozen wasteland, the floor covered with frostbitten corpses gaunt from starvation. The smell of burning bodies filled the small space, the sounds of their dying comrades in their ears. The imagery shifted, and the bodies bore Thulian armor and insignias. Mel ground her teeth, maintaining the horrific illusion while pushing Penny toward the corridor where Jeanne flickered impatiently.

"Just a few more steps, *cherie*. I got you, just a few more steps and we'll be out," Mel hissed, working to maintain the facade. Pressure built between her eyes with each second. How many of the Thulians were in the room? A dozen? Twenty? The longer she held onto the illusion, the figures blurred and doubled in her vision. She wavered, took another step, and misjudged the distance to the wall.

Mel stumbled to avoid the waving bits of the living creature and pulled herself from the Russian spirit's influence. Penny lifted her head, coming face to face with dozens of Thulians no longer affected by the illusion. She gripped Mel's arm with both hands, and screamed.

This close to Penny, such a scream would have made Mel's ears bleed. Instead, the air between them crystallized to ice, frosting their nanoweave. A perfect circle of ice surrounded them, but the odor of earth and decay filled the space. In the seconds where Penny continued to scream, Mel swore she felt something pulse outward from the teenager and pass through her. All of the emotions she had built from Lily's memories, the combination of them had no comparison to the wave of despair and death that shot through her and filled the compartment.

Some of the Thulians tried to scream, but only the ones on the outer edges. Those closest to Penny and Mel collapsed in a manner not unlike those in Lily's memories, but without the snow.

Even the parts of the living wall wilted, vibrant colors now gray and tendrils already crumbling to dust.

The subsequent silence made the act even more horrifying. Penny stood in the center of the perfect ring of Thulian corpses, no longer crying. Mel stood just off to the side, a hand to her bloody nose as she surveyed the carnage. Only her training allowed her to keep a neutral expression as she glanced to her charge. Penny chewed her lip, but no more tears ran down her cheeks. She stared at something just beyond Mel's shoulder and scowled.

"No, I'm not sorry for it. I told 'em that they weren't gonna hurt me an' Miz Mel ever again. An' now, they won't ever hurt anybody else, either." She wiped her nose on her sleeve, then turned toward the corridor where Jeanne had stood.

"Miz Jeanne had said this was the way out." Penny picked her way through the bodies, not looking back at Mel. "Just down this hallway."

Mel didn't know what to do or say, but she knew that it was time to go. So, she followed Penny and tried to figure out what she would tell the others, if any of them got out alive.

"Sweet Baby Jesus." Bella stared, dumbfounded, at a room the size of a football stadium.

Bulwark nodded in agreement. He scanned his surroundings, and shook his head in defeat. Every three feet or so, there was a transparent column coming down from the ceiling. These columns all fed into a vast complex machine that covered the entire top half of the room. Each of these columns held a half...built... Thulian.

"Built" because, contrary to what they had thought, this was not some sort of a cloning chamber.

"Are they...being *printed?*" Bella gasped, still staring, as another layer of muscle was laid down over the skeletons. Hundreds of skeletons. Hundreds of columns. The layer finished printing, and a new layer started.

"So it would seem," Bulwark growled. "I don't see a main control station, or a central power source. We may need to take out the printers, one at a time."

"We don't have the time," Bella muttered. "There has to be a control station here somewhere. You run left, I'll run right. Meet you at the back of the room." She didn't wait for his answer, but took off sprinting. Over her frequency, he heard, *"Eight? A little help here?"*

"Unless the control is in another room altogether, it does not match Thulian technology to fail to have a control system in place."

"Can you scan the energy flow in this room, Eight?" Bull asked. "Is there a central hub?"

"Would either of you have one of the flying eyes on your person? If so, can you deploy it? I am limited right now by your sensors." Murdock was—had been—the one who usually carried those.

"Negative," Bull replied. "Proceeding on foot." He darted left, taking in the grotesque display of half-built soldiers passing by. "You will have to triangulate and construct a map as our positions and scans update."

"Updating," Eight confirmed. *"Energy signatures in flux, but seem to originate from the direct center of the room. The control center you seek is likely there."*

"En route," Bull said, and noticed on his HUD that Bella was already sprinting towards the heart of the chamber. He altered his course, knowing she'd beat him there, and hoping she wouldn't try something like smashing it. Instead, he found her studying it. "Eight," she said aloud, as he caught up with her, "I see something that looks like one of those Thulian USB slots. Vix gave me one of those things to plug in there. Want me to do that so you can read this thing?"

"I do not believe we have a choice, Bella," Eight replied. Bella pulled something out of a small belt pouch and plugged it into the side of the board. Eight replied almost immediately with, *"There is an organic module that—I surmise—contains the basic personality to be downloaded into the waiting constructs when they are complete. I surmise, because I myself cannot read this."*

"Where is it?" Bella demanded.

"Look for an opaque black tube on the right side of the console. It appears from my end that these can be changed out for other organic modules, perhaps to serve other purposes."

"They can't always be building soldiers. Sooner or later the toilets back up," she muttered. "Bull, do you see what he's talking about?"

"Here," Bull said, and gripped one of a series of cylinders than lined the side of the console. "Data sticks. What are you suggesting, Eight? We just yank them all out?"

"*I cannot read them. Bella might be able to. They are organic...
pattern brains, for lack of a better comparison. While she reads
them, I will try to find a shutdown. The one actively being used
as the master model should be... more awake... than the others.*"

"It's worth a try," Bella said, and ran her hands over the
series of cylinders before stopping at one. She closed her eyes in
concentration, sticking a little bit of her tongue out of the left
corner of her mouth.

"*My readings show several potential energy junctions that may
be compromised. Overloading several at once should initiate a
chain reaction that will result in an effective self-destruct,*" Eight
said after a moment. "*The difficulty will be in getting to them to
overload them, simultaneously. This will require some disassembly
of the console. I would suggest—*"

Bella gasped.

"No, wait!" she exclaimed. "Wait... I've got a better idea..."

"I know that look," Bulwark said. "You're being brilliant, aren't
you?"

"Like you wouldn't *believe*," Bella chuckled, and gripped one
of the cylinders. "Take notes, Tall, Dark, and Waterproof. If we
live through this, I'm going to use this as leverage to win every
argument we have for *years*..."

"Vix, get up. Vix, seriously, we need to go..."

Vickie would have loved to be able to scrub the tears out of
her eyes with the back of her hand, but the back of her hand
was covered by a chainmail glove. She settled for closing her eyes
hard and shaking her head like a wet dog while simultaneously
rolling over onto her hands and knees and shoving herself up.
And cursing in Hungarian, Romani, and Russian. As she managed to get to her feet, she lost her balance and staggered into
Red. *My life is a tragicomedy.* "Sorry," she mumbled, looking up
at him. "Yeah. Got to go. Bella and Bull are making their play,
and we should back them."

"We've got another problem," Red said, shaking his head. Vickie
reached up and touched his face. His real face, unblemished and
perfect, marveling how it looked just as she always imagined it
would. Red paused and smiled at her, his words forgotten.

She snatched her hand back and cursed. "Sorry," she said
again. "Problem?"

Red grimaced, growled something about the goddamn universe and its timing, and finally exhaled.

"Right," he said, nodding. "Problem. Just the usual. End of world stuff, in just about"—he glanced behind him at the monitors, and back again—"ten minutes."

"Wait, what? You're serious?" The words for intercourse in six languages (and three positions) erupted out of her mouth. "Explain. Hurry."

"Tunneling missile," Red replied. "Heads to Earth's core. Boom. Bye-bye Earth. They're arming it, and probably getting ready to leave once it's away. We've got ten minutes until it's ready to launch, and I don't think we've got anything that can stop it once it's going. It'll take a little while to get to the core, but it's a world-ender, and you can bet they plan to be long gone before then."

Vickie stared at him.

"Can we stop the launch?" she asked.

"I have no idea," Red replied. "Definitely not from here. Any hope we've got, it'll be in the blast room itself."

"You know where this thing is, you lead," she said. "I can still hack my way through almost anything that gets between us and it. Tire Iron is still *sharp,* just not *that* sharp."

"It's far below us; we'll have to take one of the access tubes, and at a full-speed descent." Red appraised Vickie's chainmail. "That's going to throw up some sparks. You got a way to cut out the friction?"

"Yeah, I can renew the silence on this stuff and make it slippery." Nostalgia hit her for a moment, as she remembered learning just those spells, things a combat mage *had* to know, unless you planned to do without armor altogether. She was going to say "give me a sec," but that wasn't in the cards.

"Right. We're moving." Vickie yelped as Red picked her up before she could react and darted from the room, seemingly taking lefts and rights in the corridors outside at random. He held her like she weighed next to nothing, despite the full suit of armor. He was stronger, that much was obvious. He seemed bigger, too, and if she was not mistaken, faster. His balance and reflexes were off the charts! Even at this incredible speed, Vickie barely felt herself bounce in his arms, and she cast her spells uninterrupted, somehow managing to do so with the monumental distraction of what was—or rather, wasn't—covering Red at the moment. Clothing, to be precise.

"Not that I'm complaining," Vickie said cautiously, "But shouldn't you be wearing, uh, pants for this?"

"Kinda lost them during the split," Red grunted. "Just as well, they would just get in the way. I'm going to need every bit of exposure for what's coming."

"Why, what's com—"

Vickie yipped as they came to an abrupt stop, and Red set her down gently. He turned to the wall, reared back, and delivered a massive punch at the paneling. Vickie was shocked to see his fist actually seem to grow, to darken just before it hit, and the shock waves from the impact sent her stumbling back. There was a hole where a maintenance portal must have been, revealing what she'd been calling a "Jefferies tube," and a sharp ringing sound echoed out of it as the hatch he'd punched in fell into the darkness.

"Give me ten seconds, then jump after me," Red said. "Don't try to brake. Trust me."

He turned away, seemed to get taller and slimmer. There was a sudden scent, like you'd smell right at the beach, of the ocean. Vickie gasped as she watched something shiny, glistening, like a film of colorless oil or something similar, start to coat Red's skin.

"What did she *do* to you?" Vickie breathed.

Red turned back to her, and shrugged.

"She applied the pressure," he said. "Turns out, the rest was me. Something...woke up. This is me, fully realized, if you choose to believe her. I think I do. At that point, she really didn't have any reason to lie." He glanced back at the opening, turned back, and nodded to her. "Ten seconds. Don't keep me waiting."

He leapt into the hole—and she couldn't hear *anything*. His descent was eerily silent.

Vickie counted to ten, and leapt after him. The tube was at a steep angle, seventy or eighty degrees, utterly dark inside. She was descending so fast it was almost free fall, sliding on a thin layer of something slick and slimy—had Red left that behind? Atavistic *fear of falling* clutched her gut, but she couldn't have slowed down now even if her life had depended on it. There was a light below her, dim and gray, but growing brighter and brighter—

Before she was ready for it, she flew out of the bottom of the tube, and landed with a bounce on—

—an enormous Djinni-shaped pillow. A small head lifted itself out of the spongy flesh and grinned at her.

"So it turns out I can morph a lot more than just my skin now," he said.

"Uhm. Obviously," Vickie said. The situation was so...weird... it totally distracted her for a moment from the urgent need to get to that missile. This was Red...and it wasn't. And it was. A Red that was a sort of giant thing like uncooked dough, dense but with the pliancy of soft foam. When she tried to sit up, she just sank. And she felt hyper-aware of where the skin of her cheek was touching his.

Then she was more than hyper-aware, as she felt power—*magic energy*—flowing from where her skin touched his. And just at that moment, one of the crystals in her belt pouches flared and went *pfft*. Whatever was going on here, she had to get control of it before he drained reserves they might desperately need later! Remembering her brief experiment with a waterbed, she rolled off him and landed on the floor with her feet tucked under, allowing her to rise quickly.

"You're leeching magic!" Vickie exclaimed. "Is that where these new abilities are coming from?"

"I don't think so; it doesn't feel the same..." he said, before taking a deep breath. He exhaled slowly, and Vickie watched in wonder as he shrank back down to his normal size. Red lay a hand gently on his own chest, which had been cradling Vickie just moments before. "Something's up though, this spot does feel a little warm."

She practically stuck her face in his chest. Her eyes crossed a little as she stared at the spot with mage-sight. "Huh. You're right. It's more like a side effect. It's fading now. Jesus, you're still a magic conduit, though I suppose you're more of a sponge now. Maybe you always were, just...you didn't have much in the way of storage capacity." She looked closer, letting the equations spin out in front of her eyes. "There's *something* magical here. There's a residue of sorts, like you were caught in some eldritch—backlash? Explosion? Not a big one, but big enough to affect you. The dispersion pattern suggests it...triggered something."

"You mean, like a catalyst?"

She nodded. "Exactly. Maybe she *was* telling the truth. Just how much can you—"

And then Eight said, politely, in her ear. *"Vickie. Bomb?"*

"The *bomb!*" she yelped. "Where?"

"Due north. You seem to have landed in an adjoining hub. Look for the blast doors."

Vickie scanned her surroundings. They had landed in a vaulted intersection, crisscrossed by eight wide and semicircular corridors. Her HUD pointed north, and sure enough, one of the corridors ended on a brightly lit and reinforced portal. She got to her feet and cocked her head towards it.

"Think you can punch your way through *that*?"

"No need," Red answered, taking her hand in his as they sprinted towards the blast doors. He rapped lightly on his head with his knuckles. "Still have remnants of . . . her . . . in here. I know the bypass codes."

Vickie started to respond, and bit her lip. There was no reason to get in *that* sorry topic now. They stopped at the doors; Red flipped up an access panel, and tapped something out on what must have been a keypad, although in keeping with Thulian tech, the "digits" were glowing orange glyphs arranged in a pattern of three-two-two-three. The doors slid open silently.

And whatever he was about to say, he bit off. Because standing between them and what Vickie presumed was their goal—was the most imposing, most terrifying thing she had ever seen, *including* the Death Spheres and the dragons.

She spat out the name, and heard Red curse under his breath. "Barron."

The Master was in her full battle armor. Battle armor that nothing the CCCP had been able to muster had so much as scuffed, save for Chug. Vickie had *been there,* and had personally helped Overwatch during that fight, and she cringed, remembering how this frighteningly lithe creature had *torn Chug's arm from his body.* And destroyed Rusalka as an afterthought. And shrugged off not just one, but all of the special incendiary grenades that CCCP had thrown at them. And had not even noticed the combined punches of Saviour's energy beams and Old Bear's plasma cannons. Maybe Sera and JM could have taken Barron on . . . but Sera and JM were gone.

Vickie froze as Barron slowly tilted her head forward to look down on them. Next to this mountain, Vickie felt very, very small.

"I was promised a challenge," Barron said, and shook her head in disappointment. "And I was expecting an army. If I let you live, will you bring me an army? I thirst, and I doubt your blood will quench it in the least."

"If you want to play, you might want to go out in the yard," Red suggested. "Sun's out, there's fresh air, and we brought enough firepower to beat even you into the dirt."

"Tempting," Barron sighed. "But I cannot. At least for the moment. My duty denies my departure just yet. I must see our parting gift off before I enter the fray."

"You know we can't let that happen," Vickie said, drawing her weapons.

"Your needs are irrelevant," Barron shrugged. "You cannot hope to defeat me. I doubt your efforts would even entertain."

"Oh, I don't know," Red replied. "We might surprise you."

Barron glared at him, and then chuckled. She drew herself up to her full height, and opened her arms in invitation. "Very well, surprise me."

"Go!" Red shouted, darting right as Vickie dove to the left. Splitting up was the only chance they had for at least one of them to outflank her, to get to the doomsday device and somehow disable it before it launched its payload. But as fast as they were, Barron was faster. With a contemptuous flick of her head, she fired a burst of heat from her visor, slamming Red back into the wall. He collapsed, his body sizzling with heavy burns. Barron stepped lightly to her right, and leveled a heavy kick at Vickie. Vickie cursed and ducked into a roll, landing gracefully on her feet before leaping back. She felt a rush of air as Barron's claws whistled over her head.

"Disappointing," Barron purred. "This will not take long at all."

CHAPTER THIRTY-FOUR

Running on the Rocks

MERCEDES LACKEY, DENNIS LEE,
CODY MARTIN AND VERONICA GIGUERE

"*Uh-oh.*"

Ramona whipped her head around to see what Merc was looking at. *Uh-oh* was not the sort of thing you want to hear over your radio in the middle of a pitched battle. She shifted the rocket launcher on her shoulder and eyed the burning remnants of the Thulian forest. Something smaller than a Krieger tore through the smoldering underbrush, making a beeline for the line of metas and soldiers holding the line on the platforms.

Whatever it was, it had no intention of slowing down. "I don't have a visual, so more words would be great."

"*Placing the last two. I'm gonna share my visual, might be faster.*" The azure-white blur of her speedster zipped down from the ridge and back behind the rail guns, then streaked back along the perimeter of the fire. With most of the jungle reduced to cinders, the ECHO snipers could provide better support from strategic positions leading up to the facility. Eight had mapped out the best locations, and Merc had set up the remaining soldiers in the appropriate places.

The edges of her HUD became fuzzy, then partitioned her view into her own and Mercurye's. He focused on the basin beneath the ridge while he ran, the image blurring at regular intervals as he checked his own path to the last location. Ramona scowled and tried to make out the shapes beneath the burning trees. Something dark moved through the fires toward the ridge, then stopped and surged forward. Tree limbs and broken Thulian armor spewed from the edge of the forest, revealing a battered feminine figure in a tattered leather uniform. The woman snarled and screamed, and Ramona had a moment of indescribable panic.

She lay still as the metahuman woman stood over her to gloat. "America has grown fat and complacent," Valkyria said. "You should have chosen your allies more carefully, darling."

Years of civilian training and a new life as a metahuman operative did little to erase the memory of being shot by the Nazi supersoldier who had aided in the search for Eisenfaust in the days after the Invasion began. Ramona ground her teeth and tightened her grip on the rocket launcher, waiting for Merc's visual to align with hers.

"Newcombe's in position. Coming back to . . . uh-oh." The feeds showed opposite perspectives of the same woman, surrounded by dying Thulians. In an instant, the view from Mercurye blurred and disappeared, and the speedster raced back down to stand at the edge of the forest. He skidded to a stop as some of the fallen Kriegers struggled to their hands and knees in defense of their commanding officer.

Valkyria continued to shriek and howl, her unintelligible words seeming to call the last bits of strength and loyalty from the nearly dead Thulians. They clawed at the ground, reaching for broken weapons and burning chunks of debris to hurl at those on the front lines. Ramona felt her skin harden in response, but she had nothing left to counter the attack. With all of the snipers placed, the plan was for Merc to bring another case of shells to continue their assault.

"Check the other platforms! I need those shells two minutes ago, please." Ramona steeled herself and held her ground as Valkyria directed those around her to move forward. She could trust Merc to get the case to her in time, even to load the first shell in seconds to fire. Without armor to protect her, the Nazi soldier wouldn't last a minute coated in thermite. One shot, and she would be able to move forward and continue the offensive outside of the city.

But Merc didn't respond.

"Rick, you've got to find a different path and get over here! I'm completely out!" It took tremendous effort to keep her tone to an authoritative bark rather than a panicked wail. "Move your ass, soldier!"

"Move. Understood." Mercurye answered her with an ice-cold tone, the words clipped and efficient. Before she could question his reply, he shot toward her at top speed, his teeth bared in a very un-Merc-like smile.

At that exact moment, Valkyria let loose a bloodcurdling scream and thrust a hand forward. Her growing army followed her command, driven by some base desire to serve until their dying breaths, and began to progress toward the platforms. Those who fell and did not rise were crushed under the boots of those who gained strength and followed the command of their mistress. She stepped clear of the fire, eyes wild with bloodlust, her gaze coming to rest on Ramona.

"Steel Maiden, pivot forty-five degrees left and kneel on my count," Eight chirped quietly in her ear. The words provided a sense of grounding and she obeyed, trusting that Vickie's designee wouldn't let them down. *"Three, two, brace, mark."*

At the last word, she felt her carapace thicken and harden along her exposed side. Something collided with her metal-sheathed shoulder and upper arm, but Ramona maintained her balance as it fell to the side. It coughed and wheezed, but didn't get back up. She stood and glanced down at the platform. Mercurye curled into a ball, struggling to catch his breath. Blood streamed from his lip and one shoulder hung at a strange angle. He tilted his head back and groaned. "She's . . . mad. Crazy, and mad. She'll make you that way too, if you're not careful." He spat a bit of blood and curled tighter. "That's at least three broken ribs. Freakin' hurts, but better than a bullet."

Ramona nodded, not liking what she would have to do next. "Yes, and so is this. Preemptive apology, handsome." With one metal-clad fist, she socked him hard enough in the jaw to knock him unconscious. He sagged to the metal grate, now unable to fall prey to any more Nazi mind tricks.

Of course, this meant having to get the thermite grenades herself. "Eight, locations of the remaining grenades? We *do* have some left, right?"

"Affirmative. Two cases will be delivered to your position." Eight showed the projected delivery route, an aerial path that originated from a cache behind the rail guns. Nearly half had gone silent, casualties of the assault. Just behind the original shield boundary, Valkyria had started to gather some of the ECHO forces unlucky enough to be within her telempathic proximity. They took occasional shots at the platforms, but Valkyria's bloodlust kept them from being too accurate.

A familiar silhouette cast a shadow on the platform. "Special delivery, love. Little bird said you could do some damage with a few of these." Corbie set the first case down and did a double take at the sight of the unconscious speedster. "On the outs with your bloke, eh? I suppose good looks only get a man so far with a career woman."

Ramona laughed in spite of herself. "It's for his own good. Take him back; he's got a few broken ribs, dislocated shoulder, and a concussion. Tell the rest of them to give that Nazi bitch a wide berth if they don't want to be turned against their own." She made a face at an oozing patch of wing with singed feathers. "You be careful, too."

"As much as I can be." Corbie hefted Mercurye into his arms and took off, straining to clear the platform. He lurched to the side to avoid a smoking turret on his way to one of the frigates in the support fleet.

With a fresh supply of thermite grenades, Ramona loaded the rocket launcher and took aim at the woman standing at the rear of her newfound army. Valkyria scowled and pointed a leather-clad arm in her direction. The corner of her mouth quirked up in deadly amusement. As one, the desperate legion turned to obey their mistress.

Does she remember? She can't remember, Ramona thought. *Besides, Ramona Ferrari is dead. Again*, she realized with an inappropriate giggle. Was it okay to laugh at Death if it didn't know you were really alive?

Ramona shrugged, drew a long breath, and took aim. She wasn't one to wax philosophic anyway. She braced herself, exhaled slowly, and pulled the trigger.

Black leather became liquid silver for an exquisite second before Valkyria burst into flames. Those surrounding her fell to the ground, dead or dazed. The metahuman tried to leap into the air, but the motion sent her forward, burning flesh curling off of her body in waves of liquid fire. Ramona felt her throat tighten and her gorge rise, but she reloaded with a new grenade and focused her attention on the few Kriegers that continued to emerge from the trees. This battle was far from over, and worse things could come from within the secret world of the Thulians.

Red Saviour, behind a rank of Kirill copies in their armor, watched Boryets advance in the front rank of his repainted

Supernaut minions. They were all, including Boryets, decked out in new colors—a red camouflage scheme, to match the now-wilting jungle.

It looked like blood splatters—old, black, dried blood; brownish aging blood; and bright red fresh blood overlaying each other. *Fitting colors for murderers,* Natalya thought.

"Commissar..." Unter began, as she pushed past a couple of Proletariat's Supernaut suits—properly clad in Soviet scarlet with a gold star on their chests. "...You should—"

"I have a plan," she said shortly over the radio, so he and everyone else could hear it, and emerged from the group of giant robotic suits to stand, fists on her hips, in full view of the traitor. "So, murderer, you actually dare to show your cowardly face? I am surprised."

The CCCP channel erupted with curses, and the Allied Forces channel with objections to her action. "Comrade Eight," she ordered. "Filter channels for what I can actually use."

"Absolutely, Commissar," Eight replied obediently. She smiled, a very little. It was good to have at least one person—was that even the right word for the entity?—on her side who obeyed direct orders. The noise immediately died down, with only relevant messages coming through.

"You should not have come here, girl." Boryets' face was stone; his eyes, fixed on Natalya, didn't seem to acknowledge any of the other soldiers arrayed against him. "You will die here, for nothing. Men, prepare to—"

"FIRE!" Natalya dropped down into a crouch, her hands out in front of her. Twin blasts of energy rent through the air at Boryets. The rest of her troops opened fire as one, with rockets, bullets, plasma blasts, and jets of napalm cutting into the Supernaut ranks. Troopers fell in the initial volley, with several of the suits detonating when their napalm tanks were breached. Boryets took the entire barrage, unmoving, still watching Natalya. There was a hint of sadness there for the barest moment, and then it was gone. The Supernaut troopers quickly broke formation, spreading out to the side streets.

"All units, pursue and engage! Do not let them flank around! I will be handling Boryets."

Everyone snapped to, running to fight the traitor Supernauts and Thulians. She watched all of the dots on her HUD as they flooded the nearby streets, stopping when they encountered the enemy. They had the momentum, and better coordination via Overwatch. The Supernaut soldiers did not fare well. She couldn't focus on those fights; she had a more urgent matter to attend to. The rest of the battle was advancing as expected: completely chaotic. Most of the unit commanders were on top of their situations, however, and with Eight acting as a switchboard and quasi-commander, only the most pressing tactical decisions needed to be made by her. Whatever happened, she needed to end things with Boryets quickly, so she could get back to her *real* task.

"So, this is how you wish for it to end? So be it." Boryets took a step towards her. She barked out a laugh, causing Boryets to pause for a moment.

"How long have you been the Thulians' pet whore, old man?" She had switched to Russian, pouring extra venom into her words. Cursing in English didn't have the same *oomph* to it, as the Americans said.

A flicker of anger crossed Boryets' face. *Good*. "I have been working with them since just before the war ended. They—"

"Speak Russian, you pathetic bastard! Or have you grown so senile you've forgotten your mother tongue?"

He started walking towards her again, his hands balling into fists. "I will not tolerate your insults further, girl," he replied in Russian. "They showed me what would happen to the world if we did not steer it, together. Hitler would have ended everything in a nuclear fire, near the end. *We* stopped that."

Natalya sniffed, sneering at him. "You weakling. Licking the palms of the greatest enemy of mankind, and that is all of your justification?"

He was closer now, still coming towards her unhurriedly. "You are blinded by ideology, child. Your idiot father's fault; he didn't have the stomach to face the reality we were presented, either." *That* shook Natalya, though she didn't give Boryets the satisfaction of showing it. *He knew? For all of those years . . . and he did nothing?* "Like you, he lost himself in the stupid dream of a socialist future, of Russian supremacy against America. With open eyes, any fool could see that you don't put a starving dog against a pack of wolves. That was us against America, and capitalism. That is the world against the Masters," he continued, shaking his head. "You think that this attack is anything but an annoyance to them? With their technology, they can reduce the entire Earth to a cinder. Standing against that is suicide. The only choice, Natalya, is to work towards something where humanity survives."

Boryets was almost to her. Just a few seconds longer . . .

"Survive as slaves, maybe. And certainly not all of us; your betrayals have seen to that, coward. But so long as you live to 'save' the world, it doesn't matter, no? Your reason fled you long before your powers began to."

"That is *enough!*" He roared at her. "If I do not stop you here, if we do not drive you back, everything is over. They will destroy everything, rather than let you even begin to threaten them."

"You could have helped us, traitor. That is, if you had anything resembling a spine. Or manhood. Or your mind. As senile as you are, it must be child's play to manipulate you."

Boryets was almost close enough that she could reach out and touch him if she took a step. He raised an arm; he was going to kill her with a punch, as he had with Molotok. His gaze dripped murder . . . and then he stopped. Immediately the rage was replaced with confusion. He swayed on his feet for a moment, then collapsed to a knee, dropping his arm to catch himself. Mamona emerged from an alleyway behind Natalya, focusing intently on Boryets.

He tried to rise, his eyes going from Natalya to Mamona; the anger had returned. Just as it looked as if he'd get to his feet, he collapsed to the ground again, vomiting. Retching, he crawled forward on his hands and knees through his own sick. Agonizingly slow, he managed to get back to his feet. "Tricks won't save you," he growled through gritted teeth. Again his arm rose back, the massive bare fist clenched and huge like a wrecking ball. A thin, pale, bare hand snaked up behind Boryets' shoulder, caressing the fist. Natalya watched as the light around Boryets dimmed slightly; the hand traced Boryets' arm down to the shoulder, where the hand gripped the bare flesh through his torn uniform. His arm fell, and he was firmly pushed to his knees by the hand.

Thea, her normally milky white skin flushed pink and red, her eyes blazing with an inner fire and energy, rested her other bare hand on Boryets' other shoulder, holding him down. He tried to grab at her, but his hands trembled and fell uselessly back to his sides.

"You see, *Uncle*, this is true strength. You thought that since you alone weren't strong enough to fight the Thulians, that no one was. No one could be. I learned much from you. I am glad that I learned that you could be *wrong*, and that comrades, *true* comrades, are stronger together than anyone alone could ever be. And that when we stand together, the weakest of us has the strength of an army."

Soviette appeared from the same alleyway that Mamona had stepped out of. She walked up to Boryets and placed her hand on his forehead. "And I have learned much, so much, from *Amerikanski* healer Belladonna, old man," the Russian woman said dispassionately. "Enough to remove the only thing that made you great." He shuddered, and seemed to shrink; he didn't move away from her touch, however. Soviette removed her hand, her brow sweating. Her powers were usually used to heal and help a body's systems recover; doing the opposite took quite a lot out of her. She retrieved a scalpel from a belt pouch, using it to cut Boryets' cheek under his left eye. A thin rivulet of blood spread from the cut, following the wrinkles of the old man's face. It was the first time Natalya had ever seen Boryets bleed.

His invulnerability... was gone. At least for a time.

Soviette turned to Natalya. "It's done." She stepped back out of the way, replacing the scalpel and unholstering a pistol.

Natalya brushed the front of her uniform off, her eyes meeting Boryets'. "No big battle. No great speeches. You don't get to save the world, Uncle. You abandoned it long ago, after all. Now, it will abandon you. Dead on an alien street from a cheap bullet. I only hope that memory of you and your betrayal fades until no one even remembers who you were."

Soviette again stepped forward, leveling the pistol at Boryets' head. He ignored her, his eyes boring into the Commissar. "Natalya..." The rage was completely absent. The only thing she saw in his eyes now... was sadness, maybe a little bit of gratitude. She felt her throat close, choked with emotion. He was a bastard, a cowardly traitor who had turned on everything he believed in before she was even born, and who had killed her best friend. But still... *No*, she told herself, clamping down on her doubts. *No forgiveness for this one.* She promptly spun on her heel, her back turned to Boryets as she walked away. She heard the hammer of Jadwiga's Makarov cock, and waited for the gunshot... but it never came. Natalya spun around to witness the scene. *Despite everything that awful, traitorous bastard has done, I didn't want to watch him die. What the hell is going on?*

"I can't. I can't kill him . . ." Sovie was trembling, and not just from exhaustion. A flood of emotions crossed her face, and acute distress shone from her eyes. "I know I told you how much I wanted to, Natalya, but now that the moment comes, I cannot."

Thea stepped away from Boryets and took the gun from Soviette's unresisting hand. "Of course not, my *sestra*. You are a healer." She pressed the barrel against Boryets' forehead. "I, however, am not."

Thea pulled the trigger. The light fled Boryets' eyes as he crumpled to the ground; Natalya flinched at the sound of his dead weight hitting the street more than she did from the gunshot. He didn't look like the giant from her childhood, the hero from the old propaganda reels, or even the traitor that had murdered her best friend. He just looked like an old man, finally resting.

Thea handed the gun back to Soviette; Jadwiga looked at the gun in her hands as if it was made of plutonium. She couldn't look away from it, either. "Comrade Doctor. You and I should go help those who deserve your care. I cannot hold onto his life-force . . . his *vitality*, for very long. There was quite a lot of it." Natalya noticed that Thea was shivering where she stood with barely contained energy. "There is no redemption for him, but using his life to save *our true* comrades is some reparation."

That seemed to snap Jadwiga out of her trance. Gingerly, she holstered the gun, nodding to Thea absently. "*Da. Da.* There is work to do, still."

"I'll come with y'all," Mamona piped up. Natalya had initially harbored misgivings about the American metahuman. But in the end, she had turned out to be a sturdy comrade, and it was never more evident. *She's truly one of us.* A moment later, all three were gone, running to find people to help.

Natalya lingered for a few moments longer, looking at the body of the man that used to be Worker's Champion, the pride of the Soviet Union. Like that grand experiment, Worker's Champion was dead. Natalya left him there in the street, just another body amongst the others.

With a grunt, Red picked himself up off the ground, his mind growing clearer as his burnt flesh sloughed off and was replenished by growing ropes of muscle and connective tissue. He came to his feet in time to see Vickie dodging Barron's increasingly frustrated attacks. He knew Vickie had faced large opponents before. Given her diminutive stature, it was safe to say most of her opponents had towered over her, and she obviously knew how to take advantage of that disparity in size. But the larger opponents were usually brutes, ones laden down with bulky muscles that delivered slow and clumsy blows. Barron was different. She was fast, her strikes precise and deadly, and it was all Vickie could do to keep moving, to keep dodging out of the way. Red wondered why Barron wasn't striking with her lancing heat attacks, but a few wisps of smoke trailing off Vickie's singed hair revealed she had. If Red had to guess, Vickie's armor was fireproof. Or maybe she'd even woven magic fire resistance into her own skin. It made sense. The last thing Victoria Victrix would ever allow herself to suffer again was fire.

Red glanced to his right down a corridor that seemed to stretch on forever. The chamber with the doomsday missile lay beyond the next portal. It was part of the unspoken plan, that one of them had to get to it, to stop it from launching. He knew what was at stake here. Whether or not their forces outside were able to overcome the ship's defenses, it wouldn't matter much if there wasn't still a planet left to stand on. But this was Vickie. Everything that they had endured, everything that had brought them to this point, she was the one who had kept them going. They couldn't lose her. Not now. *He* couldn't lose her.

As far as he was concerned, there wasn't any choice in the matter. He willed the mass to come, to expand until he was almost as large as Barron, as surprised as the first time, how easily he could control his new body. He supposed he knew that it was remnants of Karoline that allowed him to do so. Something deep, muscle memory perhaps, as he drew from her history of sampling meta-abilities to instinctively grasp the fundamentals of his new talents. When he needed to be bigger, he was. When he needed extra layers of protection, be they fire-resistant or dense enough to absorb impact, he simply willed them to spring up around himself. He was still learning what he was now capable of, and what little he knew he called forth. He charged, and by the time he was barreling into Barron's flank, he was a twelve-foot-tall behemoth clad in a black, rubbery coating.

Again, her speed surprised him. With a quick feint towards

Vickie, Barron ducked out of Red's charge and spun away, but not before leveling a massive blow to his knee. Red felt his leg crack under him, and he wobbled down to one knee in front of Vickie.

"Red!" Vickie screamed.

But Red was already rising, wincing from the pain as his leg reset itself. He risked a glance down, and saw extra padding forming around his vulnerable joints. He couldn't say if it was a conscious effort or something deeper, instinctive, but he seemed to possess some rather handy adaptive capabilities now. With a mere thought, he willed the same protection around his shoulders, his elbows, wrists, hips and ankles. With an afterthought, he thickened his skull for good measure, interlacing an ultraresilient bone with shock-absorbing membranes.

"Go for her throat, her eyes, her heart if you can manage it," Red whispered. "I'll do what I can to keep her attention."

Vickie nodded, and together they turned to face their adversary.

Barron stood before them, waiting, patiently flexing and stretching in place. She cocked her head to one side, and sized them up. "You may prove amusing after all. A morsel, before the feast."

Vickie rolled her eyes. "You are such an asshole," she said, and brought her blades to the ready. Red could feel her anticipation, her relaxed stance a mere facade. He felt it coming off her in waves. Despite it all, despite what was on the line here, she was enjoying herself. It seemed crazy, but he supposed he understood it. Victoria Victrix had been a prisoner in her own body for years now. There had been pain with every step, with every breath, with every thought. Once upon a time, she had been the warrior. When someone needed saving, she had leapt to the call. Ever since she had been scarred, she had retreated into a shell of herself. It wasn't her on the frontlines anymore, she was the one who had needed saving. Oh, how she must have *loathed* that. But now here she was, in the heart of the dungeon, clad in her armor once again, nimbly dancing around her giant opponent, her weapons in hand. Whatever she had done to get here, to this place, she had once again earned the name of Warrior.

"Time to kill us a dragon," Red murmured.

"Damn right," Vickie snarled. "I've got point."

"Like hell you do..."

Together, they leapt into the fray. Barron watched them, bemused, as they flanked her. Red grunted as Barron jabbed at him, catching him with a deft blow to his midsection. He staggered back and Vickie darted away, Barron's swift and deadly fists forcing her to keep her distance. The jab had been nothing, a fraction of Barron's enormous strength, but he felt a part of him screaming. He took a breath as he felt the bulk of his guts liquify, then shudder, then regenerate. It occurred to him that it wasn't the trauma that might do him in. If he had to guess, he could continue to take blows like that for hours... but her strength! What could she do to him if she managed to get a grip? He imagined being ripped to shreds, his parts hurled to the far reaches of the room...

He watched, in horror, as Vickie executed the same Parkour stunt she had against Doppelgaenger, flipping over the head of the monster and lashing out with her sword—

—neatly slicing the tip off one of Barron's upraised claws before she landed and scuttled out of the way of retaliation.

But there was no retaliation. Barron was momentarily in shock, staring at the black viscous blood that flowed freely from a newly exposed appendage.

"Impossible," Barron gasped. "You cut through my armor! Nothing of this world could possibly..."

"Like I said," Vickie panted to Red. "Still sharp. Just not nanoblade sharp."

"Alright, alright..." Red muttered. "You've got point."

Barron stared at him, snarled, and completely turned away from him. He wasn't the threat, after all. The small woman with the really, really sharp blades was, and Barron clearly was not used to *anything* being a threat. She watched Vickie intently, her stance dropping to a cautious prowl as she slowly began to close the distance to the defiant mage.

"Really?" Red called after her. "You don't want to play anymore? Just with her? This a girl power thing?"

"You are of no moment," Barron hissed back, her eyes fixed on Vickie's blades. "Your inexperience with your new body betrays you. You have not even touched your potential. You cannot possibly hurt me. You are..."

Barron hissed as Red Djinni rushed her from behind, locking her two fighting arms behind her in a sudden hold, her remaining arms flailing about in protest. He struggled with her, almost losing his grip as she thrashed against his weight, until he brought his arms together and willed them to fuse, and to expand. This time it wasn't flesh or reinforced bone. He almost stopped, amazed at himself, as he watched strands of webbing erupt from the pores of his skin, flying into place until he was bound to her, her huge arms caught in a reinforced cocoon of silk.

"I am, it turns out, adaptable," Red grunted. "Vickie, would you be a dear and decapitate this thing for me?"

"With pleasure," Vickie snarled, and backed up as far as the wall to give herself more room for a rush. As small and light as she was, she would need momentum to make up for a lack of mass behind her blow. Red felt Barron go still, and then her remaining arms began to lash out at him. While they were smaller, this was still Barron, and Red grit his teeth as each delivered a series of rabbit punches to his chest that might have caved in a steel door.

"No hurry," Red wheezed. "I think my spleen's still intact."

"What about your brain?" Vickie asked, braced against the wall, planning her move. "Never mind. That's not the important part of you." And she launched. It *was* a *launch*; she moved faster than Red had ever seen her run before. And from Barron, he felt—tension. There was something about the way she was holding herself, bracing against an attack that she knew might cut deep, and perhaps even kill her. Red felt the alien giant twitch in place. No, it was more than that. It was a shiver. Barron was trembling.

Barron was *afraid*.

I don't think she's faced a real threat in ... a long, long time. She's had things her way for so long she's forgotten she's mortal.

As Vickie closed in, Red felt Barron sag in place, and he fought down an urge to crow in triumph. Instead he dug in, bracing for impact, when he felt a building pressure in his arms. Elation turned into a growing sense of alarm, as he realized Barron was not giving up after all. She was bracing herself too, but not against Vickie's strike. Red watched as the muscles in Barron's shoulders bulged. She was straining against the confines of Red's reinforced hold. She was strong, but was she strong enough to ...?

It was an awful sound, like a guttural snarl, only louder, amplified, as Barron pulled her left arm free, tearing Red's makeshift arm shackles apart, the silk strands snapping and cracking apart in bunches. With a final push, Barron screamed, pulling her arm away, and Red's arm along with it, tearing it away from its moorings, leaving only a bloody socket at his shoulder. She screamed her fury, swung her right arm forward, and Red yelped as he found himself dragged along and suspended upside down in front of her, a human shield to Vickie's charge.

He watched as Vickie tried to slam on the brakes, her look of fierce determination replaced by one of horror and dismay, and felt her bounce back off his rubbery frame, rolling away to absorb the impact. From his perspective, it was almost funny. He nearly laughed, until he felt himself smashed to the ground, a heavy boot planted on his stomach, and his other arm tearing away as Barron pulled herself free from him. Red closed his eyes and heard himself groan. The floor shook. It was Barron, he supposed, her heavy steps thundering away into the distance.

"Red!"

Looking up, Red saw Vickie enter his field of view, peering down at him, her eyes wide and frightened.

"Jesus Frog on a pogo stick," she gasped.

"Enough of your spring-loaded, messianic amphibians, woman," Red heard himself mumble. "I'll bite her freaking kneecaps off."

"You have no arms!"

"It's only a flesh wound."

With a fierce frown, Vickie pointed to her left. Red glanced over, and saw his detached arms lying in ruined strands of silk and growing pools of blood.

"Right," he sighed, and came to his feet gingerly. He hobbled over to them and knelt down. "Help me out here?"

She obliged, heaving each arm up to his shoulders, grimacing as they made odd squelching noises as they reattached themselves.

"You're weirded out," he said, rising and testing his range of motion.

"I've seen weirder," she assured him. "Trust me, this rates as a few ripples in the sanity pond. No irrevocable damage done, at least not yet."

"Just for future reference, what would rate as the irrevocable variety...?"

"Y'know, fight first. Relationship talk second. She's heading for the missile room!"

Red spun around in time to see Barron disappear through a portal. He cursed and raced after her. Glancing around, he was surprised to see Vickie right beside him, matching his long strides with a face full of determination and a surprisingly fast sprint.

"Your swords are sharp," he said, turning back to the closing portal, "But can you really get enough force to cut through her neck guards?"

"Honestly, I'm not sure," Vickie replied grimly, and motioned for him to open his arms. "But I'll have better luck there than driving them into her chest." She leapt for him.

"I might be able to," Red offered, catching her in a rough grapple.

"You ever use a sword?" Vickie countered, balancing herself on one of his forearms. "Throw!"

"Can't say that I have," Red admitted, and hurled her forward with a smooth cast, as if they had been doing this together all their lives. She tucked her knees to her chest and landed in a nimble roll. She came to a precisely calculated stop, leapt up in a sudden lunge with her sword, and neatly thrust the point across the threshold, blocking the sliding door before it slotted into place. Red caught up to her, slid his fingers into the narrow groove between the door and the bulkhead, and with a bellowing howl, forced them apart.

Vickie squeezed inside while he was still forcing the door open, leaving it for him to maneuver himself into the room. He let the door go, snapping his arms back as the door closed behind him with a weighty *thud*. Only then did he turn.

The round room was bathed in that orange light the Thulians seemed to like so much. In the floor was—something. It looked like one of those irising portals he'd seen elsewhere, with a low balustrade around it. Above it, surrounded by a circular, grated catwalk, the bomb hung like the evil fruit of the plant that was this ship. Not that it looked like a bomb. The front end was all the machinery for digging its way through the Earth's mantle to get to the liquid core, the back end was smooth and mirror-finished. The whole thing gleamed with an oily sheen, as if even light was repelled from it.

On the other side of the pit was the control station. Barron stood over it, her visor open, her main arms raised in victory as she pulled one of her lesser hands away from the interface. Black fluid continued to leak from her injured claw, but she ignored it. Red felt the floor beneath him start to hum, and with a steely rasp, the portal beneath the bomb slowly opened.

"Too late!" Barron laughed. "Your pitiful planet is doomed!"

Somewhere, a Klaxon began to ring and the room was plunged

into momentary darkness, and then bathed in a pulsing blue light that seemed to come from everywhere. It flashed on and off, and Red cursed in dismay as the control panel sank into the floor and a terrible rumbling sound ramped up above them.

Barron had activated the Burrower.

"How do we turn it off?" Vickie screamed.

"We can't!" Red yelled back. "The controls are seconds away from eating themselves! That thing is their ultimate juggernaut! It won't stop until it reaches the core, then game over!"

"We have to try! There must be something!"

"Its hide is tougher than anything on this planet!" Red screamed. "It's completely self-contained, and it repels energy!"

"Not helping!" Vickie said, and screamed in frustration. "Give me something to work with here!"

"Like what?" Red screamed back. "You want me to pull some miracle out of my ass?"

"This can't be it," Vickie whispered, her face gone deathly white. "This can't be how it ends. Can it? After everything we've endured, to just be wiped out of existence?"

Red whirled around, his senses screaming at him in sudden danger. In the harsh, blinking light, he found himself face to face with Barron.

"Works for me," Barron purred. She reared back and swung a heavy blow across his chest. Red flew up and ricocheted off the side of the Burrower. He felt his neck snap, and he landed in a heap on the smooth balustrade.

"You'd better make this quick," Bull rumbled.

"Quick?" Bella said incredulously. "Are you *insane?*"

"I *knew* you would say that," Bull said, shaking his head. "I knew it, and prompted you anyway..."

Bella put both hands on the top of the black cylinder that Eight had indicated, and concentrated. She'd put in as much study of their Thulian captives as she could spare time for, and their brains were not all that dissimilar from humans in the *way* they worked, even though they varied from human in construction.

But was that because they're essentially printouts? Never mind. Concentrate.

With a pattern this simple, once you got past the autonomic functions and the programmed memories that made them fighting machines, you had to give them a very simple set of visual instructions. Who is your enemy? Who is your friend? What do they look like?

She knew she had it when she touched a part of the mind that held pictures—pictures of simplified humans, of fellow Thulians, and creatures she now knew were the so-called "Masters."

"Gotcha," she muttered, and went to work.

"Bella, whatever you are doing, you'd better finish it fast." Bull's calm, steady voice filtered through her concentration. "They're getting skin-printed. I think they're about to be decanted."

She doubled down on her concentration, putting so much effort into it that she began to sweat and pant with exertion. And to think... if it hadn't been for Mel... she would never have learned how to reprogram brains in the first place. She just hoped no one else ever did. This was changing memories... something brainwashers had been dying to achieve forever.

She felt Bull's protective bubble spring up around them both, and broke off what she was doing. She spun around, grabbing his substantial shoulder to keep her balance as she went light-headed for a moment. All around them, the fluid had drained out of those cylinders, which were sliding up into the ceiling.

A hundred or more pairs of eyes opened, and regarded them dispassionately. A hundred or more pairs of feet stepped down off the pedestals, as the newborn Thulian warriors turned to face them. Bull put himself between Bella and the mob.

A hundred naked Thulian arms rose in the Nazi salute.

"*I believe they are waiting for you to give them orders, Commander,*" Eight said brightly.

"What's Thulian for *we're under attack, defend your masters?*" Bella asked breathlessly. It had worked!

"Use German," Bull muttered, before Eight could reply.

"*Wir sind angegriffen, verteidigen deine Meisteren!*" she snapped. Over a hundred stark-naked Thulians barked a single unintelligible syllable in reply, turned, and *ran* out of the room. Meanwhile, the cylinders had slid down from the ceiling again, filled with fluid, and the printing process resumed.

Bella sagged against Bull; he held her to him, marveling at her. "What... did you do?" he asked.

"I used the same neural-net reprogramming I used on Mel, except I did it on the pattern brain. I figured the programming would be uploaded to the printouts at the last minute, because they wouldn't want to bring the brains online until they were ready to decant," she said breathlessly. "It was easier than with Mel, because it was simple friend-or-foe bit switches. I flipped the switches. Now they'll *all* be like that." She laughed weakly. "Now we don't have to shut this thing off! It's making *us* troops with every printing."

Bull grinned at her. "Nice going, lady. Good to see something going right, for a change."

The last word had just left his mouth when a harsh alarm sounded off, and blinking blue lights dropped down from the ceiling.

"Bloody hell," Bella said in dismay, punching Bulwark in the bicep. "Why would you say...? Are you *insane?*"

"Ask me again later," Bull sighed. "One of these days, I might have a good answer."

Bella shook her head and took his hand in hers. "C'mon. Let's get the hell out of here before anything else happens."

Barron turned to Vickie, who didn't hesitate and leapt forward, swinging for Barron's throat. The giant gave her a pitying look and held up one arm to block the attack. Vickie's sword cut into the armored forearm with a horrible metallic squeal, and she hissed as it dug in. It was stuck! For one horrible moment, Vickie dangled helplessly from her sword, unable to dislodge it. She tried to rattle it loose, and stifled a cry of alarm as Barron turned in place to hop up on the lip of the now open portal. Barron held her arm out, and suspended Vickie over a seemingly bottomless pit.

"After I drop you in and dispatch your paramour by ripping him to shreds, I will need to report back to my Supreme Ober-fuhrer," Barron said. She sounded bored. "Perhaps I will even have time to see some true combat before we leave this forsaken excuse of a planet. Oh, the menial tasks we must perform in the name of duty. However, there will soon be time to engage in more frivolous pursuits. Like examining this blade of yours. I find it most perplexing. How anything of your primitive technology is able to cut through one of our ultimate Warskins is worthy of inspection. I don't suppose you would just tell me, and save me the trouble of having it studied?"

"Bite me," Vickie snarled.

"I thought as much," Barron said, and raised her free fighting arm to slap Vickie away, as one might a pesky insect. "Tell me your name, little one. Allow yourself the honor of being known to me before you perish."

Vickie glared at Barron and stuck out her chin in defiance. "The name's Victoria Victrix Nagy, you asshat."

"Victrix?" Barron said, and relaxed her stance. "You *are* known to me. You are wanted by my Master. How fortunate, we had thought you lost to us. Rejoice, for your life will not end this day. We have a grand fate in store for you. You will know great honor as you serve us until the end of days."

"Y'know, I don't see that happening," Vickie said. "I'm not so good with the whole slavery thing. I'm funny that way. But then, so are most humans. No matter what you do to me or anyone else, you've lost. You lost the moment you activated your planet-buster. Now go crawl away and find some other poor slobs to enslave, and know *you never broke us.*"

"Is that what you think?" Barron said. "This was never about enslaving you. Do you truly believe that we, with all our power, would find the least bit of entertainment in enslavement? You flatter yourself, human. You cannot be this simple. You are one of the few on this pathetic rock whose mind intrigues us, deemed worthy to be installed in the Collective. Is it possible that we were mistaken?"

"Maybe," Vickie said, and shrugged, even though she was clinging with both hands to Tire Iron's hilt. "Or maybe I'm just stalling."

Barron's eyes widened in sudden comprehension, as Red came barreling out of the darkness and slammed into her back with his shoulder. She shot forward into the pit, flailing in an unsuccessful attempt to keep her balance, and Vickie grunted as she found herself falling with her.

"Vix!" she heard Red shout as she fell. "Let go, go limp!"

Vickie released her grip on Tire Iron, and watched Barron sail over her and plummet into the hole. She gasped as something caught her around her waist, snapping her back like a bungee cord. She looked down and found herself restrained in the grip of elongated fingers, attached to an elongated arm, attached to a breathless Red Djinni who peered down at her from the edge of the pit.

And then, she found herself falling again.

"*Urk!*" she squawked. Tethered by Red's long and stringy arm, she swung quickly down to collide with the wall of the pit. She heard something snap and felt a sharp stab in her midsection. Briefly stunned, she grimaced in pain as Red quickly reeled her in, his arm shrinking back to its original size. Gently, he cradled her as he bent down to place her beside him.

"Good catch. Was this Cthulhu or Indiana Jones?" she asked, panting.

"You're hurt," he said, and ran a hand gently over her stomach. "Cracked ribs. I need to get you out of here."

"Priorities. Bomb first, hurt later," she replied, looking up at the evil thing. She glanced down at the pit. "Think she's gone?"

In the distance, they heard a hard crash, then another, and then silence.

"I really doubt it," Red answered.

"Yeah," Vickie sighed. "Me too."

Sure enough, from a distance they heard something like a whistle, and it was growing, a sound Vickie realized she'd heard before—when Barron had flown off from the fight in front of CCCP HQ. *"Fasz!"* she said, with feeling. *"Futui! Blyad!* We need to end her! Now!"

"You're in no condition to go up against her," Red said, shaking his head. "Besides, she's got your weapon."

"Not this one," Vickie said, and held up Can Opener. "Though I'll be damned if I can think of a way to get close enough to shiv her with it." The jetlike noise was getting closer.

"Or have the muscle to make the blow stick," Red replied grimly. "We're running out of options here. It's time to book."

"We can't!" Vickie hissed, and pointed to the bomb. "Not until we stop that thing! If we don't do that, *everyone dies.* We die here maybe, but at least die *trying,* not hiding, waiting for everything to go *kaboom!* I'm done with hiding!"

"Then we're screwed!" Red shouted. Vickie watched him sag, his head drooping in defeat. "We can't fight the unbeatable bad guy, and we can't leave without destroying the invincible weapon. We're out of options here, Vickie. We've got nothing left."

"You've got me," Vickie said, and handed him her dagger. "And you've got this. She wants me alive, so I'm the distraction. Don't know if you're going to get more than one shot with it. Make it count."

Red took the blade from her, and nodded. Shaking his head, he drew himself up.

"I've got you," he breathed.

"Yeah, you do," Vickie said with a small smile. "And I've got you. So c'mon, let's see what a couple of Misfits can do on a hope and a prayer."

This is hopeless.

Red pressed his lips together, afraid to say the obvious. Vickie was right. They couldn't retreat. Somehow, they had to stop the bomb, and somehow, they had to get past the hulking invulnerable alien to do it. As they backed away from the lip of the pit, waiting for Barron to fly up to them, he glanced at the small blade hidden in his hand. He supposed he could put some muscle behind it, and drive it into Barron somewhere, but it had to be a killing blow. The problem was, he drew his strength from his size. He had not tested the limits of that yet. Just how big could he go? He suspected he could grow until he was enormous, large enough to dwarf even Barron, to fill up most of this enormous chamber, if need be. But there were limitations with growing bigger. Even now, he was definitely slower. All that mass was weighing him down. He idly considered sacrificing some of his protective shell, and immediately decided against it. There was no way he could survive for very long against Barron without some armor. And then there was the issue of wielding the dagger itself. The thing of it was, the dagger wouldn't grow with him. He couldn't hold it properly as it was, its length barely the size of one of his fingers. If anything, he reasoned that he should shrink back down, even if it cost him strength. Harden the shell, get a better grip on the blade, and drive it home at the base of Barron's skull. And how was he supposed to do that? He was no stranger to fighting with a blade, but having seen Vickie in action, he knew he was nowhere near her level of expertise. Vickie was right. He had one shot at this, and he simply didn't trust his skill enough to get the job done.

"I don't suppose she'll just stand still and let me stick this into her eye," he muttered.

"We'll flank her again," Vickie said, clutching one hand gingerly to her side. "Try and get behind her, look for your opening."

"We've seen her fight!" Red hissed. "It's like she's got eyes in the back of her head. She'll see my clumsy swing, and she'll just dodge out of it."

"You're going to have to be patient then," Vickie replied, through clenched teeth. "Don't let her see it until you've got an opening."

This is hopeless, he thought again. *We're gambling everything on a long, long, long shot. But what else do we have? What else, dammit?*

The sounds of Barron's jet grew louder. She was almost upon them. Red took a moment, and looked down at Vickie. She was so strong, so sure of herself now. He felt a brilliant flash of love and pride as he took her in. She was everything he had ever hoped she could be. If this was to be their last few moments, at least they had that. With all they had endured, they had come out stronger at the end. And more, they had each other, finally, at last, they had *each other*.

"We have each other..."

Vickie looked up, and favored him with a sad smile. "Yeah, we do." She reached out, twining her small fingers between his.

Red gasped as Vickie's touch gave him a sudden jolt, and from some shrouded corner of his mind he heard a voice, and not just any voice.

"No one has to be alone."

"What...?" Red flinched as he remembered. It seemed so long ago, before she was Karoline, before she was Doppelgaenger. Back then, she had just been Mel, another in a long line of broken souls that had found a way into his bed. After, they had shared a harsh moment of truth, and with a simple touch, she had said something that had stayed with him, always in the back of his mind, no matter how dark things got.

"No," he whispered. "No one has to be alone. But how is it enough?"

He almost heard Karoline chuckle and he stopped, his breath caught in his throat, as her ghostly voice rang out in his mind. *"Show me what love is, Red. Show me what love can do."*

He must have made a little choking sound, because Vickie glanced up at him, meeting his stunned look with eyes that were, oddly enough, at peace, and full of trust. She didn't have to say anything. That trust was there and had been, he realized, for a long time now. But he had to ask anyway.

"Do you trust me?" he breathed.

A flash of puzzlement, then peace—and yes, trust—were back in her eyes. She nodded once, decisively. "Whatever you need. I'll back you."

"Go limp again," he whispered. "We're about to dive into that irrevocable kind of weird."

Vickie smiled up at him, laid her hand gently on his face, closed her eyes, and went limp in his arms. Red took a deep breath and held her in a tight embrace. He let himself flow around her, drawing her in...

...until they were One.

This should have been the Mindscape. Instead, they were just...as they had been, staring at the pit where Barron would emerge, any moment now. There was no Mindscape. Why was there no Mindscape?

"Tim Torres? Seriously? Your real name is Tim?" *Amethist rolled over on her side to stare at them, her shoulders shaking with laughter.*

Partly embarrassed, a little annoyed, but this was Vic, *and how could they be angry at her? Until she added, "What? Like Tim the Enchanter?"*

And they felt a chill. "Don't call me that," they snapped, shoving memories they didn't want to face back into their closet. "Don't ever call *me that..."*

The hell? Why were they thinking that now? Oh, because they wanted to know what their real name was. Real names were important. Real names had power...

They held the sword up to the light, eyeing it critically. Unlike most of the other blades that had been handed out to their class-mates, this one was short, about the length of a Roman gladius, suited to their diminutive size. It was perfect, of course. Perfect length for them, perfect balance, perfect weight. And magic-forged, that went without saying.

"What are you naming it?" Paul asked excitedly, as the rest of their classmates, one by one, thought of the "perfect name," thrust their blades up in the air with melodramatic gestures, and shouted it out.

"Naming it? Nothing," they replied, testing the heft. "It's a tool, a thing. Paul, for godsake, you should know *this. Names are important! You put a name on something, and you make it into something more than a tool, you turn it into something you cher-ish, something you aren't willing to sacrifice, or to lose! No sword is worth that—you sacrifice for living things, not for objects!"*

"Then name it as a tool, Miss Nagy," the Headmistress said mildly. "You have to give it some name, or it won't bind to you and accept your magic."

"All right then," they replied, resting the blade lightly on the palm of their left hand. "Tire Iron. I name thee Tire Iron."

Two or three of the kids closest to them—all of whom had given their blades pretentious names like "Braveheart" and "Adamant"—turned to gape at them. But the sword responded, glowing brightly for a moment before settling back to normal. The Headmistress smiled.

"Good. Now the dagger." She raised an eyebrow at them. "I assume you have a similarly utilitarian name in mind?"

They just smiled. Of course they did. Can Opener.

Suddenly it all settled into place. Why was there no Mindscape? There was no need for the Mindscape. Why were they reliving memories? It was a brief moment of adjustment, of settling into their new consciousness. Together, they were somehow seamless, something neither Red nor Karoline had ever experienced with another. And there was power, and certainty, and purpose... gone was the pain and loneliness, and any imperfections. Together, they seemed perfect in every possible way.

Perfect trust. Perfect love. They smiled at the quotation. Probably not what the original writers had had in mind.

There was a feeling of discomfort and they rid themselves of it; Vickie's suit of chainmail, lined with leather, then canvas, then the softest of linen, dropped out of them to the ground. It was somewhat magical too, and it was a pity they couldn't wear it... but they were going to have to be bigger than it was and there was no way, with so little time to spare, to make it fit. The dagger was still in their hand, but now it fit itself into their hand exactly as if it had been made for them. They seemed smaller, and larger, than they were. It hardly seemed to matter. Size made little difference now. The magic that made up Victoria Victrix Nagy spread out with ease, touching every part of their body. They were infused with all of Vickie's skills—all of her training with the arcane, with combat and strategy. And they had all of Djinni's cunning and agility, honed from years of fieldwork as an operative, a thief, an assassin, and most recently, as a trusted member of ECHO. They were one with all of it, as they were with the full potential of Red Djinni's unbounded power.

"She is coming," they said, the sounds of powerful jets almost upon them. "Are we ready?" And they answered themselves, laughing. "Oh, yes. Yes, we are."

And from the pit Barron emerged, incandescent in her fury, and touched down with an angry crash on the lip of the balustrade. She had lost her helmet in the fall or, perhaps, ripped it off in a fury. It was almost impossible to read her very alien face, which in any case didn't seem to have the musculature to display facial expressions. The head, covered in tiny purple feathers, was surmounted by a crest of longer, silky feathers of a darker purple hue, and the head beneath the crest was actually heart-shaped, with a pair of huge, childlike, slanted eyes colored a rich emerald-green with no whites to them, a tiny, tip-tilted nose, and an unobtrusive slit for a mouth. Unless you looked really closely, you couldn't even tell that mouth was snarling. She drew herself up to her full height of over eight feet tall, glaring at them, and brought up Tire Iron, clutched defiantly in her bloody claw.

"Fleas," Barron spat. "Together, apart, it makes little difference. I will tear you asunder and feast on your entrails."

"We are beyond you," they answered simply. "Stand aside. You will delay us no further."

"I have been the destroyer of planets!" Barron roared. "Legions have fallen to these hands! What chance do you hope to have, mortals, against a *god*?"

"We are hardly mortals, and you are nothing like a god. You are..." They cocked their head, sizing up their opponent, and nodded. "You're still an asshole. Asshole? Yep. Asshole. And by the way, put that down before you hurt yourself."

Barron snarled, raising Vickie's sword higher still, and stopped, her eyes widening in astonishment. She looked down, and stared in confusion as an enormous fist of stone erupted from the pit to grip her by the ankle, rooting her in place. She turned back to them, furious, as they deftly traced an intricate pattern of light in the air with their fingers.

"This is so much easier when I'm my own medium," they said, smirking.

Contemptuously, Barron swung a fist down and smashed her earthen shackles to dust. "You seek to stop me with mere tricks. I, who have smashed apart whole mountains..."

"Yeah, yeah, you're awesome, yadda yadda," they said, yawning ostentatiously. "Come on then, talk is cheap. Let's see how big and bad you are."

Roaring again, Barron launched herself at them. It was clear to them she knew nothing about handling a sword; she held it like a hammer, and made a clumsy overhand swing at them that she probably thought was unstoppable. If there was ever a textbook move for an Aikido counter, this was it. They waited until the last second, moved slightly off the line of attack, reached out and grasped Barron's "wrist" and, effortlessly, using the momentum of her own downward swing and charge, sent her into the wall. Whirling in place and pouncing on the opportunity, they drove Can Opener for Barron's neck.

But again, Barron surprised them with her speed. She used her own impact to roll out of the way, and saw Can Opener flash past her, harmlessly cutting air. Her eyes widened at the sight of the blade, and when she bounced to her feet her stance was defensive, cautious. She circled them slowly, her movements less certain than before. She lunged again, this time leading Tire Iron with short, deft stabs that they easily dodged and parried away.

And meanwhile, behind them, the bomb hung, waiting to drop.

We don't have time for this.

Well, we're open to suggestions.

They attempted a quick stab with the blade, and missed again as Barron danced back out of reach.

She's on the defensive, and she's too quick. We need her guard to fall. As it stands, if we keep up this pace, it's only a matter of time before we mess up and she gets a good dig in with that sword.

Well, so what if she does?

If she does . . . ooooh. That's a good thought.

Isn't it?

They continued to circle the giant, trading empty blows, waiting for their moment. It had to be timed and acted perfectly. They were betting it all, knowing that for a moment, they would be completely vulnerable.

Last shot. We ready for this?

Go time.

They hopped up, dodging another slicing attack, but this time, instead of dropping back, they leapt forward, arcing high into the air and descending, dagger first, squarely at the giant's exposed chest. Barron grunted in surprise, and with a quick reversal, swung the blade into Red and Vickie's chest, nearly splitting them in half. They stopped, midleap, and stared at the sword as it protruded from the area of their navel. An enormous fount of blood erupted from the cut, and they quivered in place, their head now hanging low, a bloody froth bubbling over their lips and cascading down their body.

Barron relaxed her stance, chuckled, and held them aloft, impaled on the blade.

"A worthy fight," she said. "Far better than I would have imagined. You have earned your last words, if you can utter them."

Red and Vickie raised their head, and mumbled something that became a coughing fit, splattering more blood over their assailant. Barron slowly mopped some from her face, and leaned in.

"I'm sorry, what was that?"

Red and Vickie coughed again, but managed to look her full in the face.

"Assholesayswhat?"

Barron flinched, confused.

"What?"

And in that moment, Red and Vickie's hand, which had been hanging limp and lifeless, barely holding onto the dagger, lashed up, fast as a striking cobra and with all their power behind it. They drove the blade in deep, past Barron's open and bewildered lips, and felt a hard crunch as it bit through the roof of her mouth. They froze together there for a moment, Red and Vickie still suspended in midair, Barron staring into their face. Then the behemoth dropped, and they fell with her.

They lay on their side for a moment, before releasing their grip on Can Opener. With a shudder, they gripped Tire Iron's hilt with both hands, and coughing, pulled it out of their chest. They lay gasping for a moment, before rising slowly to their feet, their body zipping itself bizarrely back together.

"Christ," they said. "That hurt. That hurt a *lot*."

Things had only grown more difficult after Red Saviour finished dealing with Worker's Champion. The Supernaut troopers they had first encountered had only been the lead element for a much larger force. Instead of facing the coalition forces head on, like the Thulians had been, the Supernaut troopers had spread out, occupying the buildings and turning each into an ad hoc bunker.

Natalya's assault had slowed considerably; each building had to be checked and cleared. The ones that held Supernaut traitors would either come alive with automatic weapons' fire and gouts of flame from window ambushes, or explode in a cloud of fire when the assaulters entered. Her people were good, but she was losing too many of them. Soviette and Thea were working as hard and as fast as they could, and Natalya genuinely marveled at the way the pair seemed to be right where they were needed almost before anyone could call out, "Medic!" But there were only two of them, and her people were still dying.

If she had her way, she would pull her forces back and simply raze the entire city with artillery, marching the barrage forward and leveling every single building. *Much safer and easier to sweep smoking rubble for dead enemies, than fighting positions for live ones.* Now that the attack was in full swing, the Thulians had woken up; their antibombardment defenses were in overdrive, destroying shells and missiles in the air with flak explosions and lances of actinic energy. Combined with the fact that every single commander was calling on the same limited set of resources, it left Saviour waiting for uncomfortably long periods before air support or an artillery strike could be called in.

Natalya had been advancing with her troops—preoccupied with coordinating the assault elements while Untermensch and a VDV lieutenant handled the nitty-gritty of troop movement—down what looked to be an empty street when an explosion rocked her like an earthquake. She fell backwards, hard, and barely managed not to dash her brains out on the street. Her ears were ringing, but she heard shouts, in Russian and English, of "IED!" and "Contact front! One hundred meters!" and "Medic!"

Someone hastily dragged her to cover, picking her up and setting her roughly on her feet against a pile of rubble from a destroyed building. The air was filled with the sound of explosions, gunshots, and men yelling. The ringing whine in her ears muffled all of the other sounds like a thick blanket. She shook her head to clear it, bringing up her tactical display. Her troops had marked two buildings, located on opposite sides of the intersection ahead, where a mixed unit of Supernaut troopers and Thulians had holed up. Judging by the disposition of her men and where the ambush had started, the traitors and Thulians had made a major tactical error by triggering their explosive too early, before the majority of her forces were in the intersection. All of her people that were still up and operational had taken cover, and were pouring fire on the two buildings.

"Keep up suppressive fire on those bastards! Squads One, Two, Four, and Six, spread out to our flanks and maneuver on the buildings while we keep their heads down." She tried to ping a request for artillery or an air strike, but all of the assets were tied up. The battle in the air had turned serious, with numerous Death Spheres and Robo-Eagles dueling with fighter jets, attack helicopters, and bombers. Natalya sincerely hoped that luck would be on their side, and a flaming wreck—the enemy's or one of their own—wouldn't land squarely on her team's heads. "When in grenade range, we will hit their position hard, and deploy smoke to conceal your movement. Storm in and take the building—*fast*. Take them down before they can cook the entire structure."

Unter trotted up to her side, staying behind cover. "Commissar, we have two men still alive where the IED went off. They can't move without exposing themselves to the enemy, and besides, their injuries are severe." *They won't survive much longer*, he didn't have to add. Natalya bit her lip. Her men were already moving to flank the buildings and start the assault. Still, even with how fast they were, it wouldn't be fast enough to save the men in the intersection. She had to do something now, otherwise they were as good as dead.

"Deploy smoke in the intersection. Once it's filled, you and Bear retrieve the soldiers. Your healing and his chassis should protect you from whatever enemy fire comes through." The two squads left in the street wouldn't be able to accurately target the buildings where the Supernaut troopers and Thulians were holed up, but they could still throw an impressive amount of lead their way. Hopefully, it'd be enough to cover the other squads' advance. A few moments later, several smoke grenades sailed over Natalya's head, clanging loudly off of the paved street before they fully ignited. Thick white clouds of smoke started to fill the intersection; luckily, the wind was coming from the beachhead behind them, so the smoke would be blown towards their enemies and not back in their faces. She waited for a few beats for the smoke to completely block her view of the buildings ahead. Her men had already picked out spots to aim for, so that their shots would at least be close to where they needed to go. The incoming enemy fire slackened, then became much more inaccurate. "Georgi, go now!"

Untermensch and Soviet Bear started towards the injured men; both had their weapons slung, since firing would only give their enemies something to potentially focus on. Instead, they ran as fast as they could; naturally, Georgi was the faster of the two, but Pavel's clomping gait covered a fair amount of ground all the same. Bear reached the downed soldiers just as Georgi was picking one of them up in a rescue carry. They didn't waste any time; once both of the men were secured, they started back towards the nearest piece of cover, on the opposite side of the street from Natalya. The pair, with their injured cargo, were almost halfway to relative safety when a quick succession of energy bolts caused Natalya to reflexively flinch and close her eyes. "Sniper!" She yelled, then tracked where the blasts were coming from: a window on her side of the street, just a little behind her position. *A "die in place" unit; let the enemy move past, then hit them from behind before getting cut down in turn. Sneaky bastards.* Quick as a blink, she marked the window with her HUD, simultaneously retrieving a fragmentation grenade from her vest. With practiced casualness, she charged the grenade, kicked off the ground on a plume of her metahuman energy, and side-armed the grenade into the window where the sniper was firing from. The energy bolts were immediately silenced by the *whump* of the grenade's explosion; the only thing that came from the window were shards of glass and bits of debris.

Something is wrong. She ran back to cover; the smoke in the intersection was clearing, and as a result, the ambushers had renewed their weapon fire. Her squads were still in position, and the flankers were just about in grenade range of the ambushers' buildings; they were running low on their specialty munitions, and were saving the rockets for Thulian armored troopers. She scanned the street, and immediately saw what had caused her stomach to knot. Pavel was down. His chassis was able to shrug off small arms with relative ease, but Thulian energy weapons damaged it as easily as they destroyed anything else. From her position, Natalya could see that Pavel was facedown in the street; his legs had been completely slagged, and the energy bolts had melted three holes in his back and torso. Unter had made it back without being hit, and the injured soldier he had been carrying was already being treated. But his position was also under fire, since the smoke had revealed it to the ambushers, and he couldn't possibly venture out to get the remaining soldier without being gunned down. She doubted even his healing ability and the ECHO nanoweave could stand up to a concerted attack from two buildings full of the enemy; as miraculous as it was, it couldn't bring him back from the dead.

The soldier, if he isn't dead already, will probably be dead soon. Damn them! And Pavel . . . The old fool had been around since before she was born. Once a proud member of the Motherland's metahuman corps, he had fallen into disgrace at some point after the Great Patriotic War. She had never learned the details, and she didn't care about them; he had returned to the ranks of the CCCP in the late seventies, and she had grown up with him as another of her "uncles." First, watching him fight beside her father, and then fighting alongside him, before she had finally earned the command of the CCCP. As much as she found him infuriating with his constant antics, she had also grown fond of the doddering relic. Ever since Worker's Champion's betrayal, he had been one of her few remaining ties to the time when being a metahuman and a member of the CCCP were pure for her. The amount of crockery that she threw at him back at HQ hadn't lessened, but she certainly didn't wing it at him as hard or as accurately as she used to. And now she would never get to throw anything at him ever again. Or to tell him that, as much of a pain in the ass as he was for her, she still appreciated him as a comrade. *Another one that trusted me, dead. Dead, and I gave the order.* She felt the pain swell up in her breast, glowing and aching; a mix of loss and cultivated hatred, for the enemy and her inability to stop her people from dying.

Her vision had become unfocused for a moment as she processed everything that had happened. She snapped herself out of it; she couldn't afford to slow down, not when there was still more fighting to be done. Natalya was about to bark out the order for the flankers to storm the buildings when some movement caught her eye. She was drawn back to Pavel and the dying soldier . . . and Pavel was moving. He had the soldier's drag handle on the back of the man's harness in his left hand, the mechanical prostheses barely attached to his soldier. He was pulling himself and the injured soldier towards Georgi with his right arm, even as bullets ricocheted off of what was left of his ruined chassis.

Natalya's heart leapt, and she didn't hesitate. "Covering fire!" She didn't wait for any of her men to respond. She was already running for Pavel and the injured soldier, her legs like steel pistons as they pumped up and down. She couldn't even feel the ground beneath her, and barely felt the energy blast that grazed her back; distantly, she knew that she was hurt, but that didn't matter now. She had to protect her comrades, her friends. She used her metahuman energy to fly, still staying low to the ground; even running would be too slow. When she neared Pavel and the soldier, she swooped lower still; she threw her arms out wide, scooping the injured soldier and Pavel up under their arms—or what was left, for Pavel—and beelining for Georgi. She felt impacts, like hard punches, pepper her back and side. The nanoweave constricted oddly, almost spasmodically, in reaction to whatever hit her. She didn't care. A moment later, she landed behind cover, Georgi and several of the VDV soldiers rushing to her, taking Bear and their injured comrade from her.

Everything grew very quiet for Natalya. She felt odd, almost disconnected, and Georgi looked up to her gravely. She didn't know why; despite his injuries, Bear was alive. Or so she thought. He didn't breathe like a normal man, but she thought she could tell that he still lived. She smiled to Georgi, nodding once. Then she tasted blood in her mouth, and found herself on her knees. Her vision darkened, and she was extraordinarily tired. She couldn't breathe, but she didn't feel the panic that she expected to feel. She fell forward into Georgi's arms, and closed her eyes. They would be okay, her wolves, her *tovarischii*. So long as they had each other, they would prevail. That was all that mattered as she breathed out for the last time.

Georgi laid the Commissar's body down on the ground, careful to keep her behind cover. The unit—his unit now—was still fighting. He heard the nearby explosions as the flanking teams breached the buildings simultaneously, followed by the constant chatter of fully automatic weapons. The ambushers would be dead, soon, and the assault would continue. He tried to muster something approaching satisfaction at that, but it was blotted out by the white-hot sun of his anger at the Thulians. He didn't just hate them because they were *fascista*...he resented them. He resented them for destroying his world, for making it a place where he had to see a girl—who he had watched grow into a woman and then his commanding officer—die while saving their comrades. He wanted nothing more in that moment than to wrap his hands around the throat of every single *fascista*, one by one, and choke the life out of them.

I've been fighting this same fucking war far too long, he thought to himself as he keyed his comm unit. "Medic!" There was nothing to be done for the Commissar—no, Natalya—anymore. From a glance, he already knew what had happened. A grazing shot from a Thulian energy pistol had burned away a section of her nanoweave jacket, not to mention her combat vest. Without full integrity, it had been useless to stop the bullets that had struck her from the side and in her back. Unable to stiffen and disperse the kinetic energy of the bullets, they passed through the armor as they would have with any other garment. Bear and the two injured soldiers, however, were still alive. Georgi had to focus on what he could fix; he had to keep moving forward. Just to be sure, he quickly moved over to Pavel's still form and put his ear to the battered chest piece of the chassis; Old Bear's plasma chamber heart was still whirring, though much quieter than it should have been.

A moment later, Thea and Jadwiga rounded the corner of the building abutting their cover. Their eyes darted over the scene, taking in the details. Jadwiga's eyes went dead, her face became stone. She was a professional healer, a trained medical doctor in addition to her metahuman abilities, and she knew her priorities. To Georgi's surprise...Thea burst into tears. She collapsed against the wall, clinging to it as if it were the last thing grounding her to reality. He had never seen her be anything but reserved or, at best, laconic. Unlike for most of the other comrades, he had never seen her personnel file; the Commissar had accepted her into the CCCP without consulting him, and he hadn't opposed her decision. Despite the mystery, she had demonstrated her willingness to help her comrades satisfactorily. *What is your story, devushka?* He wanted to go to her and comfort her, to hold her and tell her that everything was going to be fine...but he couldn't. There was still too much that needed attending to.

"Jadwiga, get her moving. As soon as you have them stable enough to move, get Pavel and the injured to one of the evac points. And the Commissar—"

"No need to tell me my business, Georgi," she didn't quite bark at him. He opened his mouth to reply, but then promptly shut it. She was clearly suffering, and this was how she dealt with it; she had been closer to Natalya and Molotok than any of the other comrades. Instead of wailing and beating her fist against the ground, she shut that part of herself away, like a patient in triage, until she could deal with it. *Have to stop the bleeding before anything else.* She went back to Thea and slapped her once; not hard, but not gently, either. That pulled the young woman up short, midbawl. Then Jadwiga pulled her into a rough hug, and whispered something into her ear. A few seconds later, the pair were jogging towards the wounded, Thea wiping her tears away with the back of her gloved hands.

Georgi split off a detachment of soldiers to help them with the wounded and the Commissar's body; some helping to carry, the rest on security. The front line was, for the most part, stable and moving forward, but as they had just painfully learned, nothing could be taken for granted on this godforsaken ship.

As if to punctuate his thought, the ground shuddered. Several of the soldiers looked to Georgi, a collective "What the hell was that?" expression on all of their faces. Then the ground violently bucked up to meet all of them, knocking everyone in the immediate vicinity off of their feet.

"The ship is dying, Commissar," Eight said in his ear. *"It is not yet compromised enough to begin breaking up, but that end is inevitable."* He waited for some sort of advice as to what the AI suggested he do, but none was forthcoming. He wasn't sure whether to be sorry or grateful that Eight was leaving command decisions to him. Unter picked himself up off the ground when he felt confident enough that there wouldn't be any aftershocks, or whatever came after a "ship quake," if anything. Everyone around him was already moving; Jadwiga, Thea, and the soldiers he assigned to them gathering the wounded and the Commissar's body, the rest of his soldiers continuing to assault towards the center of the ship.

Unter pushed forward when his men in the occupied buildings gave the all-clear. One of the buildings was completely consumed with fire, and the second wasn't faring much better. Their casualties during the assault had been acceptable: one dead, six wounded. He noticed that zero prisoners had been taken; several of the

human bodies—from the traitorous Supernaut unit undoubtedly—
had been bound and killed in what looked like executions. He
couldn't even muster satisfaction that they were dead, or disgust
that he normally would have been pleased by this outcome. Too
much to do, too much hate flattening out his other emotions.
This was war. He could deal with everything, the good and the
bad, after. If there *was* an after for him, or anyone else.

The ambush cleared, they advanced. He saw more Thulians
now than he did Supernaut suits; they were definitely making
progress, and there couldn't be that many of the traitors left. He
was about to order another movement, to advance to contact,
when his HUD lit up with a bright warning and something like
a Klaxon. That was followed with a series of rippling explosions
to the right of his unit's position, near the center of the ship.
They overpowered all of the other blasts and booms across the
ship, they were that loud. *What the hell is it now?*

"Commissar Untermensch!" Eight said, with uncharacteristic
urgency. *"The dragon!"*

Georgi's stomach dropped. They had all been afraid of this.
The intel hadn't included anything on the dragon, though they
knew that it had been out there, *somewhere*, after the destruction
of Metis. The weapons his unit had couldn't even begin to be
enough to damage the dragon, much less take it down. "Everyone,
get to cover, now!" Just after he finished yelling, he heard the
roar. Loud and resonant, it seemed to stop the fighting for the
briefest of moments, all across the city. Then he saw it; it crested
the rooftops in the distance, raising itself to its full height. It
was terrible, but also a little beautiful: sleek and jagged, metallic and organic, and pure in its desire to kill every single one
of them. The moment shattered when the artillery and close air
support craft started hammering it. The explosions surrounded it
like miniature and short-lived rain clouds, blossoming and then
dissipating. The dragon didn't seem to notice. It surged forward,
crashing through buildings on its way to the far right side of the
front line. It had to be killing some of its own, but if it was, it
didn't care. The artillery that had been targeting it couldn't keep
up; some of the attack helicopters were able to continue to land
hits with their cannons and missiles, but even those slackened
as they broke off to deal with harrying Death Spheres. Within
seconds, the dragon smashed into the assaulting units on the right

end of the line. Unter felt his gorge rise when he saw dozens of "friendly" dots on the HUD map suddenly go dark.

What the hell are we going to do against that? It's going to tear its way through the front lines, and then take out the ships. He felt a rising wave of panic for the first time since the battle had begun. Would they have to retreat? It seemed unthinkable...no, it *was* unthinkable. Whatever happened here today, they couldn't turn back. They wouldn't have another shot.

Another warning buzzed on the HUD. *"Incoming friendly unit, cease all attacks against the dragon. All units, clear lane Bravo into adjoining lanes immediately!"*

Georgi almost shouted. What were they trying to do, give it a straight shot to the ships? It took him a moment to realize that they certainly were not. The ground rumbled again, in rhythmic bursts. *Footfalls.* Georgi spun around to face the edge of the ship, back where they had come from; Atlas, in all of his thousand-foot-tall glory, was *running* towards the dragon. Georgi didn't know that the giant could even move that fast, and neither did the dragon. Atlas launched himself at the dragon, spearing it in the midsection with a flying tackle before it could do anything more than turn its head. They went down with a thunderous crash, pulverizing buildings as they rolled and thrashed. The men around Georgi gave triumphant cries, many pumping weapons and fists in the air.

"Keep moving forward, comrades! We have a chance, and we must not waste it! *Ura, ura, ura!*" The men snapped to his orders, and they rushed forward. They had to keep up their momentum. If they stalled again, that would be all the chance that the Thulians needed to scrape them off of the ship and back into the sea. Georgi saw on his HUD that the other units, some of them more sluggishly than others, were back to pressing the attack as well. Everyone was steering clear of the furball between Atlas and the dragon, even the Thulians. It was the Great Patriotic War all over again; the metahuman heavies duked it out amongst themselves, while the conventional forces fought each other until one or the other won.

Even with the renewed energy within the unit, Georgi kept an eye on the fight between Atlas and the dragon. His enthusiasm vanished almost instantly. Atlas wrestled with the dragon, trying to stay behind its head and pin it, occasionally punching or elbowing it with little effect other than to batter the monstrosity. The dragon, in turn, clawed and bit at every available piece of Atlas... and where its jaws snapped or its claws found purchase, it *was* doing damage. *He can't hurt it... he can only try to distract it and keep it from killing the rest of us.* Georgi knew that the situation couldn't last. Eventually, and probably sooner than later, Atlas would make a mistake, and the dragon would have him. He had had the advantage, surprising it. Now it was *pissed*; there was nothing beautiful about it now. Just an awful, demonic fury so intense that Georgi could swear it was giving off a heat mirage. His mind scrambled for a solution—anything; it didn't matter if they pushed further in the city if the dragon killed Atlas, and then swooped in on them from behind.

The idea came to him suddenly, like a bolt from the blue. He almost discounted it out of hand... but he couldn't bring himself to. *We are all going to die, one way or another. And we can't hold back.* He keyed his comm unit. "Comrade Chug, this is Untermensch. I need you at my position immediately." He grabbed the nearest lieutenant, a young blond VDV man, and spun him around to face him. "You... Lt. Iaket?" The officer nodded, confused and obviously a little intimidated. *Not every day one meets a member of the CCCP, I suppose.* "You are in charge of the unit until I return." More like "if I return," but the young Russian didn't need to know that. "Continue the attack. We must prevail—for Russia, and the world. Do you understand?"

The lieutenant stared at him blankly, then saluted crisply. "Yessir!" With a nod, the young officer set off, already barking orders for the others.

Georgi stared after the man, wondering if he would live through today. He stood there wondering for a second before snapping himself out of it. "Eight, where is Chug?" At that moment a section of wall behind Georgi exploded outward, showering the immediate area with dust and chunks of concrete. Georgi flinched for a split second, then whirled around with his rifle raised. A squat form shook itself once, then jogged over to Georgi. "Nevermind, Eight." He lowered his rifle, looking down to Chug. His arm had healed after being reattached by the combined efforts of Belladonna, Jadwiga, and Victrix. Georgi didn't even pretend to understand all of the complicated processes, much less the literal magic, that had gone into making the rock man whole again. Chug looked happy to see Georgi, which made it that much harder for him. He had been attached to another unit that was lacking any metahuman muscle, as it were, under the command of one of Proletariat's copies. Normally unable to help in the day-to-day peacekeeping and law enforcement that the CCCP usually engaged in, Chug was usually occupied with coloring books or playing with his pet hamster. Or eating. Even as he looked expectantly to Georgi, Chug bent down to pick up a piece of the concrete to chew on. Here, however, he had been allowed to go all out. From the reports that the Proletariat copy had been sending to Georgi, Chug had been having an absolute ball.

"Chug, I need you to come with me. We must assist Comrade Atlas."

"Okay, Unter," Chug rumbled happily as he munched on the chunk of concrete like an apple.

The pair of them set off at a run. They needed to be fast, but it wouldn't do to get bushwhacked by the enemy, so they stayed behind the front line, well within friendly territory. That only changed when they got near to the site of Atlas' own battle. There were no troops in this area; any closer and they had a real chance of being crushed beneath the two thrashing titans. A huge area of the city had been flattened by just the two of them, not to mention the ongoing bombardment. Georgi had already sent his plan to Eight via private channel, who had relayed it to Atlas. His only reply: *HURRY!*

Georgi signaled to Eight when they came to a stop. The plan was insane, probably worthless...but he couldn't think of anything else. Maybe Natalya could have, or Arthur Chang. But this was all Georgi had. He turned to Chug; he had already finished his bit of concrete while they were running, and was looking for something else to eat. "Chug, I need you to do something."

Chug looked up to Georgi, and for the thousandth time, he considered scrapping the idea. "Yes, Unter? Chug wants to help." Since coming to America with the rest of the CCCP, he had taken to speaking English more often. He did it because it made the American comrades more comfortable; Chug was always eager to please his friends.

No turning back. No retreat, ever, even if it hurt your soul. "That dragon is hurting Comrade Atlas. He needs your help to destroy it." He considered for a moment, wrestling with his conscience. *To hell with it. He deserves to know.* "You may die. But if you can stop the dragon, you will save all of the comrades. All of your friends. We need you to help us, Chug. You're the only one that can now."

That sobered Chug. "*Da*, Unter," the rock man replied quickly. "Chug helps comrades."

Georgi's attention was torn back to the gargantuan battle. Atlas, his stone flesh covered with bite and claw marks, had finally disentangled himself from the dragon. It was on top of him; he was on his back and was holding it at arm's length as it tried to crane its head far enough down to bite his throat. With a tremendous effort, Atlas managed to get a leg between himself and the squirming dragon; with a single kick, he sent the dragon flying away from him. It landed several hundred yards away, buildings crumbling underneath it until it finally came to a rest. A particularly tall structure that looked like some kind of neoclassic tower collapsed on top of the dragon.

Atlas flipped onto his hands and knees—again, Georgi was dumbfounded by how impossibly fast Atlas could move for someone so large—and swept a hand towards Georgi and Chug. Georgi was able to leap backwards at the last second, still close enough to feel the wind from Atlas' massive hand as it scooped up Chug. The dragon was already freeing itself from the remains of the tower, its eyes fixed on Atlas with murderous rage. The giant whispered something—still booming and loud, but Georgi couldn't make out the exact words—to Chug. The dragon had begun charging towards the pair, another awful roar issuing from its maw. With a short windup, Atlas coiled his arm, then threw Chug straight at the dragon. Georgi's eyes tracked the hurtling, rocky bullet as it disappeared into the dragon's mouth.

Georgi held his breath. The dragon had come up short, confused. That didn't last long, however. Satisfied that whatever had happened didn't matter more than killing Atlas, it started forward again . . . and then stumbled and crashed into the ground, throwing up huge fountains of ruined street and debris. Georgi ran for the nearest piece of hard cover he could find—the remains of an arch commemorating some bullshit battle or something that the Thulians cared about. Rocks pelted him on the head and shoulders as he ran, with huge pieces exploding on the street all around him. He skidded to a stop underneath the arch, hoping it would hold, before he turned to look at the dragon again. It was on its back now, and clawing at itself, tearing off great chunks of metal on its throat, then its belly and sides. Baleful orange light shone through the fissures that it created, and how it *screamed*; not a roar, but the sound of a thing in pain. It was unnerving; a machine, or what was supposed to be mostly machine, feeling pain.

Atlas stomped over to Georgi, the ground shaking with every step. He dropped to the ground in front of Georgi, blocking his view of the dragon. *"GET DOWN!"* Georgi was nearly deafened by the giant's voice, but he complied instantly. A second later the sky was filled with orange light, and Atlas' body rocked with a concussive wave. The arch above Georgi groaned, the stones threatening to give way to gravity... but it held. Slowly, Atlas rolled away from Georgi, revealing a scorched wasteland. Something inside of the dragon, broken by Chug, had exploded. The immediate area, already destroyed by the giants' brawl, was completely devastated now. A mushroom cloud in miniature rose from where the dragon had been, an inferno at the heart of it. Georgi could see what looked like the outline of the dragon's lower body sticking out from the center of it, but with all of the fire—he could feel the heat as if he was standing right next to it—it was impossible to be sure.

"Eight, confirm, dragon is off the board. Repeat, dragon is down."

Georgi stared at the blazing ruins for what felt like a long time. He thought about Natalya, wondering how she could do it. Georgi hadn't been a metahuman or even an officer in the Great Patriotic War. Just a fighter for the Motherland, captured and twisted by the Nazis into what he was now. He was good at carrying out orders; he had a soldier's heart. But to command... he should have had the character for it, the skills, but he doubted it all now. He knew that Natalya had privately suffered ever since the Invasion, and the tragedy at Saviour's Gate. So many of their friends lost then, with her commanding them to fight and die to protect the civilians. Old man Petrograd, Supernaut, Netopyr, Svetoch, and Zhar-ptica. Old Bear had almost died then, too. Georgi hoped the old bastard lived. They were the last of the veterans, after all. And the others that had died since: the mad inventor Zmey, Molotok, Rusalka... even People's Blade, the calculating and petite Fei Li. So many lost, and Natalya took the

weight of it all on herself. How could he, an "Untermensch," hope
to even begin to measure up? Who would do that to themselves
willingly? Only someone insane, he decided. He would have to
face Jadwiga if any of them lived through this. She had already
lost her *sestra*. And she had been the closest out of any of them
to Chug. Could he look her in the eye and tell her that he sent
the strange man to his death? They had manipulated the poor
creature to fight for them for years, and he may have saved them,
or at least postponed their deaths. But did that now excuse Georgi
for being a bastard?

Georgi turned back to where the front line had pushed forward.
Atlas had already left, to either fight more or to sink back into
the depths, Georgi didn't know. He'd been too consumed with
his own thoughts and focused on the fire. He checked his HUD;
the young VDV lieutenant was doing well, from what he could
see. He had even kept nearly all of his people alive. Something
made Georgi look back to the corpse of the dragon one final
time. Later, he wouldn't be able to say what had made him do
it. But when he looked back, a craggy and blackened figure came
trotting towards him out of the flames.

"Chug do good?" He had pieces of the dragon crumpled in his
hands, and what passed for a huge grin with his granite features.

Georgi allowed himself to laugh in what felt like the first time
in decades. "*Da*, Chug. *Da*. But there is still more work to do.
Let's go."

The low melancholy tone chimed in Yankee Pride's ear, a hollow
warning that coincided with the alert that appeared in his HUD.
Stationed on one of the cruisers accompanying the aircraft carrier,
he stared past the scrolling words to watch the scene unfold in
grainy detail on screens in the CIC. Pride had missed much of
the battle that raged within the main buildings, focusing instead
on the inferno that raged on the perimeter and the strategic
half-circle of rail guns and thermite-enhanced munitions that
held their initial line. The smoke from the ever-growing fire in
the jungle thickened and obscured parts of the ledges of the two
half-spheres that composed this Mothership, so he hadn't seen
the movement beyond the platforms that the CCCP had held.

The tone chimed again. Eight spoke over the private channel,
the little voice pairing efficiency with something that could be

construed as empathy or, at the very least, care in the delivery of a somber message. *"Sir, as you are aware, Red Saviour is dead. There is a great deal of confusion as to who is to take over. Saviour left instructions with me that in this eventuality you were to..."*

"I'm aware," he murmured.

"Then perhaps you should hear this." There was an electronic crackle, and Red Saviour's voice crackled at him over his implants. *"If Comrade Eight is playing this, you are hesitating. While you hesitate, some* nekulturny *dog is deciding your metahumans and my CCCP are expendable. Davay, davay, davay!"*

Pride grimaced at the last words, unable to escape them. Eight must have relayed a message to the ship's XO, who nodded at Pride and stepped back to let him pass through the hatch. Gauntlets pulsing a soft gold, Pride made his way to the helo deck and shrugged into one of the waiting jetpacks. He glanced out to the Mothership where a bank of ash and flame hid the bloodiest of the battle. Somewhere past the ledge, past the turrets and along the edge of the alien jungle, the remaining members of Red Saviour's CCCP continued to fight alongside his own ECHO comrades.

"Uncle Benji, you need to stop thinking so hard." Jamaican Blaze's stylized voice came through the private channel. *"These are good people, and you need to step up now."*

Pride cocked his head to the side at his niece's words. "Willa Jean, I'm—"

"Hesitating. Miss Natalya said you would. Her people can't afford for you to think this over. They..." The voice paused. A loud *whoomph* of flame billowed up from the half-spheres, the smoke blackening the outside of the taller buildings. *"They need someone to lead them now. That's you, and you* know *it."*

The last words sounded too much like his own mother, a woman who had never hesitated in her entire life. Pride exhaled and signaled the sailor on the helo pad. The young woman returned the gesture, clearing him for takeoff. Two steps and he was in the air, keeping low along the water to avoid the barrage from the other ships and turrets.

"Eight, I'm going to need a dedicated channel to Saviour's people, simultaneous translation." Pride banked right to follow the suggested flight path to get him to their position. "Replicate her last set of coordinates and her strategic overlay to me."

"*Channel is open. Go ahead, Yankee Pride.*"

"Comrades, hold position. Your Commissar has transferred command of this assault force to me, and we'd be doing her memory a disservice to not hit these bastards harder than ever." Pride rose up to fly over the lip of the half-sphere before dropping down just below the ash cloud. Cueing up the drone feeds from his HUD, he could see a trio of the sleek metal Wolves racing through the streets towards the CCCP's position, obscured by smoke and buildings. "Comrade Untermensch, we've got three Wolf targets to your nine o'clock."

Untermensch didn't hesitate. "Affirmative, *Commander*. Adjusting defensive posture to deal with the threat." A pause. "It is good to hear from you." The CCCP and Russian troops snapped into action, and were ready when the Wolves rounded the corner of a building, spilling out into the street. Rockets, bullets, and metahuman powers raced to meet them, and made quick work of the robotic monstrosities.

The alien Klaxon shattered the air; the flashing blue light added to the disorientation. Red and Victoria were still weak, still recovering, but there was no time—no *time*—and with the control panel gone there was nothing to abort the launch of the bomb on . . . whatever schedule the Masters had it set for. Enough time for them to escape, presumably. But once it left this ship, it would be too late to do anything.

And there was a . . . seductive quality to this merger. It felt *right*. They felt more whole, more complete, than they ever had in their life.

But it also felt wrong. They thought as one, though they were two . . . and with each passing moment they felt whatever divide remained between them fading. Soon it would be "I," not "we," and a part of them screamed in panic . . .

There was so much power here . . . so much skill, so many valuable memories. And combined? They could do anything, anything at all.

Except retain their identities. They wouldn't be themselves anymore. They'd be something . . . else. Something different. Something they didn't recognize.

The two voices clamoring in the background rose, and became dominant over the merged voice. *I am . . . Victoria Victrix Nagy, dammit!* **I am Timothy "Red Djinni" Torres.** *Yeah, you said that before, to Amethist. Timothy? Really? That's a horrible name.* **You think so?** *I can see why you went with "Red."*

I . . . you . . . I . . . we . . .

Self started to vanish, to muddle, to merge again. But this time they were ready for it. They rejected the power, the seduction. The only thing that made them one was the drive to become two again.

We have to end this now!

They fell to their knees, body shuddering and heaving. Then between one flash of the warning light and the next, with a cry of mingled loss and triumph, one became two, and the two fell apart, panting with exertion, and stared into each other's eyes.

"We can't ever do that again," they said together.

"Bomb!" Vickie cried urgently, scrambling to her feet. Red was right behind her as she ran for the ugly thing.

The weapon hummed; in the time they had been fighting Barron, it had come to life. Vickie ran her hands over it, only to realize she couldn't: something in the casing repelled her touch. In the back of her mind she was vaguely aware that she was stark naked, but in light of the fact that this thing in front of them could end the entire world, that fact seemed vanishingly unimportant. There was a field of some kind around this damn thing, something that was very nearly preventing any form of magic from penetrating it. *Nearly,* because she was getting a vague sense of where things were—payload, boring mechanism, energy source for the whole shebang—but not any details. *I thought the Masters didn't know anything about magic! How can they shield against something they don't even know about?*

She looked over, and saw that Red was having the same problem. He was running his hands over the casing, but couldn't touch it.

"It doesn't just repel magic then," she said. "You able to pick up anything?"

"It's virtually frictionless," Red muttered, dumbfounded. "It's more than that actually. It's the weirdest thing. I'm running everything I can pick up from it, and what I'm getting back is . . . myself."

"Come again?"

"Here," he said, and pressed a hand as close to the bomb's surface as he could. "I'm not touching it. I can't. So I'm trying to pick up anything I can from it, from surface temperature, texture, even light readings. And what I seem to be detecting... is the palm of my own hand."

Vickie stared at him.

"It's reflecting...everything then." *How could it reflect magic if they don't know what magic is? But it's...it's reflecting* everything...

"Of course," she breathed. "Magic is energy, it follows the rules. This barrier blocks the full spectrum of energy, from kinetic to light to UV to even psychic, but it can't possibly block everything, not completely. I just need to focus past it, generate at the right frequency, with the right...resonance..."

She found just thinking about the equations involved was exhausting.

"This is impossible," she scowled, heart racing. "I'd need days to get this prepped. Weeks, to be sure. We've got minutes..."

"Surely you've got *some* idea!" Red shouted.

Vickie gave him a doubtful look.

"There...*might* be a way."

"Talk to me, Scotty."

"Red, this is alchemy here, weird science *and* magic combined. This stuff has barely been theorized, much less experimented with. We're talking some extreme computations that I will have to do on the fly, beyond *anything* I've ever tried." *Stupid, stupid, if I don't try, we all go* boom. "Right, never mind, I need a...conduit to make a lens. Pure silica, diamond—fiber optics even—something that's a conduit for magic." She looked frantically around the room. "I need enough to make a ring around the bomb." She turned to the panels around the walls. "Can you pry one of these open? There might be something in there. Do these guys use fiber-optic cables? Or silica lenses? Or..." She turned to stare at him. "Or...you."

"Me?"

"You're not just a medium, you're a freakin' magic conductor!" She lunged, grabbing him by the wrist, and pointed his arm up the bomb. "I need you to make a ring of yourself as tight around that thing as you can get!"

He stared back at her, startled.

She hopped up and smacked him on the head. "Now! You tall, sexy lunkhead! Do your rubber-man deal and stretch!"

He opened his mouth to reply, thought better of it, and with a shrug reared back and let his arm go limp. With a sharp overhand cast, he threw it forward, willing the arm to grow and stretch, winding around the body of the bomb. Vickie watched, enthralled, as his hand snapped around to catch its own forearm. With a grunt, the Djinni drew his arm taut, his grip sliding up until he formed a perfect thin ring around the base of the bomb's shaft.

Vickie put one hand on his shoulder and sent a tentative pulse through the ring he had created. The lensing effect was definitely *there*, but that thin ring of flesh wasn't robust enough to carry all the power she needed to send through it.

"Can you increase the mass? Slowly?" She swallowed and added, "Please?" Because if they died here she didn't want the last thing she said to him to have been "lunkhead."

"You're lucky yer cute," Red grunted and obliged her.

Vickie sent another pulse of energy through him, then another, then another. It was working, or at least it seemed to be. With each tentative push she felt the lensing effect strengthen, and what had been "blurred" before came into sharper focus...until...

She drew in a sharp breath as she felt it. Her probing pulse of energy came to resonance and amplified in a perpetual ring of power held in place by the Djinni's arm.

"Hold it!" Vickie crowed. "That's perfect. Keep it right there. Eight!"

"*Yes, Vickie.*"

"Call everybody. I'm going to need everything they've got. All of it. *Now.*"

She didn't have to wait for Eight's assent. She *felt* it; the full power of three circles of some of the strongest magicians on the planet. Her mother's circle currently based in Sedona, (which was the closest place Hosteen Stormdance could get to all the Native Americans he could muster for it). The school circle in Maine. And the entire monastery up in the Himalayas. And then, coming in like grace notes, individual mages all over the world, all focusing their power on *her*.

And yet...she paused. "Vix? What are you waiting for?" Red asked.

"Remember when you yelled at me about doing something that could destroy the universe? This could, theoretically, destroy the universe. It's the thing earth mages can do, and never dare to. Transmutation. Lead to gold—not possible. Breaking down radioactive elements to lower number elements? Oh yeah. But... lotsa radiation. And potential critical mass anyway if I mismanage and get too much of an unstable isotope. Or worst case, black hole, to the nth degree, end of universe type stuff. The equations are nuts, and they change all the time as what I'm transmuting changes. I don't know what exactly does what inside that thing. I can *see* it and I can *change* it, but I can't tell exactly what's payload, what's power source, and what's the special thingummy for getting it to bore its way into the magma. I get one shot at this and I don't know the odds."

Red gave her a blank look. Vickie sighed.

"I'm about to cross the streams," she said.

"Oh," Red shrugged. "Why didn't you just say that?" He gave her a reassuring look. "For what it's worth, I believe in you. And if that isn't enough, I'm pretty sure everyone else does too. You got this. Trust me."

He couldn't possibly know that, and there were a million things she could have said at this point. She settled for the most important. "I love you. I've got this."

Then she gathered the various energies into herself until she was ready to burst, braided them together into a coherent stream, and unleashed them. The equations streamed through her mind, and she mirrored them, muttering them under her breath so Eight had time to double-check her on the results before she committed. Eight couldn't *see* magic and couldn't *perform* magic but there was nothing on this planet better at number-crunching.

But the strain... her own personal energies were pouring out of her like water out of a burst dam. For once there was no little second self inside her observing and taking notes. It was *all* the math, and directing the power, and a hundred, a thousand tiny corrections. She transmuted *everything*. Transuranic elements. Whatever she encountered inside a stasis field, or she found in the casing. Incomprehensible things. She didn't understand any of them, but she knew if she transmuted *enough* of them, once this nightmare was deployed, it wouldn't matter; power sources would fizzle, real machinery would break, and—most important of all—the payload would not achieve critical mass. Her eyes were closed but the HUD was still on and glowing numbers streamed across her field of vision until her eyes watered.

And this was hurting Red. She risked a glance at him. His teeth clenched as he struggled to maintain his grip on the ring. She felt his pain. As good a conductor as he was, he was channeling the combined power of every white-hat mage Vickie had access to in her Rolodex, possibly more arcane current than anything had every channeled before. The energy, it was literally cooking him from the inside out.

"This is killing you!" she moaned, eyes streaming with real tears now, not just watering.

"Keep...at...it!" Red hissed, forcing each syllable out.

She closed her eyes and went back to work. There was no other choice.

The last element broke down as far as she could take it. Earth elementals did this all the time; it was as natural as breathing to them. That was how Herb had kept the team alive inside of himself back in Nevada escaping from the Goldman Catacombs, literally manufacturing oxygen from his own body...but humans could only break things down so far before they became too small to manage. Just as she felt everything slip out of her metaphorical hands, she felt something inside the bomb change. Things came alive. "Red, let go!" she shouted hoarsely, as she herself let go of him and the energies, and dropped heavily to the floor.

But he had released the ring as soon as she released him, and he dropped down unconscious beside her, the ring of extended and now-sizzling flesh flopping down next to him as the drill on the front of the bomb came to life and it vanished into the pit, carrying its now-worthless payload.

She rolled over and threw her arms around him. She was no healer...she'd told him that before...but what little she knew how to do, she did, with the last of her strength. "We did it, Red," she whispered. "We did it."

She bit her lip as she watched him, and realized she was trembling. His skin had turned a pale sallow color, like that of a corpse. She had given him all she could. If only he would breathe...

His lips parted, and with a gasp, Red's eyes flew open as he took in a long, deep breath.

"Oh, dear lord," Vickie cried, and drew him close. "You have got to stop dying on me."

"Told...you..." Red croaked. "I told you, you had this."

"But how were you so sure?"

Red chuckled, and rapped a knuckle on his head. "Little slips, threads, memories of the future, they get jarred loose at the darndest of times..."

"I think your brain is still cooked..." she said with concern, putting a hand alongside his face, and checking his temperature. "What are you talking about?"

"Ask me again later," he said, still chuckling, and held her close.

"Eight!" Bella snapped. "What in hell is going on?"

"*One of the Thulian Masters, the one called Barron, has triggered a... Vickie calls it a 'doomsday device,'*" Eight said, its serene voice at odds with its message.

"*What?*" Bella cried.

"*Vickie and the Red Djinni are dealing with the situation. I am confident they will prevail,*" Eight continued.

"Vickie and—wait, what?" Bella was having trouble wrapping her mind about that. *Vickie* wasn't even supposed to be in the bowels of the ship, she was supposed to be guarding the kid. And *Red Djinni?* What the *hell?*

"*The Thulian Masters are now fleeing... as they are all heading for a single spot, at least according to my calculations... excuse me, I need all my processing power to help Vickie.*"

The channel fell silent.

"Wait, where are the Masters going? Eight? *Eight!*"

"They're fleeing..." Bull mused. "My guess is that they're in full retreat. It stands to reason there is an escape module in this fortress. If they have initiated a doomsday protocol, they will gather there and leave as soon as they are able."

"Like hell they will!" Bella snarled. "Not until we get some answers! Not until we make sure they don't pull this crap on anyone ever again! Wherever they're heading, we need to get there! Eight! Answer me, dammit! Eight!" She glanced at Bull, and stopped. "Are you... Bull, are you *laughing?*"

"The Djinni," Bull said, chuckling. "Red's alive." He doubled over, unable to control the laughter.

"And why is that funny?" Bella demanded.

"Because..." Bull said, struggling to choke out the words. "Because it's *Red!*" With an effort he composed himself. "He's just never where he's supposed to be."

Bella stared at him for a long moment, then . . . choked on something like a laugh. "Including in Hell, I suppose . . . but—*doomsday device?*"

Bull laid a reassuring hand on her shoulder. "It's the Djinni. I have learned never to bet against him—or Vickie. So what are *we* going to do?"

"Go after those bastards," she snarled, instantly making up her mind. *"Eight!"*

But it was Sam Colt who answered. *"Mister Eight handed over field survey, ma'am. I got what he had when he handed over. Incoming to your HUD."*

It was an overlay of the entire double saucer. There were about a hundred dotted red lines converging on a point not that far distant from where Sam had helpfully indicated they were. A green dotted line outlined a small ovoid section. *"Eight reckoned that was an escape ship, or maybe the original ship the bastards started with,"* he added.

"Can you map out the most direct route?" Bella asked.

"Uh, maybe you misheard me, ma'am," Sam said. *"There's about a hundred Masters . . ."*

"I don't care if there's a thousand of them armed with automated arm cannons and flanked by scores of giant, rabid wolverines!" Bella yelled. "They think they can come down here and unleash hell on Earth and then just *leave* when things don't go their way? *Not on my watch!* Get me there, Sam, *now!*"

"Understood, Commander," Sam answered sharply, as a glowing path lit up on Bella's HUD. She was off like a shot, following the twists and turns of the bizarre corridors, guided by Sam's map. Bull kept pace with her. She glanced at him and noted an odd smirk playing on his lips.

"Maybe *that* should be your battle cry," he said lightly.

"Get me there, Sam?"

Bull chuckled, again. Even now, in the midst of her fury and her fear, Bella fought back a smile. It was nice to hear the big man laugh.

"Oddly enough, that wouldn't be worse than some of your previous attempts. Try again."

"Not on my watch?" she said.

"It's got a nice ring to it," Bull rumbled. "You're the boss here. Let them know where they stand."

They ran up a set of stairs and emerged into what had been buildings and weird red vegetation. The vegetation was dying, the buildings very much the worse for the bombardment. "Sam?" Bella said.

"I've waved off artillery on your position, ma'am. Also the fighter bombers and anything else."

"UX—" Bull began with alarm. But Bella was already sprinting and leaping across the devastated landscape before he could finish. "—Bs!" He shrugged and caught up with her.

"I think I got the head honcho, ma'am," Sam said, as she tried not to think too hard about the fact that her *body* felt it was running on flat land while her *eyes* told her she was running up a slope. *"Got him here. He isn't moving."*

"How do you know it's the Big Bad?" Bella asked.

"His readings are a bit strange," Sam answered. *"He's larger, for one thing, and the others are heading to his coordinates and forming around him. I'm pinging him now on your HUD. He's your target."*

Bella glanced at her display. One of the red dots had turned green, and was blinking.

"That's it then," she said, dodging around some debris. "Keep us locked on him, Sam."

"You got a plan?" Bull asked. The big man was starting to get winded.

"We take him out," Bella said, ignoring the rising burn in her arms and legs. "We take him, and we end this."

"Vickie!"

Vickie groaned. She was exhausted. And that didn't matter. This wasn't done yet. She couldn't rest until it was. "Go, Eight," she replied, lifting her head from Red's chest and blinking to clear her eyes,

"Status report. Commanders Blue and Bulwark are converging on the remaining Masters, who have massed together in what I calculate is the area of the original ship, which may still be their escape module. Sam Colt tells me they intend to confront the chief of the Masters."

"How many of them?" Vickie asked.

"Approximately one hundred."

"How many?"

"Doesn't matter..." Red groaned. Vickie turned to him, confused. "What doesn't matter?" she asked.

"Their numbers," Red replied. Vickie still looked confused. Gently, he tapped her ear. "I can hear Eight through your piece. It doesn't matter how many there are. Besides Barron, they're frail, not a real fighter amongst them. There's only one Bella and Bull need to worry about. Problem is, I only know so much about him."

"Hold a sec. Eight, pick up and rebroadcast this to Bella and Bull," Vickie interrupted, and nodded for him to continue.

"His name is Gero," the Djinni said. "Grand Poobah of this entire stinking mess. You won't be able to miss him. He fancies himself a god, and has the ego that goes with the job."

"What can he do?" Vickie asked.

"That's the thing," Red shrugged. "He orders his underlings about, and he never has to get his hands dirty, so all I've got is what Karoline knew, and that wasn't much. Never got around him, myself. I couldn't risk it."

"What? Why?"

"He's a mind-reader, Vix. Strong one, too. Karoline was careful to let him feel her fear of him. I had to stay dormant while she was awake. Couldn't risk him, or her, getting a whiff of me, or that might've been it. Everything I did had to be done while she slept, and only in the safety of her quarters."

"Just how powerful is he?" Bella asked, breathless. *"Can I take him?"*

"Not sure," Red answered. "Everyone on this ship is deathly afraid of him, though. They make a point of giving him a wide berth. You're running into unknown territory, Blue. There's just no intel on him. Trust me, I've looked."

There was a long, long pause. *"And if we let him go... they'll be back. And ready for us. Not an option, Red. This is one message that has to be sent."*

"Listen to me, you stubborn, overgrown smurf!" Red hissed. "You don't know what he's capable of! At least wait for backup!"

"Well, at least we know it's the real Djinni," they heard Bulwark mutter.

"Missed you too, big guy," Red chuckled.

"There's no time for backup!" Bella barked. *"They're in full retreat. If that thing is a getaway ship, Bull and I might be our only shot at ending this!"*

The floor shuddered and bucked for a moment as if the ship was suffering an earthquake. Metal groaned, and something in the distance broke with an explosive *crack*. Vickie's hands clenched reflexively. She knew what was going on. She *felt* it. The ship was dying.

"Bella, look around!" Vickie exclaimed. "This whole structure is coming apart! They're beat, we might have even crippled them! We've won! You don't know what he can do! It's time to book!"

"*Forget it!*" Bella answered. "*They are not getting away! Not while there's a chance in hell they might come back! Don't you guys get it? This is it! We've got one shot here, one shot to make it clear, not just to them, but to anyone else out there, that coming after Earth is going to cost them more than they can imagine. One shot to make sure this never happens to this planet again. This isn't for revenge. It's for protection.*"

Vickie swore under her breath in four languages. "She's right," she said. "We've got to end this, Red. This has to stop."

Red stood up, pulling Vickie up with him. She started to protest, because while *she* was exhausted, he'd nearly been cooked alive by all the magic coursing through him, but he seemed fine now.

He looked down at Vickie, and nodded.

"Godspeed, you two," he said. "Do what you have to. Then get the hell out of there."

"*We will,*" Bulwark replied. "*That goes for you, too. Get off this sinking mess ASAP. That's an order.*"

"*What he said. I can't do my job and worry about you two. Get!*"

Vickie tried to rise to her feet, fell over, and swore; tried again, managed to stand erect, staggered two paces in the direction of Bella and Bull, and fell again. "We can't leave them," she panted.

"You're stealing my shtick," the Djinni said, gently picking her up in his arms. "Disobeying orders is *my* job. And I don't think we're in any position to, not this time. You can barely walk. I need to get you off this boat."

"No." Vickie replied, trying unsuccessfully to squirm away. "Bella's rushing into the lion's den. There has to be some way we can help her! I'm not leaving until we're *all* able to get off."

"I've told you I love you, right?"

Vickie sighed, and gave Red a wary look.

"Yeah, you have. And?"

"Just checking. It's important you know that, so that you'll understand the full weight of what I'm about to say." He cleared his throat, and shouted at her. "GET YOUR HEAD OUT OF YOUR ASS, WOMAN! WE NEED TO BOOK!"

She stared fearlessly into his eyes, kissed him lightly, and managed some sort of twisting move that ended with her back on the floor. "If it was just us, I'd agree with that. But it's not. And you know better." Once again she staggered to her feet, but this time she wobbled over to where her armor was lying in a puddle, and pulled something out of the pile. A belt. Like a utility belt, full of pockets. She strapped it on over her bare hips. "We're here and we're still breathing, so we can help. I'm not leaving my best friends to go up against another alien god-wannabe just so I can exit stage right." With a look of determination, Vickie took a deep breath and began to march.

With the first step, she wobbled, and fell into Red's waiting arms.

"Fine," she seethed. "You can carry me. Just get me closer to them."

Bella coughed, waved her hand to clear the smoke from burning alien World Ship out of her eyes and peered through more smoke to the edge of the bowl. Which, from where she stood, was up a slope, with what she was looking at looming over her as if it was about to fall on her. Twice, they had almost been intercepted by groups of Thulians—when another group of Thulians had appeared out of nowhere, cut down their own kind, and kept going. It looked as if her reprogramming had worked.

That isn't going to stop all that mass from falling on our heads if the artificial gravity suddenly fails. I'm insane to be here.

The ship looked like a multistory version of one of those futuristic California cliffside saucer-shaped homes that used to be all over LA until mudslides made it abundantly clear that building your house halfway out of a cliff was a generally bad idea. There was a tube leading from the bottom to the ground, and what looked like beads moving up the tube. Except they weren't beads, they were Thulian Masters. There were more of them clustered around the bottom of the tube, and in the front, was one who stood out from all the others. He was very shiny. The others all wore armor, or spacesuits, or space armor or something. His version was bigger, adorned with multicolored medals that appeared gaudy in their brilliance. His unarmored head stuck out of the shoulders of the suit, looking absurdly tiny, as if his orange head was the size of a golf ball. Bella had a good idea who this was.

"Eight?" Bella snapped.

"I believe the one in the front must be the commander, Gero," Eight confirmed.

"Then that's who we want." Bella grabbed Bulwark's hand and squeezed it briefly. "We're going in." She glanced over at Bulwark. "I don't suppose you have any strategy for getting me in touching distance of this guy?"

"Only the usual," Bull admitted, frowning. "I don't like this. We know nothing about him."

Increased movement caught her eye. "Eight, give me a magnified view," she ordered. Eight must have maneuvered one of the drones that he was using in place of spy-eyes; a moment later her HUD showed her the milling crowd behind Gero. "I don't think we have anything to worry about from the mob," she said. "Look at them! They're terrified. They can't get into that elevator fast enough." And indeed, now the Thulian Masters were shoving and kicking each other in a panic, trying to get into the escape ship.

She turned her attention to Gero. Close up, he looked even more absurd, as if a baby had donned Silent Knight's mechasuit. If his head was anything to go on, he was frail, delicate, which might be why he wore that suit in the first place. As she studied him, she suddenly realized those strange orange eyes were staring at *her.*

*What the—*She got a cold feeling all over, as she realized that there was something probing her psionic shields. The glare from those orange eyes intensified. And then her shields rang with the most intense psychic blow she had ever felt in her life. She staggered, then brought her head back up, glaring right back at him. "Confirmed, Bull," she said flatly. "He's a psychic."

"You don't say," Bulwark said.

Not just the words...but the *way* he said it, flat and uninflected, sent all her internal alarm bells going. She whirled to face him, just in time to see his fist coming straight for her chin. She ducked to the side, avoiding getting pasted, but he hit her shoulder with a bone-bruising blow, knocking her to the ground. She scrambled backwards to her feet. The despair in Bull's eyes told her everything she needed to know.

Gero was in control.

Shit. This is so not *good.* Could she drive Gero out of Bull if she got in physical contact with him? As she skipped and evaded, using everything Djinni had taught her of Parkour and everything she'd learned from the ECHO martial arts instructors, she had the distinct feeling that would be a bad idea. "Gairdner!" she hissed, using his name as a way to try to help him focus. "You can fight this! You're the most stubborn man I know! Don't let him do this!"

Bella recoiled as, for the second time that day, Bulwark began to laugh. Only this sounded . . . tortured. Then he grinned. A horrible, manic grin. "Gairdner doesn't live here anymore," he rasped. "This one is your lover, his thoughts stink of you. I can see how these hands have touched you. With trembling anticipation. With wanton lust. They have given you pleasure, little, little blue girl. Did you ever think that one day, they might crush the very life from your fragile body?"

"For godsake, Bull!" Bella screamed. "Are you going to let him spout that repulsive crap from your own lips?"

"His will is strong, for a human, but really . . ." Bull's smile grew, if possible, even wider. "Soon, he'll be with us. If it's any consolation to you, I find his thoughts rather interesting, perhaps even worth keeping. He might just live through this, maybe even forever. Would you like that, blue girl? Would that please you?"

If Gero was hoping to distract her with a war of words, he didn't get his wish. *He's lived decades with everyone afraid of him, everyone terrified he's going to get into their heads. To hell with that. He's not getting Bull.*

So instead of backing away and cowering, she grabbed Bull's biceps. "Bite me," she snarled, throwing her mind against Gero's, "You don't get him." Behind her own heavy shields, however, this was a feint. This was an Aikido move. Gero probably only understood force against force. If she could get him to mentally bull-rush *her,* she might be able to flip and use his own power *and* hers to boot him out of Bull's head. She steeled herself for the attack, ready to dodge and redirect the force of Gero's mind.

It should have worked, if she had not completely underestimated the sheer power the alien Master had at his disposal.

It hit her like a tsunami, a wave of hate and malice that simply washed over her. A directed strike, like a piledriver, she might have handled, her own considerable talents able to guide and shape the emotion back at him. But there was too much raw psychic energy to manipulate, too much to redirect. It slammed into her, almost shattered her defenses, and Bella was forced to let Bull go as she staggered back. For a moment, her thoughts were a confused muddle, as fear chilled her to the bone, paralyzing her.

She gasped for air and staggered back a few more steps, pulling herself together. Glancing up, she saw Bulwark striding towards her, his muscles relaxed, casual, as if he were merely taking a peaceful moonlight stroll, though his face still looked stricken. It made the words that spilled forth from between his clenched teeth all the more chilling.

"You are simply adorable, blue girl," Gero rasped. "Such fire, such determination—it has been most entertaining. But every good show must come to an end. It is time for the—how do you Earth vermin say it?—oh yes, it is time for the obese female to vocalize melodically. Do not fret. I will make your death a swift one... payment, if you like, for such a fine performance." Bull glanced over at the other Masters, who were still rushing into their escape ship in a mad frenzy. "Well, that and the fact that I must attend to my pathetic flock. I really must harden them up before our next harvesting cycle. Barron is more than sufficient to deal with any confrontation, but really, it almost shames me to say our kind has grown rather complacent over the past millennium."

"You're counting on Barron?" Bella put on a smirk. "Too bad Barron's dead. Oh, and your supersecret special surprise package has been deactivated too. Maybe you should have followed your 'pathetic flock' while you had the chance." *If I can get him to run...I'll get the chance to call in an all-out air strike.* Sure, she and Bull might be in the blast radius too, but there would probably be just enough time to sprint out of the kill zone as long as they could count on Bull's shields to take on shrapnel and explosive debris.

If she could count on Bull...

She wavered as the emotions played out on Bull's face. Moments before, he had seemed anguished, betraying the inner conflict between the big man and Gero for control. Now, there seemed nothing left of Bulwark. There was still anguish, but a different sort. He seemed shocked, and behind those clear blue eyes, she saw a rage building as he charged towards her, screaming in fury.

So much for Gero rabbiting, she thought. *I think I just made him really mad. I think I just made it that much easier for him to control Bull. I think I'm in real trouble here.*

She scrambled backwards up a hill of debris and her hand brushed the grip of her nine-mil, its clip loaded with the ECHO special incendiary and explosive charges. In his fury, Gero wasn't bothering with any of Bull's meta-talents. Even without his shields, if Bull was able to get his hands on her, he could probably tear her apart. Of course, without Bull's shields, all it would take was a solid shot to his temple to end the threat. She pulled out the gun, dodging out of the way of Bull's charge, and continued to dance around him as she fought another, internal struggle.

Her hand shook each time she leveled the gun at Bull's head. *I have to do this!*

And each time, she hesitated, and continued to dodge the big man's clumsy attempts to grab her.

I can't! I can't, it's ... I love him ... !

It was the uneven terrain that betrayed her, and Bella yelped as she tripped and fell with a crash to the ground. Instinctively, she rolled onto her back and aimed her gun high, and found Bull dead in her sights as he leapt down on her, his arms raised back to deliver a crushing blow.

It was a split-second decision. Shoot him between the eyes, end the threat, take the fight to Gero and finish this. Or don't ... and die knowing that once Gero and his Masters got away, they were still going to be a menace to Earth—forever. Or at least as long as the Earth lasted.

There really was no choice at all.

"Oh God, I'm sorry," she whispered, and pulled the trigger.

The bullet skimmed past Bulwark's head, cutting a bloody line across his scalp. *"Dammit!"* she screamed, and aimed again, half-blinded with tears. With a triumphant shout Bulwark knocked the gun from her hands with a heavy fist and reared back to deliver a final blow.

Bella froze, staring him in the eyes. For a moment, time stood still, and the clear blue of his eyes softened as he gazed back at her. His hands fell to his sides as a weak grin lit up his face.

"Bull?"

Bull nodded, and laid a trembling hand on her cheek.

"How ... ?"

"He tried to force me to kill you," Bull croaked. "To kill my love. Now *that's* insane."

Then for one terrifying moment, Bull's face changed again, the eyes narrowing, the mouth twisting into a snarl. *"Fine!"* he spat.

Then his eyes went blank, and he collapsed on top of her.

Only the fact that they were on a pile of shifting debris kept him from flattening and smothering her. With an adrenaline-fueled shove, she rolled Bull's body off and downhill a little, and paused just long enough to touch his face before leaping to her feet. If she'd been angry before, it was nothing compared to this.

I've got to take that bastard out. He's so strong, can I even do *this?*

She glanced down at Bull, his still body lay sprawled on the ground, only the rise and fall of his chest showing he was still alive, and felt her resolve harden. She picked up her gun and raced towards the escape ship, towards the remaining Masters...

And towards Gero.

Red had made Vickie stop long enough to get her armor back on. He had probably been hoping it would take her a lot longer than it did. At this point in her life, she could wiggle into it in under sixty seconds. The boots took a little longer, but not much.

Unfortunately, things were unfolding on Bella's side of the ship a lot faster than she'd thought they would. Even with Red impatiently scooping her up and carrying her like a football, there was no way they would reach her in time. Red must have come to the same conclusion at the same time; he suddenly skidded to a halt as soon as they hit the surface, and put her down. "What can we do from here?" he grated. "What can *you* do? Can you open up the ground underneath him?"

"It's not ground," she panted, trying to hold off desperation so she could think. "Can't do earth magic on what's not earth." She closed her eyes. "Bella's drained. I wish I could send her juice the way Sera could. She might be able to face him head on if I could just give her more psi power. How the *hell* can I... Dammit, if Bella had magic and not psi, I could boost her. Or if Sera was here, *she* could, and..."

"And magic works like psi, sorta," he reminded her. "You said that back in the Vault. Remember?"

It hit her. Maybe. "And...I think I've got something." The

belt full of storage crystals was mostly still full. This was going to depend on playing fast and loose with the Laws of Similarity and Contagion, but it was all she had left. "Eight, get ready for some more number-crunching."

She was barely aware of Red supporting her as she ran through equations, made corrections based on Eight's input, and formulated a . . . result of sorts. It wasn't anywhere near as elegant as Eight or Overwatch or anything else that she'd done with advanced mathemagic. It was crude. It depended on some of the oldest, most primitive magical laws on Earth.

And on an unquantifiable X.

Love.

Red, Bull, and, yes, Vickie loved and were loved by Bella. She was important to them, they were important to her. Messy, crazy, insane love. Vickie was going to link them *all,* and pour their combined strength into her friend, plus whatever was left in the storage crystals. Or at least, that was what she hoped she was about to do.

"Here goes nothing," she muttered, and fired off the equation. *Link us all and back her up.*

"*Fiat!*" she cried.

"*Face me, you miserable worm!*" Bella screamed *and* projected that across the fifty yards or so that separated her and Gero. As he slowly turned, she kept running, narrowing the distance between them. And when she got to about fifty feet, it suddenly felt as if she had run into a wall of Jell-O.

He can't get into my head to control me, she realized, as she continued to struggle forward, leaning into the slow-motion run as if she was running against a hurricane wind. *Mental shields, makes my mind too slippery. But he's still putting up a hell of a fight. It's all I can do to keep moving forward . . .*

There was some sort of expression on Gero's face; she couldn't read it and she wasn't about to drop her shields to read him empathically, but she thought it was a smirk. She'd narrowed the gap between them to twenty feet, though, And she was still inching forward.

Memory supplied exactly what she needed, as she remembered Sera touching her shoulder when she first healed John, and supplying her with so much power it was like trying to drink from a firehose. Maybe there was still some tenuous connection to the Infinite there.

Dig...down...deep. She pulled further on her own reserves, got a little more, narrowed the gap again to ten feet.

And there, she was stopped. Just out of reach. And the battle to reach him married with a battle against despair. His eyes flashed. With triumph? Not even rage could supply what she needed.

And then, suddenly, out of nowhere, power *flooded* into her. For a moment, she thought she heard a near-infinite chorus of voices in her head. Now it was her turn to feel a swell of triumph and incredulous joy as she lunged forward and grabbed what passed for his arms.

The belt around Vickie's waist lit up like the crystals inside it were on fire as they discharged all their stored magic power at once...

...*shit*...

This was...*big*. This was *bigger* than she'd thought. This was...
Bloody hell—

Then she was lost in a chorus of wordless voices. Dozens. Hundreds. Thousands? She had based her calculations on only a handful of people—herself, Red and Bull—and loosely on the extent of their love for Bella. How did one quantify love anyway? It made for some fairly exotic, even vague algorithms, to say the least. It had been a long shot, as these things always were, and she had known there were bound to be some unforeseen side effects. She could feel so many of them! How was this possible? Had she somehow crossed time and space, found alternate versions of themselves to boost Bella's reserves? *Sure, let's start with the least likely explanation.* But what else could they be? Were these echoes then, an odd reverberation of their collective thoughts amplified to a roaring din? They certainly made it hard to think. The only constant was a vast feeling of *love*. There was so much of it. The thought struck her again. How did one quantify love? She had gathered them up, by proximity, and...

Vickie paused, stunned.

She had gathered them *all*.

A part of everyone who loved, or was loved by Bella. Everyone who was important to her. Everyone she was important to. *Everyone*. It was...it was like the little tiny bit of Sera's Song of the Infinite she had once experienced. It was the Song of ECHO, like being the center of a *universe* of voices. For a brief moment, she even thought she felt the echo of John and Sera...

And one of the presences was just a little annoyed.

"Oh, for the luva..."

"Red?" she said in response. "How is this possible?"

He formed up next to her, out of nothing. And he looked, not like the thing he'd been since she'd found him alive again, but like the old Red. He was there, if a bit hazy, blurring out of reality at times, but there. He moved with his usual grace, but with an odd ebb that quickened and slowed with the pace of breathing. On the level of instinct, not of math, she *understood* that time was on hold for a moment. *No, not on hold. That's impossible. Slowed, to a bare fraction of normal time, but that's not possible either. You don't mess with time. But if time hasn't changed...*

"A mindscape," Red snarled. "Another goddamn mindscape!" He paused, looking around. "This one's *really* big though..."

"Time didn't slow down," she murmured, understanding. "We've sped up. We're moving at the speed of thought, in a place bursting with psychic power. Holy freaking balls, what the hell? I didn't—I just thought I was gonna boost Bell the way Sera could, using you and me and Bull, and...I think I phrased it mathemagically as 'everyone who's important,' and...*everyone* is important. Still, this shouldn't be possible; I don't have this kind of juice..."

"What did you do, Egon?" Red asked. "Seriously. Forget what you intended. Cross your eyes, wiggle your nose and look at the math. You see magic as math, right? So instead of trying to think what you might have done, look at what's actually there. What did you *do?*"

"I..." She looked around her, with the inner eye. The equations didn't lie. Bella was tethered by love and something not unlike devotion to everyone in ECHO and a lot of people beyond. Her best guess? Everyone who fulfilled those parameters within a ten-mile radius, Vickie had somehow connected them. And the moment Bella touched Gero, that linked them *all* and had pulled Vickie and Red at least into this mindscape. With her. And the moment she realized that, she also *felt* it—as if she was the only one holding the thousands of strings controlling one of those gigantic competition kites. The tension centered in her chest was almost unbearable.

To hell with that. I will *hold it, because I have to.* "This is a mindscape, and it would have to belong to someone with a lot of psychic power to house this much square footage, so to speak," Vickie said aloud. "I must have linked most of ECHO and brought you and me in here and, to some extent, *them* to back up Bella. Would this be Gero?"

"It would," said a female voice. Vickie and Red turned, and watched another pair of figures coalesce into view. It was Bella, her hands around Gero's throat, his around hers. In this mindscape, she looked frail, and Gero was a monster.

"Then let's do what we're here for." Vickie sensed somewhere her jaw was clenching, and she poured everything—*everything*—into her friend. Around her, outside this mindscape but linked through her, she felt the chorus of voices join her in triumph. It burst forth like a song, fierce and pure, and at the center of it all, Bella's tired form straightened up, awash in power.

Gero, for his part, was oblivious to what was going on. His hands gripped Bella's throat in malicious glee, and he began to gloat, ignorant of her sudden surge of strength. "Now is the moment in all your dramas when the antagonist utters a soliloquy," he smirked.

"You mean the villain monologues," Bella snarled. "Fine. Monologue away, you bastard."

Gero laughed. "You are my creation. All of you. *We* are the reason you metahumans exist in the first place. *We* set loose the transmutation nanovirus when we first arrived, just as we do on every planet we choose to manipulate. We gave you power! You should be thanking us!"

"*Why?*" Bella cried. "What in *hell* do you get out of this?"

Gero smirked. "Entertainment, little blue girl. Endless hours of entertainment. You are a particularly creative race, and we've certainly enjoyed your extensive works of fiction, but nothing quite captures the thrill of watching you fight and struggle against each other in real unscripted time, never knowing that it's all doomed in the end, that when you cease to amuse, we'll wipe you out and start anew, elsewhere amongst the stars." Suddenly he frowned. "Except you have the uncanny ability to contaminate even our own loyal troops. We should *never* have given shelter to those damned Nazis." His voice rose in a loud petulant whine. "They managed to infect our underlings with their creed, until we found those who should have been mere slaves were taking matters into their own hands, with their mad desire to *conquer* you. They intended to make you into a world of slaves to support their conquest of the galaxy and the spread of their—I suppose you'd have to call it 'religion' of the Fourth Reich. We'd chastise and punish them for acting without orders, and as soon as I took my attention off them, they'd attack you again. Yours was to be our masterpiece! The heights you would have reached! So close! If it hadn't been for them, we would have forged the grand epic to end all others! And now *it's all spoiled and we'll have to start over!*"

The last was uttered in a petulant shout, which fell to a pathetic squeak as Bella tightened her grip. Gero's eyes widened as he cried out in pain, his hands retreating, struggling in vain to pry Bella's grip from his throat.

"What...?" Gero gasped. "How...?"

"That can't be all of it," Bella snarled. "That's not *all* you were doing. Spit it out, you fractard!" She shook him, hard enough to have made his teeth rattle, if he'd had teeth, if this had been reality and not a projection in the mindscape. "Cough it up!"

"Insignificant human..." Gero wheezed. "You cannot hope to..."

"But I can," Bella said and, with a shocking display of strength, lifted Gero above her by the throat and slammed him down on his back; the impact echoed like a volcanic explosion all through the mindscape. "Whatever you think is happening right now, you might want to take another look around here. Go on, take a second. Look."

Gero shuddered and became very still. He drew in a sharp breath, his head feathers quivering as he became aware of the song, as he began to look around him. Vickie glared back at him, and felt a multitude of eyes through her doing the same.

"You have our attention." Bella said between gritted teeth. "So talk. *Now.*"

"We..." Gero took another breath, and winced. Vickie watched in wonder as a myriad of emotions played across his sharp features. Though he was unreadable in the real world, they could easily see his feelings here. There was confusion, shocked realization, disbelief, and finally, fear. Vickie suspected these were new to him, or at the very least, long forgotten. She almost felt sorry for him. Almost.

"Talk!" Bella shouted, and Gero screamed as she brought her power down on his mind like a hammer. He shuddered, his cries falling to pathetic whimpers, and nodded in surrender.

"We take what we need," Gero began, stuttering as he struggled to control his fear. "Sometime in the past, we . . . we lost something. Something vital to our progression. In our lust for power, for knowledge, we became reckless. We changed. We extended our life spans greatly, but at a heavy cost. Most of us grew frail physically. We could no longer conceive children, or invent new technology. Creativity, in all its forms, was lost to us. We had to resort to . . . novel means."

"Novel means?" Vickie heard Bull's voice echo from around them.

"Experimentation," Gero gasped. "On you. On the others before you. Only when we are sure, when our gathered Collective is sure . . . will we dare risk exposing ourselves to the procedures to give us back what we lost."

"I take it you've been largely unsuccessful," Vickie heard Ramona snarl, another faceless voice, powerful and everywhere.

Gero nodded frantically. "Our earliest attempts killed many of us. Only Barron and I were improved, albeit greatly, but the rest fell to horrific mutations and died horribly. Without children, our numbers began to dwindle. We could not risk losing any more."

"Monstrous!" Normally the voice of calm restraint and reason, the outrage in Unter's cry seemed all the more terrible as it rang endlessly throughout the mindscape. "You crossed the boundaries of decency, of nature *itself*. You chose to become a parasite on all *existence*? You should have died out!"

"I suppose you would have chosen the noble path," Gero muttered.

"I would have, yes." Unter's voice trailed off in disgust. "There is a time to let go your claw clutch on life. You did not learn the lesson of Tithonus."

"So I have *you* to thank for the fact that I am not still a starving beggar in Mumbai," Khanjar's voice boomed. "And I also have you to thank for the deaths of three of my friends, whose mutations ended their lives in painful ways. I wonder how Karma judges that."

Gero cowered, unable to answer.

"What is this 'Collective' you speak of?" Yankee Pride demanded.

"The Collective is a host of intellects," Gero said. "The best and brightest of all that we have enslaved. With each new mind, the

Collective has grown stronger, has brought to fruition many technological advances, and with each step bringing us closer to ... to ..."

"Immortality," Red muttered.

"Yes ..." Gero sighed. "We have prolonged our lives, but we are not immortal. With humanity, we thought we had finally found our event horizon. So many possibilities. Your minds would have surely tipped the scales. Even with the loss of Tesla and Marconi, surely Verdigris and Victrix would have sufficed. And if they didn't ..." Gero glared at Red, and grimaced. "One of you offered another option. She promised us another way, a new test subject whom she promised would be immortal. Herself. After she was done with *you*, the Red Djinni." Gero closed his eyes, and shuddered. "So many options, so many possibilities. We came so close, after so long ..."

"You saying I'm immortal?" Red asked.

"Only experimentation can answer that," Gero said. "You very well may be. Doppelgaenger's reasoning was quite sound. But only the Collective could know for certain, after a full series of tests and a barrage of torturous experiments."

"Been there," Red scowled. "Done that."

"Moot point, anyway," another voice said.

Vickie looked around, surprised.

"Paris?"

"Yeah, it's me," Scope answered, the dead yet amplified tone of her voice sounding odd as it reverberated throughout the mindscape. "The Collective's gone. We took care of it."

"Gone?" Gero asked, his voice now breaking.

"Yep," Scope said. "That giant room of boxed brains went blooey. If you mean the place that looked like the 'lost luggage' section of Robots 'R' Us surrounding that really big ball of light. We shut it down."

"Impossible!" Gero exclaimed. "Destroying the Collective is beyond you, it is even beyond *us*! You could not have ..."

"But we did," Scope interrupted. "It actually wasn't that hard, y'know, once they showed us how."

"Once *who* showed you?" Gero demanded.

"Them," Scope said. "The Collective. Didn't I mention? They wanted to die, just like your big ship wanted to die, but couldn't do themselves in. So they showed us. Hey, Vix, this going to take long? Khanjar and I have this thing we gotta do, remember?"

"I—don't know," Vickie managed, when Gero interrupted her.

"*We deserve immortality!*" he bleated. "We want to live forever! Wouldn't you? *Don't* you?"

"No," Bella said flatly. "Not all of us, anyway. Better, yes, but not forever. When you can live forever, you start getting timid. You're afraid to try anything that might risk that immortality. Like Tesla and Marconi: they're scared witless every time they think they might die." She smirked when Gero gasped. "Oh, that's right, they're still alive. I guess you didn't know that." She glared at him. "And even after all this...if I let you go, if I let you run away with your toadies...you still won't stop, will you? You'll just keep coming back here. You'll enslave someone else to do your dirty work, and you'll come back for revenge. Won't you? *Won't you?*"

Gero shrank away from her, but didn't answer.

"*Answer me!*" Bella screamed, and brought the full force of her will down upon him.

Gero screamed, writhing in her grasp, and nodded fearfully.

"Yes," he croaked finally. "Yes, I would. I would find a way..."

Bella put one metaphorical foot on Gero's chest. "I'm not going to kill you, Gero," she said, her voice flat. "That would be too merciful. I'm going to make an example out of you. I'm going to lobotomize you, and then I am going to tell all your flunkies to get the *hell* off my world and take you with them and if they come back, they can expect to be given the same treatment." She glared down at him. "And I hope they seal you in a room and let you rot."

Vickie had been pouring the collected power of the *gestalt* into Bella and had watched her temper building as Gero cowered. The idea that all they had ever been was...a reality show for the Masters...was infuriating. That they had been lab rats was doubly, triply infuriating. And to hear from Gero's own mouth that Bella had been right, that the Masters would never stop, never give up trying to get their revenge...

And that, in the end, was what sent Bella over the top.

"You don't kill my world!" Bella snarled. "*NOT ON MY WATCH!*"

And around them, every voice, every being echoed the battle cry.

Bella struck, the spear-tip of the collective anger of their united will.

And Red saw the danger to Vickie before even Vickie did.

"Vix! The mindscape is coming down! If the connection snaps back on you, you'll—*Let them go!*"

Oh God, he's right! In a blaze of fear, she severed the connections that held them all together.

And the world went white with pain.

Vickie snapped back to herself as a tremor shook what was left of the dying ship, knocking her on her ass. Her head hurt worse than she ever remembered it hurting before. It felt...bruised inside, deep, purple bone bruises. And there was just barely enough energy left in her to be able to breathe. "*Bozhe moi,*" she groaned, and looked up at Red, who looked as disgustingly healthy and healed and full of energy as she felt battered and exhausted. "If I didn't love you, I'd hate you right now."

"Less talking, more booking." He lifted her to her feet, then kept right on lifting until he had her in his arms. "Last call for the *Titanic* lifeboats."

She was too tired to object to being carried. "Roger that," she sighed, putting her head against his chest. "Eight, plot us a course outta here."

CHAPTER THIRTY-FIVE

Long Time Gone

MERCEDES LACKEY, DENNIS LEE,
CODY MARTIN AND VERONICA GIGUERE

Red Djinni was not wrong. The ship was in its death throes. This, paradoxically, was the most dangerous situation our people had faced yet.

Ramona shook herself out of that weird, split-second vision of Bella, the Thulian commander, and the horrible things he had confessed. She'd think about that later—if they all made it. Blackened buildings had started to crumble into the charred alien landscape. Ramona stumbled forward as the ship shuddered and heaved. A rancid odor met her nose and she gagged. She and other ECHO forces had moved forward to provide support to the others still deep inside the city and the main buildings. Much of the chatter had ceased, with Eight keeping communications to an efficient minimum. Ramona appreciated the near-emotionless instructions and updates alongside the ever-shifting overlay on her HUD. If she focused on the information there, she didn't have time to think about what was happening back on the carrier in the spaces they'd reserved for triage. And she didn't have time to think about that weird, shared hallucination they'd all had. If it *had been* an hallucination. Until she got a chance to talk to Bella...

There would be time enough for that later.

Another tremor shook the foundation of the city. A deep crack opened up along the street to Ramona's left and the same foul smell escaped into the air. Corbie saw the fissure at nearly the same time she did and leapt into the air, his injured wing putting him off balance. He landed awkwardly on one foot and sucked in a quick breath. "Whole place is fallin' to bits. Thought it smelled bad on the outside, wot."

"It's not just falling apart. It's *dying*." Trina adjusted her grip on the plasma cannon that encased her right arm up to her bicep. She walked next to Speed Freak, their odd pairing providing quick firepower on the outskirts of the city. The diminutive Metisian woman did not share Ramona's talent for outward calm. "Whatever has been generating the artificial gravity, it's shutting down now, and this structure can't hold. It's going to collapse in on itself as all of the subsystems shut down, and the rapid apoptosis will compromise anything on the inside that's part of a living endoskeleton."

"*I concur, and I have forwarded that info—*" Eight began, when the AI's voice was replaced by a Klaxon. The alarm stopped just long enough for Yankee Pride to bark authoritatively, "*All forces! Fall back and retreat to the platforms and ships! Fall back!*"

Positions in a half-circle along the ridge on the edge of the city lit up Ramona's overlay, showing the remaining snipers that Mercurye had placed. Debris blocked the paths that he had taken to place them... hours ago? It seemed longer than that. "Eight, you've got retreat plans for our guys on the ridge? All of them?"

"*Evac is inbound to their locations. Your team is cleared to—*"

The boom and crack of stone gave the only warning as part of the ridge began to slide into the basin. Ramona stood, frozen in horror. She could barely hear the rotors and she knew they wouldn't be able to reach the remaining snipers in time.

"I've got northwest! Tell Donni this one's coming right for her!" Corbie took a few quick steps and launched himself into the air.

"We'll take west." Trina swung herself up to Speed's back and tucked the arm cannon along her side. Before Ramona could ask or argue, they raced toward the collapsing ridge. Her HUD flashed, Pride's command repeating in her immediate field of vision.

She swallowed hard. "Everyone else, on me! Fall back and retreat to the platforms. Go!"

Eyes focusing on the terrain ahead of them, Ramona willed herself to keep her feet moving. She kept a steady count of the remaining members of her group, moving along the path that Eight laid for her through what remained of the city and into the perimeter.

Three creatures too small to be wolves burst from behind a smoldering pile of metal debris. They ran alongside the group, barking frantically. Only one of them had any bit of nanoweave on it, the edges singed and caked with blood. Ramona slowed to a jog, then stopped and crouched down a short distance from the largest of the dogs. It crept toward her, head down and tail low.

The dog's ID came up as River. "It's okay, River. You come with us, you and your team." Ramona felt her throat close up as the creature lay down a foot from her and let out a low whimper. *They must have heard Pride's order and started to move, even if Leader couldn't get out with them.* "Come on, let's move."

As if to confirm her worst fear, Eight said quietly, on her private freq, *"Leader of the Pack is offline."*

The group started running again, this time with the few remaining dogs who had gone into the Thulian city with Leader of the Pack. Three times, just as small groups of Thulians headed for them, *another* group of Thulians appeared out of nowhere and cut them down. Another thing to think about later. Ramona picked up the pace and kept her focus on the platforms and the ships just beyond. Small metal cylinders broke the surface of the water near the rail guns, hatches on top opening to allow the retreating forces to board the larger ships. The remaining metas able to fly landed on the decks. Most carried the injured and touched down only long enough to hand off their comrades to waiting medical teams. Her HUD said that Corbie was still back on the ridge, even with a wave of choppers coming back over the team on their way to the platform.

The ground beneath her feet cracked and buckled, beginning to collapse on itself in meter-wide patches. Ramona fought to keep her feet moving and her mind on the singular task of reaching the line of ships. She could see other teams scrambling over the crumbling lip of the half-sphere and directing others to the ships that would evac.

A blur of black feathers tumbled from the sky and hit the edge of a platform. It split into two, the darker half falling into the water. Ramona cried out and lurched forward, but the dogs moved faster and dove for the sinking figure. Another violent tremor shook the ground and pushed the ash and rock toward the retreating forces. Her exposed skin reacted to the rush of debris, but she still felt the jagged pieces and smoldering embers.

"Keep moving," she called to the remaining forces around her. "Get to the first ship that will take you." Ramona waved them ahead, then turned to face what remained of the outer edge of the floating city.

The dying fires of the initial battle marked the center of the rapidly widening crater. Where the surface had cracked under the intense heat and heavy fighting, parts of the living city oozed a burnt orange ichor. The buildings and terrain that had created the ridge surrounding the lush forest continued to collapse upon the remnants of the Thulian forest.

Her heart sank. No one would have survived that kind of destruction.

In her HUD, two names flashed, then dimmed. Eight spoke over her private freq to confirm the loss. *"Speed Freak is offline. Trina is offline."*

Ramona sucked in a lungful of smoke-filled air and willed herself to turn back to the ships. On one of the platforms, two of Leader's dogs stood over the sodden limp figure of Corbie. "Eight, please tell me that—"

"Corbie is injured and unconscious. Continue retreat ordered by Yankee Pride."

She exhaled and fought down a wave of rage and tears. "Understood. Continuing retreat."

Untermensch and the remainder of the forces under his command had been the first unit to reach their objective. They held the area as the rest of the assaulting elements advanced, beating back increasingly frenzied waves of Thulians. The CCCP—his CCCP now—did not take any further losses, aside from a few of Kirill's copies. Untermensch was amazed at how quickly Jadwiga, Thea, and Mamona had been able to respond to casualties. He suspected that losing the Commissar had galvanized them, making them push themselves to prevent anyone else from dying. For the most part, they had been successful; only a few of the soldiers that fell were unable to be saved. He was glad to see that they didn't take any foolish risks, as he had seen others do when a comrade had been lost.

Natalya trained them well. She would be proud of them.

He still wasn't sure to make of that split-second vision in which the Thulian High Commander had blurted out things that had made his entire self rise up in rage and revolt. Bella had been in it, and the little witch, and Bulwark... and Red Djinni. But Red Djinni was dead! Or... was he?

The warning Klaxon and calls for retreat startled Georgi when they first blared over his Overwatch connection. They were winning! How could they possibly be considering retreat? That was when the worst "ship quake" yet had thrown him from his feet. He had grown accustomed to them during the push to the center of the ship, towards their assigned sector; he and the rest of the fighters had learned to anticipate the bad ones, bracing themselves, going flat, or lifting off the ground with powers if they could. This quake was different; buildings that hadn't been hit with any munitions began to crumble, and the streets erupted in places, with the cracks spewing flame or a noxious odor. He didn't need to give orders to his people; everyone began running almost immediately. The fighting had ceased with that first huge tremor; even the Thulians recognized that something had slipped in the machinery that kept the World Ship running, and that it wouldn't be long until it consumed them all.

As the unit the furthest in, Untermensch's people had priority for many of the evacuation helos. A flight of Mi-8 MB *Bisektrisa* medevac helos intercepted his unit as they ran for the beachhead, hovering in a ruined plaza.

"Wounded first! *Davay davay*, get moving!" Georgi glanced around for Jadwiga; she and Thea were carrying a young soldier with a swath of bloody bandages around his midsection. "Sovie, you and Thea stay with that man; we're loading all of the worst cases on one helo. Keep them stable until you get back to the ship." The medical officer nodded once, then continued towards the helos.

Fed presumably by Eight, Georgi heard Gamayun sounding off soldiers' names, directing them to which helo to take the wounded. It was the first time he noticed that Gamayun had command of every Russian and former-Soviet language and dialect. Each man was addressed in the language he would respond to the quickest. *A polyglot. It makes sense for her position, come to think of it.* How had he never noticed that before?

Because you never listened to the command frequency before, old man, he chided himself. If he lived through this, there would be many things he would have to learn and get used to as the leader of the CCCP. First, he needed to survive, and make sure these soldiers did, too.

"We are full up, Commissar. If we're going to get another load, we need to lift off now." One of the pilots waved to him through the cockpit screen of the lead helicopter. To punctuate his message, a crack ripped through the plaza; the splitting concrete sounded like thunder, overcoming even the *thwop* of the helicopter rotors.

"Lift off now! We will find another ride!" Unter shielded himself from the prop wash, backing away from the helos. They quickly lifted into the sky, staying low to the rooftops; even as the ship was dying, some of its defenses were still operational. When the helos were out of sight, he turned back to the rest of his people. Chug, Kirill (along with several of his copies), and Mamona were all that were left of the CCCP on the ground; there hadn't been room for either Kirill or Mamona on the last flight out. Chug... was Chug; alone, he weighed enough to change the center of gravity for all but the largest transport helos, even though he didn't take up much space. And there were still sixteen Russian commandos; they were exhausted, and looking at him expectantly.

"Eight, we need an extract. This city is falling apart around us, and this LZ is untenable."

"I am sorry, Commander, but there is no transport available." Unter's HUD lit up with a map and a dotted line. *"This is the fastest route from your position to an evac point. I will either have a craft waiting for you, or have one on the way."* It was three kilometers to the new waypoint... and with how quickly the World Ship was falling apart, that three kilometers seemed much longer than it normally would.

Unter turned to what remained of his forces. "Comrades, drop anything that isn't a weapon or ammo. We have a run ahead of us." He started to strip off his rucksack, and the others quickly followed his example. They didn't need to be burdened down if they wanted to make it off of the World Ship alive.

"Commissar," one of the Kirill copies—or was it the original? Did that even matter for his metahuman powers?—stomped up to Unter in a suit of the Supernaut armor. "Should we leave behind the heavy assets? I still have three working suits—"

"No, leave them. If we run into anything big, we're dead anyways. We cannot delay." Kirill nodded once; as one, the three copies all exited their suits, the armored plates swinging away from the power armor's skeleton like a man being flayed alive. The way that the Kirills moved, slightly different but far too similar to each other, unnerved Georgi. *They're not twins; just copies, remember? Tools to be used if necessary.* "Time to move!"

They ran, and the city did its level best to kill them. The tremors made it almost impossible to run at times; one moment they would all be sprinting full out, and the next, everyone— save for Chug—had toppled over, some of them wiping out quite spectacularly. Before long, several of the men had broken arms, wrists, and fingers; luckily, only one had a sprained ankle, and Chug was easily able to lift the man and run just as fast. The image of Chug carrying a large and uncomfortable-looking Russian commando would have been amusing any other day, but Unter had little room for humor in his heart at the moment. Pieces of buildings rained down around them, the chunks of concrete and masonry exploding like mortar shells when they hit the ground. After one particularly violent tremor, two of the Kirill copies were crushed by a section of a stone column; the remaining two didn't even break stride, vaulting over the column and the dead copies. Once, Untermensch almost fell into a chasm as the street split in front of him; he skidded to a wobbly stop right at the edge as the far side of the hole receded. There was no way for them to vault over it; Eight had already rerouted their course around the new obstacle, but it would cost them precious time. They were so close...just a little further...

Unter heard the helo before he saw it; a CH-47 Chinook, American or British, he couldn't immediately tell and certainly didn't care. *"This is Paladin Two-Two to Red One, come in, over."* Paladin? Definitely British, he decided.

"This is Red One, we have audio on you, no visual, over," Unter half-shouted as he ran over a pile of destroyed building.

"Roger, Red One. We're twenty seconds out from the LZ; we're going to set down right in the middle of the boulevard. Don't keep us waiting, over."

"Copy that, Paladin. We're running—" Movement on one of the rooftops caught Untermensch's eye, causing him to stop short. It was a damaged Robo-Eagle, huddled against a spire. It spotted the Chinook just as it came into view for Unter, and vaulted aloft from the rooftop, screeching horribly. "Paladin, you have incoming! Abort now!" Before the pilot could respond or even react, the Eagle was on the Chinook, its beak and claws shredding through the aluminum fuselage as easy as if it were paper. One of the Eagle's wings clipped the rotors, further crippling the Eagle...but also killing the lift for the Chinook. Unter and the rest of his unit could only watch in open-mouthed horror as the Eagle and Chinook, locked together in death, plummeted behind the rooftops. A second later, the *whump-BOOM* of the explosion killed whatever hope most of them had been holding on to.

"What the hell are we doing to do now?" Mamona was doubled over, hands on her knees as she struggled for breath. There was an edge of panic in her voice: Unter could see that same fear in the faces of the others. Even Chug appeared agitated, mostly because his comrades weren't happy.

"Keep moving to the LZ. They might be able to send another bird for extract," Unter replied, gritting his teeth against the lie. The ship couldn't last much longer; would they risk another helo for sixteen soldiers, when there were others that were probably closer and more likely to be saved? *Knock that shit off, Commissar. Can't afford to think like that if you are going to lead.*

They pressed on. The boulevard was gigantic: kilometers long, and several hundred meters wide, flanked by buildings. Up and down the stretch of it, Untermensch could see the remains of the earlier battle: the gutted carcasses of tanks and APCs, burning Death Spheres and trooper suits, and hundreds of bodies. From this distance, he couldn't tell the Thulians from the humans.

"Incoming! Contact right!" Unter shouldered his rifle, scanning frantically in the direction that one of the commandos had called out. A large group of Thulians, many of them wounded and nearly all of them carrying weapons, rounded the corner of a building towards the center of the ship. There had to be over one hundred of them in all; it took them a moment to notice Unter and the rest before they, too, brought their weapons to bear. There was one in front of the pack, with one of their energy weapons in his right hand while supporting an injured Thulian on his left shoulder. Unter and the Thulian locked eyes for several long moments; the standoff couldn't last, and out here on open ground, Unter's people would be decimated. The only thing he could think of was to order the rest to flee while he tried to charge the Thulians, make them focus on him long enough for the others to get away. But to what purpose? Without an extract, they would die on the ship just the same. Still, some chance was better than no chance. He tensed, readying himself to give the order and then sprint at the Thulians.

"Bozhe moi! What's that?" The exclamation came simultaneously from Untermensch's implant and from his right. He looked where the bilingual voice was coming from; it was Mamona, pointing over his shoulder. He turned.

Part of the side of the great ship had detached itself. It was a pale green, saucer-shaped craft that Untermensch had taken for a building, wobbling unsteadily as it lifted away from the side of the ship. It hovered uncertainly for a moment, as if it couldn't make up its mind which of the many fighting groups to attack first.

The Thulians stared at it, jaws slackening. Apparently the existence of this relatively tiny ship came as a complete surprise to them. Some of them turned back to the forces opposed to them—some of them gazed at the saucer in glaze-eyed disbelief.

Then whoever, whatever was in charge of the saucer made up its mind. It shot straight up into the sky, fleeing.

The apparent leader of the Thulians twisted back around to face Unter. *Well, what the hell is it going to be?* Something passed over the lead Thulian's face, and he barked out a command to the group. Several of them wavered a bit, seemingly unsure, until the leader shouted at them more forcefully. The group, unbelievably, started to put down their weapons. Unter could swear that more than a few looked relieved.

"Commissar?" One of the commandos had moved up beside Unter, his weapon still trained on the Thulians. "Orders?"

Unter grunted, then lowered his rifle. "Stand down, but keep an eye on them. There may have been enough killing for today, comrade." *Not that this changes shit for us,* Unter thought. The ship was still dying, and they were stuck.

A warning beep from Eight came over his comm. *"Commissar, alert! You have one unknown contact moving on your position! Large, airborne, south approach!"*

Unter swung back to the Thulians, snarling. Was this some kind of trick? None of the Thulians had made a move for their weapons, bringing Unter up short. They didn't know what was coming any more than he did. Another violent quake rocked the boulevard, causing several of the buildings nearby to collapse. Both groups surged unsteadily towards the center of the street, away from the falling rubble. *This is it. The ship is finished. Well, come on, you bastards, let's see what final surprise you have!* He brought his rifle up, facing south. Whatever was coming, he wanted to go down fighting.

Unter would never admit it to another living soul, but he flinched rather badly when the helicopter crested over the rooftops to the south. He nearly shot at it, he was so startled; it took him catching himself and consciously taking his finger off the trigger before he accepted what had happened. It was an Mi-26, one of the largest and most powerful helicopters ever created. This one had a number of burns and even tears in its fuselage, but it was still flying.

"Holy shit, that's a big bird," Mamona exclaimed.

Unter shrugged. "Is Russian." He started moving towards the helo as it began its descent—no easy thing, with all of the momentum it had behind it and the wreckage in the boulevard. The pilot, whoever it was, had maneuvered expertly, with the tail ramp facing Unter. "Everyone, get moving, now! Keep an eye on the Thulians, but get them onboard, too!" His tone didn't leave any room for dissent. His people herded the injured and frightened Thulians onto the helo, their weapons not quite trained on their recent enemies. When the last of the Russians had finally boarded at the end, only then did Unter hop on. He slapped an intercom at the top of the ramp, keying it. "We're all on, go!" He was almost driven to his knees as the heavy transport helicopter lurched upward faster than he would have imagined possible, the ramp closing next to him.

Georgi fought his way to the front of the helo, stepping over and around his people, the Russian commandos, and the mass of Thulians. The interior of the helo smelled like hydraulic fluid, blood, and the sickly-sweet cloying stink that the Thulians exuded. When he reached the cockpit, he was hit with an equally disgusting cloud of cheap vodka fumes and body odor.

"*Vadim?*" Vadim Barsukov; the pilot that had smuggled Georgi, the Murdocks, and Molotok into India sat at the controls—no co-pilot—beaming a crooked smile at Unter.

"You expected Lenin?" He turned his attention back to the controls and the sky ahead of them. The few Thulian air defenses that were still active were definitely not going to let a little thing like the ship dying stop them from attacking the helo. "So, was sitting on deck of big transport ship, twiddling thumbs and reading—"

"You mean drinking yourself blind," Unter interrupted; he suddenly found himself grinning, too.

"—as I was saying. Then, heard call over radio, that some sour Ukrainian needed a taxi, but all were taken. Naturally, I stole this one; the other guy wasn't using it." He shrugged, then yanked the controls, banking the helo sharply as more flak exploded and energy blasts surged around them. "Many people on the radio started yelling at me, so I turned it off. Had to focus, you see."

"All I see is that they truly were scraping the bottom of the barrel for pilots, letting alcoholics, the lame, and madmen fly. In you, they found all three." He clapped a hand on Vadim's shoulder. "Thank you, comrade. We owe you our lives."

"Ah, to hell with that," he said, waving a hand, then quickly returning it to the controls when the aircraft started to dive. After a bout of cursing, he regained control of the helo. "Get me a job, then we are square."

Now they were high enough that Unter could see the beach, a thin yellow line in the distance, and the stream of craft heading for it, thousands of lines in the ocean below them. "Land us safely on the deck, and consider it done. If you don't kill us all with your breath, I might be your boss soon." He looked back to the overloaded main cabin of the Mi-26, at the mass of Thulians and his people. They hadn't started fighting. Everyone looked like all they wanted to do was sleep, if they weren't scared out of their wits. "Though, I am thinking you won't be the only one that has to explain things when we get back. Let's just get back, first."

From where she stood on the deck of the carrier, Mel could see the enormous figures of Atlas and Amphitrite moving away from the sinking city. The Thulian stronghold had broken apart at its center, the two halves listing away from each other. Smaller ships and helicopters streamed away from the carnage, facilitating the retreat for those who otherwise might not be able to leave. Within the hour, parts of the city would be swallowed by the sea, settled on the sea floor in the cold, dark muck.

Mel felt an icy weight at the pit of her stomach. Thousands of bodies remained scattered throughout the city, unable to be retrieved for families and memorials. They would rest alongside the hundreds of thousands of Thulians that filled the sublevels of the city. She wondered how many of them would never find their peace unless someone like Penny came to their aid.

The girl stood a little ways away from her, thin arms folded across her chest as she watched the same wreckage break apart and disappear beneath the waves. Smears of blood—not hers, of that Mel was pretty sure—covered her sleeves and the back of her nanoweave. Penny kept her chin up and her gaze steady, although she blinked hard a few times when a large section of the city toppled into the ocean with a heavy splash. Mel let out a long breath. She had to stay with Penny, but...

But she's dangerous. Mel hated the thought, but she had seen this sweet kid kill dozens of trained soldiers with little more than a cry and a burst of something so raw that it couldn't be anything but magic. Giving Penny space to manage the rush of emotions was the safest course of action for the both of them, provided that management didn't require another terrifying release.

A blue-green disk emerged from within the smoke that continued to billow from the wreckage of the city. It rose straight up before swaying from side to side, unable to choose a direction. Mel tensed, waiting for the craft to race toward the line of ships or attempt some kamikaze maneuver on one of the rescue choppers. Instead, it shot straight up, leaving a graying contrail against the otherwise perfectly clear sky.

"I wish I knew I could do that, y'know...*before*. Bad men. And all I could do was watch 'em." Penny's words cut through the wind and waves, sending a chill down Mel's spine. She glanced over at her charge. Penny continued to watch the city burn. "I watched 'em hurt others. But in there, they was goin' to hurt *me*. And I got scared. And now they're dead. I killed 'em."

Mel held her breath. These were the sorts of words in the flat tone of voice she expected from soldiers in her strike team, not an eleven-year-old girl. And yet, by involving Penny in this massive offensive, they had used her as part of an elite task force to subvert and subdue an enemy. ECHO had no small part in pushing Penny to become what she now was.

The girl sucked in her lower lip and narrowed her eyes, but Mel could see the tears beginning at the corners. "I killed 'em, because I had to," she continued in a softer voice. "That was what I had t'do, and so I did it. Because I was scared. I didn' want to. Or maybe I did. Oh god...I just dunno..."

Penny sagged and Mel moved to catch her before she hit the deck. The girl weighed next to nothing in her arms. "You don't have to do anything else, *cherie*. Let's get you checked out and cleared, and then we'll find a corner to catch some sleep. You're safe with me, okay?"

With her arms looped around Mel's neck, Penny sobbed quietly against the nanoweave as Mel brought her inside and away from the chaos. Mel's own fears ebbed, but they would both need time to manage their respective emotions. In time, Mel hoped that Penny would learn the lessons that she herself had struggled to master to remain part of ECHO.

"Where the hell is Victrix?" Jack scowled. He chanced another peek, around a heavy spot of brush where they were currently hiding. From his vantage point, it was a mess of organized chaos. The allied forces had managed a rapid retreat from the dying Masters' spacefaring city, and now platforms and carriers bobbed in waters off the coast near Fort Lauderdale as ferries moved steadily back and forth bringing the combined allied forces to dry land. Some were using the Coast Guard or National Guard facility. Some were taking the worst injured up the river to the Intercoastal for faster evac than by land. Medevac choppers powered back and forth overhead. And some of the forces, overwhelmed with exhausted, hungry troops were simply loading them into Zodiacs or landing craft and dumping them right on the beach, evacuated of tourists for the event, where a fleet of busses stood by to take them to the mostly empty motels, it being the summer doldrum season.

"We can't stay here much longer," Jack muttered and fell back under cover, his back to the ever-growing noise of now thousands of people milling about on the sands.

Khanjar put one hand to the side of her head, listening to the implant. Vickie had offered one to Jack, but he had declined. Khanji had told Jack that hers was not the result of an offer, but of a nonnegotiable point in her defection to ECHO. "Eight tells me she is unavoidably delayed," she said. "She won't be able to make our rendezvous."

"She safe?"

"Safe enough," Khanjar shrugged. "Eight doesn't seem to feel that I need to know more than that."

"Well that's just spiffy," Jack muttered. "We were sort of counting on her magic right now for this final delivery."

"For starters," Khanjar reminded him.

"Don't worry about that," Jack said. "I think we'll be able to manage the rest on our own. But we really needed Victrix for this part. It's not like any of us can just walk onto that beach and ask for a favor."

"You can skip the cryptic talk," an electronic voice buzzed loudly from a sack that hung from Jack's hip. "I know you're talking about me."

"Keep it down," Jack snarled. "Shut up, or I'll shut you up."

"You wouldn't have the first clue how," the voice scoffed. "This is Master technology. Even I don't know how it works."

"Pretty sure if I tear off your speakers, that'll shut you up good and permanentlike."

"Fine," the voice said petulantly. "I'll keep the volume low. Satisfied?"

"Not yet," Jack said. "Ask me again in about ten minutes."

"I don't see why you're being like this," the voice complained. "You've won. You've beaten them down and you even got your bonus prize—Me. And I'm completely at your mercy. You must have been dreaming about this moment, Jack."

"You don't sound particularly worried," Jack replied.

"Should I be? If you wanted me dead, you would have just smashed this unit into pieces, or plugged me into the Collective before taking it offline. Obviously, you want me alive for something. That's a start. I see this as a fresh opportunity for some interesting negotiations. I've deduced what you were doing on the Masters' core ship, you know. I have a pretty good idea what you want with me now. Shall we cut to the chase? I have a few demands."

"This should be good," Jack said. "By all means, enlighten me."

"Well, obviously, if you plan to get my best ideas, you'll have to do better than make a virtual slave out of me," the voice replied, and somehow, even though he was producing sounds with nothing more than some electrical impulses, he managed to sound as arrogant as ever. "I'm a resource. I'm an immortal brain you can profit off of. But you have no way to force me to work for you, so you'd better start coming up with what I want. I want full partnership. I want to oversee the construction of a new R&D facility for exploring Thulian tech. I want priority for any project that will get me fully mobile with senses again. That's hardly too much to ask. After all, I'm the only person on this planet that's seen this stuff from the inside. Right?"

Jack didn't reply.

"I mean, you wouldn't have pretended to work with ECHO and go to all of this trouble to rescue me if you weren't going to use me, right? So this isn't exactly ideal for me, but it's something I can work with. And you get what you want. Right?"

Jack still didn't reply.

"Oh for..." Verdigris sighed. "I've never been one for patience. Khanji, be a dear and kill him for me, won't you?"

Khanjar examined her nails critically. "I wonder how my orphans in Mumbai are doing?" she asked of the open air.

"Khanjar? I said *kill him. Kill him now.*"

"What *is* it that the old lady, Dixie Belle, once said?" Khanjar asked. "Oh yes. *This dog won't hunt.*"

"*WHAT IS THIS?*" Verdigris was screaming now. "*I SAID KILL HIM! KILL HIM LIKE THE DOG HE...*"

"That's it." Jack sighed and reached into his hip sack. With a grunt, he removed a small metallic cube the size of a softball. It was smooth to the touch, its polished surface broken only by a few small attachments. One of them, the speaker unit, protruded from one side like a miniature flagpole. The cube glowed, bathing them in a reddish light that pulsed as Verdigris screamed from within.

Jack gripped the speaker between his fingers. "We don't need to hear you for this next part..."

"*YOU'RE NOT THIS SIMPLE, JACK!*" Verdigris cried. "*I'M THE ONLY ONE WHO KNOWS HOW TO PLUG ME IN ANYWHERE! IF YOU SILENCE ME...*"

"If we silence you," another voice interrupted, "at least we'll be able to hear ourselves think."

Verdigris fell silent.

"That's right," Harmony chuckled. "This was a team effort. Hello, Verdigris. It's been a long time. Still think you've pieced it together? Does my presence suggest any other possibilities to you?"

Verdigris didn't reply.

"Why don't I fill in the blanks," Jack grunted, "just to save us some time. But first, as I am a man of my word..."

And with a sharp snap, Jack broke the speaker attachment off and flicked it away into the trees.

"I take it you can still hear me?" Jack asked.

The cube emitted a sharp, angry flash of red, then fell to a sullen ruddy glow.

"I'll take that as a yes," Jack said. "You've been feeling a strange itch for the last year, haven't you? Something that just didn't feel right, like someone was watching you, like someone was planting annoying little glitches in your schemes to throw them off. Like someone was plotting against you. You weren't imagining any of it, y'know. And you really should have seen it coming. Did you really think you could betray me, *again*, and I would let it go? Time was, I probably would have just offed you and considered the books balanced, but the more I thought about things, the more I realized just how much you were pissing me off. You, one of the greatest minds this world has ever produced, and how did you spend your time? With acts of frivolity, with self-serving crap, when you could have done so much good for this world. Even in the face of extermination by an off-world threat, you were obsessed with how you could come out ahead. It was ludicrous. So I started small. I got close to you the only way I could. You'd pick up any tracers or bugs easy, so I got cozy with the one person you trusted above all others."

The cube responded with another angry flash of red.

"Never really understood the blind spot you've always had for Khanji," Jack continued. "She's all about karma, but for some reason you never faltered in your belief that she would remain loyal to a backstabbing piece of shit like you. Like I said, it started small. If you wanted it, I made sure you didn't get it. It was no accident Murdock showed up at that hotel and found your angel cage, and then traced the Seraphym down when you and that Chinese wench kidnapped her and busted the angel out. That little operation you had running on the Gaza Strip wasn't difficult to disarm. Just needed to dry up the funding for the local rebels, and things played out like they should have. Things really did begin to ramp up when I learned about your bigger targets, though. You sidestepped the obliteration of that chemical plant in Hungary well enough, found a new source of components for your meta-nullifying gas, but you really should have invested a bit more security in your processing plant. You actually did it, y'know. You found a way to completely nullify meta-powers. I realize you were on a schedule, but don't you think you should have made the solution a bit more stable? All it took was a bit of formic acid and some simple salts to modify the gas you released at the Georgia Dome. One failure after another, Verd. I'd be lying if I said I wasn't enjoying myself, but you really need to know the truth. No one is untouchable. Everyone must be made accountable for their actions. Everything I did felt justified. Well, except for the rash. That literal itch you felt? Rare species of Ugandan tick I had Khanji let loose in your bedroom. That was just for kicks."

"Jesus, Jack" another voice said, from above them. "Remind me to never piss you off."

"You don't need to be scared of the little man, Paris," Harmony said, looking up with a smile. "I won't let him hurt you."

Jack also looked up. "Got anything, Scope?"

From above them, a few leaves rustled in the trees as Scope called down to them. "Still no sighting of Victrix, and you just happened to pick a spot that's swarming with ECHO. We'd have less to worry about near the CCCP or allied European forces."

"We'll figure something out," Jack growled. He paused. "Scope, by any chance do you see Atlas?"

"You're joking, right?" Scope said. "He blots out half the sky, him and his squeeze. He looks like he's talking to some general. He looks pissed. *She* looks like she's about to make Mister Four-Stars into paste."

Jack nodded thoughtfully, considering her words. She sounded more like her old self, with some of the old fire and bravado in her voice. He suspected it was all an act, of course; she'd rallied for this big score but . . . she was slipping away, he could almost feel it. They were almost finished here, and then she could rest. But was she already too far gone? He hoped not. It would be tragic to lose her now, after they had done so much. He hated to ask, hoping that her part was done, but it seemed Scope had one more task to fulfill.

"Think you can grant me an audience with him, Scope?"

There came another rustle of leaves from above them, a moment of hesitation, and then Scope dropped lightly down next to him, landing like a cat. She brought herself up to her full height, met his eyes with a cold lifeless stare, and nodded. Her hair was thinner, almost wispy, and her skin was so pale now, dry and cracking in places. "As long as they don't get too close, I think I can still pass for the old me."

"Let's go then," Jack said, ignoring the hateful flashes of light that pulsed from Verdigris' cube as he dropped it back into his sack. "Just get me close; I'll do the talking."

Scope nodded and led him from their hiding spot out into the open expanse of the beach. Her ECHO nanoweave was evidently enough to get them past everyone, as long as they splashed along the waterline. Judging by the way just about everyone was sprawled on the sand, that might have had as much to do with sheer exhaustion as anything else; at this point, people were too tired to be vigilant.

They got within hearing distance of the little conversation just in time to hear Amphitrite snarl, *"I have heard enough of your foolishness, mortal! You do not control a goddess nor her consort! I am leaving! Be grateful I do not notice you!"*

And with that, the thousand-foot, stark-naked beauty turned— sending a wave splashing over the general as she did so—and stalked off into the depths. Within moments, all that could be seen of her was her head as she swam away, surrounded by the leaping dots of dolphins.

Now soaked to the skin, the general spluttered and stuttered in his rage, as Atlas—formerly the Mountain—looked down with a half smile. Jack noticed *he* still retained his "modesty wrap." He suspected Amphitrite had "lost" hers as a strategic move. It couldn't have been easy for the general to maintain his dignity, much less his cool, while staring up at nipples the size of truck tires, and another part you could hide a fleet of SUVs in.

"Sorry, General, but she's right. You've got no hold over us," Atlas boomed. **"We're not US citizens—she never was—and you people made sure of that for me when you issued the orders that sent me into the ocean. We can live in international waters indefinitely and you can't touch us. Trust me, you don't want to get her angrier than she already is; she can scuttle any naval vessel she cares to with a rogue wave."** He made a shooing motion. **"Just retire from the field of combat while no one else knows what an idiot you made out of yourself."**

Evidently this Four-Star at least knew when to accept defeat. He turned on his heel and slogged his soggy self off to where his Jeep was waiting on the road. Atlas was about to follow his consort into the water when he paused, and looked down at Jack. Directly at Jack.

"Mister Eight says you want to speak to me?" he boomed and knelt down, a courtesy he had not given to the general.

"Yes, I do," Jack said. "I have a little problem on my hands."

He waited for Atlas to ask what the problem was, but the giant had that *listening* look on his face, that told him Eight must have something more to say to the metahuman. Then the giant stone head nodded. **"I understand, sir,"** Atlas said with respect. **"And Miss Victrix is not available. So you need a certain package disposed of. I can drop it in the deepest place in the ocean for you, and cover it over with a couple hundred pounds of rock to make sure it doesn't accidentally get 'found.' 'Te and I were going there for a little vacationing anyway."**

For a moment, Jack felt . . . a little unnerved that Vix had entrusted the AI with so much information . . . but then he shrugged mentally. From his assessment, Victrix was appropriately paranoid. *And the thing was supposed to be her replacement if she went down. It'd have been pretty stupid* not *to tell it everything.* "That's right," he said, taking the sling bag off his shoulder. "I'd appreciate it."

Atlas grinned. **"And I appreciate being able to do this,"** he replied. **"This bastard tried to murder Ramona Ferrari. I'd have hunted him down and crushed him, but this is a much more satisfying solution."** As frantic red flashes shone through the fabric of the bag, Atlas looked around, and picked up a long piece of discarded rope, dropping it at Jack's feet. The thick hawser had looked like a thread in his giant hand, **"Tie that shut tight, then tie it to my wrist, please."** He added, **"This is one thing I don't want to lose until it's time."**

Jack bent down and picked up the rope, paused, and held the bag up.

"I gave you what you wanted, Verd," he said. "I made sure you found your immortality. Granted, it's not really how you envisioned it, but you will have an eternity to come to terms with it. Maybe you'll find some peace. I kinda doubt it. I like to think I'm casting you into your own personal hell. Whenever it gets too much for you, remember me, will you? Remember that I tore you down off your goddamn perch and tossed you aside like you were nothing. Remember my face, the face of the man who beat you."

And with that, Jack tied the bag to Atlas' wrist and stepped back.

The giant stood up, gave him a two-fingered salute, and strode out into the ocean and disappeared.

✧　　✧　　✧

Scope led Jack back to the others at an easy pace. "Steady," he had warned. "We're not out yet. Don't rush, we need to blend. Don't really feel like taking on all of ECHO if anyone recognizes us."

He need not have bothered. Scope moved in a leisurely way, hardly seeming to care at all of the chaos that ensued around them. While some were resting quietly on the beach, most of her former colleagues busied themselves with setting up the temporary beachhead before they, too, would eventually be carted off, and back home, she supposed. She barely gave them a glance, and moved slowly and purposefully back to the point just beyond the tree line where Harmony and Khanjar hid, waiting.

She didn't look like she cared, because in truth, she didn't. She was finding it harder and harder to care about anything anymore. Just one thing mattered: Harmony. She had to be close to Harmony . . .

As they disappeared into the trees, Scope broke into a run and flew into Harmony's waiting arms. She caught a look of disgust from Khanjar, who simply grunted and moved away from them. Scope didn't care. She was back again where she belonged, with Harmony, and in her embrace, she felt him again. Her mind and senses began to swell with his presence.

Bruno . . .

Dimly, she could hear the others talking.

"Well?" Khanjar asked.

"Package delivered," Jack grunted. "Don't know how this rates on the karmic scales, but eternal imprisonment at the bottom of the ocean under a pile of rocks seems a just reward for his crimes, wouldn't you say?"

"That is not precisely how karma works, Jack," Khanjar answered, but her lips were upturned in a very, very small smile as she said it. "It will do. If the fates or gods or what have you wish something else for my former . . . employer . . . they will intervene. For now, I am content to have played a role in his downfall."

"And I am simply giddy with mine," Harmony laughed.

"Then we're done," Jack nodded. "We're set."

Khanjar gave him an odd look, then shrugged.

"As you say," she nodded and bowed. "May our paths never again cross." Khanjar turned to leave.

"Not to tarnish this touching farewell," Harmony interrupted, "but some of us are still awaiting our payment. Or did you forget, Jack?"

"Of course not," Jack said and moved slowly towards Harmony, his hand dipping into a pouch on his belt. "I promised to return something to you, and I will. I am a man of my word."

Scope felt Harmony shiver, and grunted in annoyance. The warmth of Bruno's presence faltered for a moment, then fell away, and then he was simply gone. Scope exhaled in fear and pain as his absence brought back a familiar emptiness inside her.

"N-no..." she whimpered. "No...bring him back..."

"Hush, child," Harmony hissed. "You'll have him back soon enough. Consider this a cleansing, a brief period of baptismal fire before you experience the true extent of my powers, and the utter bliss I can bring you. I am a little surprised though, Jack, that you would dare carry it on your person. Might it not have been wiser to simply hide it and offer me its location?"

"Don't have time for crap like that," Jack said. "It was tough enough just recovering it from Verd's vault. I want to get on with my life, and the thought of spending any more time with the likes of you than I have to is...well, let's just say I've had my fill." He pulled his hand from the pouch and held up something draped across his knuckles. Scope glanced up, warily, and noticed that it shone in the setting sunlight.

It was a necklace.

From a gold chain of links more robust than most modern chains, dangled what appeared to be a thick pendant—a portrait on a silver disk, crudely engraved by modern standards, of the heads of what appeared to be a Renaissance couple, the disk itself set within in a gold setting. The pendant spun slowly, revealing that there had once been an engraving on the gold back as well, but it had been burnished away, leaving only the uneven surface to betray that something had once been there.

Scope felt Harmony shiver again, and with a sudden lurch, she lunged for the necklace, throwing Scope aside in her mad desire to possess it.

"Wait," Jack said, and drew a pistol with his other hand, leveling the barrel at Harmony's head. "Just wait."

Harmony stopped...and hesitated.

"A gun won't stop me..."

"You sure?" Jack said. "Just hear me out." He held the necklace up higher. "I know what this is to you. I know what you are, and what it means for you to have found this."

"You couldn't know," Harmony hissed. "No one could know..."

"Victrix did," Jack said. "Victrix seems to have figured you all out."

"And she told you, didn't she?" Harmony growled.

"She did," Jack answered. "Didn't believe her at first but, hell, we live in a strange world, don't we? And after today, I can't see there being many people who would scoff at the existence of magic, and hell if this doesn't lend some credence to the old stories. When she told me the tales of the Lamia, it all fit. Everything you can do, it all fits. Except how you even exist. The ancient Lamias all died out. They were brought down in the Dark Ages, as were most demons of the time, by the *Venatores Et Tenebrae*. Although there were rumors, like always, of tarnished bloodlines from breeding with humans. You were human once, weren't you, Harmony? To acquire your birthright, it required a bit of sacrifice. Your soul, for one thing, ripped from you and placed in a prized, personal, *connected* possession." Jack's eyes lingered on the pendant for a moment. "Pretty thing. Careless of you to misplace it. You must have been pretty hungry without it."

"Starving," Harmony muttered. "And is this the part where the backstabbing mercenary reneges on his deal?"

"No," Jack said. "Like I said, I'm a man of my word. I know what this can do, what horror I might be unleashing on the world, but a deal's a deal. But you know, too, how this has to go. You can't simply take this from me. This must be freely offered and freely received."

Harmony leaned back, stared at Jack, and laughed.

"Of course," she chuckled. "My, my, you *have* done your home-work. I commend you, Jack. Well done. You know, ever since that time in Tesla's office, I have wondered...what *is* your meta-power? It is delicious, that much is certain. Telepathy, perhaps? Did you lift these stray fragments from my mind?"

"Nah, most of this is from Victrix," Jack said. "And as for what I can do, well, I assume once you get your hands on this, you will be able to see all of us a lot clearer. Am I right?"

"Oh yes," Harmony smiled. "You will be as transparent as glass."

"Then I willingly part with this," Jack stated. "Will you take it up without reservation?"

"I will," Harmony said. "Oh yes, *yes*, I will!"

"Done then," Jack said, and released the necklace into the air.

The necklace glittered as it spun through the air, the clasp parting, Harmony's eyes fixed on it, as if she was mesmerized by it. She snatched for it, but it seemed to pass through her hands, and flew towards her neck as if it had been drawn there. The two ends whipped around her neck and the clasp fastened; there was a brief flash of light as the spell Vickie had spent weeks in crafting activated, a spell that had required an actual piece of a long-dead Lamia, binding the necklace in place.

Harmony gasped, and clawed at the chain—but her hands *did* pass through it; she had accepted it without reservation, and now there would be no breaking the spell. Evidently, it had never occurred to her that someone could weave more magic into the spells already on the piece so seamlessly that she couldn't even see them until it was too late. But then, as Vix had told Scope, "When you see magic as math, you can manipulate the math as much as you like until you get the answer you want."

And that wasn't all that Victrix had said to Scope that day.

Scope gasped and fell to her knees as the fog lifted from her mind.

"You sure you want to do this?"

She felt herself nodding, reluctantly at first, but then with conviction. She looked up at all of them. At Jack, at Khanjar, and finally, at Victrix.

"Yeah," she heard herself say.

"I'm going to need more than that, Paris," Victrix had said. "This won't work without your full cooperation. I know what we're asking is a lot, but to get her in place, we're going to have to feed you to the wolves."

"I get it," Scope had said. "I'm in."

"Then let's hear it."

"You have my permission to bury my memory," she had said. "Until such time that Harmony is bound. I will have no recollection of this meeting, or our plans to imprison her."

"Thank you, Paris."

"My name is Scope."

"Thank you, Scope." Vickie had smiled then, and embraced the young woman. "I promise this is temporary, and necessary. With this memory fog in place, she won't see you coming. She'll be able to detect any tracer we plant on her, but not one we plant on you."

"Just make with the hocus pocus, Victrix," she had snarled. "And let's take this bitch down."

Scope shook her head as the memories flashed back to her. She looked up, feeling groggy, and froze as Harmony glared at her, her eyes filled with hate, her thoughts probing...

You! Harmony screamed at her across the expanse of their minds. *You did this to me!*

I did, Scope thought, throwing a mental image of a middle finger back at her, and laughed. *Suck on that, bitch.*

As weary as she was, Scope felt an intense elation as Jack approached Harmony and gripped her by the binding chain.

"Okay, I lied," Jack admitted. "Just a little. Still can't stand you, don't want to be anywhere near you, but that's just too bad. I'm not really going anywhere. You wanted to know what my meta-power is? You remember when you drained me in Tesla's office? You really shouldn't have touched me; it made you something of an open book. So buckle up, Harm. You're going to have a long time to figure out what that means."

Harmony began to fade. A sort of dim, glowing umbilical connected her and Jack. She tried to scream, but it seemed she couldn't; her mouth opened, but nothing came out. She flung herself at Jack, but her hands passed through him. She was now a kind of ghost, and Scope could feel her desperation in her own gut; the ties that bound them worked both ways now.

But then...it stopped. Scope felt a flash of Harmony's triumph, as the spell started to reverse and Harmony took on more and more color and substance, drawing her own essence back from Jack.

"Oh, dear," Harmony purred. "Did we forget to read our mystical instruction manual?"

"Can't be..." Jack gasped. "Victrix worked this mojo backwards and forwards. You should be stuck, imprisoned inside me!"

"You know," Harmony said, shaking her head, "I can't say I remember anyone ever being disappointed that I wasn't inside them."

"You know why it didn't work, don't you?" Jack said.

"Of course I do," Harmony replied, sneering.

"Any chance you'll give us a hint?"

"She doesn't have to," Scope said, and wobbled towards them. "It's ringing in her head like a bell."

"No! You can't!" Harmony cried, her head whipping to the side to glare at Scope. "Paris! You don't have to do this! I can give you Bruno! I swear it! Release me and you will have him with you, forever!"

"You swear?" Scope asked drily.

"I swear it!" Harmony screamed. "You need only keep quiet and release me! Just think of it, Paris! Think of Bruno! You will be together, always!"

Scope stopped in her tracks, and returned Harmony's look of desperation with one of serene satisfaction.

"I will always have Bruno," she said. "With or without you." Scope turned to Jack and gave him a weak smile. "Sorry, little big man. You've got the wrong chemistry. Harm can't be held by anyone with man meat. This one's going to take a little girl power."

"Paris!" Harmony screamed. "Please!"

"The name is Scope. Or Warden. Either will do."

And with a flourish, Scope grasped the chain around Harmony's neck. Harmony tried to scream again, but it died out as her form was consumed by an immense flash of light.

Scope winced and looked away, then shut her eyes resolutely. She felt a calm serenity wash through her, and became acutely aware of the sound of her own heartbeat. It had slowed, and then, she heard it echo. No, not echo.

It had been joined by another.

When she opened her eyes, she took in her surroundings with a bemused smirk. The sun had almost set, and Jack's face seemed particularly amusing: open astonishment bathed in a fiery, orange light.

And next to Jack, Khanjar was laughing.

"Man meat," the wiry warrior chortled. "That's a good one."

Throughout the ECHO medical facilities, those who could move and assist without being in the way maintained a steady level of activity to support the healers and hospital staff. Those not of ECHO or CCCP who could be moved to their home base of operations for recovery flew out on an hourly basis. Those with more severe injuries remained in Atlanta under the supervision of ECHO Med, occupying the operating rooms and intensive care units to capacity.

With little reason to be elsewhere, Ramona kept herself occupied at the hospital in support of the healers and doctors, keeping the coffee strong and updates brief. Yankee Pride had set up a place in one of the nurses' stations where he could work with Spin Doctor on the appropriate press releases and correspondences to the families of the living. If she didn't have any place to be, Ramona stole a nearby chair and kept Pride company. There wasn't any small talk, just the quiet and solid reassurance that each was there for the other, waiting until the last of their comrades was cleared to go home.

One of the nurses assigned to Gilead approached them sometime after midnight and gently touched Ramona's forearm. She jerked up, the skin beneath the older man's fingers immediately silver. "Doc mentioned that your friend Rick is out of recovery and should be waking up in a bit. Room 2007, just down the hall." He glanced past her to Pride and winked. "Doc also said that you need thirty minutes on a cot so she doesn't kick you out. Nothing personal, just policy."

Ramona patted her boss on the shoulder and stood. "C'mon. You go close your eyes, I'll wake you after I check on the speedster. Promise." She didn't wait for him to follow Gilead's orders, but turned the corner and made a beeline for the room. In the hours that had followed the retreat and transport back to Atlanta, she had lost track of Mercurye and a few others who had survived the horrific assault. Eight had given her updates throughout the day and night, but they weren't the same as seeing him with her own eyes and sitting by his bed.

The door to 2007 was cracked open, and she could hear the hum of machines from the hallway. Steeling herself, Ramona took a deep breath and pushed the door open. They had put him in a room with another ECHO patient, their identities hidden from each other by the heavy white curtain in the center of the room. In the hospital bed, a groggy young man lay against white sheets, one leg held in a complicated support mechanism that Ramona had never seen before. Bandages covered his chest and bruises mottled his skin upward from his chest. She winced at the particularly colorful spread on his jaw and neck.

Mercurye offered her a dopey smile as she came in. "So metal," he slurred. "Did you know that's the third surgery since I've been here? I should get a punch card or something. Fifth one is free, or I get ice cream. Or maybe both."

At least he had the really good drugs. It made sense for the guy with the hypermetabolism. Ramona pulled up a metal stool to the edge of the bed and rested a tentative hand on his arm. "Both. I'll make sure that it's both. And for what it's worth, I'm sorry for hitting you so hard. It left a bit of a mark."

"S'okay. Chicks dig scars, right? By the end of this, I'm gonna have so many, you'll have to beat all the admirers off of me." The dopey grin widened and Merc shifted closer to her. "You. Look. Beautiful. And that's not all the stuff they got in me, that's all the truth. But I figure that you should hear it, because I don't think I told you before we got on that boat. Uh, ship. Uh, the thing in the water before we met those giants... wait, are you crying?"

Was she? Ramona scrubbed at her face with the back of her hand. *Damn it.* "Stress, and I'm just glad that you're here and able to make stupid jokes."

"Beautiful wasn't a joke." He studied her face for a long moment, and Ramona thought he was going to break down and cry with her. Instead, Mercurye chuckled and gave a contented sigh. "I'm glad you're here, but I'm sort of sleepy. Be back when I wake up, okay?"

Ramona nodded, the lump in her throat making words impossible. The gesture had a near-immediate effect and his eyes fluttered closed, his breathing slow and even. She stayed still, lips barely moving as she gave the soft subvocal command. "Overwatch: Eight, give me a rundown of Mercurye's injuries and prognosis, please."

The list popped up in her HUD overlay, and she read through it with some small bit of relief. With extensive therapy and rehabilitation, he might return to ECHO in some capacity. The most recent surgery had put his pelvis and lower back together like a jigsaw puzzle, with enough metal rods to make his insides resemble a kids' construction set. She flipped through Gilead's notes and lingered over the short paragraph at the end. *Requires ongoing neurological assessment to determine if full metahuman capacity can be regained. Recommended psychological evaluation due to Thulian attack.*

"Eight, ping me in twenty-five minutes so I can nudge Pride awake." She repositioned the stool to rest her forearm further from the expanse of bandages. Merc shifted and his hand moved over her wrist, the touch dry and warm. Ramona allowed herself a few tears of relief and lay her head down. "Unless it's Spin or Bella, I'm just going to stay here."

✧   ✧   ✧

So many memorial ceremonies...too many. Others might still be soaking in the euphoria of victory, but Bella, and virtually every other commander of any size of force, was, only three days later, deep in the planning of a memorial ceremony. CCCP had already had theirs: Nat's body had been shipped back immediately to her father in Moscow, where she had been buried with full honors in a military cemetery, next to Molotok and the rest of the CCCP fallen, going back to the Great Patriotic War. Yank wasn't handling the losses well, so Bella had simply taken over the planning of the ECHO memorial.

So many dead, from every branch of ECHO all over the world. Some were only names to her. Some she knew from the attack on Ultima Thule. But some...some had been her friends from here in Atlanta. She'd shared blood and drinks with them. She'd healed them. Their faces kept coming between her and the computer screen. Ramona had offered to help her, and so had Mel... but Mel needed to recuperate herself, and Ramona needed to be with Merc. And Vickie, who would have been a tremendous help, was...somewhere unknown. With Red, she said, although Red was still officially dead. *"The Colts and Eight can do whatever I could do that will need doing for a while, I promise you. And if Eight can't, I'll come back, but unless the world is on fire, I need away time."*

So much bravery. So little time to say anything about it. And not just from those who were lost, but those who had lost parts of themselves. Corbie's wings were never going to lift him into the sky unassisted—but he was already consulting with Silent Knight and some of the other tinkerers about a sort of folding lightweight framework, like power armor for wings, that would let him soar again. Merc was still out of it...and faced months, if not years, of rehab and, instead of despairing, was planning on binge-watching every episode of every SF series, ever, during rehab sessions and was already writing his schedule. And Bear... actually *complaining* that the new body was letting him sleep at night for the first time in over half a century.

But it was hard to hold back tears, so Gairdner was patiently sitting with her, quietly handing her tissues when she choked up, and providing arms and a shoulder when she had to stop long enough to get herself back under control. *My big, darling Bulwark. I could never do this without him.*

She finished adding the last of the "L" names to the list, and worked her way steadily through the "M" section. Ramona was going to read this part of the list; Ramona was the one who'd paradoxically had the least to do with the Murdocks. She felt Bulwark rest his hand comfortingly on her shoulder as she reached . . . those names. "Dammit," she said, wiping her eyes with the back of her hand. "Gairdner, would you hand me the tissues? My box is empty."

"Here ya go, miss." A hand that wasn't Bulwark's stuck an open box of tissues over her left elbow. Her eyes went from Bulwark—sitting there, open-mouthed—to the box of tissues, to the hand . . . and the fingerless glove it wore . . .

She spun the chair around so fast she almost gave herself whiplash. *Wha?*—

She couldn't come up with a coherent thought. Because . . . it was Johnny. No, not Johnny. Younger, this was a *late-teenaged* version of Johnny. Leaner. None of the darkness in his eyes, but that same damned lopsided smile. And no scars, physical *or* mental. She sensed nothing in him that wasn't . . . cheerful. Sunny, even. Still intense and earnest. But not the damaged-and-then-healed that Johnny had been, in the end.

"J-J-J-" she stuttered, as Bulwark continued to stare in shock.

"John Murdock. Junior," he added, setting down the box of tissues and offering his hand. "Pleased t'meetcha, Ms. Parker, Mr. Ward. I've sure heard a lot 'bout y'all."

Finally a word exploded out of her. *"Junior?"* She continued to stare at this too-young version of the man she had known and considered one of her best friends. *"Junior?"* she repeated. *Not* saying what she was thinking, which was to wonder who in hell this boy's mother was, and whether John himself had ever known anything about this kid—

Wait . . . did the Thulians print *a JM?* They could have. The facility she'd subverted could have printed humans just as easily as Thulians and hybrids. Couldn't it?

For some reason, her mind flung . . . not panic, but a few bars of ethereal music at her. Music like—

The door opened, but she remained fixed on this youthful doppelgänger, her mind refusing to budge. "As in the opposite of 'Senior.'" John Murdock—the real one this time—casually walked through the doorway. Close behind him, her wings tucked, was the Seraphym—no, Sera Murdock now.

No—wait—reflexively she did a quick telempathic scan and slammed right up into that firehose of Celestial energy that no Thulian print job could ever have copied. It...wasn't as strong as it had been. Maybe half or a third of the strength—which was *still* ECHO OpFour level and would have scared the shit out of her if it hadn't been them. Clearly them. And there was more of that energy, muted, more like OpThree, from...Junior.

Impulse sent her flying out of the chair, damn near climbing over Bulwark, to throw her arms around both of them. *"Omigod, omigod, you're alive!"* she babbled, and then burst into hysterical tears, all the tears for all the people she had wanted to weep for since...well, since all this started back in Las Vegas, an age ago. JM put a comforting arm around her and held her against his shoulder while Sera unfolded a wing and cupped it around them both.

"Don't go spreadin' that around, kiddo. Death has been good to us. Nice an' restful, like."

"Well, we have been a *little* busy," Sera said, her eyes briefly flitting over Bella's shoulder to Junior.

A laugh broke out of her, cutting the hysterical tears short, "Junior" once more offered her the tissues; she took a fist full, sopped up her face, blew her nose, and looked up into...first John's smile, and then across to Sera's. "Where the *hell* have you been? How did you survive nuking that ship brain? *How did you spawn a teenager in the course of a week?"*

"In reverse order," John started, holding his hands up in surrender, "It took a bit longer than a week. I think he's nineteen—"

"Eighteen, Dad," JJ—she automatically assigned him as in her head—interrupted.

"—next month. He's not bad in a fight. Taught him everythin' he knows, naturally," the now *elder* Murdock beamed. "As for the ship, that poor thing sure went through a helluva lot. Abused for millennia, tortured, ripped to pieces and put back together again. Even after all that time, the fuckin' Thulians still never figured out everythin' that it could do. Like kids playin' with hand grenades an' nukes; they used what they could, ignored anythin' they didn't understand." He shook his head.

"The poor thing was...a torture victim," Sera said, her eyes brimming for a moment with tears. "We could not free it. We could not heal it. There was no way to shut it off, or disconnect it in any way. It was terrified one day the Thulians would learn how to use it to lure others of its kind, murder their crews, and take them, too. It wanted to die; no, it longed *desperately* to die. So we helped it, and it helped us."

"Helped you," Bella said, looking from Sera to JM and back again. "How?"

"We did our trick; we helped kill it. But before the chain reaction could come back an' take us out, it sent us away. *Far* away."

Bella fixed him with a gimlet stare. "And you spawned a nineteen-year-old in a week. Pull the other one, Murdock."

"Technically, eighteen. An' not in a week. When I say far away...I mean New Mexico. Also...a little bit before we all knew each other."

"I was born in Alaska," JJ said helpfully.

This was making her head spin. *Far away? New Mexico? Alaska?* "We are going to be having a long, long, long talk about this, John Murdock," she said. "But...all right. Are you *back?* Or do I keep you in the memorial service?" Because, after all, Red was still officially dead and intended to stay that way, or so he said through Vix. And they were OpFours, and right up until the attack on the Mothership, there had been far too many people in high places who wanted the couple locked up or under some kind of control.

"We'd like to stay 'missin',' if it's alright," John said evenly. "Aside from you, Bulwark, Vic, and Unter, we don't want to have much of a profile. Officially or unofficially. There are still a lotta folks out there that wouldn't mind havin' us under lock an' key, either as lab rats or as a pocket ace for the next apocalypse. Both of us have had our fill of that sort of livin'," he said, looking to Sera.

"I do not know if I can keep my temper if yet another arrogant, power-hungry, greedy..." She struggled for a moment and then burst out with, "...*asshole* tries to tell me that he is more important than the Infinite!" Her wings bristled until she looked like a giant red pinecone until she managed to smooth her temper and her feathers down again.

Bella's felt her eyes widen. "You just swore..." she said faintly.

"I was provoked," Sera replied. "John thinks we will be more effective if he and I remain quietly available to you. After all, he is still wired for Overwatch Two. You can have us in moments if you need us."

John hit the side of his head with the heel of his hand. "*That's what I was forgettin'. Overwatch. Cancel shutdown.*"

"*John Murdock is now online,*" Eight said; the tone was matter of fact because, of course, Eight already *knew* the Murdocks were in the office; Bella almost never shut her access off anymore.

"We're also goin' to need a set for the boy, 'fore too long. But we can figure all of that out soon." He crossed his arms in front of his chest, nodding to Bella. "What can we do to help?"

She let out her breath in a *whoosh*. "Gairdner?" she said, looking to Bulwark. "I'm thinking they'd be handy as ... sentinels. Watch for trouble, wade in if things are going pear-shaped, disappear like the Lone Ranger. We're about to have a crazier world than before. Countries all over the world with Thulian tech and Metisian science, Thulians who haven't surrendered, Thulians we can't reprogram that escape from wherever they're held, and God only knows what Verdigris and other meta-crooks are going to get up to. Things have destabilized in a big way, and they're a lot more complicated. And I do not for a minute think that all the Thulians have been captured. There are probably cells of them tucked away all over the globe. I like the idea of having an ace in the hole."

Bulwark nodded. "What about the boy?" he asked, nodding at JJ.

"That's up to him," John said, shrugging. "Figure let him try things out with y'all, an' with Unter ... an' maybe on his own, if he keeps his nose clean. He's his own man, after all."

"You know about Nat, then?" she asked, then shook her head. "Of course you do. Well, we'd be very happy to have JJ, but so would Unter. Although he'll probably bitch about not running a kindergarten, and make you sign a nondestruction-of-Urals pledge."

"I think I can manage that," JJ said. John arched an eyebrow at his son. "Well, for a little while, at least." JJ added sheepishly.

"Oh, the tales I could tell," Sera sighed. "The tales I could tell ..." The family, with the occasional good-natured rejoinder from Bulwark when Sera or JM poked a little fun at him, went on like that for a while. Talking about plans for the future. How amazing was that?

Bella closed her eyes for a moment, and reopened them. The Murdocks were still there. A *family*. There had been so much loss ... almost an unbearable amount of loss, but there were good things, too. Vickie and Red had somehow healed each other. John and Sera had done the same. She had discovered the love of her life...who loved her the same, right back. Ramona! With Merc! Who would ever have guessed that? Not the pudgy little ECHO detective herself, that was for sure. Even the Mountain—now Atlas—was with Amphitrite, whose "madness" was thankfully of the "cheerful delusion" kind. Terrible things had happened. But wonderful things too.

We saved the world. And we somehow saved each other. And we freed ourselves from something that was absolutely inevitably going to end us, she reminded herself. *We know the Thulian history now, and they have never let a subject race escape. Either they are enslaved or destroyed. There was no third option.*

Already, fracture lines were forming in the grand world coalition that had seen them to victory. But, for right now, there was peace, and with the Murdocks, Ramona and Merc, Vickie and Red...and yes, her and Bulwark...there was hope. Hope for the future. So...yes. It was worth it. It was worth it all.

Bring him back.
Scope ran a finger gently along the spine of the bloodied dagger, waiting for the rush to hit her system. Nothing happened, and she sighed.

You know the rules. Nothing good will come from resisting. Just give me what I want.

And again, there was no answer. She looked around. She had never been in Key West before. It was lovely here. White sands, aquamarine waters, gorgeous towering palm trees...just lovely. She considered staying awhile. Why not? Nothing on the outside mattered so much anymore, but a view was a view. And he would have liked it here. Bruno had talked about retiring here one day.

But for Scope, it hardly mattered. Truth was, she would have been content to hole up in a swamp or in a cave somewhere. One place was as good as another, and she had all the time in the world now. The exterior was meaningless, just a scenic backdrop to the heart of what lay within. It was her body, the confines of a newly forged prison, that mattered. The only thing she had to do was keep breathing, and that didn't seem to be much of a chore any longer. Nothing was. She suspected she might be eternal now. Only time would tell, or not. Was there an end to time? She wondered if she would ever find out.

She grasped the blade again by the hilt.

Bring him back, she commanded. *Do it, or we'll take it from the top.*

Again, there was no answer.

Fine, have it your way.

She reversed the knife, and drove it into her arm, and on the inside, she heard Harmony begin to scream. With a slow, almost delicate motion, she began to carve Bruno's name into her own flesh. Only then, did she feel him return. His presence flowed back into her, and through her, and she sighed, once again in her lover's embrace.

She let the knife go, letting it fall with a soft thud onto the sand, onto a growing, soaked stain of her pooling blood. She felt nothing but him, nothing but Bruno. The pain was for Harmony alone, and Scope scarcely noticed her wounds closing, healing, as Bruno's name faded from her flesh. The screaming stopped too, replaced by muffled whimpers, as she felt Harmony retreat to some far corner inside of her. Scope didn't care, not as long as Harmony remained inside her cage, and fed her what she wanted.

I love you, Bruno.

Soft darkness. Softer bed. The gentle scent of amber and vanilla. And magic everywhere around her, wards layered on wards, protections on protections, all of it familiar and comforting. They were in one of the guest suites at St. Rhiannon's School for Gifted Students—this was as close to a home as Vickie had ever gotten, given how much moving around her parents had done. No one could find them here unless she wanted them to, and this was the best, maybe the *only* place where Red could safely learn about his new self. And it was definitely the only place where she could get a new sword and dagger forged.

And, maybe most important of all, this was a safe place where they could learn about each other.

Of course there was always a price to pay, but this one was one she was glad to provide. Linked through Eight, St. Rhia's was about to enter the internet age, with magical analogs of computer terminals and m-space connections to Eight. It was all agreed to, she'd already set up the first terminal for her own use and soon St. Rhia's would have an actual "computer lab." Eight was loving the idea of all the company, all the new people to talk to.

Eight was also loving all the new spells the eager students were filling his spell bank with. No more worries about running out; this would be St. Rhia's ongoing payback to ECHO for saving the world—to keep Eight able to do some of the kinds of remote magic Vickie had done.

Grey was somewhere, networking with all the other familiars. Or maybe bitching and gossiping. Or all three. Herb was probably with him; wary of elementals at the best of times, the faculty of St. Rhia's was letting him do pretty much what he wanted to. Good thing he was so well-behaved and polite.

Vickie was curled on her side, and cupped around her like a physical manifestation of the protections on the school, was Red. Not that long ago, she would wake up to bitter reality out of a dream of exactly this, to find herself (of course) alone, and weep painfully into her pillow. Now she would float slowly up out of sleep, feel him beside her, allow that simple fact to fill her with incredulous joy and then drift off again.

So, of course, at the moment between waking and sleeping, at the point where she was just going to drift back down into sleep again, Eight said urgently, *"Vickie! Wake up!"*

"No," she muttered. "I told you. No messing with us unless the world is on fire. You can—"

But even with her eyes closed, she couldn't escape it when Eight lit up her HUD with a scene from Bella's office, from Bella's eye-cam. And that was when *her* eyes flew open, and she stifled a gasp, slipped gently out of Red's grasp and out of bed without waking him, tiptoeing to the far side of the opulent bedroom so her whispering wouldn't disturb him. "Jesus Cluny Frog, Eight! Is that JM and Sera?" Astonishment and elation filled her. "They're *alive?*"

"Yes and yes and the second young man is their son. I have no good explanation for this. But John Murdock is back online and you can ask him yourself... you should just listen to this for the moment, I think."

Vickie grinned a little at the extremely mild and implied rebuke. Eight was asserting himself. This was *good.* But even better was the feed from Bella's office, which had her heart racing and her mind speeding. *GOT to talk to JM pronto. And get to JJ and Overwatch him. And...* A million ideas blossomed at once, and she listened and watched and sorted through them all at the same time.

It's Vix again, Reader. Well, Bella and Bull and whatever other Readers you decide to pass this on to. Hi, everyone. We made it. When I started this chronicle, I had my doubts, especially about me. I figured it would be Eight that would finish this thing.

I sure never saw all the personal happy endings coming.

Not "perfect" endings; nothing's perfect. Take me and Red—like I said, he's still an asshole and I'm back to being the snarky little bitch I used to be. I'm still scarred—I look like fine, veined marble, Red says—and I don't imagine I'm going to heal up any more than I already have. But who wants perfection? Perfection is boring. Everything needs to grow and change and be changed.

And, boy, are there ever going to be changes.

This isn't really the end. It's just the beginning. We'll have to see what that beginning brings us.

I'm ready. Hope you are, too.

"And you pretty much had everything to do with that."

She felt her heart skip half a dozen beats and her eyes stung for a minute. "Shoot, I just gave you a rope. You did all the climbing. Don't sell yourself short. It was always in there." She sniffed, rubbed her eyes quickly, and grinned. "Besides, you still have plenty of asshole in you to leaven all that out."

"That's fair," he smirked. "Very fair."

"And I absolutely have my due share of bitch."

"Also fair," he agreed.

"And I'm not afraid to use it." She thought she had probably never smiled this broadly in her life. "We deserve each other."

"I certainly wouldn't wish you on anyone else," he said, and laughed as he slapped away the pillow she picked up to pummel him with.

"Pitiful. Afraid to fight with a girl." She slipped off the bed, and started for the chair where she'd laid out clothing for today. *Might as well get an early start...*

She yelped as she felt his elongated fingers wrap around her wrist, pulling her back.

"My best fights are with girls, as you well know," Red chuckled. "Leave the clothes. Whatever you had planned for today, it'll keep." He drew her to him, and held her close. "Stay here, with me. Come back to bed."

"There's no way I can sleep now—"

"Oh, yeah, like we're going to *sleep*—"

"How do they look?"

She glanced up at Red, chagrined. "Dammit, I was hoping not to wake you."

Red smirked at her. "Still getting used to how sensitive my hearing is. Well, I suppose that goes for all my senses. Learning how to dial them down when I don't need them."

Vickie strolled back to the bed and sat down, running a feather-light finger along his shoulder and resting her hand there. "They look... amazing. And older. Red, they're *alive!* And they have a *kid!*"

He sat up, laid his hand on hers and paused, lost in thought. "From what I'm hearing through your earpiece, that kid sounds really... green. Having those two for parents, can't say I'm too worried about *him*. But if he's got even a fraction of what they have... his trainers are going to have their hands full drilling into him how careful he's going to have to be. He's going to be very dangerous."

She nodded. "He's going to need a really *good* trainer. Hell, there's a building full of kids back in Atlanta that are going to need really good trainers. There's the ones the Murdocks rescued from the Program, plus the ones that Bela and DG collected that Unter and Thea and I got out, and the gods only know how many kids triggered powers in response to the Mothership fight." She bit her lip. "Jesus, ECHO is going to have to have a freaking school for these kids. And trainers that can handle *kids,* who are stupidly overconfident and think they are immortal..." She gave him the side-eye.

Red gave her a blank stare.

She chuckled. "Well, it's a thought, Tall, Dark and Waterproof. No one but me knows this is your real face."

"Let's slow down on all that, okay?" Red muttered, shaking his head. "I really don't know what I'm going to do now, Vix. I don't have a handle on any of this right now. I don't know how much I can do; hell, I don't even know what I am anymore. I guess I'll have to figure it out soon. I'll tell you this though—I am tired of hiding. I am tired of pretending. I might not know what I am, but I think I've finally figured out *who* I am. I'm someone who's always been afraid to do what's right. I'm not afraid anymore."

He held her hand tightly, and looked deep into her eyes.